Henry William Lucy, Harry Furniss

A diary of the Salisbury Parliament 1886-1892

Henry William Lucy, Harry Furniss

A diary of the Salisbury Parliament 1886-1892

ISBN/EAN: 9783741191671

Manufactured in Europe, USA, Canada, Australia, Japa

Cover: Foto ©Andreas Hilbeck / pixelio.de

Manufactured and distributed by brebook publishing software (www.brebook.com)

Henry William Lucy, Harry Furniss

A diary of the Salisbury Parliament 1886-1892

A DIARY

OF

THE SALISBURY PARLIAMENT,

1886—1892.

MR. BALFOUR.

A DIARY

OF THE

Salisbury Parliament,

1886–1892.

BY

HENRY W. LUCY,

Author of "The Disraeli Parliament (1874-80);" "The Gladstone Parliament (1880-85)."

ILLUSTRATED BY

HARRY FURNISS.

SECOND THOUSAND.

CASSELL & COMPANY, LIMITED:

LONDON, PARIS & MELBOURNE.

1892.

To the Right Hon. A. J. Balfour, the principal product of the Salisbury Parliament, these simple annals of some passages in its life are inscribed.

London, October, 1892.

CONTENTS.

CHAPTER	PAGE
I.—How Lord Salisbury came in	1
II.—Coercion and the Land Bill	8
III.—Changes and Familiar Things	14
IV.—Mr. Balfour in Harness	26
V.—Under the New Rules	36
VI.—The English Local Government Bill	48
VII.—Mr. Gladstone	61
VIII.—Ministerial Difficulties	74
IX.—Mr. Parnell pleads "Not Guilty"	87
X.—The Parnell Commission	97
XI.—The Autumn Session	108
XII.—Orators and Debaters	132
XIII.—Calm before the Storm	148
XIV.—Mr. Parnell's Day of Triumph	157
XV.—Unrest in the Commons	163
XVI.—Death of Mr. Bright	175
XVII.—Lord Randolph Churchill	179
XVIII.—Parliamentary Customs	188
XIX.—Some Noble Lords	200
XX.—Small Beer	208
XXI.—Leaders of Parties	218
XXII.—Death of Mr. Biggar	237
XXIII.—The Commons and the Special Commission	249
XXIV.—A Maiden Speech in the Lords	255

CHAPTER	PAGE
XXV.—Budget Night	259
XXVI.—The Irish Party—Old Style and New	264
XXVII.—A Vanishing Majority	270
XXVIII.—Randolph Rediviva	287
XXIX.—At an All-Night Sitting	295
XXX.—Committee Room No. 15	313
XXXI.—Paralysis of the Opposition	326
XXXII.—Death of Mr. Bradlaugh	333
XXXIII.—Pastoral Times	343
XXXIV.—Why Dissolve?	355
XXXV.—Death of Lord Granville	363
XXXVI.—Depression	371
XXXVII.—In Committee of Supply	384
XXXVIII.—The Absent Leader	396
XXXIX.—Ministers in Kell and in Dome	410
XL.—Men of the Salisbury Parliament	419
XLI.—The Recreation of Statesmen	434
XLII.—Two Dead Men	440
XLIII.—Mr. Arthur Balfour's Start in the Leadership	447
XLIV.—Hard Times for Irish Members	450
XLV.—At the Bar of the House	470
XLVI.—The Derby Day	482
XLVII.—Dissolution Imminent	495
XLVIII.—The End	509

LIST OF ILLUSTRATIONS.

	PAGE
Mr. Balfour	Frontis.
The New Chief Inspector	xii
The Speaker	4
Peter Rylands	15
Stafford Northcote	17
The Fourth Party	19
"One of the Heroes of the Civil War in Ireland"	20
Colonel Hughes-Hallett	21
The Parnellite Minister	28
W. H. Cromwell Smith	32
Sir Henry James	39
"Charley"	41
Sir Charles Russell	48
Mr. Ritchie	49
Sir William on the Offensive	51
Lord Folkestone	54
Sir William Hart Dyke	56
The Flag of Truce	59
"Mr. G."	66
The Lord Advocate	68
"A Bad Quarter of an Hour"	73
Sir Charles Forster	77
Mr. Balfour	79
Frank Hugh O'Donnell	84
O'Connor Power	85
Joseph Gillis	88
The O'Kelly, V.C.	95
Mr. Balfour's Below-the-gangway Attitude	104
Sir John Swinburne Aslowy	107
Sydney Buxton	119
Mr. Jacoby	120
"What I say is this"	124
Mr. Joseph Cowen	133
Mr. Bradlaugh	137
Mr. Sexton	141
Mr. G. and Tim	144
Mr. Chamberlain	146
The Attorney-General	150
"Not quite Bismarck"	152
"The Utility Man"	158
Mr. Gladstone addresses Mr. Chamberlain	160
The Doctor	164
James Francis-Xavier	170
"In Dressing-gown and Nightcap"	172
John Bright	175
Aitken, M.P.	183
St. George or the Dragon?	189
"A Suitable Accessory"	194
Lord Carmarthen	204
Lord Rosebery's Onus	205
Mr. Sykes	209
David Plunket	213
Sir George Campbell	214
Mr. Gladstone	230
"Ponderosity of Invective"	232
"The House's Ancient Enemy"	245
Sir Richard Webster	253
The Budget	263
Lord Elcho II.	270
"Only Forty Seconds"	284
Like, yet Unlike	290
"With Amaryllis in the Shade"	294
The Irish Leader	298
Mr. Picton brooding over Mighty Thoughts	300
Mr. Goschen	302
Dick Power	332
Justin McCarthy	335
Mr. Bradlaugh	339
The Bearded Pard	342
Dan'l, M.P.	349

	PAGE
"Jemmy" Lowther	350
An Hon. Baffey	350
The Bore	371
Lord Denman	383
Alphens Cleophas	388
"Tim"	400
"His influence accumulates though his Party decays"	402
Henry John Atkinson	404
"I don't care which it is, you know"	423

	PAGE
"Old Morality"	441
Charles Stewart Parnell	442
Nearing it	460
Cunninghame Graham	464
The Letter to the Queen	483
Mr. Maclure and the Bishop	491
Julius Annibal Picton	497
Sir William and Alphens Cleophas	505
Lord Salisbury listening to Lord Denman	509
Mr. Gladstone walks in	531

THE NEW CHIEF INSPECTOR.

A DIARY

OF

THE SALISBURY PARLIAMENT,

1886—1892.

CHAPTER I.

HOW LORD SALISBURY CAME IN.

The Short Parliament—Home Rule—A General Election—The Tory Ministry.

THE Parliament which supported Lord Salisbury in power through six eventful years was opened by Royal Commission on August 5th, 1886. With the object of preserving the continuity of this record with the two volumes that have gone before chronicling events in the Disraeli Parliament and the Gladstone Parliament, it will be convenient to glance at the events of the short-lived Parliament elected in December, 1885.

The Short Parliament. The poll placed Mr. Gladstone in a magnificent position. His followers numbered 334, whilst of Conservatives there were 250, and Parnellites 86. The Liberals were thus within two of equal number with the combined forces of the Conservatives and Parnellites. The new Parliament, the eleventh of the Queen's reign, met on the 12th of January, 1886. The Bradlaugh difficulty threatened to revive, and did actually present itself in the person of the junior member for Northampton, who came up with the rest to take the oath in the ordinary fashion. Sir Michael Hicks-Beach was prepared to reopen the old controversy— had, indeed, written a letter to the Speaker submitting that Mr. Bradlaugh should not be allowed to take the oath. When

B

the member for Northampton came to the table, book in
hand, Sir Michael interposed, and proposed to discuss the
matter; but the Speaker ruled him out of order. The new
member thereupon took the oath in ordinary form, seated
himself quietly below the gangway, and thus, in commonplace
manner, closed a memorable episode in Parliamentary life.

Although the Conservatives were in a hopeless minority,
the Government of Lord Salisbury, in office at the time of the
General Election, still held the Treasury bench, at the mercy
of any combined move that might be made by the Liberals
and the serried phalanx under the leadership of Mr. Parnell.
Whenever these two powers closed their ranks the Government must inevitably be swept away. The crisis was not long
delayed. Amongst the amendments to the Address was one
moved by Mr. Jesse Collings, in favour of the form of assistance to the agricultural labourer that came to be known as
the allotment of three acres and a cow. On a division, which
took place on the 26th January, the Parnellites voting with
the Liberals, the amendment was carried by 329 votes to 250.
The Government being thus defeated by a majority of 79,
forthwith resigned. There was no alternative from Mr. Gladstone as successor, and he immediately formed a Government.

Home Rule.   It was evident from the first that the question
of Home Rule in Ireland must be dealt with,
and the air was full of rumours of a new and momentous
departure contemplated by Mr. Gladstone. At the outset
it appeared, whatever might be the course adopted, it
would, with two conspicuous exceptions, be supported by the
undivided force of the Liberal leaders. Lord Hartington,
who had shown some restlessness at Mr. Gladstone's closer
alliance with the Parnellites, did not accept office. But Mr.
Chamberlain was President of the Local Government Board in
the new Ministry, and the gentleman who was then still Mr.
George Trevelyan was Secretary for Scotland. Mr. John
Morley was Secretary for Ireland; Sir William Harcourt,
Chancellor of the Exchequer; Lord Rosebery, Foreign Secretary; Lord Granville at the Colonies; Earl Spencer, Lord
President of the Council; whilst Sir Farrer Herschell was
raised to the peerage and made Lord Chancellor. This

post, it is understood, was in the first case offered to Sir
Henry James; but that gentleman, also shying at the Irish
question, joined Lord Hartington in withdrawal from Ministerial life.

On the 8th of April, 1886, Mr. Gladstone, in a marvellous
speech that took three hours and a half in the delivery, unfolded his scheme of Home Rule for Ireland. A week earlier
the adoption of the scheme by a majority of the Cabinet had
been ominously marked by the resignation of Mr. Chamberlain and Mr. Trevelyan. The second reading of the Bill was
moved on the 10th of May, and by this time a Dissentient
Liberal party had been regularly organised, with Lord Hartington as its head and Mr. Chamberlain as its arm. On the
7th of June the House divided on the second reading of the
Home Rule Bill, and amid a scene of wild excitement it was
rejected by a majority of 30: 311 voting for the second
reading and 341 against. Mr. Forster died just three days
before the introduction of a measure which changed the
whole face of parties, breaking up the Liberal ranks and
relegating Mr. Gladstone to opposition for a period of six
years, during which Lord Hartington and Mr. Chamberlain
actively co-operated with Lord Salisbury in maintaining the
Conservatives in power.

A General
Election.
Defeated in the Commons, Mr. Gladstone de-
termined to appeal to the country, hopeful
that he would have placed at his disposal forces equal to the
task of overriding the new and unprecedented coalition of
Liberals and Conservatives. But the event disappointed his
expectations. When the poll was finally made up, the new
House of Commons was found to consist of 317 Conservatives, 74 Dissentient Liberals, 191 Liberals, and 84 Parnellites.
The Unionists, as the allied forces of Lord Hartington and
Lord Salisbury styled themselves, thus numbered 391; whilst
Liberals and Irish National members combined could muster
only 275, leaving Mr. Gladstone in a minority considerably
over 100. He at once resigned, and Lord Salisbury undertook
to form a new Government. Before doing so he entered into
communication with Lord Hartington, proposing that he
should assume the Premiership. This offer Lord Hartington

THE SPEAKER.

declined, though, as Lord Salisbury was able to assure the Conservative party meeting at the Carlton Club, he gave distinct assurance of his desire to provide an independent support to the new Government: a pledge which, as will be seen in the course of events, was faithfully fulfilled.

The Tory Ministry. When the new Cabinet was formed, Lord Salisbury was, of course, Prime Minister, but not Foreign Secretary, as had been expected. Sir Stafford Northcote, quitting the Commons, was made First Lord of the Treasury, holding the post with the title Earl of Iddesleigh. Lord Halsbury was Lord Chancellor; Viscount Cranbrook, Lord President of the Council; Mr. Henry Matthews, on the nomination of Lord Randolph Churchill, was Home Secretary; Lord Randolph himself was Chancellor of the Exchequer and Leader of the House; Mr. Stanhope answered for the Colonies; Mr. W. H. Smith was Secretary of State for War; Lord Cross looked after India; Mr. Arthur Balfour, as little as the House knowing what lay before him in the near distance, was Secretary for Scotland; Lord George Hamilton presided at the Admiralty; an old friend, Mr. Gibson, now Lord Ashbourne, was Lord Chancellor of Ireland; Sir M. Hicks-Beach was Chief Secretary for Ireland; Lord Stanley presided at the Board of Trade, and Lord John Manners was comfortably provided for in the Chancellory of the Duchy of Lancaster.

Parliament met, as has been stated, on the 5th of August, Mr. Arthur Peel being elected Speaker, the second time within seven months — "thrice within thirty months," as he reminded hon. members, standing on the steps of the Chair and humbly placing himself at the disposal of the House. The Session did not last long, the new Parliament being prorogued on the 25th of September. Only formal or absolutely necessary business was despatched. But Lord Randolph Churchill found opportunity to display himself in a new light, bringing to the discharge of the duties of Leader of the House a courteousness of manner and a display of tact which agreeably surprised onlookers.

SESSION OF 1886.[*]

JANUARY.

12. Tues.—Mr. Arthur Peel elected Speaker.
13. Wed.—Mr. Speaker. Royal approval of His Statement (Parliamentary Oath). Members took the Oath.
14. Thurs.—Members took the Oath.
15. Fri.—Ditto.
20. Wed.—H. M. Speech. Address. First Debate thereon.
21. Thurs.—H. M. Speech. Address. Second Debate.
25. Mon.—H. M. Speech. Address. Third Debate. Amendment (Revenue of India), Mr. Hunter. Withdrawn. Amendment (State of Agriculture), Mr. J. W. Barclay. Division—For, 163. Against, 311.
26. Tues.—H. M. Speech. Fourth Debate. Amendment (Agricultural Labourers' Allotments), Mr. Jesse Collings. Division—For, 329. Against, 250.
28. Thurs.—Resignation of Ministry.

FEBRUARY.

1. Mon.—Resignation of Ministry.
18. Thurs.—Ministerial Statement. Mr. Gladstone. H. M. Speech. Fifth Debate. Amendment (Crofters), Mr. Macfarlane. Division—For, 104. Against, 291. Report of Address agreed to.
19. Fri.—Supply. Mr. Courtney took the Chair. Supplementary Estimates.
22. Mon.—Parliamentary Procedure. Rebel Committee appointed, Mr. Gladstone. East Burmah (Expenses). Resolution, Sir U. K. Shuttleworth.
23. Tues.—Imperial Revenue. Resolution, Sir J. McKenna. Employers Liability Bill. Mr. A. O'Connor. Read 1°.
24. Wed.—Tenure of Town Houses (Ireland) Bill. Mr. Crilly. Withdrawn.
25. Thurs.—Supply: Supplementary Estimates. Crofters (Scotland) No. 2 Bill. Mr. Fraudyn. Leave given.
26. Fri.—Metropolitan Police. Motion, Mr. James Stuart.

[*] By permission of Messrs. Vacher, I supplement the record of each Session with the admirable calendar of events given in their well-known "Parliamentary Guide."

MARCH.

APRIL.

MAY.

MAY (continued).

21. Fri.—Government of Ireland Bill. 2nd Reading. Fifth Debate.
24. Mon.—Supply: Civil Service Estimates. Vote on Account, &c.
25. Tue.—Derby Day. Adjournment, Mr. Labouchere. Division — For, 251, Against, 164. Government of Ireland Bill. 2nd Reading. Sixth Debate.

27. Thurs.—Arms (Ireland) Bill. Committee. Bill reported. Adjournment of House. Ventilation, Lord R. Churchill.
28. Fri.—Government of Ireland Bill. 2nd Reading. Seventh Debate.
31. Mon.—Ditto. Ditto. Eighth Debate.

JUNE.

1. Tue.—Government of Ireland Bill. 2nd Reading. Ninth Debate.
2. Wed.—Registration of Voters (Ireland) Bill. Mr. Dillon. Debate adjourned.
3. Thurs.—Government of Ireland Bill. 2nd Reading. Tenth Debate.
4. Fri.—Ditto. Ditto. Eleventh Debate.
7. Mon.—Ditto. Ditto. Twelfth Debate. Division — For, 311, Against, 341.
10. Thurs.—Ministerial Statement. Mr. Gladstone. Supply: Navy Estimates.
11. Fri.—Adjournment of House. Crofters Compensation, Dr. R. Macdonald. Supply: Civil Service Estimates. Vote on Account. Army Estimates. Vote on Account.

16. Wed.—Supply: Report. Returning Officers Expenses (Scotland) Bill. Considered.
17. Thurs.—Appropriation Bill. 2nd Reading.
18. Fri.—Ditto. Committee.
21. Mon.—Ditto. 3rd Reading.
24. Wed.—East India. Revenue Account. Resolution. Municipal Franchise (Ireland) Act. Continuance. Bill reported. Motion for 3rd Reading objected to by Mr. Speaker. Tramways, Orders in Council (Ireland) Bill. Passed. Parliamentary Returning Officers Expenses Bill. Lords Amendment agreed to.
25. Thurs.—Prorogation.

SESSION II., 1886.

AUGUST.

5. Thurs.—Mr. Arthur Peel elected Speaker.
6. Fri.—Mr. Speaker. Royal approval of. Members took the Oath. H.M. Commission. Vacancies in Royal Commission. New Writs issued.
9. Mon.—Members took the Oath.
10. Tue.—Ditto.
19. Thurs.—H.M. Speech. New Members took the Oath. Standing Orders. Division on Order, interchange of Peers, &c.—For, 138, Against, 138. H.M. Speech. Address. First Debate. Adjourned.
20. Fri.—H.M. Speech. Address. Second Debate.
21. Sat.—H.M. Speech. Address. Third Debate.

24. Tue.—H.M. Speech. Address. Fourth Debate. Amendment (Payment of Rent by Irish Tenant Farmers), Mr. Parnell.
25. Wed.—H.M. Speech. Address. Fifth Debate.
26. Thurs.—Adjournment. Sir R. Fowler's appointment, Mr. E. N. Fowler. H.M. Speech. Address. Sixth Debate.
27. Fri.—H.M. Speech. Address. Seventh Debate. Division on Mr. Parnell's Amendment—For, 181, Against, 304.
30. Mon.—H.M. Speech. Address. Eighth Debate. Amendment (Distress), Mr. A. O'Connor. Division—For, 115, Against, 202.
31. Tue.—H.M. Speech. Address. Ninth Debate. Amendment, Employers (Scotland), Mr. Esslemont. Division—For, 121, Against, 204.

SEPTEMBER.

1. Wed.—H.M. Speech. Address. Tenth Debate. Amendment (Belfast Riots), Mr. Sexton. Debate adjourned.
2. Thurs.—H.M. Speech. Eleventh Debate. Division on Mr. Sexton's Amendment—For, 127, Against, 222. Address agreed to. Debate on Report adjourned.
3. Fri.—H.M. Speech. Address. Report. Amendment (Speeches of Chancellor of Exchequer), &c., Mr. Labouchere. Division—For, 119, Against, 202. Report agreed to. Report against tax.
6. Mon.—Supply. Mr. Courtney took the Chair. Army Estimates. First Sitting.
7. Tue.—Supply: Army Estimates. Second Sitting. Ireland Inquiry Bill. Mr. Attorney-General for Ireland. Read 1st.

8. Wed.—Supply: Navy Estimates. Third Sitting. (Fourth Sitting)
9. Thurs.—Ditto. Civil Service Estimates.
10. Fri.—Ditto. Ditto. Fifth Sitting.
13. Mon.—Ditto. Ditto. Sixth Sitting.
14. Tue.—Ditto. Ditto. Seventh Sitting.
15. Wed.—Ditto. Ditto. Eighth Sitting.
16. Thurs.—Ditto. Ditto. Ninth Sitting.
17. Fri.—Ditto. Ditto. Tenth Sitting.
18. Sat.—Ditto. Report. Appropriation Bill brought in.
20. Mon.—Tenants Relief (Ireland) Bill. Mr. Parnell. 2nd Reading. Debate adjourned. Appropriation Bill. Committee.
21. Tue.—Appropriation Bill. Committee. Tenants Relief (Ireland) Bill. Division on 2nd Reading—For, 202, Against, 297.
22. Wed.—Appropriation Bill. Read 3rd.
23. Thurs.—Prorogation.

CHAPTER II.

COERCION AND THE LAND BILL.

A New Leader in the Commons—The Closure—The Parnell Commission.

1887.   THE Session of 1887 opened on the 27th of January, and, with the exception of brief recesses at Easter and Whitsuntide, sat into the middle of September. Its progress was marked by a succession of turbulent scenes, through which an Irish Land Bill and a Crimes Bill were forced. In addition, there were added to the Statute Book, at the instance of the Government, the Allotments Act, the Mines Regulations Act, the Truck Act, and the Merchandise Marks Act. Personal changes that had taken place during the recess were marked in both Houses. In the Lords, the Earl of Iddesleigh's place was vacant, his placid life having closed with a touch of tragedy. The Commons, who had separated in the autumn with Lord Randolph Churchill Leader of the House and Chancellor of the Exchequer, found the noble lord on their return a private member, seated at the corner of the bench behind his former colleagues. Tribute was paid in both Houses to the memory of Lord Iddesleigh, and Lord Randolph Churchill seized the earliest opportunity of explaining how it came to pass that he no longer served Her Majesty at the Treasury.

That the Opposition were in fighting mood was proved on the motion for the Address. A series of amendments were moved, one by Mr. Parnell challenging the policy of the Government in Ireland. This received the full support of the Opposition, and after six days' debate was negatived by 352 votes to 246, a division interesting as fixing the Government majority at this date at 106. Lord Randolph Churchill contributed to the debate the remark that the Dissentient Liberals were a kind of crutch, to be thrown aside when the Government should be strong enough to walk alone.

A new leader in the Commons.   Mr. W. H. Smith, who had succeeded Lord Randolph in the Leadership of the House, found it necessary to invoke the Closure in order to carry the

Address. Before the Session was many weeks old it became clear that the power of the Closure must be strengthened in order to make it really operative. After a stout fight it was, at the instance of the Government, agreed that the Closure might be carried by a bare majority provided 200 voted for it. It was further stipulated that before the Closure was proposed the consent of the Chairman should be obtained. The way thus cleared, the Crimes Bill was brought in, introducing Mr. Arthur Balfour in his new office as Chief Secretary for Ireland. When the new Parliament was sworn in, he had, as noted, been Secretary for Scotland, Sir M. H. Beach being at the Irish office. Ill-health compelled Sir Michael's temporary withdrawal from Parliamentary life, an accident which at this critical stage led to the momentous event, rich with unforeseen consequences, of the committal of Ireland to Mr. Balfour's care.

The Closure. The Crimes Bill led to prolonged and angry discussion, which Mr. W. H. Smith, making his first "pounce" under the new Closure rule, brought to an abrupt conclusion. When the Closure was carried, the Opposition, English and Irish, headed by Mr. Gladstone, and accompanied by Mr. Parnell, walked out of the House. The incident arose on a motion for leave to introduce the Bill, and the Opposition declining at this stage to take further part in the business, the Bill was forthwith brought in and read a first time. This abstention from debate was, however, not long maintained. The second reading was carried only after debate which, commencing on the 5th of April, concluded on the 18th, whilst the Committee was forced through only by the extreme measure of closuring debate on the sixth clause, the remaining clauses being added to the Bill without discussion.

In the meanwhile an Irish Land Bill had been introduced in the Lords, through which it quickly passed. But the Commons were not ready to take it in hand till the 4th of July, and it passed its final stages only on the eve of the Prorogation. The Session closed amid a scene of a kind which repetition had caused to pall on the taste, Mr. Cunninghame Graham and Mr. E. Harrington succeeding in getting themselves suspended on the discussion on the Appropriation Bill, the very last opportunity the Session provided.

The Parnell Commission.   The Session was memorable among other things for the commencement of the movement which led to the appointment of the Parnell Commission. On the 2nd of May the *Times* published an article accusing Mr. Parnell of wilful and deliberate falsehood in respect of a statement he had made touching his connection with P. J. Sheridan. Sir Charles Lewis, avowedly anxious that Mr. Parnell should have opportunity of clearing his character, denounced this as a breach of privilege, and moved that the printers of the *Times* be summoned to attend at the Bar. This was opposed by the Government, who suggested that the Irish members should bring an action against the *Times* for libel arising out of publication of what were subsequently proved to be forged letters, and proffering the assistance of the Attorney-General to conduct the prosecution. This offer was declined, and a motion made by Mr. Gladstone for a Select Committee to inquire into the charges of the *Times* was rejected by 317 votes against 231. Here for the time the subject dropped.

Parliament was prorogued on the 16th of September.

SESSION OF 1887.

JANUARY.

5. Thurs.—Personal Explanation. Lord Randolph Churchill.

H. M. Speech. Address thereon. First Debate.

28. Fri.—H. M. Speech. Address thereon. Second Debate,

31. Mon.—Ditto. Ditto. Third Debate,

FEBRUARY.

1. Tues.—H. M. Speech. Address. Fourth Debate.

2. Wed.—Ditto. Ditto. Fifth Debate.

3. Thurs.—Ditto. Ditto. Sixth Debate,

4. Fri.—Ditto. Ditto. Amendment (Egypt), Mr. Cæsar. Division—For, 67. Against, 210. Seventh Debate.

7. Mon.—H. M. Speech. Address. Amendment (Redress of Laws, &c., Ireland), Mr. Parnell. Eighth Debate.

8. Tues.—Ditto. Ditto. Ninth Debate.

9. Wed.—Ditto. Ditto. Tenth Debate,

10. Thurs.—Ditto. Ditto. Eleventh Debate.

11. Fri.—Ditto. Ditto. Division on Mr. Parnell's Amendment—For, 245. Against, 352. Twelfth Debate.

14. Mon.—H. M. Speech. Address. Amendment (Agricultural Holders, Northumberland), Mr. Cadzow. Division—For, — . Against, 446. Amendments; Great Britain (Local Government, Rivers, &c.), Cozens-Hardy. Withdrawn. Thirteenth Debate.

15. Tues.—H. M. Speech. Address. Amendment, Crofters (Scotland), Mr. Cameron. Fourteenth Debate.

16. Wed.—H. M. Speech. Address. Division on Mr. Commons's Amendment; For, — . Against, 253. Fifteenth Debate.

17. Thurs.—Motion for Adjournment. Jury Packing, Mr. Dillon. Ruled out of Order.

FEBRUARY (continued).

Business of House (Priority to Rules of Procedure). Resolution, Mr. W. H. Smith.

17. H. M. Speech. Address. Amendment, Working Classes (Distress), Mr. Cox. On Mr. Speaker's interposition, Question put for Closure of Debate on Amendments. Division—For, 291, Against, 41. Division on Amendment—For, [illegible], Against, 288. On Mr. Speaker's interposition, question put for Closure of Debate on Main Question—For, 290, Against, 74. Division on Main Question—For, 283, Against, 70.

18. Fri.—H. M. Speech. Report of Address; Amendments, Bulgaria, Mr. Labouchere; Barbavilla Trial; Mr. Tuite. Negatived. Address agreed to.

21. Mon.—Procedure. Rule I. Closure. First Debate.

22. Tues.—Ditto. Ditto. Second Debate.

23. Wed.—Ditto. Ditto. Third Debate.

24. Thurs.—Ditto. Ditto. Fourth Debate.

25. Fri.—Ditto. Ditto. Fifth Debate.

28. Mon.—Supply: Supplementary Estimates.

MARCH.

1. Tues.—London Corporation (Charges). Motion for Adjournment, Mr. Howell. Procedure. Rule I. Closure. Sixth Debate.

2. Wed.—Procedure. **Rule I.** Closure. Seventh Debate.

3. Thurs.—Supply: Supplementary Estimates.

4. Fri.—Procedure. Rule I. Closure. Eighth Debate.

7. Mon.—Supply: **Supplementary Estimates.**

8. Tues.—Procedure. Rule I. Closure. Ninth Debate.

9. Wed.—Ditto. Ditto. Tenth Debate.

10. Thurs.—Supply: Supplementary Estimates.

11. Fri.—Procedure. Rule **I. Closure.** Eleventh Debate.

14. Mon.—Supply: Army Estimates. Amendment (Coast Defences), Col. Duncan. Negatived.

Observations, Sir E. Reed.

15. Tues.—Procedure. Rule I. Closure. Twelfth Debate.

16. Wed.—Ditto. Ditto. Thirteenth Debate.

17. Thurs.—Supply: Navy Estimates. Amendment (Ships of War), Mr. Gourley. Negatived.

18. Fri.—Arrest of Father Keller. Motion for Adjournment, Mr. Dillon. Procedure. Rule I. Closure. Fourteenth Debate. Resolution agreed to. To be a Standing Order.

21. Mon.—Supply: Navy Estimates. Vote (Victuals and Clothing). Question put for Closure of Debate. Division—For, 207, Against, 54.

Civil Services, &c. Vote on Account. House adjourned at 1.30 p.m.

22. Tues.—Business of the House. Criminal Law Amendment (Ireland) Bill. Motion for Priority. Mr. W. H. Smith. Amendment, Mr. J. Morley. First Debate.

23. Wed.—Ditto. Ditto. Second Debate.

24. Thurs.—Ditto. Ditto. Third Debate.

25. Fri.—Ditto. Ditto. Division on Amendment—For, 180, Against, 349. Resolution agreed to.

28. Mon.—Criminal Law Amendment (Ireland) Bill. Motion for leave, Mr. A. J. Balfour. First Debate.

29. Tues.—Ditto. Ditto. Second Debate.

30. Wed.—Ditto. Ditto. Third Debate.

31. Thurs.—Ditto. Ditto. Fourth Debate.

APRIL.

1. Fri.—Outrage. Motion for Adjournment, Dr. Clark.

Criminal Law Amendment (Ireland) Bill. Adjourned Debate. Motion for Adjournment of Debate, Mr. T. O'Connor. Division on Motion for Leave—For, 251, Against, 361. Motion for Adjournment of House, Mr. Dillwyn. Division—For, 251, Against, 361. Motion for Closure of Debate, Mr. W. H. Smith. Division—For, 361, Against, 253. Bill ordered.

4. Mon.—Reflections on the Speaker by Mr. Conybeare. Question, Mr. Chaplin.

Supply: Civil Service Estimates. Harbours Loans. Amendment, Mr. Redhead. Mr. Deputy Speaker took the Chair. Committee deferred.

5. Tues.—Criminal Law Amendment (Ireland) Bill. Mr. A. J. Balfour. 2nd Reading. Amendment, Sir W. Harcourt. First Debate.

6. Wed.—Ditto. Ditto. Second Debate.

7. Thurs.—House adjourned.

12. Tues.—Mr. Speaker returned to the Chair. Criminal Law Amendment (Ireland) Bill. Adjourned Debate on 2nd Reading. Third Debate.

13. Wed.—Ditto. Ditto. **Fourth Debate.**

14. Thurs.—Ditto. Ditto. **Fifth Debate.**

15. Fri.—Criminal Law Amendment (Ireland) Bill. Mr. Healy suspended. Sixth Debate.

18. Mon.—Ditto. Ditto. Adjourned Debate. Division on Amendment—For, 370, Against, 269.

19. Tues.—Harbours of Refuge. Motion, Mr. Fox. Division—For, 91, Against, 85.

20. Wed.—Police Force Enfranchisement Bill. Mr. Bartlett [illegible]. Committed.

Land Tenure (Scotland) Bill. Mr. J. W. Barclay. Motion for 2nd Reading.

21. Thurs.—Ways and Means. Financial Statement, Mr. Goschen.

22. Fri.—Personal Explanation, The Marquis of Hartington.

Supply. Amendment (Market Rights), Mr. Bradlaugh.

25. Mon.—Ways and Means. **Resolutions** agreed to.

26. Tues.—Criminal Law Amendment (Ireland) Bill. Motion for Committee; Amendment, Mr. H. T. Reid. First Debate.

27. Wed.—Ditto. Ditto. Second Debate.

28. Thurs.—Ditto. Ditto. Division on Amendment—For, 216, Against, 341.

29. Fri.—Ditto. Ditto. Committee, First Sitting.

MAY.

JUNE.

JULY.

AUGUST.

1. Mon.—Irish [illegible] Land Bill. Committee. Sixth Section.
2. Tues.—Personal Explanation, Mr. [illegible]. Irish Land Law Bill. Committee. Seventh Sitting.
3. Wed.—[illegible] Ditto. **Eighth Sitting.** Bill reported.
4. Thurs.—Supply: Army Services.
5. Fri.—Irish Land Law Bill. Considered;
6. Sat.—Ditto. Ditto.
8. Mon.—Supply: Civil Services.
9. Tues.—Ditto. Ditto. Technical Education Bill. **Sir W. H.** [illegible] Ditto. 3rd Reading.
10. Wed.—Lunacy (Scotland) Districts Bill. 2nd Reading. Sheriff of Lanarkshire Bill. 2nd Reading.
11. Thurs.—[illegible]. Motion for Adjournment of House, Mr. [illegible]. Supply: Civil Services. Labourers Allotments Bill. 2nd Reading.
12. Fri.—Irish Land Law Bill. Consideration of Lords Amendments.
13. Sat.—Supply: Civil Services. Education.
14. Mon.—Coal Mines Bill. Committee.
16. [illegible]—Ditto. Ditto.
17. Wed.—Coal Mines Bill. Committee.
19. Thurs.—Irish Land Law Bill. Consideration of Lords Amendments.
20. Fri.—Labourers' Allotments Bill. Committee.
21. Sat.—Supply: Civil Services.
23. Mon.—Ditto. Ditto.
24. Tues.—Ditto. Ditto.
25. Wed.—Ditto. Ditto.
26. Thurs.—Irish National League (Proclamation). Address thereon, Mr. W. [illegible] Redmond. Debate adjourned.
27. Fri.—Labourers' Allotments Bill. Committee. Irish National League (Proclamation). Address thereon. Division—For, [illegible]. Against, 272. Ways and Means. Order read. Motion for Adjournment of the House, Mr. H. Fowler. Mr. Speaker's ruling. Motion withdrawn.
28. Sat.—Labourers' Allotments Bill. Committee.
30. Mon.—Supply: Civil Services.
31. Tues.—Ditto. Ditto.
[illegible]. Wed.—Ditto. Ditto.

SEPTEMBER.

1. [illegible]—Meeting, &c., Ballymena. Motion for Adjournment, Mr. [illegible] Davis thereon. [illegible]. Against, [illegible]. Supply: Civil Services.
2. Fri.—Ditto. Ditto.
3. Sat.—Coal Mines Bill. **Considered.** Read 3°.
4. Mon.—Supply: Civil Services. Labourers Allotments Bill. Considered.
6. Tues.—Supply: Civil Services.
7. Wed.—Ditto. Navy Supplies.
8. Thurs.—Ditto. Navy and Army Services.
9. Fri.—Ways and Means. Report. Appropriation Bill. Read 1°.
Registration Laws Consolidation Bill. Committed.
10. Fri.—Expiring Laws Continuance Acts Bill. Considered. Appropriation Bill. [illegible] Bill. Observations. Division on Second Reading—For, [illegible]. Against, [illegible].
13. Mon.—Appropriation Bill. [illegible] Bill. Observations. [illegible]. [Coal] Mines Bill. Lords' Amendments considered.
14. Tues.—Appropriation Bill. **Read 3°.**
15. Fri.—Prorogation.

SESSION 1888.

CHAPTER III.

CHANGES AND FAMILIAR THINGS.

After Three Years—Changes—Stafford Northcote —" Bobby " Bourke—Why
Addington?—The Fourth Party—Opening Day—Col. Hughes-Hallett—
Welcome—Disappointment—An Unexpected Friend—The Embattled Pyne
—Arresting the Wrong Man—Ominous Quiet—Gilhooly no more.

Feb. 9.—After three years. IT is not quite three years since I last sat on the Cross Benches at the opening day of the Session. Only three years, and yet how changed are the place and its conditions! When, on the 19th of February, 1885, the House resumed a Session which had opened in the previous October Mr. Gladstone was at the head of a powerful Ministry, and what seemed an invulnerable majority. Stafford Northcote sat on the opposite bench with the first of a series of Votes of Censure in his pocket, the subject being the sad Soudan. On the second bench below the gangway, on the Ministerial side, sat Mr. John Morley, not yet " right honourable," and left pretty much alone among foremost Liberals in his advocacy of Home Rule. Mr. Gladstone was supported on the Treasury bench by his stalwart lieutenant, Lord Hartington; his old friend and fellow-labourer, Mr. Bright ; his trusted disciples, Sir Charles Dilke and Mr. Chamberlain, the latter not yet having fulminated his scathing denunciation of " a stop-gap Government," at the date uncreated ; his eminent legal satellites, Sir William Harcourt and Sir Henry James. Lord Randolph Churchill was below the gangway in command of his concentrated forces—two all told for regular duty, with Mr. Arthur Balfour, unmindful of the great future awaiting him, lending occasional assistance. Just behind the Fourth Party, within convenient hand grasp of its chief, sat Mr. Tim Healy, and the rest of the " bhoys." Before a week of the new Session was over the Closure was put into operation for the first time,

and incidentally Mr. O'Brien was suspended.   There seems
nothing new in all this, except the relative position of parties.
It was Mr. Gladstone who at that time of day "pounced," and
it was the Conservatives whose diminished forces were
strengthened by the Irish vote. The only thing unchanged
is that it is still the Irish Party who are pounced upon.

Changes.   The caprice of he constituency, the call to the
                 peerage, and the hand of Death have among
them wrought many changes since the day distant, as the

PETER RYLANDS.

almanack counts, only three years. Beresford Hope, whose
familiar figure was in later times transferred from the corner
seat below the gangway to the corresponding position on the
front bench, has passed away. Newdegate, another of the
old guard, has been finally removed from his watch over the
higher interests of Church and Constitution. Peter Rylands

will never more greet with friendly slap on the back members forgathering on the opening day of a new Session. Sir William M'Arthur's place knows him no more, and never again will Colonel Tottenham, with his eye fixed on Mr. Gladstone, talk at the Irish members seated below the gangway on his left flank. Another Irish member of quite a different stamp who has joined the majority is Mr. Blake. Blake was doubtless well enough known in his own part of Ireland, but as far as reputation on this side of the Channel is concerned he belonged entirely to the House of Commons. Here he was known as the possessor of a rich fund of quiet humour only too rarely poured forth to the delight of the select few who chanced to be present when he rose in the middle of a dull debate. He will always be remembered for his story of the correspondence that took place between himself and a revered uncle who was unhappily addicted to taking six tumblers of whisky toddy daily. Mr. Blake, as early one morning he confidentially told the House of Commons, wrote a dutiful letter, urging his esteemed relative to cut off the supply, assuring him that such a course would be the means of lengthening his days. To which the uncle replied that, struck by the friendly advice, he last Friday had given up whisky toddy ; adding, " I believe you are right, my boy, as to my days being lengthened, for bedad it was the longest day I ever remember."

Stafford North-
cote.   Last, but not least, among those who sat in the House on the 10th of February, 1885, and will never be seen there again, is Stafford Northcote. He had left the House for another place before the final parting came. But his name will ever be associated with the House of Commons, where he dwelt so long, where he was so universally esteemed, and where in the very last days, on the eve of the triumph of the party he had faithfully served, he suffered so much.

> He has outsoared the shadow of our night ;
> Envy and calumny, and hate and pain,
> And that unrest which men miscall delight,
> Can touch him not and torture not again.
> From the contagion of the world's slow stain

He is secure, and now can never mourn
A heart grown cold, a head grown grey in vain.

STAFFORD NORTHCOTE.

"Bobby" Bourke. Other translations, equally unforeseen, but not so saddening, have taken place since that far-off February day.   Who would have thought, looking upon "Bobby" Bourke as he sat in modest retirement on the front bench, that when Parliament opened in 1888 he would be found grateful for the presence of the punkah, Governor of Madras, and Baron Connemara in the peerage of Great Britain?   I was reading about him the other day on a triumphal passage through his Presidency, and how the people of Pochucotta, delighting in his genial presence, agreed that "as Lord Dalhousie was the greatest of Indian Viceroys, and Lord

c

Mayo the most popular, a Governor who was the son-in-law
of one and brother of the other possessed special claims on
their regard and consideration."

Sir Richard Cross has carried his Grand Cross to the House
of Lords, and though he rules over India is happily spared to
imbue one branch of the Legislature with the light of his
bodily presence. Colonel Stanley, first partially disguised as
Sir Frederick, and then, as far as the House of Commons is
concerned, wholly obliterated as Lord Stanley of Preston,
keeps his old colleague company on the Ministerial bench in
the other House, pending his transference to the vice-regal
chair at Ottawa. Thither, too, has gone Sir James M'Garel
Hogg, whose stormy orations, read in answer to questions and
delivered with side glances of withering import, will never
more thrill the House of Commons. Even in his translation
Sir James invests himself with a subtle atmosphere of terrorism
by taking a title (Lord Magheramorne) which few can pronounce and none can spell. Gone, too, is Mr. Sclater-Booth
(Lord Basing), who, remembering the denunciation by Lord
Randolph Spencer-Churchill of mediocrities with double-
barrelled names, was careful when he changed his to take a
title of bi-syllabic construction and unassuming orthography.
That doughty border chieftain Earl Percy now figures in the
House of Peers as Lord Lovaine. He thus rejoins an old
companion (Earl Wemyss), long known in the House of
Commons as Lord Elcho, now acknowledged as the apostle to
the House of Lords of what Lord Granville wittily called " the
Cross Bench mind." We still have in the House of Commons
a Lord Elcho, as we have a Sir Stafford Northcote. But the
change is in either case complete.

Why Addington? Another old friend disguised under an unfamiliar title is Lord Addington. Why Addington, one wonders? There was an Addington well known in
the House of Commons in Pitt's time. He was once Speaker,
and developed into Prime Minister. It was he of whom
Sheridan said he flattered himself he might continue to act as
Prime Minister as he had acted as Speaker, and could say
" strangers will withdraw " when he saw Foreign Powers
annexing small States, and could arrange a quarrel over the

Rhine frontier by crying aloud, " Germans to the Right, French to the Left!" One would have understood Mr. J. G. Hubbard if, casting about for a title on being raised to the peerage and attracted by the jingle of the syllables, he should have called himself Lord Paddington. But he is Lord Addington, and a strange fate has led him in his declining years into the Chamber of the Legislature in which the Budget of the day is almost the only Parliamentary topic that may not be made the subject of an amendment.

The Fourth Party. Much has changed as far as persons and parties are concerned; but the House of Commons readily adapts itself to variety, and comes up to its work at the opening of this new Session as fresh and as vigorous as if in the meantime no one had died and no one been buried in the House of Lords. The Fourth Party is a memory. Like a comet passing through the heavens, it has broken up into

THE FOURTH PARTY.

fragments by the force of its own velocity. Lord Randolph Churchill has been a Cabinet Minister, and now, travelling on his holiday, hobs-and-nobs with the Czar of all the Russias. Mr. Gorst is " Sir John," Her Majesty's Under-Secretary of State for India. Mr. Balfour is the rising hope of Toryism, and can put an Irish member in prison at his pleasure. Sir Henry Wolff has taken his ticket for Teheran, and presently, happy in the fortuitous change, will be telling his pleasant stories in the ear of the Shah. We have a new clerk at the table, a new Sergeant-at-Arms in the Chair, a new Chief

Inspector in the lobby, a new Leader on the Treasury bench,
a new party in politics, and the same Grand Old Man eager,
restless, spoiling for the fight, in the seat of the Leader of the
Opposition. The same Mace is on the table; the Speaker
seems to wear the same wig
and gown that generations of
members have known; "the
Clerk will now proceed to
read the Orders of the Day"
in precisely the same un-
emotional manner as they
have been read since George
the Third was king, and there
is really nothing new under
the sun.

Opening day. It is the unexpected that
happens in the House of
Commons as elsewhere. The
opening of the Session
to-day was looked forward
to with the certainty that
it would be marked by a
succession of "scenes" that
should eclipse anything yet
done even upon this classic
ground. The Government,
afeared at the prospect,
issued an urgent whip, and
the alarm was so loyally
shared by their supporters
that at four o'clock, when

"ONE OF THE HEROES OF THE CIVIL
WAR IN IRELAND."

the Speaker took the chair, the House was crowded, and
the lobby held a kind of overflow meeting. Amongst the
rumours on every tongue at the opening of business was that
the Government had determined to arrest one or two of the
Irish members who are here on bail. Mr. Pyne, whose long
retirement in his castle had invested him with quite unusual
interest, appeared early on the scene, having strategically

broken through the cordon of police that more than ever
closely watch the approaches to the House. For months
of the recess he has been beleaguered in his quaint Irish
home with the trenches filled with water, the drawbridge
up, and supplies taken in by a window in the battlements,
the police, with the warrant for his arrest in their pockets,
looking on helplessly. He is so little known, that few
recognised in the high-shouldered, ill-dressed man sitting on
a back bench one of the heroes of the civil war in Ireland.
Rising to give notice of a motion, he was hailed with exultant
shouts by the Irish members.

Col. Hughes-
Hallett.

Colonel Hughes-Hallett turned up very early in
the new Session, walking in shortly after
luncheon, wearing in his button-hole the white flower of a

blameless life. Hughes-Hallett was a year ago one of the most widely-known men in the House of Commons; he knew everybody, and was always ready to chat. It was curious to see how carefully he was avoided to-day. He made no advances to anyone, and exceedingly few spoke to him. Evidently determined to brazen out the scene, he took his seat immediately behind W. H. Smith, thus constituting himself the representative of the Conservative Party closest at the heels of the leaders.

Welcome.   All through the preliminary proceedings, which were as long as they could be made, the House was in a state of expectation of the something going to happen. Prominent Ministers and ex-Ministers arrived, and met with varying receptions. Mr. Smith, who came in pretty early, blushed rosy red when a hearty cheer greeted him. It was nothing equal in volume to what Lord Hartington received from the Conservative Party, when a quarter of an hour later he strolled in with one hand in his trousers pocket and the other swinging his hat. He found only Mr. Heneage in possession of the section of the front bench appropriated by his little party. Sir Henry James, coming in later and finding no room there, took a seat on the bench behind. Mr. Balfour, oddly enough, was allowed to enter without recognition —an omission handsomely made up when later he rose to give notice of a Bill. Then the Conservatives raised a prolonged cheer, meant to be a demonstration in favour of coercion. This was good; but the loudest, longest, and most enthusiastic cheer of the sitting was reserved for Mr. Gladstone, who came in while Ministers were still tabling their notices of Bills to be introduced. He looked worried, and thinner than when I saw him last before the recess. Like Hughes-Hallett—the sole thing in common between them, it may be presumed—he wore a bunch of white flowers in his button-hole. There were quite a batch of new members waiting to take their seats, the gracious presence of Mr. Biggar being accidentally made known as he walked up to the table to introduce Mr. Kilbride.

Disappointment.   Members began to ask when the fun was going to commence. It seemed imminent when the

Speaker rose with a batch of letters in his hand and read forth the several contents, which officially informed him of the imprisonment of quite a company of Irish members. Still, except for a little burst of ironical laughter here and there, the Irish members made no sign. Now was their time or never, and it becoming evident that there was no intention of movement on their part, the House began to empty. The fact is, there never was any foundation for the scare in Ministerial circles which led to the issue of the whip. Mr. Healy, who was said to be coming over to raise the question of privilege, is in Ireland, likely to remain there for some time, being much engaged in lucrative business at the Bar. Mr. Parnell will in due time give notice of an amendment to the Address, which will raise the whole Irish Question, and, in the meantime, the Irish members are on their good behaviour.

An unexpected friend. The event of the evening, since there were to be no scenes, was the speech of Mr. Gladstone. It was seven o'clock when he rose, not a favourable hour for a great speech. When it was known the Liberal chief was on his legs, the benches, but lately empty, rapidly filled; and Mr. Gladstone had a packed audience for the first half-hour of his speech. By that time it became apparent that no fight was imminent. On the Irish Question he was trenchant, to the full expectation of the Irish members; but when he had disposed of that part of his speech, and came to the other paragraphs of the Address, he was almost grandfatherly in his patronage of the surprised and delighted Ministry. He went so far as to declare that their programme was conceived in a spirit above party considerations, and promised the friendliest consideration for their measures. After this, it becoming clearly apparent that there was no fight in the front, members rapidly disappeared, and the first night of the Session closed at a reasonable hour in a decidedly humdrum fashion.

Feb. 10.—The re-entitled Pyne. Pyne has been run to earth at last, and passes to-night in custody. He was nearly caught this morning, but got away after an exciting chase through

the silent streets. The difficulty in the way of the police is
their legal inability to arrest a member actually within the
precincts of the House. As long as Pyne remained within
the walls of Westminster he was in sanctuary; the moment
he passed outside the boundary they let slip the dogs of war,
and the police had something like the pleasurable excitement
of a fox-hunt. They missed him this morning, but were,
therefore, the more sharply on the look-out this afternoon.
Doubtless if he had been content to stop away from the House
he would still have been at liberty. He is not personally
known to the London police, and strategic efforts made
yesterday to secure for his pursuers a good look at him were
frustrated by the watchfulness of his colleagues. It has been
a funny game for a powerful Government to play, with policemen all about, peering in at doors and from galleries of the
House of Commons to catch a look at the man they were to
arrest.

Just on the stroke of four this afternoon Pyne approached
the House from Westminster Bridge, and was walking briskly
down the steps by the Clock Tower, that being the quietest
approach, when he was recognised, arrested, and instantly
marched off. A minute later he would have been in sanctuary;
he was just outside, and is now on his way to gaol. He
was quite prepared to meet his fate, which has been hanging
over him for many weeks; but he is triumphant, inasmuch
as he has carried out his full intention, which was to evade
arrest until he should be taken whilst the House was sitting.

Arresting the
wrong man. Gilhooly is another of the Irish members who
through the recess has evaded capture. He
came up for the opening of the Session, and the police have
been hot on his track. They thought they had him this
morning; but, instead, they collared poor Patrick O'Brien,
who on his own account has been sufficiently often arrested
to expect to enjoy some little immunity when in London.

Whilst amazed Patrick was being haled to prison under
the idea that he was Gilhooly, that hon. member was
comfortably eating his lunch in the House of Commons,
whither he had repaired at an early hour of the day. He is
quite safe at this moment, and can defy his pursuers till the

House is up; but it is pretty certain that when that time arrives his game will also be up. There are policemen everywhere, posted at all available egress from the building. They lurk about every doorway, and hide in the shadows of the buttresses. Gilhooly means to have a run for it, but the odds are hopelessly against him.

Ominous quiet. If it were not for this curious game going on, in some of its aspects like the policeman scene in a pantomime, the House would be an intolerably dull place. The oldest member cannot recall, certainly for the last thirteen years, any Session which opened so flatly. There are various reasons to account for this. One is the absence of the principal leaders of the Irish Party. Parnell has not been here to-night. Dillon, O'Brien, Healy, and other active spirits have not yet put in an appearance. Biggar is on guard, and his variously intoned " Hear, hear," with its manifold meanings, resounds from time to time through the almost empty House. But, as long experience has shown, Biggar is nothing when left to himself. The few Parnellites present are exclusively engaged keeping watch over Gilhooly, warning him when the bull's eye of the police is turned upon him. At the present moment the hunted member is sitting in the library writing what his humorous companions report is his last will and testament.

Feb. 17, 1.15 a.m. —Gilhooly no more. Gilhooly was arrested just now, as he left the House. Everything was arranged between Parnellites and police with comical amicability. Gilhooly, escorted by a crowd of Irish members, entered Palace Yard from the usual members' exit. As soon as he left the Yard he was arrested. But the police graciously consented to his going over to the Westminster Palace Hotel before setting forth for Dublin in custody. So the Irish members, forming a guard of honour, escorted him at a slow march to the hotel, singing by the way, " God save Ireland ! "

CHAPTER IV.

MR. BALFOUR IN HARNESS.

Mr. Arthur Balfour—Mr. John Morley—Police Protection—"Face to Face in the Commons!"—Mr. Balfour's Reply—Mr. Gladstone Angry—Mr. Goschen in High Spirits—The Fruit Arrives—The New Procedure Rules— Collapse of Opposition—Mr. Smith as Leader—Colonel King-Harman— His Salary.

THE FAVOURITE MINISTER.

Feb. 15.—Mr. Arthur Balfour. DEBATE on Address going forward. Arthur Balfour spoke. Vastly improved since Fourth Party days. He now addresses the House with the consciousness of the importance and responsibility of his position, and feels he is supported by the hearty approval of gentlemen on the benches behind. He is undoubtedly the favourite Minister of the day, overshadowing W. H. Smith as effectively, though in another way, as he was put in the shade by Randolph Churchill. That irrepressible person is completely outstripped by his former colleague and subaltern. The Conservative Party are evidently tired of Lord Randolph, and turn with favour to welcome a rising young man who they say at least has never betrayed them. It should be said, to the credit of the Irish members, that they do not spoil Mr. Balfour's opportunity by interruption. They sit wonderfully quiet whilst the Chief Secretary pegs away at them and the Land League. Amongst the various anticipations of the new Session unfulfilled was one which looked to Mr. Balfour's rising as the signal for uproar in the Irish camp. Doubtless the truce is only temporary. Mr. Balfour has not yet come face to face with the men he has actually put in prison. The arrival of T. D. Sullivan, the return of W. O'Brien, may change the scene.

Mr. John Morley. Another speaker much improved even since last Session is Mr. John Morley. It has been urged against his full success as a Parliamentary man that his speeches have about them too much of the literary essay. To-night he treated the House to a capital debating speech, the better and more effective because it was brief. He followed Balfour, taking him up point by point, of course without preparation, and effectively disposed of some of his facts and arguments. Gladstone was hugely delighted with the speech, portions of which he vigorously cheered. Mr. Morley still shows traces of his recent severe illness, and by medical advice has to live under careful restrictions. But he is evidently in good fighting form.

Police protection. The House heard to-night with a pardonable complacency that it takes not less than 155 policemen to guard its members from evil, at a cost to the nation of £300 a week, not counting the Lords, who do not come under special consideration in this matter. The allowance is nearly one policeman for every four members. This, of course, is the general average. Just now the attention of the police is somewhat unfairly concentrated upon the Irish members. It is reckoned that here the proportion is reversed, and that every Irish member has four policemen told off for his personal supervision.

Feb. 18.—"Face to face in the Commons!" Since the night, ten years gone by, when Mr. Forster, rising to move an amendment to the Vote of Credit, was interrupted by the arrival of a telegram announcing that the Russians were at the gates of Constantinople, there has been no more dramatic scene than that which shook the House to-night. The sitting throughout has been a notable one. If it ended in something like tragedy, it opened with the lightest comedy. Last night

Mr. O'Brien, fresh from his plank bed at Tullamore, had delivered his soul in a tremendous philippic.

"Here we are now face to face," he thundered, shaking an outstretched hand at Mr. Balfour, gracefully prone on the Treasury bench. The Chief Secretary listened to this speech with an unvaried smile that greatly aggravated the Irish members. When O'Brien resumed his seat they resettled themselves with savage satisfaction in expectation of beholding the Chief Secretary at the table vainly endeavouring to hide his wounds. But Mr. Balfour also resettled himself, at a slightly different angle of repose, and only smiled again when angry cries of "Balfour! Balfour!" filled the chamber.

He had "funked the challenge thrown down to him by O'Brien," so the Parnellites said. His shattered nerves required at least a night's rest before he could stand up and repel the assault. But he must speak to-night, and all the benches were crowded in varied anticipation, the Opposition looking for his abject discomfiture, the Conservatives hoping for the best.

Mr. Balfour's reply. It was a surprise, agreeable or otherwise, according to the side of the House where it was manifested, to find Mr. Balfour provokingly at his ease. He had availed himself of the interval of leisure to look up the literature of Irish vituperation, and was able by citation of some of the grotesque passages from earlier numbers of *United Ireland* to show that in his capacity as Chief Secretary to the Lord-Lieutenant he did not enjoy a monopoly of personal abuse. It was interesting to watch the faces on the Ministerial bench as Mr. Balfour proceeded through his opening sentences. There was an air of unmistakable anxiety reflected in the serried rows behind and to the right. It was all very well to scout O'Brien's speech as rhetorical rhodomontade; it had undoubtedly made a great impression on the House, and there was a shrewd suspicion that the impression would be deeper still among the multitude outside who read the penny papers. It was easy to imagine how Forster would have dealt with such a speech, or John Morley, or Sir George Trevelyan. They would have taken it seriously, and made laborious efforts to meet it point by point. Mr. Balfour is not constitutionally inclined to take that view of his duty. He laughed at O'Brien's heroics, playfully prodded him in the ribs, and, skilfully concealing the effort, lightly ignored all the graver points in the indictment. His high spirits were contagious, and from first to last he kept the Ministerial benches in a roar of delighted applause.

Mr. Gladstone was plainly indignant at this exhibition of what he regarded as frivolity. *Mr. Gladstone angry.* Time was when he used to single out Mr. Balfour for the distinction, shared with the late Stafford Northcote, of being alluded to in the debate as "my hon. friend." To-night the young Minister was coldly referred to as the "right hon. gentleman," and sometimes, with vocal inflection of chilling contempt, as "the Chief Secretary." But Gladstone's resentment only added fuel to the fire of the supreme satisfaction with which Balfour's friends regarded him. Many who had gladly sat out his long speech rose and left the House when Gladstone appeared at the table to reply. In their opinion it was unanswerable, and why waste time in hearing the Leader of the Opposition marshalling the stale arguments, and trampling the well-trodden ground of the debate? As compared with the packed benches, whose members had sat listening to Balfour's speech, Gladstone faced many gaps that might have been disheartening to a less practised speaker. As he went on, unmindful of the dinner hour, the benches to the right of the Speaker thinned more and more. Only the Treasury bench remained filled, W. H. Smith gallantly struggling against the tendency to yawn, and all his colleagues, sitting shoulder to shoulder, trying hard to look as if they were not hungry.

As soon as Mr. Gladstone resumed his seat the Speaker, detained long past the usual hour of retirement, gave the signal by promptly leaving the Chair. The Treasury bench quickly emptied, and simultaneously the Irish members below the gangway leaped to their feet, and, wildly waving their hats, cheered Gladstone. It was evidently expected that, having made his speech, he would quit the House, and the enthusiastic Opposition made as if they would escort him to the door. But as he sat there, taking recreation after

his long speech in private conversation, they stood vigorously
cheering for the space of three minutes by Westminster clock.

Mr. Goschen in
high spirits.   It seemed that in this unprecedented scene the
dramatic interest of the sitting had reached its
crisis. There was a long anti-climax, the place being so
empty as to suggest to some original mind that, on the whole,
the best way to settle the matters at issue was to count out
the House. At signal of the bell members came trooping in
from the dinner table in time to make a House, and straightway went back again. At a quarter to eleven, when Mr.
Goschen unexpectedly rose, there was the same listless, worn-
out look over the sparsely filled benches. But Goschen had
something to say; his heart was in his work, and he utterly
disregarded these depressing circumstances. Even when he
addresses the House upon subjects of which he is master he
has a curiously self-deprecatory manner. He seems to assure
members that if they will only be so good as to hear him he
will be very brief and absolutely accommodating. To-night
he was as bold as Randolph Churchill and as aggressive as
Harcourt. His voice, lifted high above its usual tone, filled
the House, was heard in the crowded lobby, and speedily
brought in members to throng the erewhile empty seats.
Encouraged by the success achieved by Mr. Balfour, confident
in the coming majority, irritated by the presence of his old
colleagues, exasperated by the cheers of the Irish members,
Goschen threw himself into the fray with a vigour that gave
a fresh access of delight to the Ministerialists. Five minutes
after he had stood up in an almost empty House he was the
centre of attraction for an eager and excited throng. Cheers
and counter cheers rang forth. Turning right or left as the
interruptions fell upon him, Goschen answered with sharp
effect. He raked the front Opposition bench fore and aft.
Harcourt, after long wrestling with growing anger, at length
jumped up, and with clenched fist smote the table, motioning
Goschen to sit down. Goschen was in possession of the
House, and resolutely shook his head. A roar of angry
remonstrance rose from the Conservative benches.

"I should like to know——" Harcourt shouted above the
storm.

But that was all that could be heard, the interval being filled in with fresh uproar. Sir William stood wildly gesticulating, Goschen still shaking his head at the other side of the broad table happily placed between the parted friends.

Harcourt had at length resumed his seat, and Goschen had commenced again, when a sudden burst of cheering once more interrupted his remarks. It was Mr. Gladstone coming back after dinner, and this was his renewed welcome from the Irish camp. At sight of him Goschen returned to the attack with redoubled force. Ringing cheers incessantly rising and falling from the Ministerial bench urged him forward. Mr. Gladstone had claimed that he had never spoken more useful —he would go further and say more fruitful—words than when he telegraphed, "Remember Mitchelstown." "Fruitful words!" exclaimed Mr. Goschen, pointing a finger of indignant scorn at Mr. Gladstone, and turning to greet the renewed storm of cheers from the benches seething with furious delight behind him.

The Fruit arrives. And lo! as he spoke and as they cheered, the fruit was at the door. Mr. Arnold Morley came running in, waving a telegram. In an instant the Irish members guessed its purport, and began to cheer. Then someone called out, " Majority over a thousand!" and it was known, as in a flash of lightning, that there had been a great Liberal victory in Southwark, where all day long a critical contested election had been fought. Once more the Irish members were on their feet, this time joined by Liberals above the gangway, and there arose a storm of cheering and a scene of waving hats exceeding all that had gone before through this memorable and turbulent sitting. Goschen stood aghast, wondering what it meant, but not long left in doubt. He struggled gallantly on through the remainder of his speech; but it was a hard fight, the like of which does not often fall to the lot of a Minister speaking at the table of the House of Commons.

For Ministerialists looking on, bravely trying to smile, there must have been some consolation in the recollection that the last time the Irish members jumped on the benches and cheered and waved their hats was when Rowland Winn

standing by the Mace, read out the figures which proclaimed
the downfall of Gladstone's Government in 1884.

Feb. 24.—The new Procedure Rules. There is at first sight nothing about Mr. W. H.
Smith that recalls Cromwell. But history will
tell how, under his leadership, the House of Commons to-
night was induced to take a step that will revolutionise its

W. H. CROMWELL SMITH.

daily life. Never since Cromwell entered the House with his
file of men-at-arms and had the Mace removed has there been
such swift and sudden displacement of ordered procedure.
It began, as momentous proceedings in the House of Commons
often do, in the quietest, dullest manner. At question time
the benches were barely filled. There were some forty
questions on the paper—rather in excess of the average in
these degenerate days. But there was nothing in them, or
developed by them, that lifted the sitting from its attitude of

commonplace. The Irish members had every other question to themselves, and now and then, Tim Healy interposing, there was a flash in the pan. But the harp that once through Westminster's halls used to ring forth angry and angering questions is now mute, or at best is capable only of a spasmodic twang.

Mr. Gladstone seemed to feel the influence of the now solemn quietness of the question hour. On Thursday night Mr. Smith, whose freshness and daring originality are the amazement of his most intimate friends, blandly proposed that the House should proceed to discuss in detail the Procedure Rules without the time-honoured ceremony of preliminary general debate. In the Autumn Session of 1882, when it was Gladstone's task to propose reform of Parliamentary procedure, and the Conservatives were in opposition, the House took the business in hand on the 21st of October, and it was not till the 10th of November that the First Resolution was carried by a narrow majority of 44 in a full House of 500 members, including the Speaker. In this instance over a fortnight had been appropriated for discussion on a Rule which had only one simple proposition. By what rule of three sum was it possible to calculate the time required to carry the bold scheme of reconstruction of the business arrangements involved in the First Rule of the new series? Mr. Gladstone's breath seemed taken away by the impetuous movement of the Leader of the House, and he insisted that there should at least be some show of general debate. If this had occupied the whole of to-night's sitting, and the amendments to the First Rule had been approached next week, it would have seemed rapid progress by comparison with early experience.

Mr. Gladstone's fighting propensities were subdued by the influence of the hour. His objections to the Ministerial programme applied root and branch. He did not think the Government were wise in placing Procedure in the forefront of their business; and if that were conceded he objected to their taking the whole of the time of private members. But he was content with this protest, spoke only for a few minutes, concluded by expressing his general approval of the Procedure Scheme, and thereafter left the House.

D

Collapse of Opposition. The Irish members, worsted in the dinner hour, sat paralysed spectators of this act of surrender. Biggar, unable to control his emotion as memories of old fights round the standard of Procedure crowded upon his mind, followed Gladstone's example and quitted the House. Tim Healy, silently poring over the amendments, sat gloomily in the corner seat whence he has so often hurled denunciation at the heads of gentlemen on the Treasury bench. Mr. Pyne and Mr. Gilhooly, temporarily out on bail, took every opportunity of bringing themselves under the personal observation of the police, who provokingly ignored their presence. The incident of an Irish member being arrested in the neighbourhood of the House has palled upon the jaded palate. But in the nightmare depression of this evening that or any other diversion would have been welcome. After a division, in which a proposal to reserve Wednesday for private members was heavily defeated, Tim Healy rose, and a ripple of expectation ran through the languid House. Perhaps the standard of revolt would now be raised, and somebody might be suspended ; but Healy, like Mr. Gladstone, had succumbed to the surrounding influences. He cooed the Treasury bench as gently as a sucking dove, only strengthening his general approval of the proposal by a criticism on the detail of the dinner hour. After this it was all over, and shortly after half-past twelve, in a single sitting of moderate length, a complete revolution in Parliamentary Procedure had been quietly accomplished.

Mr. Smith as Leader. The attitude of the Opposition greatly simplified matters, but the happy result was in no small degree due to the management of Mr. W. H. Smith. As Leader of the House he is naturally gifted with two marvellous accomplishments. He knows how to sit through long spaces of time without saying anything, and when he does interpose he says so very little that no opportunity is furnished for controversy. A fussier or more ambitious Leader might to-night have spoiled the game. Mr. Smith, the Brer Rabbit of House of Commons Leaders, "lay low and said nuffin." He has his reward in the bloodless victory by which has been established a momentous change, the effect of which will extend beyond narrow Parliamentary circles to the whole social fabric of London.

Feb. 25.—Col. King-Harman. Mr. Arthur Balfour has within the last two years done much to prove his Parliamentary capacity. He excelled himself when he invented the process of wearing Colonel King-Harman on his sleeve, as it were, for the Irish daws to peck at. It is no use being angry with the hon. and gallant member for Thanet. He is provided with a strip, sometimes several strips, of paper, on which a particular statement is written. At a signal, the calling out of a number on the ordered list, the Colonel lifts his tall head at the table and hurriedly reads out what is written for him. As soon as it is over he gets back to the seat judiciously chosen at the end of the bench, and if Irish members want to rave they have full opportunity. The Parliamentary Secretary to the Chief Secretary to the Lord-Lieutenant has read out what was written for him, and there is an end of articulate speech. A schoolboy who, having dropped a penny in one of the automatic machines at the railway stations, has drawn a damaged packet of chocolate, might as well punch the head of the iron framework as an Irish member, dissatisfied with an answer to his question, might gird at Colonel King-Harman.

His Salary. Apart from the simply mechanical nature of his duties, a tender interest still hangs around the Colonel in connection with the romantic episode of his salary. It is known that, as yet, he has not received one penny for the conspicuous services he renders the State. This Session a Bill has been brought in making due provision for him. It was not mentioned in the Queen's Speech; but it had a place side by side, or rather in precedence of, the Local Government Bill. It has appeared on the Orders day after day, and day after day the Irish members have sat and watched it safely past the hour at which it was possible to make progress. Everybody knows that the Bill is retrospective. Some day it must pass, and then the Parliamentary Secretary to the Chief Secretary of the Lord-Lieutenant will be entitled to draw arrears in a lump sum. Members think of this as time after

time the Colonel comes up to read out his answer. It is like
watching by the bedside of a fasting phenomenon. Another
day has passed, the fast remains unbroken, and the watchers
ask themselves whether the patient has been surreptitiously
served with food, and when will it all end? So members
look on while Colonel King-Harman, a chastened sadness
settling on his once jovial countenance, reads somebody
else's answers to a question put by a gentleman opposite.
Is a salary being surreptitiously advanced to him? And,
if not, when will the watchfulness of his countrymen be cir-
cumvented, the Bill passed, and the arrears (always an Irish
question) be within his grasp? Doubtless Mr. Balfour did not
think of all this when he invented the Parliamentary Secretary. But there is the result, seen again to-night, as it may
be seen every night, in the happy and successful treatment of
what was in three previous Parliaments the tyranny of Irish
questions.

CHAPTER V.

UNDER THE NEW RULES.

"The Admiral"—The Speaker's Full-dress Dinner—Tipping Members—Exit
Lord John Manners—A House of Mourning—Lord C. Beresford and the
Civil Lords—The Closure—The Oaths Bill—"Bakur Pasha"—"Salisbury's
Manners"—Mr. Chamberlain and the Queen—The Demosthenes of Peck-
ham—Under New Rules.

Feb. 27.—"The Admiral." To-NIGHT comes news of the death of Sir
William Edmonstone. Ten years ago the announcement would have created a melancholy sensation in
Parliamentary circles. Now a few lines in the newspapers
report the event, and it is only the members of the already
antique Disraelian Parliament that recognise in the full title
the old gentleman who in the Parliament of 1874 was never
known by other style than "the Admiral." He was one of
the special features of that assembly, and was in some respects
a type of its majority. He was singularly ignorant, obstinate,
and prejudiced, his sole idea of political life being to vote for

Disraeli and grunt when Gladstone rose to address the House.
And yet he was so simple-hearted, and of such unblemished
honesty, according to his lights, that he was a prime favourite
on both sides of the House. For more than six years, night
after night, and if necessary all night through, he sat on the
bench immediately behind the Leader of the House.

It is said that "the Admiral" during his long tenure of a
seat delivered only one speech. I do not remember even that
articulate effort. But there was no speech delivered from
either side of the House in which he did not take the part
of chorus. He had two orations learned off by heart, and
recited verbatim as occasion arose. One was "Hear, hear,"
which came forth with rattling persistency whenever a Conservative was speaking. The other was "No, no," which he
flung broadcast through speeches delivered from the Liberal
side, rising to the highest pitch when Gladstone was on
his legs. He was also master of an eloquent cough, which
expressed all kinds of sentiment, according to its varying
tone and vehemence. Finally, "the Admiral" had invented
quite a new fashion of commentary. With his copy of the
Orders, he used to fan himself with more or less fury, as circumstances demanded. When Biggar rose to his feet, "the
Admiral," with an eloquent grunt of disgust, turned his back
towards the member for Cavan, and furiously fanned himself.
It seemed to the Disraelian Parliament that existence would
be impossible without its "Admiral." Now he quietly dies in
obscurity, and in a new House of Commons there are few to
recall his identity.

Feb. 29. — The
Speaker's full-
dress dinner.   Lord Hartington, Sir Henry James, Mr.
Heneage, and Mr. Caine are left out in the
cold in respect of one important function of
the Parliamentary year. This is the dinner given by the
Speaker to Ministers and ex-Ministers. Last Wednesday the
Speaker entertained Her Majesty's Ministers who have seats
in the House of Commons. Next Wednesday Mr. Gladstone
and his colleagues in the late Government will be the
Speaker's guests. But Lord Hartington and his supporters
being, in a political sense, "neither fish nor flesh nor good red
herring," do not dine with the Speaker this year. They are

not Ministers, and therefore could not go with the Conservative Party; they are not Liberals, and therefore are omitted
from the Party of which Mr. Gladstone is the principal figure.

MR. HENRY JAMES.

March 1.—Tipping The Serjeant-at-Arms, giving evidence to-day
Members.   before the Committee on the admission of
strangers to the House of Commons, told how on one occasion,
having found a seat in the gallery for an applicant, the
grateful stranger tipped him half-a-crown. I knew two prominent members of the House of Commons, both now, alas!
dead, who had their politeness in the lobby rewarded by the
proffer of a coin. One was Sir John Holker, at the time
Attorney-General in Mr. Disraeli's administration. Hearing
a man in the outer lobby inquiring for Mr. Cross, as the
present Secretary of State for India then was, and knowing
that his colleague was not in the House, Sir John courteously
undertook to get the stranger an order for the gallery. He

convoyed him to the door, and on parting the man gently pressed a sixpence into the palm of his hand. Sir John used to say that he never earned a sixpence more honestly. Mr. A. M. Sullivan was more highly favoured, a shilling being his guerdon in similar circumstances. It seems quite right that when the Serjeant-at-Arms himself is enlisted in the service of the stranger the fee should run up to half-a-crown.

March 8.—Exit Lord John Manners. When Lord John Manners walked home on Tuesday he did not know it was the last occasion on which he would be privileged to sit in the House of Commons. The state of his brother was serious but not critical, and the end came with some suddenness. Many eyes were turned towards the Treasury bench when the House met this afternoon, resting upon the vacant seat where Lord John has, with intervals, sat since Young England days. He was a great favourite in the House on both sides, and his kindly presence will be much missed. Of late years, more particularly since the removal from the House of his old friend and early chum, Mr. Disraeli, he has retired from active part in Parliamentary affairs. But, when occasion has called for it, he has gallantly come to the front and delivered a speech, always remarkable for its vigour, and, sometimes, for the neatness of the points made.

No one ever seemed to take into account the possibility that Lord John might some day be Duke of Rutland. Although only seventy years of age, quite a chicken compared with Mr. Gladstone, his white hair and gaunt form lent him a venerable appearance, which did not seem easy to associate with the idea of his succeeding to the peerage. But we have seen the last of him in the Commons, and shall miss the final representative of the " Young England " school, of which Lord John was an ardent disciple, and Disraeli the founder and leader.

March 12 — A House of mourning. There was a considerable show of mourning in both Houses of Parliament to-day. It was expected in some quarters that formal note of the death of the Emperor of Germany would be taken in the shape of a vote of condolence. But there is no precedent for such procedure. Mr. W. H. Smith was amongst the most conspicuous of those in sable garb, Mr. Ritchie being also in uncompromising black. The Chancellor of the Exchequer and Lord George Hamilton were not in mourning, a circumstance remarkable in the latter case, as it was Lord George's field night, and he was the most prominent of Ministers. The Speaker being usually arrayed in black, found it difficult to fall in with the fashion set in high quarters. All he could do was to wear what are called "weepers" over the cuffs of his gown, and to substitute black rosettes for the gleaming buckles on his shoes. The Serjeant-at-Arms had more scope. The Speaker never wears his sword except at a State dinner in his own house, and on State visits to Buckingham Palace. The Serjeant-at-Arms always girds on his sword when on duty, and to-night he carried it in a black scabbard. He also wore black gloves, which, by the way, were quite the fashion in the House of Lords, adding more than usual to its funereal aspect.

Among private members mourning was not so prevalent. One marked exception was the case of Colonel Hughes-Hallett, who sat in the deepest mourning, a bouquet of white violets worn in his button-hole showing conspicuously out of the array of black. The member for Rochester has of late vacated the seat immediately behind the leader of his party, which he assumed on the first night of the Session. He now sits shoulder to shoulder with Lord Randolph Churchill, who, however, does not avail himself of the opportunity to enter into conversation with an old acquaintance.

March 13.—Lord C. Beresford and the Civil Lords. The House was occupied for the greater part of the sitting by discussion of the Navy Estimates. Lord Charles Beresford moved his amendment, which had the great merit of terseness. It declared, in the briefest possible words, that "the allocation of authority in the Admiralty requires entire reform." The most attractive part of the speech was devoted to stories and little asides. His anecdote about the Lord of the Admiralty who received a report, couched in technical phrases, of disaster to a ship, and resented it as simply bad language, was much applauded. Another success was his story of the civilian lord, who looking over a chart, and finding that a ship's return course passed, within only two inches' space on the chart, an island where castaway sailors were supposed to be sheltered, wanted to know why it could not call and relieve them. The two inches on the chart, as Lord Charles Beresford explained amid prolonged laughter, meant a distance at sea of four thousand miles.

March 16.— On the premises. The House of Commons is plodding along in excellent fashion under the new rules. It meets at half-past three, breaks up at midnight, and, what is more, does something in the interval. The great salvation of the dignity of the House and the prosperity of public business is the Closure—that expedient against which, less than six years ago, all the Conservative forces were

desperately arrayed, and which within the past month they have urged a not unwilling Opposition to adopt. It has of late been discovered that Mr. Smith has no monopoly of "the pounce." Twice this week the privilege has been exercised by private members with excellent effect. On Tuesday night, when a division on Mr. Slagg's motion touching the frontier policy in India was imperilled, Mr. Caine moved the Closure, and a division was taken. On Wednesday the angry and baffled residuum of Tories in the House of Commons tried, as a last resort, to defeat Mr. Bradlaugh by talking out his Oaths Bill. The member for Northampton, in humble imitation of the illustrious example of the Leader of the House, moved the Closure, and the House had an opportunity of declaring its opinion upon the issue. It becomes daily more and more clear that the Closure is an indispensable agent in Parliamentary procedure. Its effects are much wider than is apparent from the line in the Parliamentary reports, which states that the Closure has been moved. The knowledge that this rod is in pickle deters obstruction, for obstructionists know that they are ineffectively wasting their own time by prolonging debate. At the proper moment the Closure will be moved, and the division will be taken. It might, therefore, as well be taken early in the evening as late.

March 15.—The Oaths Bill. Mr. Bradlaugh had a great triumph this afternoon, carrying his Oaths Bill by a majority of 100. That would be a great feat in whatever circumstances it was accomplished. But in the present condition of parties in the House of Commons, the mere statement of the arithmetical fact implies the wholesale conversion of the Conservative Party. When five years ago Mr. Gladstone, then at the head of an overwhelming majority available for general purposes, attempted to pass a Bill having the same object, he was defeated by a small majority. What Mr. Gladstone, Prime Minister and Leader of a great party, could not do in 1883, Mr. Bradlaugh did to-day with a majority of 100. Mr. Bradlaugh indeed accomplished more than Mr. Gladstone vainly essayed. The Affirmation Bill of 1883 merely proposed that members returned to the House of Commons might, if they pleased, make affirmation instead of taking the oath. The Bill passed to-day extends deliverance from the oath to all the ordinary relations of public life. It provides that any person on objecting to being sworn shall be permitted to make affirmation in all places and for all purposes where and when an oath is at present required by the law. It will be strange news for Sir Henry Wolff, on his way to Teheran, to hear how matters fared in the House of Commons. It was this question of Mr. Bradlaugh being permitted to take the oath that directly led to the creation of the Fourth Party. Now, whilst the Mr. Gorst of those days is Sir John, whilst Mr. Arthur Balfour is Chief Secretary for Ireland, Lord Randolph Churchill votes with Mr. Bradlaugh practically to abolish the oath, and the Bill is carried, under a Conservative Government, by a majority of 100 !

March 21.
"Baker Pasha." When the House met at two o'clock to-day, for a morning sitting, it was much gratified by the appearance of an Irish alderman with sword and gown lodging a petition. These occasional appearances of the Lord Mayor of Dublin in State used to be great opportunities for Mr. Dawson, that typical Lord Mayor, who, when Mr. Forster, then Chief Secretary, was moving a clause of the Coercion Act endowing the police authorities with the right of search in the night-time, told him that, if he approached the bedside of Mrs. Dawson, it would only be over the dead body of her husband. Mr. Dawson, in his business relations a baker, was known among his colleagues sometimes as the "Master of the Rolls," but most often as "Baker Pasha." He belonged to a type that is dying out from among the more serious business-like men whom Ireland now sends to the House of Commons. He was brought back to recollection to-day, as he used to sit in his Lord Mayor's scarlet gown, with the chain of office glittering round his neck, and his quite inadequate legs crossed in lordly attitude of composure.

March 22.—"Salis-
bury's Manners." The Duke of Rutland to-night made his first visit to the House of Commons since he left it as Lord John Manners. The occasion of this revived interest was the appearance at the table of his son, the Marquis of Granby, who came up to-day to take the oath and his seat for East Leicester. Amurath to Amurath succeeds, and the head of the Manners family having gone up to the House of Lords, the heir-apparent takes his place in the Commons. The new member is much better known as Henry Manners, or, as he is sometimes called, "Salisbury's Manners," having for many years occupied the position of private secretary to the noble Lord. The Marquis of Granby has all the affability and the geniality of his father, and his popularity is co-extensive with the list of people who know him, and that is very long.

The new Duke of Rutland looked in good health, and everybody hopes he will live many years to enjoy his long-delayed honours. He watched with pathetic interest the instalment of his son and heir.

April 3. — Mr. Chamberlain and the Queen. Mr. Chamberlain is having a case made worthy of the photograph Her Majesty recently sent him in recognition of his services on the Fishery Commission. It is quite true Royal munificence did not on this occasion run to the extent of adding a case to the photograph, but the spiteful little story current that the photo was of the ordinary carte-de-visite size is an invention of the enemy. This special mark of personal esteem on the part of the Sovereign was no surprise to Mr. Chamberlain's old colleagues in former Cabinets. From the moment his Ministerial position brought him in personal communication, he established himself in Her Majesty's most favourable regards. No one familiar with the charm of Mr. Chamberlain's social gifts can wonder at this. In America, as in Canada, he was a favourite even among those politically opposed to him. It is said the only adverse criticism passed in social circles upon the British emissary during his stay in America was by a Washington belle whom the right hon. gentleman had been privileged to lead through the mazy dance.

"He's nice," she said, "but he doesn't know how to dance. He takes such a short step you think he must have practised on a postage stamp."

April 6. — The Demosthenes of Peckham. If the House of Commons were in other than the curious mood which now depresses it, it would have wakened up with some flicker of interest when to-night Mr. Baumann delivered his great speech. Mr. Baumann is a young gentleman with whom Peckham dowered the House of Commons at the otherwise memorable election of 1885. It would be difficult to explain why there appears a singular appropriateness in Peckham being the precise locality represented by Mr. Baumann. If the subtlety of the sensation evades description, it nevertheless makes itself felt. The speech deserved fuller recognition than it received, not because its style was new, for in truth it is at least as old as the most pretentious form of oratory in the Oxford Union. Its merit lay in the unblushing, unhesitating boldness of the flights into poesy, in the air of pleased surprise with which the orator wandered through familiar places, and made for the first time astounding discoveries. The reference to the " iron tears " wrung from the eye of humanity at the spectacle of the struggling landowner was really new, and the description of " the gorgeous robe of civilisation " was novel in its adaptation. But what made the older generation rub their eyes and live their youth again was to find Mrs. Jellaby trotted forth to illustrate a bitterly sarcastic passage aimed at the statesmanship of to-day which, with telescopic view, interests itself with affairs in Egypt and the Canadian Fisheries, looking far over the heads of "our own artisans." It was evident the member for Peckham had only just made Mrs. Jellaby's acquaintance, and older men well understood how that broadly painted picture would attract the ingenuous mind upon which it had suddenly burst.

After Mrs. Jellaby had been introduced and dismissed, Mr. Baumann, so to speak, handed round Mr. Carlyle, " the rugged sage of Chelsea," of whose "acrid satire " he was able to say an encouraging word. " Kingsley " was also passingly alluded to, with a friendly familiarity that would have soothed some of his darker moments had he been able to foresee this night. That Mr. Baumann did not mention the author of *Mangnall's Questions* was probably due to the suspicion that the attention of the select audience was beginning to stagger under the accumulated load of literary reference and the whirling rush of philosophic thought.

It was all so pretty—so Peckhamish—that the House visibly resented the matter-of-fact, business-like tone in which Mr. Stanhope addressed himself to a very brief reply. To observe the rapt expression on the orator's face when he spoke of " the skilled labourer of the country now largely living out of unemployed benefit funds ; " to watch the smile of withering sarcasm with which the still fresh form of Mrs. Jellaby was taken out of the long-neglected trunk ; and to quaver under the impassioned tone with which Mr. Baumann, turning aside for a moment from the company of the Rugged

Sage and Kingsley, looked down upon "my right hon. friend
on the Treasury bench," and expressed the hope that he
should receive a sympathetic answer—induced the belief that
the member for Peckham had put his finger on an exceedingly
sore place, and that it was no use for a convicted Secretary of
State for War to attempt to disguise his discomfiture. It
turned out that Mr. Baumann's information on political
affairs was as far out of date as his studies in light literature.
His amendment solemnly called upon the Government to
discontinue the practice of working overtime in Government
yards and factories. It turned out that what the Demosthenes
of Peckham, with folded arms, corrugated brow, and broken
voice, demanded at the hands of a trembling Ministry, had
been accomplished long ago. The practice could not be
discontinued, Mr. Stanhope drily said, because it did not exist.
Peckham was behind the age, and the birth of its member,
though long deferred, had come too late.

There was an awkward pause and the faint echo of a titter
when Mr. Stanhope somewhat abruptly resumed his seat,
having really nothing more to say. The Speaker glanced
anxiously round in search of competitors for precedence in
the debate thus started. It was difficult to believe that a discussion opened in so portentous a style should be suddenly
and swiftly extinguished. Surely someone might say something, if it were only with the object of introducing the names
of Mrs. Nickleby and Mrs. Gamp. But the House of Commons
is not what it used to be, even in the not far-off days when
the member for Peckham, in jacket and trousers, still pondered
over the pages of the interrogative *Mangnall.* Within the past
two months there has dawned upon it the long-delayed conviction that it is really a business assembly. It had sat down
in an attitude of grave attention to hear discussed a question
which seemed to have an important bearing upon the condition
of the labour market. But there had been a mistake somewhere. It had been, quite unintentionally and in good faith,
deceived. It was evidently in no mood for further trifling, and
before the considerable number of members who now had the
ground cleared for them to bring on amendments had realised
their position the Speaker had left the Chair, the mace was off
the table, and the House in Committee of Supply.

Under new rules. This happy conclusion of a ludicrous episode
which might have wasted much valuable time
illustrates the totally altered condition of affairs established in
the House of Commons under the new Rules of Procedure.
These operate not only by the restraint of their actual application, but by their influence, which dominates the whole spirit
of the proceedings. What happened to-night in respect of
the early lapse into Committee was a repetition of the
agreeable surprise which awaited Ministers at Thursday's
sitting, when the House got into Committee of Supply
ten minutes after public business had been opened. Even
with the Closure at hand there was plenty of scope for talk
on miscellaneous subjects which would have prevented
any material progress being made with the votes at either
sitting. If King Ja Ja, in his enforced retirement, has
opportunity to read the Parliamentary debates, he will
find food for reflection upon the degeneracy of the House
of Commons. Information about his Majesty and his
wrongs is a little vague, and no one quite knows why Mr.
W. Redmond should have adopted his cause. As Mr. Haumann
would probably have observed if he had had opportunity
of taking part in debate on the topic, the connection between
the two personages is as vague as that between Hecuba and
the player whom Hamlet watched. But that is quite immaterial. Mr. Redmond had an opportunity to-night of
flinging the body of King Ja Ja across the floor of the House
of Commons and obstructing the progress of business. He
refrained, and an opportunity that four years ago would
have been made to serve the purposes of a whole night of
obstruction was wantonly cast aside.

CHAPTER VI.

THE ENGLISH LOCAL GOVERNMENT BILL.

The Front Opposition Bench—How the Local Government Bill was Debated—
Mr. Jesse Collings—Sir William Harcourt and Mr. Chamberlain—Lord
Randolph Churchill wakes up—Mr. Chamberlain and Irish Local Govern-
ment—Amateur Artists—Mr. Lockwood—Ex-Whips—Lord St. Oswald—
Sir William Dyke—A Flag of Truce—The Strangers' Gallery—" Black
Rod!"

April 9.—The front Opposition bench. It is evident a dead-lock will shortly be reached in respect of the arrangements on the front Opposition bench. To-night there was a great crowd to hear Mr. Gladstone's speech. Amongst the earliest arrivals was Sir H. James, who was followed by Mr. Heneage and Lord Hartington. They somehow managed to squeeze themselves into a limited space at the end of the bench near the gangway. Presently Sir Charles Russell arrived in search of the seat he usually occupies, to-night appropriated by Mr. Heneage. Finding no room the ex-Attorney - General seated himself on the gangway steps. Presently, when the House divided, on the motion for the adjournment of the debate on the King-Harman Bill, Sir

SIR CHARLES RUSSELL.

Charles, getting back first in the race from the division

lobby, recovered his seat on the front Opposition bench. In due course Sir Henry James and Mr. Heneage dropped in. Then came Lord Hartington, last as usual. But there was no place for him. A position of profound embarrassment was relieved by Sir Charles Russell rising, who found a back seat, Lord Hartington falling into the space vacated.

April 30.—How the Local Government Bill was debated. This is the sixth night of debate on the second reading of one of the most important measures ever submitted to Parliament—the English Local Government Bill. The Government at the outset showed a disposition to curtail the conversation. This met with such a storm of angry indignation, more especially from below the gangway on the Liberal side, that Mr. Smith stepped back appalled, and the debate, which according to the original scheme should have concluded within two nights, dragged on through six.

Every evening, questions over, the lumbering figure of the Bill has been dragged on to the stage, and what is ironically called "the business of the evening" commenced. On every evening the private business of members has been to gird up their loins and flee. They had done their duty to their constituencies, their country, and their conscience in insisting that not less than six days should be given to debate on the second reading. What they liked to be assured of was that the debate was actually going on. If it had been absolutely necessary to maintain its continuance, there is not a man in the House who would not have faced

the sacrifice of remaining in his place for an hour or two.
But there was always someone there, enough to keep the
thing going, and to maintain that general sense of virtuous
satisfaction induced by the reflection that this important
Bill was being thoroughly discussed, and that Mr. Ritchie,
who really was in attendance throughout, was getting a hint
or two by which he might profit in Committee.

Mr. Jesse Collings. When Mr. Jesse Collings rose to continue the
interesting stream of reflections dammed by the
stroke of midnight on Thursday it was curious to watch the
attitude of parties. Mr. Collings's old friends and companions
dear on the Liberal benches were free from all embarrassment
They rose in a body and left the House, with even ostentatious
signs of indifference. But it was different with the hon.
gentlemen opposite. There was a time in the days of old,
when Mr. Collings was a particular object of derision in the
Conservative camp. He girded at them with all his strength,
and they were wont to be contemptuously offensive in retort.
But times have changed. If the Radical member for the
Bordesley division of Birmingham is to be cheered at all,
the shout must needs come from the Conservative side, and
when Mr. Collings rose to resume the debate cheers were freely
given. There was also borne in upon the gentlemen to the
right of the Speaker a sense of duty to remain and keep
an audience for their new ally. The Liberals would not
stop to hear him; the Conservatives should, and so said
all of them. So strong and unanimous was this unspoken
sentiment that individuals felt no hesitation in withdrawing.
One would not be missed where so many would stay. Thus
one by one they slipped away, and the wilderness to the left
of the Speaker, out of which the voice of Mr. Collings was
heard crying, presently found a parallel in the waste places
where every Conservative had honestly meant that his neighbour should remain in close attention.

Sir William Harcourt and Mr. Chamberlain. When Sir W. Harcourt rose at a quarter-past
ten there were thirty-five members on the
benches, all told. In the very first sentences he
turned to attack Mr. Chamberlain, and the effect upon the

aspect of the House was electrical. The few still present who had lived through the debate brightened up and began to laugh. The long unwonted sound was heard by groups in the lobby. The news spread in ever-widening circles through the precincts of the House that Harcourt was "giving it to Chamberlain," and before many of Sir William's treasured impromptus had been wasted on the empty benches the House was full, and the glad sounds of cheers and laughter filled the Chamber, inciting the orator to bolder flights.

It was a great opportunity for Sir William Harcourt, and he made the very most of it. As a personal attack nothing so happily conceived, so brilliant in point, and so light in touch has for years been heard in the House of Commons. The circumstances were peculiarly favourable. Mr. Chamberlain had laid himself open to attack by the tone of his speech on Monday, in which he dealt many hard back-handed blows at former friends sitting near. Sir William Harcourt did not lie under the charge of going out of the way to attack a former colleague. Mr. Chamberlain had deliberately trailed his

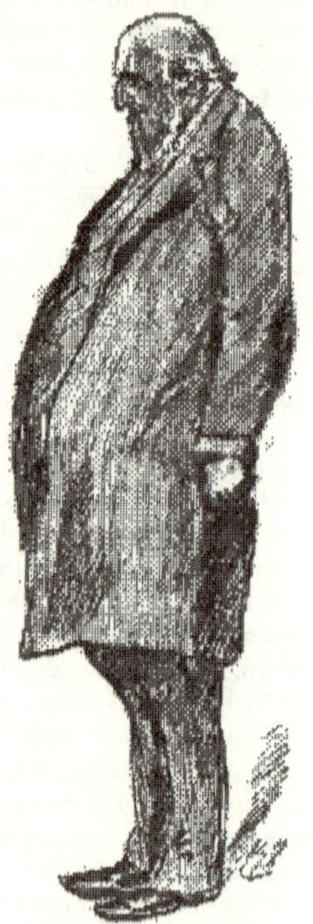

coat, and Sir William gleefully trod upon it. It is well enough, when opportunity offers, to beat about the head one of the prominent officers of the enemy, but there is a sweeter and subtler joy in turning upon an old friend and former colleague when circumstances invite the encounter. The only thing lacking in the completeness of Sir William Harcourt's enjoyment of the opportunity was the accident which prevented Mr. Chamberlain being present to hear.

Mr. Gladstone came in hurriedly, having missed but a few of the opening sentences; Lord Hartington sat and listened, the only man in the House who did not pay the tribute of hearty laughter to the mirth-provoking gambols. The speech bristled with carefully elaborated points, admirably put, and thoroughly enjoyed by the audience. Nothing could be better than the description of Mr. Chamberlain's relations with the Government as being of a conjugal character. "A man very often felt himself at liberty to find fault with his own wife who would not allow anyone else to do so." Mr. Chamberlain's diplomatic tact displayed in his mission to Washington, contrasted with his remissness in that respect at home, reminded Sir William of the witches and warlocks of old. "As soon as they crossed the water their power of enchantment ceased." The description of the head and front of Mr. Gladstone's offending, inasmuch as he had overlain that promising infant Mr. Chamberlain's draft Bill for the reform of local government, swiftly told. Perhaps most effective of all was the bitter reminiscence of the time when a Radical tail below the gangway wagged the dog who sat on the front Opposition bench—the day when Mr. Chamberlain, standing in the place Mr. Parnell now habitually occupies when he addresses the House, formally renounced the authority of Lord Hartington, and, amid ringing cheers from the Radicals, hailed him as "late the Leader of the Liberal Party."

It was magnificent, but it was not the Local Government Bill, which presently the House, accidentally remembering, agreed to read a second time.

April 25.—Lord Randolph Churchill wakes up. Lord Randolph Churchill has for some weeks remained in an ominously quiescent state. He has been regular in his attendance, and has stuck to his corner seat behind the Ministers, in spite of the fact that Colonel Hughes-Hallett, who insists upon having a leader somewhere, has permanently secured the adjoining seat. Lord Randolph has watched the increasing influence of Mr. Balfour in the House of Commons, and has heard night after night the enthusiastic cheers his gibes at the Irish people or his polished snubbing of the Irish members have elicited. It seems that after all Lord Randolph has only been biding his time, and this afternoon it came. The House had been for some time discussing a Bill brought in by the Irish members, designed to introduce an enlarged system of local government in Ireland. At the outset the attendance was small. But towards four o'clock the benches began to fill, and when Mr. Gladstone rose there was already a good audience.

The Leader of the Opposition heartily supported the measure, and, by an odd coincidence, took exactly that line of attack upon the Government which Lord Randolph Churchill followed up with crushing effect. Mr. Gladstone insisted that in 1886 the present Government had pledged themselves to deal with the Local Government question in Ireland simultaneously with its reform in England, and he openly accused them of breaking their pledge. Mr. Balfour, who followed, was as gay and as confident as ever, little dreaming of the Nemesis sitting behind, twirling his moustache and preparing a few things pleasant for his old colleagues to hear.

Lord Randolph rose just before five o'clock, not leaving himself much time for an elaborate speech. He spoke with quite unusual earnestness and decision, categorically and emphatically declaring that in 1886 he, as spokesman of the Government, and with the full approval of his colleagues, announced that the reform of local government in Ireland should be treated, as respects the English question, with "similarity, equality, and simultaneity."

This speech fell like a bombshell on the Treasury bench, lately so elate. The ingenuous countenance of Mr. Smith betrayed his perturbed feelings. Even the graceful head of Mr. Balfour drooped. The Conservatives sat silent, not knowing what to do; and again and again triumphant cheers from the Opposition benches punctuated Lord Randolph's telling sentences. There was nothing new in what he said. The facts had been declared over and over again from the Liberal side. Less than two hours earlier Mr. Gladstone had made the same statement; but everyone knew the significance of the stand Lord Randolph was taking, and felt that the Irish policy of the Government had received a serious blow.

Mr. Chamberlain and Irish Local Government. Lord Randolph's attack on the Government was taken, if not in concert with Mr. Chamberlain, at least with his full knowledge. For upwards of half an hour, in a quiet corner of the library, the two had been in consultation. Mr. Chamberlain, with an easier conscience than Lord Randolph has suddenly become possessed of, was able to vote against the Bill. But the terms on which he did so were not less significant than Lord Randolph's freer expression of dissent. Mr. Chamberlain voted against the Bill only on the assurance, which he was able to extract from Mr. Balfour's speech, that the Government had not indefinitely postponed the question of local government in Ireland. Lord Hartington, who was present during the remarkable scene, also voted against the Bill. The event has created a surprising sensation in political circles. It is felt that Lord Randolph Churchill, whether seriously meaning it or not, has made it impossible for the Government to continue their Balfourian policy in Ireland in the unmitigated form in which it has lately raged.

LORD FOLKESTONE.

April 20.—Amateur artists. It is a noteworthy and happy incident that Lord Folkestone should sit on one side of the House of Commons and Mr. Lockwood on the other. These two gentlemen have great gifts in the way of humorous portraiture, and during an important debate may be seen, one immediately behind the front Opposition bench, the other at the lower end of the Treasury bench, diligently sketching their fellow-members. Lord Folkestone's artistic industry has been somewhat interfered with by the acceptance of office as Treasurer of the Household. Still, when the cares of that important institution press heavily upon him, he finds recreation in secretly drawing Mr. W. H. Smith with monumental mutton-chop whiskers, or Lord Randolph Churchill twirling an exaggerated moustache.

Mr. Lockwood. Mr. Lockwood has more time, and one or other of his sketches is constantly being passed up and down the benches. One made from his place in the House of Commons was circulated the night when news came that the Baroness Burdett-Coutts was on board the Channel steamer *Inrieta*, reported a wreck. It was a fancy portrait of Mr. Burdett-Coutts, leaving the House of Commons in evening dress to rescue the Baroness. It was a capital likeness, and there was a dishevelled appearance about the member for Westminster that testified to his marital concern. Since then the opening of the Grosvenor Gallery has led to a development of this idea. A notable picture in the collection is a large one in the west gallery representing a noble family of Huguenot refugees shipwrecked on the Suffolk coast. Among the somewhat comical figures is an excited gentleman, bearing from the relentless waves a lightly-clad lady seated on his shoulder. It is now said that this is Mr. Burdett-Coutts in the act of rescuing the Baroness —a little bit of humour that goes a long way when circulated in dull times over the benches of the House of Commons.

April 27. — Ex- It was a curious coincidence that on the self-
Whips.   same night, whilst Lord Stalbridge, in the Upper House, made an eloquent speech, Sir William Dyke should have found himself in the other House Minister in charge of an important debate. Rarely the voice of one who has held the post of Whip is heard in either House, and here to-night were two retired Whips occupying between them the joint attention of Imperial Parliament. Good Whips before they die go to the House of Lords. But the longer their service in the outer lobby, the more rooted is their objection to speech-making. They never, or hardly ever,

knew a speech to influence a vote ; and, after all, the vote is
the thing.   Speech-making must go forward, as otherwise the
interval between the Speaker taking the Chair, or the Lord

SIR WILLIAM HART-DYKE.

Chancellor seating himself on
the Woolsack, and the rising of
the House would be difficult to
fill up. Still, a Whip, whether
in harness or out, is inclined to
leave talking to others. Lord
Hampden, though he passed
the Chair on the way to the
House of Lords, has yet to
make his maiden speech. He
sat in the Chair of the House of
Commons at the birth of the
Home Rule Party, saw the
growth of Obstruction, sat up
till dawn through many nights,
and may be forgiven if he thinks
he has had his fair share of
speech - making without contributing personal effort to its
extension.

Lord Wolverton, whose
cheery presence is still missed
from the precincts of both
Houses, was not known in the
House of Lords as an orator. That he could make a speech
was proved by some tempestuous bursts of oratory delivered
in the country.   Lord Stalbridge will remember one memorable
occasion in a home county when Whip met Whip, and the
tug of war was unusually strained. Lord Kensington preserves in the Upper House that habitude of silence characteristic of him in the House of Commons.

Lord St. Oswald. As for Lord St. Oswald, there is no man in either
          House who may with fuller sense of performing
senatorial duty sit silent.   So grave is the old Whip's
bearing, so churchlike the solemnity of his listening attitude,
that it would be an unpardonable waste of natural gifts if he

broke silence by ordered speech. Yet, when he was still Mr.
Rowland Winn, he made one brief and memorable speech
the House of Commons is not likely to forget. It was
early in the morning of the 9th of June, 1885. Through the
long night the House had been debating Sir M. H. Beach's
amendment on Mr. Childers' Budget. The debate was over;
the tumultuous division had drawn to a close, and Mr. Rowland
Winn literally took the floor. He stood at the table with the
notes of his speech in his hand, the House, stilled to a moment
of intensest silence, waiting for him to begin.

" Ayes, to the right," said Mr. Winn, " were 252. Noes, to
the left, 264."

So, as the Speaker said, the "noes" had it. The Budget Bill,
together with the Gladstone Ministry, was thrown out, and
Lord Randolph Churchill, leaping on the bench below the
gangway, hailed the sudden and unexpected birth of a Conservative Ministry.

This was the Conservative Whip's last speech in the House
of Commons, and the momentous consequences by which it
was followed surely justify the silence of an after lifetime. It
transformed Mr. Rowland Winn into Lord St. Oswald ; it sent
Sir Stafford Northcote to the House of Peers ; it made Lord
Randolph Churchill Secretary of State for India ; and it
plunged Mr. Gladstone into a morass from which he has not
yet emerged.

Sir Wm. Dyke.   Years before this historic night Sir William
Dyke had parted company with Mr. Rowland
Winn in the office of Whip. He had faithfully served his
party through the heyday of the Disraelian Parliament ; and
when the end came, and Grand Crosses were falling in showers,
it seemed something of a slight that Sir William should be
tossed a Privy Councillorship. The neglect of an esteemed and
usually grateful chief had the effect of turning his attention to
the broader stream of politics outside the Whip's room and the
lobby. He went in for statesmanship, took occasional part in
debates on Imperial topics, and when the Conservative Ministry
was formed, in the summer of 1885, he was made Chief
Secretary to the Lord-Lieutenant. It was a post that had
sorely tried some great reputations. Next to the Premiership

it was the most difficult in the Administration. Sir William Dyke probably shared the surprise of the House when it was offered to him; but the habitual reticence of the Whip prevented his making any remark. He took it, and was understood to govern Ireland for a few months. Next to the Chief Secretaryship, perhaps the most surprising office in which to find Sir William would be that which practically belongs to the Minister of Education. Accordingly, when the Conservative Government returned to office, Sir William Dyke was made Vice-President of the Council.

The exigencies of this position brought him to the front to-night. Mr. Arthur Acland had once more submitted a motion for the appointment of a regular Minister of Education, and had taken the opportunity to review the wide field of educational systems. Mr. John Morley had seconded the resolution in a luminous speech, which lifted the debate to the highest standard; Mr. Kenyon had delivered an opinion apparently confused by reminiscences of the Welsh language; Mr. Bruce had spoken for Scotland, and then the way was opened for the Minister.

The great majority of members present were in evening dress. The Vice-President of the Council, having in his charge the interests of the children in a hundred schools and the cattle on a thousand hills, had no time to dress for dinner. Another personal touch which had its effect on the watchful House was the production towards the middle of the speech of something that looked remarkably like a pair of horn spectacles. Peering through these at the accumulated notes, where some of Mr. Kenyon's remarks appeared to have been jotted down to the credit of Mr. Morley, Sir William Dyke looked every inch a Minister of Education.

A Flag of Truce. The crowning strategy, the little device which marked the old Parliamentary hand, was the disposition of his pocket-handkerchief. This he had deftly fixed in his coat-tail pocket, so as to display a liberal expanse of crumpled cambric. Whenever he came to a controversial point likely to rouse the ire of the magnates on the front bench opposite, Sir William turned round, presenting a back view to the Liberal Party. What this meant quickly pene-

trated the trained intelligence to which the hint was addressed.
Sir William Dyke, member of a Conservative Administration,
could not be expected to go so far in educational matters as
the Radicals opposite. He had the country party to think of
and conciliate. But when he was declaring that "the day had
gone by for a Minister of Education." when he launched that

striking illustration pointing to "the danger that the cry, so
easily raised, of robbery of the poor would seriously impair the
attempt to range educational machinery on what he might
call the bidder system," his back was turned to right honourable gentlemen opposite, and they recognised the flag of truce
displayed as the obtrusive handkerchief fluttered with every
gesture by which the Minister graced and enforced his oratorical flights. He must needs satisfy extreme men on his own
side; but Mr. John Morley, Sir Lyon Playfair, Mr. Mundella,
and Professor Bryce knew what the white flag portended,

and the debate closed in a general spirit of amity, which
Mr. W. H. Smith appropriately rose to express.

April 30. — The
Strangers'
Gallery.

The Committee for some time sitting to consider the question of the admission of strangers
to the House of Commons concluded their
labours to-day. With that enlightened spirit which has recently come over the House in dealing with its own arrangements, the Committee have decided to recommend a revo-
lutionary measure. There are two divisions of the gallery
facing the Speaker's chair. One is the Strangers' Gallery
proper, the other the Speaker's. The Committee this afternoon resolved to recommend the House to abolish this
distinction. Henceforth there will be no Speaker's Gallery.
One result of the change will be a much-needed addition to
the accommodation. Between them the Speaker's and the
Strangers' Galleries find sitting room for 130 persons. The
removal of the dividing line will give another bench containing thirty seats. The Peers' Gallery, and what is known as
the Special Gallery, being the front bench of the Speaker's
Gallery to the right of the clock, and the few seats under the
gallery on the floor of the House, will remain as heretofore,
specially reserved.

As to admission to the Strangers' Gallery, there will be a
partial return to the old principle under which every member
was supposed to have the right of giving a ticket for the
Strangers' Gallery. Hereafter each member will have two
tickets every day when the House sits. But as there are only
160 seats available, it is evident this will be a Barmecide feast
for many an eager constituent. After obtaining an order, the
stranger will have to ballot for a seat, and it is in this connection that the principal safeguard against the visitation of
possible dynamitards comes in. It is intended to have a ticket
office in the outer lobby, in charge of the police. All strangers
will gain admission to the gallery from the outer lobby, thus
increasing the privacy of the inner lobby.

"Black Rod!"

It is a pity whilst this reforming zeal is on,
it could not be extended to the useless, ludicrous, and, upon occasion, vexatious nonsense of the visit of

Black Rod to the House of Commons. This afternoon, whilst Mr. Balfour was on his feet answering an important question with respect to the conduct of business in Ireland, the door was flung wide open, a messenger abruptly entered, and with stentorian voice announced " Black Rod!" Even Mr. Balfour was not able to stare this intruder down, or to snub him. Without completing the sentence upon which he had embarked, the Chief Secretary resumed his seat, and amid a titter of laughter Black Rod entered, and, bowing thrice, summoned the Speaker and the House of Commons to attend at the Bar of the other House to hear the Royal assent given by Commission to certain Bills. The Serjeant-at-Arms advanced, and shouldered the Mace; the Speaker left the chair; the Home Secretary and Mr. Stanhope fell in by way of procession; amid further tittering the Speaker and mace disappeared, leaving the House with nothing to do. In little more than ten minutes the Speaker was back again, the mace was returned to the table, Mr. Balfour rose, and continued the answer thus grotesquely interrupted. But ten minutes had literally been wasted by this piece of antique tomfoolery.

CHAPTER VII.

MR. GLADSTONE.

Mr. Gladstone—An Accidental Speech—Tireless—Mr. Disraeli at Seventy—"Bobby" Boycotted—Lord R. Churchill and Mr. Balfour—The Lord Advocate (Mr. Macdonald, since Lord Kingsburgh)—Scottish Humour—Father of the House—The Reformed House—An Old Story Re-told—One Interested Listener.

May 4.—Mr. Gladstone. PERSONS who for political reasons are interested in the actual health and possible longevity of Mr. Gladstone ought to have seen him to-night, discoursing on the abstract proposal that the State should buy up the railways. The House was, naturally enough, pretty empty. Mr. Watt had read an interesting paper in support of his motion; Sir Julian Goldsmid had

chanted certain objections; Sir Bernard Samuelson, for whom
so dry a subject had an irresistible attraction, delivered a
weighty essay on the general subject; Mr. Holton, who really
knew something about the matter, had talked of it from the
railway chairman point of view; and then Sir M. H. Beach,
wearied of much speaking, had come down with the acrid
protest, that never had he heard a more important proposal
supported by weaker arguments.

The whole proceedings were curiously illustrative of one
aspect of the House of Commons. It was by chance at the
ballot box that Mr. Watt had obtained the first place on the
agenda of the sitting. Being in this position, he thought he
might as well raise a discussion on the question of the State
Purchase of Railways. Possibly, in the privacy of his chamber,
he had debated whether he should not ask the House to
consider a cognate scheme, for the building of a railway
to the moon. The two projects had precisely equal bearing upon the practical business of the House of Commons.
On the whole, perhaps, the discussion on the lunar railroad
project would have possessed the greater measure of attractive-
ness. But Mr. Watt finally decided to confine his attention
to terrestrial affairs, and therefore the House of Commons,
oppressed with the weight of urgent public business, with the
Budget Bill standing for third reading, was asked, *à propos
des bottes*, to consider the question of buying up the railways,
and running them for the public weal.

It was just one of those matters an over-burdened
statesman might welcome as an opportunity for taking his
rest. It was all very well for the President of the Board of
Trade to chafe. The question affected his department, and
since it was seriously raised he must needs, with gravity,
take note of it. For Mr. Gladstone there was no such
necessity. He was in his place at question time, vigorous
and alert, pricking up his ears at mention of King Ja Ja of
Opobo, and fixing poor Mr. Smith with searching eye when
he endeavoured to make the terms of the reference to the
Royal Commission on the National Defences look as like
as possible to those originally cited and subsequently
abandoned. Questions over, he left the House, as everyone
thought for the sufficient reason that there was nothing

going forward worthy attention or necessitating his presence. Within the space of half an hour he was back again, looking younger and fresher than ever, arrayed in dinner dress.

He was evidently going out to enjoy himself, Youth at the prow and Pleasure at the helm. Somewhere, peradventure, covers were laid for forty faithful friends, with a screen behind which a reporter sat and sharpened his pencil. Visions of an important speech suddenly sprung upon the public from some private dining-room floated before Sir M. H. Beach's troubled gaze, adding to the anger that possessed him at the lengthening of the debate. Still, since Mr. Gladstone was dining out, possibly with a speech to follow, his visit to the House was not likely to be either prolonged or provocative.

An accidental speech. It is probable when Mr. Gladstone re-entered the House he had not the slightest intention of speaking on the question of the State Purchase of Railways. It was presently recollected that the Budget Bill was down for third reading, and that, having delivered a series of important speeches on Mr. Goschen's plan, he had on Thursday night protested against this stage being taken without further debate. It was clear he had come down to fire a last shot at the Budget, and would wait with whatever measure of patience was possible, till the railway question was shunted and his opportunity came. Even up to the moment the President of the Board of Trade rose Mr. Gladstone may have intended to reserve himself for his Budget speech.

Sir Michael Beach, all unconsciously, struck a chord, response to which was irresistible. The subject naturally led him to refer to the epoch of 1844, and the great parent Railway Act then added to the Statute Book. Mr. Gladstone, sitting on the deserted front Opposition bench waiting to discuss the Budget of a man who was a puling infant when he took his seat for Newark, pricked up his ears at mention of this date. Looking across the half-empty House he may have seen, with the eyes of memory, sitting low down on the Opposition benches, "a fine-looking young man of about the usual height, of good figure, with a countenance mild and pleasant, highly intellectual expression, eyes clear and quick, eyebrows dark and rather prominent, with jet-black hair carefully parted from the crown downwards to the brow, where it is tastefully shaded," a fine-looking young man, just growing into regard as the rising hope of stern, unbending Toryism.

Mr. Gladstone knew all about the Railway Act of 1844, as he presently informed the House, chatting with it in that charming manner he, on occasional off-nights, talks of half a century past. He told how, in 1841—or was it 1842?—when he was at the Board of Trade, the question arose whether there should be a railway all the way to Scotland. At that time Hudson was King, " a bold and not unwise railway projector," Mr. Gladstone explained, for the benefit of young fellows like Sir W. Harcourt and Mr. W. H. Smith, who sat enthralled listening to his story. The boldness of Hudson prevailed over the inertia of the Board of Trade. It was decided there should be a railway, at least within touch of the Lowlands of Scotland, and it was determined the line should be built substantially, so as to last through the ages, and successfully bear the concentrated burden of Northern traffic.

These memories passed through Mr. Gladstone's mind as he sat and listened to Sir Michael Beach prosing. When the President of the Board of Trade sat down, and a discussion, much fitter for a debating society than the House of Commons, seemed to have drooped to its fitting conclusion, Mr. Gladstone appeared at the table, as fresh and vigorous as if it were still '42, and all his responsibilities limited by the range of the yet infant Board of Trade. As it turned out, the *menu* of the dinner whither he was bound did not include that new last course of the Reporter, which has of late added a fresh terror to dining out. Still he had his postscript to many Budget speeches to deliver, to tread once more the intricate mazes of Mr. Goschen's manifold Budget scheme. Being here, and finding the House talking about railways, why should he not contribute a speech? Apart from older reminiscences, the very mention of a railway train suggested rapid movement, expectant crowds at barricaded stations, speeches with head out of window, enthusiastic cheers, and ultimate downfall of a wicked Conservative Government. So Mr. Gladstone made his speech as an ordinary man might offer a casual remark

with no greater effort and no fuller evidence of fatigue when it
was over.

Tireless.　　　　He was talking the day before and the day before
　　　　　　　　that.　Last week he delivered four great speeches,
any one of which would have established a Parliamentary fame.

But it seemed that since the House last saw him he had
renewed his youth, like the eagle.　Even his voice, which
sometimes failed him, had regained its mellowness.　He spoke,
as he often does in chance debates on a Friday or Tuesday
night, in a conversational tone, free from all political acerbity

—a speech luminous with knowledge, profound in wisdom, touched here and there with flash of kindly humour. It was like Priam sitting at the Gate talking in the mellow evening sunlight to the young men around him. Only Priam was old and out of harness, a chief "who no more in bloody fights engaged;" and Mr. Gladstone was to-night as young and full of life as if it were but yesterday he talked with George Hudson about the new and startling project of building a railway all the way to Scotland.

Mr. Disraeli at seventy. In later years, when Mr. Disraeli was yet in the House of Commons, and faced Mr. Gladstone, the Tory chief was much older in manner and appearance than a comparison of almanac dates would seem to justify. Mr. Gladstone is to-day eight years older than Mr. Disraeli was on the August evening in 1876 when he walked out of the House of Commons for the last time, with the word "Empire" on his lips, the final word in the last speech he delivered in the House of Commons. But long before that, save in an occasional spasmodic playfulness, Mr. Disraeli assumed the manner of an old man. He would sit for hours on the Treasury bench with folded arms and impassive face, taking as little part as possible in debate. Mr. Gladstone's share is written large in the reports of the last fortnight. To-night his little aside on the stupendous question of the State purchase of railways was followed by an ordered speech, in which he once more subjected the Budget scheme to searching analysis, after which he lightly stepped out to his deferred dinner. There have been old men in harness before Agamemnon Gladstone—Mr. Disraeli, Lord John Russell, and Lord Palmerston. But for sustained energy, for undiminished power of mind and body, the House of Commons has never seen such a phenomenon as now nightly faces it from the front Opposition bench.

May 18.— "Bobby" boy snubbed. Much talk to-day about the Duke of Westminster. It seems that, having engaged Mr. Robert Spencer, half-brother to Lord Spencer, to dine with him, and Mr. Spencer having in the meantime accepted an invitation to dine with Mr. Parnell at the Eighty Club, the Duke sent him a curt note revoking the invitation.

There is some talk of asking Mr. Balfour whether his attention has been called to this flagrant instance of boycotting, and whether it receives the sanction of Her Majesty's Government.

Lord R. Churchill and Mr. Balfour. It is pretty to see Lord Randolph Churchill, seated on the corner bench behind Ministers, playing with his moustache, while Mr. Balfour stands at the table exponent of the views of the Cabinet Lord Randolph left in a moment of anger. It is one of Lord Randolph's peculiarities that he cannot stand any competition for the first place. He must be everything or he will be nothing. At one time he seemed to have completed his dominion over Lord Salisbury, and it was the discovery that the Prime Minister would not back him up in his peremptory efforts at snubbing Lord George Hamilton and Mr. Stanhope that caused him to quit the Ministry. Still, that Lord Salisbury should assume a position of personal supremacy is a matter for which some excuse may be made. He is well up in years, he is the head of a patrician house, he has earned the confidence of the party. What vexes Lord Randolph is that Mr. Balfour, who, a few years ago, was quite a junior member of the Fourth Party, should now, without assistance from him, and even in opposition to his wishes, have reached a foremost place in the estimation of the Conservative Party and of the House of Commons. Lord Randolph remembers the time when Mr. Balfour used to fetch and carry for him, and feel distinguished by a nod of approval. Now he lords it on the Treasury bench, confident in the assurance that with the Conservative Party, alike in the House and the country, he is absolutely the most popular Minister.

Lord Randolph, it is noted, never tries a fall with Mr. Balfour. Other members of the Ministry whom he holds indebted to him for their personal advancement suffer occasionally from his resentful lash. He has openly expressed his contempt for Mr. Henry Matthews, whom he made Home Secretary, and never misses an opportunity of giving him a little prod in debate. To Sir John Gorst, who was the most active half of the party of which Mr. Balfour was really only an outsider, he does not even speak. That he should be Under-Secretary for India, with a comfortable

salary, whilst Lord Randolph haunts the cold shades of the
Opposition, is more than an amiable spirit can bear.   Accordingly, Lord Randolph cuts Sir John Gorst in private, and in
public, as happened the other day when a question was put
on the Hyderabad Deccan business, he gives him a back-
handed slap.   He would take even more delight in striking at
Mr. Balfour if that were possible.   His abstention from active
hostility is one of the highest tributes to the position Mr.
Balfour has gained.

THE LORD ADVOCATE.

June 1. — The
Lord   Advo-
cate (Mr. Mac-
donald, since
Lord   Kings-
burgh).

The Lord Advocate has not sat opposite Mr.
Mundella for three Sessions for nothing.   He
has taken note of the remarkable effect the
member for Sheffield is able to produce at
critical occasions by a liberal display of blood-
red stocking, and is not above taking a hint from the adversary.   To-night, sitting in his accustomed corner seat on the
Treasury bench, waiting till Mr. Anderson ventured to appear
among the mussel-beds of the tidal waters of Scotland, the

Lord Advocate, with a pretty air of unconsciousness, threw one leg over the other, and flashed to and fro a considerable space of sock of sanguinary hue. This was a danger signal which any body of men less reckless than the Scots would quail before. They know the Lord Advocate by this time. To outward appearance he is a gentleman of almost monumental amiability. But behind his smiling countenance there lurk dark clouds of wrath, which are accustomed to whelm Scotch members at question time. If there is one thing the large mind and broad sympathies of the Lord Advocate cannot away with, it is a Scotch private member. Mr. Mark Stewart he can just tolerate, though he would be better pleased if he reduced by two his average of three speeches in a Session. But for hon. gentlemen opposite who are always getting up wanting to know, and even sometimes. as to-night, presume to place on the Order Book an amendment challenging the conduct of the Government or presuming to advise thereupon, the Lord Advocate, contemplating them, can only mourn the departure of the good old times when Earl William Douglas lived at Thrieve Castle, and " when the gallows knob rarely lacked its tassel."

Scottish humour. It is just six weeks since the ill-omened activity of the Scotch members as nearly as possible placed the Lord Advocate under the appearance of having made a mistake. It was on a Tuesday night, after a morning sitting, and there was quite a cluster of Scotch Bills on the Orders. The Lord Advocate had arranged in his own mind that there should be a count out. There was Professor Bryce, with his Access to Mountains Bill, and somebody else with a Scotch Liquor Traffic Bill. Of course, if the Orders were reached, it would be easy enough for the Lord Advocate to demolish the arguments of the supporters of the Bills, and disastrously rout them. But why take the trouble? Let the House be counted out, and Lowland pride receive a contemptuous rebuff.

So the Lord Advocate arranged matters, and, being in genial mood, planted himself at the glass door to watch the discomfiture of the busybodies opposite. He saw Mr. Bryce rise and almost immediately sit down. Somebody else was up—of course, moving the count. Then the member in charge of the Liquor Traffic Local Veto (Scotland) Bill presented himself, and as promptly sat down. The Speaker had doubtless called his attention to the fact that a count had been moved. But why did not the bell ring? The Lord Advocate would go in and see. So he strolled down the floor of the House, amazed to find himself loudly cheered by "the Glasgae bodies" opposite—amazement which culminated in the discovery that the two Scotch Bills he was specially deputed to oppose had passed their second reading! The canny members in charge, noting his absence, had dispensed with their speeches. Others in the plot held their peace, and there being no opposition, the Bills passed as rapidly as the question could be put from the Chair, the Lord Advocate, all unknowingly, watching the process through the glass door.

June 10.—Father of the House. During the last two or three days new members have been much exercised as to the identity of a tall, elderly gentleman who has been seen within the House of Commons or moving about its precincts. He is distinguished, amongst other things, by wearing a woollen comforter, which hangs straight down by his side to embarrassing lengths, after the fashion long ago made familiar by Trotty Veck. The stranger, as he personally is to nine-tenths of the present House of Commons, is Mr. Talbot, member for Glamorganshire and "father of the House of Commons." He is not often in his place, but came up specially on Tuesday to take part in the expected division on the operation of the Contagious Diseases Acts in India. Being here, he has every day put in an appearance for an hour or two. Mr. Talbot is the only member left who sat in the unreformed Parliament. Born in the third year of the century, he was returned for Glamorganshire in 1830, and has since, without interruption, sat for the County, a matter not only without precedent, but without approach. Mr. Gladstone, who is six years younger, entered the House of Commons two years later, taking his seat for Newark in 1832. Mr. Talbot is the only man now having a seat in the House of Commons who was present when Mr. Gladstone took the oath as member for Newark. He has no contemporaries of his first year in the House.

June 13. — The reformed House.

Thero is no doubt, as earlier pointed out, the new Rules have improved the possibilities of the House as a business assembly. It is equally uncontrovertible that they have made the assembly exceedingly dull. Frolic, once free of the place, has fled elsewhere, or only now and then ambles across the floor hopelessly handicapped. The element of surprise, indispensable to procuring the effects which once made the House of Commons famous as a place of entertainment, has disappeared. The Speaker takes the Chair at three o'clock. At half-past three questions begin. At the outside they do not occupy more than an hour. The Orders of the Day are reached, at midnight debate closes, and members sadly go home. Occasionally one moves the adjournment in order to discuss what he calls a matter of urgent public importance. But the prevalent matter-of-fact mood is not to be disturbed. The House sets itself, without emotion, to consider the question brought forward, and either divides on the adjournment or apathetically sees it withdrawn.

Old things have passed away. Mr. Biggar has become a responsible, respectable personage, who, when Blue Books and four-hours' readings are mentioned, turns the subject of conversation into the channel of the relationships between Germany and Austria. During the Session he wears black broadcloth and a gold chain, and in the recess retires to his castle in Ireland, alternating the pursuits of a country gentleman with the pleasures of a cultured statesman. Mr. Healy is a learned counsel, Mr. O'Brien is in prison or on his way thither, Major O'Gorman is a myth, Mr. Disraeli is dead, and Mr. W. H. Smith leads the House of Commons.

An old story retold.

It is a strangely transformed scene, upon which old members coming back after an interval of compulsory retirement gaze with marvel. And yet, as was shown by the sudden outburst of hilarity at the incursion of Mr. Cavendish-Bentinck, the House is much the same as of old, only lacking opportunity. To-night its spirit had been wounded afresh by a three-hours' debate, which touched a sympathetic chord in the breasts of old members. Sir Roper Lethbridge, with his three years' experience of the House, came up quite brisk with his story, sparing no detail in his

anxioty to instruct the House in a case with which it was
sadly familiar twenty years ago, when the member for North
Kensington was professing political economy in the State
colleges of Calcutta University. Sir Roper might as reasonably have treated the House to a succinct account of the
discovery of America by Columbus, or have announced with
an air of novelty the death of Queen Anne. The wrongs of
Mr. Taylor, of Patna, used to be a standing dish, comparable
in the frequency of its presentation with that other famous
case of Mr. John Clare, with which in unregenerate days Mr.
Biggar, now of Rutlerstown Castle, used to fret the soul of a
helpless House.

One interested
listener.   It is true there was one member, not the least
inconsiderable, who managed to throw into the
attitude of listener an appearance of intense, ungovernable
interest sufficient of itself to keep the debate going. Everyone was surprised to see Mr. Gladstone coming in shortly
after the House was made for the evening sitting. As already
noted, he has abandoned his old habit of sitting out debates
of whatever lack of interest. Even the Committee on the
Local Government Bill cannot chain him to his place. Midway in the morning sitting he had casually looked in, evidently
without intention of taking part in the debate. Lord Lymington by chance rose immediately afterwards, and referring to
Unionist principles as bearing upon the particular point under
discussion, succeeded in drawing up Mr. Gladstone in one of
those playfully sarcastic moods in which he is seen at his best.
In a moment he had transformed the business-like gathering
into a laughing, cheering assembly of partisans. It was, however, but a flash in the pan. Having demolished the unsuspecting and finally alarmed Lord Lymington, he left the
House, probably wending his way to the British Museum to
pursue the inquiry upon which on Wednesday afternoon he
had engaged the assistance of Lord Acton and Mr. John
Morley.

To-night he was down again, hurrying in from a hasty
dinner, fearful to lose a word of the exciting debate. Looking
at him as he tossed about the front bench, leaning forward
with elbow on knee, hand to ear, drinking in with great

intensity the prosy narrative of Sir Roper Lethbridge, the impassioned and not quite consequential harangue of Sir Henry Havelock-Allan, the pitiless criticism of Sir John Gorst, who has a quite surgical manner of dissecting a weak case, it seemed as if the one thing in the world's history that at the moment engrossed his mind was the story of Mr.

Tayler, of Patna. Home Rule for Ireland had drifted hopelessly astern; the shortcomings of Lord Hartington and the far-goings of Mr. Chamberlain were forgotten. Ayr election, by this time settled, was a matter of no consequence. Not only the whole forces of his mind and the full emotions of his soul were given up to the question at the moment debated, but every muscle of his body throbbed under the influence of the rights or the wrongs of Mr. Tayler, who thirty-one years ago did something right or something wrong in far-off Patna.

Mr. Campbell-Bannerman, who happened to drop in and

seat himself near his leader, had an uncommonly bad quarter
of an hour. As the case was carried forward, Mr. Gladstone,
with nervously extended forefinger, punctuated every point
by a thrust at the ribs of his suffering colleague. Ever and
anon he suddenly wheeled round from his listening attitude,
and, turning upon his neighbour, literally pointed the application of something that had been said. Fortunately Mr.
Campbell-Bannerman had not spent some years at the War
Office without learning the strategy of retreat. Once, when
his renowned chief was absorbed for a longer length of time
attentive to the speech in which Mr. Maclean disclosed to an
unsuspecting House the addition of a first-class Parliamentary
debater, Mr. Campbell-Bannerman, with a pretty air of
unconcern, rose, and with light footstep swiftly withdrew.
Presently Mr. Gladstone, turning round and finding the place
next to him empty, peremptorily called up Mr. Henry Fowler,
who thereafter sat privileged by a process of physical concus-
sion to learn how right or how wrong was Mr. Tayler, of
Patna. What Mr. Gladstone's views on the subject were
remains unknown to the House as a body, for, contrary to the
expectation roused by his animated appearance, he refrained
from taking part in the debate.

CHAPTER VIII.

MINISTERIAL DIFFICULTIES.

Colonel King-Harman—Ministerial Misfortune—Sir Charles Forster's Dilemma
—Mr. Arthur Balfour—Lord R. Churchill and Mr. Gladstone—Mr. Stanley
Leighton—Welsh Members—The Decadence of the Irish Members—Mr.
Biggar.

June 16.—Colonel THE death of Colonel King-Harman relieves the
King-Harman.   Government from a difficulty, for the grave
closes over all the personal feeling created in the House of
Commons against the gallant colonel in his ill-fitting political
garb. Only for its politics Colonel King-Harman would have
found life more than endurable. The big, burly ex-lieutenant

of a marching regiment was rather distinguished for muscle than brains. He was more like a character that had stepped from the pages of one of Charles Lever's novels than flesh and blood of the nineteenth century. Like Colonel Tottenham, whom he resembled in height and bulk, King-Harman when he came into his inheritance found himself possessor of a rent roll of nearly £40,000 a year. He went the pace in the jolly, reckless way familiar to the friends of "Tom Burke of Ours." He died with his private fortunes in as troubled a state as were his political. At one time he was the object of wild enthusiasm throughout Ireland. "The King," as he was affectionately called, could not walk through the streets of Dublin without drawing in his train an enthusiastic mob. The right-hand man of Isaac Butt, the idol of the Irish people, he became in his premature old age the ineffectual tool of Mr. Balfour, a target for abuse in the House of Commons, and an object of scorn in his own country.

June 22. — Ministerial misfortunes. Matters are moving fast with Lord Salisbury's Government. Only a fortnight ago they seemed to be plodding steadily forward, not brilliantly, but safely. The Local Government Bill had been entered upon, the Southampton election was beginning to be forgotten, the Opposition maintained a moderate attitude, the Dissentient Liberals backed up the Tories through thick and thin, and the prospects of winning in "the race with an old man" seemed assured. To-day the situation is suddenly changed. Within the space of nine days the Government have withdrawn, under damaging circumstances, a vital section of the Local Government Bill, and have suffered two defeats in the House of Commons. They have lost Ayr, and their coercion policy has met with a serious rebuff in the highest court of law in Ireland. Rarely in politics has a transformation scene been so complete.

Not the least curious feature in the situation is the marked manner in which Lord Randolph Churchill effaces himself. It is nearly a fortnight since his keen face was seen in the House of Commons watching Ministers from his corner seat behind the Treasury bench. He does not, as has been his wont, account for his absence by turning up in some remote

part of the country, whence he says nasty things about his
former colleagues. He does not even write letters to the
newspapers. He is content with assiduous attention upon the
heavy and unattractive duties of Chairman of the Select Committee inquiring into the Army Estimates. This is a course
of daily life so unusual and so unattractive that people are
driven to all kinds of conjecture to account for it. Two
theories pretty equally divide opinion. On one side it is said
he is waiting till the Government are even more hopelessly
entangled by circumstances, and that, seizing a favourable
opportunity, he will swoop down and destroy them. The
other hints that Lord Salisbury and Lord Randolph have come
to terms. that the noble lord will presently return to office, and
that in the meantime he is undergoing a temporary period of
seclusion by way of purging himself of recent offences.

June 29. — Sir
Charles Forster's
dilemma.

Sir Charles Forster had a very anxious five
minutes at this morning's sitting. He appeared
on the scene just when the long list of questions
on the paper had been brought to a close. It seemed that the
search to which has been devoted a long and honourable life
had been crowned with success. For a moment he stood at
the bar with his long-lost hat in one hand and a folded sheet
of paper in the other. Suddenly he advanced at the double
up the floor of the House, making straight for the Speaker,
presumably with the intention of communicating the joyful
intelligence to a sympathetic ear. But just at this time a crisis
had come. The long series of sham fights, dress parades, and
interchange of compliments between hostile camps were at an
end. The Opposition had resolved to give formal battle, and
as Sir Charles Forster presented himself, ignorant of what had
passed, his whole being suffused with joy at the happy termina-
tion of his prolonged endeavour, Mr. John Morley was waiting
to catch the Speaker's eye and the invitation to rise in order
to cast the gauntlet at the foot of the haughty First Lord of
the Treasury, seated with folded arms on the bench opposite.

When Sir Charles Forster left his anchorage at the bar,
and, with eye steadily fixed on the Speaker, made his way towards the Chair, a preliminary skirmish was going forward.
The paper bristled with questions addressed to the Chief

Secretary by Irish members. One after the other had been
tumultuously put and icily answered. Mr. Balfour, with his
back against the wall, stood at bay, parrying with light rapier
the bludgeon blows rained upon him, now and then stepping
forward and pinking an adversary with sharp, clear thrust.

But Sir Charles Forster was not thinking of any of these
things as he made his way towards the table. Perhaps, after
all, it was not the hat he was
going to deposit, but a report
of that interesting and important department of the State,
the Committee on Petitions,
over which he presides. He
had just landed safely at the
foot of the Chair, passing between Ministers and the table,
and had turned to retrace his
steps, when Mr. Balfour, called
up for the twentieth time to
answer a question, barred the
passage. It was a parlous
position for a nervous man.
The House was alive with excitement. Cheers and counter
cheers rang through the
chamber. The Chief Secretary,
with pale, stern face, but with
passionless intonation, was
delivering one of his pointed,
polished retorts, and there
stood Sir Charles Forster,

hemmed in between Ministers and the table, committing a
grievous breach of decorum, inasmuch as he was standing up
when another member was addressing the Chair. There was
the piteous look of the hunted hare in his eyes as he glanced
about for means of escape.

Mr. Balfour is, happily, brief in his replies, and when he
sat down Sir Charles, getting up steam again, started at a
terrific pace to gain his seat above the gangway on the benches
opposite. He had just skirted the mace and headed for the

gangway when Mr. Healy jumped up. To pass between him and the Chair was another offence against Parliamentary etiquette which the Chairman of the Committee on Petitions would have died rather than commit. So Sir Charles, doubling back, dropped into a vacant seat on the Treasury bench, surveying the House with undiminished alarm from this coign of vantage. Mr. Healy was down, and now was the time to get his place. Starting, again at the double, he had not crossed the floor before Mr. Conybeare, temporarily overcoming his constitutional bashfulness, rose to continue the cross-examination of the Chief Secretary.

This was too much for Sir Charles Forster. He was caught, *flagrante delicto*, interposing between an hon. member and the Chair. To go back to the Treasury bench would only aggravate his offence. So, putting on a desperate spurt, he dashed forward and sank down with a grateful groan on the lower step of the gangway. Here he remained in safety till the scene was over, till Mr. Morley had, with rare dramatic energy, declaimed the terms of the challenge to the Government, till Mr. Smith, amid a ringing cheer from the Ministerialists, had accepted the gage of battle for the very earliest day.

June 23.—Mr. Arthur Balfour.   It is a pity Mr. Beresford-Hope did not live to see the marvellous development of the genius and capacity in which he was a fervid and, as to its full extent, a solitary believer. When Mr. Balfour was a somewhat unconsidered follower of Lord Randolph Churchill—the odd man of the Fourth Party—there was a certain pathos in the admiration with which his veteran uncle listened to his rare interposition in debate. In the slim, tall youth, with his pleasant voice, his polished manner, and his picturesque appearance, the member for Cambridge University seemed to see the inchoate form of that Batavian grace of which he was himself in his prime accepted as the embodiment. The uncle lived his youth over again in watching the nephew.

It is doubtful whether even the prophetic soul of Mr. Balfour's uncle ventured to forecast the brilliant Parliamentary success to be achieved in an incredibly brief space of

time.　Whilst yet unattached Mr. Balfour was always a pretty
speaker, with a neat turn for saying nasty things.　But as he
sprawled on the bench below the gangway he was taken at

best for a Parliamentary *flâneur*, a trifler with debate, anxious
chiefly, in some leisure moments, to practise the paces learned
in the hall of the Union at Cambridge.　He was not sufficiently
in earnest or adequately industrious to take his full share in the
labours of the Fourth Party　It was all very well for Mr. Gorst

and **Sir** Henry Wolff to scorn delights and spend laborious hours over Blue Books in order to confound Mr. Gladstone, and to show either that the Khedive was a rogue and the Emperor of Russia an injured person, or *vice versâ*, according as the exigencies of the moment required. The freshness, versatility, audacity, of the new party had attractions occasionally irresistible for Mr. Balfour. On a field-night he might be counted upon to lend his aid, and Mr. Beresford-Hope, exiled to the front Opposition bench, chortled in his joy as he watched and listened to his nephew standing in his own familiar place in the corner seat below the gangway sneering at Sir Stafford Northcote and speaking disrespectfully of Mr. Gladstone. The fair-faced, languid youth, too indolent to stand bolt upright, was the very last person likely to develop into a civil Cromwell, the most unbending, thorough administrator of iron rule Ireland has known since '98. There was no trace of the mailed hand under the silken glove that occasionally dallied with questions **coming** before the Parliament of 1880.

To-day there was notable in Mr. Balfour's manner a further development of a change that has been obtaining the mastery within the last two or three weeks. He is less light-hearted than at the opening of the Session, when Southampton was still a Tory stronghold and Ayr an apparently impregnable position held for the Unionist cause. When disaster begins to dog the steps of a particular line of policy, one of the earliest and surest signs of coming catastrophe is found in the murmurings of the host behind directed against the leader in the van. Mr. Balfour was an eye-witness of the closing days of Mr. Forster's Chief Secretaryship. He will remember how the cheers which regularly encouraged that statesman when he first developed his policy gradually died away, till it came to pass that, night after night, he stood alone, an object of angry contumely from the Irish members, with not a voice raised on his own side to support him. It has not come to that yet with Mr. Balfour. But, as nothing succeeds like success, so there is nothing so depressing as indications of failure. Day by day the spirits of the Irish members, never lacking in boisterousness, are rising, and, whether through weariness or apprehension, the spirit of members opposite is

failing. Things are going wrong. Someone is to blame. Mr.
Balfour has been the most prominent exponent of the Government policy, and if it does not immediately succeed question
begins to arise whether, after all, he is a heaven-born Minister.
There is nothing so cowardly as a crowd, and the House of
Commons is (as Sir William Harcourt is said to regard himself) to a certain extent human. There is no sign of waning
resolution in Mr. Balfour. He may be counted upon to die
with harness on his back. But he is graver in his manner,
less cynical in his replies, more inclined to admit that the
representations of Irish members must receive, if they do
not deserve, some consideration.

June 29.—Lord R. Churchill and Mr. Glad-stone. Second reading of Channel Tunnel Bill moved
once more by the indomitable Sir Edward
Watkin. Mr. Gladstone, speaking on behalf
of the Bill, delivered one of those charming addresses in
which on off-days he deals with non-political questions. Lord
Randolph Churchill was in his best form. His graphic
picture, dramatically illustrative, of the present Cabinet meeting
at the War Office, and deciding who was to touch the button,
through the agency of which, according to Sir E. Watkin,
the Channel Tunnel might upon occasion be blown up, greatly
pleased the House. Even more charming was his attitude
towards Mr. Gladstone. It was the height of comedy to see
the young lordling gravely lecturing the veteran statesman on
the question of economy, gently chiding him for his alleged
ignorance on matters relating to naval and military affairs,
but still graciously holding him up as a bright example which
on the whole he hoped might find followers. It was noteworthy that, even whilst feeling it his duty to call Mr. Gladstone to task, Lord Randolph was unusually deferential in his
personal bearing towards the Leader of the Opposition, who
sat immediately opposite him with hand to ear eagerly
listening, as has always been his wont when Lord Randolph
speaks.

June 30.—Mr. Stanley Leighton. It is a pity Welsh members cannot claim Mr.
Stanley Leighton as one of themselves. He
is not the rose, though he lives near it. As representative of

the Oswestry division of Shropshire, he as nearly occupies the position of a Welsh member as is consistent with being returned for an English constituency. This geographical position happily endows him with all the gravity of the Englishman underlying the vivacity of the Cambrian. Of late the former quality has assumed the supremacy. He has been so long quiescent that his quaint incursion into to-night's debate had the additional charm of surprise. There was a time when he was always popping up, catching the Speaker's eye and (in a Parliamentary sense, of course) tearing his own and Mr. Gladstone's hair. At that epoch he represented North Shropshire, an incident which gave Lord Edmond Fitzmaurice an opportunity, happily used. "The Man from Shropshire" he called the hon. member, who, certainly, both in appearance and manner, recalled the Chancery suitor described in " Bleak House," who periodically appeared in Court, and at the close of nearly every day's business broke forth in rabid effort to address the presiding judge.

Like Mr. Ashmead Bartlett, whose earliest Parliamentary prominence was gained in a somewhat similar fashion, Mr. Stanley Leighton now leaves Mr. Gladstone severely alone, and, no other topic occurring to him, he has rather fallen out of recollection. But he reasserted himself to-night in a manner not likely to be forgotten by the few privileged to be present. As far as could be gathered with any certainty, Mr. Leighton was opposed to the motion under discussion, which was designed to place Wales on a footing of equality with Ireland in the matter of its claim to sympathy on the Land Question. But Mr. Leighton was in such a condition of brimming good humour, both with himself and members opposite, that it was with the greatest pain he dissented from anybody. In this frame of mind it was the more regrettable that he was constantly bringing up members with flat contradiction of opinions attributed to them. Over and over again Mr. Leighton, daintily toying with his *pince-nez*, "w'drew anything he might have said." When he attributed something to the hon. member for Merionethshire he had really had in his mind the hon. member for Montgomery, and when Montgomery rose and hotly denied that he "had said anything of the kind," Mr. Stanley Leighton, still sweetly smiling and toying with his eye-glasses, apologised and "w'drew."

It was just the same when he alluded to the hon. member for Monmouth. He had really meant the hon. member for Macedon, and as Macedon is not now represented in the House of Commons, Mr. Stanley Leighton was able, with a little bow to the Speaker and a simper towards the Serjeant-at-Arms, to proceed with his remarks, which culminated in the declaration that "farmers distrusted politicians who would not assist them to bring in new breeds."

July 1.—Welsh members. There are various phases of dull nights in the House of Commons. There are, for example, the colonels' nights, the admirals' nights, the East Indian nights, Scotch nights, and nights of the gentlemen concerned in the maintenance of roads. Each is delightful in its way. But there is something about a Welsh night, as illustrated to-day, that leaves them in the shade. The Welsh are an ancient nation, distinguished in war, in literature, and in music. To this day they hold their national Eisteddfodd. Yet it is a fact which has not received the measure of attention its importance and interest warrant that in the House of Commons the Welsh members have never made a mark. Numerically, as compared with other divisions of the United Kingdom, they are in a minority. With England sending 465 members to the House of Commons, Scotland 72, and Ireland 103, gallant little Wales has to struggle with the disadvantage of having only 30 representatives. Still, it has had that number for at least fifty years, and memory does not recall any Welshman who has succeeded in making a first-class Parliamentary position. It has never given any leading Minister, and though it is true in Mr. Gladstone's last Administration Mr. Osborne Morgan worthily filled the important office of Judge-Advocate-General, yet the fact remains that immediately afterwards this ancient post was dug up. There is a considerable portion of legal gentlemen among the Welsh members, and they are nearly all Q.C.'s. The limit of their attainable ambition for official life seems reached when they are appointed County Court Judges. Why this should be, who shall say?

The lack of Parliamentary "go" about the Welsh members is to be the more deplored in view of the continued decadence of the Irish member. The part he but a few years ago filled in Parliamentary proceedings is now abandoned, and the gaiety of the House of Commons is eclipsed. There is still a little badger-

FRANK HUGH O'DONNELL.

ing at question time, and, as happened on the two first days of the past week, there is occasionally a set debate on Irish affairs. But with new times we have other men and different manners. Time and circumstances have wrought grievous gaps in the representation of Ireland. Not to go so far back as the time when Baron Dowse sat on the Treasury bench, and illumined debate with the rich humour which seems to have exhausted the mine as far as his successors are concerned, Mr. Macnaghten with his shrewd speech is silent in another place. Mr. Dawson, who used from time to time to thrill the House of Commons by dealing with imperial questions, "speaking as Lord Mayor of Dublin," is no more. Captain O'Shea has carried out of the House the secret of the Kilmainham Treaty. Mr. William Shaw, whom to look at was an education in sagacity, has disappeared. Dr. Lyons no longer fights for the corner seat which Lord Randolph Churchill has now appropriated. Mr. O'Donnell has dropped his eyeglass for the last time in the presence of a howling majority. Where is "the gay and dashing Lysaght Finnigen;" the meritorious Mitchell Henry; the mellifluous Pat O'Brien:

Whisky O'Sullivan, with his rich brogue and his contempt of silent spirit; George Errington, who cast an air of cultured clothing over the somewhat ragged ranks of his compatriots: O'Connor Power, able and eloquent; the Rev. Mr. Nelson, who, temporarily freed from the limits of his pulpit, made the delivery of a speech in the House of Commons the opportunity for a perambulation; the mute Metge; P. J. Smyth, with his plain manner and his gorgeous oratory; the O'Donoghue, ever halting between two parties; A. M. Sullivan, "the eloquent member for Louth," as Mr. Gladstone once called him; Isaac Butt, bland and astute; his forlorn lieutenant, M'Carthy Downing; John A. Blake, with his confidential correspondence with his toddy-drinking uncle? All, all are gone, the old familiar faces. In their place resentful Ireland gives the House of Commons the Harringtons, the Redmonds, Dr. Commins, Mr. Tuite, and Dr. Tanner.

O'CONNOR POWER.

Mr. Biggar. Of the old band one still lingers with us, but he is sadly changed. In the responsible middle-aged gentleman, carefully dressed in black, with prosperous gold chain and still budding moustache, no one would recognise the Joseph Gillis Biggar of ten years ago, the patriot who used to read to a writhing House of Commons Blue Books for the space of four hours, who once lightly alluded to Mr. Gladstone as "a vain old gentleman," who was never so happy as through an all-night sitting, who snatched the fearful joy

of sleep stretched on two chairs in the library, and who came
back with the rising sun to assure hon. members (who rather
hoped he had gone under) that he had " returned like a giant
refreshed."   There has during the last two days been a dread

whisper that the member for Cavan is going into society.   He
has been seen in the gilded *salon* of one of the stately man-
sions which lift their heads to the east of Temple Bar.   Mr.
Biggar's carriage has stopped the way in Stonecutter Street.
When it comes to this it seems time to abandon all hope,
as far as Irish members are concerned, of the revival of the old
order of things. Society's gain is the House of Commons' loss.

CHAPTER IX.

MR. PARNELL PLEADS " NOT GUILTY."

Mr. Gladstone—At Seventy-nine—Mr. Parnell pleads "Not Guilty"—Mr. Courtney as Chairman of Committees—Mr. Ashmead Bartlett—The Parnell Commission Bill—Mr. Parnell and the *Times*—A Moneyed Man— An Irish Member.

July 5.— Mr.
Gladstone.

IN one respect Mr. Gladstone is, in fullest measure, the representative Parliament man. Several members can be as serious as he when weighty questions are to the fore, but none can equal him in the intensity of unfeigned interest in the purest trifling with forms of debate. Watching him to-night, literally bounding about on the front Opposition bench whilst the question of payment of members was under discussion, a deaf mute in the Strangers' Gallery might have been forgiven if he concluded that news had just come (as it did on a memorable night in Mr. Forster's time) that the Russians were at the gates of Constantinople. At least it might reasonably be supposed that the short, sharp fight, with its varying phases, was over, and that Home Rule, which once seemed to have finally wrecked his position, was actually within reach of his nervously extended right hand.

There are some people accustomed to find deep design in Mr. Gladstone's most ordinary action, and certainly his presence through the long hours of the debate on Mr. Fenwick's motion seems to suggest necessity for research. To ordinary men, as yet far off their seventy-ninth year, the opportunity seemed specially made for quietly going home to bed. It is true the business for which the House was summoned to meet at nine o'clock was Committee of Supply, in which a few hours might well be spent to the advantage of the public service. But there was no chance of getting into Committee. Mr. Fenwick had had the personal good fortune to bar the way with a motion, cautiously suggesting the expediency of " reverting to the ancient custom of paying members for their services in Parliament." The topic was not without interest, and was

precisely suited to that admirable institution the Kensington
Parliament.   But for the House of Commons, with the Speaker
in the Chair, the mace on the table, Supply in arrear, and the
Local Government Bill advanced only as far as its 21st Clause,
it would seem criminal, if it were not ridiculous, to devote a
night to the subject.

Yet here was Mr. Gladstone, not a passive listener, looking
in late on his way home from dinner, content to take a
preliminary doze in the House of Commons, but in a positively
electric condition from head to heel. Whoever the speaker
might be, whether it was Admiral Field below the gangway,
forging ahead under heavy press of canvas, or Sir John Gorst
immediately facing him, humorously posing as "an old Tory,"
Mr. Gladstone turned in the direction of the voices, with hand
to ear, sitting on the very verge of the bench, so as not to lose
a word of the precious utterance. It was all, at best, the
merest academical trifling, the veriest indulgence in debating
society dialectics; and here was the veteran statesman of world-
wide fame, with the weight of fifty years' public service on his
shoulders, drinking it all in with contagious avidity.

The fact that the discussion was raised on an abstract
motion did not check his enthusiasm. The House has often,
when convenience has called for protest, heard him declaim
in ardent speech against the practice of putting forth abstract
resolutions, and the unfairness of asking the House to vote
upon them. He might have found in that fact alone adequate
reason for stopping away, or, being present, of showing some
signs of impatience. Or, taking up other and quite familiar
grounds, he might have resented the whole business as un-
dignified trifling with precious time. The aspect of the
House could scarcely have been congenial to a work-worn
statesman. Nearly everyone was in dinner dress. Laughter,
hilarious cheering, and more or less humorous interjections
prevailed. If one of the gods in the gallery had put a bent
finger in his mouth and shrilly whistled, it would have
seemed all in keeping. Absence of sound of the popping of
the corks of ginger-beer bottles and of smell of orange-peel
struck the senses. The broad expanse of white shirt-front on
the Conservative benches recalled the " chappies " in another
place. It was like a big night at Evans's in old times, with

Admiral Field as Paddy Green to say "Dear boy!" and affectionately smite new comers on the shoulder.

At seventy-nine. It all proved irresistible for Mr. Gladstone. When he had, with boyish delight, watched Admiral Field stumbling through his speech, rolling head over heels through mingled metaphors, like an elderly porpoise tumbling in the sea, he showed a disposition to jump in himself. But Sir John Gorst was before him, and with undiminished interest Mr. Gladstone followed the Under-Secretary's ordered speech. Then he could wait no longer, and, springing up, plunged into the controversy. As he stood at the table, his tall, lithe figure drawn to its fullest height, turning right and left as the ripple of laughter and the roar of cheers followed his sentences, he conveyed to the House a sense of absolute youth alike of mind and body, of undiminished strength and unsapped vitality, that could not fail to make an impression even on those most familiar with his recent public appearances.

Peradventure, since the reason is hard to find in ordinary grooves, this was the explanation of his unexpected interposition. There has been talk about pitting the maximum life of a Parliament in its third Session against the accumulating years of "an old man." If any were reckoning on Parliament winning, let them look at the Old Man, springing up at midnight on the last day of a laborious week's sitting, delivering an oration of consummate skill, practically about nothing, talking for the simple pleasure of making a speech and working off some surplus energy. As Mr. Matthews pointed out in a speech which came nearer to House of Commons style than any he has delivered since a freak of fortune made him Home Secretary, Mr. Gladstone "delivered himself of a charming speech, which contained an abundance of statements, but was absolutely colourless and meaningless so far as regarded expression of opinion."

That was exactly it. Mr. Gladstone is too old a Parliamentary hand to commit himself, even in the maddest exuberance of verbosity, on a matter of comparative unimportance. He made his speech (possibly with the underlying purpose suggested) on the principle avowed by Mr. Wemmick when he led Miss Skiffins to the altar. "Hallo!" said Mr. Wemmick, passing down a street with his affianced on his arm, "here's a church; let's go in and get married." "Hallo!" said Mr. Gladstone, looking in at the House of Commons at half-past nine last night, "here's a debate; let's go in and make a speech."

July 6.—Mr. Parnell pleads "not guilty." Mr. Parnell, having been solemnly and deliberately charged with being an accessory to murder, stood up in the House of Commons just now and pleaded "Not Guilty." Although a morning sitting, every place was crowded from the floor to the galleries. A strictly judicial air prevailed. Each man looked as if he were summoned upon his oath well and truly to try the issue between our Sovereign Lady the Queen and the prisoner at the Bar. When Mr. Parnell rose a cheer greeted him from the compact body of Irish members mustered around. Mr. Biggar, with thumb reflectively inserted in the armhole of his waistcoat, stood in the centre of the throng at the Bar, with glasses astride his nose, and an air of gentle and remote interest in the proceedings charming to look upon. No one finding him there could have imagined that he was bracketed in the indictment against Mr. Parnell which the Attorney-General had on the previous day thundered forth in the Court of Queen's Bench.

For Mr. Biggar a tender interest mingled with the more tragic aspects of the story. Mr. Joseph Cowen, in the witness-box, had been led to touch upon the memorable flight to Paris in which Mr. Biggar had joined, and which had incidentally drawn him into alleged matrimonial relations subsequently investigated in a court of law. Exiles from their country, from the time of the Young Pretender down to the year 1882, have ever been inclined to seek female sympathy, and Mr. Biggar, in his brief sojourn at Paris, proved no exception to the rule.

Possibly he thought of this as he stood listening to his chief, who, with icy manner and level tones, put from him the charge of murder as if it had merely been one of using a false quantity in quoting from the Latin grammar. Throughout the brief speech the crowded House sat silent, save for an

occasional mechanical cheer from the Irish camp. When Mr.
Parnell had made an end of speaking, and Mr. Justin M'Carthy
had added a few words, the House passed to the Orders of the
Day. Nobody said anything ; but perhaps everyone thought
the more.

July 14. — Mr. Courtney as Chairman of Committees.   Mr. Courtney has achieved the rare reputation
of successfully filling a post which experience
shows was one girt about with prickly difficulties. Justice has never been done to Sir Lyon Playfair
during the period he filled the same office. He may be said
to have assisted at the birth of Obstruction, and he certainly
passed some very bad nights with the lusty infant. Between
1880 and 1883 the Irish members deliberately, and without
taking the trouble to assume any cloak of decency, "went for"
the Chairman of Committees. He had a terrible, turbulent
time, compared with which a bout with the beasts at Ephesus
was child's play. If he sometimes failed in preserving the
dignity and authority of the Chair, those who think they
could have done better are to be congratulated upon not
having had the opportunity of trying.

Mr. Courtney answers for order under quite other conditions. He is armed with disciplinary rules which did not
exist in Sir Lyon Playfair's time. The whole conditions of life
and business in the House of Commons are changed. Obstruction as it was organised in 1880 and ruled the roost up to
1885 no longer exists. It is not only that the lions of the
Parnellite Party lie down with the lambs of Liberalism, but
time has wrought soothing changes with obstructionists in
other quarters of the House whose fame once filled the land
and worried the Chairman of Committees. Mr. Cavendish
Bentinck long ago passed out of the ranks he once adorned
and sometimes led. To Dr. Tanner or Mr. Conybeare of to-
day the right hon. gentleman stands much in the same relation
as a cloaked and grizzled Chelsea pensioner bears towards a
recruit in scarlet who has just mastered the intricacies of the
goose step. Even the return of Mr. James Lowther to familiar
haunts has not succeeded in bringing back the light that once
beamed in Mr. Cavendish Bentinck's eye when Mr. Gladstone's
name was mentioned. Just as on sunny Sabbaths the worn

veteran from Chelsea shows himself in the streets, and may
with due persuasion be brought to talk of war and days that
are no more, so at rare intervals, lured by some congenial
topic, Mr. Cavendish Bentinck, rising in the mellow midnight
hour, will prattle about pictures and mumble over misplaced
monuments.

Mr. Ashmead Bartlett.   Other changes Mr. Courtney sees in persons
who when he yet sat below the gangway were
accustomed to wrestle with the authority in the Chair. Coming
later into the field, and further removed from the state of
Parliamentary dotage, these gentlemen have developed into
responsible Ministers of the Crown, or sober statesmen ready
by their weight and personal influence to support the authority
of the Chair whenever and by whomsoever attacked. There is
Mr. Ashmead Bartlett, for example. Never since the time
when that doughty champion of dockyard reform, the late Sir
James Elphinstone, was transformed by a similar process of
mutation, has such a notable change been witnessed by contemporaries in the House of Commons. When Sir Lyon
Playfair was in the Chair, Mr. Ashmead Bartlett was one of the
most constant and successful competitors for an eye difficult
to be caught behind imposing spectacles. Omniscience was
the *forte* of the then member for Eye, and Foreign Affairs his
foible. Alas! poor Civil Lord of the Admiralty. The House
of 1880 knew him well. Where be now his questions, his
motions, and his interjections that used to keep the Commons
in a roar of contumely?

The strain upon the Chairman of Committees to-day is
of a totally different character from what it was in the period
between 1880 and 1885. Still, it is of enormous weight and
constant tension. Take, for instance, the Local Government
Bill, for the smooth and business-like passage of which through
Committee the House of Commons and the country are
largely indebted to Mr. Courtney. When one of the greater
Irish Land Bills was passing through the Commons Mr.
Gladstone said he believed there were only three men in the
House who were thoroughly acquainted with its details. One
was Mr. Law, the then Attorney-General for Ireland, another
was Mr. Healy, and the third himself. Taking the Local

Government Bill, with its 162 clauses, its five schedules, and
its escort of amendments, at one time exceeding eighty
pages, it is probable that, with the exception of Mr. Ritchie,
Mr. Courtney is the only man who is able to take a clear
view of the illimitable landscape. The great body of members
whose simple duty it is to vote in divisions may occasionally dutifully sacrifice half an hour, an hour, or—before
dinner—two consecutive hours to the debate, free to go and
come as they list. A member in charge of an amendment
must needs sit it through, and then his interest lapses. But
the Chairman of Committees sits hour after hour with mind
intensely fixed not only on the immediate course of the debate,
but on the long line it has passed and the direction whither it
is tending. He must be courteous but firm, watchful and
ready; out of the Chair no more than an ordinary member,
liable to be suspended by the Speaker, in the Chair the autocrat of the hour empowered to suspend others. Above all, he
must rise beyond the faintest suspicion of political or personal
leaning, and even when the question of Proportional Representation crops up must look as if he had never heard the
phrase before, and had never taken tea with Sir John Lubbock.

All these conditions Mr. Courtney meets, and though he
rules with an iron hand, never once since he took the Chair
has a breath of suspicion of his impartiality and honesty of
purpose floated through the heated chamber.

July 15. — The
Parnell Com-
mission Bill.
In asking the First Lord of the Treasury
whether the Government had held any communication with the leading counsel for the *Times*
in the case of O'Donnell v. Walter and another, with respect
to the charges brought against members of the House, Mr.
Summers touched an explosive subject. Mr. Smith sharply
answered that there was not the slightest foundation for the
statement implied in the question. The Attorney-General,
interposing, emphasised this denial by stating that he had
received no communication from the Government on the
subject, either direct or indirect.

Mr. Sexton, varying the aspect of the topic, asked whether
the Attorney-General had given his assistance in drawing up
the Bill for the appointment of a Commission of Judges. Mr.

Smith, hastily rising to answer before the question was concluded, faced Mr. Sexton for two or three moments amid cheers, counter cheers, and cries of "Order." The Leader of the House finally resuming his seat, Mr. Sexton concluded his question. Observing that the Bill was already drawn up, Mr. Smith went on to say he declined to answer any question as to communications that had passed between any members of the Government in discharge of their duty, an announcement broken in upon by cheers and counter cheers.

The questions on the paper disposed of, Mr. Parnell, who had made several ineffectual attempts to catch the Speaker's eye, rose and asked Mr. Smith whether the fixing of the notice for leave to introduce the Members of Parliament (Charges and Allegations) Bill at the end of thirty-one Orders of the Day and five notices of motion was an indication of the importance assigned to the measure by the Government. He further asked whether the Bill would be circulated to-morrow, and whether the second reading would be put down for an early day as the first order.

Amid a scene of growing excitement, Mr. Smith went back to the formula, already familiar to the House, that it was for Mr. Parnell to say whether he would accept the Bill or decline it. If it were accepted, it would be forthwith read a first time and printed. But the First Lord did not intend to make provisions for debating the measure. He was neither able nor desirous to occupy the time of the House of Commons with discussion at any length.

Mr. Parnell, who was in a state of unusual excitement, moved the adjournment of the House in order to discuss the question as one of urgent public importance. The Speaker pointed out that there being on the paper a notice of motion with respect to the Bill, it would be out of order to move the adjournment. Mr. Parnell explained that he had no intention of discussing the Bill, only the procedure of the Government with reference to it. The Speaker again ruled him out of order, and remained standing whilst Mr. Parnell, amid angry shouts from the Conservatives and cheers from the Irish members, endeavoured to make himself heard. Finally, Mr. Parnell resumed his seat, but it was only to await opportunity.

This came when the business on the Orders was disposed

of. It was ten minutes after midnight, and the House was densely crowded. Speaking in a manner far removed from his usual passionless tone, he denounced it as "a monstrous proposition" that he should be asked to accept or decline a Bill before it was printed and before it was explained. The acceptance of the Bill was not a question for him or for Mr. Smith. If the allegations made against him were true, he whom they called "an honourable member" was dishonourable and dishonoured. Mr. Smith and the Attorney-General, who sat by his elbow, knew whether the statements were true. If they were, instead of coming down and attempting to make bargains with him, they ought to have indicted him. He would give Mr. Smith no chance of creeping out of his undertaking. He would offer no opposition to the introduction of the Bill, but in Committee he would claim his right to take the judgment of the House upon any of its details.

July 27. — Mr. Parnell and the Times. Lord Herschell and Sir Charles Russell have been consulted on the question of the desirability of Mr. Parnell bringing an action for libel against the *Times*. Unfortunately these eminent authorities disagree, and it is probable the matter will be dropped. Mr. Parnell will not go into a court of law unless he can be assured that the inquiry will be limited to the truth or falsehood of the allegations personal to him made by the *Times*, more particularly in respect of the letters he alleges to be forged. One counsel believes that can be done; the other doubts it. A third authority from another branch of the profession has stated his opinion that it would be quite possible so to conduct the case that Mr. Parnell's object of avoiding a fishing inquiry into the proceedings of the Land League would be gained. This is Mr. George Lewis, of Ely Place. Still another point raised in the consultation not yet finally closed is whether it would not be too late now to refer the matter to a court of law, and whether on the whole it will not be better to take the Commission offered by the Government and make the best of it.

July 30. — A moneyed man. Lord Leveson still sticks to the half-crown he swallowed among other delicacies at Christmas time, whilst engaged upon an amateur conjuring performance.

Everyone will be glad to know that the popular son of the genial Leader of the Opposition in the House of Lords is not a penny, much less a half-crown, the worse for the adventure. He indeed seems to thrive upon the current coin of the realm, and was never in better health.

"He has gained 11 lbs.," said Lord Granville to a youthful colleague on the front bench, who was inquiring after Lord Leveson's health.

"Ah," said the witty Peer, "that makes £11 2s. 0d."

An Irish member.   Mr. O'Kelly, the latest fish that has fallen into Mr. Balfour's sweeping net, has not been much heard of in the present Parliament. The garment of common-

THE O'KELLY, T.C.

place decorum which Irish members, including Mr. Biggar, now wear does not suit the warlike member for Roscommon. He is the kind of man who would have made an historic name had he lived in the time of Drake and Raleigh. As it is, he

has made the most of whatever opportunities have offered.
When war broke out between France and Germany he offered
his sword to the Republic, and saw some fighting on the Loire.
Next he joined the service of the *New York Herald*, on whose
behalf he proceeded to Cuba, then in a state of revolt. Mr.
O'Kelly was seized by the insurgents or the Government (I
forget which), but certainly was sentenced to be shot, and
narrowly escaped the doom. Later still he fought for the
United States against that eminent convert to Christianity,
Sitting Bull, who at the time was living in sin with all the
dignity of a Sioux chief. Coming to this country, Mr. O'Kelly
was in 1880 elected as member for Roscommon, and joyfully
entered into the nightly fray that used at that epoch to go on
in the House of Commons. He joined the Land League, made
seditious speeches, and was clapped into Kilmainham by Mr.
Forster. When he got out, the only part of the world where
war was going on was the Soudan. Thither Mr. O'Kelly gleefully went, carrying the flag of the *Daily News*, and pledged
to discover the Mahdi. But he did not get further than
Dongola. Since his return he has lived a quiet life, the world
forgetting by the world forgot, till now Mr. Balfour winds up a
cycle in his career by clapping him into prison.

CHAPTER X.

THE PARNELL COMMISSION.

"Judas!"—The Duel between Mr. Parnell and Mr. Chamberlain—Mr. W. H.
Smith's "Old Friend"—The Lord Advocate at his Post—Mr. Goschen on
his Legs—Mr. Disraeli's Hat—Mr. Balfour's Attitude—Lord G. Hamilton's
Scrap of Paper—Final Division on the Commission Bill—A Sleeping
Member.

July 30.—
"Judas!"   In Committee on Parnell Commission Bill;
much irritation in all parts of House. Rising
at five minutes to twelve, Mr. Parnell introduced a new turn
in the debate by a bitter attack upon Mr. Chamberlain, whom
he accused, when a private member, of using Irish members to

M

do work he was not inclined to assume the responsibility for, and when a Minister of betraying the counsel of his colleagues in order to maintain his secret connection with Irish members. At midnight, whilst Mr. Parnell was still speaking, the debate was adjourned by the Standing Order, and the ringing cheers with which the Irish members greeted their Leader's foray on the Dissentient Liberal camp were maintained for several minutes.

Amid the roar rose a cry of "Judas Chamberlain!"

Mr. Chamberlain, who was sitting on the front bench, sharply turned round and asked—

"What is that? What did he say?"

Mr. Biggar obligingly informed the right hon. gentleman what had been said. As soon as the Speaker returned to the Chair, Mr. Chamberlain, amid cheers from the Conservative side, called attention to the episode, naming Mr. T. P. O'Connor as having started the cry, and Mr. Biggar as having repeated it. Mr. Parnell showed some disposition to argue the matter on a point of order. But the Speaker called upon Mr. O'Connor to say whether he had made use of the language. Mr. O'Connor admitted the impeachment, Mr. Biggar being, upon the evidence of Lord Hartington, acquitted from the charge brought against him by Mr. Chamberlain. Mr. O'Connor asked leave to withdraw the words, which he admitted were out of order, and the incident, which had been eagerly followed by a crowded House, closed.

July 31. — The duel between Mr. Parnell and Mr. Chamberlain.

There was a consensus of opinion, wherever the remarkable scene which took place in the House of Commons at midnight was talked about, that Mr. Chamberlain would be bound to take notice of the terrible indictment Mr. Parnell publicly brought against him. It amounted to the charge that Mr. Chamberlain had, for his own purpose, at one period of his career used the Irish members as instruments for attacking the Conservative Government, and that later, when between 1880 and 1885 he occupied Cabinet office, he had betrayed the secrets of the Cabinet in order to maintain his relations with the Irish members. That was not the kind of charge from which any public man could run away, and even

Mr. Chamberlain's bitterest enemies, whose name just now is legion, would not accuse him of a disposition to turn his back on an assailant. Accordingly, no one was to-day surprised to find Mr. Chamberlain early in attendance. He took his seat at the end of the front Opposition bench shortly after a quarter past three, and was later joined by Lord Hartington and Sir Henry James.

If Mr. Chamberlain was ready to meet Mr. Parnell, it soon became evident that Mr. Parnell was not disinclined for the encounter. Without preface he, when the Order of the Day was reached, took up the thread of his discourse where it had been dropped on the previous sitting at the stroke of midnight. In the same passionless way in which he had in the ear of the startled House opened his accusation against Mr. Chamberlain he now continued it. He had not gone far before the Chairman interposed on a point of order, whereupon Mr. Parnell promised to reserve further statement until he came before the Commission, when he undertook to prove every one of his allegations by letters written by Mr. Chamberlain.

This was a new and quite unexpected turn of affairs, watched by the crowded House with acutest interest. Mr. Gladstone, turning round, sat forward with hand to ear, thus coming uncomfortably close to Mr. Chamberlain, who, with arms folded, sat a little lower down on the bench. Cheers and counter cheers broke in upon the statements, Mr. Parnell always waiting till the noise had subsided, and then going forward in the same quiet, business-like way, taking up the sentence and sometimes the syllable where it had been broken in upon.

Mr. Smith fumbled with his portfolio, and looked anxiously towards Mr. Courtney, evidently wondering how far this was to go. It was certainly a curious turn of events. Here was Mr. Parnell in the dock, as it were, upon a charge of complicity with murder. Instead of pleading not guilty and endeavouring to prove his innocence, he suddenly turned upon one of the principal supporters of the indictment and forced him into the position of the accused. It was not business as business was set down upon the Orders. But it was a development of bold and unexpected tactics, which left the House in a state of profound excitement.

Mr. Chamberlain next addressed the House in a manner the studious calm of which excelled even Mr. Parnell's. He was evidently deeply wounded, but had completely recovered the habitual self-possession momentarily lost at midnight, when the tumultuous cry of "Judas!" went up from the Irish camp. At first he showed a disposition to deny everything. He had not, he said, the remotest idea of the special circumstances Mr. Parnell had alluded to, but as he went along Mr. Parnell, by various interjections, helped his memory, and in the end Mr. Chamberlain admitted that he had from time to time between 1880 and 1885 held communication direct and indirect with Mr. Parnell. But—and here was the gist of his defence—he declared that every one of those communications he had made known to Mr. Gladstone, Lord Hartington, Mr. Forster, and other colleagues in the Cabinet directly concerned. In brief, what Mr. Parnell described as "the midnight conferences of a conspirator playing for his own hand behind the backs of his colleagues" Mr. Chamberlain held forth as the ordinary actions of an able and active Minister, anxious to serve Ireland, and carefully keeping his colleagues acquainted with all that had taken place in his semi-private character.

Mr. Gladstone followed with a few words, in the course of which he cautiously guarded himself against the admission that Mr. Chamberlain had told him all that had passed in connection with the Kilmainham confabulations. But as far as another branch of the intercommunications were concerned, viz., that of dealing with the proposal of national councils as the basis of a Home Rule scheme, Mr. Gladstone made haste to say that his memory confirmed Mr. Chamberlain's narrative.

Here the incident closed, having lasted not quite an hour. On the whole, compared with the short, sharp attack by Mr. Parnell on the previous night, followed up by the scene in which Mr. Chamberlain was assailed by the Irish members, it came in the form of an anti-climax. To those having any knowledge of the undercurrent of affairs between 1880 and 1885 (and there was no particular secret in the matter) there was nothing new in Mr. Chamberlain's admissions to-night, or in the colour Mr. Parnell attempted to place upon the proceedings. A part of the story that was new, and made considerable impression upon the House, was the account of the visit of Mr. Parnell and Mr. Justin M'Carthy to Mr. Chamberlain's private residence on the terrible Sunday when London was throbbing with news of the assassination of Lord Frederick Cavendish. There was something grimly comical in Mr. Parnell's outline sketch of Captain O'Shea knocking at Mr. Chamberlain's door a little later, and his chagrin on discovering that Mr. Chamberlain was not alone.

Mr. W. H. Smith's "old friend." After the Parnell-Chamberlain incident the House of Commons got to work on the Commission of Judges Bill, and made very slow progress. The electrical atmosphere of the chamber was not lowered even by the incursion of the dinner hour. On an innocent-looking amendment by Mr. Molloy, not an exciting speaker, there arose a boisterous scene, which presented the House in its very worst aspect. Sir W. Harcourt, who has thrown himself into the discussion with great vigour, brought to the front all the gossip about the interview of Mr. Walter, the proprietor of the *Times*, with Mr. W. H. Smith. That such an interview took place, Mr. Smith, driven to the wall, finally admitted. But he tried to minimise its importance by describing it rather as a morning call of "an old friend." It was a painful position for Mr. Smith, who above all things is an honest man, and is conspicuously uneasy when exigencies of State impose upon him an attitude of appearing to dissemble. Inexorably pressed from the Opposition benches, he finally admitted that Mr. Walter, in quite a casual way, *had* mentioned the Parnell Commission Bill; but that he had in any way influenced the action of the Government in drafting it Mr. Smith denied in an excited manner that was as painful to witness as it was ineffectual in supporting his case. The general feeling in the House was that if Mr. Parnell had called at Grosvenor Square, and sent in his card to Mr. Smith, the Leader of the House of Commons would, with natural politeness, have begged to be excused from meeting him under the peculiar circumstances of his official position.

Aug. 8. — The Lord Advocate at his post. Lord Salisbury, who does not visit the House of Commons so much as it might be worth his while to do, little knows what a stout bulwark his Government possesses in the person of the Lord Advocate.

Regarded solely as a physical make-weight for Sir William
Harcourt, Mr. Macdonald is an acquisition of peculiar value to
the Treasury bench. He is about the same height, would
probably weigh about the same tonnage, and brings the same
imposing presence to the table. When Sir William Harcourt
poses as the general denouncer of whomsoever may differ from
him; as he swings about in the frenzy of eloquence and to the
imminent personal danger of colleagues immediately near him;
as his voice sinks to the lowest depths of sorrowful indignation,
or is uplifted to the height of thunderous reproof, somehow
there comes back to the memory what Lamb once said of
another great man for whom he had a warm personal affection
and almost unmixed admiration.

" Coleridge," Lamb wrote, " is an archangel a little
damaged."

In his loftier moods—when, for example, he is reproving
Mr. Goschen or sorrowing over Lord Hartington—there is
something of the shady archangel in Sir William's majestic
manner. But the Lord Advocate, though he too can scold
when a Scotch member has presumed to open his mouth,
never suggests an archangel, in whatever imperfect condition.
He is a plain Scotchman, of the kind of which bailies and
provosts are made, whom a strange freak of fortune has led
to the Treasury bench of the House of Commons.

From the first the Lord Advocate appropriated to himself
the end seat by the gangway, which, with the crossbar,
is endowed with pleasing reminiscences of the corner bench
in a Scotch kirk. Here, with his broad back stiffly set against
the post, with an angry profile visible from the benches below
the gangway where certain Scotch members connive with the
Parnellites, with a benignant visage turned upon Mr. W. H.
Smith, the Lord Advocate sits hour after hour keeping the
Speaker in countenance. The awed mind shrinks from contemplation of what would happen if, by any chance, he were
deprived of this corner seat and found himself somewhere
midway on the Treasury bench, where Lord Advocates before
him usually sat.

In spite of the temporary political predominance of
Liberalism in the Scotch contingent in the House of Commons
at the present day, there is a prevalent strain of Conservatism

in the Scotch character. Probably in bygone ages, when the
Maccallum More put up posts over his estate, a forbear of
the Lord Advocate may have joined in the grateful cry, " God
bless the Duke of Argyll !" which echoed through the wilds
of Inverary. Quite unconsciously, from mere stress of ancestral
habit, the passion for having a post at his back may exist to
this day in the breast of a distinguished descendant. However
it be, or whatever be the explanation, the fact remains that
the Lord Advocate must have his back pressed firmly in his
corner seat if he is to regard with equanimity and concentrated
thought the political problems that hourly present themselves
in the Legislature.

Mr. Goschen on
his legs.
   This passion for propinquity finds a curious
parallel in the case of Mr. Goschen, who is never
thoroughly happy when addressing the House of Commons
unless he is sustained by the consciousness that the backs of
his legs are pressing against the edge of the bench from which
he has risen. If in the fervour of eloquence he momentarily
advances a step, he delights the House with some of the
gestures of the proverbial drowning man clutching at straws.
He claws at the air, passes his open hand up and down his
side, halts in his speech, loses the thread of his discourse, and
would probably break down if, in the course of his efforts, he
did not re-establish contiguity with the bench. Thereafter all
goes well again. His ideas flow smoothly, the illustrations and
arguments he had forgotten become clear to his mind, he goes
forward with irresistible force, till in an unhappy moment he
takes a step forward. The spell is broken, once more the
orator clutches at the air, spasmodically catches imaginary
flies buzzing within an inch of his nose, smooths himself up
and down with open hand, and convulsively works his way
back to the bench.

Mr. Disraeli's
hat.
   In his earlier Ministerial experiences Mr. Balfour
used to find official life not worth living unless
he could put his feet on the table. In his salad days, when
he sat below the gangway, an ornamental appendage of the
Fourth Party, he had all the floor before him where to choose
to spread his legs. He made the most of the opportunity, and

his figure sprawling half-way across the House, like a languid lily pulled yesterday, was one of the most familiar features in a debate. When he reached the Treasury bench he was hampered by a difficulty in some degree akin to that which fettered Mr. Disraeli's freedom when he went to the House of Lords. Whilst he was yet in the Commons, Mr. Disraeli, contrary to the custom of leaders of parties, always brought his hat with him, and as he took his seat carefully deposited it under the bench. The Ministerial bench in the House of Lords differs from that in the Commons inasmuch as it is planked up below the seat. For several nights after Lord Beaconsfield took his seat in the House of Lords he might have been observed making futile efforts to press his hat through the board that fringed the lower part of the bench. It was some time before he grew accustomed to the altered situation, and learned to dispose of his hat among Bills on the

MR. BALFOUR'S BELOW-THE-GANGWAY ATTITUDE.

table awaiting second reading or committee stage. So Mr. Balfour, accustomed to the freedom of space below the gangway, when he reached the Treasury bench thrust out his legs, and finding no other deliverance planted his feet on the table, which otherwise barred the way.

Mr. Balfour's attitude.

Events have worked together to assist Mr. Balfour in overcoming his tendency to bridge the space between the Treasury bench and the table. He has no time to lounge now. If, having answered a question, he were to resume his seat in the elaborately languid attitude learned below the gangway he would, before an hour passed, be physically worn out. It is all very well once or twice in a sitting to rise from a posture in which the head is carefully fixed on a level with the top of the back of the seat, an arrangement which allows an undue proportion of the weight of the body to be rested on the elbow, leaving the legs free to describe graceful curvatures. But for the Chief Secretary a question read out from the paper is the certain prelude to three or four more "arising out of the answer just given." It would personally be more convenient, as tending to save trouble, if Mr. Balfour were permitted to stand at the table all through the question hour. But since the rules of order in debate permit only one member at a time to be on his feet, Mr. Balfour must needs pop up and down whilst questions are going forward. Thus he has gradually abandoned his former attitude, and now sits on the bench with only something less of the rigid dignity with which the First Lord of the Treasury surveys the House.

Lord G. Hamilton's scrap of paper.

Before a young, and formerly little considered, interloper in the person of Mr. Balfour invaded the Treasury bench, and straightway took a leading part in its deliberations, Lord George Hamilton was wont to contemptuously view right hon. gentlemen immediately opposite through the tips of his boots set out on the edge of the table. But as it was certain that Mr. Balfour would at least begin with that habitude, Lord George, who would never have consented to smell at the same nosegay with the other King of Brentford, abruptly cut himself off from a cherished and comforting habit. He has found nepenthe in one much more original. When he takes his seat on the Treasury bench he possesses himself of a sheet of paper. Holding this between his two forefingers and thumbs, he turns and twirls and tears it till it is reduced to a slip of the length and breadth of a finger. This he folds deftly over and over till the harried paper falls to pieces. Hour after hour, with head bent down and fingers deftly working, the noble lord may be seen engaged in this exhilarating exercise. It is a little worrying for colleagues of highly-strung nerves sitting next to him; but on the Treasury bench patriotic considerations ever stand before personal prejudices. Whilst Lord George's nimble fingers are folding and refolding the pieces of paper, his mighty mind is conning problems of shipbuilding, gunnery, and dock administration, which, fully worked out, may stop the downward course of the country, and reinstate Old England in her proud position of Empress of the Seas.

Aug. 6.—Final division on the Commission Bill.

When the House adjourned a little after half-past two this morning all the proposed new clauses to the Parnell Commission Bill were disposed of. There remained a considerable number of new amendments. To-day had been appropriated for Scotch business, but Mr. Smith had no alternative from taking the Commission Bill and putting it through. This was achieved shortly before five this afternoon. Sir Wilfrid Lawson did not move his amendment to the third reading, it being, upon consideration by the tacticians below the gangway, decided it would be better not to limit the issue, but to divide on the main question whether the Bill should be read a third time or not. The total number in the division, 244 excluding tellers, shows that even up to the last, on a Wednesday afternoon just before the adjournment, a very respectable House was kept for this measure. But these figures do not represent the full number present during the discussion. When the division was called, the Irish members, led by Mr. Sexton—Mr. Parnell not putting in an appearance—walked out without voting. Two or three right hon. gentlemen sitting on the front Opposition bench also declined to vote. Thus it came to pass that Lord Hartington was left in sole possession of the front bench, and in due time voted with the Government. The Attorney-General was not present during the discussion, but came in to take part in the division; wherein he differs from his colleague in the counsellorship for the *Times*, Sir Henry James having scrupulously refrained from taking part in any of the innumerable divisions that have marked the progress of the Bill.

A sleeping
member.

A curious incident marked the closing scene in the history of this famous Bill. Sir John Swinburne, probably owing to the extreme heat, combined with the eloquence of Mr. Sexton, fell asleep, and slept so soundly that members passing him on their way to the lobby, and all the bustle that marks the preparation for a division, failed to

ASLEEP.

awaken him. One by one members sauntered forth, and still Sir John slept on. The officers began to lock up the doors. The Serjeant-at-Arms was marching 'in to take his last look round and ascertain that the House was empty, when the discovery was made of the member for Lichfield still slumbering. A friend, running back from the division lobby, woke him up before the services of the Serjeant-at-Arms could be invoked, and he went out to vote.

Aug. 11.   Sittings adjourned.

CHAPTER XL

THE AUTUMN SESSION.

A Quiet Opening—" Hansard "—Major O'Gorman—Mr. Biggar on the Watch
—Passing a Bill through Committee—Fatal Clause 10—Lord R. Churchill
in Possession—Lord Halsbury's Patronage—Mr. Gladstone's Position—
Mr. Smith makes a Joke—An Irish Bull—Mr. O'Reilly Dease's Will—A
Thrilling Ten Minutes—How Bills are "brought in"—Mr. Buxton
outrages Order—Again and Again!—Sir George Elliot takes the Floor—
The Lord Chancellor—Mr. Bradlaugh in a New Light—Lord Monk
Bretton—A Long Link with the Past.

Nov. 6.—A quiet opening. THE Commons on reassembling this afternoon presented the appearance of an ordinary sitting when Supply is the principal business of the day. There was a considerable muster of Ministers, but the front Opposition bench was deserted save by Sir William Harcourt, Mr. Stansfeld, and the two Whips. Lord Randolph Churchill sat watchful in the corner seat behind his revered leaders, and Mr. Jesse Collings had spared himself from Birmingham, albeit the town is to-night throbbing with a flood of Liberalism. Mr. Chamberlain was not in his place, neither was Lord Hartington, nor Sir Henry James. The latter may well be excused from attendance, seeing he spent the day in the Probate Court, but Sir Charles Russell, who was also there and very busy, came straight over to the House of Commons, and remained up to the dinner hour. Mr. Parnell passed through the lobby, but did not enter the House, having much business with his correspondence and constant callers. As Irish votes are not to be dealt with this week, Irish members generally have extended their holidays.

The Speaker is back in his place, looking much better in health. He may have watched with interest the early arrival of Dr. Tanner, and certainly was not long left in doubt as to whether Mr. Conybeare, whose term of expulsion closed with the first period of the Session, had yet returned. Three times Mr. Conybeare was up within the brief space of time devoted to questions. At the outset he brought upon himself

a snub from the Speaker, none the less effective because it
was quietly administered. It appears that after his suspension
in July, the attendants refused him admission to the library
and other precincts of the House. Now, after this long
interval, in the first quarter of an hour of the Autumn Session,
Mr. Conybeare, in his studiously offensive manner, asked the
Speaker whether such exclusion was in order. The Speaker
quietly remarked that it was very unusual to put such a
question in that manner, and invited the hon. member to communicate with him privately, promising him in such case all
the information in his possession. The House laughed, pleased
at this neat "letting down;" but Mr. Conybeare was up again
in a moment, giving notice of a motion denouncing, as a gross
abuse of the rules of the House, the Speaker's action in
applying the Closure to the debate on the second reading of
the Bann Drainage Bills.

Nov. 12.—
"Hansard." Visitors to the lobby of the House of Commons in recent years will be familiar with the
figure of a little elderly gentleman with white hair, who wears
a long coat of old-fashioned cut and generally carries an
umbrella. This is Mr. Hansard, the present representative of
the firm whose name has been intimately connected with
Parliamentary business for more than three-quarters of a
century. It was in 1803 that Mr. Hansard, father of the
present bearer of the name, began those Parliamentary reports
the title of which is as familiar in connection with Parliament
as the Mace, or the Serjeant-at-Arms. For more than half a
century the present Mr. Hansard has had charge of the
business, and, as Mr. Jackson bore testimony to-night, has
fairly discharged his duties. But his day is over, and
hereafter "Hansard" will disappear into the limbo of Parliamentary history, where Old Sarum and other more respectable
relics of former times lie huddled. The result of the labours
of the Select Committee which sat in the Summer Session is
that the Financial Secretary to the Treasury has decided
to throw open to competition the business of reporting the
Parliamentary debates. A maximum sum of £5,000 appears
in the votes to meet the expenses, and tenders have been
invited. This modern business way of dealing with the

matter will probably be all the better for the public service.
But it is a little hard on Mr. Hansard, who had come to think
that the British Constitution was not more firmly based than
was the permanency of " Hansard's Debates." What makes
the blow the heavier for him is the fact that the sacred
principle of compensation is not to be invoked on his behalf.

Nov. 15.—Major O'Gorman. Major O'Gorman, the announcement of whose
death appears in an obscure paragraph in the
morning newspapers, once filled a large space in the House of
Commons. He was by far the biggest man in it, and was
primest favourite. The humorist who protested that if he
asked his neighbour to pass the salt everyone laughed, had not
nearly such ground for complaint as Major O'Gorman. When
he stood up the House began to laugh. If he coughed it
hilariously cheered. When he cried " Hear, hear," everybody
roared. He was indescribably funny, the real Irishman in
flesh and blood (and a good deal of both) whom Charles Lever
used to draw, brought into close connection with the new field
of Parliamentary affairs. He was a source of unfailing amuse-
ment to Mr. Disraeli, who in the heyday of the Major's
Parliamentary fame yet led the House of Commons. It was a
study to watch the Premier with his eye-glass screwed in his
eye, and his face taking on new wrinkles with unwonted
laughter, as he watched the Major in the paroxysm of his
oratorical passion.

"The Major," as he was called in the Parliament of 1874
(there being none other like him), was a man of stupendous
girth and volcanic voice. He really took seriously to politics,
and all his little speeches in the House were delivered with an
air of deep conviction that added the last touch to their
grotesqueness. The first, and perhaps the most famous,
was delivered in debate on Newdegate's annual motion with
respect to convents. The Major as a good Catholic opposed
it, and in the course of his oration introduced some allegory
the mystery of which has never been fathomed to this day,
the last man capable of explaining it being the Major.
It was something about a nun who was supposed to be
questioned by one of the inspectors to be appointed under
Newdegate's proposed Bill. Major O'Gorman undertook to

recite what this nun would say to the inspector, and began in a tearful voice proper to a nun in distressed circumstances. But he never got beyond the opening sentence, " I had a sister. Her name was Sophia—" inextinguishable laughter from the crowded House breaking in upon his oration. ·

Once the Major took part in a thrilling scene in which the other chief actor was Mr. Disraeli. It was thirteen years ago, the House of Commons being then, as now, engaged in discussing Irish affairs. A Coercion Bill was under debate, and after long talk Mr. Disraeli rose to wind it up. The Major had been dining, and had, after his manner, sat a long time after dinner. He was in more than usually patriotic mood, and on returning to the House, finding the Premier on his feet, he marked the conclusion of one of his sentences by a resonant "No!" Cries of "Order!" set the Major off with increased ferocity. He bellowed "No, no, no!" like a bull of Bashan. Mr. Disraeli, always happy in retort, good-humouredly observed that if that ejaculation was to be taken as a reply, the hon. member was precluded from taking further part in the proceedings. Then the Major jumped up, and bellowed out—

" I have not spoken one word !"

There was a fearful uproar, over which the Major rose superior, till he was literally pulled down by the coat-tails. A few minutes later he was discovered sailing down the floor of the House in the direction of the table at which Disraeli stood. There was an anxious moment, during which the common fear possessed the heart of lookers-on that the Brobdingnagian Major was going to dispose of the fragile Premier by walking off with him under his arm. Disraeli paused and looked at the threatening advancing figure, which, as soon as it had reached the gangway, happily turned off to the right and dropped heavily into a seat.

Nov. 17. — Mr. Biggar on the watch. There were a dozen Bills on the Orders after Report of Supply, and about as many members sat in common attitude of expectation, hoping against hope that, peradventure, they might catch the enemy sleeping and advance a pet measure by a stage. This is the period of the evening when Mr. Biggar comes to the front and pervades the premises. Duties partly of a forensic character engage his attention elsewhere through the day, and prevent that regular attendance upon a sitting it was formerly his pride to maintain. But when midnight approaches, and members in charge of private Bills settle themselves in their places intent upon making progress, anxious glances cast below the gangway never fail to discover the member for Cavan at his post. With a pair of spectacles adding a last touch of benevolence to his visage, with pencil in right hand and copy of Orders firmly grasped in his left, he sits and pays off old scores. In the wisdom of Parliament it suffices at this stage of a night's proceeding that any single member, by signifying objection, may stop the progress of a measure, whether big or little. Thus Mr. Biggar is master of the situation, and avenges outrages perpetrated upon his country by Oliver Cromwell by frustrating all effort on the part of individual Saxons to pass their little Bills.

The Suffragans Nomination Bill was the first victim of his relentless crusade. What was the object of the measure it would perhaps puzzle Mr. Biggar to explain. But it was in charge of a Minister ; it seemed to have something to do with bishops ; it had certainly come down from the Lords. That was enough for the member for Cavan. His cry "I'bject" rang shrilly through the House, and a powerful Government, commanding a still unbroken majority, succumbed to his will.

Passing a Bill through Committee. For some reason that did not appear upon the face of things, a measure in charge of Mr. Haldane escaped Mr. Biggar's observation. This was succinctly described as the Land Purchase Registration and Searches Bill, and the five strangers privileged to sleep in the gallery woke up, and curiously watched the process of legislative action in the House of Commons. The motion was that the House should resolve itself into Committee to consider the Bill. The Speaker, who two minutes earlier had made solemn entry and taken the Chair in wig and gown, as if through all the eight hours that had elapsed since he departed he had been standing at the doorway, withdrew. Mr. Courtney reappeared at the table. Mr. Haldane, who had betrayed his personal concern in the measure by sitting on the extreme edge of the bench and bobbing up and down as if he had unexpectedly found it red hot, rose and said something. The Attorney-General, secure on the following day of a holiday from the Probate Court, took his seat on the Treasury bench, Bill in hand. The Solicitor-General, anxious to show that apprehension of public business being overlooked by law officers of the Crown under stress of private business was ill founded, joined his learned colleague. Mr. Courtney put in sonorous tone the various clauses, declaring each added to the Bill. Meanwhile Mr. Haldane, finding the edge of the seat hotter than ever, bobbed with redoubled energy. The Attorney-General slowly crossed the floor, Bill in hand, and Mr. Haldane, gratefully quitting his seat, met him midway, where a hurried consultation was held.

"Clause 8," said Mr. Courtney, going on with his recitative; "that Clause 8 be added to the Bill."

At this the Attorney-General and Mr. Haldane retired, and again advanced, as if it were some figure in a quadrille they were engaged upon, rather than in Committee upon the Land Purchase Registration and Searches Bill.

Fatal Clause 10. On Clause 10 something happened. Either the clause ought to have been omitted or amended, or the wrong amendment was inserted in the rapid, relentless recitative. The Attorney-General and Mr. Haldane again taking the floor, *chasséd*, hands across (with a copy of the Bill in each), down the middle and up again to their seats. A thrill of freshened interest moved the somnolent House, and the five strangers in the gallery became almost turbulent in their excitement. Something had surely happened to Clause 10, and a slight tremor in Mr. Courtney's voice showed that he was not unconscious of the mishap. But the Chair can do no wrong. There was nothing for it but to go straight forward with the clauses, which he did with increased rapidity. "Clause 14, 15, 16"—Mr. Haldane rhythmically bobbing up and down as each number was recited. Then it was proposed to take the report stage. But here Clause 10, with whatever had happened to it, was avenged. The Attorney-General, in gravest, almost funereal, manner declined the responsibility of permitting the final stage to be taken, and report was postponed till Tuesday.

All this while Mr. Biggar had sat abashed and silent, watching Mr. Haldane's gymnastics, and pondering over Clause 10. But, this measure disposed of, and proposal made to read a second time the School Board for London Pensions Bill, he found his voice, steadily objecting to this and to all succeeding measures till, the list exhausted, the House adjourned.

Nov. 20.—Lord R. Churchill in possession.

Lord Randolph Churchill was early in his place in the House of Commons this afternoon. As usual he sat in the corner seat behind the Treasury bench, which he has appropriated with more success than Mr. Forster met with when, in years gone by, he claimed his favourite seat. Since Lord Randolph foregoes the privilege of attending prayers, he has no statutory right to the place, and it was upon this ground that five years ago Dr. Lyons, coming down to prayers and securing a ticket for the corner seat, used to question Mr. Forster's attempts to appropriate it. But no one ventures to dispute Lord Randolph's determination to fill his favourite place. Whether he comes early or late he always gets his seat and sits there, incessantly twirling his moustache, an attentive listener to whatever may be going forward. He very rarely speaks to anyone, a manner differing diametrically from that familiar with him when he was still Leader of the Fourth Party. Then he was wont to buzz all over the House in search of temporary allies, whether against Mr. Gladstone or Sir Stafford Northcote. That is all changed. Having at one time, according to hostile critics, been distinguished for impudence, he now affects dignity, and sits apart in lordly self-communion.

Nov. 21.—Lord Halsbury's patronage.

The expectation that the Lord Chancellor would feel himself compelled to take notice of the grave allegations made against him in the House of Commons in debate on the vote for law charges was realised to-night. As soon as Lord Salisbury had answered a question with respect to the new German alliance, Lord Halsbury, who had been carefully nursing a bundle of notes, left the Woolsack, and, according to the manner of the

Lord Chancellor when addressing the House, stood a pace
or two to the left. From this place he read out a statement
occupying some time in the delivery, but which, as far as its
purport could be followed, delicately skirted the fringe of the
question raised in the House of Commons with that brutal
frankness which sometimes distinguishes Lord Randolph's
attacks. There was a good deal said about Lord Halsbury
on that night, but the charge that stuck in the memory
of the House, and has since arrested attention, was that
two years ago, on a vacancy occurring in the department of
the Official Referee, the Lord Chancellor had filled up the
post, notwithstanding the fact that Lord R. Churchill, at the
time Chancellor of the Exchequer, after carefully going into
the matter and finding it was practically a sinecure, had
recommended that it should not be filled up, a conclusion
arrived at, after a similar but independent investigation, by
Mr. Jackson, Financial Secretary to the Treasury. To this
charge Lord Halsbury replied in very general terms.

Lord Salisbury said never a word, whilst Lord Granville
adroitly excused himself from discussing the matter on the
ground that no notice had been given of Lord Halsbury's intention of dealing with the subject. The general impression is
that if the Lord Chancellor had nothing better to say, it would
have been wiser to have maintained the attitude of silence
with which he has hitherto met similar charges.

<table>
<tr><td>Nov. 22.—Mr.
Gladstone's
position.</td><td>It has come to pass in the whirligig of time that
Mr. Gladstone is, at this epoch, in a position</td></tr>
</table>

wherein his comings and goings arouse the
hearty cheers of his motley following. It seemed fourteen
years ago, when he wrote to " My dear Granville " from Carlton
House Terrace, that the end of his political career was reached,
and that whether he took his seat on the front Opposition
bench at half-past four or half-past seven, or did not put in an
appearance at all, was a matter of no consequence. But a
great deal has happened since 1874, and Mr. Gladstone has
once more gone through the regular stages of popular adulation and personal neglect, though the depth reached in 1886,
after the new rout at the poll, did not approach the dark
profundity that whelmed him in the spring of 1874.

Once more Mr. Gladstone is gambolling on the crest of the flowing tide, and the House of Commons waits on his utterances, watches his coming and going, as it began to do in 1879. He never cherishes personal resentment, otherwise his daily life would be a sore travail. Yet sometimes he must have a pained consciousness of the hollowness of the personal adulation which just now, as from time to time in other days, greets him in the House of Commons. He is the same man to-day he was when, in the Session of 1874, he used to sit at the remote end of the front Opposition bench, wearing his gloves and carrying his stick, with studious expression of the admission that he had really no business there, hoped he did not intrude, and would presently quietly go away. It was not quite so bad in 1886, partly because past experience had proved the danger of taking it for granted that he was finally discomfited, and largely because scores of his followers who had sacrificed their seats on the altar of his new-formed policy were not in their places to frown upon him. But circumstances change, and he haply forgets. However it be, he brightly beams upon his faithful, hopeful following when, as happened the other day, they rise to greet him with stormy cheering on his return from a triumphal tour in the Midlands.

Nov. 24.— Mr. Smith makes a joke.

As Mr. Gladstone, coming in this afternoon a little late, stood for a moment at gaze by the Speaker's chair he beheld an animated scene. The Strangers' Gallery, long empty, was crowded. The benches on both sides of the House were filled with members rocking to and fro with uncontrollable laughter and hilarious shouting. At the table stood Mr. W. H. Smith, his ingenuous countenance suffused with a deeper blush, and a spasmodic smile responding to the general hilarity. Mr. Gladstone, making haste to reach his seat, anxiously inquired into the cause of the mystery, and speedily learned the truth.

Mr. Smith had made a joke, the unqualified success of which was completed by an absence of deliberate intention.

Quite early in the course of questions the First Lord of the Treasury had displayed a sprightliness which attracted the attention of the House. Mr. Labouchere had set him off by veiled inquiry as to the possibility of a Saturday sitting.

With grave irony Mr. Smith had acknowledged the earnest desire of the member for Northampton to get on with public business, and, assuming that he was the authorised exponent of the desire of members to sit on Saturday, proposed with pretty appearance of unwillingness to make the necessary arrangements if the House so willed it. Members on both sides, entering into the spirit of the joke, hotly objected, and Mr. Smith, pausing for a moment, as if weighing the pros and cons, finally decided that a Saturday sitting was not the general desire, and therefore should not take place.

This was a little bit of comedy that presented the prosaic First Lord of the Treasury in a new light. No one was more pleased with its success than the leading gentleman, and it encouraged him to higher flights. The opportunity came after he had set forth the arrangements for the business of the Session. There followed the usual clamour of private members in charge of Bills, beseeching that exception might be made in their favour. The Irish members having been mollified, Dr. Clark came forward to plead the privilege of Scotland. Why, he asked, should the Scotch estimates be remitted to the end of the programme, coming after everything else?

"I am very sorry," said Mr. Smith, in one of those kindly apothegms which immortalise his Parliamentary speech, "that anybody should have to come after anybody else."

The House, once resolved to accept Mr. Smith as a humorist, roared with generous delight at this *naïveté*. Thus encouraged, Mr. Smith went on :—" But that is a state of things inseparable from Parliamentary life, unless we can sit in two or three Houses at the same time."

The House, quick as lightning, saw the bearing of this epigram. Session after Session, since the far-off time of Mr. Butt, the Irish members had been clamouring for the right to sit in their own Parliament on College Green. And here, in the very midst of a stormy campaign, where as yet the Home Rule flag had ever been beaten back, was the spokesman of a Conservative Ministry stumbling into an admission which surrendered the whole position! Of course Mr. Smith had not meant anything. Lured on by the passion for epigram, he had chanced upon this unlucky turn of phrase. But that added to the enjoyment of the situation, and the strident cheer, started below the gangway, was taken up along the Opposition benches, echoed by peals of laughter on the Ministerial side, finally working the House up to the state of excitement in which Mr. Gladstone found it when he chanced to look in.

Nov. 27.—An Irish bull.   Mr. Clancy, referring to-night to a disclaimer by Mr. Jesse Collings of certain conduct attributed to him, flashed forth one of those priceless sayings, not unfamiliar in the days of Sir Boyle Roche and later Irish members, but, unhappily, rare in these more prosaic days.

"Whether it is a calumny or not," said Mr. Clancy emphatically, " it is true."

Nov. 29. — Mr. O'Reilly Dease's will.   The Chancellor of the Exchequer, questioned to-night by Mr. Justin M'Carthy, admitted the truth of the romantic story of Mr. O'Reilly Dease's will. Mr. Dease, years ago, sat for an Irish constituency, and was a well-known figure in the House, though he did not take obtrusive part in debate. When the Parnellites came into power in Ireland Mr. Dease lost his seat. But he kept up his London house, and spent his days and nights in the Reform Club. He had a curious habit of talking about the wealth at his disposal, and of his difficulty as to whom he should bequeath it to, being, as he said, a lone and childless man. Somehow, when the confidential conversation had closed, his interlocutor had had it subtlely borne in upon him that if he only minded his P's and Q's, and was properly deferential to Mr. O'Reilly Dease, he might be agreeably surprised when that gentleman's will was opened. When the end came, and the will was read, it was found that Mr. Dease had left his whole fortune, amounting to something like £50,000, to the Chancellor of the Exchequer for the time being, with instructions to apply it to the reduction of the National Debt. The disclosure of the contents of the will must have been a profound disappointment to more than one member of the Reform Club whom Mr. Dease was accustomed to single out for his confidential conversation and his hints of princely legacies, conveyed by winks and nods and pressure of the hand. Now the Chancellor of the Exchequer has got the money, though Mr. Goschen almost wept when he referred to

the two nieces of the legatee, in ill-health and wholly without
means, and declared himself utterly unable to assist them.

Nov. 30. — A
thrilling ten
minutes.
Mr. Sydney Buxton is a hard-headed young
man who has thoroughly mastered the political
questions of the day, and is able to state both
sides with such perfect impartiality as to induce in the mind
of the student a condition of absolute indifference as to which
he shall advocate. No casual
observer would suspect Mr. Buxton
of tendency to perpetrate a practical joke; but it is opportunity
that creates the offender, and the
circumstances that Mr. Jacoby intended to-night to introduce a Bill
for the establishment of Tribunals
of Commerce proved too much for
Mr. Buxton's rigid morality.

STDNEY BUXTON.

Mr. Jacoby is the member who
early in the year came to the front
in *levée* dress and a lethal weapon.
Attempting to enter the House of
Commons with sword by his side
he was stopped by the Serjeant-
at-Arms, who, with reckless courage,
disarmed him and retained possession of the weapon till the hon.
member was seen safe off the
premises. He was, it was made
known in reply to earnest inquiry,
going to dine with the Paraguayan
Minister, or the representative at
this Court of some equally overbearing State, and, determined
the House of Commons should suffer no loss of dignity in his
person, had as early as four in the afternoon put on his *levée*
dress, girt on his sword, and presented himself to the view of
the amazed throng in the lobby.

To-night he was in attire more suitable for the prosaic
business with which he was charged. A velvet coat, ruffles at
the wrist, and sword at side, were all very well when the object

was to overawe the Minister of proud Paraguay; but to introduce a Bill for the establishment of Tribunals of Commerce
was quite another thing, and the ordinary dress of commerce
sufficed.   There were two Bills to be introduced at this con-

venient period of the Session, Mr. Jacoby standing second,
precedence having been gained by Mr. Sydney Buxton.   Mr.
Buxton had, however tardily, awakened to the necessity of the
better protection of sand grouse.   With a view to conciliate
opinion on the opposite benches, and with a consciousness
that he was not above suspicion of Separatist tendencies, he
had dexterously dragged in a reference to the solidity of the
Empire.   The full title of his measure was "a Bill for the
better protection of Sand Grouse in the United Kingdom."

How Bills are "brought in." Questions over, he, always keeping his eye on Mr. Jacoby, sallied forth to accomplish the important and well-defined process by which Bills are brought in after leave has been humbly asked and graciously given. From time immemorial it has been the unwritten ordinance that a member having a Bill in charge shall leave his seat, march towards the door as if about to retire from political life, halt at the Bar, and take up his position at the cross bench to the left. Here he stands until the Speaker calls upon him by name, whereupon he advances (always skirting the benches on the left), making due obeisance to the Chair, and, passing between the Treasury bench and the table, hands in a document which may or may not be the Bill. Too often it is what is known as "a dummy"—a blank piece of paper endorsed with a title, after the fashion of the hollow wooden cases imitative of books with which quaintly disposed persons sometimes fill up odd shelves of their library.

Mr. Buxton outrages order. On a memorable occasion Mr. Christopher Sykes, burdened with a measure dealing with crabs and lobsters, sadly bungled the business of bringing in a Bill. Mr. Sydney Buxton has not sat in two Parliaments without knowing all about it; but there was Mr. Jacoby to be led astray, and by a series of elaborate manœuvres Mr. Buxton successfully carried out his little plot. Starting from the cross bench before the Serjeant-at-Arms' chair, he walked down the right-hand side of the House, essaying to reach the Clerk by the passage between the front Opposition bench and the table. Instantly a shout of "Order! order!" rang across the crowded benches. The House of Commons is a body imbued with a tolerant spirit; but there are some things it will not stand. One is two members on their legs at the same moment; a second is a member crossing between the Chair and another member addressing the Speaker; a third is a member standing as much as five inches within the Bar; a fourth is a member moving a single pace with his hat on. A penny may be added to the income-tax or a declaration of war made with less outward disturbance than is created by any one of these accidents.

To see a member skirting the benches on the right-hand side

intent upon bringing in a Bill when he should have walked to the left hand was a covert attack upon the foundation of the Church and the stability of the Throne not to be passed over in silence. By the time Mr. Buxton had reached the table, and was showing a disposition to pass by the front Opposition bench, the roar had increased to a degree of ferocity before which this ordinarily self-possessed young man visibly trembled. Faltering and finally halting, he turned and made again for the cross bench by the Serjeant-at-Arms' chair.

This accomplished, he, to the added horror of the House, again set forth on the wrong track.

Again and again! The uproar, now grown deafening, began to tell upon Mr. Jacoby. That hon. gentleman—prepared to follow up the sand grouse of the United Kingdom with the establishment of Tribunals of Commerce—had happily stationed himself in proper position by the cross bench on the left-hand side, facing the Speaker's chair. Thence he watched the manœuvres of Mr. Sydney Buxton, who, with the ordinary pallor of his studious face grown ghastlier, began to look like a hunted hare. What had been commenced in jest had deepened into sternest earnest. Having reached the table a second time, again approaching from the wrong side, Mr. Buxton found his passage barred by an ex-Minister. There was nothing for it but to double again, a storm of laughter, cheers, and cries of "Order!" rendering inaudible the directions that would have guided his steps to the other side of the House. Once more he retired towards the Bar, no sand grouse in the United Kingdom more sorely in need of protection. Gasping for breath, with parched lips and the perspiration dewing his brow, he set out for the third time to bring in his well-meant Bill, and for the third time, amid terrific shouting, he was seen to make his way over the fatal track towards the passage by the front Opposition bench !

Arrived there, a friendly member pushed him over towards the other side of the table, and at last, amid hearty cheers, he was welcomed by Mr. W. H. Smith half rising from the Treasury bench, and reached the haven where he would have been. .

Attention was still fixed upon the now breathless Buxton, when Mr. Jacoby was discovered sailing down the House before he had been called upon by the Speaker. He had gained a few steps, had made his first obeisance to the Chair, when he was startled by a roar of execration even more blood-curdling than any that had rebuked Mr. Sydney Buxton. The roar of caged lions observing the tigers' daily meal carried past their den is a mere whimper to this outburst of humorously simulated indignation. Mr. Jacoby faltered for a moment, and looked anxiously round at the excited throng on either side of him. His hesitation lasted only a moment. Something was wrong; but he had to bring in his Bill, and the sooner it was over the better. Accordingly he started off at the double, making straight for the passage by the Treasury bench, the roar increasing as he moved forward. Fortunately the Leader of the House was again equal to the emergency. Throwing himself bodily into the breach, Mr. Smith stopped Mr. Jacoby's unauthorised advance, and the member for Mid-Derbyshire turned about and slowly withdrew to the Bar, peals of laughter ringing through the House. There he stood till the Speaker, in tones of awful solemnity, cried aloud, " Mr. Jacoby!" whereupon he advanced in due form and safely landed his Bill.

Throughout this scene the House of Commons had been thronged and intensely interested. Afterwards, there being nothing more important than the voting of a million and a half in Committee of Supply, the benches emptied, and to the intense excitement crowded into the space of three minutes there followed a lengthened period of paralysis.

**Dec. 7. — Mr
George Elliot
takes the floor.** There was something about Sir George Elliot as he stood to-night behind the Treasury bench discoursing on the Employers' Liability Bill that irresistibly recalled Mr. Pecksniff leaning over the banisters at Todgers's addressing the hastily gathered company at the foot of the stairs. Not that Sir George in any personal aspect resembles Tom Pinch's employer. It was more the attitude and the air of benevolent philanthropy suffusing the oration that recalled the famous scene.

" My friends," said Mr. Pecksniff, leaning over the banisters, " let us be moral."

"Gentlemen," said Sir George Elliot, leaning over the rail

of the Treasury bench, "let us not put a collar round the neck
of the working man and allow him to be guided entirely by
Trades Unions."

Sir George, as he confidentially informed the House,
"knew what he was talking about," which a genial nod of the
head, comprising in its survey the whole of the Opposition
benches, hinted was not universally the case with former
speakers. Man and boy he had been in the House for twenty

years. He had also, the earnest searcher after autobiograph-
ical truth might gather, been largely engaged in business in
which Trades Unions were somehow inextricably mixed up
with the Egyptian question.

"What I say is this," said Sir George, and the crowded
House of Commons bent forward to catch the words of wisdom
dropped in a voice so impressive as occasionally to become
inaudible. "There must be a limit to it," Sir George added,
after a dramatic pause, looking round on the listening senate
with an aspect of supremest sagacity.

The loud cheer which this dictum drew forth did not lure
Sir George into tiresome lengths of oratory. He had gained
the ear of an audience which always gladly listens to him.

He was speaking on a subject of which he is master, and was evidently in the vein. He swayed the potent House of Commons with master touch. Laughter and cheers punctuated his sentences. Moreover, unlike Mr. Pecksniff on the occasion referred to, he was not disturbed by an uneasy sense of the comparative scantiness of his garments. He was thoroughly comfortable; the joyousness beaming from his face as he thrust his left hand into his waistcoat pocket, and held out his right containing a copy of the Orders folded up like a bâton, was reflected on every countenance.

But Sir George is not the man to imperil an oratorical success by undue length. Glancing upwards at the clock, whose very face, regarding him, caught the contagion of hilarity, he observed, " I see the clock is going round : I must be brief," and then, waving his bâton, he gracefully glided into the powerful peroration in which he besought the House " not to hand over the destinies of this great country to Trades Unions."

Cheer after cheer rose from the crowded benches as Sir George, bowing and smiling and gaily waving his bâton, withdrew without resuming his seat.

The Lord Chancellor unfortunately missed this oration, which was delivered long after the dinner-hour and just upon the eve of the division. But Lord Halsbury was in time to behold Mr. Bradlaugh taking Her Majesty's Government under his friendly protection and defending it from the aspersions of men like Mr. Broadhurst. Lord Halsbury does not often return to the scene of his earlier Parliamentary triumphs. To-night's visit, extending over two hours, was the first occasion when opportunity and attraction have combined to make him a prominent figure in the Peers' Gallery. He sat in the Commons as member for Launceston up to 1885, and was not unfamiliar with Mr. Bradlaugh's interpositions in debate. He has seen him waltzing up and down the floor with the late Serjeant-at-Arms, advancing and retiring between the Mace and the Bar amid angry shouts from outraged Conservatives. With nose uptilted he has heard him, standing behind the outdrawn Bar, plead, before an implacable majority, for admission of his constitutional rights and the inalienable privileges of the electors who sent him to Parliament. Sir Hardinge Giffard, being a man of natural dignity and repose of manner, took no personal part in the exciting scenes when Mr. Bradlaugh was hustled across the lobby, down the stairs, and out into Palace Yard, where he arrived breathless, with his coat torn and his stylographic pen broken. But more than once his voice joined the chorus of execration with which, between 1880 and 1885, Mr. Bradlaugh's attempts to take his seat were met. Whilst Mr. Bradlaugh's old adversaries, united under his banner, passed the Oaths Bill, the Lord Chancellor, faithful among the faithless found, resisted the innovation.

Mr. Bradlaugh in a new light. It was but yesterday Lord Halsbury had lamented in the Lords the bowing of unaccustomed knees at the shrine of Baal. And now, straying by accident into the Commons, he sat fascinated in the gallery, looking down upon a scene the realisation of which went far beyond the wildest fantasy of nightmare dreams that may have flitted over the pillow of the late Mr. Newdegate in the early Sessions of the Parliament of 1880. Here was Mr. Bradlaugh, in attitude of studied elegance, with one foot set in the rack of the bench before him, doing battle for a Conservative Government, one of whose most important measures was attacked by a Radical faction. The Bill was by courtesy styled a Government measure; but Mr. Bradlaugh, struggling with natural modesty, was fain to confess that in all its principal clauses it was his own. He, and he alone, had done it. There were, it is true, other members sitting on the Grand Committee which had moulded the measure as it was now presented to the House, and Mr. Bradlaugh was not indisposed to share the credit with them. But a passion for accuracy required him to state that, with one single exception so immaterial that it need not be particularised, he was responsible for every suggestion made in Committee and accepted by the Government.

In such circumstances he was hardly able to repress the scorn and indignation with which he beheld the appearance on the scene of men like Mr. Burt, Mr. Fenwick, and Mr. Broadhurst, claiming to be heard on behalf of the working classes. Codlin was the true friend of the British working man, and Mr. Bradlaugh's most metallic tones were inadequate to duly ring forth his righteous indignation at the impudent pretensions of the obtrusive Short.

The Lord Chancellor, sitting in the gallery, rubbed his eyes, and pinched his ears, and gazed about in silent amazement as he heard again and again the ringing cheers that rose from the serried ranks of the Conservatives sitting at the feet of their new Gamaliel. Did he dream, or were visions about? No, it was the old familiar unmistakable place, with the Mace on the table, the Serjeant-at-Arms in the Chair, the Bar beyond which a few years ago Mr. Bradlaugh dare not advance, and the glass door that used to be flung wide open when his burly form was hustled out.

Lord Monk Bretton. Close beside him, sharing the full length of the Peers' Gallery, sat Lord Monk Bretton. He used to be Mr. Dodson in those not distant days, and Sir Hardinge Giffard had more than once paired with him through the dinner hour, when there was prospect of a division on a new Bradlaugh incident. The Lord Chancellor furtively scanned the countenance of his noble friend, hoping haply to find upon it some fleeting emotion of surprise. But Lord Monk Bretton is gifted with imperturbable self-possession. Sir Hardinge Giffard had sat opposite Mr. Dodson for years, and to-night remembered how, when the House was in a state of seething commotion at some crisis in Mr. Bradlaugh's Parliamentary career, Mr. Dodson had looked out straight over his nose with the same imperturbability as Lord Monk Bretton now gazed into space over the head of the transformed member for Northampton and the bewitched Conservative Party. As the Parisians of an older generation used to sing about the statue of Philip Augustus on the Place du Trône, the Lord Chancellor pitied Lord Monk Bretton—

> Car il est en pierre, en pierre,
> Pour lui ce n'est pas amusant.

When Mr. Bradlaugh had made an end of speaking the spell was broken, and the Lord Chancellor went out as one dazed.

Christmas Eve. Parliament prorogued.

Dec. 30.—A long link with the past.   The announcement of the death of Lord Eversley will convey as a surprise to many people the news that the Speaker who retired from the Chair more than twenty years ago was alive so recently as Friday morning. Since Lord Eversley quitted the Chair three Speakers have filled it—Mr. Denison, Sir Henry Brand, and the present occupant. Mr. Denison is long since dead; Sir Henry Brand (Lord Hampden) is living a peaceful life, chiefly devoted to dairy farming; and Mr. Peel has only just lived down the circumstantial rumour that he was about to retire to make room for the fourth Speaker whom Lord Eversley should have seen in the Chair. But the oldest of all Parliamentary Hands has dropped off at last, and Lord Eversley is dead at ninety-four.

It was only a few weeks before the prorogation that a near relative of Lord Eversley, just returned from a visit to the veteran, told me an interesting story about him. Born six years before the century, he was one of the oldest men, and certainly, for his years, the halest man, in England. He preserved to the last all his mental faculties, and his memory was, with a notable hiatus, remarkable. He could not recall events of last week or last month, or of the last few years, but going back fifty, sixty, seventy, or even eighty years, he had a vivid and accurate memory for particular incidents. One thing he remembered quite well was the visit he paid to the House of Commons when he heard William Pitt speaking in triumphant tone of the coalition he had just formed with Austria and Russia against Napoleon.

This must have been in the late autumn of 1805. In December, 1805 — the 2nd of December, a memorable Napoleonic date—Austerlitz was fought, and the coalition crumpled up. This broke Pitt's proud spirit, and in the following January he died. Thus it must have been more than eighty-three years since young Shaw-Lefevre, afterwards Viscount Eversley, heard this speech in an assembly over which thirty-three years later he was elected to preside.

It is drawing on for thirty-two years since Mr. Shaw-Lefevre stepped out of the Speaker's chair and went up to the House of Lords as Viscount Eversley. This is more than a lifetime in the political world. I suppose there are not more

than a dozen men in the House of Commons at the present
time who sat there when Mr. Shaw-Lefevre was Speaker.
A right hon. gentleman, now sitting on the front Opposition
bench, diligently turning over the pages of "Dod" has discovered that of men who sat in the Parliament dissolved in
1868 only thirty now have places in the Commons. It seems
incredible that we should but the other day have been able
to go back to the Speaker appointed in 1839 and find him
still in the flesh. Lord Eversley's last public appearance was
in connection with the Queen's Jubilee last year, when he
was able to take his part, sitting with the assembled Commons
in St. Margaret's Church, between Lord Hampden, the late
Speaker, and Mr. Peel, the present.

By an odd coincidence the death of the ancient Speaker
was announced on Mr. Gladstone's birthday. Compared with
Lord Eversley Mr. Gladstone is a mere stripling of seventy-
nine, and according to the latest accounts received of the state
of his health there is reasonable expectation that he may live
as long as the Speaker whose installation he witnessed close
upon half a century ago. Mr. Shaw-Lefevre was two years
Mr. Gladstone's predecessor in the House of Commons. He
took his seat in the year 1830 for the pocket borough of
Downton, Mr. Gladstone coming in two years later, in the first
reformed Parliament, as member for Newark.

SESSION OF 1888.

FEBRUARY.

9. Thurs.—H.M. Speech. Address thereon. First Debate.

10. Fri.—Ditto. Ditto. Second Debate.

13. Mon.—Privilege. Arrest of Mr. P. O'Brien. Complaint and Motion, Mr. Picton. Amendment, Mr. Attorney-General. H.M. Speech. Address thereon. Amendment, Mr. Parnell. Third Debate.

14. Tues.—Ditto. Ditto. Fourth Debate.

15. Wed.—Ditto. Ditto. Fifth Debate.

16. Thurs.—Ditto. Ditto. Sixth Debate. Metropolitan Board of Works. Royal Commission. Lord R. Churchill.

17. Fri.—H.M. Speech. Address thereon. Division on Mr. Parnell's Amendment—For, 220. Against, 317. Seventh Debate.

20. Mon.—H.M. Speech. Address thereon. Agricultural Depression, Mr. Chaplin. Ditto (Finance) Amendment, Mr. S. Smith. Eighth Debate.

21. Tues.—H.M. Speech. Address thereon. Scotland (Disturbance, &c.). Amendment, Dr. Cameron. Ninth Debate.

22. Wed.—H.M. Speech. Address thereon. Agricultural Depression (Scotland), Mr. Anderson. Division—For, 77. Against, 190. Address agreed to. Report made. Tenth Debate.

23. Thurs.—H.M. Speech. Report of Address agreed to.

24. Fri.—Rules of Procedure, No. 1, Sittings of the House. Agreed to. First Debate.

27. Mon.—House met at 3 o'clock. Supply; Civil Service Estimates.

28. Tues.—Rules of Procedure, Nos. II. to VIII. agreed to.

29. Wed.—Ditto. Nos. IX. to XII. agreed to.

MARCH.

APRIL.

MAY.

MAY (continued).

JUNE.

JULY.

AUGUST.

AUGUST (continued)

7. Tues.—Members, &c. (Charges, &c.), Bill. Considered.
8. Wed.—Ditto. Read 3°.
9. Thurs.—Oaths Bill. Read 3°. East India Revenue Accounts. Committee.

10. Fri.—Local Government (England and Wales) Bill. Lords' Amendments agreed to.

11. Sat.—Adjournment of the House till Tuesday, 6th November.

NOVEMBER.

6. Tues.—Supply: Civil Service Estimates.
7. Wed.—Ditto. Ditto.
8. Thurs.—Ditto. Ditto.
9. Fri.—Ditto. Ditto.
10. Mon.—Ditto. Ditto.
11. Tues.—Ditto. Ditto.
14. Wed.—Ditto. Ditto.
15. Thurs.—Ditto. Ditto.
16. Fri.—Ditto. Ditto.
19. Mon.—Land Purchase (Ireland) Bill. Mr. [illegible]; Motion for Leave.
20. Tues.—Ditto. [illegible]; Mr. [illegible]. Division—For, 246. Against, [illegible]. Bill ordered.
21. Wed.—Ditto. First Reading. Debate Adjourned.

12. Thurs.—Land Purchase (Ireland) Bill. 2nd Reading. Division—For, 256. Against, 271.
23. Fri.—Ditto. Ditto. Committee. [illegible], Mr. [illegible]. Division—For, 148. Against, 162. Bill considered. First Sitting.
26. Mon.—Ditto. Committee. Second Sitting.
27. Tues.—Ditto. Ditto. Third Sitting.
28. Wed.—Ditto. Ditto. Fourth Sitting. Bill reported.
29. Thurs.—[illegible]. Motion for Adjournment, Mr. Bradlaugh; Land Purchase (Ireland) Bill. 3°.
30. Fri.—Supply: Civil Service Estimates.

DECEMBER.

1. Sat.—Supply: Civil Service Estimates.
3. Mon.—Ditto. Ditto.
4. Tues.—Ditto. Ditto.
5. Wed.—Ditto. Ditto.
6. Thurs.—Ditto. Ditto.
7. Fri.—Ditto. Ditto.
8. Sat.—Ditto. Ditto.
10. Mon.—Ditto. Ditto.
11. Tues.—Ditto. Ditto.
12. Wed.—Ditto. Ditto.

13. Thurs.—Supply: Navy Estimates.
14. Fri.—Ditto. Army Estimates.
17. Sat.—Ditto. Civil Service Estimates.
17. Mon.—Ditto. Ditto.
18. Tues.—Ditto. Ditto.
19. Wed.—Appropriation Bill. Read 1°.
20. Thurs.—Ditto. Read 2°.
21. Fri.—Ditto. Committee.
24. Sat.—Ditto. Read 3°.
24. Mon.—Prorogation.

CHAPTER XII.

ORATORS AND DEBATERS.

Mr. Gladstone —"Joe" Cowen —The Speaker—Mr. W. O'Brien—Mr. Bradlaugh—Mr. Chaplin—Sir W. Harcourt—Mr. Biggar—Mr. Sexton—Mr. Tim Healy—His Noble Friend—Mr. Gladstone and Tim—Mr. Parnell—Mr. Chamberlain.

Dec. 31.—Mr. Gladstone.

It is a noteworthy circumstance in a picked assembly of 670 gentlemen, one of whose especial functions is to make speeches, that so few should reach the standard of oratory. Now that Mr. Bright has practically retired from Parliamentary life Mr. Gladstone stands alone, the only man in the House of Commons to whom the old-fashioned term orator may fitly apply. Mr. Disraeli never seriously aspired to it, and some fitful attempts to qualify for the position

stand out among his more disastrous Parliamentary failures.
He began by being an orator, and everyone knows the history
of his first deliberate attempt. He drifted into the more
useful position of a debater, and it was only when he had
nothing to say, or did not desire to say something, that he
momentarily returned to his earlier manner. Mr. Gladstone
holds two unique positions in the present House of Commons.
He is not simply the only orator, but with one possible exception
he is the supremest debater, two qualities which, even less
richly bestowed, rarely meet in a man.

"Joe" Cowen. The late Mr. P. J. Smyth had the oratorical
faculty developed in no inconsiderable degree.
With due preparation this shabbily dressed plebeian-looking
man was wont to rise and, in the
presence of an entranced House
of Commons, declaim glittering
passages of polished periods.
Members crowded in to listen
when "Smyth was up," sat in
something approaching devotional
attitude for a quarter of an hour,
found half an hour rather long,
and went away with a pleasing
sense of having assisted at a function. It was magnificent, but it
was not debating. Mr. Joseph
Cowen is another born orator,
whose absence the House of
Commons laments. Mr. Cowen's
oratory was nearly as ornate as
Mr. Smyth's, and was declaimed
with something of the same indication of possession of illimitable
hoard of polished sentences. But
Mr. Cowen, deeply stirred himself,
really did momentarily move the
House of Commons, though it is
doubtful whether he ever influ-

MR. JOSEPH COWEN.

enced a voto. His speech in 1876 on the Royal Titles Bill,

and a second delivered two years later on the Vote of Credit
moved by Sir Stafford Northcote under the impression that
the Russians were at the gates of Constantinople, hold high
place in the records of Parliamentary oratory.

Excepting Mr. Gladstone, I know of only three men in the
present House of Commons who have the oratorical faculty.
They are the Speaker, Mr. Bradlaugh, and Mr. O'Brien, an odd
conjunction of persons, each differing widely from the rest.

The Speaker.   Mr. Arthur Peel's opportunities of doing justice
to his natural gifts are rigorously limited by his
official position. In ordinary times the Speaker is the man
who does not speak. But circumstances arising since he was
called to the Chair have once or twice given Mr. Peel an opportunity of displaying the charm of perfected grace, force, and
dignity in public speech. No one who heard his speech on
taking the Chair upon his election can forget the impression
created. It was, as far as I remember, the most perfect surprise, the most striking revelation that ever came upon the
House. Up to that time he had been slightly known in
various Under-Secretaryships. He had answered a few questions and taken an occasional part in debate. But though a
member of long standing, he had made no impression on the
House such, for example, as had been established by his elder
brother. He was looked upon as a sort of ordinary, not to say
provincial, member, who, inheriting a great name, naturally
came in for a vacant Under-Secretaryship, took his salary, did
his office work, and would presently die and be forgotten.
Called to the post of highest dignity open to a Commoner, Mr.
Peel quietly, at a single step, assumed his natural place. His
very personal appearance seemed to have undergone a change
since last he was seen at the lower end of the front Opposition
bench. He looked taller, and had taken on an impressive
dignity; his voice sounded deeper and his intonation was more
measured.

Of course this was all fancy. The simple fact is, he had
lived in the House of Commons for twenty years, and only on
this February afternoon, when he stood up and declared that
"if elected to the Chair he would humbly and honestly try to
do his duty," did the Commons know him.

That was a difficult speech for a man to make, and its successful accomplishment was equal to a triumph. Quite another manner was necessary on a painful occasion during the present year, when the Speaker met the necessity of taking note of certain charges levelled against the impartiality of the Chair. No position could be more embarrassing than that in which Mr. Peel found himself placed. To defend himself without appearing to make excuse, to vindicate the impartiality of the Chair without appearing to admit the possibility of its fallibility, was a task the full difficulty of which can be appreciated only by those steeped in the traditions of the House of Commons. The difficulty was increased by a consciousness that there were many men whose opinion he valued who were not sure that the conduct noisily challenged out of doors had been altogether free from error. Yet Mr. Peel came unhurt out of the horny dilemma. There was just enough concession in his tone and manner to make the nice distinction that, though the Chair was infallible, and its decisions not to be appealed against, yet the present incumbent, honest in intention, was after all human, and claimed nothing more than the possession of absolute integrity of purpose.

Mr. W. O'Brien. Mr. O'Brien is one of the large body of members, chiefly Irish, who have taught themselves Parliamentary oratory at the expense of the House of Commons. When he took his seat for Mallow little more than five years ago he was even repulsively uncouth. He had a way when addressing the Chair of gnashing his teeth and clenching his hands, painfully suggestive of what might take place if he could only get within reach of the unoffending Speaker. Traces of these gestures still linger around his more impassioned speech. But by practice and perseverance he has brought them under command, so that they even lend force to his invective. He is as fluent as Mr. Sexton, as fiery as Major Nolan. Sometimes—more especially when fresh from prison, with the spectacle before him of Mr. Balfour languishing on the Treasury bench—it seems as if his passion would overmaster him and carry him away into the regions of shrieking bathos. A picturesque figure he presents, with pale set face, flashing eyes gleaming under spectacles, and long arm signalling denunciation of right hon. gentlemen on the Treasury bench.

His paroxysm is, in these later days, of limited duration. He always pulls up in time, and comes out in the end master of himself and of the critical and, to a considerable extent, hostile assembly he addresses. His speech on the Vote of Censure, moved by Mr. John Morley last Session, was a splendid sample of militant oratory of the "Ruin-seize-thee-ruthless-king" kind. In truth, in these later days, the House of Commons presents no nearer resemblance to Gray's angered bard than is found in Mr. William O'Brien on the war path. Listening to him as with a "master's hand and prophet's fire he strikes the deep sorrows of his lyre," one expects him to lapse into the Pindaric strain—

> Weave the warp and weave the woof,
> The winding-sheet of Balfour's race.
> Give ample room and verge enough
> The characters of hall to trace.

Mr. Bradlaugh.   Mr. Bradlaugh differs in all personal respects from Mr. O'Brien, except inasmuch as he has an evil habit of occasionally addressing the House at the top of a strident voice. Mr. O'Brien is ascetic looking, with something of the air of a professor not over well remunerated. Mr. Bradlaugh is plump, not to say massive, and looks as if he slept o' nights. The position he has achieved to-day in the House of Commons furnishes remarkable evidence of the ultimate success of natural ability when pitted against prejudice. As a rule the House of Commons is the fairest-minded assembly in the world. It looks to what a man is, not to what he possesses, whether in respect of advantages of birth or accumulation of wealth. Being human and English, it has natural leaning towards a lord. But, as Lord George Hamilton has discovered, that a man should be the son of a duke does not solely suffice for his acceptance by the House of Commons. It is pretty certain that had the present member for Paddington been simply Mr. Churchill, his father a Manchester merchant, a Scotch ironmaster, or something in the City, he would not so readily have achieved his present position. To discover that a young man inheriting a title, even

MR. BRADLAUGH.

though it be of courtesy, has in him appreciably more than
the average commoner, is so agreeable a surprise that the

House of Commons is always inclined to make the most of it. But it must have something more, and it does not withhold its admiration because one who deserves it was obscurely born, and has nothing but his talents to recommend him to notice.

The exception made at the outset of Mr. Bradlaugh's Parliamentary career testifies to the intensity of the distaste in which he was held. Since Wilkes was expelled from the House of Commons and brought back again and again on the crest of the wave of popular enthusiasm, there have been no such scenes in the House of Commons as once raged round the burly figure of Mr. Bradlaugh. Devout men like Lord Randolph Churchill, Sir Henry Wolff, and Mr. Gorst, had their deepest sensibilities shocked by his avowed atheism. That was an insuperable barrier to their approval of his claim to take his seat. But behind Mr. Bradlaugh stood the figure of Mr. Gladstone, just at that time (1880) returned to power at the head of what looked like an impregnable majority. A crusade led against atheism and Mr. Gladstone was a delirious delight, the more treasured since it would in ordinary circumstances have seemed a combination impossible for imagination to conceive.

Thus Mr. Bradlaugh was, year after year, barred out whilst Mr. Gladstone was leader of the House, and quietly admitted in the very earliest days of Conservative accession to power.

In the now far-off days when Mr. Bradlaugh was wont to be buffeted at the bar, with occasional processes of propulsion into Palace Yard, he made his mark as an orator. His opportunities were unique. Whilst ordinary members, desiring to take part in debate, rose in their places and struggled with others to catch the Speaker's eye, Mr. Bradlaugh had provided for him special advantages. The veritable Bar of the House of Commons, a mysterious entity rarely gazed upon in the course of a generation, was solemnly drawn out. Behind it he stood, the Serjeant-at-Arms in immediate attendance, with the House crowded from floor to topmost range of the galleries, and all London waiting outside to catch the earliest echoes of his speech. The opportunity was great, and time after time he rose to it. The audience forgot his ungainly presence in the keenness of his argument and the glowing eloquence of his appeal.

Those were his palmy days, to which he must occasionally

look back with regret as he now not infrequently rises from
the Bench below the gangway and argues with a half-empty
House, whose lymphatic mood is stirred only by occasional
applause from the Ministerial majority, or a nod of approval
from the Conservative Attorney-General. In these quieter
days Mr. Bradlaugh has had time to cultivate a new oratorical
attitude. He always addresses the House from precisely the
same place far down on the third bench below the gangway,
almost level with the line of the Bar, and so commanding the
fullest view of his audience. Beginning on two legs, Mr. Bradlaugh, as his argument advances, finds his thoughts and his
tongue run freer if he stands upon one. So, with one knee
resting on the back of the bench before him, he will stand
twenty minutes on one leg and wrestle with the convictions
and prejudices of the House of Commons.

Mr. Chaplin. Examples of the burlesque of oratory and of the
fatal tendencies of fluency are seen in diverse
development in Mr. Chaplin and Mr. Sexton. Probably if Mr.
Chaplin had never had an opportunity of studying Mr. Disraeli's manner his Parliamentary failure would have been considerably less complete. Able, well-informed, personally popular, enjoying exceptional opportunities of ascertaining the
views and feelings of the country gentlemen, he might, as their
spokesman, have achieved a position of influence and usefulness something akin to that of Lord George Bentinck. But
the temptations thrown in his way by Mr. Disraeli were irresistible. To listen to that great man uttering, in deep chest notes,
pompously conceived commonplaces, to behold him literally
filling out his cheeks with wind, to note his Jove-like frown,
and to see him fling his arms about in windmill fashion,
seemed easy for anyone with ordinary mimetic powers to
imitate. So it was. Where Mr. Chaplin made the mistake
was in believing these little mannerisms, rarely and with deliberate purpose assumed, held the secret of Mr. Disraeli's
Parliamentary success. Making due allowance for diversity of
personal appearance, Mr. Chaplin reproduces them skilfully
enough. But the House of Commons only laughs, for this is
all of the Great Master the earnest painstaking pupil is
capable of recalling.

Sir W. Harcourt. Sir William Harcourt is another frequent participator in debate who shows traces of having studied in the school where Mr. Chaplin's gifts were cultivated. The House also laughs at Sir William Harcourt when he flings about his arms and trembles with carefully cultivated indignation at the shortcomings or iniquity of some right hon. gentleman on the bench near him or on the bench opposite, as the time may serve. But Sir William Harcourt has something more than these borrowed garments wherewith to fix the fancy of the House. He has much of Mr. Disraeli's great gift of phrase-making, though he lacks the skill with which Mr. Disraeli was wont to hide evidences of deliberate preparation. Like Mr. Disraeli, Sir William Harcourt brings all his impromptus down to the House with him. But he has not Mr. Disraeli's skill in deftly removing and hiding away the little pieces of paper in which they were wrapped.

Mr. Biggar. As unconscious imitators of familiar styles, both Sir William Harcourt and Mr. Chaplin must yield to the supremacy of Mr. Biggar. Whilst they concentrate their attention upon one great *exemplaire,* he mingles with skilful touches traces of the personal manner of half a dozen. If one famous Parliamentary man predominates over the rest in his influence on Mr. Biggar's later Parliamentary style it is Mr. Bright. The traces are faint and fleeting, indescribable by the pen, but recognisable by anyone familiar with Mr. Bright's Parliamentary manner. Mr. Biggar's imitative faculty is indeed habitually called into play by immediate connections, and since Mr. Bright's voice has of late been silent in the House he has partially lost touch with him. Mr. Gladstone is always with us, and Mr. Biggar, following upon one of his speeches, is certain to show recognisable traces of his influence. He also, when opportunity offers, lapses into his Randolph-Churchillian manner; whilst if the Speaker has had occasion prominently to interfere in the course of a sitting, the member for Cavan, following at a later hour, assumes a certain dignity of manner and authority of tone which would bewray the secret to any late comer ignorant of the course of earlier proceedings. It is in this mood that he makes use of his familiar gesture—holding out his right hand palm downwards, imperiously waving it and authoritatively disposing of other members who may rise at the same moment to compete with him for precedence.

Mr. Sexton.   Mr. Sexton imitates no one unless it be Lord Castlereagh, whose likeness to a pump was discovered by Tom Moore. "Why is a pump like Lord Castlereagh?" the poet asked, and answered—

> Because it is a slender thing of wood,
>   That up and down its awkward arm doth sway;
> In one weak, washy, everlasting flood
>   It coolly spouts, and spouts, and spouts away.

The pity of it is that Mr. Sexton's flood of eloquence is not invariably weak and washy, and need never be so. Occasional passages in his voluminous discourses are flashes of heaven-born eloquence. But they are so smothered in verbiage that they have no chance either to burn or to illumine. He rarely addresses the House of Commons for less period than an hour at a stretch, hopelessly wearying it. If he were content with a quarter of an hour, or at most twenty minutes, he would be a valuable addition to its debating power.   But he is so openly and undisguisedly in love with his own gift of speech-making that he has no room for consideration of the physical frailty of his audience. Mr. Chaplin does not disguise the pleasure with which he listens to himself. The late Mr. Beresford-Hope used literally to hug himself

with delight in anticipation of a yet unspoken witticism. None of these peculiarities is so aggravating as the seraphic smile which wreathes the lips of Mr. Sexton as he listens to his own interminable talk.

To compare small things with great he recalls a criticism of Lord Thurlow's which hits off in a sentence the prevailing difference between the oratory of Fox and of Pitt. "Fox," said the Lord Chancellor, "always speaks to the House; Pitt speaks as if he were speaking to himself." The phrase may be borrowed to indicate the fundamental difference between Mr. Sexton and another well-known Irish member. Mr. Healy always speaks to the House; Mr. Sexton speaks as if he had himself for sole audience—a condition of affairs which his more prolonged harangues tend literally to bring about.

Mr. Tim Healy. Mr. Healy, out of unpromising materials, has grown into one of the most acceptable and influential debaters in the House of Commons. Of practical work accomplished by Irish members during the past five years, it is a moderate computation to say that fully one-half has been achieved by him. He can see farther through the intricacies of a Bill than most men, and is exceedingly adroit in drawing up amendments. Like some other of his compatriots, he has gained in polish at the expense of a long-suffering House. To this day he is not debarred from using a phrase because it is coarse, or following a line of argument because it is personally offensive. But he is a very different person from the one whom, eight years ago, Wexford Borough sent to Parliament. Those were the days of coercion pure and simple, with Home Rule scouted, and the Irish members a sort of guerilla force whose duty it was, between intervals of imprisonment and suspension, to make things as uncomfortable as possible for the Saxon at Westminster.

Mr. Healy entered the House with a consummate contempt and hatred for it. He once informed a listening senate that he "did not care two rows of pins whether he was in prison or whether he was in the House of Commons." In the relations which then existed between the Irish Party and their fellow-members the House probably had a preference, which it was too polite to express. When addressing the Speaker he would

not even take the trouble to remove his fists from his trousers
pockets. With both hands hidden away, with neck bent forward in slouching attitude, a scowl on his face, and rasping
notes of hatred in his voice, he scolded at large. All that is
changed. Mr. Healy is now the " hon. and learned gentleman,"
one of the leaders in debate, in open counsel, even in colleagueship, with right hon. gentlemen on the front Opposition
bench.

His noble friend. That these relations should exist with a prominent section of English members is no new
thing to Mr. Healy's experience. In the Parliament of 1880
Lord Randolph Churchill, his immediate neighbour below the
gangway, was in constant personal communication with him.
One night Mr. Healy created quite a sensation by alluding
to Lord Folkestone, one of the Conservative Whips, as " my
noble friend." These were fleeting acquaintance, arising out of
temporary tactical movements, and have no ground of comparison with the formal and regularised alliance now existing
between the Irish members and the leaders of the Liberal
Party.

Mr. Gladstone and Tim. In the last division Mr. Gladstone took part
in during the summer Session—it was on the
Parnell Commission Bill—a crowded House watched with
breathless interest a significant scene. The leader of the Opposition, strolling down the floor of the House towards the
division lobby, halted at the Bar, and, turning round, took out
his glasses and eagerly scanned the Irish benches. Perceiving
the person he sought, he retraced his steps as far as the gangway, stood there, the focus of four hundred pairs of eyes,
beckoned Mr. Healy down and, placing his arm within his,
walked out eagerly conversing with him.

Mr. Healy has risen to the full height of altered circumstances. He lives cleanly, and has almost entirely abjured
sack. Now and then he falls into his old bullyragging manner,
as when in debate on the Parnell Commission Bill he tickled
the fancy of the House with his reiterated inquiry, " Where's
Walter?" meaning the respected proprietor of the *Times*.
But for the most part he is grave, responsible, acute, weighty

in counsel, overpowering in attack, living up to his new status
as an " hon. and learned gentleman."

Mr. Parnell. Mr. Parnell is still another, not the least
striking, example of the disciplinary influence of
the House. In the self-possessed, softly spoken, courteous
gentleman who at long intervals addresses the Speaker, it is
difficult to recall the lineaments of the one time member for
Meath. A dozen years have passed since Mr. Parnell found
in Mr. Biggar his chosen companion, and, sustained by his acrid
cheer, was wont to flout the then leader of the Irish Party,

Mr. Isaac Butt, and nightly assail the authority of the Chair.
He began Parliamentary life by being in an ungovernable
passion. He promises to end it in an atmosphere of icy calm.
His coolness in debate is almost supernatural, and probably
has something to do with the secret of his supremacy over an
emotionable nation and a heterogeneous party whose leading
characteristic is certainly not repose of manner. He comes
and goes without affectation of mystery, but with all its effect.
No one can say whether he will be in his place on a particular
occasion, however specially interesting to him, and, if he comes,
whether he will take part in the debate or remain to vote.

He is the only man of prominent position who has not appropriated for himself a corner seat. When he speaks he rises
from some place midway on the bench below the gangway, in
which he has happened to drop on arriving. He has a
pleasant voice, a clear enunciation, and a pellucid style. He
never, even on the most moving occasions, attempts to rise
into the oratorical style. Having something to say—and he
never speaks till he has, a rare personal peculiarity in the
House of Commons—he says it as simply, as briefly, yet as
forcibly as possible, and sits down. For an Irish leader,
wielding more power than one has held since the days of
O'Connell, Mr. Parnell is in appearance, in manner of speech,
in tone of thought, and in all his ways, less like a typical
Irishman than any man in Parliament.

Mr. Chamberlain. Take him for all in all, I should say Mr. Chamberlain is the best debater in the House, not excepting Mr. Gladstone. He is not an orator, but rather a man
of business gifted with lightning-like acuteness and consummate
gift of lucid expression. With intimate knowledge of Mr.
Chamberlain's speeches during the last twelve years, I remember only one occasion when he permitted himself to drop into
oratory, as Mr. Silas Wegg used to drop into poetry. That was
at Birmingham in the bright June days of 1885, and the
passage itself is so remarkable, affording within brief space
so admirable a specimen of Mr. Chamberlain's more elevated
style, that it is worth citing :—

I sometimes think (he said) that great men are like great mountains, and that
we do not appreciate their magnitude while we are still close to them. You

K

MR. CHAMBERLAIN.

have to go to a distance to see which peak it is that towers above its fellows: and it may be that we shall have to put between us and Mr. Gladstone a space of time before we shall know how much greater he has been than any of his competitors for fame and power. I am certain that justice will be done to him in the future, and I am not less certain that there will be a signal condemnation of the men who, moved by motives of party spite, in their eagerness for office, have not hesitated to load with insult and indignity the greatest statesman of our time; who have not allowed even his age, which should have commanded their reverence, or his experience, which entitles him to their respect, or his high personal character, or his long services to his Queen and to his country, to shield him from the vulgar affronts and the lying accusations of which he has nightly been made the subject in the House of Commons. He, with his great magnanimity, can afford to forget and forgive these things. Those whom he has served so long it behoves to remember them, to resent them, and to punish them.

Mr. Chamberlain is supremely good on a platform addressing an applauding audience, a quality which does not by any means imply that a man will be a success in Parliament. He swiftly rose to the front rank in the House of Commons whilst yet a favourite captain in the Liberal host. As a Minister in charge of intricate Bills he displayed capacity for exposition and management not excelled by Mr. Gladstone. To see him at his very best is to watch him in the House of Commons in these days, when he stands with his back to the wall engaged in a hand-to-hand struggle with his former comrades. Mr. Gladstone in the full swing of his oratory is often disconcerted by hostile interruption, and is too easily led astray into devious paths. The fiercer the attack on Mr. Chamberlain, the more noisy the interruption, the brighter and cooler he grows, warding off bludgeon blows with deft parrying of his rapier, swiftly followed up by telling thrust at the aggressor. A dangerous man to tackle even with the advantage of overwhelming numbers—one whom it would not be safe to count as beaten, however disastrous circumstances concerning him may at a given moment seem to be.

SESSION 1889.

CHAPTER XIII.

CALM BEFORE THE STORM.

Opening Day—In the Sparrow's Nest—Mr. Balfour—Sir Richard Webster—Sir
J. Fergusson—Sir John Gorst—Wasting Time—A Useless Procedure—
Bringing in Bills.

Feb. 21.—Opening day. THE new Session opened to-day in unique circumstances. Ordinarily public attention is fixed upon the opening of Parliament to the exclusion of all other matters. To-day the inquiry before the Parnell Commission, which opened in October, chanced to reach a crisis of its dramatic run. Pigott has been in the box all day under cross-examination by Sir Charles Russell. Even whilst Notices of Motion were being piled upon the Clerk's table came news of an incident in the cross-examination that profoundly stirred the House. In one of the letters alleged by the *Times* to be in Mr. Parnell's handwriting, the word hesitancy was spelt "hesitency." Sir Charles Russell, with nice affectation of meaning nothing particular, asked Pigott to write down at his dictation a brief sentence in which the word hesitancy appeared. Pigott blandly consented, and a thrill went through the crowded Court when it was known that the third syllable of the word was spelled with an *e*.

It was of this incident, and of what might be expected to follow upon it, that the crowd gathered in the lobby of the House of Commons was eagerly talking, to the neglect of ordinary topics. Still the crowd of members gathered as heretofore.

In the Sparrow's Nest. The movement of Mr. Heneage, who, on first entering the House, took a back seat, gave some colour to the report that the leaders of the Dissentient Liberals

had resolved to refrain from further forcing their company upon
the adversary's camp. But when the House met again for the
despatch of business, Mr. Heneage took up his old quarters on
the front bench, and was presently joined by Mr. Chamberlain.
The latter gentleman was the recipient of many congratulations, chiefly from the Conservative side, on his marriage, which
has taken place during the recess. Mr. Chaplin was peculiarly overjoyed in contemplation of the domestic event.
Coming in a little after Mr. Chamberlain had arrived, he
crossed over and shook the bridegroom's hand, slapped him
on the shoulders, and made other boisterous demonstrations
of congratulation. Lord Hartington, as usual, came in late,
not arriving till six o'clock, when that plumed knight, Sir
John Colomb, was on his legs, seconding the Address. He
took his accustomed seat at the end of the front bench, where,
the House being at this time nearly empty, there was plenty
of room.

Mr. Smith arrived just before half-past four o'clock, the
hour at which to-day's public business commenced. He had a
hearty reception, to which many members on the Opposition
benches lent their voices. It was not a sharp, ringing, exultant cheer, such as that which greeted Mr. Gladstone half
an hour later. It was a friendly, even warm, reception, testi-
fying to the high esteem in which the Leader is held by the
House of Commons. Sir Horace Davey, at last returning to
Parliamentary scenes, was welcomed with a cheer by the
Liberals.

Mr. Balfour. There was one more outburst of cheering,
perhaps the most significant and dramatic of
the series. It was noted that among the crowd of Ministers
on the Treasury bench the slight, graceful figure of Mr. Balfour
was lacking. Half-hour after half-hour sped, but still he came
not. At length, just when the long list of Notices of Motion
was drawing to a close, and the hands of the clock pointed to
half-past five, a sudden, sharp cheer went up from the Conservative benches, and the Chief Secretary was discovered
striding into his place at the gangway end of the Treasury
bench. The Irish members made a hostile demonstration;
one or two of them even hissed, though not in a tone so loud

as to attract the attention of the Speaker. This, of course,
added fuel to the fiery enthusiasm of the Ministerialists, and
again the cheer rang forth as Mr. Balfour dropped into his
seat, and tried to look as if both demonstrations were intended for someone else.

Sir Richard Webster.   One of the plumpest, healthiest, and most
pleased-looking men seen on either side of the
House on this day of meeting is the Attorney-General. Considering he is fresh from the fifty-fourth day of the Parnell
Commission, of the work of which he has done the lion's share,

it is little short of a miracle. I passed a fortnight of my life in the Court from its opening day, and never in any experience felt brought so near to the verge of the grave. It is true the fortnight was almost exclusively occupied by delivery of the Attorney-General's opening speech, a peculiarly terrible ordeal. Still, fifty-four days, with whatever pleasing variations, are a serious matter. Yet it is no exaggeration to say Sir Richard Webster looks really better in health and is brighter in manner than when he started. He is a man of powerful constitution, with an inexhaustible stock of good health, so that he thrives and blooms amid circumstances that sap the vitals of an ordinary man. Sir Henry James is looking haggard; Sir Charles Russell is visibly older; even the florid countenance of stalwart Frank Lockwood is beginning to be sicklied o'er.

But the Attorney-General seems to draw nourishment from the Probate Court, and to blossom like a rose in what to others is a wilderness.

Last Friday night it happened the Attorney-General had a dinner-party at his house. Friday was a most exciting day in the Court. Mr. Soames had been under long examination, and Mr. Macdonald had followed. It was the crisis reached at last, and even the invulnerable Attorney-General might have been expected to show some traces of anxiety and seek for some interval of rest. But he was as cheerful and fresh as if he had been lounging in a library all day, or out with his gun. After dinner someone laughingly asked him for a song. Nothing would please him better. He gave one song, then another, and another, singing for nearly an hour and a half, as if he had not been talking for the greater part of the day.

It is an odd coincidence that both the Attorney-General and the Solicitor-General in Lord Salisbury's Government are gifted songsters, each regarding the other's endowments with secret rivalry.

"Capital fellow, Clarke!" says the Attorney-General, "only he *will* sing."

"Excellent fellow, Webster!" says the Solicitor-General, "but we all have our weakness, and he thinks he can sing."

Feb. 22.—Sir J. Fergusson. "I am obliged to listen to particularly tasteless speeches out of the mouths of uncommonly childish and excited politicians, and I have, therefore, a moment of unwilling leisure which I cannot use better than in giving you news of my welfare." Thus Bismarck wrote to Mr. Motley, in 1863, from his bench in the Reichstag. Sir James Fergusson is not quite Bismarck; has not been anything like him since he was Governor of Bombay. But thus he might have written as he sat to-night forlorn on the Treasury bench listening to Mr. Bradlaugh lustily declaiming on foreign politics. It is one of those nights on which leaders of a party find engagements elsewhere, leaving the cares of State to Under-Secretaries. At last night's sitting it had been formally resolved that battle should be given on

the paragraph of the Address echoing the complacent reflections about Ireland that figured in the Queen's Speech. Mr. John Morley's amendment was fixed for Monday, and for all practical or useful purposes the House might as well have adjourned till that day. But there were Thursday and Friday to be filled up. The Speaker was in the Chair, the Mace on the table, and, as was proved before the hour of adjournment, there were explosive elements lying scattered about which might at any moment blaze forth.

One peculiarity of the situation was that whilst the comprehensive mind of Mr. Bradlaugh had by chance selected foreign affairs as the subject of his tremendous oration, tho

Under-Secretary, having already taken part in the debate,
was precluded from speaking. He had to sit there and
listen, with that air of profound sagacity which assisted to
strengthen the hold of the British Crown on Bombay. But
he might not speak.

"THE UTILITY MAN."

Sir John Gorst. Fortunately, Sir John Gorst had also been "kept
in," and Sir John, as has been shown on many
occasions, is equal at briefest notice to represent the Government view on any question arising in connection with what-
soever department. He is the utility man of the Treasury

bench, at home in the Soudan or Syracuse, Thibet or Thessalonica. Macaulay somewhere tells a story about the (to him) amazing ignorance of the Duke of Newcastle, for thirty years Secretary of State and during nearly ten First Lord of the Treasury. "Oh, yes, yes, to be sure; Annapolis must be defended," said the Premier; "troops must be sent to Annapolis. Pray where is Annapolis?" Sir John Gorst would have been invaluable in the Duke of Newcastle's Ministry, as, to tell the truth, he is in that of Lord Salisbury.

Wasting time. It was a dull five hours that followed on the resumption of the so-called debate on the Address. It was mercifully designed in the interests of the stranger in the gallery, whose mind had earlier been wrought up to a dangerous pitch of excitement, being privileged to witness the time-honoured, but, as far as the public is concerned, very little known, process of bringing in Bills. Last year the opportunities for legislation by private members were wofully curtailed, and, if report is justified, the coming Session will be arranged on similar, if not more severely-drawn, lines. Nevertheless, over a hundred members, casting about, have found as many subjects urgently calling for legislation. Last night over an hour of time reputed to be valuable was occupied in the business of balloting for places. This is a process useful, even necessary; but there is no reason in the world why it should not be carried out by the Clerks in the *quasi* privacy of one of the Committee Rooms. The equally ancient custom of verbally giving notice of questions, and of subsequently reciting the terms of the question, has happily been abolished by the action of the Speaker. There is no reason apparent why licence should be permitted on the first night of the Session, and public time occupied by an interminable string of members rising in their places to announce the title of a Bill they propose to ask leave to introduce, or the terms of a resolution they mean to submit.

A serious procedure. But if some indulgence might be claimed for the opening night, there is nothing to be said in favour of the monotonous, soul-depressing process which appropriated one of the earlier hours of to-day's sitting. The

Speaker, taking in hand the long list of notices given yesterday, calls the names of the members in succession, and this is what the stranger in the gallery beheld.

The Speaker calls out " Mr. Murphy :"   Mr. Murphy raises his hat, whereupon the Speaker says, " The question is that leave be given to bring in a Bill to provide for the vesting in the Commissioners of Public Works in Ireland Royalties, Foreshore Rights, and Water Rights connected with lands sold under the Purchase of Lands (Ireland) Act."   The Speaker reads out this description of the Bill with the perfect elocution of which he is a master.   Not an accent is lost, not a syllable slurred.   His sonorous voice and emphatic intonation invest the Royalties and Foreshore Rights (Ireland) Bill with a new grace even in the eyes of its author, and Mr. Murphy sits blushing and smiling.   " Who is prepared to bring in this Bill ?" asks the Speaker (it is the ninety-fourth measure), with precisely that air of personal interest and preparation for being surprised that he has managed to throw into each of the ninety-three precedent interrogations.   Then Mr. Murphy rises and reads out the names of members who endorse his Bill, and the Speaker goes on to the next on the list.

Bringing in Bills. This is only a portion of a Parliamentary proceeding of which the newspapers give no account.   As the Speaker approaches the end of the list the stranger in the gallery, craning his neck over the rails, will discover a gathering throng of members at the Bar.   Gradually nearly every seat on either side is vacated, and members struggle for places at the Bar.   The Speaker calls on Mr. Bradlaugh, whose name heads the list.   Mr. Bradlaugh is very well acquainted with the locality between the Bar and the table on which lies the Mace.   In days gone by he has waltzed up and down with the late Serjeant-at-Arms hanging on to the lappels of his coat what time three-fourths of a crowded House, not all seated on one side, yelled and roared.   Now Mr. Bradlaugh, having been favoured with the first place in the ballot, brings up unmolested a Bill to " Abolish Prosecutions for the Expression of Opinion on Matters of Religion," and making the circuit of the Speaker's chair goes quietly back to his place below the gangway to gather up his

papers and scan his notes for the instructions he will presently
deliver to Her Majesty's Ministers for their guidance in
Foreign Affairs.

The Speaker calls on the next member on the list, who,
making his way through the throng at the bar, advances
towards the table holding a piece of folded foolscap in his
hand. This is understood to be the Bill he is bringing in, and
nothing done under the eye of the stranger in the gallery
dispels the fiction. But the member himself has the guilty
knowledge, shared by the imperturbable Clerk at the table,
that the piece of paper carefully folded and elaborately endorsed is nothing but a blank sheet. The text of the measure
will be deposited in the Bill Office at some future convenient
date. The Clerk, carefully concealing his knowledge of the
little fraud, respectfully takes charge of "the Bill," recites its
title, and observes to the member,

" Second reading ?

" Eighth of May," says the member.

" Bill read second time eighth of May," says the Clerk at
the table.

" Read second time eighth of May," echoes the Speaker in
the chair, giving quite new point to the observation by his
impressive tones. Then Member No. 2 disappears behind the
Speaker's chair, and so on through all the hundred.

This is all very well if the House of Commons has nothing
better to do; but for a barbarous, futile waste of time it must
take the palm. To-night it did not greatly matter. The
House was bound in decency to sit till midnight, and for all
other useful purposes served this wearisome and ridiculous trotting up and down of members with pieces of waste paper in their
hands was just as good a way of spending an hour as any other.
It was, in truth, exhilarating as compared with what followed
with Sir James Fergusson sitting on the bench ready to coach
Sir John Gorst, with Mr. Goschen flitting uneasily in and out,
and Mr. Smith showing himself now and then with a pen
stuck behind his ear to let the Under-Secretaries know that,
though he might not be actually in his place as Mr. Disraeli
was wont to be on similar nights in days long since dead, he
was hard at work in his room, caring for the destinies of the
nation.

CHAPTER XIV.

MR. PARNELL'S DAY OF TRIUMPH.

The Flight of Pigott—Mr. Gladstone and Mr. Chamberlain—Mr. Parnell's Hour
of Triumph—A Memorable Scene—Then and Now.

Feb. 25.—The Flight of Pigott. THE news of the flight of Pigott, which burst
through the Probate Court into the crowded
Strand this morning, rapidly spread over the Metropolis.
By eleven o'clock it was known in the clubs, and very shortly
afterwards the evening papers came out with specially early
editions. In the lobbies and in the Chamber itself the
House of Commons is literally buzzing with the news.
Those in the councils of Mr. Parnell and his legal advisers
have for some time spoken of surprises in store which should
exceed anything hitherto disclosed in the court. It need
hardly be said that this sudden and dramatic disappearance
of the mainstay of the case for the *Times* was not alluded
to. It came as a great shock upon the crowded court, and
was the occasion for a profound disappointment on the part of
Sir Charles Russell, who had come down bright and early to
carry forward his terrible cross-examination. But Mr. Pigott
had had enough of it; and when the officers despatched in hot
haste from the court visited Anderton's Hotel, they found the
nest empty.

Never in the history of a nation not without moving annals
has there been so dramatic an episode. If the whole procedure
of the Commission had been arranged with a view to this
climax it could not have been more skilfully done. There
were the long weeks and months of monotonous serving-up of
ancient history. It is easy enough now to understand the
coyness with which the Attorney-General approached the
consideration of the letters. Every day spent in trotting out
policemen and emergency men to describe the state of Kerry
or Galway was twenty-four hours' further postponement of
catastrophe. Then, abruptly, on the long drawn out scene the
stout, flabby-faced figure of Pigott slinks. There is a day or

two of breathless suspense while Sir Charles Russell equals even his own great reputation in cross-examination; and then, without a word of warning, Pigott vanishes into space.

March 1.—Mr. Gladstone and Mr. Chamberlain. House still debating Mr. John Morley's Amendment to the Address challenging the Irish policy of the Government. This is the fifth night of talk for the most part dreary. But a fillip is given to the business by the expectation of Gladstone's interposition. He found his opportunity as early as half-past four, the House crowded in every part. His appearance at the table was the signal for a prolonged outburst of cheering from the Opposition, jubilant at the turn events had taken before the Parnell Commission. He looked in perfect health. As is his custom when delivering an important speech, he wore a flower in his button-hole. During his opening sentences Mr. Chamberlain entered and took his seat at the end of the front Opposition bench, an attempt to hail his arrival by a general cheer on the Conservative side not proving a success. A quarter of an hour later Lord Hartington arrived, any difficulty in finding room for him on the crowded bench being avoided by Mr. Heneage relinquishing the corner seat he had secured when the Speaker took the chair.

At the outset Mr. Gladstone turned his attention to the speech Mr. Chamberlain delivered on the previous day; and to his former colleague, who sat close at his left hand, he directly, and with animated gestures, addressed such remarks as personally referred to him or his friends.

Mr. Chamberlain had expressed a desire to see the Irish Land Question settled, and Mr. Gladstone, listening to him, had, he said, thought it easy to foretell his next sentence. Of course he would appeal to the Government actually in office, and in possession of official information, forthwith to submit a scheme dealing with it.

"But he turned to me," Mr. Gladstone exclaimed, with dramatic tones and gestures that caused much laughter on both sides; "me, forsooth! the leader of a discomfited and discredited minority."

Placing his hands behind his back, and bending down towards Mr. Chamberlain, he asked amid renewed laughter,

"Am *I* the person who is so happy as to possess the political confidence of the right hon. gentleman?"

The Government, he proceeded to argue, were the persons to produce a plan dealing with the Land Question. Mr. Morley's amendment was an invitation to the majority to take that course, and if they disregarded it they would show once more the utter hollowness and the shallowness of the pretexts

with which in 1886 they had gained the control of the destinies of the Empire.

These passages were delivered with a joyous animation of manner and a wealth of gravely humorous gesture that delighted the crowded House. From this point Mr. Gladstone proceeded in more prosaic style to deal with various aspects of the question at issue. Dealing with the alleged decrease of crime under the " salutary " influence of Mr. Balfour's administration, he showed that the returns were so prepared that they did not afford any proof of the decrease of crime within the meaning of the Crimes Act. He commented on the treatment of prisoners under the Crimes Act, comparing it with what was meted out to O'Connell. He drew an instructive picture of

the state of Ireland between 1835 and 1840 under the beneficent Chief Secretaryship of Mr. Drummond ; and finally led
up to a fine peroration, delivered with thrilling energy.

"You may," he said, "deprive of its grace and of its freedom
the act which you are asked to do, but avert that act you
cannot.   To prevent its consummation is utterly beyond your
power.   It seems to approach at an accelerated rate.   Coming
slowly or coming quickly, surely it is coming.   And you your-
selves, many of you must in your own breasts be aware that
already you see in the handwriting on the wall the signs of
coming doom."

These sentences were declaimed amid profound silence,
broken in upon, as Mr. Gladstone fell back in his seat, by
tremendous cheering from the Opposition, many members
standing up and waving their hats.

Mr. Parnell's
hour of tri-
umph.

Mr. Gladstone resumed his seat at half-past six,
having spoken for two hours.   Thereupon the
House emptied.   At one time the attendance
sank so low as to suggest to some ingenious mind the idea
that the best way out of the business was to get the House
counted, and so home to bed.   This, of course, failed, and
members trooping in at the sound of the bell, thereafter remained in numbers sufficient to give some appearance of life
to the temporarily languid debate.

When Mr. Asquith rose it was a quarter past ten and a dull
night.   But gradually, as the young barrister went forward,
with a speech marked by conspicuous debating power, and
illumined with felicitous phrases, the benches rapidly filled,
and when he sat down the House presented the eager, restless,
almost tumultuous, appearance which marks it only two or
three times in a Session.

One thing beyond the persuasiveness of Mr. Asquith's
oratory which served to muster the eager throng was the expectation of Mr. Parnell's appearance.   There was no man
in the House more interested in the debate, which had
already lasted five days ; and he of all men had been persistently absent.   The Irish leader has a great gift of subduing,
and even effectively concealing, his personal interest in public
proceedings, whether taking place at Westminster or in the

Probate Court.   It was quite on the cards that he might not come at all.   No one had seen him about the House. Eleven o'clock was drawing near, and before midnight the debate must needs close and the House be cleared for the division.

A loud, hearty, and prolonged cheer paid tribute to the excellence of Mr. Asquith's oratory.   As it was dying away, and members were looking round to see who might follow, a sharp ringing cheer from the Irish camp drew all eyes in that direction, and behold! there was Mr. Parnell, rising from an obscure place midway down the second bench below the gangway, with pale set face turned towards the Chair.

A memorable scene. — When he stood up, the Irish members near him began to cheer.   Then they rose to their feet. The enthusiasm extended beyond the gangway, and sedate English Liberal members sitting behind the front bench also uprose, a thing never seen before in the House of Commons in honour of an Irish member.   But there was more to follow.   Mr. Gladstone stood up, and turned to face with welcoming countenance the representative of Ireland.   In a second, ex-Ministers right and left of him followed his lead, and resounding cheers filled the House, whilst Mr. Parnell, pale to the lips, stood waiting till the cheering subsided.

On the front Opposition bench only one figure remained seated—Lord Hartington, immobile at the end of the bench. It was some minutes before Mr. Parnell found an opportunity of speaking, the cheers rising again and again, with waving of hats and clapping of hands.

All the while Mr. Gladstone and his colleagues stood with their faces turned towards the animated group below the gangway.   The Conservatives refrained from those ironical counter-cheers with which they are wont to greet ebullitions in favour of Ireland.   When silence was restored, Mr. Parnell proceeded with his remarks in his ordinary quiet, self-possessed manner, with unbroken voice, as if nothing particular had happened. He spoke for twenty minutes in a studiously moderate tone, only once referring to the events before the Commission of Judges, and then contenting himself with the remark that he would not stop to consider the means adopted by the

Government and their friends to pass the Coercion Act, or deal with the conspiracy that had assisted them.

This was a well-understood reference to the fact that the *Times* had held back the publication of the forged letter till the morning preceding the division on the second reading of the Crimes Bill, the alleged disclosure materially increasing the majority for the Bill.

Then and now. Mr. Parnell received this ovation standing by his usually obscure seat below the gangway. Leaders of sectional parties and leaders without parties usually affect a corner seat, a coign of vantage whence they may with proper authority and due distinction address a listening senate. At one time, when Mr. Parnell first emerged into prominence, having Mr. Biggar as his constant companion and *alter ego*, he dropped into the fashion amongst Parliamentary claimants of addressing the House from a corner seat. That was many years ago, and the preference was not long displayed. Now he has no seat especially connected with his personality as has Lord Randolph Churchill, Sir Walter Barttelot, Mr. Dillwyn, or that other guerilla chief, Mr. Chaplin. Somewhere about the middle of the second bench below the gangway, any seat that happens to be vacant, or anywhere where room may be made for him in this quarter, suffices Mr. Parnell for his rare and, of late, historical addresses to the Commons.

Here he stood one summer night in the sitting which saw the suspension of thirty-seven Irish members. From this very place he expressed a "doubt whether it was really of any use addressing the House," noting that the English nation was in the habit of bullying and oppressing weaker nations, "much in the same way," he added parenthetically, "as I am subject to menaces from members of this House." Twice in the same sitting his words were "taken down," and the House solemnly agreed that "Mr. Parnell having wilfully and persistently obstructed public business is guilty of contempt of this House, and that Mr. Parnell for the said offence be suspended from the service of the House till Friday next." It was from this seat that, after years of incidents akin to this, he rose last Session to denounce as forgeries certain letters which had of late appeared in the *Times*.

Perhaps in the few minutes' pause imposed upon him to-night, whilst the Opposition enthusiastically cheered him, and whilst he looked on the unprecedented scene of the veteran statesman on the front Opposition bench rising to do him honour, his thoughts turned back to the days that are no more.

CHAPTER XV.

UNREST IN THE COMMONS.

Dr. Tanner's Escort—The New Lord Radnor—A Missing Document—Sir Wm. Harcourt in Saddened Mood—Mr. Biggar—J. F. X. O'Brien—Mr. Courtney's Mistake—A Sitting of the House of Lords—An All-night Sitting—Worried Ministers.

March 2.—Dr. Tanner's escort. As Big Ben tolled forth half-past twelve this morning, Lord Beaconsfield, gazing out from his pedestal in Parliament Square, looked upon a strange scene. On the stroke of the half-hour there issued from the corridor by the carriage entrance of the House of Commons a densely-packed body of men. They spoke in low tones, moved with slow step, and, under the tolling of the bell, suggested a funeral procession. Slowly they marched across Palace Yard, shoulder to shoulder, almost tumbling over each other in their undisciplined effort to keep their square unbroken. As they passed out of the Yard their steps quickened; there was less anxious closing up of the serried ranks, and as the procession passed beneath the statue of the late Premier, there rose up on the stilly midnight air the strains of the Irish Marseillaise—

> "God save Ireland!" say we all,
> "Whether on the gallows high, or on battlefield we die,
> What matter if for Ireland dear we fall?"

This was the escort of Dr. Tanner, bent upon the desperate but vague purpose of somehow or other delivering him in safety at Westminster Palace Hotel, and so baffling the Chief Secretary's myrmidons. Dr. Tanner has hitherto successfully carried out his little scheme for bringing authority into disrepute.   After evading for a month the magistrate's warrant for his arrest under the Crimes Act he last night with dramatic effect burst in upon the assembled House of Commons on the very eve of the division which challenged the existence of the Government. He had had a boisterous reception; and now "the boys" were taking him home—a stern, resolute body of men as they emerged from the sanctuary of the House and faced the unknown terrors of Palace Yard.

What would happen who could tell? Would the police bear down upon them báton in hand and wrest from them their precious convoy? Would the Yard bristle with bayonets, its dark recesses illumined by the flash of rifle fire? No one could tell; but Mr. O'Hanlon, who had almost tasted blood on the previous night when under the gallery he wrestled with Sir Henry Havelock-Allen, and magnanimously gave him "a minute to think," was among the throng of members who grimly set their teeth and prepared to meet the worst. *Ex pede Herculem.*

Nothing came of it in Palace Yard; nothing in Parliament Square, only the familiar figure on the pedestal looking down with that inscrutable glance with which some in the procession were familiar when Mr. Disraeli used to gaze across the floor of the House at the tumultuous group below the gangway. Then among

THE DOCTOR.

them the stupendous form of Major O'Gorman towered. Then "dashing Lysaght Finigan" was still to the fore (where is

Lysaght now ? Married a wealthy widow, they say, and retired from politics), Then well-meaning M'Carthy Downey was distraught between his devotion to Mr. Butt and his desire to mingle in the scrimmage led by lighter spirits such as Frank Hugh O'Donnell and Joseph Gillis Biggar.

As the procession passed the broad space by Westminster Court House and neared the hotel, a depressing thought simultaneously possessed the mind of the gallant band. What if, after all, no attempt should be made to arrest Dr. Tanner ? Irish members sometimes bitterly say Mr. Balfour lacks a sense of humour. Supposing he were suddenly to develop it in this ruthless way and spoil the sport by leaving the procession severely alone ? Footsteps lagged ; a ripple of laughing conversation succeeded the measured chant of the song ; the crowd halted forlornly at the open doors of the hotel. There had been the usual policeman or two about the gates of Palace Yard, but they had taken no notice of the procession, had not followed it, and were not now anywhere within sight. There was evidently nothing to be done but for Dr. Tanner to enter his hotel as any ordinary late comer might, to disappear, and go to bed, perchance to sleep.

Before the curtain fell the doctor, standing bareheaded on the topmost step, delivered a speech, the best (because the briefest) ever heard from him since his Parliamentary career commenced. Then he went in, the door closed ; the escort having, regardless of personal danger, performed their duty, went boldly home, and Dr. Tanner was nabbed—ignominiously nabbed in the smoking-room of his hotel, with scarcely any to see save a waiter, whose sympathies were sapped by the consciousness that he had been unduly kept out of his bed.

March 14.—The new Lord Radnor. The death of the Earl of Radnor incidentally removes a familiar and favourite personage from the House of Commons. Lord Folkestone, his heir and successor to the peerage, is something more than a Conservative. He is one of those thorough-paced Tories whom modern concatenation of political circumstances makes increasingly rare. But he is so bubbling over with the quality described by the untranslatable word *bonhomie* that he is as

much liked on the Liberal side as the Conservative. He
has been in the House of Commons for upwards of fifteen
years, and has throughout voted steadily against every one of
those reforms Mr. Gladstone and his colleagues have been
instrumental in bringing forward. His reward has been the
appointment of Treasurer to the Household, which came to
him in 1885, the year he was returned for the Enfield Division
of Middlesex, severing his long connection with South Wilts.
It is well known among Lord Folkestone's intimate friends
that when the Conservative party came into power in 1886 he
looked for the appointment of Chief Whip, which he would
have admirably filled. Nominally he has never been Whip,
but during the time the Conservatives were in Opposition he
did all the drudgery of the office.

March 18. — A **Mr. Beaufoy**, the newly-elected member for
missing docu- Kennington, was during question-time under
ment. the gallery, in the seat allotted to members
waiting to take the oath. It was naturally expected that as
soon as questions were over he would walk to the table, and
the crowded state of the Opposition benches promised an
enthusiastic welcome. It presently turned out that, owing to
some unaccountable accident, the return to the writ of election
was not to hand, and the Speaker ruled that, failing its arrival,
Mr. Beaufoy might not take his seat. The delay is, of course,
accidental, and of no particular consequence, since no critical
division is on to-night. But it is unpardonable, seeing the
considerable space that has intervened since the election
was determined. There has been no similar case since the
year 1848. The nearest approach to it was in 1877, when
the present Lord Chancellor, then Sir Hardinge Giffard, after
many defeats managed to get elected for Launceston. When
he arrived at the table, and was asked to produce the return
to the writ, he could not find it. This was a dozen years ago,
but no one who was present can forget the ludicrous scene,
which lasted several minutes, during which the new member
frantically fished in every pocket, turning out heaps of papers,
vainly searching for the document. It was finally found on
the bench under the gallery where he had been sitting awaiting the call to the table.

March 22.—Sir Wm. Harcourt in saddened mood. The little scene in which Mr. J. F. X. O'Brien to-night involuntarily figured supplied a grateful relief to the over-wrought feelings of the House of Commons. For an hour and a half Sir William Harcourt had mingled his tears with those of gentlemen who deplore the short-comings, or the too far-goings, of the Attorney-General. Sir William's oratorical manner may be roughly classified after the manner of an interesting page of the morning paper, which announces deaths in one column and marriages in another. His more familiar manner is marked by the boisterousness of the happy bridegroom. But there are times, happily rare, when he assumes the habiliments of mourning, and laments at large. Such an occasion presented itself to-night, when it fell to the lot of this distinguished man to indict the Attorney-General for his private practice in connection with the Parnell Commission. He was oppressed with a sense of his responsibility, borne down with the weight of commiseration for his "right hon. and learned friend" at the other side of the table.

At the very outset he, with instinctive dramatic art, assumed an attitude of almost limp depression. As a rule, he stands with head erect and lissom figure poised, so that he may, at a moment's inspiration, the more readily and easily launch forth in that convincing gesture by which, with arms flung abroad, he turns rapidly upon his heel and literally rounds off a telling sentence. To-night his arms hung listless at his side; his massive shoulders were bowed; his head drooped. Unconsciously he assumed the attitude of the principal accessory, who usually stands at one of the corners of a monumental piece, and drops a stony or metallic tear over departed Youth, or Valour, or Domestic Excellence. His voice was attuned to his attitude. He hardly once uplifted the tones of his righteous scorn or ridicule, familiar in ordinary circumstances. He plodded along in melancholy monotone, rarely raising his eyes from the brass-bound box on which lay the manuscript that entombed the annotation of his spontaneous regret. It was a touching spectacle; but, perhaps, regarded through the space of an hour and a half, a little monotonous. If the Attorney-General had not been quite so wicked, or the three months' ex-Solicitor-General

had been a little more hopeful of the ultimate destination
of his learned friend, the crowded House would have been
thankful. Sometimes, towards the end of a week, the House
of Commons begins to think it has had a little too much of
Sir William Harcourt as *L'Allegro;* but the punishment of
his *Il Penseroso* is apt, after the first sixty minutes, to grow
insupportable.

Mr. Biggar.   It was this made the House grateful to
Mr. Courtney for the diversion he presently
created. The Irish members, relieved from the incubus of
Sir William Harcourt's lament over the iniquity of his right
hon. and learned friend, showed a tendency to be a little
uproarious with the Attorney-General.   For one or two
among them it was a great opportunity. Mr. Biggar, for
example, had for days and weeks and months sat silent in the
Probate Court whilst the Attorney-General had laboriously
unfolded his case before the Commission of Judges. Occasional attempts to find vent for overcharged feelings had
been sternly repelled by the Court. Now, here was the
Attorney-General at bay in the open field of the House of
Commons, and Mr. Biggar's spirits rising to the height of the
occasion, he joined lustily in the ironical cheers and running
comments with which Sir William Harcourt's speech was
punctuated. Once his excitement reached such a pitch that
the Chairman, addressing him with studied courtesy, observed
"If the hon. member for Cavan finds it impossible to
restrain his emotion I must ask him to retire." Mr. Biggar
smiled grimly; but the hint was not thrown away, and his
subsequent contributions to the uproar below the gangway
were made with judicious furtiveness.

Still the noise was continuous. The Attorney-General,
encouraged by the cheers with which his friends had welcomed his appearance, and desiring to present some contrast
to the funereal manner of Sir William Harcourt, was, when
he came to reply, unusually animated. For the nonce he had
abandoned his level *nisi prius* style, and with uplifted voice
and commanding gestures he met and repelled the charges and
allegations levelled against him. One interruption he met
with the remark that he left his case not to hon. members

below the gangway (this with a contemptuous gesture of his
ready right hand), but to the judgment of any honourably-
minded man—a nice distinction which drew from the turbulent ranks of the Irish members a roar of angry resentment.

Mr. Courtney sprang to his feet, and, amid a scene of
growing excitement, ruled the expression out of order.

Then the shouts of exultation below the gangway rose to
stormier pitch. Members flung themselves about as if the
floor were upheaving in earthquake throes. Above the din
Mr. Courtney was heard shouting "Order! order!" After a
while the Irish members, supposing the Chairman was about
to continue his interrupted rebuke to the Attorney-General,
became partially hushed, and through the undertone of eager
talk sounded forth the injunction—

"I must order the hon. member for South Mayo to retire."

J. F. X. O'Brien. The member for South Mayo is the many-
initialled O'Brien, who holds a position of peculiar eminence among Irish patriots. Most of them have at
one time or another been in prison; Mr. J. F. X. O'Brien was
nearly hanged. Twenty-two years ago he was tried for high
treason and sentenced to death. Almost at the last moment
the hand of amnesty was extended, and James Francis-Xavier,
a brand plucked from the burning, survives to this day to live
in Fentiman Road, Lambeth, and represent South Mayo in the
House of Commons. For one with such a history the member
for South Mayo is a disappointing personality. He is probably the mildest-mannered man ever sentenced to death for
the crime of high treason. Since his appearance in the House
in 1885 he has taken no prominent part in its proceedings.
A grey-haired, kindly-faced, unemotional-looking man, one
meeting him in the corridor or crossing the lobby would
think he was a stranger, who paying his first visit to the House
of Commons, had strayed from the Strangers' Gallery. That
he of all men should have been fixed upon by the Chairman
and ordered off for immediate sacrifice as atonement for the
uproarious conduct of his colleagues had about it something
familiarly comic in its bearing. It is an old trick on the
pantomime stage for the policeman called in to quell a
street riot to pounce upon the smallest, most inoffensive boy

on the skirts of the crowd and hale him off to the nearest
dungeon. Whatever may have been Mr. O'Brien's degree of
complicity in the events of 1867 he was certainly innocent
enough of any prominent participation in the uproar that at

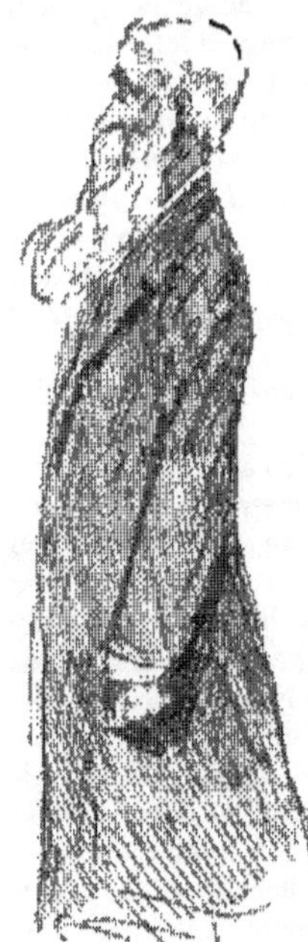

JAMES FRANCIS-XAVIER.

this particular juncture hampered
the progress of the Attorney-
General's speech. Breathless with
indignation, almost inarticulate with
conscious innocence, he gasped forth,
"I did not open my lips." Members near him bore testimony to the
accuracy of his denial, and the temporarily played-out storm below the
gangway burst forth again.

Mr. Courtney's mistake. This was a difficult
position for Mr. Court-
ney. He had made a mistake, innocent in intention and natural enough
in the circumstances. But a mistake
from the Chair is a serious matter,
fatal if persisted in, exceedingly embarrassing if acknowledged. Here
was Mr. O'Brien persistently on
his feet plaintively stretching forth
the curiously long neck once in such
imminent peril, and insisting that
again he had been wronged. He
was under orders to withdraw, and
the next word was with the Chairman.
If he insisted on his withdrawal
Mr. O'Brien would have suffered a fresh wrong in his unduly
chequered life. If the Chairman admitted he had made a mistake his authority at a critical epoch would be sorely shaken.

Mr. Courtney was equal to the occasion. Having accused
Mr. O'Brien of doing something which it was shown he had
not done, the Chairman accepted his "disclaimer," bargaining
at the same time that Mr. O'Brien should not deny having
repeatedly interrupted in a loud voice earlier in the evening.

This was not a very logical position. It was not lacking

in suspicion of introducing into diets from the Chair the
principle of the occult science of Proportional Representation.
Mr. O'Brien, it was admitted, had not been guilty of disorderly
interruption at the particular moment he was arraigned and
sentenced. But he *had* been guilty at some earlier period,
and a proportion of his offence extending through later sections
of the proceedings had suddenly, at a given moment, assumed
a magnitude which authorised the Chairman to order him to
withdraw. This, perhaps, does not seem very clear when
written out; but its effect upon the mind of Mr. O'Brien as
he stood facing the Chairman and the excited House was, on
the whole, successful. He opened his parched lips, turned
his head slowly round in search of enlightenment, and, finding
none, dumbly dropped into his seat.

Then the Attorney-General went forward with his speech.

March 13.—A sitting of the House of Lords. The House of Lords met this afternoon with all
its ordinary pomp and ceremony. The Lord
Chancellor, in wig and gown, took his seat on
the Woolsack; the Mace was laid on the table; and the
Pursebearer reverentially deposited his burden. The only
thing lacking to add dignity to the proceedings was
some work to do. There was positively none, except the
third reading of the Hythe Corporation Bill, a private measure
which has quietly gone through earlier stages. The Lords
meet at a quarter past four, and public business is not opened
till half-past. The Hythe Corporation Bill was disposed of in
the interval, after which the Lord Chancellor sat on the Woolsack twiddling his thumbs. The few Peers present sat looking
at each other. The clerks at the table scribbled away, and
the strangers in the gallery looked on awestruck. Not a word
was spoken till the clock struck half-past four, when the Lord
Chancellor rose and solemnly observed—

"The question is that the House do now adjourn."

No one opposed this reasonable procedure. Lord Halsbury—who, arrayed in wig and gown, always looks like the
comic man gone astray from a music-hall—walked down the
floor of the House, preceded by Black Rod, and followed by
the Pursebearer. A few Peers quietly walked out, the galleries
emptied, and the sitting was over.

March 22.—An all-night sitting. Matters have come to a pretty pass in the House of Commons when in these mad March days the Speaker takes the Chair at two o'clock in the afternoon, and leaves it at ten minutes to four in the following morning, with delusive interval of a couple of hours for dinner. It is true that on this particular occasion the Speaker was not uninterruptedly on duty. At the morning sitting, and for an hour after the House resumed in the evening, the question before the House was that it should resolve itself into Committee, in which case the Speaker is in the Chair. Once in Committee Mr. Courtney takes the lower chair at the table, and thence sees the long night through. But though the Speaker is free from actual attendance on the House whilst it is in Committee, he must needs be within call. The Chairman of Committees may not adjourn the House, and the Speaker must be fetched up out of bed to perform that formal business. If he could only stalk in in dressing-gown and night-cap, the operation would be useful as bringing strongly home to the House the absurdity of its sitting up all night to scamp important business that should be carefully despatched at more reasonable hours. But the Speaker must needs put on wig and gown, walk in with his stately stride, and make belief that he has not had a wink of sleep, but has been sitting at the door through the night awaiting the summons. The deadlock is peculiarly painful to Ministers. If it came about through ordinary accident or by deliberate obstruction they might find some means of consolation. But they know too well—the fact is absolutely beyond dispute—that the whole affair is due to their own action.

IN DRESSING-GOWN AND NIGHT-CAP.

Their curses of Mr. Parnell and his colleagues in the representation of Ireland have come home to roost. That fateful Commission of Judges they insisted on appointing, in the sure and certain hope that it would prove the destruction of Mr. Parnell, and with him of Mr. Gladstone, Home Rule, and the Liberal Opposition, looms darkly over the Chamber. Every day as the question hour comes round the Chief Secretary and the Home Secretary are set up against the wall and pelted with questions as to their connection with the *Times* and its various agents, from Mr. Pigott to Mr. Soames, from Mr. Houston to the Attorney-General.

Worried Ministers. Poor Mr. Smith is terribly worried, and is too honest-minded a man to succeed in disguising his condition of hopeless disappointment. There is talk about his throwing up the sponge, seeking the more placid atmosphere of the House of Lords, and so bringing about a reconstruction of the Ministry. There is not any more foundation for this story now than there has been at any time during the last eighteen months, when it has periodically cropped up. Mr. Smith will probably be garnered to the House of Lords some time in the late autumn. But he will undoubtedly stick to his post through this Session.

Not a very strong man himself—his strength, indeed, such as it is, lies in his weakness and in the friendly patronage with which he is therefore shielded from both sides of the House—he is not assisted by his colleagues. Mr. Balfour, infinitely the strongest, is just now tainted with the breath of the departed Pigott. Mr. Goschen, from whom so much was expected, is rather a source of weakness than of strength. He has this week succeeded in accomplishing one of the rarest feats of the least habile Minister. He has "got up the backs" of the Scotch members, turning a habitually peaceful section of the House into an exasperated and almost desperate company. He is listened to with dislike by the party he has deserted, and without respect by the party he has joined. The only Minister who, having made a position, keeps it, is Mr. Ritchie, whose adroit and resolute dealing the other day with the Board of Works has given him another lift in the opinion of the House of Commons.

CHAPTER XVI.

DEATH OF MR. BRIGHT.

Mr. Bright Dying—Mr. Gladstone and his Old Friend—Death of Mr. Bright—
John Bright in the Commons—Bright and Kenealy.

March 20.—Mr. Bright dying.   THE sad tidings of the state of Mr. Bright's health were a leading topic of conversation in the House to-day. The near approach of the end was no news to the generality of members. His brother and his son have been in constant attendance at the House, and they have not from the first attempted to hide their conviction of the hopelessness of the case. Either of the two diseases which had attacked Mr. Bright was necessarily fatal. With the combination the marvel is he should so long have withstood the assault. None has been more surprised than his medical attendant at the prolongation of his life. Dr. Hayle privately expresses the opinion that it is Mr. Bright's tremendous brain power that has had an appreciable effect in delaying the end. He determined that he would not give up the contest with his deadly disease, and for a period that at the outset seemed impossible he has held his own.

Mr. Gladstone and his old friend.   With respect to Mr. Gladstone and his old friend and colleague, they had in these last months renewed their ancient relationship. When Mr. Bright was first stricken down, and was, as it seemed, at the gates of death, Mr. Gladstone sent him an affectionate message, to which he promptly responded, and since then, though Mr. Bright himself has not been able to write, several messages have passed between them. This is a happy change from the state of things formerly existing.

A little more than a year ago an honourable baronet who sits for a southern constituency told me he had been in communication with Mr. Bright with the object of bringing about, apart from all political differences, a personal reconciliation. He proposed that the two old friends should

meet at his country house. The negotiation did not go so far
as to elicit from Mr. Gladstone a personal reply, but a member
of his family who possesses in peculiar degree his confidence

JOHN BRIGHT.

was sounded on the matter, and expressed the confident belief
that nothing would please Mr. Gladstone better. The next
thing was to approach Mr. Bright. Mr. Bright, who was then
in tolerably good health, and in occasional correspondence

with stray people on the iniquities of Mr. Gladstone,
brusquely refused to have anything to do with the project.

March 27.—Death of Mr. Bright. There was no difficulty in making a House in
the Commons to-day. Members came down
unusually early in anticipation of proceedings in connection with the death of Mr. Bright, news of which reached
London shortly after ten o'clock. Mr. Smith was promptly
in his place, accompanied by about half a dozen of his colleagues, Mr. Balfour and the Home Secretary being among
the absentees. Mr. Goschen was in his seat, and as soon as
prayers were over crossed to the front Opposition bench to
speak to Mr. John Morley, who, with one exception, was the
sole representative of the Liberal leaders.

Before business commenced Mr. Smith approached the
table, and alluding to the great loss sustained by the country,
proposed that, pending the arrival of Mr. Gladstone, further
observations should be postponed. Mr. John Morley expressed
what is the general feeling on both sides of the House—a deep
sense of the considerateness and good taste displayed by Mr.
Smith. Everyone felt it would have been an irreparable loss
if the temporary absence of Mr. Gladstone should have prevented him from paying a last tribute to his old friend and
companion in arms. Nothing is more difficult in Parliamentary oratory than to pronounce a panegyric. Mr. Bright
was one of two men in the House of Commons of recent
years capable of worthily performing the task. The other is
Mr. Gladstone, who, hurrying back to town from the grave
of his elder brother, will on Friday be in his place to cast
flowers on the coffin of one who was almost his oldest political
friend.

The shock that would in ordinary circumstances follow
upon the news of the closing of so great a career has been
modified by the slow but certain approach of the end. Mr.
Bright's old companions in the House of Commons have
known for weeks, even months, that he was marked for
death. Still, now the end is accomplished a great sorrow has
fallen on the Chamber in which he for many years filled so
large a place, and nothing is heard but words of personal
esteem for the great Tribune and admiration of his noble

career.   Mr. John Morley, in his brief remarks this afternoon, did not refrain from touching upon the division which had parted the dead statesman from his lifelong friends.   But, as was well said, that has not in the smallest degree impaired the gratitude, the veneration, and the affection felt for him.

March 29.—John Bright in the Commons. On Tuesday next it will be twenty-four years since Mr. Bright stood at the table of the House of Commons and spoke a few broken words about his dead friend Cobden.   Lord Palmerston was at that time Leader of the House, and Mr. Disraeli Leader of the Opposition.   Both had delivered their eulogy on the apostle of Free Trade, and as they resumed their seats all eyes were turned upon Mr. Bright.   He rose, spoke half a dozen sentences in a voice scarcely audible, and then sat down.

Now the years have passed—nearly a quarter of a century—and to-night Mr. Gladstone, who on that April day went down to Lavington with a great contingent from the House of Commons to stand by Cobden's grave, rises to lament the death of John Bright.   On the other side of the table in place of Disraeli stands Mr. W. H. Smith, with Mr. Gladstone still a link with the far-off past, mourning afresh one of the now innumerable friends and colleagues who have passed before him.   There are few men in the world, perhaps none other, for whom the grave holds so many distinct memories as it does for Mr. Gladstone.

For this Parliament of 1886 John Bright was rather a tradition than a realisation.   As far as memory goes he had but once or twice entered its doors since they were thrown open in August, 1886.   For him the times were out of joint, and he had no more pleasure in a place where his deathless triumphs were won.   It is, in truth, nearly twenty years since he was a commanding figure, a motive power in the House of Commons.   He came back to the Parliament of 1874 in shattered health.   He took his seat at the remote end of the Treasury bench, where on dull nights he chatted in low tones with Mr. Gladstone, who had just written that famous letter from "Carlton House Terrace" announcing to "My dear

Granville" that " at the age of sixty-five, and after forty-two
years of a laborious public life, I think myself entitled to retire
at the present opportunity." He seemed beyond doubt an
extinct volcano. But one night the House discovered to its
partially-delighted surprise that the old fires were not dead,
but only sleeping. It happened early in the Session of
1875, of all subjects in the world, on a turnpike debate.
Sir George Jenkinson—another ghost of past Parliaments—
had brought forward his annual motion dealing with this
entrancing subject. It was a Tuesday night, and the House
was almost empty, but, in accordance with their wont, Disraeli
and Bright sat in their several places as attentive to the
course of debate as if the life of the Ministry depended upon
it. Mr. Bright suddenly interposed. It was his first ordered
speech since his return to public life, and as the word went
round the wondering lobbies that Bright was "up" the
Chamber swiftly filled. Mr. Bright, bowling along the hitherto
placid turnpike, dashed at the Tory Party in general and
Disraeli in particular, heaping on them a sudden outburst of
contumely and scorn. The attack brought Disraeli promptly
to his feet, and in a few flashing sentences he replied.

It was all over as swiftly and as suddenly as it had
commenced, and the House going back to Sir George Jenkinson and the turnpike roads got itself counted out. The
incident was taken to heart as showing that for all his
stooping shoulders, his halting manner when he approached
the table, and the broken music of his once clarion voice, John
Bright, regarded as a factor in Parliamentary debate, was not
safely to be disregarded. Later in the life of this triumphant
Tory Parliament he spoke oftener in sufficiently aggravating
tone. He was always listened to by the party he lectured
with a feeling of respect and admiration, miraculously merging
at last in that strange concatenation of circumstances that
placed the Anti-Corn Law League agitator of 1843 on the
highest pedestal of Conservative adulation.

Bright and
Kenealy. I well remember the first appearance at the table
Bright made in the House of Commons on return-
ing to political life. It was in 1875, and he was moved thereto
by one of those generous impulses that marked his life. It was

at the time Dr. Kenealy was to the fore.   He had just been re-turned for Stoke, and on this February night had walked up the floor of the House of Commons with his hat in one hand and a good stout umbrella in the other.   He was a sort of pariah. No man, except poor Mr. Whalley, would hold converse with him.   He had been returned for Stoke by an overwhelming majority.   A huzzahing multitude had brought him down in triumph to the gates of the House of Commons.   Within he stood alone—alone with his gingham umbrella and poor, half-cracked Mr. Whalley.

It is requisite that a new member coming up to the table shall be escorted by two sitting members, who vouch for his identity.   When Kenealy got as far as the table and showed premonitions of desire to hang his umbrella on the Mace whilst he signed the Roll of Parliament, the Speaker interposed and observed that it was customary for a new member to be accompanied by sponsors.   Were there two members of the House prepared to introduce the elect of Stoke ?

There was a dead silence, and Dr. Kenealy's Parliamentary career seemed cut off thus early on the threshold ; when from his modest seat at the end of the front Opposition bench John Bright rose and said that, out of deference to the will of the large constituency that had elected Dr. Kenealy, he would himself, if the hon. member would accept his companionship, be glad to walk with him to the table.

As he stood at the table in the thronged and excited House, thus breaking the silence of many Sessions, Mr. Bright trembled like an aspen leaf, and his once magnificent voice was so beyond his control that it hardly penetrated as far as the cross benches.   Through succeeding years, certainly up to the close of this Parliament, he never entirely mastered his curious nervousness.   I have often seen him sitting on the front Opposition bench hour after hour, taking notes with evident intention of delivering a speech, and failing to muster courage to rise.   Whenever, at this period, he did speak, he began in a nervous, hesitating way, which would have well become a modest young member making his maiden speech. As he went forward he regained his self-possession and his mastery of his audience.

What in those days used to be his salvation was the sight of the Conservative Party massed opposite him; Disraeli on the Treasury bench, with folded arms, head bent down, and brown eyes watchfully fixed on his ancient adversary. As Bright shook a contemptuous finger at them or a clenched right hand, his voice rang out with its old metallic sound, and the inimitably clustered words sprang spontaneously from his lips.

All his life Bright has been angry with some one. In his latest days it was with Mr. Gladstone and the flower of the Liberal Party. Once it was the Tories, Mr. Disraeli and Lord Salisbury, their hate of him being equalled only by their fear. For a man of peace, of Quaker parentage, he was desperately aggressive. Of all the millions of words that have been spun about him through his long life, and now, with added force, at the day of his death, I do not think a briefer or more graphic summary has been uttered than is to be found in the remark of Lord George Bentinck.

"If Bright," he said, "had not been a Quaker, he would have been a prize-fighter."

CHAPTER XVII.

LORD RANDOLPH CHURCHILL.

Lord R. Churchill and the Representation of Birmingham—The Chairman of Committees in the Lords—Mr. Chaplin and Lord R. Churchill—From Bad to Worse.

April 2.—Lord R. Churchill and the representation of Birmingham.

A REMARKABLE political episode was brought to a conclusion at five o'clock this afternoon by Lord Randolph Churchill's declinature of the invitation to contest Central Birmingham, the seat vacated by the death of Mr. Bright. Some weeks ago, when the vacancy which has now taken place was known to be imminent, negotiations were opened with Lord Randolph on behalf of the Conservative committee of the constituency. There was no difficulty in ascertaining his personal views on the matter. The fact is, it has for years been the dearest object of his political life to represent Birmingham. He fought it in 1885, and almost won, even against so supreme a candidate as Mr. Bright. He has no sympathy with the villadom of Paddington, nor do his constituents regard with unqualified satisfaction the vagaries of his Parliamentary career. He believes that in Birmingham he would find the very constituency that would appreciate and sympathise with his Democratic Toryism, and when an opening was presented to him to succeed Mr. Bright he jumped at it.

Everything was practically settled, and the deputation that visited London to-day came assured of being able to carry back his formal assent. So complete was the understanding that arrangements had been made for holding a meeting at Birmingham on Friday, which Lord Randolph was to have addressed as the Conservative candidate. He saw the deputation at his house this morning, and promised to hand in his formal reply at five o'clock this afternoon. This delay was the response to signs of uneasiness which had reached him from the quarter where Lord Hartington and Mr. Chamberlain sit together. Mr. Chamberlain had won over Lord Hartington to his view that the appearance of Lord Randolph to compete for a seat recently held by a Dissentient Liberal would be fatal to the prospects of the alliance between Dissentient Liberals and Conservatives. If, it was pointed out, on the very first opportunity where the Conservatives seemed to have the pull, a seat were snatched out of the grasp of the Dissentient Liberals, there would be an end of all confidence, and the Dissentients would clearly perceive what was in store for them when the day of dissolution came. It is quite possible, and is freely asserted this afternoon in Conservative circles, that, apart from this consideration, Mr. Chamberlain was influenced in the course he has taken by the unwelcome character of the prospect of sharing his throne in Birmingham with so active and popular a person as Lord Randolph Churchill.

After seeing the deputation this morning, and promising them an answer, Lord Randolph had an interview with Sir Michael Hicks-Beach, the only member of the present Ministry with whom he is on terms of intimate friendship. Sir Michael repeated to him representations that have been made to the Government by the Dissentient Liberal leaders, and pointed out the gravity of the situation. Lord Randolph finally consented, if Sir M. H. Beach would meet Lord Hartington and Mr. Chamberlain, and confer with them upon the situation, to accept the unanimous decision of the three. This was given shortly before five o'clock, and was against the candidature. Lord Randolph loyally accepted the decision, though he himself frankly admitted that the disappointment is very bitter.

Whilst Lord Randolph Churchill is in a mood of profound depression, the deputation of Birmingham Conservatives left in a very angry frame of mind. It was in the Conservative Whip's room at the House of Commons that the decision was conveyed to them, and they openly told Mr. Akers Douglas that if a Dissentient Liberal candidate were put up they as Conservatives would not vote for him. If this be more than idle threat Mr. Chamberlain's peremptory interference will have disastrous consequences for the Ministerial Party. The incident has engrossed attention here throughout the sitting of the House, and has excited much feeling between the two divisions of the Ministerial forces.

Between Lord Randolph Churchill and Mr. Chamberlain there is not even the appearance of a patching up of old friendship. Lord Randolph is not a man to take half-measures with his personal acquaintances. He is either on terms of friendship with them or he declines to hold intercourse with them. He has reached the latter stage in respect of Mr. Chamberlain, and what at one time seemed in a fair way to become a notable political alliance is now drifting into a condition of personal antagonism. Lord Randolph in his private conversation does not mince matters. He plainly traces the upsetting of an arrangement on which he had fixed his heart to the machinations of Mr. Chamberlain, who, he says, was thinking not of the interests of the Unionist Party, but of his own. Mr. J. A. Bright, an amiable gentleman dowered with the heritage of a name popular in Birmingham, but himself not a strongly-marked character, will suit Mr. Chamberlain as his colleague in the representation of Birmingham much better than would Lord Randolph Churchill,

whose personal popularity in the town is already embarrass-
ingly great.

April 4. — The Chairman of Committees in the Lords. When Lord Granville entered the House of Lords to-day he was asked by a friend from the Commons whether there was any chance of his carrying the election of Lord Morley to the Chairmanship of Committees.

"Not the slightest," said Lord Granville, and so said everyone else concerned.

There is no question on either side which is the better man for the post. But Lord Salisbury had championed the cause of Lord Balfour of Burleigh, and it was taken as a foregone conclusion that he would be elected to this snug berth. He has been already provided for, being Under-Secretary to the Board of Trade, at a salary of £1,500 a year. As compared with the Chairmanship of Committees, an appointment for life at a salary of £2,500 a year, it would be an easy and agreeable sacrifice to give up this berth. Lord Balfour accordingly put forth every effort to win the prize. His friends worked hard for him, and his election seemed a certainty.

The result is a surprise to everyone. In a fuller House than has been seen for some weeks Lord Morley was elected by a majority of 10. Last time he was put up he was defeated by a majority of 18. It is cheering to know that, however leniently the Lords may look upon a family and political arrangement in connection with other departments of the State, they will not sanction a job when their own immediate interests are at stake.

April 5. — Mr. Chaplin and Lord R. Churchill. For a period now fast running into ten years Lord Randolph Churchill has been a trouble to Mr. Chaplin. There was an epoch when the member for Sleaford used to regard the stripling with that measure of languid interest with which Goliath might have looked upon David before his attention was directly called to him by a personal challenge. Mr. Chaplin, who shares with true greatness the feeling of kindly interest in ambitious youth, was wont to be in his place on the night, which came but once a year, when in the Parliament of 1874 Lord Randolph Churchill, seated on the heights of mediocre respectability immediately behind the Treasury bench, repelled the attacks of Sir Charles Dilke on unreformed Corporations. Lord Randolph was then, as Mr. Jacob Bright would say, " member for Woodcock," and his little family borough being included in the vigorous attack of Sir Charles Dilke, at that time a member seated below the gangway, Lord Randolph was drawn out of his indolent retirement into the forefront of debate. The House was startled and delighted with the freshness, vigour, and originality of these speeches, which relieved the dulness of a Tuesday evening. Mr. Chaplin, turning round from his throne below the gangway, nodded approvingly at his young friend, who might one day, if he diligently studied an attainable model, rise to some position in Parliamentary debate.

After a while Mr. Chaplin, his mind occupied with more urgent matters (including from time to time the preparation of a speech), lost sight of his young friend on the back seat behind Ministers. Sir Charles Dilke intermitted his annual attack on Woodstock and similar anachronisms, and nothing else, not even the proposal to make the Queen Empress of India, stirred the languid pulses of Lord Randolph. Then came the General Election of 1880, which transferred parties in the House of Commons, and somehow Lord Randolph turned up on a seat below the gangway. This locality had been selected in the first instance by Sir Henry Wolff as offering certain strategical advantages in connection with resistance to the incursions of Mr. Bradlaugh. As that gentleman began about this date to display a disposition to present himself at all unguarded moments and make a dash for the table, it was found desirable in the interests of the Constitution that someone should be at a convenient place where he might throw his body across the pathway of the intruder. Mr. Bradlaugh by frequent *reconnaissances* had acquired the precise range of the table. He knew exactly in how many swinging strides he could reach it. For the Defender of the Faith, the Champion of the Constitution, to be on guard midway on a back bench would obviously place him at a disadvantage. Before he could get down to plant himself in

Mr. Bradlaugh's path that gentleman would be already at the table, and well through the speech that always began with the perhaps unnecessary exordium " I am here——"

So Sir Henry Wolff, the real pioneer of the Fourth Party,

planted himself on the front bench below the gangway, and to him presently gathered Mr. John Gorst and Lord Randolph Churchill, with Mr. Arthur Balfour still in the dim and distant future.

Mr. Chaplin was able, on the whole, to approve the policy pursued by Lord Randolph Churchill when he took the full command of the Fourth Party. Occasionally he himself deigned to enter the lists and buffet Mr. Bradlaugh. He also turned a friendly countenance upon the little party when they wrestled with Mr. Gladstone, collogued with Mr. Parnell, Mr. O'Donnell, and Mr. Biggar, and made things generally uncomfortable for the Government. This sort of guerilla warfare was very useful in its way—always assuming that in reserve there stood one or more responsible gentlemen of commanding presence, oratorical gifts, and some position in the country, who might be counted upon to deliver set orations on field nights of debate.

When Mr. Chaplin first began to look with uncertainty upon his young friend was when, intoxicated with the success that had attended his nightly appearance on the political stage, Lord Randolph began to turn upon his pastors and masters. As early as the Session of 1882 the young man was known to speak disrespectfully of Sir Richard Cross, G.C.B. Mr. Chaplin was present one night in the Autumn Session of that very year when, some amendment being under discussion without having been placed upon the paper, question arose as to its precise terms. Sir Richard Cross, always precise, had jotted them down on a piece of paper, which he, with engaging smile, handed to Lord Randolph, who was complaining that no one knew what was under discussion.

Lord Randolph took the memorandum and, holding it disdainfully between finger and thumb, turned a glaring countenance upon Sir Richard, and said, "A pretty pass we've come to in the House of Commons when we have to consider amendments passed about from hand to hand on dirty bits of paper."

From bad to worse.

After that Lord Randolph went entirely to the bad, followed by the troubled gaze of one who would fain have gathered him under his wings and clucked affectionately in his ear. He threw all authority to the winds, made the life of Sir Richard Cross a burden to him, was responsible for fixing on the countenance of Mr. W. H. Smith a wavering inconsequential smile, and fatally disturbed the placid course of Sir Stafford Northcote's existence. Mr. Chaplin, shocked and estranged, came again and again to rescue and reprove. But even a worse thing happened. Lord Randolph Churchill, with whom even the equator would not be free from the risk of disrespectful reference, was known to turn scornfully on Mr. Chaplin, and in the sight of a pained House of Commons prod him with ill-timed thrusts of so-called humour.

All this happened in the Parliament of 1880. What followed in 1886, when Mr. Chaplin, overlooked in the disposition of offices, rubbed his eyes and beheld his quondam young friend promoted to the Leadership of the House of Commons, is a matter of familiar history. That Lord Randolph should, after a brief enjoyment of office, suddenly throw up his position and entangle his colleagues and his party in the most embarrassing position, was no surprise to the Nestor of the Conservative Party. But what puzzled Mr. Chaplin then, as it had astonished him before and annoys him at this day, is the question why should the party and the country be so interested and even absorbed in the vagaries of this presumptuous young man ?

Take the latest evolution—that which has during the past week disturbed the mind of Mr. Chaplin, and incidentally justified, or at least utilised, the outbreak of cattle plague in Germany. Supposing a respected member of the Conservative Party, a man of high intellectual attainments, one who possesses quite peculiar gifts of Parliamentary oratory, a scholar, and a country gentleman—supposing Atticus had announced his intention of resigning his seat, for, say, the Sleaford Division of Lincolnshire, and contesting Central Birmingham, what would have happened ? Would a leaf have stirred in the Parliamentary atmosphere ? Probably not. But because it was whispered that Lord Randolph Churchill, abandoning Paddington, was about to present himself as a candidate for the suffrages of Central Birmingham, a sudden storm bursts forth in the political world which obscures all other interests. The strong places entrenched by the Unionist forces tremble with dismay. The Treasury bench is perturbed; Lord Hartington, temporarily aroused from his mood of lethargy, hurriedly consults Mr. Chamberlain; the President of the Board of Trade is selected as the plenipotentiary of the Government; meetings are summoned;

conferences are held; and all the world waits breathless at Mr. Akers Douglas's door to learn Lord Randolph's decision whether he will go to Birmingham or whether he will refrain.

These things are past Mr. Chaplin's comprehension. He has on an earlier occasion turned aside from contemplation of the phenomenon to plunge into the entrancing study of bimetallism. But the personality of this troublesome person has thrust itself even into the quiet glades where bimetallists walk and take counsel together. Providentially there is the cattle plague, and Mr. Chaplin, sternly shutting out from his mental view Lord Randolph Churchill and all his works, has bent his mind to the task of obtaining the slaughter at the port of arrival of cattle which, though ostensibly coming from Holland, may have contracted infection in Germany.

CHAPTER XVIII.

PARLIAMENTARY CUSTOMS.

The Lamp Bill—A Curious Dilemma—Mr. Sam Smith—Sir John Gorst—Sir R. Temple—Mr. Balfour and the Boers—Ancient Parliamentary Customs—The Letter to the Queen—Gunpowder Plot—"Who goes Home?"—"The Usual Time!"—An Interesting Library—Mr. Disraeli—Sir R. Peel—Mr. Gladstone—An Historic Letter.

April 8.—The lamp bill. THE spirit of economy which animates the present House of Commons manifested itself afresh to-night in the fierce controversy that raged around the lamps supplied to the House of Commons, which figure in the Estimates for no less a sum than £2,000. Considering that the House does not sit more than seven months in a year, and these the summer months, £2,000 for lamps over and above the gas bill is a little stiff. What makes it worse is the fact that of late the electric light has been introduced into many parts of the building. Nevertheless, the lamp bill remains the same. It should be understood that lamps are burned in very few parts of the building, not in the House itself, but in the Committee rooms and some passages. As the Committees sit in the daytime, the consumption of oil obviously cannot be much. Moreover, in addition to the assistance from the electric light, the consumption of oil must have materially decreased since the twelve o'clock rule came in. In spite of these various considerations, the contractor will have his £2,000, though it is plainly discernible from the breeze that sprang up in the House to-night when the subject was incidentally mentioned that this nice little perquisite, worth even more than a canonry, is not likely to last longer than the term of the existing contract.

April 18.—A curious dilemma. To-day the House of Commons, following in the footsteps of the more easily wearied Lords, adjourned for the Easter holidays. The final moments of this section of the Session were marked by a little comedy, of which only the barest indication is found in the Parliamentary Reports. Just before six o'clock the Irish members decided that a last word must be said about Donegal. Mr. Sexton had another speech ready, and felt it must be got off before the House did. Accordingly, negotiations were opened with the Ministerial Whip, who, for a consideration, sold the last hour of the sitting. The price paid was two votes in Class 2 of the Civil Service Estimates. These being granted, it was agreed that progress should be reported at six o'clock, and that the Irish members should have the remaining hour in which to discourse.

Mr. Arthur O'Connor made a commendably brief speech, introducing a telegram despatched by Mr. Conybeare, Mr. O'Brien, and Mr. O'Hea, describing the latest condition of affairs in Donegal. Mr. Balfour had pooh-poohed the story; Mr. Sexton had appropriated for his speech fully one-half of the possible limit of time; and Mr. Waddy was haranguing when the hand of the clock touched ten minutes to seven, and the Speaker, rising, called "Order, order!" in intimation that the debate must now close.

This was a surprise to the Irish members. They had understood that they might talk up to seven o'clock, the moment when the morning sitting would lapse. Mr. Sexton, delighted at the opportunity of again coming to the front, put this view before the Speaker, who pointed out that under the orders that rule debate the last ten minutes of a morning sitting are reserved for unopposed business.

And now the fun of the situation developed itself. There was no business, opposed or unopposed, on the paper. There sat the Speaker in the Chair, and there sat members facing each other, the flood of talk peremptorily stopped. It was expected that the Speaker would leave the Chair, and the sitting come to an end. But the Speaker might not go till seven o'clock, and so members sat in solemn silence staring at each other. After a moment's pause, Dr. Tanner rose. Time was with him a more than usually precious commodity. His hours were numbered. When the House met again he would be in gaol, and here were ten precious minutes running to waste! So Dr. Tanner proposed to utilise them, and had got as far as the declaration that the policy being carried out in Ireland was murderous, when the Speaker interposed. But Dr. Tanner was desperate.

"Am I to understand," he said, "that the House, having still eight minutes before it, and the Chief Secretary and Solicitor-General for Ireland being in their places, we are to sit doing nothing?"

"Yes," the Speaker said, that was about it.

Dr. Tanner subsided, and there was another pause of awesome silence, broken once more by the irrepressible doctor, to whom a bright idea had occurred. If they could do nothing else, why not count the House? He moved a count, and hurried out so that when the Speaker counted he should not add a unit to the numbers present and peradventure make a quorum. The Speaker sat motionless and unresponsive, and there was another interval of silence, through which a subdued titter could be heard. The pauses might be counted in seconds, but they seemed terribly long.

Sir Wilfrid Lawson next broke silence.

"Is the House sitting, Mr. Speaker?" he asked in bewildered tones, "or are we not sitting; or which?"

Then the Speaker executed a strategic movement. It was too grotesquely comical for him to be presiding over a silent and impotent assembly. Yet he could not declare the adjournment till seven o'clock, and it was now five minutes to seven.

"There is," he said, "no business before the House, and to show that is so, I will leave the Chair."

So he stepped down and sat on the Treasury bench, talking in low voice to Ministers who clustered round this unwarranted, I believe unprecedented, visitor to their preserves.

The five minutes slowly passed, members conversing in awed whispers, the Chair empty, the Mace on the table, the Serjeant-at-Arms with sword by his side in his chair, the astonished strangers looking on, and members wondering what would come next, or how this curious sitting would close. At seven o'clock the Speaker rose, and, always stately, dignified even in these circumstances, walked up the steps to the Chair, faced the House, cried "Order! Order!" and then, turning, left the Chair, slowly passing out of the House.

Thus the sitting was adjourned, and members, relieved of the terrible tension of the past ten minutes, broke up in a buzz of laughter.

May 3.—Mr. Sam Smith. Somebody who remains unknown varied the dull routine of life in the House of Commons to-night by a graceful act. He—or was it she?—taking advantage of the clearance of the House for the interval between the morning and evening sitting, flung upon the end of the Treasury bench where the graceful figure of Mr. Balfour is known to lounge a spray of pale blush roses. The flowers lay unnoticed whilst Mr. Samuel Smith, encouraged by his victory of Tuesday night, once more assailed the Government. Then it was India and the liquor traffic. To-night it is China and the opium trade. "Let us be moral!" said Mr. Pecksniff on a memorable occasion, looking down from an upper landing on the company at Todgers's, assembled in haste and alarm at the foot of the stairs.

"Let us be moral," said Mr. Samuel Smith to the natives of India, who do not usually drink brandy and soda, and to the countless population of China who, whilst they eschew whiskey, occasionally eat opium.

John Gorst. It was an interesting speech, instinct with amiable intention, eloquent with moral reflections. It will, perhaps, be chiefly memorable to those who sat out the long debate, as drawing from Sir John Gorst

one of the most neatly-constructed and effectively-delivered
bits of banter heard in the House of Commons in recent times.
No newspaper reports it, though if it had chanced to have
been delivered by the late Mr. Disraeli—and, perhaps, no one
else could have done it quite so well—every one of the exqui-
itely framed sentences would have been preserved, and the
passage would have become historical.

It was a very old text Sir John preached from for the
edification of Mr. Samuel Smith and Sir Joseph Pease. It
was set forth ages ago in the injunction about extracting
the beam from one's own eye before devoting kindly endeavour
to removing the mote from one's brother's. Hudibras later
summed it up in the ironic injunction to—

> Compound for sins you are inclined to
> By damning those you have no mind to.

Into the old theme Sir John managed to throw a brightness
of wit, a delicacy of thought, and a dexterity of expression
not often met with towards midnight at an evening sitting
devoted to Indian topics. Rarely has the Hudibrastic satire, to
which Mr. Sam Smith probably to this hour remains impervious,
been put in a more effectively humorous form than in Sir
John's lightly sketched picture of himself confronted in far-off
New Zealand by native chiefs, who, not above suspicion of
cannibalism, reproached the representative of Western civilisation with an inexplicable and repulsive taste for decayed cheese
and "well-hung" birds.

Sir R. Temple.   It was, probably, the scent of the floral tribute
laid at Mr. Balfour's feet that inspired Sir John
to this successful flight. But though the spray of roses was at
this hour of the debate generously passed from hand to hand
along the Treasury bench, it did not reach Sir Richard
Temple, and cannot be held to account for *his* exceptional
success. When Sir Richard first appeared in the House of
Commons, fresh from ruling Bengal, he made the serious
mistake of attempting to coerce the House into listening to his
speeches. A year or two earlier the central provinces of
India had lain prostrate whilst he spoke, and in Bombay there
was not an *aide-de-camp* who was not thrown into a condition

of uncontrollable emotion by his Excellency's eloquence. It was a sad, swift change to the blunt manners of the House of Commons. The Chief Commissioner of the central provinces of India, when at last he caught the Speaker's eye, was after his first speech met with angry cries for the division. The Lieutenant-Governor of Bengal was "booed" at as if he were simply Secretary to the Lord-Lieutenant, and the Governor of Bombay was actually laughed down. This was a strange and painful experience, not at once to be grasped. For some time Sir Richard Temple struggled against the House, which only grew angry at his persistent interposition. At last he recognised a force superior even to that of a Chief Commissioner or Lieutenant-Governor of a Province, and retired into comparative obscurity, while men possessing not one tithe of his natural ability were permitted to discourse at large.

Sir Richard has lived down the contumely of the crowd, and now, speaking less frequently, finds bestowed upon him at least some measure of the attention he deserves. Blossoming in this balmier breeze, he has developed lighter gifts not suspected under his statesmanlike aspect. On Tuesday, gallantly coming to the assistance of a Government that has never shown itself disposed to recognise his capacity, he created a diversion which, for a moment, checked the advance of the Temperance party. Mr. Samuel Smith, Mr. Caine, and other advocates of the repression of the drink traffic in India, had piled up statistics and marshalled facts in support of their argument. Sir Richard Temple, lightly stepping into the arena, quoted by the yard extracts from the works of native poets, which showed that the gods of ancient India were not averse to the blandishments of the

wine cup. That should have settled the question for the
House of Commons, and it was only a perverse and accidental

"A SUITABLE ACCESSORY."

majority that subsequently, in
the division lobby, defeated
the Government. To-night Sir
Richard, in even lighter vein,
buffeted that other great Anglo-
Indian, Sir George Campbell

"I feel," he said, at the
conclusion of a sparkling passage, "as if I had taken part
in an encounter between St.
George and the Dragon."

The House laughed con-
sumedly, delighted with the
uncertainty of identity with
which the illusion was charged.
There is an old familiar and
not very kindly-meant House
of Commons story about a
well-known member and his
wife being likened to a conjunction of Beauty and the
Beast, and the husband, on
hearing it, resenting the impu-
tation upon his wife's good
looks. Thinking of this, and
listening to Sir Richard's
simile, members laughingly
asked which was St. George?

Mr. Balfour and the roses. It was whilst Sir
Richard Temple
was speaking that Mr. Balfour
came in, and, dropping into
his seat, became aware of the proximity of the spray of roses.
Perhaps if there had been time to think the matter out, and
opportunity had been available, a branch of lilies would have
been more suitable. In tempestuous times, when the roar of
members below the gangway opposite is most threatening, Mr.

Balfour never loses the languorous grace with which he droops over the notes of the speech he may be delivering. If the customs of the House permitted it, a branch of lilies, such as is depicted in the hands of a tall, slim young man, who figures in many stained-glass windows in Continental churches, would be a suitable accessory for Mr. Balfour when answering questions addressed to him by Mr. Sexton, Mr. Harrington, or Mr. Swift MacNeill. Failing that, the pale blush roses did very well.

Mr. W. H. Smith had been in his place for an hour before the Chief Secretary arrived, and there lay the roses unregarded. With Supply in a backward state, the Scotch Local Government Bill not yet read a second time, and the Sugar Bounty Convention Bill threatened on all sides, the First Lord has no time for dalliance with the flowers that bloom in the spring. He turned with a wearied look on his young colleague toying with the roses, and when they were passed across him in response to the eager request of Sir John Gorst, he made no sign of desire for closer acquaintance. Sir Richard Temple had made an end of speaking; Dr. Farquharson was now on his legs, giving gratuitous advice to an interested House, on the circumstances which, strictly observed, might make opium not a curse, but a blessing. Sir John, listening and awaiting his turn, sniffed eagerly at the roses. Sir James Fergusson, who sat next to him, was no more interested in the flowers than his respected Leader. He had had a bad time on Thursday when the Foreign Office had been persistently assailed for a space of eight hours. Roses pleased him not, nor daffodils either. But the Home Secretary, not without his crosses, is ever susceptible to the influences of grace and beauty. He reached across the immobile Under-Secretary to take the flowers from Sir John's hand, and, having gracefully sniffed them awhile, passed them back till they were restored to the keeping of the favoured Minister for whose delight they were originally designed.

May 11.—Ancient Parliamentary customs.   When at twenty minutes past twelve this morning Mr. William Redmond rose to continue the debate on University Representation, Mr. W. H. Smith promptly possessed himself of a sheet of paper and commenced his letter to the Queen. The Leader of the

House of Commons is the most courteous and long-suffering
of men. He is ready at any time to sacrifice his personal
inclination and comfort to the calls of duty. But there really
did not seem any particular occasion why he should longer
defer his concluding task of the day's round in order to
master the reasons which, presenting themselves in logical
sequence to the mind of Mr. William Redmond, brought him
to the conclusion that the Parliamentary representation of
Universities was an anachronism. If it had been King Ja Ja
it would, of course, have been different. Mr. William Redmond is an authority in respect to all that concerns that
interesting potentate, just as of old Mr. Delahunty was on the
subject of pound notes, and Mr. Chaplin is to-day on bimetallism. But the head of King Ja Ja could not by any
force of ingenuity be dragged into the controversy about the
representation of Universities which Mr. Robertson had raised,
and to which the new Solicitor-General for Scotland contributed an interesting speech.

So when Mr. William Redmond, after several efforts, finally
succeeded in catching the Speaker's eye, gracefully posed
himself and commenced the exposition of his views, the First
Lord of the Treasury bethought him of his letter to the
Queen, and began to write it.

The letter to
the Queen.   There are several peculiarities about this function
of the Leader of the House of Commons. Not
the least striking is that it should continue to be exacted.
When George III. was king it was all very well for Pitt or
Addington to send to His Majesty at the close of every sitting
of the House a succinct account of what had taken place. In
those days the penny newspaper was not, and the science of
Parliamentary reporting had not had birth. The King
naturally wanted to know what his faithful Commons had
been at, and no one was better qualified to inform him than
the Leader of the House. But things are vastly different
to-day. Mr. W. H. Smith's letter, concluded just before one
o'clock this morning, could hardly reach Windsor before the
second postal delivery. By that time London morning papers
would have been hours in hand at the Castle, and Her Majesty,
anxious to know how Mr. Jackson had fared in Committee of

Supply, or what Mr. Raikes had said in defence of the Parliamentary privileges of his University, would have had full opportunity of reading the accounts, writ large and full in type.

Gunpowder Plot. But for these hundred years back the letter has been written to the Sovereign whenever the House of Commons sits. In some of its aspects and habits an assembly which has passed several Reform Bills, introduced the Ballot, disestablished a Church, and almost enfranchised the land, is obstinately conservative. For example, after discovery of the Gunpowder Plot it was ordered that at the commencement of every Session the cellars below the House should be searched. This very year, on the day before the Session opened, the Serjeant-at-Arms, escorted by a strong and resolute bodyguard, perambulated the subterranean passages of the Houses of Parliament, determined at any risk to frustrate the evil purposes of any nineteenth century imitator of Guy Fawkes. No one would venture to affirm that any useful or practical purpose is served by this annual perambulation. But the order was made in 1606, it has never been rescinded, and it is solemnly obeyed to this day.

"Who goes home?" Another quaint and less well-known custom is that which marks the conclusion of every day's sitting, whether the House rise at six o'clock on a Wednesday evening or at some far advanced hour of the night. In the days when George III. was king, London, ill-lighted and insufficiently policed, was not a particularly safe place for honest people to be out o' nights. Members going home after a late division were accustomed to depart in squads, half a dozen or a dozen living in Bloomsbury or other fashionable quarter seeing each other home. Thereupon it was directed that as soon as the sitting was adjourned the doorkeeper, standing well out in the middle of the lobby and uplifting his voice, should cry, " Who goes home ? "

At ten minutes past one this morning, when the House adjourned after rejecting Mr. Robertson's motion depriving Universities of their Parliamentary representation, the old cry echoed through the vaulted lobby, disturbing the shades of the innumerable company of old Parliament men back to the days of Walpole and the first Pitt, who have long ago and for ever "gone home."

"The usual time!" Still another ancient custom pertaining to this period of Parliamentary business is fulfilled by the principal janitor. It has from time immemorial been the custom that the hour for the next meeting of the House of Commons shall be officially declared. It is now set forth on the Orders circulated in printed form, and delivered every morning at the private residence of members. But in early days, when matters were not carried forward with such regularity, it was found convenient that members mustering in the lobby preparatory to seeing each other safely home should learn what time they were expected to resume their labours on the following day. The doorkeeper was, under some forgotten rule, directed to announce it, and to this day his successor in the chair scrupulously fulfils the duty.

The Speaker having left the Chair, members dispersing, the lights going down, and the echoing cry of "Who goes home?" having died away, the doorkeeper again uplifts a sonorous voice and cries aloud, "The usual time!"

An interesting library. It is probable that somewhere stowed away are the manuscript letters written for more than a hundred years by the Leader of the House of Commons to the reigning Sovereign—Pitt and Fox and Lord Liverpool to George III., Canning to George IV., Lord Grey and Lord Melbourne to William IV. Certainly there are at Windsor Castle, in handsomely bound volumes, the manuscript letters written amid varying scenes from the House of Commons to Queen Victoria; a series four years long from Sir Robert Peel, five years by Lord John Russell, whole volumes from Lord Palmerston, a number extending over six years from Mr. Disraeli, and tomes innumerable from Mr. Gladstone.

Mr. Disraeli. When, in February, 1874, Mr. Disraeli found himself Premier and Leader of the House of Commons, he devoted himself with pleased assiduity to the task of nightly communicating with his gracious mistress. An air of added solemnity stole over his face as he reverentially took up his pen, and, straightening out the paper on his knee, began to " present his humble duty."

Sir R. Peel. It is a peculiarity connected with this important Ministerial function that the letter shall be written on the knee with the assistance of a blotting-pad. It would appear more convenient that the Leader of the House should repair to his own room and, with the luxury and convenience of a writing desk, despatch his letter. More than fifty years ago Sir Robert Peel coming in with his first Ministry, and being as much hurried as was possible with one of his temperament, began to write the letter on his knee seated on the Treasury bench. His successor imitated him ; Sir Robert coming in again in 1841 returned to his early habit, and so it became established.

Mr. Gladstone. Mr. Gladstone introduced a characteristic variety into the practice. In the laborious sittings of the Parliament of 1880 he adroitly availed himself of the opportunity of successive divisions to get his letter written. Beginning it on the Treasury bench, whilst the question was put and the House cleared for the division, he with youthful alacrity headed for the door as soon as the tellers were appointed, and planting himself at one of the writing tables in the division lobby went on with his work whilst his followers trooped past. The division over he returned, bringing up the rear, happy in the consciousness that he had utilised ten minutes which would otherwise have been lost.

A historic letter. No one who was present on that night in June, 1885, when the Government were unexpectedly defeated on Sir Michael Hicks-Beach's Budget amendment, can forget how Mr. Gladstone wrote his letter to the Queen. It was half-past one in the morning when he resumed his seat after winding up the debate in an angry speech. When the House was cleared for the division he hastened out with his writing-pad and sheet of letter-paper, coming back with his letter half written. Whilst members streamed in from either wide, and the buzz of excitement grew to stormy heights, Mr. Gladstone went on writing, "presenting his humble duty to the Queen," informing Her Majesty how matters had thus far fared.

Before he had finished Lord Randolph Churchill was standing upon the bench below the gangway, hat in hand, wildly cheering, and the Premier, still going on writing, was enabled to add to his budget the interesting item that in a House of 516 members Her Majesty's Government had been defeated by a majority of 12.

CHAPTER XIX.

SOME NOBLE LORDS.

In the Wrong Shop—The House of Lords—Oblivious of Pending Doom—Mr. Labouchere's Motion—Mr. George Curzon—Heirs-apparent—Lord Rosebery's Guest—"The late Sir James Hogg."

May 16.—In the wrong shop. LORD GRANVILLE tells with keen enjoyment the story of his adventure on Monday, when, strolling along Pall Mall with half an hour to spare, he thought he would step into the Reform Club and look at the evening papers. He inadvertently walked into the Carlton Club, and had proceeded to make himself at home when his error was pointed out to him. It was the Duke of Abercorn who, coming within Lord Granville's view, suggested to him that there must be something wrong. The mistake will, it is hoped, induce Lord Granville to renew a closer acquaintance with his old Club, the Reform, where he has not been seen since the night of the Jubilee ball.

May 17.—The House of Lords. At eighteen minutes past five this evening the House of Lords tranquilly adjourned. It had met at the usual hour with the accustomed pomp and circumstance, and had discharged its ordinary duties as if no chasm yawned. At a quarter past four the Lord Chancellor, preceded by the Mace, with Black Rod in attendance, and that mysterious entity the Serjeant-at-Arms hovering near, had glided down the House and taken his seat on the Woolsack, a high position to which Lord Halsbury lends habitual grace and dignity.   The Beverley and East Riding Railway Bill had been read a third time and passed, and the Kettering Water Bill had gone through the same ordeal. Certain Provisional Orders made by the Board of Trade relating to St. Ives Gas, Otley Gas, Pocklington Water, and Marlow Water Bills had been considered and decided upon.   Lord Salisbury had been in his place, his shoulders slightly stooping under the cares of Empire.   Opposite him Earl Granville, that *preux chevalier* of politics, a statesman who combines the courtliness of the best type of Frenchman with the strength of the typical Englishman, diffused an air of geniality over the scene.   There was some conversation on various topics, including the Arch-deaconry of Cornwall; and then noble lords dispersed to dress for dinner with as light a heart as beat within Ollivier's breast when France declared war against Germany.

Oblivious of pending doom. It were idle to suppose noble lords were ignorant of what was pending in another place. It is one of the pretty fictions of our Legislature that one branch is ignorant even of the existence of the other. No member with any self-respect, speaking whether in Lords or Commons, would allude to remarks made at the other end of the corridor, save by dark allusion to something said " in another place." When the present Houses of Parliament were built the ingenious and sentimental architect so planned the structure that the Lord Chancellor and the Speaker should for all time sit *vis-à-vis*. If when both Houses are at work all the doorways were flung open, the Lord Chancellor looking straight before him would catch the Speaker's eye, and Mr. Peel might learn a lesson in deportment by watching Lord Halsbury on the Woolsack.

But no one minds the dead-and-gone architect and his pretty but forgotten fancy. The splendid brass doors of the House of Lords remain closed, shutting out the view beyond, and the Commons come and go through their lobby without even a thought of the privilege, carefully secured for them under quite possible circumstances, of standing at their own bar and gazing upon the assembled House of Lords. To the Commons the House of Lords is "another place," and no one knows what wealth of scorn this simple formula may contain till he has heard it used by Lord Salisbury when the exigencies of debate have compelled him to make reference to remarks offered in the Commons.

Mr. Labouchere's motion. Yet what with equal euphuism is known in Parliamentary parlance as "the usual channels of information," must have brought to the knowledge of noble lords dallying with the Pocklington Water Bill the fact that before midnight the House of Commons, at the invitation of Mr. Labouchere, would have discussed and decided the question whether or not the House of Lords should continue to exist. Probably the magnificent air of indifference with which Lord Brabourne and Viscount Cross regarded this attack upon the ancient privileges of their order was safely assumed with the certainty that there was within the House of Commons itself a body of resolute young men, not unconnected by ties of kindred, who might be depended upon to give a good account of the assailants. There is a scene in Corneille's *Horace*, which Boileau always delighted in, where Horatius is lamenting the disgrace he supposes to have been brought upon him by the flight of his son in the combat with the Curiatii.

"*Que voulez-vous qu'il fît contre trois?*" asks Julie; and the old man passionately replies, "*Qu'il mourût!*"

What could the thirty eldest sons of peers having seats in the Commons do against six hundred clamouring for the destruction of the House of Lords?

They could die.

Mr. George Curzon. It was only apparently disheartening that Mr. Curzon, who stood in the front rank of the defenders of the House of Lords, should have dissembled his love. Mr. Labouchere asked the House to agree to the proposition that it is contrary to the true principles of representative government, and injurious to their efficiency, that any person shall sit and vote in Parliament by right of birth. Mr. Curzon denied this, but admitted that existing hereditary legislative rights might with advantage be modified by extending the principle both of life peerages and representative peerages in the House of Lords. This, as the late Major O'Gorman once shrewdly observed, was opening the door to the thin end of the wedge.

But it was only Mr. Curzon's art, a strategic broadening of the ground of defence. His amendment, if carried, would not prevent his taking his seat in the House of Lords when he succeeded to the peerage, whilst even in his present condition as eldest son of a peer, he might stand a chance of election to that august assembly.

Heirs-apparent. Besides, it is well not too sedulously to cultivate overweening pride. A Session or two ago, before Mr. Labouchere found opportunity for his annual motion, the heirs-apparent having seats in the House of Commons took upon themselves to put their father's house in order. There were solemn meetings at which Mr. Curzon and Mr. Brodrick took counsel with the Marquis of Carmarthen as to what steps should be taken to keep the House of Lords going till they came into their heritage. They drew up a resolution, circulated among and extensively signed by elder sons, who through this medium gave their fathers and grand-fathers to understand that something would have to be done. The document was formally brought under the notice of Lord Salisbury, who received it with grave courtesy, though a brief minute drawn up in his own hand, descriptive of his feelings on the occasion, would be a priceless contribution to our literary possessions. Nothing came of this movement except that the Premier, entering with grim humour into the spirit of the joke, introduced a Bill proposing to add to the House of Lords thirty life peers, chiefly drawn from the classes which General Goldsworthy and Admiral Field severally adorn.

It was, doubtless, owing to the limited time available for debate to-night that so few of the next-of-kin to the House of Lords took part in it. The Marquis of Carmarthen probably accepted Mr. Curzon as the exponent of the feelings that welled in his breast as he listened to Mr. Labouchere's elaborate sarcasm, and watched Dr. Wallace trampling through the thicket of hereditary privileges with hearty

manner, suggestive of a rhinoceros among the saplings. Mr.
Brodrick had his mouth closed by his official position, and
Lord Lewisham, with his ever-ready book in hand, was too
deeply engrossed in trying to remember who had promised to
dine in the House, and who had pleaded imperative engage-

LORD CARMARTHEN.

ments elsewhere. Lord Wolmer and Mr. Marjoribanks have
active duties in the same line, which preclude them giving
full attention to matters savouring of personal interest. Lord
Hartington's prospect of inevitable translation to the House
of Lords, and consequent comparative effacement from
political life, is not a subject calculated to draw him into
conversation except under pressure of imperative necessity.

But the House would have liked to hear Lord Lymington.

There is about the future Earl of Portsmouth a happy mingling of youth and middle age—the playfulness of the kitten combined with the gravity of the judge and the erudition of the professor—that makes precious his too infrequent contributions to Parliamentary debate.

Lord Cranborne took part in the discussion with a freshness, vigour, and originality that give high promise of gifts that some day—long distant everybody hopes—will illumine the House of Lords. Earl Compton delivered a good *bourgeois* speech, and Mr. Arthur Balfour, in one of his polished, sparkling addresses, gave the House of Commons an opportunity of reflecting with pleased complacency on the happy accident of birth that leaves one of its chiefest ornaments unthreatened with removal to another place. Mr. Balfour is the nephew, not the eldest son, of a peer; in this case, happily, not the rose, though he lives near it.

But where were other older sons—Lord Baring, the Lord of Burghley, the Earl of Cavan, Lord H. Cavendish-Bentinck, Mr. Cochrane Baillie, Mr. W. H. Cross, Lord Curzon, Lord Ebrington, Lord Elcho, Mr. Gathorne-Hardy, the Marquis o' Granby, Mr. Grimston, Mr. Hubbard, Mr. Kenyon, Mr. Plunket, Lord Weymouth, Mr. Rowland Winn? And where was Mr. Bernard Coleridge, that he should have neglected this memorable opportunity of showing how sweet a flower will some day bloom in the Paradise of the House of Lords?

May 20.—Lord Rosebery's guest. A story is told about Lord Rosebery which one hopes is true. It certainly is not improbable. The other night Lady Rosebery was " At Home " in Berkeley Square, and nearly everybody in London who is anybody was bidden to attend. On the day before the party took place, Lord Rosebery met in Piccadilly a Scotch farmer whom he had occasionally seen at election times in Midlothian. Following his natural impulse of kindness, he invited the Scotchman to the evening party. He arrived in due time, and in a costume which, whilst broadly following the regulation for evening dress, was of a cut never before seen in Berkeley Square. He walked about, looked at the company, and finally found his way to the supper-room, where were spread all the delicacies of the season.

The Scotchman had not been in the room ten minutes when bang went a lobster salad, half a chicken, a handful of meringues, and a large plate of jelly.   After this he began to trifle with the good things on the table.   Seeing a glass dish of olives, he, full of trust in the results of his general

LORD ——'S GUEST.

sampling, took a spoonful, thinking they were something in the confectionery line.   The result was not satisfactory, and he slyly deposited the *débris* under the table.

He had noticed the ladies all about eating, with evident delight, a pleasant-looking thing, pink or cream coloured, served in saucers.   He asked for one of these, and the servant gave him a bountiful supply of ice cream.   He took a big spoonful, and conveyed it to his mouth.   A look of painful surprise crossed his countenance, but he was not going to disgrace his host.   He closed his eyes, shut his mouth firmly, and with a few spasms swallowed the ice.

That was all very well for him. He was a strong man, accustomed to difficulties; but he felt that to avoid pain to others someone should know about this. Looking round he saw Lord Rosebery talking to a group of ladies and gentlemen. Sidling up to him with a saucer of ice cream in his hand, he plucked him by the sleeve.

"I don't suppose you know it, my lord," he loudly whispered, "but I think I ought to tell you. There has been a mistake somewhere, and *this pudding's froze.*"

Lord Rosebery grasped the situation in a moment. With perfect courtesy and with a pretty appearance of critical inquiry, he tasted the ice cream.

"So it is," he said; "that's very strange."

He went off to speak to one of the servants, and, returning, said, "It's all right; I am told that this is a new kind of pudding they freeze on purpose," and, taking his friend's arm, he led him from the room.

May 30.—"The late Sir James Hogg." Mention of the not lately heard-of title, Sir James McGarel-Hogg, recalls a story not yet embalmed in print. Shortly after the Chairman of the Metropolitan Board of Works was raised to the peerage, he accepted an invitation to dine at a house he had been accustomed to visit in the days of his baronetage. The butler preceding him, with the evident intention of announcing him by his old title, Lord Magheramorne observed the precaution of mentioning his new style. The butler looked at him dumbfounded, made an audible attempt to pronounce the name, and miserably failed. He nevertheless held on his way to the drawing-room, where, flinging open the door, he announced to the assembled guests, "The late Sir James McGarel-Hogg."

CHAPTER XX.

SMALL BEER.

Patient Listeners—Mr. Sykes—Mr. H. Matthews—Mr. Biggar—Mr. Rathen—A Critical Moment—Smart Answers—"Fearful Creatures"—The New Whip —Sir Wm. Dyke's Misadventure—A Stranger in the House—A Death-bed Story.

May 21.—Patient Listeners. THERE are some men to whom the House of Commons is attractive in all or any of its moods. Conspicuous among these is Mr. Gladstone, and only less so was Mr. Bright. The difference between these two old Parliament men is that whilst Mr. Gladstone is equally interested when the House is stirred to its profoundest depths, Mr. Bright used, in later years at least, to find fuller joy in the long level plain of quiet hours that intervene. During the first one or two Sessions that followed the collapse of the Liberal Party in 1874 Mr. Bright was accustomed to sit through the dinner-hour on the front Opposition bench, as attentive to the comparatively obscure members carrying on the debate as if he were the Leader of the House. Mr. Gladstone also has this gift of patient listening, and has been known to encourage with strained attention a member who, by his prolixity, has driven nearly everyone else out of the House.

Mr. Sykes. Mr. Christopher Sykes experiences, in common with these greater statesmen, the yearning after the duller delights of Parliamentary life. When political controversy runs high, when the clash of arms reverberates through the corridors, and the fate of Ministries hangs in the balance, Mr. Sykes holds aloof almost up to the hour of the division, and then watches the closing struggle from a remote corner of the side gallery. To-night, drawn by an irresistible impulse to the Legislative Chamber, he found it admirably attuned to his desire. Mr. Pickersgill had obtained the first place at the evening sitting for a motion demanding the appointment of a Royal Commission to inquire into the inequality of penal sentences. This enticing dish had been served up after a sultry morning sitting spent in the delivery of four speeches in so-called debate on the Scotch Local Government Bill. Members who had survived that walked sadly back again at nine o'clock, and made a House for Mr. Pickersgill.

Mr. Sykes, entering shortly after ten o'clock, found the Home Secretary on his feet explaining ,the view of the situation taken by the Government. There were fully a score of members present, scattered here and there over the benches in something approaching devotional attitude. There was plenty of room for newcomers, and Mr. Sykes selected a seat far down on the back bench below

MR. SYKES.

the gangway—a happy position that combined the fullest opportunity for observation with perfect immunity from contact with other members.

Mr. H. Matthews. Mr. Matthews, addressing his speech personally to Mr. Henry Fowler, who had all the front Opposition bench to himself, was painfully deferential. It seemed only by a masterful effort of self-control that he baulked his evident inclination to address the right hon. member for Wolverhampton as "my lud." He spoke in hushed tones as if he were in church. Indeed, the whole

o

atmosphere of the place was suggestive of afternoon service.
Mr. Esslemont, from time to time resisting the tendency to
drop asleep, appeared to miss the familiar smell of peppermint
that permeates the kirk in far-off Belhelvie. Once when Mr.
Matthews paused in his address and bent his head in examination of his notes, Mr. Molloy, sitting at the corner seat below
the gangway, instinctively put his hand under the bench as
if he were feeling for the box committed to his charge as
" sidesman," and now was the time to make the collection.

Mr. Biggar.   The holy calm which brooded over everything
             settled with sweetening influence upon Mr.
Biggar, as he sat in the corner seat once appropriated by
Isaac Butt. Through the almost empty chamber sounded
the hushed voice of the Home Secretary as, in his curiously
apologetic manner, he excused the judges who allotted too
heavy sentences, and minimised the shortcomings of those
who gave too little. There were few of Mr. Matthews's colleagues in the Ministry present to keep him in countenance.
The Attorney-General had come down to keep an eye on the
debate, and had kept it in such fixed condition that he had
gone fast asleep. Mr. Ritchie, ostentatiously arrayed in light
morning suit in protest against the prevalence of evening
dress, sat and listened. He had gone through the Scotch
debate at the morning sitting, and felt himself in admirable
training. Near him sat Lord George Hamilton, folding, refolding, and tearing up bits of paper.   .

Mr. Raikes.   Mr. Raikes was there too, and presently took
             part in the debate, though what he did in this
galley was not precisely clear. The Postmaster-General's
personal interest in penal sentences is presumably limited to
consideration of what are the precise deserts of an hon.
member who, in season and out of season, pursues him with
questions about the parcel post, the postal rates to Timbuctoo,
and the reason why a letter sent to far-off Orkney should cost
only a penny, whilst, with much less generous consideration
of weight, twopence-halfpenny is charged for its despatch to
Calais. It was not difficult to guess whom Mr. Raikes was
thinking of, as a wistful smile illumined his countenance

when Mr. Henry Fowler described the tendency of a judge at
Stafford to pass sentences involving long periods of seclusion
from active life, Parliamentary or otherwise.

From time to time Mr. Akers-Douglas looked in, hovered
awhile at the Bar, and then disappeared. At intervals the
columnar figure of Lord Arthur Hill appeared in support of
the doorway, was withdrawn, and presently discovered supporting some other archway. These were the only signs of
active life about the premises, the only representatives of the
Whip brotherhood. "Bobby" Spencer, whose cheery presence
is not unfamiliar on occasions like these, had fled in affright.
Even Mr. Jacoby had put on his hat and walked away. The
pulses of political life beat so feebly as to be almost imperceptible.

The most remarkable testimony to the influence of indo-
lence that prevailed is found in the fact that no one even
attempted to move a count. When Mr. Matthews made an
end of speaking Mr. Neville, in a sharp voice that had a
momentary effect in stirring the languid audience, took up
the story. Then Mr. Raikes struck in, skimming round the
subject, discussing sentences adequate and inadequate, and
never once alluding to Mr. Henniker Heaton. So it went on
till Mr. Conybeare and one o'clock arrived, when, it being
impossible to go beyond this combination, a division was
taken, and members wearily sauntered out into the still
sultry air.

May 21.—A crit-
ical moment.
The irruption of the Irish members upon the
ordered business of the House of Commons
to-night, and the postponement of the division till close upon
the dinner hour, led to an event almost tragic. An hon. and
learned member who sits for a northern constituency, and
enjoys well-deserved popularity on both sides of the House,
had a dinner engagement at a place fully half an hour's drive
from Westminster. Long experience of the House of Commons
had convinced him of the uncertainty of events, and, as a
precaution against contingencies, he had brought a change of
clothes with him, and had secured the loan of the private room
of a member of the Ministry, meaning to dress at his leisure
and set forth in good time. As the debate to-night proceeded

upon the abortive attempt of Mr. Smith to bring about the
closure, the hon. and learned member began to grow uneasy.
When the Solicitor-General for Ireland succeeded Mr. Gladstone things looked desperate, and when Mr. Parnell rose he
felt that something must be done. The only thing was to
rush off and dress, return to take part in the division, and
hurry off as soon as the doors were unlocked.

After sitting listening awhile to Mr. Parnell, he at length
made off to the Minister's room, and began his toilet, feeling
certain that the Irish leader would occupy at least a quarter
of an hour. At an exceedingly critical moment, when he had
divested himself of his morning suit of clothes, the division bell
rang. There was no time to get back into his morning dress,
or to fully array himself in evening attire. Still less could he
enter the House in the transition state in which he was caught.
Then a happy thought occurred to him. The Minister's room
is close by the cloak room, and, huddling on some clothes, he
managed to signal the janitor, and begged him to borrow an
overcoat that would cover his *déshabille*. One was brought,
but the learned member is more than usually portly, and the
coat would not button. A desperate rush was made to the
cloak-room, and another coat produced, which just buttoned
across, though rather tight about the chest. In this borrowed
garb the hon. and learned gentleman, displaying remarkable
agility, managed to reach the lobby before the door was closed,
took part in the division—everyone wondering why on a comparatively warm night he was so closely wrapped up—got
safely back to the Minister's room, completed his toilet, and
went off to dinner only a little late.

May 30.—Smart   Two Ministers questioned in the House of
answers.   Commons to-night delivered the smart answer
which rather provokes than turns away wrath. The first to
fire off was Mr. Raikes, who was questioned by Mr. Henniker
Heaton as to the feasibility of the scheme of advertising
on the back of postage stamps and telegrams. Mr. Raikes
answered soberly enough to begin with, indicating that the
matter had been under the notice of the Post Office department. Mr. Heaton concluded a lengthy question by asking
whether the Postmaster-General had consulted any advertising

agents with a view of ascertaining what revenue might be
forthcoming from this source.   To this Mr. Raikes replied—
   " No, sir; I have not.   The fact is, it does not appear to be

so much a question of advertising agents as of advertising
politicians."
   The House laughed at this little hit, and Mr. Heaton
would have done well to take the same course. He, however,
brooded over the reproof for the hours through which the
remaining questions ran, and then appealed to the Speaker
whether the dignity of the House was served by such answers.

The Speaker, however, ruled that no harm had been done, and Mr. Raikes still remains Postmaster-General.

"Fearful crea- A neater and much more enjoyed bolt was
tures."   shot by Mr. Plunket. Mr. John Ellis and
Mr. Cavendish-Bentinck had been asking questions about the stone carvings of birds and beasts placed by way of ornamentation on the new staircases in Westminster Hall. Mr. Plunket had replied to these questions, which appeared on the paper, when Sir George Campbell interposed, and was, as usual, greeted with a howl of humorous protest from the House. When the noise had subsided, Sir George, in his emphatic manner, asked whether Mr. Plunket was "responsible for these fearful creatures." The First Commissioner, coming back to the table, smilingly said, with a genial nod towards Sir George—

SIR GEORGE CAMPBELL.

"No, I am not responsible for the fearful creatures in Westminster Hall, or in this House either."

This is a good-humoured hit at Sir George Campbell which can only be thoroughly understood by the House of Commons. It was enjoyed so uproariously that questions were interrupted for several moments, whilst everybody—not least delightedly Mr. Gladstone—roared with laughter.

May 31.—The new It is but a few months since Mr. Jacoby under-
Whip.   took, in conjunction with Mr. Philip Stanhope,
the duties of Whip. So quietly was the arrangement entered

upon that a large majority of the House learned the fact from
observing the hon. member for Mid-Derbyshire habitually
perambulating the lobby without his hat. It is one of the
unwritten laws of the British Constitution that the Whip of a
party shall never be seen in the lobby with his hat on. Lord
Lewisham and Mr. Robert Spencer add to this sartorial peculiarity the right of turning up their trousers well over their
boots. That is, however, not obligatory, and up to the present
time Mr. Jacoby has not followed it. He is content to know
that, whilst a Whip *must* go hatless from the time the Speaker
takes the chair till he leaves it, he *may* turn up his trousers.
When it was discovered that Mr. Jacoby had become a Whip,
further inquiry brought out the facts that he had a colleague
in Mr. Philip Stanhope, a titular Leader in Mr. Labouchere,
and a party which, all told, was said to muster seventy votes.

Still young in a profession that has enriched the peerage,
and but lately filled the Chair of the House of Commons, Mr.
Jacoby has achieved an unparalleled personal triumph. He
has actually whipped into the Opposition lobby a member of
Her Majesty's Government, who for many years held the
office of chief Government Whip!

This happened in the division on the vote for the Office of
Works. Mr. Storey had moved to reduce the amount by the
sum of £1,100, and insisted on taking a division. Mr. Smith
and his colleagues on the front bench walked out into the
lobby serenely confident. They had had a prolonged struggle,
but the end was in view. The vote for the Board of Works
would be carried, and there would remain time for Mr. Balfour
to bring in his Drainage Bills. Mr. Jacoby, with a suspicious
gleam in his eye, watched them go, whipping up "Our Party"
into the "No" lobby. It was a long process, but in due time
the doors were locked, and the "Ayes" and the "Noes" were
cooped up in their respective lobbies, pressing towards the wicket
and as eager to get out as they were anxious to get in. The
House was deserted even by the Chairman, who had seized the
opportunity to take a stroll behind the Speaker's vacant chair.

Sir Wm. Dyke's misadventure. Suddenly a shout of surprise was heard in the
"No" lobby. It rose again, now become an
exultant cheer. Mr. Smith and his friends in the other lobby

pressed anxiously against the wicket gate, marvelling what this might portend. Again the cheer rose, coming muffled through the closed door, but unmistakable in its almost fierce triumph. Then there were sounds of an altercation ; a slight pause ; an unlocked door ; and next was beheld the spectacle of the Right Honourable Sir Wm. Hart Dyke, Vice-President of the Council, some time principal Whip of the Conservative Party, running for dear life across the passage by the doorway of the House, heading for the other lobby. The door was hurriedly unlocked, and a welcoming cheer from the Conservatives testified to their joy at this happy deliverance.

Mr. Jacoby, dexterously getting his men together, had actually drawn Sir Wm. Dyke into the wrong lobby.

In those interesting little memoirs which illumine the pages of *Dod*, Sir Wm. Dyke is self-described as a Conservative, " but not opposed to those moderate changes which altered circumstances render necessary." To find himself in the same lobby as a collection of Radicals bent upon reducing a vote for the salary of one of his own colleagues was " altered circumstance " indeed. But it could scarcely be regarded as a moderate change, such as it was a statesman's duty to make the best of. So Sir William thundered at the lobby door till the affrighted messenger opened it, and the new Whip's prey escaped.

June 17. — A stranger in the House.

The liveliest episode in to-night's sitting had no place in the programme. Shortly after five o'clock, whilst the Home Secretary was explaining the Tithe Rent-charge Bill, members sitting below the gangway on the Conservative side were horrified to discover a stranger climbing over the front of the pews under the gallery where a few privileged strangers sit. He had alighted on the other side, and was proceeding to dispose himself comfortably on a cushioned bench on the Ministerial side, when a temporarily paralysed doorkeeper, recovering himself, rushed forward, seized the man, and escorted him out of the House.

Brought to the Serjeant-at-Arms, the stranger explained that he had never been in the place before, and had not the slightest idea there was any breach of order in changing his seat. He could not hear Mr. Matthews very well, and being

deeply interested in tithes, thought he would go and sit a
little nearer to him. The Serjeant-at-Arms took a lenient
view of the offence, and gave the stranger an order for a seat
in the remoter Strangers' Gallery, whence a descent upon the
House is practically impossible.

June 20. — A death-bed story. The Rev. Henry White, Chaplain of the House
of Commons, tells a gruesome story. Once,
many years ago, when Mr. White was a curate
living at the East End of London, he was rung up in the dead
of the night and urgently implored by a woman at the door
to come and see her husband, who, she said, was dying.
Mr. White hastily dressed, not forgetting to fasten his watch
in his waistcoat pocket, and went out into the dark streets.
The woman led him by many tortuous passages till they came
to the door of a squalid house in a court. Mr. White, going
about his Father's business, had no fear or hesitation. Following the woman's lead he entered, went upstairs, and found,
lying on a wretched bed in a corner of the room, a man of about
forty years of age, already within touch of the hand of death.

Glancing round the room, the young curate was surprised to observe some articles a little out of place with
such surroundings. There stood on the table a silver dish of
considerable value; clothes of good style were heaped about
the room; and there were one or two small pictures which it
seemed a strange thing the man and his companion should
buy. But this was no business of Mr. White's. He bent over
the bed, talked to the man, and offered to pray with him.

As he spoke he observed a sudden gleam in the man's eyes,
and noted that they were fixed on his watch chain. He went
on talking of things past and things to come, and then, as the
woman stood near sobbing her heart out, the young curate
prayed. When he finished he found the man was dead, and
rising from his knees discovered that the fingers of the corpse
were clasped in his watch-chain.

The man was a noted burglar and lifelong thief. Even as
he was dying the sight of a gold watch chain in the possession
of a pre-occupied man was too much for him, and as Mr.
White prayed to God to forgive him his sins, the dying thief
tried to pick his pocket.

CHAPTER XXI.

LEADERS OF PARTIES.

A Quiet Time—Sir George Campbell's Strategy—Mr. Balfour at Leisure—Royal
Grants—Mr. Gladstone's Dilemma—Disappointed with the Atlantic—Mr.
Smith as Leader—The Division on the Royal Grants—Mr. Bradlaugh—
Dividing!—Mr. Biggar—"The Grand Old Man"—Sir W. Harcourt as
Leader of the Opposition.

June 21.—A quiet
time.

A SINGULAR quietude just now prevails in Parliamentary circles. There has not been seen anything like it these fifteen years. The nearest parallel is found
in the Session of 1874, when Mr. Disraeli came into power at
the head of a substantial majority. The country, weary with
the turbulence of the triumphant Radicals under the leadership of Mr. Gladstone, turned with thankful heart to the *laissez
faire* policy the new Premier inaugurated. The House of
Commons from a bear garden was transformed into a temple
of ease. The Irish Nationalist Party was not yet born; the
Fourth Party was undreamt of; the Liberal Party was shattered; Mr. Disraeli was omnipotent, and, accurately gauging
the public desire and the chief necessities of the case, he let
heroic legislation alone, made the passing of Supply the chief
business of the Session, and the House of Commons was
steeped in an atmosphere of languorous rest.

A somewhat similar condition of affairs, brought about
under different circumstances, once more prevails in the
House. There has been a general sheathing of swords, a
proclamation of truce. All unruly elements have temporarily
withdrawn. Mr. Gladstone has not been seen in the House
since Monday, when he benignly expressed approval of the
arrangements for the business of the Session announced by
Mr. Smith. Lord Randolph Churchill, after terrifying Lord
George Hamilton with threats of what would happen when
the House got into Committee on the Navy Estimates, went
off to Norway, and the Navy Estimates were passed in a
couple of nights. Lord Hartington has spent the week at

Ascot. Mr. Chamberlain has effaced himself, and only Mr. Heneage, big with the fate of the Board of Agriculture Bill, has braved the indignation displayed by Mr. Osborne Morgan on finding at the far end of the front Opposition bench right hon. gentlemen who do not believe in the infallibility of Mr. Gladstone.

Even the Irish members have felt the subtle influence of the situation. The first time for many years they have trafficked with the Leader of the House for conveniences of debate. On the understanding that the Irish votes should not be taken in the first week after the holidays they have stayed away, and public business has advanced by leaps and bounds. On Monday, when the full influence of Mr. Smith's statement had not yet crept over the House, Mr. Labouchere uplifted a defiant voice, and more than hinted his intention of pursuing the familiar habit of debating and dividing on every vote. But the member for Northampton had over-estimated his own invulnerability. Slowly but surely the spell worked upon him also, and though on Monday night he spasmodically resisted its influence it was with steadily failing energy. By Tuesday he had completely yielded, and was silent through twenty-seven votes.

Mr. Jacoby, weary of piping when none will dance, has given up sending out four-lined Whips. Though he still refrains from the ultimate, irrevocable course of resuming the wearing of his hat during the time the House sits, he wanders listlessly about the lobby, thinking of days that are no more.

Even the incorruptible aggressiveness of Mr. Conybeare has yielded to the sweet influence of the prevailing Pleiades. It is true that on Monday night he protested against Mr. Smith's suave suggestion that the prorogation should take place at an unusually early period. Why should the House not sit till September? growled the member for Camborne, with hands in pockets, lowering brow, and head bent down with that curious gesture which suggests to the timid mind that he contemplates driving home his arguments by physically butting the unconvinced. It was at once perceived that in this matter Mr. Conybeare was not absolutely impartial. Whether the House rises in the first

week in August or sits to the end of September it cannot
matter to the member for Camborne, who about that period
will be safe in prison under a warrant issued under the Crimes
Act.*

There are some people who, being themselves in compulsory confinement, would find compensation in the knowledge
that the House of Commons was also "kept in" through the
glad autumn months. But the House is naturally inclined
to take another view of the matter, and Mr. Conybeare's
suggestion was openly scouted.

In ordinary times such a demonstration would have had
the effect of aggravating the manner of the member for Camborne; but just now he, too, must yield to the witchery that
enslaves the House. Content with having offered the suggestion he did not press it, nor take those means open to him,
not unfamiliar in his hands, of contributing to his desire by
delaying the progress of business. There is no kink in the
chain, no discordant voice in the harmony. The wolf of
obstruction lies down with the Ministerial lamb, the young
lion below the gangway and the fatling on the Treasury bench
dwell together, and Mr. W. H. Smith leads them.

June 22. — Sir George Campbell's strategy. The House of Commons, spending a long night
in Committee on the Scotch University Bill, was
indebted to Sir George Campbell for a pleasing
episode cunningly devised to divert the over-weighted mind.
That the Bill immediately under discussion specially dealt
with matters concerning the kingdom of which Kirkcaldy is
the hub afforded no particular reason why Sir George should
take a prominent part in the debate. The House is too
familiar with his authoritative omniscience to be surprised at
his interposition on any miscellaneous question that may
present itself. Where his native originality triumphed was in
the novel conditions amid which he pursued his disquisition
on Scotch Universities and the proposals of the Lord Advocate.
Ordinary members taking part in debate are accustomed to
rise from some particular seat they have secured at the opening

* On the 8th of July the Speaker informed the House he had received a
letter from Judge Webb, announcing that Mr. Conybeare had been committed to
Londonderry Gaol for three months.

of the proceedings. How to-night Sir George Campbell managed to secure the favourable attention of an utterly fagged House was by the variety and rapidity of his movements. Whilst the echoes of his voice discussing Clause 5 still resounded above the gangway he would be discovered animadverting upon Clause 6 from a bench below the gangway. After a while, the House having had brief opportunity of forgetting his existence, Sir George's white hat was discovered gleaming under the shade of the gallery, and his voice heard discussing the proposition whether the assessors elected by the *senatus academicus* should be four in number or three. Anon, he upstarted from the bench consecrated to the memory of Mr. Newdegate, and delivered his opinion as to the propriety of holders of the highest degree with honours in any faculty being recognised (subject to carefully considered regulations) as teachers for the purposes of graduation in such faculty. Ariel, when at the bidding of Prospero the sprite boarded the King's ship,

> now on the beak,
> Now in the waist, the deck, in every cabin
> I flamed amazement,

suggests the nearest approach to the peripatetic member for Kirkcaldy distilling wise counsel before the heavily moving steps of the Scotch University Bill.

Mr. Balfour at leisure. Mr. Balfour, lounging on the front bench, watched Sir George's movements through half-closed eyes. As if the Chief Secretary had not enough to do in connection with Ireland, he appears to be told off to watch the course of Scotch legislation. It is true that just now the pressure of work in his own particular department is lightened. Several Irish members, including Dr. Tanner, are in prison; others, including Mr. Gill and Mr. Cox, are *en route;* still others, Mr. O'Brien and Mr. John Dillon, are recovering from the effects of imprisonment, and are making holiday away from Westminster; others, again, like Mr. Healy, are more profitably engaged in pursuing their private business in Ireland than in worrying the Chief Secretary at Westminster. Mr. Sexton is in attendance, and, in accordance with long-established habit, opens the proceedings by a little series of ornate speeches ill-disguised in the form of supplementary questions. Mr. Balfour, having conceded the expected tribute of alluding to him as "the right honourable gentleman," the Lord Mayor of Dublin retires for the rest of the evening.

Mr. Biggar, once so formidable an adversary, has abjured sack, and become a reformed character. His constant attendance upon the Probate Court has imbued him with a certain judicial air incompatible with his former eccentricities. He now treats the Speaker with as marked respect as if he were presiding over a Court of Justice, and once, taking exception to an attempt made from the Conservative benches to proceed after midnight with contentious business, he alluded to the Solicitor-General for Ireland as "my learned friend."

July 4. — Royal Grants. Mr. Smith, moving to-night for a Committee to inquire into the question of Royal Grants, was from the first apologetic in his manner. All he hoped for was that, "at this stage at all events," in consideration of Her Majesty's most gracious message, the House would be unanimous in the conclusion arrived at. He was not unconscious of *laches* in connection with delay in submitting the proposal for a Committee. But for that shortcoming he only was to blame.

"I am," he said, "personally responsible, and I take it entirely upon myself if any blame is to be attached to anyone."

This move, simple as it seemed, was in reality profoundly skilful. The Radicals below the gangway raised their first fierce cry of angry resentment when Mr. Smith alluded to the failure to fulfil a pledge given many Sessions back. When he chivalrously, as Mr. Gladstone promptly admitted took on himself the full measure of responsibility, the most relentless sectary was mollified. The hand uplifted to strike drew back disarmed by the peaceful, lamblike bearing of the proffered victim. When a short time after Mr. Smith lapsed into that touching eulogy of domestic life, beginning " Around the sentiment of family is clustered all that is good and pure in the Constitution of this country," he had brought the turbulent House into so gentle a mood that if it had been

possible forthwith to submit the vote it would undoubtedly
have been carried without a dissentient voice.

Mr. Gladstone's dilemma. Mr. Gladstone seconded the motion in one
of those speeches he alone can make. If he
had not commenced with the simple statement that he
rose to second the motion, the crowded House, following the
tortuous windings of his speech, would, up to the closing
sentences, have been in doubt as to which of two courses he
had resolved to take. He had so much to say in support of
the proposal, and so many considerations to put forth of its
possible inappropriateness, that the bewildered mind, hurriedly
weighing one with the other, was by no means certain how the
scales would fall.

When later he rose again to speak on the amendment moved
by Mr. Bradlaugh, he had become aware of the exceedingly
strong feeling on the part of fully one-half of his followers
hostile to the proposal to vote additional grants for the Royal
Family. His task was to support the Government, and yet
not to offend his own supporters ; to make two and two seem
five, yet in result to bring out the addition as simply four ; to
hint that a colour was black, whilst acting on the assumption
that it was white ; to agree with Mr. Picton as to the iniquity
of the practice of giving doles and dowries, and to vote with
the Government in support of the Gracious Message of the
Queen.

These were the tasks to which he devoted himself with
an intellectual delight that sparkled through his elaborate
endeavour. He had had no time for preparation to meet
the serious turn events had taken. The consequence was
that his discourse partook of the character of a soliloquy.
He was thinking aloud, arguing with himself, arbitrating
between his dual character of ingrained Conservatism and
Leader of a political party largely infused with Radicalism.
He had made up his mind to vote with the Government at
whatever cost. The object of his speech was to minimise the
cost, if possible to find reasons for less intellectually agile
followers to support the Government, or, failing that, to make
them regard with the least possible resentment his temporary
alliance with the Powers of Darkness.

He spoke for only a few minutes, but rarely has he presented so interesting a psychological study. Now he walked a little on the left-hand side of the road, comforting his own friends with assurance that the instruction to the Committee as it stood would secure for them the right to inquire into those, possibly imaginary, hoards of money Mr. Labouchere had gloated over. Then, turning to the right, he walked for a while in company with the First Lord of the Treasury, protesting that "it would be unfair that he should be required at a moment's notice to give his impression as to what the motion contained and what it did not contain." In the end, his dubious course eagerly watched by three hundred pairs of eyes, he sat down, having succeeded in vaguely conveying the impression that whilst he would give his vote with the Government, his sympathies were with hon. gentlemen below the gangway on his own side.

July 5.—Disappointed with the Atlantic. I wonder if anybody knowing Sir Wilfrid Lawson could hit upon a near guess at his favourite poet? Talking with him at dinner the other evening, the conversation turned upon poets, and he made confession. The poet he most delights in is Byron, probably the last that would have occurred to the mind in such connection. I do not remember hearing him quote Byron in any of his speeches in the House or out of it. This is not for lack of knowledge, as he proved by recital of a whole stanza of "Childe Harold." But Sir Wilfrid Lawson, unlike Mr. Bright, and, in one of his meditative moods, Mr. Chamberlain, is not prone to drop into poetry. His great forte is story-telling, and of stories he has a wonderful collection, keen insight into their appropriateness, and rare gift of recital.

On the particular night I refer to he had heard from a friend travelling in Ireland of a little adventure Sir Wilfrid related with contagious glee. The English tourist, a member of the House of Commons, was travelling in the West of Ireland, and found himself in the train with two priests. He learned that they were stationed at Kilkee, in County Clare, a rift in the coast on which the Atlantic beats in sublimest beauty. The priests complained that it was very dull there:

"Ah," said the M.P., thinking of the Atlantic in its many moods, "but you must have a beautiful view?"

"Divil a bit," said one of the priests testily; "there's nothing between us and Ameriky."

July 8. Mr. Smith as Leader. It is no secret that Mr. Smith was selected for the office of Leader of the House of Commons not because he was at the time regarded as the best man, but because he was recognised as the best possible man. His character was prophetically drawn in a couple of lines written years ago:

> "Here comes a young person of excellent pith,
> Fate tried to disguise him by calling him Smith."

Mr. Disraeli, a swift and excellent judge of character, had discovered in him this unobtrusive endowment of character, and when he came to power in 1874, made him Financial Secretary to the Treasury. There was, as everybody admitted, an absolute fitness about the state of things. It was putting the square man into the square hole, and Mr. Smith justified the selection by proving himself, in a comparatively obscure, but really important, office, a model Minister. Everybody agreed he was the right man in the right place, but if everybody had been polled there is little doubt it would have been further agreed that he had reached the height of his possible fame.

The more intimately acquaintance was formed with his capacity, the fuller was the appreciation. Whenever a man was suddenly and imperatively required to fill a post in a moment of difficulty, there was W. H. Smith. At the end of the Session of 1877, when a reconstruction of the Ministry became necessary, and Mr. Gathorne Hardy went to the House of Lords, Mr. Smith was made First Lord of the Admiralty, and, with fuller opportunities, added to his reputation. After the stirring scene in the House of Commons in the Session of 1885, that saw Mr. Gladstone's great majority dissolved into thin air, he was made Secretary for War, an office he resumed after the General Election of 1886. When in the same year Lord Randolph Churchill disturbed the Christmas festivities at Hatfield and elsewhere by throwing up his portfolio, Lord Salisbury turned, in his dilemma, to his plain, unadorned,

unobtrusive colleague, and, whilst the political world was still
perturbed with the news of Lord Randolph's resignation, it
learned the fresh marvel that Mr. W. H. Smith was nominated
First Lord of the Treasury, and Leader of the House of
Commons.

He has now held the post through three Sessions, and has
worked upon the House of Commons the same charm which
operated to his advancement in the inner councils of the
Conservative leaders. The House, it is true, sometimes laughs
at him. But there is nothing malicious in the merriment, for
it recognises in him an honest, kindly, able man, who, free
from all pretension, unaided by personal prestige or family influence, has conducted the business of the House of Commons
with a success that will bear comparison with any equal period
of time under more famous leaders.

July 28.—The di-
vision on the
Royal Grants.

Probably never since Parties were formed was
there given such proof of personal supremacy
as is supplied by the acquiescence of the Irish
members in their Leader's tactics on the Royal Grants. Often-
times has this anti-type of O'Connell, this almost morose
recluse, in striking ways brought into orderly line the turbulent
spirits that follow him. That he should succeed in taking
them into the division lobby in opposition to Mr. Labouchere
and his friends, in support of the colleagues of Mr. Balfour,
seemed a feat beyond the range of his necromancy. Yet the
report that he would do so, current for forty-eight hours, was
not contradicted.

As the serried masses that waited on either side to hear
the question put slowly rose and parted right and left, all
eyes were turned below the gangway where Mr. Parnell sat,
sternly silent. Parties and sections of parties mingled and
divided. Mr. Gladstone went out to support the Government
in their resistance to the Radical revolt. Lord Hartington,
lingering awhile to talk to Sir William Harcourt, strolled
out in the same direction with his old colleague, shoulder to
shoulder. Mr. John Morley, happy in the final deliverance
of his amendment, followed, more slow-footed, in the same
direction. Mr. Mundella went the same way. Of the crowd
on the front Opposition, only Sir George Trevelyan, deeply

wrought, but bent on following what seemed to him the
right course, at whatever wrenching of personal relationships,
turned his face towards the other doorway, amid a murmur
of ironical cheers from the watchful Ministerialists.

It was an enormous gathering for a July night, with the
shadow of the Prorogation already overhanging the Session.
Including the tellers, 518 members voted, many more than
could find seats on the floor of the House. They stood in a
throng at the bar; they sat on the steps of the gangway; they
were huddled together behind the Speaker's chair; they filled
the galleries on either hand. It was a splendid audience, worthy
of something better than the closing speeches of the debate.

Mr. Bradlaugh. When the House met, Mr. Bradlaugh had secured the prized opportunity of addressing it in
the freshness of its gathering, and had prepared one of those
stupendous, tinkling-cymbal speeches which mark his decadence. Like Mr. Sexton, Mr. Bradlaugh mars the gift of
oratorical power by a too-prevailing sense of his own worthi-
ness. Whilst omniscience is his forte, legal erudition is his
foible. He is ever posing before the House in plaintive chest
notes as a poor layman struggling against the trained hosts of
titled and salaried legal luminaries. Beneath his melodramatic
humility in presence of the Attorney-General, the House
discerns a self-conviction that, save for the absence of wig and
gown, he is more than a match for all the Inns of Court. He
digs among the sepulchres of Statute Books with patient industry, and frequently brings to light some forgotten Act that
should have the effect, not always attained, of upsetting modern
judgments. To-night he rolled under his tongue as precious
morsels the 9th and 10th of William the Third, revelled in
"Crown Lands" and "hereditary possessions." He was
great on a statute of William IV., and contemptuous of
a Committee who, in the sixth paragraph of their Report,
had entirely misapprehended the bearings of "small branches."
This was very imposing, but delivered for the most part in a
strident voice, with much complacent pursing of the lip and
conclusive thrusting forward of the right shoulder, it grew a
trifle tiresome, and the House hailed with a shout of delight
Lord Randolph's happy, Disraelian whisper of the suspicion

that the hon. gentleman's legal erudition was derived from diligent study of that popular authority, *Every Man His Own Lawyer.*

Mr. Bradlaugh had, especially at the outset of his speech, a full House, and a still fuller audience followed Lord Randolph Churchill through his sparkling speech, in style and manner perhaps the best in a long series of Parliamentary triumphs. After this the company fell away, and to an almost empty Chamber Sir Hussey Vivian, pink of political respectability, struggled to explain to diverse audiences, present at Westminster and listening in the Swansea District, the grounds upon which he should, at this stage at least, support the Government. Nor was Sir W. Lawson so happy as usual in keeping the table in a roar; whilst Mr. Goschen, hampered with abundance of notes and shortness of time, halted terribly.

Dividing!   Whilst Big Ben was tolling midnight overhead the division bell rang through all the corridors, and members, waiting the signal, trooped in. A rush was made for the division lobby by members anxious to be out first. The crowds in the side galleries poured into the House till the multitude that had peopled the benches thronged the broad passage between. Midway met the two streams, one passing towards the doorway behind the Speaker's chair, the other, much smaller, making for the doorway under the clock. Still the Irish members tarried in their places, and many members on the benches opposite remained seated, waiting till the passage was clearer, and watching how the Irish would go. They went at last, passing Mr. Labouchere in his corner seat, he regarding each familiar face with a glance of poignant regret. They had all passed out with slow step, disappearing in the Government lobby. Still the Ministerialists, clustered on the benches opposite, sat watching and waiting.

Mr. Biggar.   Then there was a ripple of laughter, a burst of cheering, and Mr. Biggar was discovered strolling all by himself in a casual way into the lobby through which the figure of Mr. Balfour had but a few moments earlier disappeared. An uneasy smile flickered over his flushed face as the cheers and laughter grew in volume. It was noted

that on this supreme occasion he was dressed with remarkable
care. The imitation sealskin waistcoat, which in years gone
by he used to spread in defiance of whatever Ministers sat on
the Treasury bench, has long ago disappeared with his increasing political and social importance. Of late he has not
disdained the lighter attire affected by the man of fashion in
summer-tide. To-night he had put away these vanities.
Draped in deepest mourning, with no gleam of colour save
the flush in his cheek, the white shirt-front, and the gold
watch-chain, he followed with slow, sad steps the majority
that went to crown the triumph of the Ministry.

Looking at him, a sombre figure amidst the boisterous
hilarity of the scene, it was impossible to resist the impression
that Joseph Gillis was walking out to the funeral of his old,
dead self.

July 20.—"The Grand Old Man." Mr. Gladstone has had in his time many
nicknames. Ages have passed since a daily
newspaper, then endeavouring to bask in the
rays of the rising sun, lapsed into an extravagance which,
adroitly turned by the enemy, bestowed upon the popular
statesman the mock title, "The People's William." Still later,
taken in the same way, came the historic appellation, the
"Grand Old Man," perhaps the most widely accepted ever
bestowed upon a public man. Whilst his enemies use it with
tongue in cheek and meaning wink of the eye, his admirers
are content to adopt it as a literal description of a remarkable
individuality. The origin of the phrase is already beginning
to be lost in obscurity, but the honour of its invention
belongs to Sir William Harcourt. It will be found in one of
his early addresses to his constituents in Derby, and had its
birth amid the exultation that followed on Mr. Gladstone's
return to power in 1880, on the ruin of Lord Beaconsfield's
Government.

There is still another name for Mr. Gladstone, reserved
for the inner circle of his official colleagues. To them he
is always "Mr. G.," and the amount of expression this initial
is capable of can be estimated only by those accustomed to
hear it spoken in the varying moods in which Mr. Gladstone
leaves his colleagues.

There is only one other man in political life whose personality is so intimate in the public mind that he is invariably spoken of by a more or less affectionate diminutive. No one in ordinary conversation ever thinks of alluding to the noble

lord, the member for Paddington, as Lord Randolph Churchill, or even Lord Randolph. He is always Randolph, whether to the man in the street or to the politician at the dinner-table. Perhaps it is funniest to hear fair ladies, old and young, speak of him by his Christian name, as if he were a brother, a cousin, or a pet dog.

Aug. 16.—Sir W. Harcourt as leader of the Opposition. Concealing Sir William Harcourt's position as the Leader of an Opposition bent upon opposing, nothing could exceed the skill or the adroitness of his operations carried on throughout the week in Committee on the Tithes Bill. It has been a momentous epoch in his career, finally settling the always vexed question of the succession to Mr. Gladstone's leadership in the House of Commons. Sometimes, lacking a free hand, not quite certain of his position on his own side, and still impelled to volubility, Sir William Harcourt has offended the sense of the House by a certain ponderosity of humour and invective. Through this week he has been entirely free from these vices. No one, unless it be Mr. Henry Fowler, a kind of Parliamentary Bidder, could count up the number of speeches he has made since Monday. But it can be safely asserted by one who heard them all that never once did he descend into that swaggering, bullying mood which at other times debases his style. Quick to see a point, happy in phraseology, brief in speech, he has invariably said the right thing at the right time in the right way.

For high comedy, in which Mr. Smith played a by no means secondary part, nothing has of late been seen in the House of Commons equal to the passage in which the two Leaders fenced across the table over the dead body of the Tithes Bill. Sir William Harcourt's first business was to see that the Bill was really destroyed. This conclusion was reached as a consequence of the Speaker's ruling in reply to his question on a point of order. Mr. Smith of necessity followed with the withdrawal of the Bill, and on this 16th of August, with over eighty votes in Supply yet to be taken, and with knowledge gained through the week of the manifold opposition evoked by any attempt to deal with the question, it was physically and morally impossible to make a fresh attempt.

That quite clear, Sir William Harcourt's whole manner changed. On the instant he became the chief mourner over the still-born Bill foreshadowed by the amendments of the Attorney-General. It was the dearest object of his heart, the apple of his eye. Could it be possible that Mr. Smith, unnatural parent, was determined to refuse proffered help of a

"PONDEROSITY OF INVECTIVE."

passer-by to resuscitate the bantling?   Then came his eulogy
of this offspring of a Conservative Government sketched in

the amendments to the now abandoned Bill the Attorney-General had laid upon the table, embodying, as Sir William said they did, principles fought for through generations by Radicals—the transference of the liability for tithes from occupier to landowner, and the establishment of a universal land court in this country. The Attorney-General tossed uneasily on his seat as Sir William Harcourt turned and blessed him. Mr. Smith endeavoured to look unconcerned while he spasmodically took notes. Conservative gentlemen rustled their papers and muttered interjections. But it was not for them to interrupt a generous adversary, exhausting eulogy on a measure submitted by their own leaders, which they had assembled in unwonted numbers to support.

When Sir William Harcourt resumed his seat his triumph was complete. The Bill he had fought all the week was dead, and no one could say he had done it. On the contrary, he had extolled its merits (in its amended form), and with tears in his eyes had besought the Government not to abandon it by the wayside.

Aug. 30.   Parliament prorogued.

SESSION OF 1889.

FEBRUARY.

21. Thurs.—H. M. Speech. Address thereon. First Debate.
22. Fri.—Ditto. Ditto. Second Debate.
25. Mon.—Ditto. Ditto. Amendment (Ireland), Mr. John Morley. Third Debate.
26. Tues.—H. M. Speech. Address thereon. Fourth Debate.
27. Wed.—Ditto. Ditto. Fifth Debate.
28. Thurs.—Ditto. Ditto. Sixth Debate.

MARCH.

1. Fri.—H. M. Speech. Address thereon. Division on Mr. Morley's Amendment — For, 320. Against, 329. Seventh Debate.
4. Mon.—Ditto. Ditto. Amendment (Highlands, &c., Scotland), Mr. Caldwell. Division—For, [illegible]. Against, [illegible]. Eighth Debate.
5. Tues.—Ash Wednesday Motion. Division—For, 193. Against, 112. H. M. Speech. Address thereon. Amendment (Trafalgar Square), Mr. Pickersgill. Division—For, 105. Against, [illegible]. Ninth Debate.
6. Wed.—H. M. Speech. Address thereon. Division on [illegible] by Mr. W. H. [Smith] — For, 237. Against, [illegible]. Tenth Debate.
7. Thurs.—Naval Defence. Committee. Supply: Civil Services.
8. Fri.—Morning Sitting. Motion, Mr. W. H. Smith. Supply. Amendment, Mr. Bradlaugh. Division—For, 79. Against, 11[illegible].
11. Mon.—Supply: Army Estimates. Mr. [illegible] Motion.
12. Tues.—Morning Sitting. Supply: Army Estimates.

MARCH (continued).

8. Wed.—Prisoners (Ireland) Bill. Mr. J. O'Connor. Division — For, [illegible]. Against, [illegible].
14. Thur.—Supply: Navy Estimates; Amendment, Mr. Puff. Division—For, 61. Against, [illegible]. [illegible] considered.
15. Fri.—Salaries of Ministers. Motion, Mr. [illegible].
   Technical and Evening Schools.
17. Mon.—Supply: Civil Services.
18. Tues.—Public Business. Motion (Procedure, &c., on Supply), Mr. W. H. Smith. Division on Main Question — For, [illegible]. Against, [illegible].
   Supply. Report. Civil Service Estimates.
20. Wed.—Supply: Civil Service Estimates.
21. Thur.—Ditto. Ditto.
22. Fri.—Ditto. Ditto. Special Commission. The Statement by the Attorney-General.

23. Mon.—Supply. Report. Mr. C. Russell and The Attorney-General's Statement.
   Naval Defence. Committee.
24. Tues.—Supply: Civil Service Estimates. Slave Trade. Motion, Mr. S. Buxton.
27. Wed.—Removal of Wrecks Bill. Sir L. Birkbeck. Read 3°.
   Sale of Intoxicating Liquors on Sunday Bill. Mr. J. C. Stevenson. 2nd Reading. Division—For, 175. Against, 157.
28. Thur.—Supply: Civil Service Estimates. Army Annual Bill. Committee.
29. Fri.—The late Mr. John Bright. Remarks by Mr. W. H. Smith, Mr. Gladstone, &c.
   Payment of Members. Motion, Mr. Fenwick. Motion counted.

APRIL.

1. Mon.—Naval Defence. Committee. Report. Division (Estimate)—For, [illegible]. Against, [illegible].
2. Tues.—Supply: Civil Service Estimates. Poor in Large Towns. Motion, Mr. [illegible]. Select Committee agreed to.
3. Wed.—Trusts Investments Bill. Mr. [illegible]. Read 2°.
4. Thur.—Naval Defence. Report.
5. Fri.—Vaccination Acts. Motion, Mr. [illegible].
8. Mon.—Local Government for Scotland. Bills brought in.
   Supply: Civil Service Estimates.
9. Tues.—Supply: Civil Service Estimates. House Rate for Scotland. Motion, Mr. Clark. Division—For, 79. Against, 100.
10. Wed.—Agricultural Tenants (Ireland) Bill. Mr. [illegible]. 2nd Reading. Division —For, 103. Against, 228.

11. Thur.—Adjournment. Motion (state of Business), Mr. McNeill.
   Supply: Civil Service Estimates. River Conservancy Bill. Motion for leave. Bill to be brought in.
12. Fri.—Supply: Civil Service Estimates. Motion (Public Executioner), Mr. E. Lechmere.
   Supply: Report.
   Religious Persecution, &c., Bill. Mr. Cremer. 2nd Reading. Division—For, 91. Against, 112.
15. Mon.—Ways and Means. Financial Statement. Mr. Goschen.
16. Tues.—Supply: Civil Service Estimates.
17. Wed.—Ditto. Ditto.
18. Thur.—Business of the House. Morning Sittings. Motion, &c., Mr. W. H. Smith.
   Post Office (Savings Department). Motion, Mr. S. Smith.

MAY.

1. Wed.—Leaseholds Enfranchisement Bill. Mr. H. H. Fowler. 2nd Reading. Division—For, 157. Against, 181.
2. Thur.—Ways and Means. Budget Resolutions.
   Supply: Civil Service Estimates.
3. Fri.—Ditto. Ditto.
   Motion (Opium Trade), Mr. S. Smith. Division—For, 88. Against, 105.
6. Mon.—Adjournment. Motion (Ireland. Railway), Mr. J. [illegible].
   Naval Defence Bill. 2nd Reading. Debate adjourned.
7. Tues.—Ditto. Ditto. Division— For, 272. Against, 134.
8. Wed.—Tramways (London) Bill. Mr. Dixon-Hartland. 2nd Reading. Bill put off for six months.
   Universities (Scotland) Bill. Mr. [illegible]. 2nd Reading. Division—For, 176. Against, 140.

9. Thur.—Ways and Means. Budget Resolutions.
   Supply: Civil Service Estimates.
10. Fri.—Ditto. Ditto.
   Universities (Representation of). Motion, Mr. A. Robertson. Division— For, 155. Against, 217.
13. Mon.—Scotland, &c., Bill. Read 2°. Naval Defence Bill. Committee.
14. Tues.—Supply: Civil Service Estimates. Established Church in Wales. Motion, Mr. Dillwyn. Division—For, 222. Against, 208.
15. Wed.—Education (Wales) Bill. Mr. S. Smith. Read 2°.
16. Thur.—Perpetual Pensions. Motion, Mr. Bradlaugh. Division—For, 236. Against, 204.
   Customs, &c., Bill. Committee.

MAY (continued).

19. Fri.—Customs, &c., Bill. Committee.
    Naval Defence Bill, 3rd Reading. De-
        bate adjourned.
    House of Lords, Motion; Mr. Labouchere;
        Division—For, 160. Against, 304.
20. Mon.—Naval Defence Bill, 3rd Reading.
        Division—For, 162. Against, 101.
    Supply: Civil Service Estimates.
21. Tues.—Ditto.   Ditto.   ...
22. Wed.—Coal Duties (London) Bill, Mr. J.
        Pease, 2nd Reading. Division—For,
        284. Against, 104.
23. Thur.—Local Government (Scotland) Bill,
        2nd Reading. Debate adjourned.
24. Fri.—Ditto.   Ditto.
    Truck System; Motion, Mr. Pickersgill.
        Division—For, 55. Against, 122.

27. Mon.—Adjournment. Motion, Ireland
        (Evictions); Mr. W. O'Brien.
    Local Government (Scotland) Bill, 2nd
        Reading. Debate adjourned.
28. Tues.—Supply: Report.
29. Wed.—Poor Rate (Metropolis) Bill, Mr.
        Pickersgill, 2nd Reading. Division
        —For, 181. Against, 217.
30. Thur.—Local Government (Scotland) Bill,
        2nd Reading. Division—For, 236.
        Against, 111.
31. Fri.—Local Government (Scotland) Sup-
        plementary Provisions Bill. Read
        2°.
    Supply: Civil Service Estimates.
    Unwarranted Civil Servants (India)
        Motion, Sir R. Lethbridge. Division
        —For, 87. Against, 127.

JUNE.

3. Mon.—Light Railways (Ireland) Bill. Mr.
        A. Balfour. Read 2°.
    Supply: Civil Service Estimates.
    Board of Agriculture Bill. Mr. W. H.
        Smith. Read 1°.
4. Tues.—Supply: Civil Service Estimates.
    Elucidation. Motion, Mr. Flynn.
        Debate adjourned.
17. Mon.—Supply: Army Estimates.
18. Tues.—Supply: Navy and Army Esti-
        mates.
19. Wed.—Cruelty to Children Prevention
        Bill. Committee.
20. Thur.—Universities (Scotland) Bill.
        Read 3°.

21. Fri.—Supply: Army Estimates.
    Evictions (Ireland). Motion, Mr. J. E.
        Ellis. Division—For, 154. Against,
        198.
24. Mon.—Board of Agriculture Bill. Com-
        mittee.
    River Conservancy Bill. Second Reading.
        Division—For, 226. Against, 30.
25. Tues.—Adjournment. Motion, Mr. Channing.
    Universities (Scotland) Bill. Committee.
26. Wed.—Cruelty to Children, &c., Bill.
        Committee.
27. Thur.—Universities (Scotland) Bill.
        Committee.
30. Fri.—Ditto.   Ditto.
    Sale of Irish Estates. Motion, Mr. Lea.

JULY.

1. Mon.—Adjournment. Motion (arrest of
        Mr. W. O'Brien). Mr. Sexton.
    Universities (Scotland) Bill. Committee.
2. Tues.—Ditto.   Ditto.   To report.
3. Wed.—Cruelty to Children, &c., Bill.
        Committee. To report.
    Coal Duties (London) Bill. Committee.
4. Thur.—Prince Albert Victor and Princess
        Louise of Wales. Royal Messages.
        Select Committee appointed.
    Local Government (Scotland) Bill. Com-
        mittee.
5. Fri.—Ditto.   Ditto.
    Hop Industry. Motion, Mr. Brookfield.
        Select Committee appointed.
8. Mon.—Adjournment. Motion (arrest of
        Mr. O'Brien), ruled out of order by
        Mr. Speaker.
    Local Government (Scotland) Bill.
        Committee.
9. Tues.—Royal Grants. Nomination of
        Select Committee.
    Local Government (Scotland) Bill. Com-
        mittee.
10. Wed.—Cruelty to Children Bill, consi-
        dered.
    Intermediate Education (Wales) Bill.
        Committee.
11. Thur.—Local Government (Scotland)
        Bill. Committee.
12. Fri.—Ditto.   Ditto.
13. Mon.—Ditto.   Ditto.
14. Tues.—Ditto.   Ditto.

15. Wed.—Universities (Scotland) Bill. Con-
        sidered.
16. Thur.—Tithe Rentcharge, &c., Bill.
        Mr. Secretary Matthews, 2nd Reading.
        Division—For, 224. Against, 131.
18. Fri.—Adjournment. Motion (Magistrates,
        Ireland). Mr. Cameron.
    Light Railways (Ireland) Bill. 2nd
        Reading.
    Motion (midnight debate (Sir W. Lawson),
        not put by Mr. Speaker.
    Merchant Shipping, &c., Bill. Con-
        sidered.
21. Mon.—Local Government (Scotland) Bill.
        Considered.
22. Tues.—Ditto.   Ditto.
23. Wed.—Ditto.   Ditto.
24. Thur.—The Royal Grants. Debate on
        going into Committee. Adjourned.
25. Fri.—Ditto.   Ditto.   Division on
        Mr. Labouchere's Amendment. For,
        118. Against, 398.
28. Mon.—Ditto. Committee. Division on
        Mr. J. Morley's Amendment—For,
        134. Against, 398. Resolutions re-
        ported.
29. Tues.—Royal Grants. Bill read 1°.
    Universities (Scotland) Bill. Considered.
    Post Office Sites Bill. Read 1°.
31. Thur.—Universities (Scotland) Bill. Read
        3°.
    Infectious Houses Notification Bill.
        Read 1°.

AUGUST.

1. Thurs.—Mr. Deputy-Speaker took the Chair under S.O. No. 1. Adjournment. Motion (Mr. Tomey's ...), Mr. ... Prince of Wales's Children Bill, Committee.
2. Fri.—Prince of Wales's Children Bill, Committee. Council of India Bill, Read 3°.
5. Mon.—Prince of Wales's Children Bill, Read 3°. Supply: Education Vote.
6. Tues.—Supply: Civil Service Estimates.
7. Wed.—Ditto. Ditto.
8. Thurs.—Ditto. Ditto.
9. Fri.—Ditto. Ditto.
12. Mon.—Tithe Rent-charge Bill, Committee. Debate on Instruction thereto.
13. Tues.—Tithe Rent-charge Bill, Committee.
14. Wed.—Tithe Rent-charge Bill, Committee. Supply: Civil Service Estimates.

15. Thurs.—Supply: Civil Service Estimates.
16. Fri.—Tithe Rent-charge, &c., Bill, Withdrawn. Supply: Civil Service Estimates.
17. Sat.—Ditto. Ditto.
19. Mon.—Light Railways (Ireland) Bill, Considered, Read 3°. Supply: Civil Service Estimates.
20. Tues.—Ditto. Ditto.
21. Wed.—Ditto. Ditto.
22. Thurs.—Ditto. Ditto.
23. Fri.—Ditto. Ditto.
24. Sat.—Supply, Report. Appropriation Bill, Read 1°.
26. Mon.—Technical Instruction Bill, Committee. Appropriation Bill, Read 2°.
27. Tues.—Appropriation Bill, Committee. East India, Financial Statement. Technical Instruction Bill, Considered.
28. Wed.—Appropriation Bill, Read 3°. Technical Instruction Bill, Considered.
30. Fri.—Prorogation.

SESSION OF 1890.

CHAPTER XXII.

DEATH OF MR. BIGGAR.

Opening Day—Privilege—A Stranger in the House—Mr. Parnell—The Duke of Fife—The Parnell Commissioners' Report—Mr. Pyne's Watch—Death of Mr. Biggar—"What's That?"—Major O'Gorman—Mr. Parnell—The Four-hours' Speech—Reaction—Biggar *père et fils*—Mr. Biggar and the Admiral.

Feb. 11.—Opening Day. THE attendance of members of the House of Commons on the barren ceremony of the opening of Parliament by Commission is gradually falling away, and to-day there was a more than usually beggarly array. This was made up for two hours later, when lobby and House were crowded. Everyone was asking whether the motion on the breach of privilege would come off, and if so in what circumstances. It is to be moved by Sir W. Harcourt, and characterises the letter published in the *Times* last April (purporting to have been written by Mr. Parnell, but proved to have been forged by Pigott) "a false and scandalous libel, and a breach of privilege of the House."

Thus it came to pass that, except for the crowded benches and the teeming excitement, matters progressed for a couple of hours as if nothing particular were to the fore, and as if by-and-bye the House would be lulled by the platitudes of the mover and seconder of the Address. The front Opposition bench had mustered in full force, only Mr. Gladstone tarrying on the way. At five o'clock, when the dreary process of balloting for motions had been going forward for half an hour, the echo of a prolonged cheer was heard in the precincts of the House. This was from the serried multitude at the gates of Palace Yard, who had waited all the afternoon to greet Mr. Gladstone, and were rewarded by seeing him drive down in an open barouche.

Mr. Parnell was early in his place, looking much better than before the recess. Lord Randolph Churchill was also back, bringing his Licensing Bill with him. Mr. Labouchere sat watchful at the corner seat below the gangway, and there was quite a fight for the opposite seat vacated by Mr. Chaplin, who presently took his seat on re-election on acceptance of office as Minister of Agriculture. Mr. William O'Brien was also in the House, but he took up a position on a back bench, and was not observed till he rose to give notice of a motion, when he was loudly cheered from below the gangway. Sir William Harcourt came and went, moving solemnly to and from his place on the front Opposition bench, but his appearance gave rise to no demonstration. Mr. Gladstone, on the contrary, was hailed with hearty cheers from the Opposition.

On the other side Mr. Balfour is still the favourite, as was shown by the cheering that greeted his entrance. Mr. Joseph Chamberlain arrived long before four o'clock, full of pleasant reminiscences of his going down to Egypt. He and Sir Henry James solely represented the Dissentient Liberals on the front Opposition bench, and Sir Henry, coming in late, found uncomfortably little room. There is already evident a determined indisposition on the part of Mr. Gladstone's colleagues to put themselves to any inconvenience to find room in the centre of their camp for allies of the Government.

Privilege.   Sir W. Harcourt's speech in moving his resolution on the privilege question was in his more serious Parliamentary style. There was an expectation in the crowded House that he would enliven the debate by some of his sharp thrusts. But he was apparently weighted by the seriousness of the occasion, and resisted the temptation that sometimes besets him to raise a laugh. He was listened to throughout with engrossed attention on the Conservative side, and was encouraged by frequent cheers from the Opposition. Perhaps the most effective passage in a speech that lasted nearly three-quarters of an hour was the picture he presented to the House of the *Times*, instead of libelling an Irish member, having made an accusation of similar import against either Mr. Smith or the Chancellor of the Exchequer, timing its attack for the morning of a debate ending in a vote

of confidence in the Government.   How, he asked, would the
House of Commons have acted in such circumstances ?   That
shot went right home.

As frequently happens when the Government are in a
tight place, Sir John Gorst was put forward to deliver them.
He was less successful than usual, but, as Mr. Gladstone
generously said, he had done his best in a bad case.   How
bad it was was testified to by the fact that so trained and
able a debater gravely argued two points: the first that the
motion of Sir William Harcourt was too late, the second
affirming that it was too early.   Sir John moved an amendment, declaring that the House declined to treat as a breach
of privilege the publication of the letters and the comments
thereupon.

A stranger in the House.   The Ministerialists listening to Sir John Gorst
knew how bad a case they had, and welcomed
with disproportionate hilarity a little incident that varied the
gravity of the occasion.   This was the appearance of a mouse,
which darted from the Bar towards the centre of the House,
and then, frightened by the cries the intrusion drew forth,
harked back, stumbling against Mr. Bond, the member for
East Dorset, who happened to be standing by the Cross
Benches.   Mr. Bond is one of the most imposing figures in
Parliament, and the spectacle of the hon. member jumping
up into the air, affrighted at the attack made upon him,
convulsed the House with laughter, and for several minutes
the grave debate was interrupted by this trivial incident.

Mr. Gladstone spoke with all his customary force and
cogency, undaunted by the unwonted circumstance of almost
empty benches.

Mr. Parnell.   After this the House emptied, not to be kept
together even by Mr. Balfour's speech, which
seemed to portend the sudden close of the debate.   It was
not till half-past eleven, when Mr. Parnell rose, that the
benches once more filled.   Mr. Parnell made an impressive
speech, full of dramatic force, unassisted by gesture or uplifted voice.   He concluded by moving that the word " forged "
should precede " letters " in the amendment of Sir John Gorst.

Mr. Smith, rising to the situation with quite unexpected
readiness and adroitness, accepted this amendment, frankly
and fully declaring the detestation of himself and his party
of the tactics in which the *Times* had so disastrously failed.
The division took place just before midnight, Sir John
Gorst's amendment (as amended by Parnell) being of course
carried, but by a significantly reduced majority, 260 voting
for it and 212 against.

It was now too late to proceed with the Address, which
for the first time in Parliamentary history stood over un-
touched on the first night of the Session.

**Feb. 14.—The
Duke of Fife.** The Duke of Fife has passed an interesting,
and more or less agreeable, evening. At half-
past four o'clock, robed in scarlet and ermine, he was one of
a quaint procession in which the Prince of Wales played a
part, whereby he was re-introduced to the House of Lords in
his new dignity as Duke. An hour later he was sitting in
mufti in the Peers' Gallery of the House of Commons listening
to Mr. Labouchere, who, in his peculiarly frank manner, was
discussing and criticising the Duke's connection with a com-
mercial undertaking in South Africa. As Earl of Fife the
Duke has held a seat in the Lords since, in 1885, he was
created a Peer of the United Kingdom; but in the House of
Lords there is a considerable difference between an Earl and
a Duke, and, coming to his legislative duties in his new style,
the Queen's grandson-in-law was received with a certain
ceremony not lacking in grotesqueness.

As no one knew what was in store the House of Lords was
nearly empty. The first intimation of the event was the appearance of a little procession entering from the Bar. Under their
disguise of scarlet cloaks slashed with ermine were presently
recognised the Prince of Wales, the Duke of Westminster,
and the Duke of Norfolk. Behind them walked Black Rod
and Garter King-of-Arms. This august body had evidently
in charge the new Duke, who was also hidden behind the
folds of his peer's cloak. The novice, walking between the
Prince of Wales and the Duke of Westminster, advanced
towards the woolsack, on which reposed the classic and
graceful figure of the Lord Chancellor. Halting a few paces off

the four peers, putting on their three-cornered hats, solemnly
lifted them three times in salute of the Lord Chancellor, who,
with equal gravity, thrice lifted his. Not a word passed, and
the procession started off again. This time it made a tour of
the Clerk's table, reaching the bench on which dukes are privileged to sit. The four peers, taking their seats here, once
more turned towards the Lord Chancellor, and again gravely
three times raised their hats. Each time they did it the Lord
Chancellor raised his, the whole procession being comically
reminiscent of an essay in semaphore signalling.

This done, the Prince of Wales' son-in-law, the Duke of
Westminster, and the Duke of Norfolk, with Black Rod and
Garter King-of-Arms still in attendance, marched forth and
disappeared through the doorway. Presently the Prince of
Wales, unrobed, came back, and, seating himself on the woolsack, chatted with the Lord Chancellor, probably congratu-
lating him on the graceful manner with which he had achieved
his share in the ceremony.

The Parnell
Commissioners'
Report.

Shortly after the House met this afternoon Mr.
Parnell put the expected question to the First
Lord of the Treasury. He asked Mr. Smith
what action Her Majesty's Government intended to take with
respect of the Report of the Special Commission.

Mr. Smith's reply was awaited with profound interest.
He briefly pointed out that the report had been placed in the
hands of Ministers, only at ten o'clock last night, and that
they had not had an opportunity of determining the proper
course to take. There was a dead silence after this reply—an
awkward pause. There was a half expectation that Mr. Gladstone, intently listening, would break in, but after a moment's
hesitation he leaned back in his seat, evidently accepting the
answer as reasonable. By Monday, however, Ministers will have
had full opportunity of considering their position, and a fresh
opportunity will be afforded them of stating their intentions.

It was noted that Mr. Smith, in his brief reply to Mr.
Parnell, was particular in intimating that Her Majesty's
Government did not occupy any privileged position in respect
of early knowledge of the purport of the report. That is literally true, and it is a pleasant thing to know. The manuscript

of the report was sent to the Home Secretary, and he forthwith despatched it to the printers. Proofs were supplied to the three judges, who were placed in direct communication with the printers. Mr. Smith was, I believe, most punctilious in arranging that the distribution of copies of the report should be made to Ministers exactly on the same terms as to other members of the House. As a matter of fact, in the hurly-burly that took place at the door of the Vote Office last night, when at ten o'clock the first batch of Blue-books arrived, more than one Minister figured struggling for a copy. There was no more intensely interested reader of the Blue-book in the House than Mr. Smith, as he sat on the Treasury Bench a little after ten o'clock with the prized volume in his hands, eagerly looking over the pages.

Feb. 17.—Mr. Pyne's watch. Bearing on the question of the manner of the death of Mr. Pyne, member for Waterford (who disappeared from the deck of the Holyhead packet-boat, and was drowned), I hear a curious story. Just before starting for Holyhead he went to a colleague in the House of Commons and handed him his watch, asking him to take care of it for him. The member was puzzled at this request, but accepted the commission. When news came of poor Pyne's disappearance, what was doubtless his original intention was carried out, and the watch was forwarded to his wife. On the dial there was roughly engraved the words:

" Pay no rent."

This was one of Mr. Pyne's original devices, akin to his famous exploits in his castle. Whenever in troublesome times any of his poor neighbours came to him for advice as to what they should do in face of a demand for rent, Pyne would shake his head.

"I cannot give you advice on this subject," he said, "because Mr. Balfour says it is illegal. But I'll tell you what I'll do, I will show you what time of day it is"; and holding out his watch, the inquiring tenant read upon it the admonitory legend.

Feb. 19.—Death of Mr. Biggar. The announcement of the death of Mr. Biggar, which reached the House of Commons shortly after it met this afternoon, has created a deep and painful sensation. Probably there are not more than a dozen members in the House whose sudden removal would have given a profounder shock. For sixteen years the member for Cavan has been a familiar figure at Westminster, and last year his personality gained a wider circle of acquaintances through his daily appearance in the court of the Parnell Commission. There is something of surprise to find how strongly he was liked, and how sincerely he was respected, even by his political adversaries. There was a time when his uprising was the signal for an outburst of yells and howls. He lived that down, and had come to be regarded as doubtless oddly-mannered, but as a man of shrewd judgment, untiring industry, kindly heart, and unpurchasable integrity.

It chanced that his very last appearance in the House was in a prominent position. Just on the stroke of midnight he walked up to the table as one of the tellers in the division on Mr. Parnell's amendment to the Address, and at six o'clock this morning he was lying dead in his bedroom at Clapham. Angina pectoris was the immediate cause of his death—a disease of which symptoms had only recently manifested themselves. Before Parliament met, he had been staying at Bath, whither he had gone for the relief of some bronchial disorder. He was at the post of duty as soon as the Speaker took the chair, and stuck at it in spite of many warnings. Last week he more than once complained of a pain in his chest—a circumstance he attributed to the prevalence of east winds. Dr. Kenny, passing him in the lobby last night, and casting upon him a kindly professional eye, remarked how ill he was looking. He took him off to a quiet room and subjected him to such examination as was possible. He warned him that he was in a bad way, and advised him to leave London for at least a couple of months' rest. Mr. Biggar said he would "think about it," but Dr. Kenny subsequently saw Mr. Parnell, and urged him to use his influence with Mr. Biggar to get him away. It was quite hopeless to endeavour to get him to leave the House before the division. So he stayed, "told," in company with his friend and colleague, Dick Power, and went home saying he felt better.

At six o'clock this morning, his landlady, hearing him

breathe heavily, went into his room, and, finding him very ill, run out for help.   When she came back he was dead.

"What's that?"   County Cavan gave Mr. Biggar to Parliament at the General Election of 1874, and through the greater part of that year he sat silent, but observant.   Rising late in the Session to put a supplementary question to a Minister, Mr. Disraeli, startled by his harsh voice and his odd Ulster accent, looked up and curiously regarded him through his eye-glass.

"What's that?" he drawled to Lord Barrington, with an air of affected surprise, as if he had seen seated in the Irish quarter an ourang-outang, or some other strange creature.

After a while the House grew more familiar with Mr. Biggar, his voice, his manner, his ways, and his waistcoat—this last a fearsome garment, which, at a distance, might be taken for sealskin, but was understood to be of native manufacture. Later, when the member for Cavan had established his fame and position, Mr. Disraeli knew only too well what "that" was.   For a whole Session Mr. Biggar flitted to and fro on the skirts of his party, nominally owning the gentle leadership of Mr. Butt, and having, as yet, no fixed policy, nor any close companion.

Major O'Gorman.   In the beginning of the Session of 1875 he was attracted by the potentialities that lingered around Major O'Gorman.   Certainly after dinner the Major would go further than any man in the direction of defying the Speaker and flouting the fetish of Parliamentary decorum. The first manifestation of that Obstruction which has since played so important a part in Parliamentary history was noted in the closing months of the Session of 1874.   At that period a Coercion Act was thought so little of, that, being passed only for a year, it was included in the Expiring Acts Continuance Bill, an omnibus measure into which all kinds of matter-of-course Bills are annually shovelled.   The first stand made by the Irish Party was against this procedure, and it was thought a signal victory when Mr. Disraeli gave an undertaking that in future the annual Coercion Bill should have a place all to itself, and should be brought in early in the Session.

In accordance with this pledge, it was introduced early in the Session of 1875 and, in the month of March, Obstruction, as an organised system, manifested itself. Its organiser was Joseph Gillis Biggar, and for a while his forces consisted chiefly of Major O'Gorman. Mr. Biggar took to challenging divisions at unexpected moments, and to see him walking up the floor of the House, co-teller with the massive major, was a picture that excelled all possible travesty.

Mr. Parnell.   It was not till April, 1875, that Mr. Parnell took his seat in the House of Commons as member for Meath. At this time the Irish Party were thoroughly roused. They had begun to feel their power, even though a hopeless minority. They were always beaten in divisions, Liberals and Conservatives joining in the majority. They were, moreover, weakened by internecine conflict. Mr. Butt, steeped in the traditions of Parliament, fretted and fumed when he saw Parliamentary usages trodden down by the elephantine Major, egged on by Mr. Biggar. His authority was still acknowledged. There were meetings of the party at which he presided, and at which resolutions were submitted and agreed to. But Mr. Biggar, pulling the strings to which the Major danced, was slowly but surely gaining the ascendancy. He at least knew what he wanted, and how it was to be obtained.

He was lacking in many of the personal qualifications that go to make a leader, and in truth he had no ambition to figure as such. He would attach himself to anyone in whatever subordinate position, if only the combination would work to the end of preventing the majority in a Saxon Parliament from trampling on the liberties of Ireland. He associated himself with Major O'Gorman *faute de mieux*; but when the tall, pale, reticent, Cambridge-bred, wholly un-Irish young man, whom Meath had sent to the support of Mr. Butt, took his seat, Mr. Biggar quickly recognised in him the long-sought instrument. It was a strange combination, odder even than that first formed between the dwarf and the giant.

The Four-hours' Speech.   Mr. Parnell entered Parliament just in time to hear Mr. Biggar's historic four-hours' speech. This was delivered on the motion to go into Committee on what was called the Peace Preservation (Ireland) Bill. The member for Cavan moved a hostile amendment. The motion came on at five o'clock, at the conclusion of questions. Mr. Biggar promptly rose from a seat below the gangway, presenting himself to the view of the House from behind a barricade of Blue-books. There was nothing to indicate a prospect of anything out of the way. By this time members had grown accustomed to the interposition of the member for Cavan, and when he rose they took their ordinary course of leaving the House.

Looking in an hour later they found him still on his legs, with more or less coherence connecting long extracts from his collection of Blue-books. An hour later he was still talking; at half-past seven he read through from preamble to schedule a long Act of Parliament. At eight o'clock he was interrupted by a motion to count the House.

If the House could be counted out that would suit his purpose as well as anything else, his object being simply to interpose delay in the passing of the Coercion Act. He had not for hours seen more than ten or twenty members in the House. He had no personal knowledge of the impatient crowd outside. It might be a near thing. Suppose the Whips succeeded in driving in thirty-nine members and Mr. Biggar stayed he would make the fortieth, and so the count would fail. As this flashed through his mind he thrust on to his

forehead the glasses, with the assistance of which he had been
laboriously reading extracts, dived down among his select
library of Blue-books, filled both arms with them, took his
glass of water in one hand and his hat in the other, and made
with all speed for the door.

But it was of no avail. Upwards of a hundred members
flocked in at sound of the bell, and Mr. Biggar had only just
time to get back to his place and resume his speech, which he
carried on till nine o'clock, having occupied the time of the
House four hours less ten minutes.

Reaction. This was the beginning of a series of escapades
which, whilst they endeared him to the people
of Ireland, made him fiercely hated in the House of Commons.
But he grinned his way through contumely, hitting out when
attacked, growing to be a power by reason of his absolute
contempt and disregard for the usages which guided the conduct of an ordinary member of Parliament. As the Sessions
rolled on, his eccentricities came, by imperceptible movements,
to be regarded with indulgent eye. Members knowing him
better learned that beneath his rough exterior beat a kindly
heart ; that his hand, though coarsely grained, was generous ;
that he was a faithful friend, an ardent lover of the nationality
to the advancement of whose cause he had given up his nights
and days. So it came to pass that he grew into the position
of primo favourite in the alien assembly it had once been his
delight studiously to insult, and when, to-day, news came of
his sudden death, every member, from the Speaker to the
stiffest Tory squire, mourned for the House's ancient enemy.

*Feb. 20.—Biggar
père et fils.* It is understood Mr. Biggar has left behind
him considerable property. In addition to his
own income, derived from a large and prosperous business, his
father, who died a few years ago, left him a considerable
legacy. A coolness sprang up between father and son at the
time when the member for Cavan was received into the fold
of the Catholic Church. Mr. Biggar, senior, was a strict
Presbyterian, and heard with horror of his son's apostacy.
The correspondence which passed between the two was cited
in the House of Commons at the time. Mr. Biggar, senior,

cut out from a newspaper the paragraph announcing his son's admission to the Church, and enclosed it with the following note:

"Dear Joseph,—Is this true?—Yours, J. B." Our Mr. Biggar wrote on the fly-sheet—

"Dear Father,—It is.—Yours truly, J. G. B."

After this the father threatened to disinherit the son, but before he died relented, and did nothing worse than cut him off with £40,000.

Feb. 21. — Mr. Biggar and the Admiral. Reference is made in one of the numerous biographical reminiscences current of Mr. Biggar to the famous waistcoat he wore in the Parliament of 1874-80, a garment that used to flash through the fray like the plumes of Henry of Navarre on another field of battle. At that time sealskin was much in vogue, and a friendly, not too inquisitive, eye might (at a distance) have thought Mr. Biggar was in the fashion. The substance, however, was, as recorded, not sealskin, but a rough imitation. Whatever it was, Mr. Biggar was very proud of it, and when he threw back his coat and got his thumbs well in the arm-holes of his waistcoat Her Majesty's Government knew very well they were in for a bad hour, peradventure a repetition of the famous four hours.

Whilst everyone was susceptible to the subtle influence of this waistcoat, its generous display always had a curiously irritating effect upon another scarcely less famous character of the Disraelian Parliament. This was Sir Wm. Edmonstone, member for Stirlingshire, better known as "The Admiral," who in those days was anchored in deep water just astern of the Treasury bench. One night in the Session of 1878, at a time when Russia was at the gates of Constantinople and the British fleet had been ordered to the Dardanelles, Mr. Biggar came very near being the death of the irascible old salt.

"It's my opinion, Mr. Speaker," he said, stroking his waist-coat upwards till every hair stood forth with added aggressiveness, "that before many days have passed we shall hear that the British fleet has struck its colours, and is being towed by a couple of Russian men-of-war through the Bosphorus."

The Admiral broke forth into a very fusilade of groans and

snorts, violently fanning himself with his copy of the Orders, and tossing about from side to side, threatening every moment to break away from his anchorage, Mr. Biggar meanwhile audibly chuckling and watching him with maliciously gleaming eyes.

CHAPTER XXIII.

THE COMMONS AND THE SPECIAL COMMISSION.

The Commons and the Commission—Mr. Smith's Sermon—Mr. Gladstone's Speech—Lawyers in the House—Sir Henry James—Mr. Asquith—Sir R. Webster—Sir W. Harcourt.

March 1.—The Commons and the Commission. IT was half-past four when Mr. W. H. Smith rose to move his resolution declaring that "Parliament having constituted a Special Commission to inquire into the charges and allegations made against certain Members of Parliament and other persons, and the Report of the Commissioners having been presented to Parliament, this House adopts the Report, and thanks the Commissioners for their just and impartial conduct in the matters referred to them; and orders that the said Report be entered on the journals of this House."

He had a splendid audience, the House thronged from floor to ceiling. Mr. Gladstone was early in his place, and was supported by a full muster of his colleagues. Of the Dissentient Liberals, only Mr. Chamberlain sat out the earlier portion of the debate. Sir Henry James, who was in his place at question-time, curiously enough withdrew when Mr. Smith rose. Other counsel engaged in the great case were in their places, the Attorney-General on the Treasury bench, taking notes in a sort of duet with Sir Charles Russell, who sat by Mr. Chamberlain on the front bench. Behind sat Mr. Lockwood; and Mr. Asquith, profiting by the temporary withdrawal of Mr. Labouchere, secured for himself the favourable position of the corner seat on the front bench below the gangway.

Mr. Smith's
sermon.

Mr. Smith, to do him justice, is not accustomed to put himself forward on great occasions when speeches are to be made from the front bench. To-night his prominence was inevitable, and everybody sympathised with him in the ordeal. He had written out his speech, a tremendous bundle of manuscript, in foolscap sheets. On commencing his task it seemed physically to weigh him down. At times his solemnity was so profound that he became inaudible. He got on better when, finally abandoning all attempt to observe the rule which forbids speeches to be read, he turned to his manuscript and read boldly on, openly turning over the folios under the very nose of the Speaker. The House, though now and then it broke in upon his solemn adjuration with merry laughter, was very patient, sitting out the full hour with all the decorum born of the associations of the occasion. Nothing has been heard in recent years in the House of Commons so like a good country rector reading a prosy sermon as Mr. Smith's contribution to the debate on the report of the Parnell Commission.

Mr. Gladstone's
speech.

Mr. Gladstone, who followed, spoke for an hour and forty minutes at the highest level of his argumentative force and matchless eloquence. The only sign of his eighty years was manifested by his voice, which midway in the discourse began to show tendency to failure. But he went on quite unmindful of what seemed to listeners a painful effort, and by-and-bye, as often happens, his voice miraculously came back, and he gave his glowing peroration with undiminished vigour. It is difficult at this time of day to say anything fresh about the Parnell Commission or its Report. It may not appear, on a careful study of Mr. Gladstone's speech, that he had overcome this transcendent difficulty. What he did was—by common consent not less heartily expressed on the Conservative than on the Liberal benches—to put all the points in new position and marshal them with unequalled skill and power. Among the audience was Mr. Cunynghame, the Secretary of the Commission of Judges. He is a man who has heard more of the case than any human being who has survived its recital. He is also not open to the charge of being on the side which Mr. Gladstone to-night advocated. I met him in the lobby after the speech, and asked him what he thought of it. " Magnificent," he said ; " I shall never forget it."

Perhaps the most striking passage of a great speech was the peroration, with its subtly conceived notion of appealing to the Conservatives not as a party, but as individuals. The serried ranks sat silent as Mr. Gladstone, leaning across the table, in beseeching voice begged each man to place himself in the place of Mr. Parnell, the victim of this frightful outrage, and to give his judgment so that it might bear the scrutiny of the heart and conscience, as each man betook himself to his chamber and was still.

The audience at this moment was solemnly silent. As Mr. Gladstone resumed his seat it roused itself with a mighty cheer and with one accord made for the doors.

Amid the bustle of departure the Speaker's voice was hardly heard as he recited the terms of Mr. Gladstone's amendment, which were to leave out from Mr. Smith's resolution all the words after " House," in order to add the words, " deems it to be a duty to record its reprobation of the false charges of the gravest and most odious description, based on calumny and on forgery, which have been brought against members of this House, and particularly against Mr. Parnell ; and, while declaring its satisfaction at the exposure of these calumnies, this House expresses its regret for the wrong inflicted and the suffering and loss endured, through a protracted period, by reason of these acts of flagrant iniquity."

March 7.—Lawyers in the House. This is the fifth night of the debate on the Parnell Commission Report, and, in accordance with the rules of ordinary dynamics, it ought to have gained increased force. On the contrary, it has grown so lifeless that before nine o'clock the House was counted out. With the exception of Mr. Asquith's speech the debate had not, through the night, reached the level of exhilaration.

Sir Henry James. Last night the Attorney-General spoke for two hours. To-night Sir Henry James, not to be lacking in respect to the head of the Bar, closely imitated his learned friend in the volume of his speech. Though he did not remain at the table quite so long, it is probable

Sir Henry exceeded in number of words the prodigious commentary of the Attorney-General. For one thing, Sir Richard Webster's speech partook of the character of conversation. Two hours were occupied in its delivery, but he had not all the talking to himself. Sir Charles Russell made various contributions, and the Irish members constantly interrupted, leading the Attorney-General into fresh lines of thought, or at least into new mazes of speech. Though in Sir Henry James's case interruptions were not lacking, he had, by comparison, a fuller share of the time, and made the most of it. Some passages in his speech were delivered with a velocity that not only mocked the efforts of the shorthand writer, but made him unintelligible to the listener. At the close of Sir Charles Russell's speech yesterday—an effort which marked a new departure, and placed the great advocate in the ranks of Parliamentary orators—Sir Charles's voice faltered, and he was plainly possessed by an emotion that was communicated to his audience. Sir Henry James's speech was not lacking in evidences of solemn feeling, but the manifestations were, perhaps, a little too monotonously recurrent. There was a mechanical ebb and flow about the business that deprived it of due effect. "Sermonettes" Lord Cavan, in his extremity coining a word, calls Sir Henry James's Parliamentary disquisitions. The word, if it means anything, implies brevity, and that was not a quality Sir Henry thought proper to impart to speech.

Mr. Asquith.   When at length he concluded, and Mr. Asquith presented himself to carry on the debate, something like a feeling of blank despair settled over the benches. It was lightened by the knowledge that Mr. Asquith is rising to the first rank as a Parliamentary debater. But, after all, he is a lawyer, and on this fifth night of the debate the House of Commons has begun to recognise the truth underlying the paradox about the possibility of having too much of a good thing. It would be hard to say why, as a rule, lawyers are not successful, or at least are not popular, House of Commons debaters. It would be reasonable to expect precisely the reverse. A trained advocate endowed with natural gifts, strengthened and polished by daily training appears to be the man of all others who should succeed in the Parliamentary arena. As a matter of common fact, daily verified, and standing forth in lurid light in connection with this debate on the Report of the Parnell Commission, what Mr. Disraeli used to call "gentlemen of the long robe" are grievously handicapped in the race for Parliamentary pre-eminence. It was said of Canning by a great living statesman, who certainly is not suspected of tendency to harsh judgment in the matter, that with all his brightness, humour, and fancy, he never said in House of Commons debate a good or a memorable thing. This kind of dual life is lived at this day by some of the principal men at the Bar. In court, eloquent, brilliant, resourceful, and successful; in the House of Commons, prosy, artificial, tiresome, unconvincing.

Sir R. Webster. Sir Richard Webster deservedly enjoys the personal esteem of all who know him, and has, unaided, won his way to the highest place at the Bar by sterling ability. Yet the fondest fancy of the foolishest friend could not take delight in his speech of yesterday. No one hearing Sir Henry James in days past address a jury, or listening now to his sparkling conversation, could conceive him so dull, as far as influence upon Parliamentary debate is concerned, so vapid as he was to-night.

Sir W. Harcourt. It is curious in this connection to note how a man drifting away from the practice of law succeeds with increasing force in becoming an acceptable Parliamentary debater. Sixteen or seventeen years ago Sir William Harcourt ranked as a lawyer—was certainly appointed to the Solicitor-Generalship. In those days he and Sir Henry James hunted together, the quarry being Mr. Gladstone, the happy hunting ground, the front bench below the gangway. When their lively opposition had been blunted by appointment to office, it seemed for a while that Sir William Harcourt might sink into a mere Solicitor-General, with prospect of promotion to the headship of the Bar, and final tranquil transference to the Bench. Had his style been in fuller accord with the vastness and profundity of his legal knowledge, that would doubtless have been his career. Brought into prominence by his brief tenure of a seat on the Treasury bench, he enjoyed opportunities of catching the Speaker's eye, of which he availed himself with increasing success. Once become an accepted favourite in Parliamentary debate, he instinctively turned aside from the shadow of the courts of law. When he took office again, it was no longer as a Law Officer of the Crown, and it is quite an age since anyone alluded to him in debate as the right honourable " and learned " gentleman.

While Sir William Harcourt's career appears to prove that an acceptable House of Commons speaker does not usually possess the qualities that go to make a successful practitioner at the Bar, and while Sir Henry James's case puts the truth in another way, the thesis is further supported by the rarity of cases in which a great lawyer has been also a Parliamentary debater of the first, or even of the second, rank. In recent times the Conservative and the Liberal Party have each furnished an exception to this rule. One was Sir Hugh Cairns, the other Sir Alexander Cockburn. Lord Coleridge, whatever success he may have achieved on the Bench, is not remembered at Westminster as a great debater. Baron Dowse, on the contrary, has left behind him cherished memories. His occasional sharp, shrewd observations from the Bench, and his always sparkling humour, recall many occasions when, as the Attorney-General for Ireland, he illumined debate

with bright touches. In later times Lord Herschell is a rare
and supreme example of the combination of the qualities
which secure success at the Bar and command it in the House
of Commons. Of possibly equal promise is Mr. Asquith,
whose speeches in the House of Commons are entirely devoid
of that indefinite something that marks the address of the
lawyer.

CHAPTER XXIV

A MAIDEN SPEECH IN THE LORDS.

New Peer's Maiden Speech—Eloquent and Incomprehensible—A Rare Resolution—The Premier's Strategy—Back again.

March 13.—New
peer's maiden
speech.

EXACTLY a week ago the serenity of the House
of Lords was broken by a strange apparition.
The business of the sitting was practically over.
It had lasted fully fifteen minutes, and their lordships, like
unharnessed athletes, were stretching their weary frames
preparatory to retiring. The Lord Chancellor had half risen
to put the question of the adjournment, when a plaintive voice
was heard from the cross benches, and their lordships glancing
in that direction beheld an unfamiliar figure—a white-haired
gentleman, with pallid face just flushed by the unwonted
excitement of oratory, a tall, swaying figure, with a quaint
habit of occasionally turning his back upon the audience and
addressing an imaginary friend in the recess of the strangers'
gallery. Whispered inquiry at length made known the fact
that the new-comer was Lord Teynham, a peer but recently
inducted. The name was unfamiliar in the House, for the late
holder of the title, the sixteenth baron, born before the century,
had, previous to his decease, long remained in seclusion.

This was evidently the new peer's maiden speech, a circumstance that lent special interest to the occasion, and their
lordships, always courteous, bent forward to pay due attention
to the novice. It was observed that the new peer had chosen
the locality for his *début* with great skill. In the Lords the
cross benches stand boldly out athwart the seats on which are

drawn up the contending hosts of Liberals and Conservatives.
A member speaking thence not only has in full view the
stately figure of the Lord Chancellor, but, slightly turning
his head right or left, stands face to face, eye to eye, with
his peers.   Lord Teynham, inspired by the occasion, rose to
its fullest height.   In truth, the height proved so dizzy that
his audience could not, with most diligent effort, follow him.
Now and then, eagerly straining attention, they seemed to be
on the very verge of catching at least the drift of his remarks,
when suddenly the orator, drawing himself up to his full
height, thrusting his hands into his pockets, and throwing
back his head till his flashing eyes seemed to char the fretted
woodwork of the roof, swiftly turned on his heel, and the concluding portion of his sentence was addressed to the recesses
of the empty gallery at his back.

Eloquent and in-comprehensible.   Repetition of the word "Syria" favoured the
impression that the speech had something to do
with the Eastern Question, and this was conjecturally confirmed
by his personal address of fragmentary sentences to the Prime
Minister, who, like the rest of the House, sat in an attitude of
troubled attention.   The longer the new peer was on his legs
the more eloquent and incomprehensible he grew, and the more
excited in his gesticulations.   Just before him sat the Prince
of Wales, little dreaming how often the orator's arm swept in
perilous proximity to his head.   Other peers saw it and
trembled.   The subject was evidently growing upon the
orator, and no one could say whither it would carry him.
The most probable conclusion was that if it finally concentrated upon Lord Salisbury, he would be landed head first on
the bench where the prince sat.   Every time he came back to
the noble Marquis, he, sinking his voice to a tragic whisper,
and grasping with both hands the rail of the bench before
him, leaned over at perilous angle.   Anon, drawing himself
up to full height, closing his eyes, and forlornly shaking his
head, Lord Teynham uplifted his voice with a weird wailing,
that in a less self-possessed assembly would have made the
blood curdle.
    This strange scene went forward for a quarter of an hour,
noble lords uneasily moving in their seats and gazing askance

at each other. There were times when Lord Teynham remained in such protracted contemplation of the recesses of the strangers' gallery that it was assumed his oration was finished. But turning with swift motion he began again, his voice rising and falling like the soughing of the wind through a leafless forest. It was evident that something must be done, but who should do it?

Lord Granville looked across at the Leader of the House. The Marquis of Salisbury gazed for a moment hopefully on the Leader of the Opposition. In the Commons the solemnity of the scene would have been broken in upon in boisterous fashion. There would have been ironical cheering, noisy laughter, cries for the division, and then the swift application of the Closure. The more courtly breeding of the Lords prevented any such vulgar demonstration of impatience. Here and there a moderately young peer shuffled his feet, and one or two timidly coughed. But to the orator, aflame with his theme (whatever it might be), his audience seemed to sit entranced.

A rare resolution. Thus encouraged, the oration might have continued till Lord Teynham fell back in his seat physically exhausted, as Lord Chatham, speaking in the same assembly, had once done. The occasion was unprecedented, but happily the British race has born to it men who dare to make precedents. One of these happened to be seated on the Opposition benches in close proximity to his leader. The Earl of Camperdown, in addition to being a cornet in the Warwickshire Yeomanry Cavalry, carries in his veins the blood of Adam Duncan, who suppressed the mutiny at the Nore and destroyed the Dutch fleet at Camperdown. It is not for nothing that he bears on his shield the proud motto, *Secundis dubiisque rectus.* Rising now whilst his elders hesitated, he brusquely moved that "the noble lord be not heard."

Lord Teynham, resuming his seat on the interruption, sat for a moment literally gasping for breath at this quite unexpected turn of events. The Lord Chancellor hesitated to put the question, and, after an awkward pause, Lord Teynham, probably taking up his remarks at the point where they had been left, floated off once more, his voice having added to it a

tinge of deeper melancholy, in reproof of the hasty cutting-out
manœuvre into which Lord Camperdown had by hereditary
instincts been led. Lord Camperdown having failed, Lord
Teynham seemed master of the situation, and might go on for
another hour or so, impinging even on the sacred precincts of
dinner-time.

The Premier's strategy.   From this dire extremity the House was delivered by the happy strategy of the Leader.
Watching till Lord Teynham had resumed his favourite attitude, with his back to the wool-sack and his eyes dreamily
fixed on the strangers' gallery, the Premier moved that "the
House do now adjourn." The Lord Chancellor, with remarkable alacrity put the question, and when Lord Teynham,
roused by the bustle of departure, turned round—lo! the
benches were empty, and in the doorways he caught glimpses
of the fluttering garments of the hurrying peers.

This was all very well; but in spite of some drawbacks
Lord Teynham had so thoroughly enjoyed himself on the occasion of his maiden speech, that he determined to find
opportunity for supplementing it. He accordingly placed on
to-night's paper a notice of motion raising a point of order.
This was eagerly turned to by noble lords, hopeful that the
printed words would afford some clue to the mystery that still
lay dark over the memorable speech. The expectation was
only partially fulfilled. Last Friday Lord Granville, with the
exquisite courtesy and ready kindness which distinguish all
his acts, had endeavoured to relieve the House from embarrassment, and let Lord Teynham down gently, by pointing out
that it was not in order to bring forward a motion without
having given due notice. On this dictum Lord Teynham had
fastened, and the motion which stood in his name for to-night
proposed to add to the Standing Order some quaintly constructed sentences more or less indirectly bearing on the point
of giving notice.

Back again.   The new peer's fame had gone abroad, and when
this evening he rose, entrenched behind the
cross benches, he had an audience fuller than has been seen
since the night the Address was moved. Apparently he began

where he left off when interrupted by the abrupt conclusion of
the proceedings last Friday. In one sudden flash of connected speech the strained attention of the audience was rewarded by gaining some insight into the origin of the whole
affair. It would appear that what Lord Teynham had at
heart was to encourage Lord Salisbury by expression of his
approval of certain action taken by the Government in connection with a mission to Syria. That being all, where, he
asked, with scathing glare at Lord Camperdown, was the
necessity for him to give notice of his intention ?

"I might," he said, drawing himself up to fullest height
and holding out his hands with tragic gesture towards Lord
Salisbury, " have given formal notice of my intention of con-
gratulating the noble lord on his recovery from influenza."

The peers laughed cheerfully at this, grateful for a sentence
whose drift they could wholly gather. Encouraged by this
tribute of appreciation, Lord Teynham went on again, pouring
forth a flood of words eloquently cadenced and illustrated by
strikingly dramatic gestures. It was a pity the Bar was not
crowded with members of the House of Commons, who might
have learned a useful lesson by observing with what chivalrous
patience a body of English gentlemen, assembled for legislative
purposes, sat out this strange experience to the long-delayed
conclusion.

CHAPTER XXV.

BUDGET NIGHT.

Lord R. Churchill and the Conservative Party—Lord Cottesloe on Budget Night
—Reporters—Mr. Goschen's Dilemma—Discovery—Disaster—Mr. Disraeli's
Manchester Speech.

April 11.—Lord
R. Churchill and
the Conserva-
tive Party.
LORD RANDOLPH CHURCHILL'S slashing blows at
the Land Purchase Bill have cut the last strands
of the ties that bound him to his party. With
good Conservatives this one-time Leader is regarded with
something of the venomous personal hatred in which Mr. Gladstone used to be held during the Jingo fever, and which was

wont to hiss and splutter round Mr. Bright, till, in the closing years of his life, he accomplished what he once declared to be an impossible feat, and " turned his back upon himself."   The Conservatives hate Lord Randolph for divers reasons.   One is that his defection from their ordered ranks deprives them of a powerful force.   If he would only run in harness, giving up to party what he now wastes in isolated action, he would be an immense accession of power.   If he could only be depended upon he would be welcome to take the place that has never been filled since Disraeli died.   But the dream is hopeless.   As one of his old colleagues mournfully says, " One never knows where to have Randolph.   Whilst you are looking round for his assistance, it is ten to one he comes up from behind, boxes your ears or knocks you down."

There is some talk of Lord Randolph moving the rejection of the Bill on the second reading.   That would be another conclusion logically following on this onslaught.   But because a thing is logical it does not follow that Lord Randolph will accept it.   Rather the reverse.   Moreover, this curiously complex character has been discovered upon occasion to be lacking in courage.   He has come up to the attack with drums beating and colours flying, and just when another step forward would have brought him into actual conflict with his party, he has stepped back.   This was what happened in that memorable crisis of his political career when he was invited to contest the seat in Birmingham vacated by the death of Mr. Bright.   At the very last moment he shrank back, obedient to the order that had issued from Hatfield.   Had he carried out in the afternoon the resolution he had distinctly affirmed in the morning— appropriated the Birmingham seat and been returned to the House by the mandate of a great and populous constituency— he might have dictated his own terms to his friends the Ministers.   At the very last moment he yielded, beat an ignominious retreat, leaving Lord Salisbury and Mr. Chamberlain relieved and astonished at the victory.

April 17.—Lord Coleridge on Budget night. On some big nights in the Commons, when the benches on the floor are thronged and the galleries filled, the House is familiar with the cheery presence of the Prince of Wales seated over the clock in the Peers' Gallery. To-night, whilst Mr. Goschen was explaining his Budget scheme this favoured and prominent place was occupied by a little old gentleman, who through the longer period of Mr. Goschen's three hours' speech sat bolt upright, with pale set face turned towards the Treasury bench, intently listening. Once a year this face and figure are to be seen in the same place, drinking in, with eager, fascinated attention, the story of the Budget. When the century was still in its earliest prime Lord Cottesloe began to attend on Budget nights, though he was not then privileged to sit in the Peers' Gallery. Forty-six years ago he heard Sir Robert Peel proudly boast, as evidence of the immeasurable wealth and limitless prosperity of England, that the imposition of a single penny on the income-tax brought into the imperial exchequer the princely sum of £800,000. To-night he heard Mr. Goschen admit that every penny added to the income-tax means an additional revenue of £2,200,000.

It is a wide chasm bridged by these two epochs. To the attentive listener over the clock it was less than half a lifetime. Lord Cottesloe was born two years before the century, in the very year that General Bonaparte was at Aboukir. He was quite a young man when Waterloo was fought, and has seen the coming and going of many sovereigns since the First Napoleon sat on the throne of Charlemagne. Twice Secretary to the Treasury, once Secretary of State for War, Chief Secretary for Ireland before Mr. Balfour was born, he has personally known all the great Parliament men since Canning was Prime Minister. He has heard every one of the glowing speeches in which Mr. Gladstone has from year to year dealt with the national finances. He has heard Mr. Disraeli at length and Mr. Ward Hunt in brief. He plodded his way through Sir Charles Wood's Budget speech, and followed Mr. Lowe as he fumbled through his columns of figures, and, happily leaving them for a while, flashed forth into pointed speech. It is, in its way, a unique experience. Many men do odd things in search of deathless renown. Some fast for forty days; some swoop over Niagara in a tub; others go up in a balloon and come down in a parachute. Only Lord Cottesloe has heard the Budget speech annually delivered in the House of Commons through a course of fifty years, not missing a single Budget night.

Reporters.   What to-night seemed to interest the noble nonagenarian more than any other incident in the prolonged scene was the manner in which Mr. Goschen did not get his port wine.   In the brave days of old there was no embarrassing modesty in the matter of taking refreshment at the table of the House of Commons through the discharge of onerous duties.   Mr. Disraeli's honest tumbler of brandy-and-water was plainly in evidence during his Budget speeches, and if the scheme was intricate and the exposition prolonged there was no hesitation in replenishing it.   Mr. Ward Hunt, though he made the shortest speech on record in introducing his Budget had the assistance of a soda-water tumbler.   Mr. Gladstone was the first Chancellor of the Exchequer who prominently truckled to conventionality in this matter.   There was no secret about his sherry, with the egg beaten up.   But he temporised by bringing the compound down to the House in an uncompromising vessel which at a distance was always taken for a pomatum pot.   Had Lord Randolph Churchill held office long enough to find opportunity of making a Budget speech there is nothing in his history which justifies the suspicion that he would have displayed any embarrassment in the matter of taking necessary refreshment during the accomplishment of his task.

Mr. Goschen's   Mr. Goschen's position in this respect was, it
dilemma.   must be admitted, exceptional.   His Budget turned mainly on the drink question.   The financial year just closed had, as he frankly put it, been the most drunken year since the famous era of prosperity, 1874–5.   Out of a surplus of three millions and a quarter, two millions and a half was directly due to drink.   Some, he said, have rushed to the beer barrel, others to the spirit bottle, others to the decanter.   All classes seem to have combined in toasting the prosperity of the country—"a circumstance which must be deplored by all," said Mr. Goschen in a broken voice, as he thought of his magnificent surplus.

That was the keynote of his speech, cleverly struck to lead up to the concluding passages, in which he announced the re-imposition of the added duty on beer and the surtax on British and foreign spirits. How was he to preserve the proper attitude if, during bursts of cheering elicited by his appeals, he were observed refreshing himself out of a tumbler that obviously contained other liquid than water?

Such was the difficulty of the Chancellor of the Exchequer, a situation unparalleled in the long experience of Lord

THE BUDGET.

Cottesloe. But though sentiment is all very well, and self-sacrifice a commendable virtue, practical difficulties must be met in practical ways.

Fortunately there is an eminently practical man in Mr. Goschen's counsels. This is the Financial Secretary to the Treasury. Mr. Jackson knew that his chief had a three hours' speech to make, and recognised in it a task that might well test the strength of a more robust man. Knowing the purport of the Budget scheme, he recognised as keenly as anyone the peculiar difficulties of the situation.

But he resolved to face them.

When the Orders of the Day were reached and scouts were out in all directions hunting up Mr. Courtney, who was unaccountably caught napping, Mr. Jackson carelessly strolled in from behind the Speaker's chair, casually carrying a tumbler of dark liquid, which he placed on the table before himself. There are, of course, degrees of responsibility in these matters. Though it might not do for a Chancellor of the Exchequer, overweighted with a surplus swollen by the drink bill, full of moral reflections and stern resolutions, to be seen publicly sipping fruity port, the ban did not extend to the Financial Secretary to the Treasury.

There the glass remained for a while. Presently, when interest grew in the masterly expansion of the Chancellor's speech, and the thoughts of the crowded House were absorbed in speculation as to whether it would be Tea or the Income-tax, Mr. Jackson, leaning over and arranging the papers in front of him, accidentally, by almost imperceptible movements, moved the tumbler along till, closely nestled amid copies of the Orders, secure under the shadow of the brass-bound box and the imposing rows of volumes on Constitutional Law which fringe the table, it lay *perdu* in convenient contiguity to the left hand of the orator.

Mr. Goschen went on with a speech that raises still higher his reputation as a statesman and a financier. He had brought out in pregnant sentences the enormity of the national movement which had endowed him with his millions. Step by step, followed by the listening Senate, he had unravelled the mystery of the national ledger. So admirable was his arrangement of the multitudinous figures, so adroit his grouping of the powerful arguments, so masterful his command of the intricate subject, that it seemed quite an easy task to those who listened. But the strain was beginning to tell on the Minister. Sir William Dyke, kindly attentive, had brought him a glass of water, which he gratefully drank. Half an hour later Mr. Balfour arrived with another glass, which he set down in the customary place on the right-hand side of the box. Mr. Goschen drank again and was refreshed.

Discovery.   A quarter of an hour later, searching amongst the heap of papers on the left-hand of the box, his eye fell upon the tumbler filled nearly to the brim with the ruby elixir. There was a gleam in Mr. Goschen's eye which members opposite interpreted as a flash of natural exultation at his diplomatic triumph with Greece in the matter of the duty on currants. He made no other sign; but as he went on, sternly warning British claret manufacturers that they must not make too free use of currants, his left hand strayed downward towards the recess where the tumbler coyly lurked.

Disaster.   A smile of satisfaction overspread the kindly face of Mr. Jackson. His action was understood, and all would be well. But, alas! Mr. Goschen, his gaze fixed on the Opposition bench, missed the quarry. Instead of grasping the tumbler he knocked it over, and, amidst a scene of indescribable confusion, Mr. Jackson wildly mopped the table with ineffectual blotting-pads.

Lord Cottesloe, looking on, complacently reflected that, albeit a penny of the Income-tax yields nearly three times as much as it did in Peel's time, there were some incidents of a Budget speech better managed fifty years ago.

April 16. — Mr. Disraeli's Manchester speech.   It has frequently been stated with respect to a famous speech delivered by Mr. Disraeli in Manchester, more than twenty years ago, at the time when he was Chancellor of the Exchequer, that in the course of his oration he became evidently the worse for liquor, and that before he reached his peroration he was, not to put too fine a point upon it, decidedly drunk.

The other day I heard a contribution to the secret history of this remarkable incident which disposes of all doubt. The narrator is a member of the present House of Commons, a pillar of Conservatism in Lancashire, and was Mr. Disraeli's host on the occasion of his memorable visit. Before the Chancellor arrived in Manchester, his host, anxiously inquiring as to what the great man liked to eat and drink, learned that when he was addressing an audience he was particularly partial to white brandy, which, in addition to its other qualities, has an innocent appearance when displayed in a glass that must necessarily stand in full view of an audience. White brandy is a rare vintage on this side of the Channel, but the host succeeded in getting a couple of bottles.

When the night of the great meeting in the Free Trade Hall came he had a bottle of the brandy decanted and placed within reach of the orator. Disraeli poured out into the tumbler a pretty full allowance considering the character of the beverage, and, tasting it, smiled appreciatively. As he proceeded with his oration the tumbler rapidly emptied, observing which, the chairman, all unconscious of the true character of the liquid, filled up the tumbler again. Dizzy went on with his speech, and with what, apparently, was a glass of water. This also was emptied, the watchful chairman filling up the glass again, and Dizzy, warming with his speech and his brandy, gulped it down. When he concluded his speech he had also finished the bottle of brandy.

This is a story vouched for by the hon. member, and I would not venture to repeat it on less authority.

CHAPTER XXVI.

THE IRISH PARTY—OLD STYLE AND NEW

Mr. Gladstone in a Tight Place—Mr. Parnell at Fault—The "Old Parliamentary Hand"—Mr. Parnell's Indifference—The Irish Party; Old Style and New—McCarthy Downing—Delahunty—Captain Stacpoole—Mr. Biggar's Will.

April 24.—Mr. Gladstone in a tight place.   If Mr. Gladstone's right to carry the title "The Old Parliamentary Hand" had not long ago been established, it would have been assured to him after his speech of to-night. The House was crowded from floor to topmost range of strangers' gallery. Expectation buzzed, and Mr. Gladstone, as he stood at the table waiting for opportunity to speak when the cheers of his friends should subside, was the focus of fully six hundred pair of eyes. The occasion was one upon which it was natural he should deliver a carefully-prepared speech. The matter at issue was the critical stage of the principal Bill in the Ministerial programme. The subject was Ireland, and it involved the Land Question, a topic of absorbing interest to the great statesman and orator.

Still, the question that filled every mind was not primarily how Mr. Gladstone would deal with the main principles of the Land Purchase Bill. That problem was indeed not without its special difficulty, and, therefore, its peculiar attraction. Four years ago Mr. Gladstone had brought in an Irish Land Purchase Bill. It had been opposed by the Unionist Party, born of the struggle, and, upon appeal to the country, Mr. Gladstone and his great majority had been hustled from power. Now the Unionist Party being in office had brought in a Land Purchase Bill. They, with whatever modifications of form, were supporting the principle the adoption of which they had successfully resisted in 1886, and Mr. Gladstone had been brought by the whirligig of time to stand at the Opposition side of the table and demonstrate that whilst the Unionists were wrong in 1886 in opposing the principle of State-aided purchase of land in Ireland, they were even more hopelessly wrong, when, in 1890, they embodied that principle in a Bill, and staked upon it the existence of their Ministry.

Mr. Parnell at fault. It would take a very old Parliamentary hand so to shuffle cards as to make a winning game of this complex situation. But there was something beyond which added interest to the performance, and for the while engrossed the thoughts of onlookers. On Monday Mr. Parnell had suddenly interposed, and given a fresh and unexpected turn to affairs by proposing a plan of his own. The mystery which obscures all Mr. Parnell's comings and goings had been specially darkened over this movement. When at the outset of his speech he had announced that before he concluded he would submit an alternative scheme, men on both sides of the House set themselves to consider what was naturally supposed to be the outcome of consultative action by the Irish Party. It presently became clear from their attitude of surprised attention that Mr. Parnell's party were as much in the dark as was everybody else. Mr. Parnell had conceived his plan, jotted down its leading features on sheets of foolscap, and his first communication to his own friends was made to them in common with the listening world.

That would have been in itself an embarrassing state of things, but the situation was further complicated by the evident fact that Mr. Parnell was not quite clear in his conception of his own plan.

He had taken the unusual trouble of writing out his speech, which he brought down on folios of uncompromising size. If he had only pinned them together disaster might have been averted. As it was they got hopelessly astray, one at least bodily disappearing, carrying with it his pregnant remarks on congested districts. These were circumstances that would have fatally discomposed an ordinary man. Mr. Lowe's Parliamentary experience was longer than Mr. Parnell's, and his position as an acceptable speaker more assured. But it came to pass one night when the veteran debater found himself hopelessly entangled with his notes he threw them down on the table with piteous glance round the sympathising audience, admitted he could not go on, resumed his seat, and never again essayed to take prominent part in debate in the Chamber he had once swayed with powerful intellect and incisive speech. But Mr. Lowe, in spite of his gibes, felt a deeply-rooted respect for the House of Commons, and Mr. Parnell has none. He offered no apology for his frequent pauses whilst he tried to rearrange his dissevered folios of notes. If members found his manner irksome they might walk out. He was no more inclined to consult their prejudices for ordered arrangement than he was to conciliate members of his own party or meet the convenience of right hon. gentlemen on the front Opposition bench. If he had been fully master of his plan, or if his folios had chanced to come up in due sequence, his statement would have been marked by his usual lucidity of thought and expression. Things chancing to be otherwise, the House of Commons must needs make the best of them.

This was the added misfortune of Mr. Gladstone's peculiar position. It was bad enough for his colleague in the direction of Opposition forces suddenly to have developed a plan of his own. But at least he might have been expected to make it intelligible. If, on the eve of Waterloo, Blucher had thought out a line of independent action he would not have explained it to the Duke of Wellington in the German tongue. He would have had it fairly translated for the Commander-in-Chief's information. But, as Mr. Gladstone delicately put it, it was not possible to discuss in detail Mr. Parnell's plan, "because I am not certain that of all its details I have a perfect comprehension." Still, there it was, its embarrassing existence and probably dangerous tendencies made all the more formidable by reason of the obscurity in which it had been accidentally involved. What would Mr. Gladstone do with it? Would he take the responsibility of approving it, and so hopelessly weaken the strength of the Opposition attack on the Government Bill? or would he brave the possibility of rupture with allies below the gangway by disowning the whole affair?

The "Old Parliamentary Hand." How Mr. Gladstone got out of the difficulty appears from the printed report of his speech. But no verbatim report could suggest the consummate art of the manner in which the difficulty was rather evaded than overcome. He was fully conscious that the acutest audience in the world, gathered in crowds around him, was chiefly thinking how he would deliver himself from this quandary. He could not, as Sir George Trevelyan had done on Monday, escape from it by leaving it absolutely unnoticed. He must say something, but it must be as little as possible, without appearing to underrate the importance of the Irish leader's contribution to the controversy, at the same time without magnifying it. What watchful eyes on the benches opposite regarded as a mountain he must treat as a molehill, and yet not offend the susceptibilities of the proprietor.

It was a difficult task, but it was surmounted by the Old Parliamentary Hand with airy ease and grace. It was doubtless an accident having no bearing upon the peculiarities of the situation that Mr. Gladstone had not provided himself with the sustaining force which lurks in his famous pomatum pot. For fifteen years he has been accustomed to preface great efforts in the House of Commons by producing this faithful companion from his coat-tail pocket and placing it on the table by his notes. The duty of demolishing a new Irish Land Bill brought in by a rival firm of statesmen certainly did not in matter of importance fall below the average of occasions when the pomatum pot has appeared. But, really, having only to set aside Mr. Parnell's little error in tactics it was not worth while making special preparations, and a glass of ordinary water would suffice.

So, accidentally, as it were, stumbling on the topic at the very outset of his speech, Mr. Gladstone, in half a dozen genial sentences, disposed of Mr. Parnell and his plan, and thereafter, amid a murmur of admiration extorted from the closely-watching crowd on the benches opposite, proceeded to the accomplishment of the comparatively easy task of showing how what was right in 1886, when he was Premier, was wrong in 1890, with Lord Salisbury in power.

May L. — Mr. Parnell's indifference.

Mr. Parnell too evidently does not care what a great statesman in a classical sentence once described as "a twopenny damn" for anything that may be said about him in the House of Commons. Mr. Chamberlain's speech of Monday night on the second reading of the Irish Land Bill was heralded by obviously authorised hints that it would be chiefly devoted to discussion of the plan Mr. Parnell had, to the surprise of friends, not less than of enemies, flung on the floor of the House. It was even said, with truth, as events proved, that the member for Birmingham would express his approval of some of its main principles, and would hold out his hand across the gangway to the Irish leader. Politically as well as personally that was an attractive, at least an interesting, prospect. Suppose Mr. Parnell had accepted the invitation to confer with Mr. Chamberlain, and these two statesmen had worked out a scheme of Land Purchase and united in pressing it on the acceptance of the Government. That would have been a momentous turn in affairs, certainly one worth the deference of passing attention.

Mr. Parnell did not even take the trouble to be in his place on Monday to hear Mr. Chamberlain, nor was he more curious to-night. Yet through the long hours of the sitting the most languid pulse beat with expectation of possible development. The curious game going forward through the fortnight, with its succession of surprises, was nearing its close. At this sitting, somewhere between five o'clock and midnight, the leading trumps would be thrown on the table. How they would be played was a question that thrilled an assembly packing every available seat in the House of Commons.

For Mr. Parnell it had an interest of special bearing. But whilst the House was crowded in every part, men looked in vain for the Irish leader in the obscurity of the seat he affects below the gangway. Mr. Balfour delivered a speech which strongly marks his uninterrupted progress as a Parliamentary debater. Like Mr. Chamberlain, he has the gift of making capital out of interruptions that would embarrass a less ready speaker. He steered his way with ease and skill between the Scylla of Mr. Parnell's plan and the Charybdis of Mr. Chamberlain's commentary. By comparison, his attitude was more friendly towards the Irish leader than the English ally. It was at least odd that so self-possessed a speaker, one so little prone to unguarded slips, should, to the unconstrained delight of the Irish members, have stumbled upon that phrase about the coming of "a leader who knew not Joseph."

When Lord Hartington had made an end of speaking the tangled position was cleared. Everybody knew how everybody else stood, and there remained nothing to do but to vote. The whisper had gone round that Mr. Parnell was not even coming for the division. He certainly was not in the House at this last moment. His place was empty when the question was put; but he must have been within hearing of the Speaker's voice, for, lagging behind as the Opposition trooped in from the division lobby, he made his way to his customary seat, yawning amid the enthusiastic cheers with which the Ministerialists hailed the passing of the second reading of the Bill by the unexpected majority of eighty.

<table>
<tr><td>May 9. — The Irish Party; old style and new.</td><td>In one prominent respect it is a far cry from the House of Commons of 1875 to the House of 1890. In both the Irish Party fill a</td></tr>
</table>

large space; but how different are the men! It would be difficult to find two persons more diametrically opposed than the Irish leader of 1874 and he who now, from behind an impenetrable covert, imperiously controls the Irish Party. Mr. Butt was of the order of sleek-headed men, such as sleep o' nights. "Yond Cassius has a lean and hungry look; he thinks too much." Mr. Butt was always ready to bubble over with mirth; Mr. Parnell is rarely known to smile.   Mr. Butt knew "Gosset's room," where he was ever a welcome guest; Mr. Parnell never entered that sanctuary, for frequenters of which he had an unconcealed contempt.   Mr. Butt, even in his most militant days, overflowed with the milk of human kindness: Mr. Parnell, though in these latter days not lacking in a certain air of high courtesy, conveys the impression that his fathers had eaten sour grapes.   Mr. Butt was always ready to discuss Irish policy with his followers over a jorum of whisky; Mr. Parnell scorns the adventitious encouragement of a social cup of tea.   Mr. Butt was "hail fellow well met" with the humblest member of his motley party; Mr. Parnell's followers would more readily face the responsibilities of breaking in upon the privacy of the Grand Lama than of approaching the presence of their leader without special invitation.

In truth the difficulty often is to know where to find him at a given moment.   The Irish members are too loyal to make open complaint, but the embarrassment created during the changing scenes of the debate on the second reading of the Land Purchase Bill by their leader's habits of seclusion, extended beyond their circle.   No one knew what he thought about a particular turn of events.   No one could say what he would do, no one, in fact, knew where he was, when he might turn up, or whether it were safe to expect him at all.   Mr. Butt had his periods of disappearance, but they were not without a certain regularity; and when he came back he wore a comically apologetic air that won forgiveness.

McCarthy Downing. This wide divergence between the personality of the two Irish leaders is equally strongly marked in the characteristics of the party.   There have always been notable Irishmen at Westminster since the date of the Union: never was there such a coruscation of native genius as had its birth in the throes of the Home Rule Party in Mr. Butt's day.   Some who seemed to have stepped straight out of the pages of Charles Lever, justifying the novelist from charges of exaggeration.   The present generation knows

nothing of Mr. McCarthy Downing with his curiously scared
appearance, alternating with magisterial manner.   Mr. Downing was invested with a certain air of authority, inasmuch as
he was reported to control the editorial utterances of the
Skibbereen Eagle.   It was the *Skibbereen Eagle* which checked
Napoleon the Third in the very height of his power.   At the
time when the French colonels were ramping at Chalons,
jingling their spurs, clanking their sabres, and clamouring to
be led *à Londres*, the *Skibbereen Eagle* came out one Saturday
morning with a leading article commencing: "We have
long had our eye on the Man of Destiny at the Tuileries."
Mr. Ronayne always said McCarthy Downing had written
that article.   Perhaps he never did; possibly it was never
written.   But it was talked about "in Gosset's room," where
McCarthy Downing sometimes sat with a delightful consciousness of trifling with valuable time and great opportunities.   This and other legends created around him an air
of occult authority, brought to bear with great effect upon
debates in the House of Commons.

Towards the end life darkened over poor McCarthy
Downing, and he grew to look more than ever like an eager,
ill-fed bird, that had worn away its plumage in places by
fluttering against the bars of its cage.   When the political
conflict grew serious, when the stern, implacable spirit that
dominated Mr. Parnell began to gain ascendency, the genial
kindly, scholarly, doughty Isaac Butt was driven to the wall,
and with him, to his honour be it said, went McCarthy
Downing, faithful and fluttering to the last.   There came a
time when Butt publicly washed his hands of the Parliamentary practices of which Mr. Biggar was the original in-
ventor and principal exponent.   The old man, broken in spirit
and failing in health, crossed the gangway and took his place
among the Saxons.   There, in a corner seat, with his grey head
bent on his hands, he sat whilst Mr. Biggar shrilly gibed at
him, Mr. Parnell hissed scorn in his ear, and forgotten men
like Fay and Finigan scouted his authority.   Only the faded
faithful McCarthy Downing accompanied him, and sometimes, rising with faint reminiscences of his old magisterial
manner, rebuked his countrymen amid unwonted, and
perhaps unwelcome, cheers from gentlemen on the benches

opposite, varied by howls of contumely from his former colleagues.

Delahunty.   Of quite another type was Mr. Delahunty, who, genuinely anxious for the welfare of his country and the re-establishment of the old kings of Ireland, was warped by his preference for one-pound notes. It is odd to think how in these days, years after the once familiar member for Waterford is dead and forgotten, a Chancellor of the Exchequer of the respectability and responsibility of Mr. Goschen should be known to have seriously taken into consideration the policy of issuing one-pound notes. But wisdom is not unfrequently justified of her children. Mr. Delahunty was sound on Home Rule, a faithful follower of Mr. Butt; but once a year, as the ballot favoured him, he brought forward his motion and demonstrated to the delight of a crowded House that if only you had one-pound notes the sun would always shine, wages would go up, prices would go down, and an era of universal happiness would spread over the face of the United Empire. Amongst his local distinctions Mr. Delahunty had for many years filled the honourable office of Coroner, not only for the borough, but for the county, of Waterford. Circumstances connected with the peregrinations in the discharge of his duties had induced the habit of carrying about with him a small black bag containing an assortment of toilet necessaries. After he had resigned his coronership the habit and the bag stuck to him. He always brought the latter down to the House, utilising it among other purposes for storing data bearing upon the question of one-pound notes.

Who that was present on a certain Wednesday afternoon back in the dim Disraelian days can forget the part this bag played in debate? Mr. Delahunty was standing in his place below the gangway moving his resolution affirming the desirability of re-establishing the currency of one-pound notes. He had occasion to quote some figures that would clench his argument. The folio containing them lay, with many others, in the recesses of the black bag. Diving in whilst the crowded House looked on attentive, he fished out the first thing that came to hand, which proved to be a hair-brush decidedly the worse for wear. Undisturbed by the shout of laughter that greeted the misadventure, he proceeded in his search. There appeared in succession a soiled collar, a bottle that may have contained hairwash, and finally a single stocking. Members tossed about in tempest of laughter, but the member for Waterford, "without haste, but without rest," pursued his search till he came upon the desired folio, and, repacking his bag, read out the conclusive figures.

Another estimable member of the Butt Party whose name is perhaps unknown to the present House was Captain Stacpoole. Like Mr. Delahunty, while the gallant Captain was sound on the Home Rule question he had his special panacea for the wrongs of Ireland. What he desired to see was a member of the Royal Family in residence in his country. He was always drawing up resolutions which, under pledge of secrecy, he showed to friends, and with his hands partially thrust in his trousers pockets (his little fingers being left outside toying with the seam), his hat well set on the back of his head, he asked in a confidential whisper what they thought of *that!* In even more confidential moments Captain Stacpoole used to confess that he was a Whig. His great model of a statesman was Lord Palmerston—Pam, as he was privileged to call him.

" Ah !" he used to murmur, sorrowfully tapping his little fingers on the seams of his trousers, " I wonder what Pam would say if he were alive now !"

Captain Stacpoole has long ago joined Pam and the majority. Gone, too, is Dr. O'Leary, in whom Disraeli, on the eve of a critical division, judiciously discovered a personal likeness to Tom Moore, and whose vote thereafter was always at the service of the Government where the interests of Ireland did not clash. Gone is Major O'Gorman, noblest Roman of them all ; and gone, too, latest though not less endearing, the sturdy, honest, unpurchasable—acrid in manner, but kindly at heart—Joseph Gillis Biggar.

Mr. Biggar's will is a very characteristic document, more especially in respect of the provision made for his son. The late member for Cavan always had an urgent desire that this youth should become a solicitor. To that end he had him educated regardless of expense ; but unfortunately when he came up for one of the preliminary examinations he was plucked. Mr. Biggar took this unexpected disaster with his usual imperturbability, but he let the younger Joseph clearly understand that the success of his scheme was inseparable from an originally intended distribution of his property. No solicitorship, no fortune. This resolve, of which he made no secret in conversation with his personal friends in the House of Commons, is sternly carried out by the provisions of the will. "My son Joseph" is to have £100 a year until he shall be admitted as a solicitor, thereafter coming in as residuary legatee of the handsome estate, the personalty of which exceeds £37,000. But if "my son Joseph" fails, the money goes elsewhere, leaving him that bare pittance of £100 a year.

CHAPTER XXVII.

A VANISHING MAJORITY.

"Very Blind and very Deaf"—Sir Wilfrid Lawson Identified—The Queen's Gossip—Two Lord Elchos—The First—The Second—Mr. Gladstone saving himself up—A Close Shave—Prince "Eddie" takes his Seat in the Lords—Place and Precedence.

May 20.—"Very blind and very deaf." THERE was a scene in the House of Lords to-night which has its pathetic as well as its comic side.

Lord Denman moved the second reading of his Municipal Franchise (Ireland) Bill, a measure he brings in session after session, to the great annoyance of noble lords. He spoke for twenty-five minutes in his rambling fashion, sometimes muttering to himself in so low a tone of voice that the purport of his sentences could not be caught. The Peers are long-suffering with one of their own order, which can of course do no wrong nor betray any human infirmity. But twenty minutes of Lord Denman exceeded their patience, and there were cries of "Agreed" and "Divide"—quite unwonted

interruptions in this serene atmosphere. Lord Denman took
no notice, and was further proceeding when the storm rose.
He paused, and looking round the House, said—

"My lords, I am very blind and very deaf, but I try to do
my duty."

Then he groped his way back to the cross benches.
Here he sat whilst the question was put, and, not a voice being
lifted in support of his Bill, the second reading was negatived.
When the Lord Chancellor announced the result, Lord
Denman hurriedly approached the table and began another
speech. This, of course, was a breach of order, and there arose
what, for the House of Lords, was a veritable hurricane of
cries of "Order! Order!" After facing the storm for a few
moments the old peer said—

"My lords, it is you that are disorderly," and with this final
blow returned to his seat.

May 21.—Sir Wilfrid Lawson identified. Sir Wilfrid Lawson has a rich fund of anecdotes
with which he illumines his public speeches.
There is one he retains for private conversation,
though it is by no means lacking in point. A short time ago,
Sir Wilfrid, visiting at the house of a friend, made the acquaintance of a bright little boy some ten years of age, with whom
the genial baronet talked and romped. After a while he said—

"Well, my boy, we have been great friends; but it's odd
we were never introduced. I don't know what your name is,
and I am sure you have not the slightest idea who I
am."

"Oh yes," said the small boy; "I know very well. You
are the celebrated drunkard."

May 30.—The Queen's gossip. It is well known that the late Lord Sackville
left a large portion of his estate to certain Maids
of Honour. The legacies were disputed by his heirs-at-law,
and the case was finally settled out of court, the Attorney-
General acting for one of the parties, and Sir Henry James for
the other. The late Lord Sackville was an intimate acquaintance
of the Queen. Nearly fifty years ago he was appointed to be
Gentleman Usher. After that he became successively Groom
of the Privy Chamber and a Groom-in-waiting. In this last

capacity he saw a good deal of the Queen, who admitted him
on terms of unusual intimacy. Lord Sackville married a
second time some seventeen years ago, and whilst he was at
Windsor or Osborne Lady Sackville remained at Knowle. Her
husband wrote to her every day long letters giving minute
accounts of palace life, telling all that the Queen had said to
him, and what he said to the Queen.

These letters were carefully preserved by Lady Sackville,
and in the course of the investigation carried on by the
Attorney-General and Sir Henry James they came under their
consideration. Of course infinite pains will be taken that they
do not see the light of day in the present generation, but if
they survive to appear in book form they will afford a new
generation a curiously graphic account of the inner life of
Osborne and Windsor. The Queen has almost sternly withdrawn from participation in social life outside her own family
circle. But this correspondence shows that she preserves a
keen womanly interest in all that goes on in the various circles
that surround the Court. Lord Sackville brought her all the
news of the day, some of it not lacking in piquancy, and in
these letters to his wife he sets forth his story as told to the
Queen, together with Her Majesty's commentary.

June 6. — Two
Lord Elchos.

Lord Elcho, standing the other night at the corner
of the front bench below the gangway, cracking
jokes on the subject of Derby Day, made the oldest inhabitant
of the place feel young again. Mr. Villiers was not present,
nor was Mr. Gladstone. Otherwise in their minds' eye they
would have beheld themselves seated in a Parliament, now
fifty years dead, to which had come straight from East
Gloucestershire a tall youth with easy manner and fluent
speech, known as Lord Elcho. A stripling who knew better
than to be a Tory or a Liberal, his independent mind liked to
make selections. So taking a bit here and a bit there, he
called himself a Liberal Conservative, voted for Lord Derby's
Reform Bill in 1859, and vindicated his impartiality by voting
against Lord Russell's Reform Bill in 1866.

Lord Elcho we had long with us, always in this corner seat
till the Fourth Party, to whom nothing was sacred, bundled
him out.

The first.   Lord Elcho—the one who is now Earl Wemyss —was of the class of men who never grow old. As he was born three years after Waterloo, he must have been pretty well up in years as men count age when, only the other day, he stepped lightly across the corridor and took his place in the House of Lords. But to elderly people like the Earl of Rosebery and Lord Cadogan there seemed quite a breezy boyishness about the new peer. After the interminable series of speeches he had made through the course of nearly half a century in the Commons it might reasonably have been expected he had uttered all he had at heart. But amid novel scenes, touched by new associations, the Earl of Wemyss renewed his youth like the eagle, and the House of Lords speedily found a common ground of sympathy with the House of Commons.

During this present Session there has flitted mysteriously over the Orders of the House of Lords a motion in the name of Lord Wemyss calling attention to "the Socialistic legislation of past Sessions." Nobody had the slightest idea what this meant. It was a sort of prize conundrum with the attraction of the prize left out. At first he coyly declined to name a day for bringing on the subject. The notice appeared for weeks among the list of motions "for an early day." Then when the subject had burned itself, as it were, upon the brain of noble lords a day was fixed.

There was nothing original about this. It was, perhaps rather obviously, founded on the practice of advertisers who placard the walls of the town with bills containing blank spaces and the invitation to "keep your eye fixed on this." After a while the blank is filled up, and the public are invited to buy a particular soap or use a special make of bed-room candle. Lord Wemyss, though not disdaining the practised art of the advertiser, went a bold step beyond him. Having named the day, having drawn down to Westminster an audience of palpitating peers, having risen in his place at the call of the Lord Chancellor, he with a graceful sweep of the arm pointed to the empty seat of the Premier, and protested that in his absence he could not think of delivering his discourse.

That was a novel proceeding which probably would be found inconvenient in a business assembly if its adoption became general. But the House, secretly glad to escape the discourse on any terms, offered no protest, and Lord Wemyss had another day specially set apart when the Premier was in his place, and at last, like tardy rain falling on parched pastures, he discoursed by the hour on the tendency of Socialistic legislation.

The House of Peers, insatiable of supreme excellence, have appropriated the Lord Elcho who was familiar to the Commons through eight Parliaments. But the wind is tempered to the shorn lamb, and the House of Commons feels, not without a thrill of pride, that, though the Lords have the Earl of Wemyss they have Lord Elcho. It is questionable whether the Lord Elcho of the present day is not an improvement upon the member, first for East Gloucestershire, then for Haddingtonshire, who lent countenance in succession to the Ministries of Sir Robert Peel, Lord John Russell, Lord Derby, Lord Aberdeen, and Lord Palmerston; who filled a large space in the House Mr. Disraeli led, and who proved a thorn in the side of Mr. Gladstone in the triumphant days which dawned for him in the Session of 1880. As an old member the former Lord Elcho rather presumed upon his opportunities. When he had once caught the Speaker's eye he showed a strong disinclination to let the next man have a chance. There were few speakers who so undisguisedly delighted in the sound of their own voice. Only very hard-hearted, unsympathetic people could refrain from sharing his pleasure in his own speech. His style of oratory lent itself readily to the exigencies of the occasion. He could go for an hour, and generally did. But if he had stopped midway, or at the end of the second twenty minutes, the symmetry of his discourse would not have suffered in appreciable degree.

The second.   The Lord Elcho of to-day is not, as his father grew to be, a chartered institution of the House. He has his way to make, and must be careful of his opportunities. In his speech on moving the adjournment of the House over the Derby Day there was not lacking evidence of the influence of heredity in the direction of garrulousness. If he had foregone five, or even seven, minutes of the time

appropriated, his effort would have been attended with fuller
success. As it was it was excellent, conceived in the true
spirit of the occasion, cleverly phrased, admirably delivered.
The likeness to his father grew as he gained confidence amid
the laughter and applause that greeted successive sallies. It
was a, perhaps not undesigned, coincidence that for this
occasion he should have secured
the very seat from which his
forbear had risen to enlighten
successive Parliaments.

Mr. James Lowther has
secured the reversion of this
corner seat, but in grateful recognition of much intellectual
pleasure and sound information received in years gone by
from the lips of Lord Elcho's
father he gracefully conceded
it to the son for one night
only. As the youth stood there,
with little movements of arms
and legs precisely identical with
those that graced his father's
speech, the hand of Time
seemed suddenly put back. Sir
Robert Peel was in the height
of his power; Lord Lyndhurst
was Chancellor, Sir James
Graham Home Secretary, Lord
Aberdeen Foreign Secretary;
Mr. Gladstone was still the
rising hope of the Conservative
Party; Mr. Disraeli had just been elected member for
Shrewsbury; Mr. W. H. Smith had not yet been heard of
outside the Strand. The young member for East Gloucestershire (Lord Elcho) had all his days before him, and had no
thought that in the race on which he was just confidently
started he might be beaten by his young contemporaries
then representing Newark and Shrewsbury.

Looking and listening to the mover of the adjournment

over the Derby Day, all this might have been. But it was not. The Lord Elcho of 1841 has gone to another place, and a great deal more has happened in the intervening half-century since he made his maiden speech.

June 13.—Mr. Gladstone saving himself up. In the matter of Parliamentary excesses Mr. Gladstone is quite a reformed rake. There was a time not many sessions back, when no power or influence could induce him to work in moderation. He was in his place early and late, primed through long hours with dangerously explosive materials. At one time, during his Ministry of 1880-5, there was grimly humorous talk of a conspiracy by which on the stroke of midnight he was to be seized by his faithful retainers and carried off to bed *vi et armis.* In those days, living in Downing Street, it was his boast that he could go home, eat his dinner, and be back in his place within 35 minutes. Night after night through fierce fights he did this, sometimes beating the record. Every-one knows what happened. He broke down, and was for a time compulsorily absent from his post.

He is older and wiser now, and despatches his Parlia-mentary duties upon quite another plan. He is pretty regular in his attendance, but he strictly limits it. He comes in for questions, not always at the commencement, remains through-out an attentive listener, and if any debate of interest is going forward, stays till half-past seven. If he intends to speak he interposes between five and seven. Then he goes off to dress for dinner, dining out at least four nights a week, and thereafter going straight off to bed, his reappearance in the House after dinner being an exceedingly rare occurrence. He is, he says, "saving himself up," and looks uncommonly like as if he would succeed.

June 19.—A close shave. The Ministry to-night narrowly escaped what would have been a particularly embarrassing defeat. The hotly-contested Licensing Bill was in Committee. At four o'clock Mr. Akers Douglas, anxiously looking round the House, knew that, supposing the challenge were promptly given, the Government stood in a hopeless position. The clubs were scoured for members, and they came dribbling

down in twos and threes. But a strong contingent was at
Ascot, not expected back before half-past six. As soon as
this skirmishing was over, the House would go into Committee,
the question would be put that Clause I. stand part of the
Licensing Bill, and if it were true, as rumour had it, that a
strategic movement had been devised—no one rising from the
Opposition side to resume debate—the division would forthwith
be called, and the Government must be beaten. To be beaten
on this first clause meant the destruction of the Bill. It might
be due to an accident, or to a trick; but the clause once
rejected in Committee could not be reinstated, and the Bill
must go.

It was just twenty minutes past five when, questions over,
Mr. Courtney took the chair and put the question "That
Clause One stand part of the Bill." In the ordinary course
of events Mr. Storey would have risen to continue the speech
interrupted by the stroke of midnight on Tuesday; the ranks
of the Opposition would have fallen in; and for the rest of the
sitting, or till the Closure had been invoked, this clause, already
talked over through many nights, would have been re-discussed.
No one rose, and the Chairman of Committees put the question
that the clause be added. There was a cry of "Aye!" from
the Ministerial benches, swiftly answered by a thunderous
"No!" from the crowded benches where the Opposition sat
radiant with the hope of victory. Only three minutes more,
during which the bell rang through all the empty corridors,
in the deserted reading-room, through the forsaken smoking-
room. When the sands in the glass on the table ran out the
doors would be closed, and the fate of the Bill would rest
with the seething crowd shut up in the House. Mr. Akers-
Douglas was out in the lobby now, standing by the swinging
door of the corridor leading to the cloak-room, whence, peradventure, help might yet come. Only a minute and the last
grain of sand would pass. Lord Hartington was descried, with
one hand in his pocket it is true, still hurrying at a pace unprecedented in his Parliamentary history. Just behind him toiled
Mr. Chaplin, with a scared look on his face, having heard the
news from the scout at the outer doorway. It would be a pretty
thing for a Cabinet Minister, the first Minister of Agriculture
with which a happy State had been endowed, to be absent, even

at Ascot, from a division upon which the fate of the Ministry might depend. Whilst Mr. Hornby made the running with Lord Hartington a good second, Mr. Chaplin came in third, Mr. Maclure not being placed. But the massive member for Sleaford managed to struggle past, and when the door closed on the breathless four the Ministry had their majority.

This could not be known as a certainty, and in truth the Ministerialists went out to the division lobby with the conviction that they were beaten. At half-past four heads had been

carefully counted, and it was known that the Opposition were in a majority of between thirty and forty. Since then members had struggled in on either side, the preponderance evidently being with the Government. But count had been lost, and the general impression was that Ministers were beaten by something between five and ten votes.

Slowly the severed throng came back, Ministerialists from the doorway under the clock, the Opposition from behind the Speaker's chair. The excitement grew in intensity as the benches filled. There murmured through the chamber that buzz of eager talk heard only twice or thrice in the career of a Ministry. The tellers for the Government were back first, a stream of the Opposition still trickling in from the "No" lobby—almost certain sign that

they were the larger number. All eyes were eagerly bent
upon the clerk standing at the corner of the table, having
written down the figures from the "Ayes," waiting for the
record from the "Noes." If he handed the paper to Mr
Akers Douglas it was a sign that the Bill was saved. If
he gave it to Mr. Labouchere the day was lost. Whilst
the clerk was writing down the second tale of figures Mr.
Akers Douglas was observed taking his position on the right-
hand side of the muster of tellers, a movement which to the
keenly watching throng proclaimed how the contest had gone.
A ringing cheer went up from the Ministerialists, repeated
when the paper was handed to the Government Whip, and
continued so boisterously that the figures of the Ministerial
muster were not heard. It was only when the Chairman of
Committees recited the figures it became known that 228 had
voted for adding the clause to the Bill, 224 against. Thus
the measure to which a powerful Ministry have in their fifth
session pinned their fortunes was saved by a majority of four.

June 23.—Prince "Eddie" takes his seat in the Lords. The House of Lords received an addition to its
numbers in the person of his Royal Highness
the Duke of Clarence and Avondale. The
fact that the ceremony was fixed to take place this evening
was not generally known, and the attendance of the public
was not greater than at ordinary sittings. From the side
gallery facing the Ministerial bench the Princess of Wales,
accompanied by Princess Victoria and Princess Maud, looked on.

Shortly after four o'clock the royal procession entered,
led by Black Rod. Behind him came Garter King-at-Arms,
then the Prince of Wales, the new peer and his uncle the
Duke of Edinburgh, the rear being brought up by the
Hereditary Grand Marshal the Duke of Norfolk, and the
Lord Great Chamberlain, Lord Aveland. The royal princes
wore the scarlet and ermine robes donned by peers on cere-
monial occasions, the officers of State who accompanied them
being also *en grand tenue.*

On entering, the procession, marching in single file in the
order indicated, approached the Woolsack, where the Lord
Chancellor sat expectant. The new peer proffered him the
writ of his return as a Peer of the Realm, which the Lord

Chancellor by a gesture invited the Reading Clerk to take.
The procession then grouped itself round the corner of the
table, Mr. Betholl, the Reading Clerk, intoning the document which made the royal prince a Peer of the Realm.
This done, the oath was administered, the Roll of Parliament
produced and signed. Then the procession once more,
always in solemn silence, began a new peregrination. Advancing towards the Woolsack, each one bowed. The Lord
Chancellor acknowledged the salute of the Officers of State
by bending his head; but as each Prince passed and saluted
him, Lord Halsbury, with that graceful manner with which
he adorns the Woolsack, raised his three-cornered cap in
salute.

The new peer was led past the Woolsack towards a row of
three State chairs set to the left of the throne. Black Rod
kept in close attendance, but with the exception of the Prince
of Wales and the Duke of Edinburgh the others fell back.
With the Prince of Wales standing at his right hand and the
Duke of Edinburgh on his left, the Duke of Clarence took
his seat in the centre chair. The Lord Chancellor, wheeling
round on the Woolsack, replied to his salute by again uplifting
his cap. After a moment's pause the new peer left the chair
of State, and walking forward to the Woolsack, was presented
to the Lord Chancellor, who now shook hands with him.
There was more raising of hats and bowing, and the royal
procession filed out by the doorway behind the throne, the
Princess of Wales and her daughters leaving the side gallery
and joining them below.

<table>
<tr><td>Place and pre-
cedence.</td><td>The Committee on Privilege in the House of
Lords appointed to consider the place the Duke</td></tr>
</table>

of Clarence and Avondale shall occupy in the House have
been chiefly guided by the precedent established in the case of
the Duke of York, grandson of George II., the last occasion
when the eldest son of the heir-apparent took his seat as a
peer during the reign of a grandparent. It is settled that
his Royal Highness shall have place and precedence in the
House next after the Duke of Connaught and before the
Duke of Albany, the Duke of Cambridge, and all other Dukes,
not to mention the Archbishop of Canterbury. It is a curious

matter that in the settlement of this important case the Duke
of Edinburgh is entirely left out of consideration. He of
course sits in the Lords, though not a very frequent attendant
upon his Parliamentary duties. Presumably since the Duke
of Connaught is to take precedence of his nephew, the Duke
of Edinburgh cannot be placed in a different position. But
the fact remains that the Duke of Edinburgh's name does
not appear in the formal resolution passed by the Committee
on Privilege.

CHAPTER XXVIII.

RANDOLPH REDIVIVUS.

A Monster Petition—Mr. Chamberlain and Pitt—The last Chairman of the
Metropolitan Board of Works—Mr. Chamberlain and the Liberals—"Black
Rod!"—Lord R. Churchill and his Tutor—A Ladies' Man—Lord Randolph
and the Ministry—An Old Member.

June 27.—A monster petition. MEMBERS coming down to the House this afternoon, eager to learn the latest phase in the
moving history of the Compensation Bill, were seized by a
strange alarm. There was nothing unusual in the aspect of
the outer lobby or its approaches. But within the doorway
members were confronted by what appeared to be a series
of colossal packing cases, stretching up to the Mace itself.
Mr. Picton, hurrying in, intent upon the privilege of attending
prayers and, incidentally, securing the corner seat below the
gangway, possession of which gives an orator exceptional
command of the House, was for a moment lost to view. After
anxious pause Mr. Jackson, in early attendance on the
Treasury bench, observed the top of Mr. Picton's head as he
moved cautiously round one of the great cylinders, and having
safely made the tour proceeded to his accustomed seat—a
place once filled by John Bright, and for a time tenanted by
the long-forgotten Mr. Horsman.

These gigantic cylinders, borne in by six stalwart House
messengers, whose united ages exceeded four centuries, contained a petition through which six hundred thousand citizens

breathed their earnest prayer that "Your Honourable House" would not fail to pass the Local Taxation (Customs and Excise Duties) Bill. Never before had such a phenomenon varied the level course of Parliamentary proceedings. The whole business of petitions to the House of Commons is eminently unpractical. Constructed with anxious care, much trouble, and occasionally involving considerable expense, petitions are hurried through an almost empty House during the time of private business, before the overburdened Press begins its duty of recording events. At the left-hand side of the clerk at the table hangs a sack into which petitions are thrust. When it is full it is carried out, its contents strewn on the floor of a storehouse, and there is the beginning and end of the influence of petitions upon the labours of Parliament or on public opinion.

For a while members stared dumbly at the towering height of the bulky cases, covering the space on which in days gone by Mr. Plimsoll performed his historic feat of standing on one leg and shaking his fist at the Speaker. Mr. Picton, having mounted the gangway and reached the corner of the second bench, could, standing on tiptoe, catch a glimpse of Sir Walter Barttelot on the topmost bench above the gangway opposite. But Mr. Labouchere, Sir Wm. Plowden, Sir Thomas Esmonde, and other members seated on the front bench below the gangway, could see nothing but the wooden framework of the cases on the floor, with the coils of petition nestling within. A voice filled the Chamber discussing the provisions of the Overhead Telegraphs Bill. It was familiar enough, and was recognised by members sitting *perdu* on the other side of the cases as belonging to Mr. Bartley. But honourable gentlemen lost the advantage of observing the mobile features of the member for North Islington as he developed his argument, and were deprived of the guidance of his eloquent gestures as he approached a knotty point.

It was indicative of the intensity of the situation that the first protest should have come from Sir Wm. Plowden. Sir William, trained in the rigid discipline of the Bengal Civil Service, hardened by his experiences on the Imperial Census Commission, has cultivated an imperturbability of manner which stands him in good stead at crises that shake the

frames of men who have been less happily circumstanced in
earlier life.   But these new conditions of Parliamentary
debate were too much even for this cast-iron man.   After
vain efforts to catch the Speaker's eye round the corner of
the third cylinder he abruptly rose and asked how long " this
arrangement " was to hold possession of the floor ?

The Speaker, with quite unwonted meekness, pleaded that
it was all owing to the framework. He had been asked
whether there was any objection to the petition being rolled
in in sections, and he had thought not. But he had not
taken into consideration the surrounding woodwork, and as
soon as private business was over he would give direction
that " the obstacles " should be removed.

The innate respect for the high authority of the Speaker,
much strengthened of late by Mr. Peel's masterly and dignified
conduct at critical epochs, had its momentary effect.   Mr.
Bartley, first standing on tiptoe and peering over the cylinders
to see if Sir William Plowden had resumed his seat, went on
with his speech, his voice strangely echoing round the open
trellis-work of the miles of folios which bore the signatures of
six hundred thousand citizens, all aglow with desire that the
interests of the licensed victualler should be conserved. Ten
minutes later, Sir Thomas Esmonde, rising on his crutches,
plaintively pleaded that not only could he not see hon. members opposite, but he could only faintly catch the purport of
Mr. Bartley's speech. The member for North Islington
blushed with honest pleasure at these quite unwonted evidences
of interest in his views on current topics. The members hidden
behind the cases on the Conservative side acknowledged with
a murmured cheer the compliment paid them. Long as they
had sat there, face to face with the Radicals, they had never
learned how cherished was their presence till now it was
accidentally obscured.

Mr. Sydney Buxton suggested that Mr. Bartley should
continue his speech from the Treasury bench, where by a little
manœuvring members at the upper end of the benches below
the gangway could see him. Mr. Labouchere improved upon
this by suggesting that the member for North Islington should
scramble on to the top of one of the cylinders and thence
address the Senate At length the front Opposition bench,

LIKE, YET UNLIKE.

habitually slow to take the lead in popular movements, was stirred to action, and Mr. Childers, temporarily occupying Mr. Gladstone's place, entered a protest against what Mr. MacNeill had irreverently alluded to as "these vats."

The Speaker, yielding to pressure, ordered their removal. The six messengers, whose united ages seemed, after their earlier struggle with the vats, to exceed four centuries, reappeared. Amid breathless excitement the petition was trundled out, and an hour later the First Lord of the Treasury, rising in his place, dismissed the Licensing Clauses to join it.

June 30.—Mr. Chamberlain and Pitt. Strangers making their slow way to the gallery of the House of Commons are privileged to sit, sometimes by the hour, in the outer corridor awaiting their turn of admission. The corridor is lined with statues of eminent Parliament men, really lifelike presentments as statues go in this country. There is one of Pitt, which no one can look at without being struck by its remarkable likeness to Mr. Chamberlain. At Knole, the other day, walking up the broad staircase to the deserted rooms in which history was made, and in which Tudor Queens and Stuart Kings sometimes slept, I came unexpectedly upon another bust of Pitt, of much earlier date and considerably finer workmanship. Here the likeness was even more striking. There is the same keen face, the slightly tilted nose, not perfectly straight, and, with rare exactness, the same formation of mouth.

It is a curious resemblance, even more striking than one I discovered in the room at the Vatican, where are stored busts of dead Emperors and others who made ancient Rome. There is one there of Julius Cæsar, which recalls with striking force the face and head of Mr. John Morley.

July 4. — The last Chairman of the Metropolitan Board of Works. Lord Magheramorne, who was buried to-day at Brompton Cemetery, distinctly faded out of public life after he went to the Lords. The closing years of his public life were saddened by the discredit that finally killed the Metropolitan Board of Works, of which he was, for nearly twenty years, Chairman. Personally, no charge rested on his character in connection with the scandals brought to light by the Royal Commission. But to a gentleman of his temperament it must have been galling in the extreme to have had it made known that such things could take place under his nose and he all unconscious. In the House of Commons, where, with brief interruption, he sat for twenty-two years, he was a familiar figure. Not that he took prominent part in political events. It was sufficient for him to sit assiduously, vote regularly, cheer his leaders, and shake his head over the excesses of the Irish members. As Chairman of the Metropolitan Board of Works, he was a personage, and was marked by some of those little eccentricities which the House is quick to see and prone to delight in.

The Chairman of the Metropolitan Board of Works was one of two or three private members to whom it is permissible that questions may be addressed in the House of Commons on subjects concerning the body they officially represent.

When, as pretty often happened, inquiry was raised as to some procedure at the Metropolitan Board of Works, it was delightful to see Sir James McGarel Hogg—the bud from which Baron Magheramorne blossomed—rise from his familiar seat immediately behind the front bench on which the Conservative leaders sit.

Following the example of great Ministers of State when delivering important answers on imperial subjects, the Chairman of the Metropolitan Board of Works always had his answer written out on large foolscap in a clerkly hand. When he rose he turned to the impertinent questioner, casting upon him a terrible glance of mingled scorn and anger. Then, starting off in loud tone of voice, he began to read, punctuating the usually exceedingly commonplace passages of his reply by searching glances at the culprit, increasing in intensity. The House looked on and merrily laughed. But Sir James was stern and impassive, and nothing in the written word was nearly so eloquent as his gesture when he resumed his seat, which said plainer than words could utter—

"Here is a person who has presumed to call in question an action of the Metropolitan Board of Works; but I have crushed him."

July 7. — Mr. Chamberlain and the Liberals.

The strong personal feeling against Mr. Chamberlain which exists below the gangway, where he first sat when he entered the House of Commons, found sharp expression this evening. Coming in during the interval whilst the Speaker had gone to the Lords to hear the Royal Commission read, Mr. Chamberlain passed round by the Treasury bench to take a copy of the Orders on the table. As he stood there, quick eyes below the gangway caught sight of him, and immediately a sharp, angry shout was raised of "Stay where you are!" Mr. Chamberlain appeared not to hear the remark, and having found what he wanted, took his accustomed seat on the front Opposition bench.

"Black Rod!"

The entrance of Black Rod with a summons to attend in the other House to hear the Royal assent given by Commission to various bills, led to another and even more animated scene. It happened that Mr. Gladstone was on his feet addressing a question to the Attorney-General for Ireland. In the middle of a sentence, the doorkeeper, advancing to the Bar, shouted at the top of a stentorian voice, "Black Rod!" Thereupon Mr. Gladstone, in accordance with the ridiculous custom that makes such a thing possible, resumed his seat, leaving his sentence unfinished.

In ordinary cases this familiar episode would have been greeted with laughter, but the mere fact of Mr. Gladstone being peremptorily and rudely interrupted in his remarks by the entrance of an antiquated gentleman with white wand brought home to members not only the absurdity, but the unbearableness of the situation. They raised an angry roar of contumely, before which the doorkeeper judiciously retreated.

Poor Black Rod was bound to carry out his mission. A gallant Admiral and a Grand Commander of the Bath, he may be assumed in his time to have faced fearful odds. It is to be hoped for the credit of the navy that he did it with better heart when in command of his ship. This evening he managed with difficulty to walk up to the table. Arrived there, with that angry shout still ringing in his ears, his tongue clove to the roof of his mouth. For an anxious moment it seemed as if he were struck dumb, but at last he struggled into speech, and in tremulous voice invited the attendance of " this honourable House."

His withdrawal, walking backwards, was watched with keen anxiety by the House, no one sure that the venerable and gallant Admiral might not come to grief on the way. He, however, reached the door in safety, and formed part of the procession that accompanied the Speaker to the other House. Later, Mr. Waddy, amid loud cheers, called attention to what he described as an abrupt and unseemly interruption. The Speaker undertook to see what could be done to prevent its repetition.

<table>
<tr><td>July 14. — Lord
R. Churchill
and his tutor.</td><td>I hear a pretty story about Lord Randolph Churchill's Oxford days which ought to be true. It appears that when at Oxford he</td></tr>
</table>

developed a strong objection to compulsory attendance at chapel. After many warnings, his tutor sent for him, and entered upon a serious discussion of the matter. It was a chilly day, and when Lord Randolph entered the tutor was standing with his back to a cheerful fire. The discussion went on in animated form for some ten minutes, at the end of which time another delinquent was ushered in, and found, to his unconcealed amazement, that Lord Randolph was standing with his back to the fire, his coat tails comfortably uplifted, while the unfortunate tutor was arguing away out in the cold near the door.

"WITH AMARYLLIS IN THE SHADE."

July 16.—A Sir Richard Temple is the *preux chevalier* _ladies' man._ of Parliamentary life. With characteristic mastery of detail he has elevated to the rank of a fine art the pleasing duty of conducting ladies to the privileged recess by the glass door whence they may gaze upon the Commons. Others are content, having led their charges to the bench and pointed out Mr. Balfour, Mr. Bradlaugh, Lord Randolph Churchill, and Mr. Picton, to lead

them back into the lobby and take their leave. Sir Richard
Temple is not accustomed to deal in half-measures. Having
shown the ladies to the bench, he is concerned that they shall
be witnesses of the nice conduct of a member in passing to and
fro about the nation's business. So, whilst the ladies stand at
gaze, Sir Richard enters, advances slowly up the floor, halts at
the turn of the gangway, makes low and stately obeisance to the
Speaker, marches to his seat behind the Leader of the House,
puts on his hat, cries " Hear! hear!" and having sat for a while
conscious of the four pair of eyes fixed upon him at the doorway, rises, halts again at the turn of the gangway to bow low
to the Speaker, and marches out to receive the congratulations
of the ladies on the bench.

July 29.—Lord
Randolph and
the Ministry.
The sensation of the week in the political world
has been the sudden upheaval of Lord Randolph
Churchill. Whilst other politicians and statesmen have been busy at Westminster, working their way
through the Session, Lord Randolph has been enjoying his
new bent at Ascot and Newmarket, and has, I hear, been more
fortunate on the racecourse than of late he has been in the
political arena. Then, the racing drawing to a close, he
comes back, takes his familiar seat at the corner bench
behind his dear friends the Ministry, tugs at his moustache
through question time, goes his way to dinner, and does not
trouble to come back as poor Mr. Smith must do. Lord Randolph's comings and goings, the few persons who speak to him
in the House, the fewer still with whom he stops to chat in the
lobby, are all noted. On Monday the Prince and Princess of
Wales dined with him and Lady Randolph at Connaught Place,
among the guests bidden to the feast being Mr. Gladstone.
Earlier in the season it will be remembered he entertained at
the Junior Carlton Club another, and, it is said, a livelier party,
also to meet the Prince of Wales. Last night, returning for a
while to the arena of politics, he sat the honoured guest of the
Conservative Club in St. James's Street, and afterwards
delivered a eulogy on Conservatism, with some remarks on
its present official chiefs. In these last days of July people
get tired of reading political speeches; but everyone turns
this morning to see what " Randolph " has to say, and more

especially to know what may chance to be his personal attitude towards his former colleagues in the Ministry.

These things indicate one of the principal points of difference between Lord Randolph and the ordinary run of political personages. He is an interesting personality. Whatever we, in varying mood or from different points of view, think of him as a statesman, we are all interested in him, read what he has to say, watch what he does, and talk about him. In the House of Commons he is practically without a following. Mr. Jennings, once faithful among the faithless found, now sits silent and repellent on the bench behind his old friend, unforgetful of and unforgiving that curious incident which suddenly snapped their friendship. There is no doubt that if Lord Randolph pleased he might form a party, which, not numerically strong, might give the Government occasional check, proving a constant thorn in their side. But he has not manœuvred in that direction, has indeed treated Ministers with an amount of consideration that has seemed to suggest some private underground connection. There have been crises in the history of the Government during the present Session when it only needed Lord Randolph Churchill, with his quick insight and his bitter tongue, to make a diversion that would have finally upset them. But he has stayed away, or kept silent.

Now, it is said, negotiations are definitely on foot with the object of restoring him to the fold. The movement is based on an intelligible principle. The Ministry, as difficulties thicken about them, grow more insistent in their demand that Lord Hartington should join their ranks. That is all very well for them. But it would be a long step for Lord Hartington to take, and would greatly embarrass those still shrewder politicians, Mr. Chamberlain and Sir Henry James. They would like to see the Ministry strengthened, would in all reasonable ways assist at the bolstering up of the bulwark that is to keep Mr. Gladstone out of power. But there is something dearer to them even than personal hate, and that is self-preservation. If Lord Hartington goes over bag and baggage to the Tory camp the thin substance of the Dissentient Liberal party will disappear for ever. Some would imitate Mr. Caine, returning humbly to the Liberal fold. Others would follow their leader, and would take the Conservative shilling, enlisting finally in the Tory ranks. In such case what would become of Mr. Chamberlain and Sir Henry James ? That is an embarrassing question which need not arise if the Government were to receive an accession of personal strength that would serve instead of Lord Hartington's adhesion. The only man capable of strengthening it is Lord Randolph Churchill. Therefore Mr. Chamberlain and Sir Henry James, having put their heads together, are moving heaven, earth, and Lord Salisbury to get Lord Randolph Churchill invited back to the Cabinet and the Treasury bench.

July 21.—An old member. The announcement of the death of Mr. David Davies creates scarcely a flutter of interest in the present House of Commons. To more than one half the former member for Cardiganshire was an unknown person. Yet he sat in two of the most memorable and representative Parliaments of this reign, the Disraelian Parliament of 1874 and its Gladstonian successor of 1880. Mr. Davies was the architect of his own fortune, being personally connected with the growth of the railway system of Wales. He was reputed to be immensely wealthy, a conclusion no one would draw from his personal appearance or from listening to his homely speech. In the House of Commons he always had that uncomfortable appearance which the average British workman wears when he dons his Sunday clothes. He did not often address the House; but when he was on his legs he had an attentive and interested audience.

Mr. Disraeli particularly delighted in him, listening with a curious approach to a smile as the member for Cardiganshire, with one brawny hand hidden in the capacious pocket of his squarely-cut coat, the other wagging an explanatory forefinger, discoursed on the topic of the hour. Whatever it might be it almost invariably brought him back to confidential statements relating to his private business, to the number of workmen he employed, the wages he paid them, the work they did, what he thought of them, and what they thought of him. All this, told in colloquial tones, with a rich, rare Welsh accent, the mass occasionally lighted up by sudden flashes of humour, much delighted the House of Commons, and made the Montgomeryshire magnate a general favourite.

CHAPTER XXIX.

AN ALL-NIGHT SITTING.

Mr. Parnell—His Secretiveness—His Influence in the House—Mr. Goschen and his Budget—*Pas de Charge*—Mr. W. H. Smith—"A Band of devoted Gorillas"—Sir George and the Dragon—A New Procedure—Land at Last—Liberal Leaders—Mr. Labouchere.

July 27.—Mr. Parnell. HAD anyone twenty years ago evolved from his inner consciousness a type of a successful leader of the Irish people, Mr. Parnell would probably have served in almost every personal peculiarity to illustrate points to be avoided. The popular idea of a man who could sway an emotional people like the Irish was realised in O'Connell, and found much to satisfy it in Mr. Butt. There were circumstances that prevented Mr. Butt acquiring a position of dominant power either in Ireland or the House of Commons. O'Connell fully filled it, being as prominent a personage at Westminster as he was for a while omnipotent in the affection of the Irish people. It is doubtful whether O'Connell's personal influence was in its effect on practical politics as great as is Mr. Parnell's to-day. And the two men were in every respect—physically, mentally, and by temperament—wide as the poles asunder.

O'Connell lived under the broadest light of day. He delighted in publicity, courted society, and was as popular at the dinner table as he was in the streets of Dublin. Mr. Parnell is the mystery man of modern political life. On rare occasions there appear in the newspapers paragraphs stating that he dined under more or less obscure circumstances "to meet Mr. Gladstone" or some other of his former adversaries in the Liberal camp. Once the political world was riven to its centre by the intelligence that at the house of a famous advocate he had met not only Mr. Gladstone but Lord Randolph Churchill. These are exceptions to the rule, their infrequency helping to make them memorable. For the average political personage, dining out during the Session is

as much a part of his business as is sitting or voting in the
House of Commons. It is one of the happy incidents of
English political life that two men who have, amid excited
party cheering, crossed swords on the floor of the House of
Commons between five and seven in the evening may at half-
past eight find themselves
sitting side by side engaged
in the friendly converse of
the dinner table. Mr.
Parnell is never met at
the social gatherings
where, night after night
through the Parliamentary
Session, partisans meet
and mingle, sometimes
driving down to the House
together to recommence
the struggle over a ques-
tion that has stirred party
to its profoundest depths.

His secretiveness. Ono difficulty
in the way
of including him in the
average dinner party is
the doubt about his
address. A great journal,
still a factor in European
politics, once devoted a

THE IRISH LEADER.

prominent paragraph to the announcement of the discovery of Mr. Parnell's temporary abode. The name of the
lodger was not that by which the member for Cork is
ordinarily recognised. But the journal pledged its great
reputation that it was no other than he. The daily papers
cannot be always reckoned upon to be thus successful in
their enterprise, and the particulars of Mr. Parnell's private
address are through appreciable spaces of time whelmed in
the darkness of night. It is true that the House of Commons
is a standing address for all members. But Mr. Parnell's
visits to the House are rare and eccentric. Moreover, his

(relatively) intimate acquaintances complain that he does not think it necessary to open his letters on the day they reach his hand. Once a week, or at longer intervals, suffices to whet his curiosity as to the contents of the piles of letters that reach him, a process which has its convenience, inasmuch as in the interval many of the communications answer themselves.

Even with highly civilised nations like the Irish or the English a shadow of mystery brooding over a man greatly adds to whatever controlling influence he may have established by sterling ability. It would seem at first sight a hopeless condition of leading a party that the party should always be playing hide-and-seek with its leader, should never know where to find him, or when to expect him in its midst.

When Mr. Parnell is looked for in the House of Commons he does not come. When no one is looking for him his tall figure is seen flitting across the lobby. He speaks to no one, presses steadily forward, may disappear through the corridor and be seen no more, or may presently be found on his feet fluttering an astonished House with an unexpected speech. Banquo's ghost was not more fitful in its coming and going, nor did its appearance create more consternation, than sometimes follows on the sudden discovery in the House of Commons that Mr. Parnell is on his legs joining in debate.

His selection of a seat, and his very way of reaching it,

are all in keeping with the mystery that surrounds him. As
leader of an important party his natural position is the corner
of one of the benches below the gangway. When Lord
Randolph Churchill sat in that part of the House and led his
famous party, everyone knew where to find him—in a corner
seat now occupied by that other leader of a guerilla force, the
junior member for Northampton. On the corner seat behind
Mr. Picton sits and broods over mighty thoughts, and thence
he rises to read those thrilling orations which shake an empty
Treasury bench and chill the blood of Ministers hiding in
their closets. On the corner seat of the bench Mr. Parnell
frequents during his rare visits Mr. Tim Healy is generally
found, sharing the coign of vantage with Mr. Dillon.

All these eminent statesmen going to their place walk up
the floor of the House, seen of men. Their coming and going
is noted, and one desiring to find them knows where to look.
Mr. Parnell quietly reaches his place, midway down the bench,
passing behind the chair of the Serjeant-at-Arms, or, by
preference, entering by the door in the corner under the
gallery approached from the division lobby.

His influence in the House. Thus he entered at some unnoted hour when
discussion was going forward in Committee of
Supply on the vote for the Chief Secretary's salary. The
House, wearied with the iteration of personal abuse, was
almost empty. Mr. Balfour sat alone, languid on the Treasury
bench. It seemed that the level flood would flow on all
night, and there was nothing to do but to bend the head
and let it pass over as little noted as possible. Someone
sat down, having made an end of speaking; someone would
follow, it did not matter who, since it was certain the strain
would be unvaried. Then a clear, familiar voice struck
on the wondering ear, and, looking up, the few members,
marvelling, discovered that Mr. Parnell was in his place, and
was addressing Mr. Courtney.

In a moment the whole aspect of the place changed. Mr. Balfour sat attentive; members listening with dull ears to what had
gone before, turned with steadfast gaze to the bench below the
gangway, where the tall, slight figure with the pale face and
the gestures of restrained energy stood and talked. The tide,

steadily ebbing all evening, stopped and turned. Rapidly
yet silently the benches became tenanted, and before Mr.
Parnell had been on his feet ten minutes the empty chamber
was filled with a listening Senate.

Aug. 1. — Mr.
Goschen and
his Budget.
It was on the 17th of April Mr. Goschen brought
in his Budget, in a House densely crowded and
profoundly interested.   Here at last was a
Chancellor of the Exchequer with a bountiful surplus.   Some

MR. GOSCHEN.

said it was four millions, others fixed the sum at three.
Mr. Goschen in due time proudly announced that the precise
sum was £3,549,000. The House, put in a good humour by
this, listened with admiration to a speech three hours long, so
skilfully managed, so lucid in its arrangement, that it seemed
to take but little more than an hour for the unfolding of the
scheme.   The Chancellor of the Exchequer sat down a happy

man, exhilarated by the cheers that had followed his speech, and crowned with the compliments showered upon him. At worst it was said that, though not a striking Budget, an effect impossible to attain conjointly with its wide range over a multitude of subjects, it was a masterful, and likely to prove a popular one.

Alas! alack! Mr. Goschen, straining his eyes in backward glance to that bright evening in April, sees the pathway strewn with the wreckage of his Budget. His reward has been all kicks, unvaried even by occasional ha'pence. Attacked vigorously, even viciously, in the matter of his licensing proposals, the tea drinkers, who profited by his scheme to the extent of twopence a pound, have stood sullenly aside. The Volunteers, who had £100,000 placed at their disposal, have made no strategic movement in his defence; the promised reduction of seaborne postage has shed no soft light on the gloom of his condition; currants have not comforted him, nor the gold and silver smiths either. Not a word has been said on his behalf by the householder of £60 rent and under, who has had his house-tax considerably reduced. The good he has done has been written in water, whilst his errors have been engraven in brass.

Pas de chance.　The bitterest reflection for the Chancellor of the Exchequer in these closing days of a disastrous Session probably is that if anyone else had done exactly what he has achieved the result would have been quite otherwise. A few years ago the French newspapers were enchanted with a waif-and-stray brought up before a police magistrate, who appeared in the dock with a strip of paper pasted on his forehead, having written on it the legend *Pas de chance.* The man told a moving story of ill-luck persistently dogging his wearied footsteps. A model of moral rectitude, intellectual force, unremitting industry, and general aptitude for affairs, misfortune ever pursued him. The stars in their courses fought against him. He had no chance; and so, somehow, apparently without looking upon the wine when it was red, he got drunk; without stretching forth a hand he found himself in possession of other people's property. Full of human kindness, he discovered to his horror that he had unlawfully struck a neighbour, and, draggled, dishevelled, a helpless martyr to circumstances, he stood in the dock for the twentieth time, with his pathetic protest against ill-fortune bound about his forehead.

There is no parallel in Mr. Goschen's case except that, looking back over a Session through which he has gallantly struggled, displaying in his adversity all the qualities that made his way from a desk in the City to a seat in the Cabinet, he has had no chance. It is, perhaps, reasonable enough that a dead set should be made against him by the party he quitted. The pity of it is that he has not been sustained by a corresponding measure of personal enthusiasm in the party he joined.

Mr. W. H.
Smith.

In the meanwhile another Minister whose personal reputation has fallen into shadow is the First Lord of the Treasury. If Mr. Smith had retired from the Leadership of the House of Commons last Easter he would have carried with him a reputation not exceeded by some more famous predecessors in the Leadership of the House of Commons. Had he sailed away in the *Pandora* at Whitsuntide and returned to Parliamentary life only by the portals of the House of Lords he would have been remembered in the Commons as a Leader phenomenally successful through an epoch of unique difficulty. But, animated by a prevailing sense of duty to his Queen and country, Mr. Smith, broken in health and weary in spirit, returned to his post after Whitsuntide, a date since which disaster has daily dogged the footsteps of the Ministry. Up to that period, certainly up to Easter, they were as lucky as during the last two months they have been luckless. They made occasional mistakes, for, as Mr. Smith himself has observed, to err is human. But nothing did them any particular harm, or materially diminished their majority. Suddenly, without the force of attack seeming greater or the power of resistance less, the stronghold began to totter. The Ministerial majority was steadily reduced. The assailants grew in audacity, the defenders became disheartened, and at the end of a campaign that opened with the brightest assurance for the Government there is talk of forced capitulation.

The reputation of Mr. Smith as Leader of the House of

Commons, even if his term of office should close with the present Session, will certainly recover from the depressing influence of current events. The shrewdest and the fairest judge to which a man could submit his character and career is the House of Commons. For four years Mr. Smith has lived under its microscopic gaze, and he may cheerfully leave his reputation in its charge. It was a bold step, savouring rather of the originality of Lord Beaconsfield than of the character of Lord Salisbury, to nominate Mr. Smith to fill the place hotly vacated by Lord Randolph Churchill. If one were a possibly good Leader of the House of Commons, it seemed an inevitable corollary that the other would never do. Mr. Smith evidently had some doubt on the subject when he modestly took his seat in the place filled in rapid succession by Lord John Russell, Lord Palmerston, Mr. Disraeli, and Mr. Gladstone. But, as everyone knows, he turned out a heaven-born Minister for the time and place. No one else could have filled it—which was, indeed, the reason he was inducted.

He was essentially a safe man, whose lot in public life had hitherto been to fill up odd places vacated on sudden emergency. When in 1874 Mr. Disraeli singled him out for office in the comparatively obscure but really important post of Financial Secretary to the Treasury, people were good enough to say that, though this was a considerable advance for an untried man, he might do very well, and was lucky thus early in his Parliamentary career to be pitchforked into what was regarded as the highest office open to him. When, in 1877, the death of Mr. Ward Hunt made a vacancy at the Admiralty, the public learned with mild surprise that Mr. Smith had been selected for promotion to Cabinet rank. When what Mr. Chamberlain once called "the Stop-gap Government" of 1885 came into power, there being some difficulty about claims to the reversion of the office of Secretary of State for War, they were settled by Mr. Smith's taking charge of the Department, an office to which he returned when a Unionist Government was established by the General Election of 1886. He was quietly at work there when Lord Randolph Churchill flung all the fat in the fire by his secession, which, opening up interminable difficulties for the Government in tho future, peremptorily faced them with the problem of the succession to the Loadership of the House of Commons.

The situation was one calculated to appal the boldest spirit. Leader of a party that could maintain its supremacy only by the assistance of allies of strong individuality, linked by a single chain and liable to be drawn asunder by a dozen tendencies, pitted against the greatest orator and Parliamentarian of the age, not supported by any transcendent ability among his colleagues, Mr. Smith assumed the Leadership of the most critical, restive, and exacting body of men in the world. He succeeded in a manner that won for him in unprecedented degree the personal esteem of men in all parts of the House; and he has in exceptionally troublesome times done his party and his country a service that will be remembered when the vexatious incidents of the last two months drop into their due place in the proportions of the history of the present Parliament.

Aug. 8.—"A band of devoted gorillas." Sir George Campbell is momentarily under a cloud. For some days of the week he blazed forth with an oratorical effulgence that astonished even those long familiar with his gifts. Last Saturday's sitting he had had almost entirely to himself, Mr. Storey and Mr. Conybeare interposing to give him occasional breathing spaces. On Monday night he had made twenty-three speeches, and on Tuesday he had fallen only a little short of this record. It was on Wednesday he stumbled in a chance place. Rising to say a few last words on the Police Bill, he reviewed the situation with intent to show how valuable and patriotic had been his own services in debate. Generously desirous of including in the eulogy some other members, doubtless Mr. Storey and Mr. Conybeare, he had meant to make reference to "a band of us devoted guerillas." The Kirkcaldy accent, tempered by long familiarity with Hindustani, somewhat boggled over the Spanish word, and what the House heard was a reference to "a band of us devoted gorillas."

That was the end of this particular address. Even Sir George Campbell could not withstand the uproarious and prolonged laughter that greeted the phrase, and he was obliged to resume his seat without making clearer his pronunciation. Subsequent attempts to correct the impression conveyed were baulked by renewed outbursts of laughter; and for two sittings Sir George did not venture to reappear on the scene.

Aug. 10.—Sir George and the dragon. One gleam of sunlight was cast upon this afternoon's dreary sitting in connection with Sir George Campbell, though perhaps it need hardly be said it was not Sir George who dispensed the beam. He was making one of his incessant series of speeches, renewing for the twenty-eighth time his protest against the use of the familiar stamp of St. George and the Dragon on the backs of sovereigns. No one rose to offer reply or observation in continuance of his remarks, and the Chairman was putting the question, when Sir George hotly jumped up again and insisted upon his right to receive a reply. Mr. Smith with ponderous humour answered that, in asserting that the use of this die passed an insult upon Scotland, Sir George had brought a serious charge against the Chancellor of the Exchequer, and invited him to exhibit the articles of impeachment, so that Parliament might fully consider the serious gravity of the charge. Sir George insisting that St. George and the Dragon should not be represented upon any new coinage, Sir Wilfrid Lawson interposed, and gravely suggested, as a compromise, that a die should be cut representing *Sir* George and the Dragon; at which the House laughed the more heartily as it was the last word in the conversation.

Aug. 12.—Land at last. Land is visible at last across the stormy sea of the Parliamentary Session. To-night the last vote was taken in Committee of Supply, and there now remains only the process of the Appropriation Bill. This is jealously ordered, and must run its deliberate course though the Heavens fall and the House empties. There is the first reading, the second reading, Committee, and third reading, each stage having its own particular day. When it gets to the Lords the pace is sharpened, they bundling it through all its stages at the time they take the second reading. In the Commons the safety of the Constitution demands that there shall be no undue hurry, and thus it comes to pass that

the prorogation is always postponed by a week after the last
vote is taken in Committee of Supply. It is an old habit,
going back to Stuart days, when such precautions were need-
ful. Till the Appropriation Bill is passed money voted cannot
be paid out of the Treasury for the services of the State. So
the Commons keep their grasp on the neck of the purse till
they have had their last word with the Ministers who represent the sovereign.

Aug. 14.—A new procedure. An all-night sitting fighting round the Light Railways (Ireland) Bill. There were long stretches of
dulness, as usually happens when the House sits all night, but
there was one moment when the fun rose to almost screaming
pitch, though the laughter was all on one side. It was
about five o'clock this morning, when Mr. Conybeare moved
to report progress. The Chairman declared the motion to
be an abuse of the rules of the House, and put it without
opportunity of discussion. Having put the question, the
Chairman stated he thought the Noes had it. Upon this
ruling being challenged he declared in the phraseology of the
new rule, that the division was vexatiously claimed, and
directed the Ayes to stand up in their places. Sixteen members
promptly rose, and the Chairman counted them, whereupon they
sat down again, believing it was all over. But this was only
the beginning. Mr. Courtney, insisting upon their standing up
again, sent out for the clerks to come in and take down their
names. The clerks were fast asleep, and had to be wakened
up. Then they had to find their cards containing the list of
members, which they tick off at the wicket of the division
lobby. All this while the sixteen members were standing
glaring at the majority opposite, who, under apprehension
of a rebuke from Mr. Courtney, were ineffectually trying to
smother their laughter.

At length the clerks were brought in, and, standing at the
Bar with the large boards in their hands, began their task of
ticking off the names of the sixteen. It unfortunately happened that two of them were recent additions to the staff. They
did not know the members, and consequently could not tick
off their names. There was whispered consultation amongst
the little group at the Bar, fingers pointed, and heads nodded.

On this the laughter broke forth with uncontrollable force from the Ministerial benches, Mr. Healy furiously demanding whether they were there to be insulted, as well as to be counted. Mr. Courtney did his best to keep the scene within bounds, but it was irresistibly comic, and had something to do with the toning off of the opposition. There was only one more division challenged in Committee after this, and though Mr. Courtney permitted it to be taken in the usual manner, the minority did not know at what moment they might not be called upon again to stand up and go through the process of having their names ticked off by the sleepy clerks.

Liberal leaders. In these last days of a critical Session the House has been a dull place, tempered by occasional explosions. Mr. Smith has stuck gallantly to his post, though deserted by several of his colleagues who, like Mr. Raikes, have found it necessary to anticipate the recess. On the other side the flight of leaders has been a constant process, till to-day there is absolutely no one left on the front Opposition bench. That is a circumstance against which the Liberal Party is able to bear up with equanimity. Its possession in the way of leaders is indefinitely rich. Perhaps if it has a weakness it lies in this abundance. When Mr. Gladstone went Sir Wm. Harcourt and Mr. John Morley took turn about in leading the Opposition forces. When they departed Mr. Childers had a turn, and, sitting in Mr. Gladstone's place, found opportunity to reflect how in these later years he has been passed in the race, giving way to men who were not in the House when he was a Cabinet Minister, at the head of a great department, the state of his health a matter of profound public interest.

Mr. Labouchere. Mr. Childers has gone. But we still have Mr. Labouchere. Like the poor he is always with us. He is bound for Wiesbaden, and now is the height of the season in that charming town. But, as Mr. Labouchere puts it, his duty to his Queen and country keeps him in town as long as the doors of Parliament are open and there is any chance of Her Majesty's Ministers doing mischief. He was in his place to-night when Mr. Brookfield apostrophised Mr.

Conybeare, and he took up arms in behalf of the member for Camborne, bringing down on himself the attack of the enemy. It is eminently characteristic of Mr. Labouchere that he should have warmly resented an attack made on Mr. Conybeare. But that is his way: he sticks to a political friend, however personally unpopular he may be, and no one who does not live in the House of Commons can imagine how successful Mr. Conybeare has been in getting himself disliked. When in the dim and distant past that now (on the Tory side) eminently popular person, Mr. Bradlaugh, was an object of contumely, Mr. Labouchere stuck to him closer than a brother. Privately he would not hesitate a moment in saying what he thinks of Mr. Conybeare, and his opinion would doubtless be in accordance with that generally held. Publicly, when a Conservative attacks him, Mr. Labouchere promptly "goes for" the assailant, striking out as if he were resenting attacks on the most charming, inoffensive, and personally delightful member of the party.

Aug. 18.   Parliament prorogued.

SESSION OF 1890.

FEBRUARY.

11. Tues.—The *Times* and Mr. Parnell. Privilege. Motion, Sir W. Harcourt. Amendment, Mr J. Stuart. Division—Ayes, 312. Noes, 260. Main Question agreed to.

12. Wed.—H.M. Speech. Address. First Debate.

13. Thurs.—Ditto. Ditto. Second Debate.

14. Fri.—Ditto. Ditto. Amendment (Ireland), Mr. Parnell. Third Debate.

17. Mon.—Ditto. Ditto. Fourth Debate.

18. Tues.—Ash Wednesday Motion. Division—Ayes, 207. Noes, 108. H.M. Speech. Address. Fifth Debate. Division—Ayes, 246. Noes, 307.

19. Wed.—Ditto. Ditto. Amendment (Scotland), Dr. Clark. Amendment to the Amendment, Mr. Everingham. First Division — Ayes, 112. Noes, 274. Sixth Debate.

20. Thurs.—Ditto. Ditto. Amendment, Mr. Balfour, made to Mr. Crawford's Amendment. Division (harbour)—Ayes, 141. Noes, 191. Amendment (Distress and Parochial Councils), Mr. Mayrick. Seventh Debate.

21. Fri.—H.M. Speech. Address. Division—Ayes, 181. Noes, 254. Amendment (Free Education), Mr. A. Acland. Division—Ayes, 166. Noes, 232. Eighth Debate.

24. Mon.—Adjournment. Motion (Evictions, Ireland), Mr. Sexton. Division—Ayes, 164. Noes, 196.
H.M. Speech. Address. Amendment (Welsh State Department), Mr. Alfred Thomas. Withdrawn. Amendment (Hours of Labour), Mr. C. Graham. Division—Ayes, 86. Noes, 198. Address agreed to. Ninth Debate.

25. Tues.—Business. Motion (Supply this day and Friday next), Mr. W. H. Smith. Division—Ayes, 290. Noes, 131. Supply; Civil Services. Supplementary Estimates.

26. Wed.—Poor Law Guardians (Ireland) Bill. Mr. Ritchie. Bill put off six months.

27. Thurs.—Supply. Civil Services. Supplementary Estimates.
Western Australia Constitution Bill. House in Committee (committed). Companies (Winding up) Bill. Sir M. H. Beach. Committed.

28. Fri.—Supply. Vote on Account. Mr Labouchere's amendment.

MARCH.

3. Mon. — Ireland. Special Commission. Motion, Mr. W. H. Smith. Amendment, Mr. Gladstone. First Debate.
4. Tues. — Ditto. Ditto. Second Debate.
5. Wed. — Ditto. Ditto. Third Debate.
6. Thurs. — Ditto. Ditto. Fourth Debate.
7. Fri. — Ditto. Ditto. (House counted out.) Fifth Debate.
10. Mon. — Ditto. Ditto. Division on Amendment — For, 30[?]. Against, 2[?]. Debate on Main Question adjourned. Sixth Debate.
11. Tues. — Ditto. Ditto. Amendment, Mr. Caine. Division — For, [?]. Against, [?]. Main Question put and agreed to[?].
12. Wed. — Land Tenure (Ireland) Bill. [2n]. Committee. Bill put off six months.
13. Thurs. — Supply: Army Services. Amendment (Volunteer Equipments), Sir R. Reardon. Agreed to. Supply considered.
14. Fri. — Supply. Parliamentary Grants. Motion, Sir [G.] Trevelyan. Division — For, 100. Against, 175.
17. Mon. — Supply: Navy Services. Ships of War. Motion, Mr. Conolly. Withdrawn.
    Navy Supplementary Estimates.

18. Tues. — Rights of Way (Scotland). Motion, Mr. Buchanan. Ayes, 110. Noes, 97.
19. Wed. — Bankruptcy Bill. Sir J. [Lubbock]. Read 2°.
20. Thurs. — Supply: Civil Services. Vote on Account.
21. Fri. — Hereditary Legislature. Motion, Mr. Labouchere. Division — For, 160. Against, 201.
24. Mon. — Purchase of Land (Ireland). Mr. A. J. Balfour. Bill ordered. Allotments Act Amendment Bill. Read 2°.
25. Tues. — School Supply (York, &c.). Motion, Mr. [Newdin]. Division — Ayes, 11[?]. Noes, 1[?].
26. Wed. — Parliamentary Elections (Scotland) Bill. Dr. Clark. Division — Ayes, 12[?]. Noes, 1[?]. Bill put off six months.
27. Thurs. — Tithe Recovery Bill. Sir M. H. Smith. Debate on 2nd Reading. Adjourned.
28. Fri. — Ditto. Ditto. Division on 2nd Reading — Ayes, 2[?]. Noes, 1[?].
31. Mon. — Customs Department. Motion, Mr. J. [Clough], negatived.
    Supply: Civil Service Estimates.

APRIL.

1. Tues. — Supply: Civil Service Estimates.
14. Mon. — Supply: Civil Service Estimates.
15. Tues. — Hansard. Report of Supply and Ways and Means. Motion, Mr. W. H. Smith. Morning Sittings appointed. Ayes, 194. Noes, 102.
    Post Office Telegraphists. Motion, Earl Compton. Ayes, 106. Noes, 142.
16. Wed. — Rating of Machinery Bill. Mr. Winterbotham. Bill committed.
17. Thurs. — Ways and Means. Financial Statement, Mr. Goschen.
18. Fri. — Emigration. Motion, Mr. S. Smith. Division — For, 87. Against, 181.
21. Mon. — Purchase of Land (Ireland) Bill. Debate on 2nd Reading Adjourned. First Debate.
22. Tues. — Ways and Means.

South Indian Railway Purchase Bill. Committee.
Supply: Civil Services.
Labour and Capital. Motion, Mr. Burdley. Withdrawn.
23. Wed. — Intoxicating Liquors (Ireland) Bill. Mr. Lea. Division on 2nd Reading — Ayes, 34[?]. Noes, 72.
24. Thurs. — Purchase of Land (Ireland) Bill. 2nd Reading. Second Debate.
25. Fri. — Supply: Civil Services.
28. Mon. — Purchase of Land (Ireland) Bill. 2nd Reading. Third Debate.
29. Tues. — Ditto. Ditto. Fourth Debate. Licensing Law Amendment Bill. Lord Randolph Churchill. Bill read 1°.
30. Wed. — Marriage (Deceased Wife's Sister) Bill. Mr. H. Gardner. Division on 2nd Reading — Ayes, 272. Noes, 155.

MAY.

1. Thurs. — Purchase of Land (Ireland) Bill. Division on 2nd Reading. Fifth Debate. Ayes, 348. Noes, 26[?].
2. Fri. — Allotments, &c. Bill. Committee. Disestablishment (Church of Scotland). Motion, Dr. Cameron. For, 214. Against, 294.
5. Mon. — Customs Bill. Division on 2nd Reading — Ayes, 192. Noes, 115.
6. Tues. — Allotments, &c. Bill. Committee. Land Authorities (Acquisition of Land). Motion, Mr. Reid. Amendment, and agreed to.
7. Wed. — Charitable Trusts Bill. Mr. Buxton. Bill committed.
8. Thurs. — Customs Bill. Committee.
9. Fri. — Contagious Diseases (Animals) Bill. Committee.
    Education (Payment by Results). Motion, Mr. S. Temple. House counted out.
12. Mon. — Local Taxation (Customs) Bill. Mr.

[2nd] R. Amendment, Mr. Buxton. Debate on 2nd Reading adjourned.
13. Tues. — Ditto. Ditto. Second Debate.
14. Wed. — Ascension Day. Motion agreed to. Agricultural Labourers (Ireland) Bill. Dr. Fox. Bill committed.
15. Thurs. — Local Taxation (Customs) Bill. Division on Mr. Caine's Amendment — For, 248. Against, 252. Bill committed.
16. Fri. — Customs Bill. Committee. The late Sir W. Palliser. Motion, Col. Nolan. Division — For, 83. Against, 10[?].
19. Mon. — Customs Bill. Committee. House adjourned at 3.55 a.m.
20. Tues. — Ditto. Ditto.
21. Wed. — Ditto. Ditto.
22. Thurs. — Ditto. Ditto. Bill considered. Supply: Further Vote on Account.
23. Fri. — Business (Priority to Government Business). Motion, Mr. W. H. Smith. Customs Bill. Read 3°.

JUNE.

1. Mon.—Supply: Civil Services.
2. Tues.—Adjournment. Motion, Prosecutions (Metropolis), &c. [illegible], Derby Day. Motion, Lord [illegible]. Ayes, 102. Noes, 123.
   Supply: Education Votes.
3. Thurs.—Channel Tunnel Bill. Sir E. [illegible], Division—For, 153. Against, 234. Bill put off three months.
   Tithe Rent-charge Bill. Instruction, &c. [illegible]. Division—Ayes, 141. Noes, 241. Debate on Committee adjourned.
6. Fri.—Supply: Education Votes.
   Supply: Report.
9. Mon.—Instructions. **Mr. Speaker's Statement.**
   Adjournment. Motion (Pulleys in Cashel, &c.), Mr. [illegible].
   Western Australia Constitution **Bill.** Committee.
10. Tues.—Local Taxation (Customs) Bill. Committee.
11. Wed.—Infectious Disease Prevention Bill. Considered.
    Directors' Liability Bill. Considered.
12. Thurs.—Local Taxation (Customs) Bill. Committee.
13. Fri.—Ditto. Ditto.
16. Mon.—Ditto. Ditto.
17. Tues.—Adjournment. Motion, State of Public Business, Mr. Labouchere.

   Local Taxation (Customs) Bill. Committee.
18. Wed.—Directors' Liability Bill. **Further** considered.
19. Thurs.—Local Taxation (Customs) Bill. Committee. Division on Clause 1—Ayes, 215. Noes, 234.
20. Fri.—Supply: Civil Services.
23. Mon.—Railroad Bill partly considered. Select Committee, Mr. W. H. Smith.
    Local Taxation (Customs) Bill. Committee.
24. Tues.—Burglary Robbery Bill. Prohibition and Reading—Ayes, 172. Noes, 131.
    Mr. Speaker's Statement. Appropriation of Public Money.
    Adjournment. Motion, Public Meeting (Northampton), Mr. Labouchere.
    Housing (Working Classes) Bill. Mr. Ritchie. Read 2°.
25. Wed.—Directors' Liability Bill. **Further** considered.
26. Thurs.—Barracks Bill. Committee.
    Western Australia Constitution Bill. Committee.
27. Fri.—Police Bill. [illegible]. Bill considered.
30. Mon.—Barracks Bill. Considered.
    Western Australia Constitution Bill. Committee.

JULY.

1. Tues.—Western Australia Constitution Bill. Reported.
   Police (Scotland) Bill. The Lord Advocate. Read 2°.
2. Wed.—Directors' Liability Bill. Read 3°.
3. Thurs.—Adjournment. Motion, The Maharajah of Kashmir. Mr. Bradlaugh.
   Supply: Army Services.
4. Fri.—Western Australia Constitution Bill. Read 3°.
   Supply: Army Services.
7. Mon.—Supply: Civil Services.
8. Tues.—Ditto. Ditto.
9. Wed.—Bankruptcy Bill. Considered.
   Public Health Acts Amendment Bill. Committee.
10. Thurs.—Supply: Civil Services.
11. Fri.—Ditto. Ditto.
14. Mon.—Ditto. Ditto.
15. Tues.—Ditto. Ditto.
16. Wed.—Ditto. Ditto.
17. Thurs.—Ditto. Ditto.

18. Fri.—Ditto. Ditto.
21. Mon.—Housing of the Working Classes Bill. Considered and passed.
    Census (England, &c.) Bill. Read 1°.
    Savings Banks Bill. Debate on Second Reading adjourned.
22. Tues.—Census (England, &c.) Bill. Committee.
    Supply: Army Services.
23. Wed.—Supply: Civil Services.
24. Thurs.—Anglo-German Agreement Bill. Debate on 2nd Reading adjourned.
25. Fri.—Ditto. Ditto. Read 2°.
28. Mon.—Ditto. Ditto. Committee. Bill passed.
    Local Taxation (Customs, &c.) Bill. Committee.
29. Tues.—Ditto. Ditto.
30. Wed.—Ditto. Ditto.
31. Thurs.—Ditto. Ditto.
    Supply: Civil Services.

AUGUST.

1. Fri.—Local Taxation (Customs, &c.) Bill. Considered.
   Supply: Civil Services.
2. Sat.—Police Bill. Considered.
4. Mon.—Public Health Acts Amendment Bill. Considered.
   Police Bill. Further considered.
5. Tues.—Ditto. Ditto.
6. Wed.—Police (Scotland) Bill. Read 3°.
   Census (Ireland) Bill. Committee.
   Supply: Civil Services.
7. Thurs.—Ditto. Ditto.
8. Fri.—Ditto. Navy Services.

9. Sat.—Ditto. Army Services.
11. Mon.—Ditto. Civil Services.
12. Tues.—Ditto. Ditto.
13. Wed.—Ditto. Ditto.
14. Thurs.—Appropriation Bill. Read 1°.
    East India Financial Statement.
    Railways (Ireland) Bill. Committee.
    House adjourned at 7 a.m.
15. Fri.—Appropriation Bill. Read 2°.
16. Sat.—Ditto. Committee.
    Ditto. Read 3°.
18. Mon.—Prorogation.

SESSION 1800–1.

CHAPTER XXX.

COMMITTEE ROOM No. 15.

Mr. Parnell—Surprise—Depression—In the House—The Debate on the Address
—Mr. Gladstone's Ultimatum—Mr. Gladstone and the Irish Members—
Suspense—The Parnell Manifesto—Committee Room No. 15—Still Fighting
—Off on a Fresh Scent—Business in the House—Mr. Parnell Scores.

Nov. 25.—Mr. Parnell THE ceremony of opening Parliament by Royal Commission, always a dull affair, to-day lacked the grace and dignity of the presence of the Speaker. The illness under which everyone regrets to know Mrs. Peel is suffering kept the Speaker at home, and his place was taken by the Chairman of Committees. The usual procession was formed with the Mace carried by the Serjeant-at-Arms in the van. But Mr. Courtney walked without wig or gown, attired in the evening dress in which, even at morning sittings, he presides over the deliberations in Committee.

When at four o'clock, after a brief adjournment, he quietly stepped into the Speaker's chair the House presented a different appearance. Every seat was crowded, and there buzzed an excitement which portended more than ordinary interest in the opening of a new Session.

Mr. Parnell crossed the lobby shortly after two o'clock. Doubtless accidental, his arrival was well-timed if it was designed to avoid notice. It happened that at this moment the members of the House of Commons were in the Lords listening to the Queen's Speech, and the lobby was almost empty. An hour and a half later he appeared again, the lobby now crowded and the House full. In the meantime an important event had happened. The Irish members' meeting to consider the political situation, more especially with reference to Mr. Parnell's position as leader in view of recent proceedings in the Divorce Court, had unanimously and enthusiastically confirmed him in his post, and Mr. Parnell had accepted the mandate.   The news flashed through the crowded lobby before Mr. Parnell reappeared on his way to take his seat.   It was at first received with incredulity, but as the Irish members who had been present at the conference trooped in there was no longer room for doubt.   Questioned on the subject, they, whilst declining to state the grounds on which their decision had been arrived at, agreed on the main fact.

Surprise.   It would be difficult to exaggerate the sensation created by this unexpected turn of events. Last night it was so confidently expected that Mr. Parnell would save the Home Rule cause at whatever personal sacrifice, that some authorities were encouraged to put forth statements categorically affirming he had so decided, and that the business of the meeting to-day would be confined to receiving and registering the decision.   To the Ministerialists the unexpected news came as a flash of sudden light in darkness.   They, too, had been led to believe that even at the last moment Mr. Parnell would hesitate to sacrifice the cause for which he has done so much.   If he promptly stepped back the Home Rule position would be left intact.   To learn that he had decided to stay was for them all the more joyful intelligence since it was absolutely unexpected.   Mr. Chamberlain, who was in the lobby shortly after the news was made known, positively beamed with delight, and the Conservatives went about as light-hearted as if they had already won the general election.

Depression.   Amongst Liberals the feeling is almost over-whelming in its depression, disappointment, almost despair.   One hears on all sides admissions of the inevitable fatal consequences of the decision.   One well-known Liberal, on learning the decision, declared that Home Rule will be unattainable for the present generation.   Everyone agreed that if by any chance or manœuvre the Government could force a general election now they would obtain a majority.   A Scotch member showed me a letter received this morning from a gentleman whom he described as hitherto his principal supporter in his constituency, informing him

that if Mr. Parnell remained in alliance with the Liberal Party
as leader of the Irish the writer would never again appear
on the same platform as his friend the sitting member.

Some members clutch at the hope that things are really
not so bad as they look to-night. They have convinced
themselves that Mr. Parnell, having received the mark of
supreme confidence on the part of his supporters shown in
the passing of the vote to-day, will find an early and convenient opportunity of withdrawing himself from public affairs,
delegating his office to another. In conversation with some
of the Irish members who were at the meeting to-day, I find
no confirmation for this expectation.

In the House. Entering the House some minutes before Mr.
Courtney took the Chair and called on notices
of motion, Mr. Parnell took his accustomed seat below the
gangway in token of his acceptance of the position of leader
of the Irish Party, in which he had just been confirmed. No
demonstration, hostile or friendly, greeted his arrival, which
was not generally noted.

When a whisper went round that he was there, all
eyes were turned upon him. Usually he sits silent, taking
no notice of his neighbours. To-day he talked almost
effusively to members of his party sitting near him. Mr.
Gladstone, looking ill and distressed, was received with
a mighty cheer when he arrived, a similar compliment
being paid from the other side to Mr. Balfour when he came
in, the third cheer of the new Session being reserved for
Mr. Smith, who looked decidedly thinner in the face than
when he went off for his holidays. Lord Hartington came in
late, as usual, and was evidently in restless mood, passing in
and out several times. Once in skirting the front Opposition
bench he stopped to shake hands with Mr. Morley, whom Mr.
Chamberlain had already warmly greeted.

The debate on the Address. The rapidity with which the Address was agreed
to was not due in any measure to the mover,
who threatened never to finish his elaborate oration, which was
assisted to a conclusion by eloquent signs of impatience. He
and Mr. Forrest Fulton, who was comparatively brief, pretty

well succeeded in emptying the House. When the word went round that Mr. Gladstone was on his feet the benches rapidly filled up. It soon became clear that there was no fight left in the old leader. He rapidly passed over the various topics of the speech, notably declining to discuss Irish questions at the present juncture. He reserved his hostile remarks for the proposal of Mr. Smith to appropriate for Government measures all the time of the House up to Christmas, and sat down after quietly talking for three quarters of an hour.

Mr. Smith took his cue from this speech, being careful to avoid controversial subjects, and readily promising to find an opportunity for Mr. John Morley to have it out with Mr. Balfour about Tipperary. He spoke through the dinner hour to a scanty and inattentive audience. Mr. Parnell had commenced his new term of leadership by leaving the House as soon as it approached business, not even paying Mr. Gladstone the compliment of staying to listen to his speech. This example was largely followed, and by ten o'clock the whole thing flickered out, and, to the crowning joy of the elate Ministerialists, the Address was agreed to.

It is many Sessions since the Address was agreed to on the opening night. But it is many years since Parliament met in such queer conditions as environ parties to-day.

Mr. Gladstone's ultimatum.   Late to-night it was made known that Mr. Gladstone had written a letter indicating his position in respect to Mr. Parnell and the leadership of the Irish Party. The following is the text of the communication, addressed to Mr. John Morley.

1, Carlton Gardens, November 24th, 1890.

MY DEAR MORLEY,—Having arrived at a certain conclusion with regard to the continuance at the present moment of Mr. Parnell's leadership of the Irish Party, I have seen Mr. McCarthy on my arrival in town, and have inquired from him whether I was likely to receive from Mr. Parnell himself any communication on the subject. Mr. McCarthy replied that he was unable to give me any information on the subject. I mentioned to him that in 1882, after the terrible murder in the Phœnix Park, Mr. Parnell, although totally removed from any idea of responsibility, had spontaneously written to me, and offered to take the Chiltern Hundreds—an offer much to his honour, but which I thought it my duty to decline.

While clinging to the hope of a communication from Mr. Parnell, to whomsoever addressed, I thought it necessary, viewing the arrangements for the commencement of the Session to-morrow, to acquaint Mr. McCarthy with the conclusion at which, after using all the means of observation and reflection in my power, I had myself arrived. It was that, notwithstanding the splendid services rendered by Mr. Parnell to his country, his continuance at the present moment in the leadership would be productive of consequences disastrous in the highest degree to the cause of Ireland. I think I may be warranted in asking you so far to explain the conclusion I have given above as to add that the continuance I speak of would not only place many hearty and effective friends of the Irish cause in a position of great embarrassment, but would render my retention of the leadership of the Liberal Party, based as it has been mainly upon the prosecution of the Irish cause, almost a nullity.

This explanation of my views I begged Mr. McCarthy to regard as confidential, and not intended for his colleagues if he felt that Mr. Parnell contemplated spontaneous action. But I also begged that he would make known to the Irish Party at their meeting to-morrow afternoon that such was my conclusion, if he should find that Mr. Parnell had not in contemplation any step of the nature indicated.

I now write to you in case Mr. McCarthy should be unable to communicate with Mr. Parnell, as I understand you may possibly have an opening to-morrow through another channel. Should you have such an opening I beg you to make known to Mr. Parnell the conclusion itself which I have stated in the earlier part of this letter. I have thought it best to put it in terms simple and direct, much as I should have liked, had it lain within my power, to alleviate the personal nature of the situation. As respects the manner of conveying what my public duty has made it an obligation to say, I rely entirely on your good feeling, tact, and judgment.

Believe me, sincerely yours,
W. E. GLADSTONE.

Nov. 26. — Mr. Gladstone and the Irish members.

Various accounts are current of the incidents which led up to the issuing of Mr. Gladstone's ultimatum, and the subsequent history of that document. I have had the opportunity of ascertaining the facts at first hand, and am permitted to state them. Mr. McCarthy received on Monday a communication from Mr. Gladstone inviting him to call. Mr. Gladstone, in the course of the conversation, entered fully into his views on Mr. Parnell's public position as affected by recent proceedings in the Divorce Court. He plainly declared that if Mr. Parnell did not retire, it would be fatal to Home Rule. The next general election, whenever it came, would be lost by the Liberals, and, Mr. Gladstone added, as far as he is concerned, that would be his last chance, as at his age he could not look forward to another opportunity of taking part in the struggle.

He made no declaration of his determination to retire into private life if Mr. Parnell persisted in holding the leadership, nor did he make any reference to his having written a letter on the subject to Mr. John Morley. As a matter of fact, Mr. McCarthy did not know of the existence of the letter till eight o'clock last night. Consequently, the statement put forward this afternoon, to the effect that he possessed the knowledge, and whilst communicating it to Mr. Parnell withheld it from his other colleagues at yesterday's meeting of the Irish Party, is absolutely without foundation.

There was evidently some lamentable bungling in dealing with the letter. Mr. John Morley saw Mr. McCarthy at his house yesterday some hours before the Irish Party met, but did not make any reference to the letter, which must then have been in his possession. Mr. Parnell learned of it only after the meeting. I gather the opinion from several members of the party that had the contents of the letter been within their knowledge at the time the meeting took place the result would have been different. Its influence is seen in the meeting to-day, which has been further adjourned till Monday, when it is expected Mr. Healy will be present, and means will have been taken to ascertain the views of the members now in the United States. Up to to-night Mr. Parnell absolutely declines of his own free will to withdraw from the leadership. The attitude he takes up is that it is for the members of the party to decide.   At Monday's meeting a vote will be taken on the issue.

Nov. 27.—Suspense.   As soon as the House rose the Irish members proceeded to another consultation on the matter agitating the public mind. This more formal gathering was supplementary to a series of consultations held in the lobby and within the House. There is nothing particularly new to-day, everybody waiting till communication is received from Mr. Dillon and Mr. Wm. O'Brien absent in America. It is felt to be a particularly unfortunate thing that this crisis should find the Irish Party so ill-represented in London. It is better now Mr. Healy has come over, for he is a tower of strength. But there is no disguising the fact that the majority of members here are men who have been drawn from obscurity by the personal intervention of Mr. Parnell, and it is, of course, particularly awkward for them to range themselves against him. As far as they have spoken, all the principal men of the party have declared in favour of Mr. Parnell's retirement.   Mr. McCarthy, Mr. Healy, and Mr. Sexton speak with one voice, and one of them tells me to-night that nothing that can happen will induce them to swerve from what they regard as the path of duty.

Mr. Dillon, whose counsel is deservedly weighty in the councils of the party and the ear of the country, had not up to the adjournment of the House made known his view. But Mr. O'Brien, speaking as yet in guarded language, has cabled a message in favour of retirement. As for Mr. Parnell, he is immovable. It is reported, in explanation of what is on the part of so clear-sighted a man an amazing error of judgment, that in the course he has taken he is dominated by the personality that has through the last nine years exercised so malign an influence on his career. He insists that there is nothing in Mr. Gladstone's letter to Mr. John Morley that conveys a determination to retire if he (Mr. Parnell) continues to hold office. All through the evening he has been in active telegraphic communication with Ireland, it is understood in connection with efforts to be made to force the hands of his colleagues by a series of mass meetings, to be held on Sunday, declaring in his favour.

Nov. 24.—The Parnell manifesto.

The announcement that Mr. Parnell is about to issue a manifesto addressed to his constituents, but meant for the people of Ireland, has aroused the bitter resentment of an important section of his colleagues. They regard it as a fresh breach of faith, it being understood that between the adjournment on Wednesday and the meeting on Monday no step was to be taken beyond ascertaining the opinion of the members of the party at present in America. The adjournment on Wednesday was itself brought about by one of those tactical movements for which Mr. Parnell is famed. It was evident on counting heads that if the motion to rescind the election which had taken place on the previous day were then put Mr. Parnell would be beaten by two to one. In these circumstances he put up Mr. Richard Power to move the adjournment, a step which at least averted defeat. But it was an honourable understanding that the delay was not to be used by either side for any campaigning movement, an undertaking strictly observed by the section of the party led by Mr. Healy, Mr. Sexton, and Mr. Justin McCarthy.

Mr. Parnell has not been in the House to-night, and, as usual, nothing is known of his movements or intentions. Possibly his manifesto may appear in the morning. He was determined to send it out last night, and was deterred only upon the urgent representation of Mr. McCarthy that in the circumstances such a step would be regarded as a breach of faith. He would not do more than promise to delay its issue for twenty-four hours. To-night, in expectation of the step being accomplished, a meeting was summoned of members of the party who, in view of Mr. Gladstone's position, are determined that Mr. Parnell shall retire from the leadership. They must await the issue of the manifesto before taking definite steps; but they have resolved that its appearance shall be immediately followed by some action on their part.

Discussing in private conversation the probable effects upon Home Rule of severance from the Liberal Party, Mr. Parnell states that when he paid a visit to Hawarden Mr. Gladstone communicated to him the outlines of his Home Rule scheme, and they were so unsatisfactory from the Irish point of view that alliance with him was not a matter of real value. It is thought possible, though it seems incredible, that some statement of this kind may appear in the manifesto.

Dec. 1.—Committee Room No. 15.   The interest pertaining to the House of Commons has to-night been centred upon the committee room upstairs where the Irish members have been in session, rather than in the chamber where the Tithes Bill is under discussion. When, in the continued absence of the Speaker, Mr. Courtney took the Chair, the benches below the gangway where Mr. Parnell and his followers usually sit were conspicuously empty. The contagion of absence spread to other parts of the House, notably the Conservative side. The Treasury bench was the only one to the right of the Speaker that was filled. Mr. Gladstone was not in his place during question time, and Sir William Harcourt and Mr. John Morley, sitting shoulder to shoulder, seemed to indicate that there was no expectation of his arrival. When he is looked for his seat between his two lieutenants is usually kept vacant. But about four o'clock he turned up, Sir John Gorst, who was on his legs answering a supplementary question, being interrupted by a sharp cheer from the scantily-occupied benches on the Opposition side.

Mr. Gladstone looked well, and has evidently quite recovered from the mental and physical depression into which he was plunged last Tuesday by the news of the position taken up by Mr. Parnell. One of his colleagues who has come into close communication with him during the last few days tells me that not from the first, even to this aggravated last, has a single word passed his lips showing personal animus against Mr. Parnell. " Poor fellow, poor fellow," he says when some new development of what, in the House of Commons, is charitably regarded as the Irish leader's madness, is brought under his notice. He seems genuinely troubled in consideration of the distress in which he assumes Mr. Parnell is steeped.

The Irish members summoned to decide on the question of the leadership met punctually at twelve o'clock, adjourned an hour later for luncheon, and up to six o'clock, when a

second adjournment took place for an hour, remained in
session. The proceedings have been carried on in strict
privacy, but to members and others passing to and fro along
the corridor there was plain evidence that the proceedings
were of an exceedingly animated character. Rounds of
cheering frequently echoed along the passage, and familiar
voices were heard raised in excited controversy. Shortly
after the House met information leaked out that Mr. Parnell,
resolved at any cost to thwart the majority, had instigated a
motion for the adjournment. This was resisted by the
majority, but the minority, not unpractised in obstructive
tactics, succeeded hour after hour in preventing a decision
being reached.

Just before midnight the long struggle in the committee
room ended by a compromise, the meeting standing adjourned
till to-morrow. To-morrow will see the fight renewed, not
without a prospect of the triumph of physical force directed
with absolute unscrupulousness by Mr. Parnell, who completes
his outrage upon the usages of public meeting by presiding
over a court summoned to decide upon his own fate.

Dec. 2.—Still fighting. The Irish members met again at noon to-day,
under the presidency of the man upon whom
they are convened to pass judgment. They sat all through
the afternoon, and have sat through the evening up to eleven
o'clock, the same obstructive tactics which yesterday proved
successful in averting a decision being renewed. No one sees
Mr. Parnell's game with clearer vision than his old colleagues,
Mr. Healy, Mr. Sexton, and Mr. McCarthy. Every day's delay in
postponing judgment is of advantage to him. Something, no
one knows what, may turn up. However that be, it is certain
whenever a vote is taken it will go against him, and he is
resolved to put off the fatal moment as long as possible.

To-day's protracted meeting was not less excited than
yesterday's. Mr. Parnell, a master of obstruction, kept the thing
going as long as possible, but even for him there was an
end of objection, and close upon eleven o'clock Colonel
Nolan's motion adjourning the meeting to Dublin three weeks
hence was put to the vote. It turned out that Mr. Parnell's
adherents mustered twenty-nine, whilst those against him

counted up forty-four. This majority of fifteen in so small a party is pretty conclusive. Mr. Parnell, talking to a friend in passing out of the committee room, was quite elate at the result. He had reckoned that at least fifty members would be polled against him. There still remains the main question of the retention of the leadership, which will be dealt with at the meeting to be held to-morrow, when Mr. Parnell, pleased at his success, will still endeavour to gain time.

Dec. 3.—Off on a fresh scent. A cloud of mystery has suddenly descended upon the proceedings in Committee Room No. 15. I hear two versions of what happened. One is that Mr. Clancy, instigated by Mr. Parnell, submitted a resolution, by way of compromise, proposing that the leadership should remain in commission for a specified period, Mr. Parnell meanwhile withdrawing into retirement, thereafter returning to take charge of affairs. The other report is that Mr. Clancy's resolution was drawn up with the object of pledging all the Irish members to declare that no scheme of Home Rule would be satisfactory which did not hand over to the Irish Parliament the control of the police and the direction of the working of the Irish Land Act.

What this has to do with Mr. Parnell's conduct brought to light in the Divorce Court, or even with the more definite question raised by the majority of the members whether Mr. Parnell shall any longer remain leader, it is difficult to see. In ordinary circumstances it would be incredible that permission should be given to go off on this by-scent, but it must be remembered that Mr. Parnell is in the chair, and the published accounts of his demeanour in that capacity prepare the public for anything. Whatever be the nature of the amendment, it is evidently regarded by the Irish members as a new and important departure. It was arranged, upon the motion of Mr. Sexton, that an adjournment should take place shortly after four o'clock, the sitting being resumed at noon to-morrow.

Business in the House. If the Irish members do not shortly begin to make more rapid progress, they will find themselves sitting alone at Westminster. The extraordinary progress made with public business has entirely changed the prospects of the Session. When the House met eight days ago it was expected to sit certainly up to Saturday, the 20th of December, and might possibly run into Christmas week. Matters have been so ordered that the neck of the work appointed for the Session preceding Christmas is already broken, and the adjournment for the recess cannot be far off. It may take place this week. It will certainly be accomplished early next week.

The news which came down to the House of Commons just before six o'clock this evening, that the Irish members had unanimously adopted Mr. Clancy's resolution, was at first received with natural incredulity. It seemed impossible to believe that the able and experienced men who lead the opposition to Mr. Parnell should have permitted themselves to be thus hoodwinked. Called upon to decide the simple question whether, in the interests of Ireland, Mr. Parnell should or should not be permitted to retain the leadership, having had one division which demonstrated their numerical supremacy, and just strengthened by the support of the bishops' manifesto, they chose this very day for succumbing to Mr. Parnell's wiles, and yielding to him the victory, which must be all the more precious since it has been snatched out of the depths of what a day or two ago seemed hopeless defeat.

Mr. Parnell scores. What happened this afternoon was that an offer was made on behalf of Mr. Parnell that if Mr. Gladstone, in response to a demand made upon him in the name of the Irish members, should consent to include in his Home Rule Bill provisions placing the constabulary, the appointment of the Judges, and the control of the Land Act, in the hands of the Dublin Parliament, Mr. Parnell would forthwith retire from the leadership of the party. Mr. Healy and Mr. Sexton permitted themselves to be drawn into this audaciously planned side issue, and in the end it was agreed that a committee should be appointed, drawn from both sides of the controversy, and should wait upon Mr. Gladstone and obtain his views. To-morrow the Irish Party will meet again, and will receive the report of this committee. There is a unanimous feeling among influential members of the party that Mr. Gladstone is not likely to be drawn into the meshes of any such net. Even if it were reasonable to suppose that at this particular time, under the circumstances of the hour, he should with a pistol at his head deliver up pledges to a Home Rule Bill to be brought in at some indefinite period, who is to guarantee that next week, or the week after, or a month hence, Mr. Parnell may not resume the leadership?

However things turn out, it is clear Mr. Parnell has heavily scored. He poses before the Irish people as the patriot ready to sacrifice himself and his prospects if only good terms can be made for Ireland. In the exceedingly improbable circumstance of Mr. Gladstone falling into the trap, the Mr. Fox of the Divorce Court would temporarily retire with flags flying and drums beating. If Mr. Gladstone declines to be a party to the comedy, what will Mr. Parnell do, and in what position will the majority be who have to-day fallen into this astounding error? These are questions put in the House to-night without answer being forthcoming to the latter one. As to the former, there is no doubt Mr. Parnell, strengthened in the popular view in Ireland by the position taken up on the coming Home Rule Bill, will sit tighter than ever, and will doubtless weary out his adversaries, retain the leadership, break up the alliance with the Liberal Party, and so indefinitely postpone the realisation of Home Rule for Ireland.

CHAPTER XXXI.

PARALYSIS OF THE OPPOSITION.

Mr. Gladstone and Irish Members—The Parnell Blight—In the Absence of the
Irish Members—Mr. Labouchere—Collapse—The Divided Irish Party.

Dec. 5.—Mr.
Gladstone and
Irish members.
THERE is general approval in Liberal circles of
the attitude assumed by Mr. Gladstone in his
interview this morning with the delegates of
the Irish Party. That he should have consented to the interview is quite another thing. Sir William Harcourt in particular was hotly opposed to holding any communication with
the Irish members arising out of the initiative of Mr. Parnell.
To use Sir William's phrase, the Liberal allies of the Irish
Home Rulers have eaten dirt enough in connection with Mr.
Parnell, and it is time they peremptorily closed their mouths.
Mr. Gladstone is above all things courteous, and when application was, in respectful terms, made to him by a number of
members of the House of Commons asking for an interview
he did not refuse it.

But when the delegates produced Mr. Clancy's resolution,
which set out with a preamble referring to different versions
of the conversation that took place at Hawarden between Mr.
Gladstone and Mr. Parnell, he, in dignified but resolute
manner, declined to discuss the matter so introduced. The
delegates, thus firmly though courteously rebuffed, retired, and
reported the result of their mission to the Irish members once
more assembled in Committee Room No. 15. It was resolved
that an attempt should be made to meet Mr. Gladstone's views,
and by eliminating the objectionable phrases induce him still
to discuss the matter with them. As soon as the House met
this afternoon it was known that the negotiation had reached
this stage, and that the Irish delegates were at that moment
endeavouring to arrange another interview with Mr. Gladstone.

There is, amongst Liberals, a strong disinclination that Mr.
Gladstone should budge a step further. It is clearly seen,

though the Irish members of course deny it, that up to now
Mr. Parnell has triumphed all along the line.   He is, it is true,
prepared to retire; but he dictates the circumstances under
which his withdrawal shall take place, and has so arranged
matters that should Mr. Gladstone, out of desire to serve the
majority of the Irish members, make any statement acceptable
from their point of view on the Home Rule question, the Irish
people will give all the credit to Mr. Parnell.   English Liberals
agree with Sir William Harcourt in asking why, after all the
abuse levelled upon Mr. Gladstone, he should be called upon
to deliver the majority of the Irish members from a position
into which they have been drawn by a momentary irresolution
and lack of judgment surprising to contemplate.

Dec. 6. — The   It is the unexpected that happens, especially in
Parnell blight.   the House of Commons.   No one, not even
Zadkiel, could have foreseen the precise turn of events which
have made the past fortnight in Parliament memorable amid
its moving annals.   Six weeks ago, when the Midlothian
Campaign was in full blast, the prospects of the new Session
seemed so definitely assured that precise plans of action were
sketched on either side.   It seemed certain that the Ministry
would return to their labours in dejected spirits, to face an
Opposition aggressive with the near prospect of final victory.
Mr. Balfour's action in stirring afresh the muddy waters of
Irish politics by arresting Mr. Dillon and Mr. O'Brien had been
looked upon askance even in the most loyal Ministerial circles.
It was openly doubted whether he had not unnecessarily gone
out of his way to inflame the Irish Party on the eve of the
meeting of Parliament.   Whilst these things were talked of
Eccles was being fought, with result that shed an effulgent
light over Mr. Gladstone's pathway across Midlothian.

Opposition speakers and writers could scarcely contain
themselves for joy at the prospect of coming conflict in the
Commons.   There was high talk of a resolution, to be moved
from the front bench, calling upon the Crown to dismiss a
Ministry that no longer possessed the confidence of the country,
and to dissolve a Parliament that successive bye-elections
showed did not represent its views.   Short of that there would
certainly be an amendment to the Address, and a pitched

battle with some further reduction of the Ministerial majority.

What happened on Tuesday, the 25th of November, when Parliament met, is already a matter of history. The mighty militant host of the Opposition shrank and shrivelled into impotent nothingness. Mr. W. H. Smith, rising up early on the morning of the intended battle, looked forth on the host of the Hawarden Sennacherib, and, behold! they were all dead corpses.

Never was there such swift, sudden, complete collapse of a political party. It had all come to pass between a Saturday morning and sunset, and, as often happens in the best laid schemes of man, it was a woman who had done it. The dramatic concatenation of circumstances that fixed the opening of a famous divorce case so that its conclusion should take place on the very day preceding the meeting of Parliament had been viewed with sublime indifference by the party to which, as it turned out, it was a matter of life and death. To the Liberal faith in these later days had been added a new article, embodying absolute belief in the dicta of Mr. Parnell. He had been made the co-respondent in an action in the Divorce Court, and it was acutely perceived that if he should come out of the ordeal besmirched it would be an exceedingly awkward thing for a party of the State whose foundations were deeply set in strata of morality and respectability. But Mr. Parnell, smilingly shaking his head, had said there was nothing in it. It was a weak invention of the enemy, the machination of political perfidy.

"Davitt," he had said in one of many similar conversations, "you may tell our friends in Ireland that I shall come out of this matter without a stain."

Honest Mr. Davitt, glowing with generous triumph, had flitted about on his triumphant errand. It is at this moment curious to reflect what absolute authority a simple affirmation from Mr. Parnell carried in certain circles up to ten o'clock of a day only a fortnight old this very morning. Mr. Davitt told Mr. J. Morley; Mr. Morley rushed off enthusiastically to convey the glad tidings to Mr. Gladstone; an archbishop heard the news with quiet assurance of its indubitable authority; and through the allied Home Rule camp there breathed a holy

calm, a sweet assurance that there was still another triumph
in store for a persecuted man, and that the bolts of calumny,
the shafts of slander, would once more rebound and strike
the guilty breasts of those who had launched them.

Mr. Parnell, as to-day he reviews his new position, and
finds himself a pariah in the household where he was of late
enshrined, must reflect with bitter feeling on the childish
credulity now given place to uncompromising distrust.

Dec. 8.—In the absence of the Irish members. "It is an odd and striking result of the private
peccadilloes of the Home Rule leader that
during the last fortnight the country should
have been privileged to watch in dual aspect the practical
operation of the Home Rule scheme. Ever since Parliament
met we have had working side by side an Irish Home Rule
Parliament and a British House of Commons practically
relieved, as it was to have been under Mr. Gladstone's Bill of
1886, of the presence of Irish members. As an object lesson
the experience has been of priceless value. The Irish Parliament have been discussing what, if they were established at
College Green, would be their first duty. They have been
engaged in the choice of a President or, as he would be called
in Parliamentary phrase, a Speaker. With what calmness of
demeanour, what dignity of bearing, what interchange of
courtesy, this little matter can be arranged by Irish gentlemen
meeting in circumstances entirely of their own conception,
arrangement, and control, all the world has been privileged to
witness. How in their absence business has gone forward in
the House of Commons corresponding columns of the morning newspapers record." Thus a well-known Conservative
member, writing to a friend.

Mr. Labouchere. It has been, to tell the truth, a trifle dull. Even
the spirits of Sir George Campbell have flagged,
and he has delivered fewer speeches in a given space of time
than the House of Commons has enjoyed in its recent history.
The effect on Mr. Labouchere has been almost pathetic. He
is a man of natural imperturbability, trained by constant
care and inured by daily habit. When the storm burst and
everybody was shuddering under the shocks of thunder and

sheltering their eyesight from the flashes of forked lightning,
he came up smiling, asking in deliciously drawling voice what
was the matter? The new Session, as he had not thought it
necessary to hide from the knowledge of hapless Ministers,
was to be for them one of final disaster. Hitherto they had
been saved from perdition by an unaccountable hesitancy on
the part of right honourable gentlemen on the front bench
(who had themselves been in office) to depart from certain
trim, old-fashioned, and ineffectual methods of Parliamentary
warfare. Constrained by inborn reverence for authority and
respect for veteran leaders, Mr. Labouchere had held his hand.
The time had come when further trifling with the situation
would be a crime, an act of treachery to his country. Ministers
were to be smitten hip and thigh, assailed day and night, admitted to no quarter, driven persistently and remorselessly to
find refuge and escape in a dissolution.

In the first hours of the new Session Mr. Labouchere was
as good as his word. He began at the beginning, meeting
Mr. Balfour's motion for leave to introduce the Land Purchase
Bill by a hostile amendment. But the result chilled the energy
even of this undaunted soul. His words echoed through a
nearly empty chamber. Behind him, where was wont to sit
the phalanx of Irish members applausive of attacks on Mr.
Balfour, there yawned a great and dolorous gap. Mr. Gladstone, who might be supposed to have something to say on a
new Irish Land Bill if time and opportunity were fitting, sat
silent on the front bench, eloquently inert, significantly listless. It is hard work for a man accustomed to set the table
in a roar to look round and find a quiet, sober circle, with here
and there an empty chair. Mr. Labouchere was unusually
brief, and the House, grateful for this kindness, generously re-
pressed a yawn as he resumed his seat. Sir Wilfrid Lawson
followed amid surroundings growing increasingly funereal, and
when he sat down no other rose. Sir George Campbell moved
uneasily on his seat, cast an agonised glance round the House,
half rose to his feet, and despairingly fell back. It was a great
opportunity, a sore temptation. To find an opening as early
as five o'clock on the second day of a new Session to discuss
the principal measure of the Government was a joy not often
within his grasp. On reflection he thought it were not well

to grasp it. So the debate flickered out, and on a division the Ministerial majority suddenly leaped up to the long unfamiliar figures of one hundred and fifty-one.

Collapse. Since that night Mr. Labouchere has practically effaced himself, and with his retreat has disappeared the last trace of anything like obstruction. There has, indeed, been scarcely anything approaching debate on the various measures brought forward by the Government, albeit these have included topics round which last Session controversy fiercely raged. The Tithes Bill, which the Welsh members were sworn to resist to their last gasp, was read a second time after a lifeless conversation that died before the end of a single sitting. The Land Purchase Bill, which the Government after strenuous efforts were last Session compelled to abandon, passed the same critical stage after debate had, for decency's sake, been carried over from Tuesday into Wednesday's sitting. Mr. Balfour's scheme of Irish relief, involving expenditure the limit of which he judiciously declines to define, was confirmed without a division, leaving time at the same sitting to carry into Committee the Tithes Bill, and to pass through its final stages one of those Irish railway Bills which within the present year revived the memories of an all night sitting. In brief, the Government have accomplished all their appointed work, and a section of the Session expected to last up to Christmas Eve, with probably inadequate result, is already within sight of adjournment.

Dec. 9.—The divided Irish party. The section of the Irish Party under the leadership of Mr. Justin McCarthy have promptly got into action. They held a meeting this afternoon before the assembly of the House, and took various supplementary steps to constitute themselves a party absolutely distinct from Mr. Parnell's leadership and following. A committee was appointed to confer with Mr. McCarthy on all matters affecting the affairs of the party. It includes Mr. O'Brien and Mr. Dillon, Mr. Sexton, and Mr. Healy, and is thus specially designed to prevent a recurrence of that personal dictatorship which has shaken the party to its foundation. Another step taken was the election of a Whip to fill the vacancy created by Mr. Richard Power's fidelity to Mr. Parnell. Mr. Deasy, who has long been Mr. Power's colleague, will now be the first Whip of the newly-formed party, and Sir Thomas Esmonde his assistant.

DICK POWER.

Mr. Parnell has been in the neighbourhood of the House during the greater part of the day, and, as usual, no one knew what step he would be likely to take in connection with proceedings. The McCarthyites accordingly determined to take possession of their old quarters. As soon as prayers were over they marched in, filing along and filling the second and third benches below the gangway, where for many years, whether Liberals or Conservatives were in power, the Parnellites were accustomed to sit. As they mustered thirty-eight, they made a goodly show, Mr. Parnell's contingent being represented solely by Colonel Nolan, who sat on the front bench, by the chair of the Serjeant-at-Arms.

December 9. Adjourned for Christmas recess.

CHAPTER XXXII.

DEATH OF MR. BRADLAUGH.

Reassembling—Rip Van Winkle—New Members—The Original Irish Party—
Death of Mr. Bradlaugh—Lord Randolph Churchill's Beard.

Jan. 22, 1891.—
Reassembling.

MR. PARNELL was early in his place on the re-assembling of the Commons to-day after the Christmas holidays. He is determined that Mr. McCarthy and his friends shall not repeat the strategic movement successfully carried out after the break up of the conference in Committee Room No. 15, when they appropriated all the seats in the Irish quarter. Mr. Parnell secured his own, modestly situated half-way down the bench, where for more than ten years he has occasionally sat, coming in unexpectedly and going off without leaving a trace behind. There was notable among other changes recent events have brought about a decided improvement in his personal appearance. His eccentricity of dress used to be remarkable. To-night he is as spruce and well dressed as if he were about to become a bridegroom. As soon as opportunity offered he struck

JUSTIN McCARTHY.

in, in the character he insists on preserving as leader of the

Irish Party. Just before the House adjourned for the Christmas recess, Mr. McCarthy, acting as leader, gave notice of a motion calling attention to the action of the Executive in Ireland, with special reference to the cases of Mr. John Dillon and Mr. O'Brien. That was at the time counted one to the newly-constituted party. To-night Mr. Parnell, calmly ignoring the existence alike of Mr. McCarthy and his resolution, gave notice of a motion identical in purport, adding that he will ask the Government to set aside a day for its discussion. This is an adroit move, which may have the effect of embarrassing the newly-linked friendship and admiration of the Constitutional Party for Mr. Parnell. Mr. Smith can hardly be expected to grant the favour asked, whereupon Mr. Parnell will be able to pose before the Irish people as the patriot leader again rebuffed by a Saxon Government.

Jan. 29. — Rip Van Winkle. Rip Van Winkle slept for twenty years in the ravine of the Kaatskill mountain where he met the stranger carrying the keg, and everyone knows how marvellous was the transformation scene he beheld when at length he stumbled down to revisit his native village. It is nearly twenty-five years since Pope Hennessy was last privileged to sit covered in presence of the Speaker of the House of Commons. As to-night he (now Sir John) walked up the floor to renew his oath and once more take his seat he must have felt much as Rip Van Winkle did, hastening through the altered street of his village home and gazing on the strangely familiar but curiously altered faces. Much in the exterior view is the same as when he passed out of the House a quarter of a century ago. There are the gas-illumined roof, the benches on either side, with men old and young lounging about. Straight before him is the table, with its brass-bound boxes, its recumbent Mace, and its volumes of *Hansard*. At the farther end are the three clerks in wig and gown diligently writing, as he had left them. Behind is the canopied Chair, in whose recesses sits a stately gentleman in wig and gown. The electric lights about the passages and under the galleries within the House itself are, truly, new. For the first time, as Sir John heard, there is a strangely bright illumination over the arched doorway that gives entrance

to the chamber. Electric lights cunningly set in the stone-
work of the arch spread an effulgent light, which gives the
prosaic doorway an appearance curiously stage-like.

This is certainly new, but having passed it, as under an
illuminated triumphal arch raised to celebrate his happy
return, the Parliamentary Rip Van Winkle feels quite at home.
Everything is there save the old familiar faces, and of these
only one is present to bid him good evening and wonder where
he had been all these years.

New Members. The new member for Kilkenny, considering his
long public career and his manifold services to
mankind, has preserved even unto this last a certain air of
mature youthfulness. Representing his Sovereign in various
more or less salubrious quarters of the Empire, he has
acquired for State occasions a certain dignity of mien
worthy the traditions of our proconsuls. New members
enter the House of Commons in various fashions. There
is the new member who, having handed to him the printed
form of the oath, kisses it at the conclusion of the Clerk's
recital instead of saluting the book which the Clerk holds
ready for him. There is the member who always wants to
walk off before he has signed the roll. There are still more
who, having signed, turned round to march back before being
presented to the Speaker, and are captured by the wary Clerk
ere they have passed the Mace. There are quite a number
of members who when on their arrival at the table the Clerk
holds out his hand to receive the return to the writ effusively
shake it. There was one member a few Sessions back who,
being cheered by his political friends and ironically applauded
from the other side, fell a step behind his escort, and, folding
his hands before him, advanced with leisurely pace, bowing
first to the right and then to the left, with smiling visage, elate
at the unexpected universality of his welcome.

Sir John Pope Hennessy, an old Parliamentary hand, fell
into none of these errors on his reappearance on the
Parliamentary scene. If fault were found with his manner it
might be objected that it was a little haughty. Whilst Mr.
McCarthy and Mr. Sexton, walking on either side of him, approached with the regulated obeisance to the Chair, the new

member, with head erect and shoulders squared, advanced as
if he were approaching the cannon's mouth.   He was not unmindful of the dignity of the House, or of what was due to the
Speaker.   But long habit learned in Labuan, fostered in the
Bahamas, developed in the Windward Islands, cultivated at
Hong Kong, and finally matured in the Mauritius, had thrust
its fibres deep.   The Imperial mantle was not at a moment's
notice to be lightly cast aside like an old cloak.   Much was due
to the Speaker, but something to the Governor of a succession
of Colonies.   The proconsul whose dignity is now merged in
the membership for Kilkenny disdained to lower his crest even
in the presence of the Mace.

The Original
Irish Party.

To be led to the table by Mr. Justin McCarthy
and Mr. Sexton was of itself an event that
marked much that had happened since the old-time member for King's County had last approached the Speaker's
chair.   These were representatives of the very latest development of the Irish Party, born but yesterday.   When
Mr. Pope Hennessy represented King's County *he* was the
Irish Party.   Since then there have been a series of
editions of that great work.   It is quite ancient history
to go back to the time of Mr. Butt; yet he flourished
some seven or eight years after Mr. Pope Hennessy disappeared from the Parliamentary arena.   During the long
interval of Rip Van Winkle's sleep Mr. Parnell had risen into
fame, had run through a chequered career, and even now was
commencing another and not the least striking chapter of it.
Last time the gentleman now member for Kilkenny had approached the Treasury bench he would have found Lord
Palmerston sitting there, with Mr. Gladstone Chancellor of the
Exchequer, Sir George Grey at the Home Office, Lord John
Russell looking after Foreign Affairs, Sir Charles Wood at the
India Office, and Sir Robert Peel *fils*, having recently succeeded
Mr. Cardwell as Irish Secretary, meditating his resignation
because he found the post a sinecure.   Mr. Gladstone still
tarrying at Hawarden, not a single man seated to-night on
either front bench had the right to sit on the Treasury
bench when Rip Van Winkle was here last, and only a few
had seats elsewhere.   The Serjeant-at-Arms is new; the

Speaker is many times removed in succession to the gentleman to whom Rip had made his farewell bow.

Only one face, watching the scene from the doorway, recalled to the awakened sleeper days and nights that are no more. Of three intimate companions in the frolics of aforetime only this one is left. One has joined the majority. The gentleman known to the House of Commons of a quarter of a century ago as Mr. Frederick Lygon, sometime Lord of the Admiralty and anon Lord Steward of the Queen's Household, is now Earl Beauchamp, a peer sobered by the recollection of having several times sat on the Woolsack as one of the Royal Commissioners. In those far-off days Mr. Lygon used to figure prominently in the little party of four whose antics Lord Palmerston watched with rare manifestation of impatience. This was the original Fourth Party; these were the true inventors of obstruction. Before Sir John Pope Hennessy's return only one was left in the House, still with something boyish in his appearance, and with a disposition to break forth from his later judicial demeanour when staircases whose architectural structure he does not approve are placed in Westminster Hall. But Mr. Cavendish Bentinck is, alas! no longer young; and Rip Van Winkle, coming back to the old scene, and looking on the furrowed brow and the strangely scanty hair of his old companion, feels that his sleep must indeed have been prolonged.

<table><tr><td>Jan. 30.—Death of Mr. Bradlaugh.</td><td>It is almost exactly nine years since Lord Randolph Churchill, rising amid an animated scene, moved a resolution declaring that Mr.</td></tr></table>

Charles Bradlaugh, having taken his seat without having taken the oath, "is as dead." That Mr. Bradlaugh was at the moment very much alive was a circumstance of which the House had fullest evidence. He was sitting under the gallery with folded arms and a smile of triumph on his face. He had just made a fresh and startling move in the campaign he through the long life of the Parliament of 1880 carried on against religious and political intolerance. He had swooped down on the unsuspecting House after it had passed another of the long series of resolutions declaring the elect of Northampton incompetent to take his seat either after oath or affirmation. Appearing suddenly at the table, where his burly figure with the Serjeant-at-Arms literally dancing attendance had long been familiar, he produced a book out of his breast pocket—it was later discovered that in ex-

MR. BRADLAUGH.

treme of punctiliousness he had furnished himself with a copy of the then just issued revised version of the New Testament— and murmured some words, finally kissing the book with a lusty salute that reverberated through the silent and astonished House. Then, nothing omitted in his preparation, he took out a slip of paper, signed his name, and deposited the sheet in convenient contiguity to the Clerk, so that he might at his leisure add the signature to the Roll of Parliament.

"Is as dead," and now lies dead indeed, having in the interval since Lord Randolph Churchill wrote his epitaph won his way by sheer ability and force of character to a recognised position in an assembly wont to storm contumeliously at his appearance, and which once thrust him bodily forth. It is a striking coincidence in a memorable career that Mr. Bradlaugh lived just long enough to succeed in having expunged from the records of the House the resolution that stood there through eleven years declaring him ineligible either to take the oath or to make affirmation. This was a final act of justice upon the accomplishment of which he had set his heart. A motion to that effect had stood in his name upon the paper through every Session of the present Parliament. But he had not succeeded in bringing the question to an issue. Only in this, his last Session, was he favoured at the ballot-box, obtaining the first place on the agenda of last Tuesday's business. His strident voice was not heard in the discussion; but, lying in the shadow of death he yet pleaded with added force, and the motion Dr. Hunter moved in his place was unanimously carried.

Mr. Bradlaugh's stormy and dramatic conflict with the House of Commons began in the earliest days of the Parliament of 1880, with what far-reaching effect upon the course of business and upon the fortunes of political parties is a matter of history. When, on the 3rd of May, 1880, the newly-elected member for Northampton came up amid a batch of new members and claimed the right to make affirmation, he was to all but some two or three known only by name. He had written things that profoundly shocked the religious convictions of Sir Henry Wolff; and when, at a later course of the proceedings, Lord Randolph Churchill had occasion to cite from a collected edition of his works, the noble lord found relief from his outraged feelings by flinging the volume on the floor of the House, as Burke once cast the dagger.

A taste of Mr. Bradlaugh's quality as debater and orator was first given when, towards midsummer of that year, the House having by a majority of forty-five declared that in no circumstances should he be allowed to take his seat, leave was grudgingly given that he might be heard at the Bar. That was a memorable scene, never to be forgotten by those who witnessed it. It was a Wednesday afternoon, but some move on the part of Mr. Bradlaugh, in response to the vote taken shortly after midnight, was expected, and the House was crowded in every part, in itself an unwonted sight on a summer afternoon. The brass pole, shut up in telescope fashion within the range of the cross benches, was drawn out amid a thrill of excitement. The House was still young and eager to make acquaintance with all forms of Parliamentary institutions. Even to many old members this line of gleaming brass, flashing in the sunlight across the familiar gangway, was something new. Presently Mr. Bradlaugh was ushered in and conducted to the Bar, the Serjeant-at-Arms standing at his side with sheathed sword, his nervousness in marked contrast with the colossal calmness of the burly man in square-cut black clothes, looking much more like a street preacher than the author of the book that had shocked Sir Henry Wolff and made Lord Randolph Churchill's fingers tingle with uncontrollable indignation.

It presently began to dawn on the majority that, quite undesignedly, they had furnished Mr. Bradlaugh with an enormous personal advantage. Ordinary members addressing the House speak from the place whence they rise, facing only a portion of the audience, with their backs to some, other sections sitting to the right and left. Here was Mr. Bradlaugh standing in the place where the tribune would be if one were erected, with his audience full in view, subject to every oratorical influence he could bring to bear. It was a rare dilemma, developing a unique opportunity such as no other new member had ever possessed. The maiden speech forthwith delivered was a success the brilliancy of which even the outcast member's bitterest opponents admitted. He spoke for just twenty minutes, a limitation displaying profound judgment and remarkable instinct. The matter of the speech was as powerful as its delivery was eloquent. He indulged in no recrimination, only occasionally in declamation. With that legal acumen and debating skill the House had many subsequent opportunities of enjoying, he sought to establish his position as one suffering under an illegal act performed by no less illustrious a body than the House of Commons.

"What are you going to do with me?" he finally asked, dropping his voice from the stormy height of passion to which it had momentarily risen. That was a crucial question, against which the House of Commons impotently strove through the remaining Sessions of this Parliament. It forthwith tried to answer it by sending him to the Clock Tower. This was done on the motion of Sir Stafford Northcote, at the conclusion of the afternoon's proceedings. The next day the right hon. gentleman came down and, amid inextinguishable laughter, moved that "Mr. Bradlaugh be now discharged." Later, the House invoked the assistance of the police, ran him out of the lobby, thrust him down the staircase neck-and-crop, and delivered him, panting and ragged, on the footpath of Palace Yard. More than once Mr. Bradlaugh resigned, was triumphantly re-elected, presented himself to take his seat, and was denied admission. So things went on till the Parliament of 1885 met, when, his old adversaries not being desirous of letting a smouldering question further burn, resolved that they had done enough during Mr. Gladstone's first term of office to vindicate Christianity, and Mr. Bradlaugh was quietly permitted to take his seat.

Under altered circumstances he became a changed man. No longer bullied, he refrained from attack. He round whose body disorder had been invoked in the cause of order became one of the most respectable and redoubtable champions of precedents. In late years it has come to pass that Mr. Bradlaugh found his most attentive and appreciative audience on the side of the House that nine years ago combined to chivey him off the premises. At peace with the world, at rest from old adversaries, he lived long enough to mellow into something approaching staidness of Parliamentary position. He spoke often, but not too frequently; for he had always something useful to say, some new light to throw on the points debated. He was listened to with respectful attention, the House not only admiring his ability, but convinced of his honesty of purpose. He was essentially a working member, bringing to the consideration of all subjects a clear head, sound judgment, and remarkable breadth and depth of knowledge.

The House of Commons papers, in members' hands to-day
bear testimony on many pages to his energy and industry.

It was to be a busy Session for him, and already, on the threshold, he is finally shut out. Still in the prime of life, with an honourable position won against what seemed overwhelming odds, with hands full of work he meant to do, he has, in sad pathetic way, made answer to the cry " Who goes home?" that every night as the lights go down echoes through the lobby and the corridors of the House of Commons.

Feb. 3. — Lord Randolph Churchill's beard. Lord Randolph Churchill is back to-night, and has created considerable excitement by presenting himself with the adornment of a beard. This is rather hard on the caricaturists, who have made the public familiar with his clean-shaven chin and cheeks and his somewhat formidable moustache. He sat in his old place, and pursued his old habit of resolutely tugging at his moustache, entirely ignoring the latest development. He looks in much improved health, but did not find inducement to remain long in the House.

CHAPTER XXXIII.

PASTORAL TIMES.

Mr. Gladstone—In Sunny Weather—A Peaceful Household—The Radicals at Rest—The Boulogne Negotiations—Mr. Balfour and the Irish Members—"Jemmy" Lowther—An Old-time Manner—In Time of Fog—Lord R. Churchill's Recreations—A Link with the Past.

Feb. 4. — Mr. Gladstone. Mr. GLADSTONE'S speech in moving the second reading of the Religious Disabilities Bill was an indirect but conclusive answer to rumours recently current asserting his intention of retiring from the political arena. Probably no one believed the reports, the latest and most circumstantial not being even well invented. The least credulous would be those who come into most intimate personal relations with the marvellous octogenarian. Mr. Gladstone's public life, his attendance on the House, his frequent speeches there, his incidental orations in passing to and from Hawarden, his incessant letter-writing, form a task sufficient to exhaust the energies of an average man. He lives all day at the same glowing heat, lending upon the smallest relation or incident of ordinary life an energy that is superhuman. He has developed in these later days the character of an indomitable diner-out. After an amount of miscellaneous work sufficient to the day thereof he comes down to the House, listens to the long list of questions, bestowing upon each attention that could scarcely be more absorbing if it were the topic of the day; probably delivers a speech that would, if it stood alone, establish a Parliamentary reputation; and then, going off to dinner, becomes for two or three hours the centre of attention, holding in easy thrall a listening circle. To some men half his age the desirable conclusion of a day such as he lives through would be a quiet dinner at home, a placid evening, and an early bed. Mr. Gladstone's stock of energy is inexhaustible, and when others, after the final task of dining out, call their carriages and roll sleepily home, he as a rule prefers to button up his coat, take stick in hand, and walk off at a swinging pace.

Mr. Gladstone is probably looking forward with restless desire to the time when he shall once more be in charge of public affairs and sit on the bench at the other side of the table, in the place now anxiously filled by Mr. Smith. The passage, into whatever fortune it may lead him, will certainly be out of the pleasantest and most desirable epoch of his life. He has been in office many times and has struggled through long periods of Opposition. Never before has his personal estate been so gracious. He cannot forget, and the memory is not too pleasant for the House of Commons, jealous of its own reputation and careful for the fame of one of its most illustrious members, the state of things that prevailed in a similar period dating from 1874 to 1880. In Opposition then he was the mark of venomous contumely and a kind of personal hatred happily rarely manifested in English politics. The mob in the streets broke the windows of his private residence, and the mob in the House of Commons, assembling in the division lobby, hooted him through the glass door as he walked past to record his vote. His interpositions in debate were interrupted in unmannerly fashion without precedent since the days of

Dr. Kenealy. The hapless dog that darts down the course at Epsom on the eve of the race would not, if it possessed full opportunity of comparison, have changed places with the great orator rising to address the House of Commons in the Sessions of 1876 or 1877.

In sunny weather. All that is changed, and Mr. Gladstone, basking in sunnier weather, takes on a mellower mood. His personal preponderance in the House was never greater even at the time when he was master of an irresistible majority. Differences of political opinion are in no sense less acute. It is in the personal relations established between himself and the House that the change is notable. If he is enthusiastically cheered by his partisans the Ministerial majority sit in silent, respectful attention, now and then not withholding the tribute of a cheer. Liberals, Conservatives, Unionists, whatever they be, the House is all one in admiration of the genius of the great Parliamentarian. On Wednesday he had ventured upon a topic well calculated to stir the depths of ancient animosity. The situation was not soothed by the apparent gratuitousness of the irruption. No one has been able to discover any adequate reason why, just now, Mr. Gladstone should turn up on a Wednesday afternoon with a Bill calculated to raise once more, in whatever subdued tones, the old "No Popery" cry. Had he incidentally taken such a step fourteen years ago the House would have been aflame with indignation. The Fiery Cross would have been lighted at Ballykilbeg, and would have been passed from hand to hand till it filled the House of Commons with sulphurous flame and blinding smoke. On Wednesday Mr. Gladstone spoke to a crowded House, with the cheers of his supporters not once disturbed by a discordant note, whilst the tribute due to the power and dignity of his eloquence was rendered from the Treasury bench, first by the Leader of the House, and next, a much more noteworthy sign of the times, by the Attorney-General. As for Ballykilbeg, Mr. Johnston, with whatever tingling of the blood, sat silent in his seat, subsequently finding relief for overcharged feelings by issuing his mandate to Belfast, addressed, not to the disparagement of Mr. Gladstone, but to the boycotting of Sir Henry James, who spoke and voted in favour of the Bill.

A peaceful household. It is well to cherish while it lasts this pleasant interlude in Mr. Gladstone's long political life. It is not likely to survive many months after the possible triumph at a general election. Now is the placid period of expectation; then will be the rugged reality of responsibility. Mr. Gladstone is exceptionally happy, among other circumstances, in the peace that dwells among those who are of his own household. As Mr. Forster lived to learn, the Treasury bench with a Liberal Administration is not a cushioned seat. Just now on the front Opposition bench rivalries do not exist, and if any right hon. gentleman is disturbed by anxious thought it is for the personal advance and aggrandisement of his brother. The danger threatening from the domestic difficulty in the Irish camp has had the effect of drawing closer the bonds that unite the brotherhood of ex-Ministers. With disunion in the allied camp all would be lost if they, at least, did not stand together. The arrangement by which Sir William Harcourt and Mr. John Morley share the leadership during Mr. Gladstone's frequent absence works admirably. Sir William has, in truth, this Session developed a sweet equability of temper perhaps a little portentous.

The Radicals at rest. In other parts of the House to the left of the Speaker the same happy state of things prevails. There are at the present time absolutely no caves inhabited, no tea-room parties muttering revolt over their muffins. Doubtless here, as on the front bench, it is the influence of the threatened danger in the Irish camp that is responsible for the closing up of the ranks. However it be, the fact deserves recognition. Mr. Labouchere is still to the fore, but has not nearly so much State business on hand as has been his wont. Even at the worst of times he has tempered insubordination with a personal allegiance to Mr. Gladstone not always common in other cabals within the Liberal ranks. Nothing is now heard of the Radical section, the identity of whose leader was doubtful, there being several Richmonds in the field, but which last Session had a distinct organisation and the regulation number of Whips.

Mr. Gladstone primarily profits by this unusual concaten-

ation of circumstances, and for the while lends a life of rarely
equalled freedom from anxiety. Whilst Leader of the
Opposition, with an unquestioned authority never before
enjoyed by him, he is free from the petty cares and exhausting
labours of the office. Though regular in his attendance at the
commencement of the daily sittings, alert, watchful, brimming
over with energy, he is seldom seen after dinner. He can
leave with the restful assurance that in his absence one or
other of his trusty lieutenants will be on guard to the end.
This is a condition of affairs happy for him and conducive to
that steady advance of public business just now the marvel of
Parliamentary life. It is a period of peaceful pasturing that
some who browse unconcernedly through it will in tumultuous times not far ahead look back upon with fond regret.

Feb. 12.—The
Boulogne ne-
gotiations.
For a long time the Irish camp has been in a
desolate, disorganised state. The business at
Boulogne, where Mr. Parnell has with supreme
tactical skill been playing with his former colleagues,
whatever other effect it might be hoped to accomplish,
paralysed the energies of the Parliamentary Party. Only
Mr. Tim Healy had been able to show signs of bearing up
against it, and he in spasmodic inconsequential style differing widely from his former inveterate activity. An influence
resembling that of a wet blanket, or, to be more precise, of a
tear-damped pocket-handkerchief, lay over the once lively
party. The influence of Mrs. Gummidge on the Peggotty
household was as predominant as, strictly considered, it was
weak. For nearly two months the Irish Party have had their
Mrs. Gummidge, sitting in a comfortable hotel at Boulogne
" thinkin' of the Old 'un," "a lone lorn creetur and everythink
goes contrairy." Mr. William O'Brien's wails, sobbing over the
responsive Channel, have reached Westminster, and have
sapped the strength and vivacity of what at one time was an
irrepressible party.

There is, perhaps, none of the Irish Party who will serve
exactly to represent other members of the Peggotty family.
In kindness of heart and simplicity of manner, Mr. Justin
McCarthy is not lacking in reminiscences of Dan'l. But he
wants the robustness of figure, the seadog bearing, the rough

pea-jacket, and the knee-high boots of the old fisherman. Mr. Healy, in his directness of speech and steadfastness of purpose, recalls Ham. But he, too, falls short of all resemblance in certain personal particulars. About the Mrs. Gummidge of the household there is no mistake, more especially in the singular patience and forbearance with which her damping influence has been endured. When, more than two months ago, the majority of the Irish members quitted Committee Room No. 15, after formally deposing Mr. Parnell from the leadership, there was an end of the business as far as they were concerned. Mr. Parnell might struggle against his doom, and might even prove the victor. At least it seemed probable that the fight would be an open one, he on one side of the field, and they on the other. Some time after hostilities had actually commenced, when Mr. Parnell had drawn first blood in the crowbar expedition against the offices of *United Ireland*, and had subsequently received a knock-down blow at Kilkenny,

DAN'L, M.P.

Mr. O'Brien suddenly and unexpectedly appeared on the scene, pocket-handkerchief in hand, and there commenced the long series of depressing interviews of which Boulogne in winter time was made the appropriate stage.

It would have been so easy for sturdy Mr. Peggotty, with or without Ham's assistance, to bundle Mrs. Gummidge off the premises, entreating her to carry elsewhere her tears, her unavailing regrets, her fond reminiscences of broken idols, and let workaday people get on with their business under the actual conditions of the hour. But as Mrs. Gummidge was

permitted to sit in the most comfortable corner by the fire-side
mopping moist eyes whilst she thought of the Old 'un, so Mr.
O'Brien was suffered at Boulogne, whilst he enlarged in lachry-
mose tones upon the infinite virtues and graces of the lost
Leader, whose utter casting away he sought to avert.   It
would have been easy for the Parliamentary Party, keenly alive
to knowledge of whose game the supersensitive member for
North-east Cork was unconsciously playing, to go their own
way unmindful of his plaints.   But human nature is the same
whether on Yarmouth beach or Boulogne strand, and Mrs.
Gummidge is still a power in the land.

Feb. 13. — Mr. Balfour and the Irish members. Mr. Balfour has his varying moods on the
Treasury bench.   Sometimes, happily most
often, he is dangerously playful, stingingly
deferential, smilingly contradictory. To-night, fresh from a
storm-tossed passage on the Irish Channel—" not the least
invincible of Irish difficulties " he is reported to have said—he
sat in his seat, pale, stern, implacable, portentously busy with
the contents of his despatch-box. Mr. Healy broke in upon
his labours with question roughly phrased and truculently
delivered as to " when any portion of the fund for the relief of
distress would be handed out ?"   Mr. Balfour paused, looked
up from his papers, put his head on one side as if pondering
what this could possibly mean, and then coldly answered, " I
do not know what fund the hon. gentleman refers to."

" Lord Zetland's fund," Mr. Healy obligingly explained.

Then the lightning flashed forth and the thunderbolt
fell.

" The reason I asked the question," the Chief Secretary said,
turning aside from Mr. Healy as if it were impossible to hold
further conversation with him, and explaining the matter to
the bystanders, " was that I could not believe, unless it were
specifically stated, that he would ask me across the floor of the
House about a private fund with which this House has nothing
whatever to do, and with which he has nothing to do."

Even Mr. Healy had no ready response for this reply, by
reason of the manner and tone of its delivery ten times
more crushing than it reads in print. He sat silent, whilst
the gallant Swift MacNeill, who, owing to a variety of

circumstances, has not tasted the Chief Secretary's blood for many weeks, rushed in with tumultuous question, the words of which tumbled over each other with the noise and something of the coherency of the waters at Lodore.

"No, sir," said Mr. Balfour by way of reply; and the chilling negative for the time froze the furious assailants, who presently turned their attention to the more accessible Home Secretary.

"JEMMY" LOWTHER.

Feb. 14. — "Jemmy" Lowther. — Mr. James Lowther has begun in these later days to take on an air of grave statesmanship at variance with memories of his earlier Parliamentary life, and with flashes that sometimes struggle beneath his judicial air. The stars in their courses have fought against "Jemmy." He was a favourite with that keen judge of men, Mr. Disraeli, and was from the first marked out by him for promotion. He held a minor office in the last months of the Conservative Ministry, broken up by the inrush of Mr. Gladstone and the Liberals in 1868. When, in 1874, Mr. Disraeli came into power as well as into office, Mr. Lowther was advanced to the position of Under Secretary for the Colonies, and four years later became Chief Secretary to the Lord-Lieutenant.

That was the turning point of his career, and the turning

took a downward course. Personally, he was popular with
the Irish members, as he is with most classes of men. As
Chief Secretary he was marked out for their especial reprobation. When he offered himself for re-election at York in
1880, Mr. A. M. Sullivan, an irresistible platform orator, went
down and directed the campaign against him, with the result
that he was defeated. He returned to the House in the
following year, and sat in Opposition till the 1885 election, when
he was defeated at Louth. That blow he might have survived,
but in 1886, when the Conservatives unexpectedly returned to
the Promised Land, he was defeated at Eskdale. Had he won
a seat in that year he would naturally have taken his place on
the Treasury bench. When, after some years' exile, he
managed to get into the House of Commons he found the
Treasury bench filled up, and no place but a seat below the
gangway for the tired pilgrim.

An old-time
manner.   This is a hard fate, accidentally imposed, and
borne with dignified patience. What is Mr.
Lowther's loss is gain to the House. He succeeds in investing
the quarter where he sits with a certain flavour of old Parliamentary manner otherwise sorely lacking. There is no
member of the House, even of much higher standing, who has
exactly the oratorical manner of Mr. Lowther. It is much
older in its flavour than Mr. Gladstone's. He, always in the
House, and being of impressionable character, keeps touch
with its changing humour. Mr. Lowther, his Parliamentary
career peremptorily cut short, emerges from retirement with
all his old associations strong upon him. Moreover, there is
no doubt that an episode in his extra-Parliamentary life has
helped to mould his character. When, in a famous case
interesting at Newmarket, he presided on a judicial bench he
did not actually wear wig and gown. But those who saw him
there will remember how he seemed to lack only these adjuncts
to complete the bearing of a judge of twenty years" practice.
The case did not last very long, and was merely an episode in a
busy life. But the influence and associations of the Bench im-
pregnated Mr. Lowther, and he has never been quite the same
man since. When now he rises to address the Speaker the quips
and cranks that were wont to set the Parliament of 1868 in a

roar are hushed. He is almost preternaturally grave in his manner, slow in his speech, strictly judicial in his view of the question before the House. He seems, indeed, hampered by a disposition to allude to the preceding speaker as "my learned friend" and the phrase "my lud" trips to his tongue when he should be addressing Mr. Speaker. But he masters these passing temptations and goes forward with his speech, which supplies new-comers with a rare and interesting opportunity of studying the Parliamentary manner of former days.

There is no one quite like Mr. James Lowther on the Conservative side, and none at all on the Liberal benches. There are old stagers like Mr. Dillwyn and Mr. T. B. Potter. They, too, in measure like Mr. Gladstone, have remained through successive Parliaments, and their manners and ways of thought are subdued as is the dyer's hand. The last man who sat on the Liberal benches having the peculiar flavour of Mr. Lowther's style and manner was Mr. Horsman. Perhaps Mr. Villiers, if he ever chanced to speak, might disclose its possession; it certainly is manifested in the too infrequent interpositions in debate of Sir Rainald Knightley. But Mr. Lowther is the chief and most prominent depository of the subtle and doubtless unsuspected secret. He is the Grand Young Man of a dead-and-gone Parliamentary school.

Feb. 24.—In time of fog. Far down in the recesses of the House of Commons, beneath the feet of unsuspecting senators, is a spectacle which, if it could be exhibited in a public place in London, would send a thrill of horror through the community. It is a vast layer of what at first sight looks like cotton wool that has been first dragged through the Thames mud, and finally sprinkled with ink. A few hours ago it was a mass of virgin-white cotton wool, but at the time I saw it it had for several hours served as a filter through which the air supplied to the House of Commons is purified. For many years the resident engineers have been battling with fog. They have modified its effects within the House, but never till now have they succeeded in absolutely conquering it. To-night, while the fog outside has been so dense that the lights at the other side of Palace Yard twinkled like half-extinguished matches, the atmosphere in the House is very much as usual.

The process now in use is a further development of what has been tried through several years. A layer of cotton wool is prepared, and the air from outside is driven through it by force of a steam fan. The bed of cotton wool is 6 in. thick, and the area in use this week has extended over 800 square feet. The effect of the process on the wool is startling. If this filth had not been arrested by the layer of cotton wool it would have passed into the House and into the lungs of members. As it is, the foul particles in the air are imprisoned, and the House of Commons breathes comparatively pure air.

Feb. 23.—Lord R. Churchill's recreations. Lord Randolph Churchill's expedition to South Africa is, as he cheerfully says to his friends, " in search of gold." There is, however, one other reason really more influential. Though in much better health than last year, Lord Randolph is not yet thoroughly strong, and, acting under the advice of his doctor, is careful to knock about in the open air, and to avoid the concentration of thought which devotion to active politics demands. It was in obedience to this impulse that he first took up racing, but he has always had on hand some pursuit or other designed to divert his mind. In 1880, when he first came to the front as the creator and leader of the Fourth Party, Lord Randolph, beginning to find his health suffer, set himself with characteristic energy to play chess. He has always been fond of chess, having played it when at Oxford. When he came to London he joined the St. George's Chess Club, and in the summer of 1880, when the Bradlaugh debate was at its height, he engaged Mr. Steinitz, the famous chess-player, to visit him at his house and practise with him. They generally began at ten o'clock, and played for some hours, after which Lord Randolph would go down to the House like a giant refreshed, attack Mr. Bradlaugh, undermine the authority of Mr. Gladstone, and slily prod Sir Stafford Northcote. He kept up the practice with almost breathless vigour through the Session of 1880, but in the next year gave it up, as he gives up many things.

Feb. 26.—A link with the past. Lord Beauchamp was buried to-day, and in his grave has been put away all that remains of a man whose remarkable character was less widely known than

z

its peculiarities would seem to warrant. In the House of Commons, where he sat in Lord Palmerston's time, he was a prominent personage, more particularly towards midnight. He was then the Hon. Francis Lygon, and, in conjunction with Sir John Pope Hennessy, originated that organised system of obstruction which, as already shown, the Conservatives are accustomed to attribute to the Irish members. Mr. Lygon was a particular friend of Mr. Disraeli, who then led the Opposition to Lord Palmerston. Even in those comparatively early days, Dizzy had formed the habit, much noted in the Parliament of 1874, of abstaining from conversation on the Treasury bench, a habit in marked contrast with Mr. Gladstone's vivacious companionability. In 1874 Dizzy reserved all his conversation on the Treasury bench for Lord Barrington. In the long Parliament of Lord Palmerston Mr. Lygon was the chosen confidant.

A member of that Parliament, just returned to a seat in the present one, tells me that in the many divisions that took place, Mr. Disraeli had a habit of getting early into the division lobby, standing before the fireplace with his coat tails comfortably spread, and there chatting with Mr. Lygon till the way was clear to pass through the wicket.

When Mr. Lygon succeeded his brother and went to the House of Peers as Lord Beauchamp, he, though always voting with the Tories, was not restrained from an occasional sneer at Lord Salisbury. The Land Transfer Bill brought in, he, with a shrewdly-aimed blow that mortified Lord Salisbury and secretly delighted Mr. Chamberlain, warned the House to be careful to ascertain "whether the scheme had been coined at Hatfield or at Brummagem." He had in later years a particularly haughty manner, thinking so much of himself that he had no room left for appreciation of other people. He sneered and snapped all round, and was always ready for a fight, even with such redoubtable swordsmen as the Prime Minister or Bishop Magee. With the thread of his life is broken another far-reaching and interesting connection with the Palmerston epoch of Parliamentary life.

CHAPTER XXXIV.

WHY DISSOLVE ?

The Working Man—Misapplied Energy—Mr. Asquith—A New-comer to the
Episcopal Bench—Mr. Parnell and his Old Followers—Lord Strathedon and
Campbell—Peace in our Time—Three Potatoes—Why Dissolve ?

Feb. 27.—The
working man.

THE shadow of the Working Man lies dark over
the House of Commons, blighting its natural
grace and brightness. The horny hand is at its throat, compelling the disgorging from conveniently filled pockets of Royal
Commissions, Select Committees, and Bills designed in various
ways to counteract the historic malign influence which drove
blue bottle flies into the butchers' shops. This, like much
else, is Mr. Parnell's fault. If he had not been found out
we should have been just as near the inevitable period
of the General Election, but the House of Commons would
have been otherwise affected. Quite unknown to him when he
was clambering down the fire escape, Mr. Parnell was bringing
the British Workman into the front of home politics. Had
things gone forward this year as they were left when the prorogation took place in August there would have been scarcely
room for that person on the political platform. Her Majesty's
Ministers might, doubtless, have endeavoured to drag him on
the scene in order to supplant the Irish Question. But with
a united Irish Party, and a host of Liberals encouraged by the
result of a series of bye-elections, their success would have
been only partial. Now, with the Irish members hopelessly
disunited, with the Liberal Opposition checked in full cry
for Home Rule, there is a fair field and universal favour for
the Working Man, whose vote at a General Election that
cannot now be long delayed will, properly directed turn
the scale.

Mar. 3.—Misap-
plied energy.

This afternoon, whilst the House was discussing
with unexpected prolixity the Parochial Boards
(Scotland) Bill there were gathered on their knees in a room

in an hotel within a stone's throw of Palace Yard certain devout women praying that the second reading of the Sunday Closing Bill might be carried to a happy issue. The Sunday Closing Bill stood third on the Orders, and even had the Scotch debate not been so unexpectedly prolonged, the Rating of Machinery Bill, which came next, was safe to occupy the whole of the sitting. But the ladies, not seeking advice in mundane quarters, knew nothing of this. The Sunday Closing Bill appeared on the Agenda of Wednesday's business, and they took it for granted that before the sun went down on Wednesday the fate of the measure would be sealed. So they met punctually at noon, and fell a-praying till six, when, full of faith and not unduly anxious to learn a result that must be certain, their messenger came in with the startling news that the Sunday Closing Bill had not even been approached.

Mar. 4. — Mr. Asquith. Mr. Asquith has so thoroughly identified himself with affairs in the House of Commons, and has gained so prominent a position, that it seems hard to believe he took his seat so recently as 1886. But that is the case. From the delivery of his earliest speech Mr. Gladstone marked him out with favouring glance, and he has since gone on gaining the good opinion of the House. It is an odd but familiar fact that success at the Bar, achieved in whatever degree, does not necessarily imply triumph in the House of Commons. The fact is, indeed, directly the contrary. Sir William Harcourt is essentially a House of Commons man; but Sir William's position at the Bar did not rival that of Lord Eldon, for example. Sir Henry James made his way at the Bar by force and sheer ability, and in his younger days took some pains to make a reputation in the House of Commons. But he never came anywhere near the front rank of Parliamentary debaters or orators.

Why a man, convincing when he stands in wig and gown arguing a difficult case before three judges, or appealing to the passions and prejudices of a jury, should when he divests himself of his robes and speaks in the House of Commons utterly fail to carry weight, is one of those interesting problems that have never been solved. Human nature is absolutely alike whether confronted in a Court of Justice or in the House of

Commons. In both there are the actual elements of Judge and Jury; and yet the successful barrister is rarely a power in the House of Commons.

There are, perhaps, only two exceptions in recent years, and the rarity of the cases proves the rule. One was the young barrister who came into the Parliament of 1874 as member for Durham city. The other is Mr. Asquith. There is sufficient similarity between the legal and Parliamentary style of Lord Herschell and Mr. Asquith to justify the opinion Mr. Gladstone is known to hold, that the latter will in time go quite as far as the former. Both commanded the attention of the House by their maiden speech, and succeeded as the Sessions passed in strengthening the favourable impression. Whilst both bring to Parliamentary debate the orderly arrangement of matter and the lucidity of expression acquired by legal training, neither has the *je ne sais quoi* of the Bar manner and tone. As they join in Parliamentary debate you do not " almost hear the rustling " of their stuff or silk gowns.

Mar. 2.—A new-comer to the Episcopal bench. The Bishop of Wakefield, whose turn upon the rota has come for taking his seat among the Peers of Parliament, was introduced this afternoon. The procedure in respect of the introduction of a new bishop is something less grotesque than that which marks the ceremony of new peers taking the oath and their seat. Garter King-at-Arms, with his coat of many colours, is not brought on the scene, and there is nothing of that dodging round benches which to this day tickles the fancy of peers who have witnessed its recurrence for many years. There, however, is one part of the formality pertaining to ordinary peers retained for the use of the bishops. They are led up by their sponsors to the Woolsack, where the Lord Chancellor sits, and there, dropping on one knee, hand in their summons to the House. It was odd the other night to see the stately Archbishop of York dropping down before the squat figure on the Woolsack. Having paid one visit to the Lord Chancellor, the new bishop goes to the table, signs the Roll of Parliament, is again presented to the Lord Chancellor, and so passes on to the Bishops' bench, where he salutes the Lord Chancellor, and is thereafter a Peer of Parliament.

Mar. 11. — Mr.
Parnell and his
old followers.

Mr. Parnell somewhat unexpectedly turned up in the lobby of the House of Commons just before the House arose. Almost simultaneously appeared Mr. McCarthy, detachments of both parties following their respective leaders. They had come over together from Ireland, having had a pretty lively passage, which, other things apart, was sufficient to prevent interchange of conversation between the ancient friends. Mr. Parnell, amongst his other more or less innocent assumptions, always goes on the principle that the friendship which for so many years existed between Mr. McCarthy and himself remains undisturbed. He always shakes hands with him, and when, as occasion even yet arises, he writes to him, he never varies from the old friendly "Dear McCarthy." Mr. Healy, on the contrary, he honours with his uncompromising displeasure, taking no notice of him when they chance to meet or find themselves, as happened in debate on Mr. John Morley's resolution a week or two ago, sitting side by side in the Commons.

Mar. 13. — Lord
Stratheden and
Campbell.

The House of Commons is composed of six hundred and seventy members. It seems as if there were only four members of the House of Lords—Lord Salisbury, Lord Granville, Lord Stratheden and Campbell, and Lord Denman. Lord Stratheden and Campbell is, perhaps, the most profoundly wise-looking man in either House. The nearest approach to him in the Commons is Sir James Fergusson, whose profundity becomes bottomless when, as sometimes happens after he has read out an answer prepared for him at the Foreign Office, an inconsiderate interrogator puts a supplementary question which he ventures to hope the Under-Secretary will answer right off. Standing up in their respective places, and addressing either House, there is hardly a pin to choose between Sir James Fergusson and the noble lord. But when it comes to peregrination the Under-Secretary is nowhere. To see Lord Stratheden and Campbell walking along the corridor that (amongst other things) severs the House of Lords from the House of Commons is to acquire a liberal education in the mystery of Foreign Affairs. Perhaps it is the designs of Russia upon Constantinople that may, at the moment, be occupying his mind. Peradventure he has

gone further afield, and is ruminating on the aspect of affairs
in Central Asia. The Newfoundland fishery may claim his
attention, and his thoughts may be roaming at large among
the lobsters. It may be the difficulty in the Behring Straits
that engrosses his attention. Whatever it be, the casual
person whom he passes by seems in some subtle fashion to
take in knowledge of Foreign Affairs by the pores, as Joey
Ladle absorbed his employer's liquor. It is not only the face,
the high shoulders, and the head bowed as an over-full head
of corn bends over, that strike the awe-struck observer
There is something impressive in the long stride, some suggestion of diplomacy in the quiet footfall. He habitually walks
on tiptoe, with thoughtful intent, as has been said, to prevent
Campbell from disturbing the reverie of Stratheden.

His lordship's journey towards the House of Commons,
though thus foreboding in its gait, carries him upon a very
simple errand. The House of Lords has an inconvenient habit
of adjourning five minutes after the Lord Chancellor has taken
his seat on the Woolsack, suggestive, if peers were not the pink
of courtesy, that that was quite as much of Lord Halsbury's
company as they cared for. Between five and six o'clock Lord
Stratheden and Campbell finds it conducive to the interests
of the Empire that he should take forty winks. As the House
of Lords is closed and the House of Commons handy, he wends
his way thither, and, stepping up to the Peers' Gallery, takes a
back seat and goes to sleep. The House of Commons, grown
accustomed to his visitation, likes to have him there. He
diffuses over a considerable area a sense of profundity of knowledge and of trained judgment which seems to elevate the
character, and certainly increases the self-respect, both collec-
tively and individually, of the Lower House.

It may be that Lord Stratheden and Campbell is fresh from
one of his periodic conflicts with Lord Salisbury. He feels
that he is an embarrassment to his noble friend at the head of
the Government. He has a consciousness that when Lord
Salisbury is penning a dispatch, whether to Mr. Blaine, or to
Lord Lytton for the information of the French Government,
he pauses at intricate passages, and asks himself, "What will
Stratheden and Campbell say to *that!*" It is not altogether a
pleasant duty to fulfil, this mission of keeping one's eye upon

the Foreign Office in its manifold transactions with the affairs of an Empire on which the sun never sets. But Lord Strath-eden and Campbell is not the man to shirk a public duty on private considerations. He might, perhaps, be a little less sudden in his springing of mines. He has a way of handing in at the table a motion for papers on some momentous and far-reaching question, the springs of which lie deep, as it were, amid the heart-strings of nations. Lord Salisbury, suddenly called upon to stand, is made to deliver his opinion, with the knowledge that all the world is listening at the doors, weighing every word he utters.

Mar. 21.—Peace in our time. Mr. Smith, sitting on the Treasury bench and looking across the slumbering figure of the Attorney-General at the empty space below the gangway, may well marvel that there should still be people talking about the possibility of a premature dissolution. Why should the Government hasten by an hour the dispersal of an assembly so admirably adapted for its purposes? Never since the early days of the Parliament of 1874 has there been known at West-minster a state of things similar to that now existing. With the exception of Sir William Harcourt there is practically no Opposition. The Irish members are as completely effaced as if Mr. Gladstone's Home Rule Bill of 1886 had been carried in its integrity, and the doors of the British House of Com-mons closed against them. Certain events happening last November in Committee Room No. 15 seemed to promise that the energy of Irish members would, when the Session was re-newed, break out in a fresh place. The prophetic soul beheld the rival Irish leaders lying in wait to trip each other up whilst their followers constantly engaged in contumelious con-versation. There were to be alarums and excursions, Donny-brook Fair revived below the gangway. When on the only set Irish debate that has happened this Session Mr. Potter interposed his portly form between Mr. Justin McCarthy and Mr. Parnell as they sat on the third bench below the gangway, every one recognised the calm heroism of the action. The rival leaders were thus literally kept at arm's length. The process of reaching across Mr. Potter's body, supposing either was in a moment of passion impelled in that direction, was so

serious an undertaking that before it was accomplished a man
would have time to reflect on what he was doing, and might
withdraw his hand before it had committed actual assault—
except, incidentally and undesignedly, upon Mr. Potter.

AN HON. BUFFER.

Three potatoes. This strategic and self-sacrificing manœuvre of
the member for Rochdale on the night of the
debate on Mr. John Morley's motion proved unnecessary.
Even when Mr. McCarthy stood up with a paper in his hand
Mr. Parnell made no attempt to snatch it from him, and the
proceedings were on the whole rather weighted by dulness
than inspired with vivacity. Since then nothing has happened
to revive the ancient glories of the Irish quarter. Mr. Parnell
never shows himself there, nor does Mr. Tim Healy. The
question hour is appreciably shortened by the absence of Mr.
Sexton. Mr. Swift McNeill made a desperate effort to galvanise
the debate on Irish distress by producing from his waistcoat
pocket three painfully inadequate potatoes strung on a wire.
This, in any one of its possible developments, would at one
time have sufficed to give a fillip to the debate and would
have brought a crowd of angry Irish members shouting at the
heels of Mr. Balfour. What precise purpose Mr. McNeill's
exhibition of the three potatoes was designed to serve was left

a little obscure.   But the demonstration was a dismal failure, and Mr. McNeill re-pocketed the potatoes with a depressed air that eloquently testified to his appreciation of the altered conditions of the Irish Party.

Why dissolve?   Whilst the question of Tithes has failed to disturb the somnolency of the dying House, other promising questions have not proved more efficacious.   On Monday the Irish Constabulary vote was agreed to within the space of half an hour.   The Vote on Account, covering a hundred controversial points, passed in a single sitting that terminated at one o'clock in the morning.   Tokar touches the House not, nor Behring Straits either.   The question hour is strictly limited, and wholly unmarked by acrimony.   Supply is in a more forward state than it has been at any corresponding period since 1875, and Government Bills pass successive stages with regularity and dispatch.   According to the statute law, this Parliament, having met in August, 1886, may sit till July, 1893.   Why, as far as Ministers are concerned, should its term of natural life be shortened?   Even suppose a General Election were certain to give them an equal or even an increased majority, what would it benefit them?   A new Parliament comes to Westminster with its withers unwrung. Eager, restless, flushed with young life, it insists upon having work found for it.   The present House of Commons has reached a time of life when it chiefly desires to do nothing. For the sake of peace it will agree to any proposition the Government may make, even the appropriation of Tuesdays and Fridays for morning sittings as early as the middle of March.   It would be ungrateful as well as unwise to reward this docility with dismissal, and Mr. Smith, turning over the leaves of the Orders gently (so as not to awaken the Attorney-General) smiles again when he hears people asking whether the dissolution will take place in the autumn, or whether it shall be daringly postponed till the spring?

CHAPTER XXXV.

DEATH OF LORD GRANVILLE.

Death of Lord Granville—Cavendish-Bentinck—An Out-and-out Tory—A Challenge to Mr. Parnell—Lord R. Churchill as Special Correspondent—The Leader of the Opposition in the Lords.

April 1.—Death of Lord Granville. THERE is probably no one living whose death would elicit such universal lament as that uttered to-day by all sorts and conditions of men over the body of Lord Granville. There were greater statesman before him, and he has left some behind; but there was none more widely loved, more warmly esteemed. A stout politician, he has for twenty-three years fought side by side with Mr. Gladstone, identifying himself with every political action of his friend and chief. Yet not the faintest reflection of that personal animosity with which Mr. Gladstone is to this day pursued fell upon him. Everybody liked Lord Granville, and those who knew him best loved him most. Physically a martyr to gout, he bore its pangs with unruffled temper. Nothing damped the gaiety of his spirits. He was always playful whether at home or abroad, in the House of Lords or at the dinner-table. One evening last season, a friend meeting Lady Victoria at a crush, asked her if her father was there.

"No," she replied, "he said if it was a ball now he would be there, but since it was only an 'at home' he would go off to bed." Lord Granville was one of the best *raconteurs* of the age. Everything suggested to him a story, and the story seemed made to illustrate the particular turn the conversation had taken. But he did not depend upon his recollection for his jokes, frequently flashing forth gleams of wit that lighted up the table. I heard one that dates back all the way to the birth of the present Mr. Browning, the artist. When Robert Browning the poet and his wife were sojourning at Florence a child was born unto them.

"The funniest, oddest thing you ever saw," a lady reported to Lord Granville."

"Ah," said his Lordship with a smile, "then there will be not two incomprehensibles, but three incomprehensibles."

Lord Granville will be much missed in the neighbourhood of Ramsgate. He was greatly attached to his residence at Walmer Castle, upon which he spent large sums of money. He had been adding to and improving the place almost ever since he was appointed Lord Warden. He once told me a story about his first acquaintance with the place. When, in 1865, he married a second time, he and his bride set out to spend the honeymoon in Italy. They halted by the way at Dover, and being there, Lord Granville, who confessed to always having a curiosity about Walmer Castle, proposed that they should pay it a visit. Lord Palmerston was at that time Lord Warden, but did not happen to be in residence, and Lord and Lady Granville, roaming about the place, talked of what they would do supposing it were theirs. They continued their journey, and had not been long in Italy when news came of the death of Lord Palmerston. This was promptly followed by a letter from Lord John Russell, who had succeeded to the Premiership, offering to Lord Granville the Wardenship of the Cinque Ports, with its appanage of Walmer Castle.

No one outside the family circle will feel the loss more keenly than Mr. Gladstone. Between the two there has existed for nearly half a century the closest intimacy, and since 1868 the most intimate colleagueship. Dukes and earls, and even humble barons like Lord Brabourne, have fallen away from Mr. Gladstone, as with increasing energy and rapidity in these later years he strode onward. Lord Granville always stuck to him. It was pretty to see the two veterans gaily chatting across the dinner-table, where, in one house or another, they frequently met. Both were hard of hearing when ordinary people spoke even in uplifted voice. It was a peculiarity of their sympathy and close companionship that each could hear the other with perfect ease and without special effort.

When, sixteen years ago, Mr. Gladstone, at "the age of sixty-five, and after forty-two years of a laborious public life," thought himself entitled to retire, it was to "My dear Granville" he turned to address his valedictory words. Now the old friend of his youth and manhood lies silent in his chamber, and the "worn-out" statesman of 1875 is still to the fore,

eagerly awaiting an opportunity of accomplishing the crowning
act of a unique career.

Leader in the Lords The genial presence of Lord Granville will be
missed from many places in public and private
circles, but nowhere will his death make a wider gap than in
the House of Lords. It is no exaggeration to say his loss to
the Liberal Party in his capacity of leader of its cause in the
House of Lords is irreparable. It had been his fate for five-
and-thirty years to lead the party in office and in Opposition.
He has always been the captain of a minority. He has in
succession had two tasks to perform, and it would be difficult
to say which was the more arduous. In office, with a large
majority backing up his chief and his colleagues in the House
of Commons, he has had to obtain the assent of a hostile
majority for measures peculiarly obnoxious to them; in Opposition he has had to make some decent show of resistance in
a hopeless fight the issue of which was assured beforehand.

He has always been equal to the difficulty in whichever
phase it presented itself. Whatever was before him, an overwhelming defeat in the division lobby, or a sullen retreat of
the majority, he literally "came up smiling." No one remembers an occasion when the sweet equability of his temper
was ruffled by an incident in the House of Lords. Yet it
would be a mistake to suppose this suavity of manner indicated weakness of character. He could upon occasion be
prompt and even stern. On more than one occasion when
under the unbusinesslike rule of the House of Lords it was
found possible for two peers to be standing on their feet at the
same moment, each insisting on his right to speak first, Lord
Granville has taken on himself the task of restoring order by
moving that Lord A. or Lord B. "be now heard." Lord
Denman, too, has felt the iron hand under the silken glove,
Lord Granville more than once cutting in upon his wandering
speech with a motion that "the noble lord be not heard."

In these later times the muster of Liberal peers on party
divisions has not far exceeded thirty, a state of things that did
not tend to make the leadership exhilarating. Almost up to
the last Lord Granville was at his post, even if he had the
front bench all to himself and the Duke of Argyll frowning

behind him.   Though one of the most charming after-dinner
speakers of the day, he did not rank as an orator in the Lords.
But he was an excellent debater, quick to see a weak point in
the armour of the adversary, skilful and effective alike in parry
and attack.   In late years he was handicapped by increasing
deafness, and often rose to reply to a speech only a portion of
which he had heard.   No one unacquainted with his infirmity
would suspect its existence, his colleagues on the front bench,
who knew all about it, admiring the skill with which he surmounted the difficulty.

Lord Granville was perhaps seen at his best in the little
duels of question and answer fought across the table between
the leaders of parties.   He had a gentle, inoffensive way of
saying awkward things that greatly added to the damage done.
He never wielded the two-handed sword in Parliamentary
debate.   With him it was all rapier play—swift, skilful, quiet,
but none the less effective.

At a crisis in the history of Lord Beaconsfield's Government,
when the fleet had been ordered to the Dardanelles and there
were rumours of resignation of Cabinet Ministers, the House of
Lords was crowded as it rarely is in anticipation of a scene.
It opened with Lord Carnarvon explaining in a long address
the circumstances under which he had felt it his duty to
resign office.   Lord Beaconsfield followed, and somewhat
sharply traversed several of his late colleague's statements of
fact.   Then Lord Granville came to the table, and the crowded
House was hushed to hear what he would have to say in this
delicate situation.

" I do not rise," he murmured, with that slight approach to
a lisp that added to the innocency of his remarks, " for the
purpose of continuing the discussion entered into by the noble
lords opposite."

Discussion is, of course, a Parliamentary word, but the
slight emphasis upon it, and the smiling face he turned upon
the parted colleagues, pointed the seriousness of the situation,
wherein two Cabinet Ministers disagreed on material matters
that had happened only the other day, and plainly though
politely hinted that, to quote a phrase much in vogue just then,
" a lying spirit was abroad."

There was no intellectual treat more full of enjoyment than

that presented when Lord Salisbury and Lord Granville were
engaged in one of their little fencing bouts. They were foes
each worthy of the other's steel, and the House looked on
delightedly at the encounter of wit, knowledge of affairs, rare
felicity of phrase, and almost deferential courtesy of manner.
During the negotiations for the transfer of Heligoland, Lord
Granville was particularly anxious to ascertain what means
had been taken to learn the views of the population on the
question of the transfer. Lord Salisbury replied that it was
impossible to make any statement on the subject, since the
documents containing the information were of a confidential
character.

"Confidential with the population?" Lord Granville
quickly asked, even Lord Salisbury joining in the laughter
evoked by this palpable hit.

Lord Granville's personal popularity was by no means confined to the political party he has so long and so unselfishly
served. The Liberal minority mourn the loss of a leader.
The House of Lords is united in keen appreciation of the void
created by the removal of a statesman who, taking him for all
in all, was its brightest ornament.

April 3.—Caven-
dish-Bentinck. The announcement of Mr. Cavendish-Bentinck's
death came as a surprise to the House. There
was not current even a rumour of his illness. He was in his
place just before the recess, and though he looked somewhat
pallid, there was no sign that the end was near. It is a curious
and characteristic fact that his last speech in the House of
Commons was personally directed against Mr. Gladstone,
who, through all his political life, has been the object of
his unbounded distrust and embittered denunciation. This
did not particularly matter, and the House was inclined to
rejoice in it, since it was the occasion of many scenes enliven-
ing the dulness of the Session. Some members, in less degree
now than used to be the case, have the gift of moving Mr.
Gladstone to quite unnecessary wrath. Mr. Chaplin has more
than once succeeded in this direction, and Mr. Ashmead-
Bartlett's success was his earliest step towards fame. Cavendish-Bentinck only amused Mr. Gladstone. He was able to
join in the ripple of laughter with which the member for

Whitehaven's diatribes, sometimes impassioned to the point of
incoherency, were listened to. When he followed he always
turned with smiling face upon the irate adversary, and gently
chaffed him.

An out-and-out Tory.   There was no one quite like Mr. Bentinck in the
House, and he was almost the surviving repre-
sentative of a type rapidly growing extinct. He was an out-
and-out, uncompromising Tory, never tampering with the evil
thing of Radicalism. During the Parliament of 1868, when
Mr. Gladstone was engaged in one of his greatest campaigns,
disestablishing the Church, freeing the Irish land, spreading
education, and introducing vote by ballot, Mr. Bentinck distinguished himself by the vehemence of his opposition. He
was one of the earliest practitioners of the modern art of obstruction, finding a worthy companion in Mr. James Lowther.

Disraeli made him Judge - Advocate - General. It was
always regarded as a kind of saturnine joke, and that ancient
and honourable office did not long survive Mr. Bentinck's incumbency. He was not a great Parliamentarian, and for thirty
years did his best to stop the progress of the political enfranchisement and the amelioration of the lot of his countrymen. But he was endowed with fine artistic taste, and could
not " abear " the new staircase in Westminster Hall.

April 15. — A challenge to Mr. Parnell.   The storm which always rumbles below the Irish
camp flashed forth this afternoon. It arose
in debate on the Bill for making Sunday closing in Ireland permanent, and extending the rule to the
five cities which hitherto have had a monopoly of Sunday
trade. This is a question on which the opinion of the great
mass of Irish members has been repeatedly declared. Division
after division has shown that of the 102 members for Ireland
not more than fourteen or fifteen oppose the Bill. Mr. Sexton
however, cannot afford to go against the will of the Dublin
publicans, and he this afternoon uplifted his voice against
the Bill. Mr. Parnell, seeing his chance of dividing Mr.
McCarthy's following on this point, almost fulsomely compli-
mented Mr. Sexton on the line he had taken, and on " the able
and eloquent argument " with which he had supported it.

Mr. Maurice Healy had been an attentive listener to the speech. When Mr. Parnell resumed his seat, Mr. Healy and Sir C. Russell rose together, but members, spying sport, called for Mr. Healy, to whom Sir Charles gave way. Mr. Healy's fragile, shrinking figure does not seem designed to brave the wrath of Mr. Parnell. If it had been his brother Tim, what followed would have been reasonable enough. Speaking in a voice that accorded with the general mildness of his appearance Mr. Healy made a speech which was one of the briefest and most immediately effective heard in this Parliament.

" Neither on this nor on any other public question," he said, " does the hon. member who has just sat down represent the people of Cork. If he has any doubt on the subject, let him note my acceptance of his challenge to bring about a test election."

Half-way through this declaration a burst of cheering came, oddly enough, not less from the Conservative than from the Opposition side. It was some moments before Mr. Healy found the opportunity of concluding his little speech. When it was all said he sat down, and there was another burst of cheering, amid which Mr. Parnell sat pale and defiant with folded arms, looking straight before him, as if he heard nothing.

April 15.—Lord R. Churchill as special correspondent. Lord Randolph Churchill, who has been down at Newmarket all the week, returned to town this evening. He spoke to a friend of his intention to look in at the House, but has not put in an appearance. He will certainly be in his place once more before he starts on his journey. The *Graphic* have proffered him princely terms for the correspondence he has undertaken to send from Central Africa. They give him 2,000 guineas for twenty letters, each to run to the extent of 4,000 words. This is 100 guineas a letter, something more than the average pay of the ordinary special correspondent in foreign parts. But Lord Randolph did not accept the highest offer. The *Daily Telegraph* offered him £100 a column if he would write for them, whereas 4,000 words will run to something pretty near three columns. Lord Randolph, however, preferred the *Graphic* proposal, and is looking forward cheerfully to his new experience.

April 16.—The
Leader of the
Opposition in
the Lords.

The decision not to appoint a successor to Lord Granville in the Leadership of the Liberal Party in the House of Lords came as a surprise in Liberal circles. It was taken for granted that Lord Spencer would succeed, anticipating the time when he shall assume the position of Liberal Prime Minister. It is said the arrangement was come to as the result of a chivalrous contest between Lord Spencer and Lord Rosebery. There is no doubt the latter is the predestined successor to the heritage of Leadership of the Liberal Party, not only in the House of Lords but throughout the country. In him would be found a peculiarly worthy successor to Lord Granville. He has the lightness of touch, the sense of humour, the genial manner of the late peer, with, superadded, certain qualities of sterling statesmanship that even exceed Lord Granville's mark. But Lord Rosebery is young in years and can afford to wait a while. If he assumed the post of Leader in the Lords just now it would be difficult for Lord Spencer to supersede him when he comes into the heritage of the Premiership.

It is no secret that, as far as Mr. Gladstone and the inner Council of the Liberal Leaders, as at present constituted, can control future events, it is settled that Lord Spencer is to be the Liberal Premier in succession to Mr. Gladstone, leading the House of Lords whilst Sir William Harcourt leads in the Commons. It would seem natural that he should seize the opportunity presented by the lamented death of Lord Granville to get into training. That he should stand aside is a little unfortunate as suggesting undetermined counsels. Lord Kimberley is a much more able man than is estimated by the outside public. He possesses in peculiar degree the confidence and esteem of his colleagues. But he has none of the qualities of a popular leader, and his appearance in the seat of Lord Granville, whilst it is carefully announced that he does not bear the title or exercise the functions of Leader of the Opposition, is a little *finesse* of tactics more curious than assuring for the future of the party.

CHAPTER XXXVI.

DEPRESSION.

A Bore from Scotland—A Budget Speech—Mr. Jackson's Device—Where the Chancellor put Tobacco—Depression—Mr. Parnell—Lord Warden of the Cinque Ports—Sunshine on the Treasury Bench—Visitors from afar—A Toothsome Bit—The Duke of Argyll—Lord Denman.

April 17.—A Bore from Scotland. MR. SEYMOUR KEAY is one of the curious developments of human life which from time to time are sent to Westminster from remote corners of Scotland. Elgin and Nairn combine to produce him as a member of the House of Commons, a canny arrangement which leaves the direct responsibility undetermined. Elgin may say it was Nairn. Nairn, denying the soft impeachment, may accuse Elgin. It does not lie in the mouth of a Southron to determine the nice question. All we know is that eighteen short months ago Elgin and Nairn, called upon to fill a vacancy created by the death of the sitting member, elected Mr. Seymour Keay.

The new member lost no time in giving the House a taste of his quality. He made his maiden speech within a few hours of taking his seat. The House of Commons, the pink of courtesy, the pearl of patience, listened

for some time, regarding with curious interest the remarkable figure just added to its collection. Mr. Keay, pleased with the attention, discoursed at length, and on the following

night repeated the effort to please.   He had evidently made a
hit.   The House of Commons, the most august assembly in
the world, had sat silent, at his feet as it were, whilst he
descanted on things present and to come.   It evidently expected more, and Mr. Keay is not the man to baulk desire
when it takes that direction.   Accordingly, on the earliest opportunity, he presented himself again, and was received with
such a howl of anguished derision that after struggling through
a few embarrassed sentences he resumed his seat, and was
silent for a full fortnight.

Then Mr. Gladstone, heedless, probably unconscious, of the
consequences, reckless of his doom, interposed and inflicted
Mr. Seymour Keay upon the House in what promises to be a
permanent form.   The member for Elgin and Nairn had
written a book, upon what topic no one just now remembers,
except dimly that it had something to do with a statistical
question.   Mr. Gladstone, perhaps the greatest living authority
on financial affairs, having read through the copy of "the
brochure" the author had been careful to send him, had
recognised in it the work of a born financier.   With the
generosity of genius he had acknowledged a brother, and had,
in view of an envious and carping House of Commons,
straightway held out to him across the gangway the right
hand of fellowship.

In grasping Mr. Gladstone's hand, Mr. Seymour Keay resolved that he would, in spite of flouts, and gibes, and sneers,
prove himself worthy of the notice extorted from his eminent
friend, and would speedily advance the time when the House
of Commons *should* hear him.   The hour struck with the
Committee stage of the Irish Land Bill, and behold the Man!
Mr. Keay, as has been mentioned, has not been in Parliament
more than eighteen months, but he has so far mastered its
ways and traditions as to appreciate the value to a rising
statesman of a corner seat.   The time has not yet come when
he could claim one without going through the soothing, but
not always convenient, exercise of prayer-time.   On the
Liberal side there is always what may be called "a corner" in
corner seats.   The Liberal Party is a volcanic orb, in its
hurried course ever throwing off brilliant fragments which, so
to speak, set up in business for themselves.   Each independent

captain hankers after a corner seat, below the gangway by preference; and as there are only four, and as the Irish hold one and Mr. Labouchere another, late-comers fare badly.

But the flowing tide is with Mr. Seymour Keay. The corner seat on the second bench below the gangway was habitually through the early portion of the Session graced by the manly form of Mr. Picton. Rising from this historic quarter, where once the meek white head of Mr. Lowe gleamed under the gaslight, and whence Mr. Bright has thundered eloquent denunciation of a guilty Government, Mr. Picton, with some of Mr. Lowe's sarcasm and all of Mr. Bright's dignity, has wrestled with the Chancellor of the Exchequer and guardedly approved the First Lord of the Treasury. If Mr. Picton were still at his post, Mr. Keay would have to remain in the obscurity of the lower end of the bench. But it chances that Mr. Picton is just now musing amid the classic ruins of ancient Rome, and so Mr. Keay, giving up the whole of the early portion of the day to the purpose, is enabled to be down so early for prayers that no one has the opportunity of snatching from him the coveted corner seat.

Here he stood in the closing half-hour of this morning's sitting. On Clause L of the Irish Land Bill he had crowded the paper with amendments that gave pause to the most experienced debater. They look uncommonly like coherency, bristling with common fractions and imposing references to "the Consolidated Fund," "temporary advances," "mortgages," and "the Chancellor of the Exchequer." Mr. Keay had opened the ball with one amendment. After he had delivered several speeches recommending it to the notice of the House, Mr. Courtney gravely invited him to explain it. This would have offended some people. Mr. Keay was delighted to oblige. The House roared in despairing protest. Mr. Keay, both hands full of notes, turned, mildly expostulatory, and reminded hon. gentlemen opposite that the Chairman had invited him to explain what his amendment meant, and he was doing so. Mr. Gladstone happened to be on the front Opposition bench, the only incident in the proceedings that gave satisfaction. Everyone was thinking of his fatal encomium on Mr. Keay's literary effort, and all hoped that Mr.

Gladstone had it in mind. Since Frankenstein succeeded in his task no such retribution has fallen upon presumptuous man as that which now weighs down the author of a heedless eulogy.

April 24. — A Budget speech. To-night Mr. Goschen accomplished the delivery of the longest speech and the presentation of the simplest Budget of modern times. The purpose of the Budget might be described in a single short sentence. Mr. Goschen occupied three hours less twenty minutes for its exposition.

In the quiet and repose of his office at the Treasury he had neatly arranged his notes in a series of volumes. One dealt with his estimates of last year, and traced their realisation. Another detailed the expenditure under the Barracks Act, the Naval Defence Act, and the Imperial Defence Act. A third covered all that was to be said about the reduction of debt. A fourth tabled figures connected with the relief of local taxation; and so on through the successive heads of the far-reaching subject of national finance.

Each volume was neatly stitched and endorsed on the back. When Mr. Goschen had exhausted a topic he put the volume of notes on one side and took up the next from the pile that stood on his desk at the left-hand side. Close by him on the Treasury bench sat Mr. Smith, anxiously checking off the figures as they were recited. Next to Mr. Smith was Mr. Jackson, his attention divided between the duty of following his chief's speech through its intricacies and keeping his right hon. friend's tumbler filled with what Mr. Goschen in one passage of his speech distantly alluded to as "a minor alcoholic beverage." Mr. Jackson had not forgotten the disaster with the tumbler that thrilled the House last Budget night. But he is a man of infinite resource, and had hit upon what he justly regarded as a happy device. Mr. Goschen in the heat of his eloquence always forgets on which side of the desk his tumbler has been placed. If it is on the right side, in full view of a sympathetic House, he, in search of it, fumbles furiously on the left, upsetting ink-pots and hopelessly ravaging stationery. If it is plainly visible on the left-hand side, he pursues his investigations in the opposite quarter.

Mr. Jackson, kindly observant of this little eccentricity, had conceived the notable idea that if the Chancellor of the Exchequer whilst delivering his Budget speech had a tumbler on either side of his desk all would be well, and there would be no possible complication of circumstances. Accordingly, before the speech commenced, he, with kindly forethought, placed a big tumbler, brimming with minor alcoholic beverage, on the right-hand side of the desk, and another on the left. Then he took his seat close by to watch the result. At first it threatened to have disastrous consequences. Mr. Goschen, after explaining in a thrilling passage how " tea, too, plays a happy part in the history of the last year," hastily brought his hand down on the right-hand side of the desk and found the tumbler. Refreshed by a mighty draught of its contents, he calculated that every ounce of tobacco fills twelve pipes; duty was paid last year on nearly three million ounces of tobacco more than in the year before; *argal*, under a Government whose first sacred duty is the preservation of the Union, the working man had been able to smoke thirty-six million more pipes of tobacco in twelve months than he had ever before done in a similar period. Amid the outburst of genuine applause elicited by this calculation, Mr. Goschen came down on the left-hand side, and, behold! there was the tumbler out of which, as it seemed, he had lately drunk, full to the brim. He visibly started, and half raising the glass put it down again untasted.

It was on looking at the clock and discovering how time had sped and how much there yet remained to be done that the duality of the tumblers operated with fatal effect. In one of his hurried movements Mr. Goschen had unconsciously got both the tumblers on the left-hand side of the desk, close by his pile of still unused notes. Turning from the clock to look at his notes, his eye fell on the two tumblers where only one had been before. Intending to readjust matters, and put one of the tumblers on the other side, he in the flurry of the moment seized the top volume of his notes and placed *that* on the right-hand side of the desk. It was the volume containing the figures of the detailed estimates for certain sources of revenue, and came next in the exposition of his plan. But, being removed under the misapprehension described, Mr. Goschen took up the next volume in order and began his catalogue. "I now," he said, "proceed to give the figures of my estimate of the revenue for the coming year. I have said that I put the Income-tax at £13,750,000; I put tobacco," he went on, opening his volume of notes and glancing hurriedly up and down the pages, "I put tobacco——" he continued, furiously turning over the leaves—"I put tobacco——" he repeated in tones tremulous with excitement, whilst the House looked sympathetically on.

Evidently he had put tobacco where he could not find it. Mr. Smith, his kindly face furrowed with anxiety, bent over his column of figures, hoping peradventure that he might find at what the Chancellor of the Exchequer had put tobacco. Mr. Jackson hurriedly poked about among the volumes still piled to the left of the box. Mr. Goschen, with the wrong note-book held close to his nose, violently turned over the leaves. In one of his anguished movements his eye fell on the growing heap of note-books on the right, and grasping in despair at the top one he discovered himself on the right tack. Opening the book he found all his figures fairly set forth. "I put tobacco," he cried, triumphantly, "at two per cent. above the present figure." The House boisterously cheered; but Mr. Goschen never got over this accident, floundering on through morasses of figures till, at length, looking up at the patient but puzzled House, he said, "I hope my figures will be understood when you see them in the morning"—surely the most pathetic aspiration ever uttered by a Chancellor of the Exchequer on Budget night.

June 5.—Depression.

There is no withstanding the reproach that the House of Commons has degenerated into deepest dulness. The octopus of the Irish Land Purchase Bill has through the week enveloped it in its folds, and small wonder if on the fifth night of the almost unintermitted embrace the hopeless subject is in a state of coma. Scarcely any of the men accustomed to take a prominent part in debate now show themselves. Mr. Gladstone's absence through the week has been accidental, but when he is in ordinary attendance he is never seen after the dinner hour, and up to that time is content for the most part to sit silent, though watchful. Lord Hartington sometimes looks in midway through the questions, sits for a while, peradventure sleeps, goes his way, and is seen no more through the sitting. Mr. Chamberlain has effaced himself with almost equal completeness, though occasionally this Session—generally on some comparatively small measure in which he is personally interested—he has interposed, and new members learn what a loss the House suffers from the temporary withdrawal from its conferences of this keen intellectual force, this perfect master of lucid speech. Even Sir Richard Temple neglects to confer the grace of his presence on the scene. If he would only sit in his usual place and go to sleep with his customary animation, it would help to people the void. But the trained endurance of the Chairman of the London School Board cannot withstand the soul-sapping influence of the kind of debate that takes place on this measure, and Sir Richard withdraws to toy with Amaryllis in the shade, and show Neaera over the corridors, the library, the terrace, and other precincts of the House of Commons open to the fair stranger.

Mr. Parnell. Oddly enough, at this time, in these circumstances, Mr. Parnell comes back and sits by the hour attentive to the debate. He is punctilious in claiming the very seat in which he sat through the years when he was still the leader of a united party. Its precise situation makes it peculiarly embarrassing. It lies in what is now the centre of the camp of the enemy, and there being no room for any of Mr. Parnell's scanty following, he sits there with Mr. Healy and Mr. Justin McCarthy on one side, and on the other Mr. Sexton. No word or sign of recognition passes between He-Who-Was-Once-Obeyed and the old colleagues who have cast off their allegiance. He sits there in haughty silence; and they, scorning to be embarrassed by his presence, talk to each other and across him as if he were, as in truth he looks, a stone figure. It would be so easy for him to arrange it otherwise. He might sit on the front bench between the robustious Colonel Nolan and the unctuous Sir Joseph McKenna. These, still faithful among the faithless found,

would pay him the deference that once he coldly accepted
from the whole party. To do that would be to admit a
change in circumstances and in his personal relations thereto.
As Leader of the Irish Parliamentary Party, uncrowned King
of Ireland, he always sat in this particular seat. Nothing has
altered nor anything suffered sea change. Certain " gutter
sparrows " have turned and pecked at the hand that fed them.
There have been secessions from his party which, regarded
upon ordinary arithmetical principles, leave him in a miserable
and impotent minority. Once the arbiter between the two
great British parties, holding the fate of Ministries and
measures in the hollow of his hand, he is now angrily flouted
by one side and used for their own purposes by the other.
His position is shattered, his prospects blighted. Since
Lucifer fell there has been no such abrupt, complete, appalling
destruction of a career.

That is how it may strike the outsider. Mr. Parnell, with
whatever secret anguish of mind, affects to know no change.
He is exactly the same man he was this time last year, and
at whatever cost he will not abate one shade of his former
custom or habit.

June 8.—Lord
Warden of the
Cinque Ports.

A happy chance has temporarily delivered Mr.
Smith from attendance on this dreary scene.
The House of Commons, which delights in its
Leader, and by some curious twist of mind insists upon regarding him from a humorous point of view, was overjoyed to discover him suddenly and unexpectedly withdrawn from its
midst. Only on Wednesday he was in his place suffusing the
Treasury bench with a subtle sense of solidarity and safety for
the British Constitution. He had moved a resolution in his
capacity as Leader of the House, and was even prepared to
take part in the consequent division. Then a warning voice
of authority reached him, and he learned, with a start of
surprise, that though he was Lord Warden of the Cinque
Ports he was no longer member for the Strand. When he
rose from the Treasury bench to move the pious provision
which would permit members serving on Committees to
attend church on Ascension Day he was an intruder. The
Serjeant-at-Arms would have been justified in gently, but

firmly, leading him forth and barring further entrance to the chamber. A little fiction has been invented which post-dates his formal acceptance of office under the Crown, and so left him free through Wednesday to exercise the functions of a member of the House. What is quite certain is that, immediately after submitting his motion, Mr. Smith, with scared face, stole forth on tiptoe behind the Speaker's chair, and his place on the Treasury bench knows him no more.

June 10.—Sunshine on the Treasury bench. Opposition is just now effaced, the question hour is reduced to the narrowest limits, and all the real work of successive sittings takes place in Committee, which is fortunate, since it brings Mr. Balfour to the front, and leaves in his strong hand the actual direction of affairs. There was a time, not far gone, when the question of the devolution of the Leadership seemed urgent, and the merits of certain assumed candidates for the office were frankly discussed. Mr. Smith's retirement and admission within the serene atmosphere of the House of Lords were spoken of as a contingency that might any day arise. He was ill and worried, and, having weathered the storm with a skill not fully recognised because it is unobtrusive, it seemed only reasonable that he should find his haven of rest. Happily Mr. Smith's health has improved, whilst Ministerial prospects, at least within the House, have steadily brightened. The alliance with the Liberal Unionist wing has proved to be so firmly welded as to withstand any force brought to bear against it. Ireland is quiet; the country is prosperous; the Parnellites are riven in twain; and Lord Randolph Churchill has set out for Mashonaland. It is doubtless true that all the old fires in the House of Commons are latent; but the furnace is banked up, and emits only that stream of thick yellow smoke dignified by the name of debate in Committee on the Land Bill. There is no pressure on the Treasury bench, nor any reason why Mr. Smith should not through the full term of Parliament remain in the position of Leader. The House rejoices in his new advancement, and thinks kindly of him standing resolute on the Kentish rampart, scanning the horizon in search now of a possible invader, anon of any flotsam and jetsam in the way of wreckage that, in accordance with ancient law and usage, may be claimed as the perquisite of the Constable of Dover Castle, Lord Warden of the Cinque Ports.

June 12.—Visitors from afar.   One would like to know the private impression of our Parliamentary institutions acquired by the two dusky visitors who to-night stared forth at the House of Commons and the House of Lords. Halulula was the almost familiar name of the elder, and Umfete his companion. They were emissaries of the musically named South African King Gungunhana, hither bent on a mission to the Great Mother, hoping, after the fashion of African and Eastern princelings, that she would order up her redoubtable warriors to cut off some-one's head, so that her humble petitioner might reign in his stead. The Zulu envoys had learned that in the strange country they visited there was a power behind the Throne stronger than the Great Mother herself. This was Parliament, and if only they could get round Parliament all would be well with their Sovereign (temporarily deposed) Lord the King. So they engaged a four-wheeler, and, in company with the interpreter, who is to them, as they say, for the time both ear and mouth, betook themselves to Westminster.

Halulula is a man advanced in years, with grey hairs bristling on his sunken cheeks. He looked round the bustling scene in the lobby of the House of Commons with startled, wondering gaze. His companion, Umfete, a younger, stronger, somewhat bull-necked Zulu, also surveyed the scene, but with more rapid, eager glance. As he watched Sir Richard Temple crossing the lobby escorting two fair ladies, his right hand twitched, and one who has seen the assegai hurled seemed to divine his hidden thoughts. Both were luxuriously attired in Western clothing, evidently bought ready-made in the district of Whitechapel. Apparently they had revolted against the crowning grace of the tall cylindrical hat, and had accepted as a compromise a broad-brimmed soft felt head-covering, which Umfete set a little on one side, thereby assuming a comically rakish air. When Halulula bared his head to salute a new acquaintance, lo! there gleamed from under the Whitechapel wideawake the shining coil, "the Zulu ring," our men saw amid smoke of rifles and shower of assegais at Isandula and Rorke's Drift.

A curious concatenation of circumstances when we come to think of it—this Whitechapel wideawake and the Zulu head-dress.

A toothsome bit. Umfeto was no more abashed in the House of Lords than he had been in the lobby of the House of Commons. His bold eyes roved round the almost empty chamber, till, resting on the figure of the Lord Chancellor, seated in wig and gown on the Woolsack—a perilously plump and tempting target—once again the fingers of his right hand twitched, as they had done when, all unconsciously, Sir Richard Temple had passed him by. Halulula looked forth out of his soft dark eyes with the same troubled, anxious, wondering gaze. Was this the Imperial House of Parliament, this almost empty chamber, with here and there an elderly gentleman sitting at ease on the red benches? Was this the power that launched a thousand ships and burned the topless towers of Cetewayo?

The Duke of Argyll. It was almost a pity the envoys had lingered so long in the lobby across the corridor. Had they entered the Lords half an hour earlier they would have carried back to their waiting King—the "Mr. G." of their South African territory—a very different impression of Parliamentary force. Hardly as they entered had the echoes of the voice of the McCallum More died away through the awed rafters of the chamber. It is not often in these degenerate days the Duke of Argyll condescends to impart counsel to his peers. To-night he was on his feet for upwards of an hour, thoroughly enjoying himself with a disquisition on the lamentable condition of the heedless population of the Isle of Lewis "a people characterised," as he said in a fine passage, "by the lowest condition of ignorance and absolute impecuniosity," and yet so profoundly steeped in indifference to economic laws and all sense of propriety that they persisted not only in having families, but in rearing them.

If the gentle spirit of Halulula had been reticent on the subject, Umfeto would not have had the slightest hesitation in telling the Duke of Argyll how the trouble of congested districts would be met, supposing they were situate in the land over which King Gungunhana desires to rule.

But the Duke of Argyll had finished his great oration when the African envoys looked in on the Lords, and they did not hear the tone of hopeless despair and withering indignation with which his Grace recorded the damning fact that, whilst in 1818 the population of Lewis was only 25,487, the census just completed showed that this shameless population now numbered 27,486 ! The lessened unit showed some glimmering of proper feeling, some sense of what was due to their betters. But it was a mere flicker, hopelessly excluded by the increase in the thousands.

Also Haluluha and Umfete were spared the pain that must have wrung even the savage breast at the Duke's disclosure of Wordsworth's lamentable, almost incredible ignorance. One day the Duke was, with the courtly condescension that makes him charming in all relations of life, walking through the fair scenery of Westmorland in company with the somewhat overrated poetaster. Wordsworth was in deep reverie possibly thinking of the mighty city on the Thames, which he once looked at in the early morning from Westminster Bridge, when the very houses seemed asleep. Peradventure, his thoughts nearer home, he was ruminating on Peter Bell and his incomprehensible indifference to the particularity of the primrose. The Duke, breaking in on his reverie, and pointing to a hill, abruptly asked—

"Whose land is that ?"

The poor poet made answer that he never heard it was anybody's land.

"And this," cried the Duke of Argyll, throwing back his head with familiar gesture, and fixing his flaming eye on Lord Lothian, whose official position in connection with Scotch administrative affairs made him in some remote connection responsible for the dead poet's *bêtise*, "this is the man who, with reference to sheep and shepherds, wrote beautiful lines, probably known to some of your lordships."

Lord Denman.   It was quite another scene on which the dusky envoys gazed, with the sheen from the sunlit windows gleaming on the Zulu ring. The Duke of Argyll, flushed with his new oratorical triumph, that eclipsed the fame of Lord Chatham's most loudly trumpeted effort, had carefully

rearranged his voluminous manuscript, and marched forth.
The audience, witched by his eloquence, had melted away.
Only half a dozen peers remained, the murmur of their conversation mingling with the sound of a deep though broken
voice that filled the chamber as with a wail of pitiful entreaty.
Standing in the very place at the table where lately through
a long hour had swayed the figure of the McCallum More,

surging with the stream of his
own eloquence, was seen a very
different figure—an old man,
with pale, furrowed face, scanty
hair, bent shoulders, arrayed in
garb whose seediness contrasted
with the brand-new clothing of
the Zulus. An ancient, ill-
fitting, sun-faded, grey overcoat
hung loosely on his shoulders;
in his right hand—brim upper-
most, in the way a beggarman
extends his hat for alms—he
grasped an old white hat with a
narrow band that had once been
black. In the other hand was a
crumpled handkerchief that
had once been white, and with
it he held a stick.

It was difficult to catch the
full meaning of the words intoned as the rich voice rose
and fell. The tones seemed full

of tears, and were well attuned to the pathetic figure standing
there in the proudest assembly in the land, with inalienable
right to speak and vote, and yet with none to pay the deference of even seeming to listen. Some Bill had been introduced,
dealing, as far as could be understood, with the status of
sheriffs. The peer in the rusty grey coat was opposing its introduction: one of the sentences, caught amid the confused
murmur of his speech, invoked the memory of his father, a
famous lawyer and statesman, champion of Queen Caroline in
her distress, and, nevertheless, in later time Lord Chief Justice

of the King's Bench. Suddenly, the voice rising to impassioned
heights, the peer, drawing himself up to his full height, and
waving his white hat, declaimed the pathetic lines from
Horace—

> " Vixere fortes ante Agamemnona
> Multi ; sed omnes illacrymabiles
> Urgentur, ignotique longa
> Nocte carent quia vate sacro."

Then, sinking his voice to a whisper, the old man, feebly
sitting down, in humble voice begged their lordships to excuse
him if he had unduly occupied their time. The Lord Chancellor adroitly seized the opportunity to put the question that
the Bill be read a first time, and, there being no more business
before the House, it forthwith adjourned, the Zulus watching
with glistening eyes the stately procession of the Lord Chancellor, preceded by the Pursebearer and Mace, going forth
to disrobe.

CHAPTER XXXVII.

IN COMMITTEE OF SUPPLY.

"Jemmy" Lowther again—Some Chief Secretaries—The Latest—The Wool-
wich Infant—A Fall of Snow—Mr. Morton—A Civic Guard of Honour—
Colonel Hughes's Plan—The O'Gorman Mahon—Choosing a Diplomatist—
A Model Under Secretary—The Premier's Son—The Son of Jesse.

June 19. —
"Jemmy"
Lowther
again.

EVEN to this day the House of Commons has
not mastered the thrill that runs through it
when Mr. James Lowther interposes in debate.
It is not a matter of frequent occurrence, which probably adds
to its effect. It is—as happened to-night—always sudden and
unexpected. There sits the right hon. gentleman who once
presided over a judicial inquiry instituted by the Jockey Club,
and was, earlier, Chief Secretary for Ireland. It is so long
since he entered the House that it is almost permissible to
imagine him to be getting up in years. He is, at least as the
almanack counts, past the first flush of headlong youth ; and

yet there is ever about him a boyishness with difficulty overcome even when he presided over the important judicial
tribunal referred.

Nevertheless, it is a quality of almost supernatural gravity
that makes him a kind of Mystery-Man to members whose experience of House of Commons life commences with the date
of the present Parliament. Wild traditions linger round the
name of the right hon. gentleman whom to-day it seems almost
sacrilege to allude to as "Jemmy" Lowther. The memory of
some goes back to the far-off night when Sir Charles Dilke,
seconded by Mr. Auberon Herbert, presumed to call in question the provisions of the Civil List. Whilst Mr. Auberon
Herbert was struggling vainly against the uproar which for-
bade him to speak, someone "spied strangers," and, the
galleries cleared, the struggle went forward for another hour
undisturbed by the presence of onlookers. Mr. James Lowther,
jealous for the dignity of the Crown, led the riot, being ably
seconded by the late Mr. Cavendish-Bentinck. Indeed, it was
reported at the time that the latter right hon. gentleman at a
critical period of the fray went out behind the Speaker's chair
and crowed thrice. This he has publicly denied, and it is
evident that in the mental disturbance arising out of the riot
misapprehension arose.

Cock-crow was certainly heard at an untimely hour, and in
an unusual place ; but it was due to the vocal effort of some
other Royalist.

A great deal has happened since then. Mr. Cavendish-
Bentinck has passed away, and current advertisements
announce the dispersal of the treasure-trove of a long life.
Mr. Auberon Herbert, the Radical, almost the Republican of
the early '70's, now writes good Tory letters to the *Times*.
"Jemmy" Lowther has become the Right Honourable James
and sits at the corner seat below the gangway, a little distrust-
ful of gentlemen on the Treasury bench, who are prone, under
pressure of circumstances, to introduce Radical measures with
Conservative labels.

<table>
<tr><td>Some Chief Secretaries.</td><td>In the meantime, Mr. Lowther has travelled far and undergone many vicissitudes. The election</td></tr>
</table>

of 1885 left him high and dry, and it seemed through several

Sessions that the House of Commons would know him no more.
But the Isle of Thanet, which had supplied a resting-place for
the foot of poor King-Harman, hunted out of Ireland, was hos-
pitable also to Mr. James Lowther.   He has come back to the
scene of his lusty young Parliamentary life and of his later
Ministerial labours.   But it would seem that ambition is
satiated, the springs of political desire sapped. "Jemmy"
Lowther, the buccaneer of the 1868 Parliament, has become a
staid, almost elderly, gentleman, who now and then rises, and
in an unfamiliar tone and manner checks the headlong pace
of modern Conservatives like Mr. W. H. Smith. His very
style of speech is unfamiliar to the present generation.   It has
a quaint, old-fashioned, somewhat pedantic stiffness that arrests
attention.   All his life long Mr. Lowther has been in antagonism with Mr. Gladstone, and now in these days they have
this point in common, that both may claim to be historical
monuments.

It was in 1878 that Mr. Disraeli, who had a keen eye for
capacity, however environed, made "Jemmy" Chief Secretary
for Ireland.   He did not hold the office long, but whilst there
he achieved a measure of success forbidden to men of higher
standing in political life.   Mr. Forster's life and career were
shattered at the Irish Office. Sir George Trevelyan visibly
grew grey under the eyes of the House as night after night
he battled with the Irish members. Only two men holding
the office of Chief Secretary since Home Rule reared its head
have left it without, as Mr. Lowther might say, turning a hair.
One is the right hon. gentleman who has now found a haven
of refuge in the Isle of Thanet, the other is Mr. Campbell
Bannerman.   Round them, as round predecessors and successors, the stream of vituperation and contumely surged.
But, thanks to a peculiar temperament, they sat smiling and
unmoved, minding it no more than Dungeness cares for the
raving of the English Channel when storms rise and ships are
wrecked.

The latest.   In time the Irish members, quick-witted and
sympathetic with pluck and sangfroid, aban-
doned their hostile attitude, and Mr. Lowther and Mr. Campbell Bannerman had a moderately comfortable time during

their incumbency of office. Mr. Arthur Balfour is left out of the enumeration of Chief Secretaries who have not turned a hair whilst in office, since the description would not be literally accurate. He differs from Mr. Lowther and Mr. Campbell Bannerman, inasmuch as they were passively indifferent, whilst he, upon occasion, is actively aggressive. They sat smiling on the bench whilst Mr. Parnell hissed hate at them, Mr. Biggar jibed, and Mr. Healy brought his ready shillelagh into play. They were to all appearances as much amused and personally quite as indifferent as the lookers-on. That is not Mr. Balfour's way. If coats are trailed before him, he treads on them. Something like a truce reigns now. He and the Irish members have often measured swords, and they have learned to respect his skill and strength of wrist. But at the end of a fifth year this fighting habit tells upon a man. It is still possible to find Mr. Balfour's face lighted up by the swift gleam of an almost boyish smile. But when he sits on the Treasury bench in charge of a Government measure his face is both hardened and aged compared with the day when, amid doubtful smiles among friends and open jeers from enemies, he tripped up to the Treasury bench to take charge of Ireland.

Doubtless he will renew his youth like the eagle, when, in the time now not far distant, he will find himself temporarily relieved of the cares of office, and may take up that discourse on the "Life and Work of John Stuart Mill," the notes for which he cherishes in the pigeon-hole of his private desk. It was pretty to see him on Tuesday night lounging far forward on the Treasury bench, with his shoulders brought so low that he could just rest his head on the top of the bench. That is an attitude familiar enough at one time, but into which he has not dropped since the Land Purchase Bill was introduced. It meant that as far as this Session is concerned his work is done, his long labour finished. To sit and listen to Sir Wm. Harcourt discreetly discussing Manipur must be an intense luxury for a Minister who for more than thirty nights, wrestling with a manifold Opposition, has piloted through narrow and tortuous channels a Bill which, like the maid who dwelt beside the banks of Dove, there were few to like and none at all to love.

Colonel Hughes has sat for Woolwich through two Parliaments, and there is something about his build and generally warlike appearance that has suggested for him the bye-name of the Woolwich Infant. This arbitrary connection with a famous piece of armament and his title of Colonel seem to be his only connection with warlike pursuits. Looking down from the Strangers' Gallery upon his massive presence, and hearing him addressed as " Colonel," a German visitor might think with envy of an army whereof the member for Woolwich is probably an average specimen.

But though the Colonel's foible may be war when practised by the 2nd Kent Artillery Volunteers, his professional pursuits are essentially peaceful, not to say prosaic. As he informed the House to-night, he has for thirty years been a vestryman —nay, he holds office in vestry administration, being at this moment Vestry Clerk of Plumstead and Solicitor to the Woolwich Local Board of Health. Had he been born in France he would have been idolised by the Parisians as a model of *le Bon Pompier*. Born at Droitwich in the year of the Reform Bill, he was in early manhood drawn by matrimonial relations into some sort of relations with Woolwich Arsenal. These fired his mind with martial aspirations, and slowly, but irresistibly, he won his way to the front in the rank of England's soldier sons, and the Vestry Clerk of Plumstead fastened on his burly shoulders the epaulettes of the Colonel of the 2nd Kent Artillery Volunteers.

No one but a gentleman enjoying Colonel Hughes's varied experience could have made the speech with which to-night he delighted a jaded House. Any section of party can produce, and any constituency may return, a colonel, and any other may, if it please, be represented in Imperial Parliament by a Vestry Clerk. But to Woolwich alone it is given to produce the phenomenon that combines both.

Undoubtedly the particular question that happened to be before the House to-night supplied the member for Woolwich with a rare opportunity. How to grapple with, a fall of six inches of snow impartially distributed over the area of the metropolis ? That was the question with which the business branch of the Imperial Legislature was on this midsummer night posed.

A fall of snow.   Mr. Bartley, who the other night gallantly led a storming party of ten against the entrenchments of the Government, did not regard this subject as unworthy of his consideration. He had, he said, made a calculation which led him to the appalling conclusion that in order to deliver London from such an incubus there would be required the services of carts, horses, and men sufficient to remove twenty-five million loads. Mr. Ritchie, who had for some hours been piloting the Public Health (London) Bill through this critical stage with that *bonhomie* which only partially disguises rare Parliamentary skill, collapsed in presence of this stupendous fact. For idle members, able to enjoy discussions on the subject merely as an intellectual treat, this procession of twenty-five million cartloads of snow was a luxurious contemplation with the thermometer at ninety in the shade and not a breath of wind stirring. It was a different matter for the President of the Local Government Board, at whose door, so to speak, this vast accumulation of snow actually lay.

ALPHEUS CLEOPHAS.

Mr. Morton.   From the corner seat below the gangway, where once the tall figure of Mr. Newdegate was wont sadly to rise, and whence a solemn voice echoed through the House some new story of Jesuitical device, Mr. Morton grimly looked on. For him in these later years life takes on a new access of pleasure. There is, perhaps, no human comfort so enviable as that possessed by a man who in the closing hours of a Friday night can look back on a well-spent week. For most of us this pleasure is limited by opportunity. We have not all the diverse channels through which the energy of Colonel Hughes expends itself. Mr. Morton has not the gallant Colonel's especial wealth and variety of official position. But he is favoured by one fortuitous circumstance of which he has keen appreciation. The Corporation of the City of London meet in the daytime; the House of Commons, assembling in the late afternoon, sits till midnight. Alphous Cleophas Morton, being a member of both, can step lightly from Guildhall to Westminster, taking up, with light, firm touch, the tangled threads of business in either supreme assembly.

A civic guard of honour. It was only the other day he compassed within a period of twelve hours a triumph unique in the history of famous Englishmen. At the meeting of the City Council in the morning he had genially twitted his colleagues with going on their knees to the County Council in order to secure their goodwill and favour. A mere passing observation, but somehow it grated on the sensibilities of the City Fathers. They howled at Mr. Morton till he might have thought he was in the House of Commons hinting dark things about the Duke of Cambridge. To that he was used; but the scene that followed was not lacking in freshness. When business was concluded and the Lord Mayor rose to retire, the City Fathers, regarding him as the representative of Corporate dignity just outraged and insulted, rose to their feet and accompanied him with tumultuous cheering to his carriage.

Returning, they came upon Mr. Morton, umbrella under his arm, making his way out. Him they conducted to the doorway with jeers and groans and hisses, and so saw him off on his way to Westminster. Arrived there, he found himself just in time to put one or two disagreeable questions to Ministers, and before the sitting closed had the House yelling at him for ten minutes whilst he stood on his feet attempting to show that in his dealings with the volunteer service the Secretary of State for War, suborned by Royal influence, was misleading the House of Commons, and was traitorous to the country.

The memory of a glorious day like that should be sufficient to mellow a man, and make him accessible to tender influence and kindly thought. For the ordinary Londoner the place to spend a happy day is Rosherville. Mr. Morton is distraught

between the counter attractions of Guildhall and the House
of Commons, and diligently endeavours to make the best
of both. Now was his opportunity, with the hapless
President of the Local Government Board under this twenty-
five million cartloads of snow which Mr. Bartley's fecund fancy
had conjured up.

Colonel Hughes's plan. He rose quickly to his feet, and had begun to
say something pleasant, when from the other
side of the House came a thunderous voice, a noise like to
the rolling of many drums, or to the waters coming down at
Lodore. It was Colonel and Vestry Clerk Hughes, who had
something to say about the snow, and was disposed to say
it without reference to any intention cherished by Mr.
Morton. The member for Peterborough continued through
a sentence or two, but finding that no one, least of all Colonel
Hughes, took any notice of him, he sat down, and the Colonel
had the field to himself.

The Colonel's proposal was, as might have been expected
from him, soldierly and business-like. Suppose, he said in
effect, London goes to bed at night and wakes in the morning
to find six inches of snow on the streets. The block was too
enormous to be dealt with either by the Vestries (of which he
spoke with all respect) or by any other sanitary authority.
But there was one way out of it. Let a bell ring, a drum beat,
or a trumpet sound. Then let every family, from the head to
the boy or girl who had passed the sixth standard, muster in
the hall, march forth, shovel and brush in hand, and clear away
the snow before their own door and window ways. "Why,"
said the Colonel, glancing triumphantly round his rapt
audience, "in an hour the pavements would be clean as a
billiard board." Then the Colonel sat down, Mr. Morton got
his chance, and a few strangers in the gallery were more than
ever pleased with their privilege of being present at deliberation in the High Court of Parliament.

June 27.—The O'Gorman Mahon. A picturesque personality is removed from the
House of Commons by the death of The O'Gor-
man Mahon. As a matter of fact, it has been
withdrawn from a date shortly after his return to the House,

upon the vacancy for Carlow created by the death of Mr.
Blake.   The O'Gorman, as he was usually called, had reached
a patriarchal age, and, though his constitution was singularly
robust, he was not equal to the stress of Parliamentary
duties.   It was the custom of his colleagues to entertain him
at dinner on his birthday.   Last year the party was held as
usual, but the principal guest's seat was vacant.   The O'Gorman
Mahon sent word to say he was not quite well enough to turn
up on that particular night, but he promised the "bhoys" that
he would be with them on his next birthday.   Now he is dead,
and the present House of Commons, which had few opportunities of becoming acquainted with his personal appearance, will
know him no more.   He was one of the few men living last
week who had a seat in the unreformed Parliament, and it was
characteristic of him that he was unseated on petition.   He
passed a roving life in Chili, fighting indifferently on sea or
land, and, Mr. Butt used to say, with equal indifference on
either side of a quarrel.   Mr. Gladstone took a strong interest
in the old warrior, who had a cheerful little custom of sitting
on the front bench whenever he found Mr. Gladstone there,
and chatting with him at length.

June 29.—Choosing a diplomatist.   Mr. Labouchere is a man of wide sympathies and
singular experience.   If omniscience be his
foible, diplomacy is his *forte.*   As he has not infrequently mentioned in the House of Commons, he was himself at one time in the diplomatic service.   There is hardly
any phase of foreign politics which does not suggest to him
a draft upon his reminiscences.   In the discussion initiated to-
night on the Foreign Office vote he told a comparatively new
story illustrative of how the service he once adorned is re-
cruited.   A young gentleman, who the Committee was given
to understand now occupies the first rank in diplomacy, submitted himself for examination for the earliest appointment.
He knew absolutely nothing of the themes submitted to him,
and appears, with the lightheartedness peculiar to Mr. Labouchere's contemporaries in diplomatic career, to have gone in
for his examination merely for the fun of the thing—a kind
of process whereby a dull hour between breakfast and luncheon
might be whiled away.   To his unbounded surprise he found

himself not only passed, but placed at the head of the list. A day or two later he met the examiner, and, with the freedom apparently permissible in these early days of diplomacy, asked him upon what possible consideration he had been passed, seeing that he was absolutely ignorant on the points on which he was examined.

"That is just it, my dear fellow," said the great man ; " we saw you knew nothing, but your manner was so free from con-straint under what to some people would have been peculiarly embarrassing circumstances, that we said to each other : ' That's the very man to make a diplomatist'; and so we gave you a start on your career.'

A model Under Secretary. The little story was introduced to Sir James Fergusson's notice by way of prelude to Mr. Labouchere's genial declaration of personal belief that Under Secretaries for Foreign Affairs, and members of the diplomatic body generally, are of all men the most ignorant.

This is a discipline Sir James Fergusson is able to bear with provoking equanimity. If he were Mr. Labouchere's sole audience even the irrepressible spirits of that gentleman would flag. For all immediate effect observable, the member for Northampton might as well go out to Egypt, sit down before the Sphinx, tweak its nose, pull its ears, and attempt to dis-turb the equanimity of centuries by quips and cranks. Sir James Fergusson has not succeeded in impressing the House of Commons with conviction of singular ability, or even of ordinary capacity, as it is looked for in one of Her Majesty's Ministers. But as Under Secretary for Foreign Affairs he is heaven-born. His stolid imperturbability is of greater value to his chief and his colleagues than would be any measure of scintillating brilliancy. Under existing circumstances, with a strong and capable man holding the threads of Government and of Foreign Affairs from his place in the House of Lords, what is wanted in the House of Commons is the equivalent of a telephone. Doubtless, in other conditions, Sir James Fergusson could command the admiration of the House by lightness of touch, wealth of fancy, and flexibility of fence. He is content to sink all considerations of personal prominence in obedience to that sense of duty to his Queen and country of which the great exemplar sits on his right-hand side on the Treasury bench.

It is easy to understand the embarrassment that would disturb social and business life if a telephone engaged by the half-hour or five minutes were to vary an interview by interposing casual observations of its own. Sir James Fergusson knows better than that. When Mr. Labouchere, Mr. Picton, or Mr. Morton, places on the paper addressed to him questions affecting foreign policy, he rises slowly, deliberately selects a document properly labelled, and with stolid manner and unruffled voice reads out what is written for him.

In early stages of his Parliamentary career he was apt to be entrapped by persistent interrogators, who sprang upon him supplementary questions. That is a course of procedure much to be deplored. When a question is written down and circulated with the votes, it is easy enough for a chief clerk, in the leisurely retirement of the Foreign Office, to write out an answer on foolscap. It is obviously impossible to foresee contingent questions and prepare suitable answers. Suddenly assailed by a supplementary question, Sir James Fergusson, new to the office, was wont to rise, gasp out a sentence of clouded meaning, and, whilst the baffled inquirer was endeavouring to master its intricacy, the Speaker came to the Minister's rescue by calling on the next question. Sir James does better than that now. The other day, to the delight of an unexpecting House, he neatly floored Mr. Labouchere, who had put to him a carefully constructed question about the Triple Alliance. Sir James read to him an answer full of sonorous words signifying nothing.

"Am I," asked Mr. Labouchere in his most insinuating voice, " to understand that the right hon. gentleman means so-and-so ? "

"The hon. member," said the Under Secretary, momentarily rising to the height of his great chief, " is not to understand me to mean anything more than I have said."

Sir James Fergusson is not always as good as that. But his average value to Her Majesty's Government, his beneficent agency in saving the time of the House of Commons, and maintaining the peace of Europe, is incalculable.

June 29.—The Premier's son.

Lord Cranborne is in many respects the very reverse of his father. He has nothing of the massive, black-bearded visage of the Premier, being, on the contrary, slight in figure and boyish-looking in the face, making only the mildest attempt at cultivating a moustache, and that up to the present time not a full success. Although he has been in the House for some years, he still is affected by Parliamentary fright. Last night, when he naïvely proposed the adjournment of the debate at a quarter to twelve, and, the motion being resisted from the Treasury bench, he learned from the Speaker that he was imperilling his chance of subsequently taking part in the discussion, he was so overcome that he could hardly speak. Addressing the House this evening his nervousness was almost painful to the onlookers. He rubs his right hand up and down his ribs and chest even more persistently than does Mr. Goschen when he is withdrawing a Bill or explaining away a portion of his Budget scheme. He loses all command of his voice, and sometimes leads to outbursts of laughter by declaiming a truism or a commonplace in tragic tones. This evening, when in thunderous accents he announced the familiar and incontrovertible fact that "after the second reading there comes committee," he could not understand why the House should laugh. As an oratorical effort the speech was not a triumph, but the House recognised in it an independent and painstaking effort to grapple with an important question, and cheered him accordingly.

June 30.—The son of Jesse.

There is a pretty story current in the House to-night, repeated on the authority of Mr. Chamberlain. A lady, examining her Sunday-school class at Highbury, asked a promising little girl, "Who was David ?"

"Please, ma'am," said the child, "he was the son of Jesse Collings."

CHAPTER XXXVIII.

THE ABSENT LEADER.

A Pitcher that went too often to the Well—A Prophecy—The Irish Leaders—
Mr. McCarthy—Mr. O'Brien—Boulogne—Mr. Sexton—"Tim" Healy—
John Dillon—Mr. Chamberlain—Mr. Atkinson—Mr. Seymour Keay—Mr.
Caldwell—His Great Speech—No Answer!

July 14.—A pitcher that went too often to the well. MR. SMITH was again absent from his place in the Commons to-day, and is not likely to return unless special occasion demand his presence, which is not likely. He has made a gallant fight against illness, faithful even to his own detriment in his performance of his duty to his Queen and country. A fortnight ago, in rarely hot weather, when summer coats and light waistcoats were *de rigueur*, Mr. Smith brought in his carriage rug, and pathetically sat on the Treasury bench with this protection round his knees. One of Lord Salisbury's guests who sat near him at Hatfield yesterday tells me he looked more like a corpse than a living man.

There is no doubt he would be well content to retire at the end of the present Session, satisfied with the high position he has won for himself by his Leadership in the House of Commons. But next Session is positively the last that even the present Government can hope to stretch the existing Parliament into. It would be exceedingly awkward to be faced by the necessity of changing the Leader at such a juncture. It is no secret that Mr. Smith wanted to retire last year, and even the year before. Each time he was asked to defer his decision, and being to a considerable extent brought round by the rest acquired during the recess, he again undertook the task. But, as he is reported to have said to Lord Salisbury a fortnight ago when his health began to show signs of again breaking down, " A pitcher that goes often to the well will be broken at last," and he may with just reason demand the rest and quietude he has well earned.

A prophecy.   In view of the possibility of a vacancy in the Leadership it is noticed that during Mr. Smith's temporary withdrawal Mr. Goschen takes his place, which would seem to imply a settlement of the succession to the Leadership. That is an assumption, however, that goes too far, as disposing of the claims of Mr. Arthur Balfour. The Chancellor of the Exchequer is a Minister who, except at certain times or when the Budget is in preparation, has less work to do than any other of similar rank. That is why in ordinary circumstances the functions of Leader of the House are usually joined to the office of Chancellor of the Exchequer. Mr. Balfour, with Ireland on his hands, could scarcely undertake the duty of being in his place from question-time till the Speaker leaves the Chair, as is expected from the Leader. Whenever the time comes for final decision as to the Leadership to be made, Mr. Balfour will come to the front, impelled by the support of the vast majority of the Conservative members. These are willing enough to use Mr. Goschen, but they do not like him, and would never willingly follow him.

July 22. — The Irish leaders.   Mr. John Dillon and Mr. William O'Brien, having seized the earliest opportunity of clearly defining their attitude towards their formerly revered chief, have temporarily withdrawn from the political arena. Mr. Dillon has retired to a watering-place to recruit, and Mr. O'Brien has settled down in the Irish county which, it is announced, is to be the scene of his next novel. His first was scarcely so good or so successful as to suggest an early return to the field. It was marked by the failings which handicap his platform and Parliamentary eloquence. It was occasionally turgid, often dull or utterly devoid of perspective. All his minnows (supposing they were on the right side of the Irish Question) disported themselves as whales, and the thread of the story, attenuated at best, was apt to be lost, while Mr. O'Brien talked political parables. People bought and read the book because the author was just out of prison or just going to prison, or had just baffled Mr. Balfour's myrmidons and got safely away to Havre, after a perilous passage in an inadequate barque. At the time Mr. O'Brien was a personage, and so his novel was asked

for at Mudie's, and some people, it is said, read it through.
But the public is very fickle in those matters, and Mr.
O'Brien's next novel will have this disadvantage, among
others, that its author has fallen from his high estate in the
political world.

Mr. McCarthy.   Mr. O'Brien's personal decadence will have its
        effect upon a far more important problem than
the success or failure of a three-volume novel. Mr. Justin
McCarthy, as everyone knows, is Mr. Parnell's successor
only *pro tem.* No one unfamiliar with his personality and
with the circumstances of his daily life knows what a sacrifice
he made when he accepted the invitation to set up as leader
of the majority of Irish members who preferred patriotism to
Parnellism. He was nominated for the office, not because he
is a heaven-born leader, but because he would least divide the
party. That arrangement was always understood to be a
temporary one, and when, next Session, the Irish members
foregather, it will be with a new captain, whose appointment,
it is intended, shall be permanent.

Mr. O'Brien.   Who shall it be ? If the question had arisen a
        year ago, or Mr. O'Brien had been available as
a candidate when, last November, the vacancy was created,
there is no doubt the choice would have fallen on him.
Under Mr. Parnell's leadership he took a more prominent
part in Parliamentary debate than did Mr. Dillon, nor was
the proportion disturbed in their little tours through
Ireland. They often hunted in couples, but it was noteworthy, and seemed natural, that when they appeared on the
platform Mr. O'Brien should speak first, Mr. Dillon falling
into the second line. It was the same in the House of
Commons, though with that audience, whose judgment of
men is never at fault, Mr. Dillon, from the first, carried the
greater weight in debate.

Boulogne.   The crash that overwhelmed Mr. Parnell found
        Mr. O'Brien in America, and he came home *via*
Boulogne. That was the fatal step in his career from which
he has not yet recovered and probably never will. His

hysterical sobs transmitted by cable under the melancholy
ocean, his waving of a tear-stained handkerchief in assurance
that, faithful as Mrs Micawber, he would " never desert " his
old chief, presented his character in a new light. He had
always been regarded as emotional ; this was maudlin.
When at length he reached Boulogne, he arranged a series of
interviews and congratulations with stealthy comings and
goings, stage whispers and blue lights that better fitted a twopenny theatre than the stage of real life. The farce was
redeemed from puerility only by the pale, set face, the impassive figure, and the cool, calculating gaze of Mr. Parnell.
Before Mr. O'Brien appeared on the scene the member for
Cork had seemed to be utterly defeated. Now, by the operation of motives which puzzled the public, he was set up again
with another chance, and with consummate skill made so
much of it that for a while, even in what had seemed the
hour of assured victory, the fate of Ireland again trembled in
the balance, and the enemies of Home Rule, looking on,
audibly chuckled at this unexpected diversion in their favour.

Mr. Sexton.　　　Apart from Mr. Dillon and Mr. O'Brien there
　　　　　　　are two members of the Irish Parliamentary
Party who might well be considered in running for the
leadership. One is Mr. Sexton, the other Mr. Tim Healy.
The former, owing to the absence of other prominent members
of the party, enjoyed last Session unusual opportunities of
coming to the front, and he certainly made the most of them.
In the debate on the Land Purchase Bill he displayed a
mastery of details second only to that of Mr. Balfour.
He was assiduous in attendance through the Committee
stage, unwearying in his efforts to introduce amendments,
some accepted by the Chief Secretary as improvements on the
Bill. If he were only gifted with a modicum of modesty, his
position in Parliament would be a very different one, and
there is no reason why he should not be Mr. Parnell's
successor. Mr. Sexton is unhappily afflicted with a mor-
bid, exorbitant self-conceit, which makes him personally
unpopular with his colleagues, and inflicts sore suffering on
the House of Commons. He is so in love with the sound of
his own voice that when once he falls under its seductive

influence time and space are annihilated, and no one can say
when he will give others a chance of being heard. His
speeches all run to seed for lack of timely cropping. An able
debater, occasionally capable of rising to the height of eloquence,
this fatal facility of word-spinning has been his ruin, and
there is no sign in recent times of any determined effort to
manfully grapple with the weakness.

"Tim" Healy.   For quite other reasons Mr. Tim Healy is passed
over when the question of Mr. Parnell's successor
is discussed. Since the Irish Party are chronically in Opposi-

tion, "Tim" would, if it suited
his circumstances, make a model
leader. With Sir William Harcourt leading from the Treasury
bench, Mr. Balfour in charge on
the front Opposition bench,
and Tim Healy below the gangway, captain of the Irish contingent, there would be no more
room for the complaint of dulness in party proceedings. Mr.
Healy has other qualifications
for the post than that of com-
bativeness. He is singularly
well acquainted with the forms
and precedents of the House, as
Mr. Goschen learned last year
when he upset his Budget
scheme on a point of order
arising out of the proposed distribution of the grant in aid of
publicans. He is an agile debater, with a wonderfully quick
eye for a flaw in a Government
measure. He knows the Irish Question *au fond*, and in
spite of a manner occasionally, and, I believe, deliberately,
coarse, he is liked and respected on both sides of the
House. People may, and the great majority do, differ from
him on matters of opinion. No one except Mr. Parnell,

whoso standard of honour is unworkably high, ever threw a doubt on "Tim's" honesty of purpose. But Mr. Healy has other claims upon him. He has within a few years established a large and growing practice at the Bar, and though he never shirks his duty as a member of Parliament, often withdrawing from lucrative business for weeks at a time in order to watch an important Irish measure through, he is not disposed to abandon his profession and devote himself to political life with the completeness that would be necessary for anyone but Mr. Parnell in the office that gentleman lately held.

John Dillon. In these circumstances Ireland is happy, and the House of Commons will be fortunate in the possession of the services of Mr. John Dillon. For eleven years, with intervals occasioned by ill-health and residence in jail, Mr. Dillon has lent to the Irish Parliamentary Party a character and dignity sorely needed in view of the personal standing and public eccentricities of some of the late Mr. Biggar's "lambs." He has gone as far as any of his colleagues in his defiance of authority in the House of Commons and elsewhere. On a memorable occasion he stood with folded arms and flashing eyes angrily denying the Speaker's right to interrupt him, for which unprecedented breach of order he was presently "named" and suspended from further attendance till purged of his offence. But the House of Commons will forgive anything to a man in whose honesty of purpose it believes, and it never for long quarrelled with John Dillon. His succession to Mr. Parnell would be a tower of strength for a sorely badgered party.

July 24. — Mr. Chamberlain. Mr. Chamberlain's absence from the Prince of Wales's dinner party last night was due to the fact that he has set out on a visit to Germany and the Tyrol. He will have opportunity in the course of his holiday to reflect with satisfaction on the position he holds in public life. He, though the cherished companion of marquises, dukes, and a' that, is still plain Mr. Chamberlain, a private member in the House of Commons, where once he stood a powerful Minister, with the succession to the leadership of the party apparently assured. He has this year taken little part in

A A

political warfare, whether in the House of Commons or on the platform. If he has plunged anywhere, it has been into the vortex of social life. Amongst the various phases of his remarkable and interesting career none has been so striking as his success in the social world.

In reaching the position Mr. Chamberlain now commands

he had to battle with personal opposition in high places that at one time reached the force of frenzy. Up to the summer of 1885 he was the mark for the especial obloquy of those gentlemen of England amongst whom he now ranges himself, and with whom he is almost as acceptable as if his grandfather had been a duke. At that period even the bitter personal hatred of Mr. Gladstone existing amongst the Conservatives yielded to the height and depth of the abhorrence in which Mr. Chamberlain was held. The very process by which Mr. Chamberlain's political aspect was metamorphosed atoned for his former obnoxiousness, and straightway endeared him to what were wont to be regarded as his hereditary and natural foes. At a sudden crisis he turned sharply on Mr. Gladstone, became his bitterest and most powerful adversary, and thereby endeared himself to the Conservative mind.

Mr. Chamberlain is personally a more potent influence in political life to-day than he has been at any earlier period of a busy and prosperous life. The political principle he avows is every day loosening its hold on the section of the country that once avowed it. Bye-election after bye-election has dealt him and his party a series of heavy blows. Such demonstration of public opinion taking practical effect in cutting off his following would seem to point to the gradual weakening and final decay of the power of the principal personage in the party. As long as he could command some seventy votes he was, naturally, a power in the House of Commons; with the party diminished in numbers, it would be reasonable to look for some lowering of the leader's crest, some indication of the undermining of his power. Mr. Chamberlain's personality is so strong, his ability so conspicuous, and his generalship so brilliant, that his influence accumulates though his party decays. It has been shown this Session in the fact that, in spite of the deeply-rooted dislike of the Conservative Party, and in face of the desperate struggle of Mr. Goschen, he has imposed upon the Conservative Government the task of introducing and carrying so thoroughly Radical a measure as the Free Education Bill.

July 28.- Mr. Atkinson.
Mr. Atkinson, in a white waistcoat and a voluminous, carelessly-tied neckcloth of palest salmon colour, gave quite a summer aspect to the House to-night. He had a breezy way of suddenly turning up in various quarters of the House which lent a new charm to his presence. When he rose to make his earliest objection to the Railway Rates and Charges Bill he presented himself from his accustomed seat immediately behind Ministers, a position usually indicative of exceptionally close adhesion to the

Government of the day.   Anon the pale salmon necktie flamed from below the gangway, and presently it was seen streaming forth as Mr. Atkinson flashed through the doorway on one of his numerous retreats *pour mieux sauter.*   The member for Boston has led through the week a somewhat tumultuous life. For months he disappeared from Parliamentary ken, and just at the time when people had forgotten his existence he was discovered sitting in consolatory contiguity to his leaders on the Treasury bench.   Taking into account the interval of his absence, it seemed to have occurred to him that it was his duty

HENRY JOHN ATKINSON.

to make up the average, and in these closing days of the Session he has set himself to the task with an energy that has already succeeded.

Mr. Seymour Keay.   It is a happy coincidence, illustrative of the resources of the House of Commons, that whilst the Opposition have their Alpheus Cleophas Morton, the Ministerialists should have their Henry John Atkinson.   It is true the Opposition can also boast their Seymour Keay, for whom there is no parallel on the Ministerial benches, or indeed elsewhere.   But Mr. Keay, after a promising opening, has, so to

speak, gone under. In the Committee stage of the Land Purchase Bill, whilst Mr. Atkinson was at Prague, and Alpheus
Cleophas was comparatively quiescent, Mr. Seymour Keay was
a leading personage in debate. He was vaguely credited with
having discovered some serious default in the financial
arrangements of the Bill He had privately called on Mr.
Gladstone and explained the whole matter. Some authorities
went so far as to say that Mr. Gladstone understood it. However it be, Mr. Keay summed up his criticism in the form of
an amendment, which possibly might have presented some
glimmering of sense and ordered purpose if, unhappily, he had
not undertaken to explain it.

This he did in quite a series of speeches, which under-
mined even Mr. Gladstone's belief that he had grasped the
hon. member's main intention. After a while Mr. Keay was
stricken with influenza, and temporarily withdrew from the
Parliamentary arena. When he came back the Land Bill was
through Committee ; and though he brought up his amendment again on the report stage, and spent some fresh hours in
explaining it, the bloom had gone off it, and Mr. Keay could
not fail to be aware that the House of Commons was indifferent to the prolongation of his remarks.

On Thursday the Land Bill came once more before the
House of Commons for consideration of the Lords' amendments. Mr. Keay, who had observed with secret chagrin Mr.
Morton's prominence in debate, and had more openly resented
the volatile manner of Mr. Atkinson, saw his opportunity and
prepared to seize it. He was down early, and secured the
corner seat below the gangway, bringing with him a pile of
papers, including notes made for the series of speeches in Committee, closured by the influenza. The point in the Bill to
which—at least to commence with—he desired to call attention had reference to the automatic action of the Sinking
Fund and the "cancellation of stock." Mr. Keay looked linger-
ingly at the vacant seat that had been filled by the member
for Mid-Lothian when last he delighted the House with
those evidences of financial ability which indicate where
a Chancellor of the Exchequer may be found when the
country is ripe for a successor worthy of Mr. Gladstone. Sir
William Harcourt was in his place, but Mr. Keay is not

without suspicion that the right hon. gentleman regards him, if not with impatience, at least with a lack of full appreciation. Indeed, though Sir William Harcourt has for a brief period filled the post of Chancellor of the Exchequer, Mr. Seymour Keay shares Mr. Goschen's scepticism as to his complete mastery of the science of finance. However, he might learn something now if he would give up his engagement to dine at Marlborough House and listen to Mr. Keay on the Sinking Fund, and the provisions of the Bill as to holdings subject to purchase annuity.

When Mr. Keay rose Sir William Harcourt rose also and left the House, regardless of the opportunity provided for him. There remained at least eight other members, and to these, and to the world listening at the doorway, Mr. Keay proceeded to present his views. He got along very well till the accident of Mr. Balfour's looking in reminded him of something the right hon. gentleman had said seven or eight weeks ago, which, whatever may have been the intent, was not laudatory of the member for Elgin and Nairn. This was "the attack on me by the Chief Secretary" to which many references had been made in the pre-influenza period. Now Mr. Keay thought it would be convenient to go into the matter thoroughly, presently returning to take up the thread of his discourse on the Sinking Fund.

Putting on his pince-nez, the more fully to enjoy the writhing of the Chief Secretary under the lash, he proceeded to administer it. He had not got through many sentences when the Speaker interposed with a threatening cry of "Order!" Mr. Keay thereupon adroitly harked back to the Sinking Fund; but after a while something reminded him again of the Chief Secretary's attack, and he again proposed to answer it. Once more the Speaker interposed with increasing severity, and Seymour, with incredible rapidity, shunted himself on to the purchase of annuity line. When, a third time, the Speaker had occasion to interpose, Mr. Henniker Heaton was encouraged to throw out the suggestion that motion should be made to the effect that the member for Elgin and Nairn be not heard for the remainder of the Session.

The House, waking up, cheered this enthusiastically; and the Speaker, whilst ruling it out of order, adopted a tone and manner that indicated the possible approach of a time when such a motion might be made. Under this portentous threat Mr. Keay subsided, listening with a ghastly smile to the Chancellor of the Exchequer, who alluded to his erudite speech as " a long rigmarole."

That he knew was mere jealousy.

July 31.—Mr. Caldwell. The closing days of a memorable and useful Session were shadowed to-night by an untoward incident. The Scotch votes at length reached, the Scotch members were determined to show that, with opportunity given, they did not fall short of the Irish members in oratorical gifts. The vote had, indeed, been approached at an early hour this morning, and Mr. Caldwell had been notified by the Chairman of his opportunity. But the member for St. Rollox is not the kind of man to tempt Providence by such flinging away of opportunity. There was no use disguising the fact that he had come down prepared to deliver his oration. He had the notes for it actually in his possession, in proof whereof he tugged out of his pocket a small bale of goods which at first sight members were inclined to surmise contained a sample of the art of calico printing, which, when not engaged in Parliamentary duties, Mr. Caldwell carries on at sweetly-named Milton of Campsie. These were truly the notes of his speech, and as he waved them to and fro he carried conviction to the mind of hon. members that, seeing it was already half-past two in the morning, it would be well to postpone delivery of the oration.

Mr. Caldwell had occasion this afternoon to congratulate himself on the success of his early morning ruse. As he sat and surveyed the benches at question-time, his face beaming with satisfaction and his pocket bulging with notes, he contrasted the appearance of the House with that presented at the hour when the unsympathetic Chairman of Committees had called upon him. Then the Chamber was more than half empty, and the audience altogether weary. Now, considering the lateness of the Session, there was a brimming House, probably brought together by the expectation of hearing a carefully-prepared lecture on the Educational Condition of Scotland.

Everything comes to an end, even questions in the House
of Commons, and when the last had been disposed of, Mr.
Caldwell beheld his opportunity within reach.   The House
went into Committee of Supply, and the Lord Advocate explained, in one of his lucid and compendious speeches, how
Scotland stood in the matter of education.   His statement
bristled with figures and information.   It roamed over the
whole field, and those who cared to listen were placed in possession of full information on the subject.

The number was not inconveniently great. Questions over, the
audience had swiftly melted away.   Still there were a score or
two listening with intelligent interest to the unvarnished tale
of the Lord Advocate, which took exactly twenty minutes to
tell.   That was brief for a Scotch member cognisant of the
existence of special wires in connection with the local papers.
It is only in Scotland that the dwindling practice of Parliamentary reporting exists in its ancient ruthless vigour.   The
Scotch are a "dour" race, capable of reading six or even
seven columns of a day's ordinary proceedings in Parliament.
Even if some weaker brethren do not really enjoy the exercise,
they remember that, in many cases, before they obtain a newspaper bang goes a penny, and they like to have a pennyworth
provided.   The House of Commons suffers from this national
characteristic, inasmuch as it leads to ruthless competition
among Scotch members for the lengthiest speech of the night.

In the painful scene which followed later on the delivery of
Mr. Caldwell's oration he pointedly alluded to the fact that at
that moment representatives of the Scotch papers—a curiously
short-lived race—were diligently plying pen or pencil taking full
notes of the speeches, and that they would all appear in print
on the following day.   Ruthless and remorseless, in memory of
the slight passed upon him, Mr. Caldwell hinted that his own
speech would, in addition, be reprinted and circulated in convenient pamphlet form, suitable for sale on excursion steamers
cruising about the Kyles of Bute, and at other places of holiday
resort.

Mr. Caldwell, however, at this time unconscious of his
doom, recognised in the brevity of the Lord Advocate a
gracious and appropriate tribute to himself.   Whilst Scotia
and the isles and continents there adjacent were awaiting his

deliverance, why should a mere Lord Advocate occupy the time of the House?

His great speech. It was close upon five o'clock when the Lord Advocate resumed his seat. Mr. Caldwell rose, and, steadying himself on his legs, once more produced the bale of notes. Its reappearance had an effect not less marked than was observed in the dead of the previous night. In all parts of the House members rose and hurriedly fled, till by the time Mr. Caldwell had settled down into a level pace the audience dispersed over the benches before him consisted of one Lord Advocate, one Scotch member below the gangway awake, and one Scotch member above it asleep.

This was inexplicable; but Mr. Caldwell presently grew so interested in his disquisition that he seemed hardly to notice it, being probably buoyed up by expectation of a verbatim report in the *Scotsman*, to be followed by the reprint that would presently fall like sunshine on the watering-places of Scotland.

Quarter of an hour stole on after quarter, and still Mr. Caldwell went on. The Scotch member who was awake rose and guiltily stole forth. His hon. friend above the gangway slept on. The Lord Advocate nodded approval with suspicious regularity. Six o'clock struck, and still the impressive figure stood behind the empty front Opposition bench, and the monotonous voice filled the hapless chamber. It was like printing so many miles of calico at Milton of Campsie. Steam was up, and the engine would go round till the last yard of material was stamped.

At last this was done. The engine stopped with a jerk, and the Scotch member above the gangway opposite, awaking, discovered Mr. Caldwell re-seated and collecting the folios of his notes preparatory to re-baling them. Many a man after such an effort would retire for some refreshment or a walk on the terrace. Mr. Caldwell knew the Lord Advocate would reply, and felt that since the greater part of his rejoinder must have reference to his speech it was only courteous to remain to hear it. So he sat expectant—and when the Lord Advocate attempted to wind up the debate the right hon. gentleman, replying lightly but effectively to other speakers, said never a word about Mr. Caldwell and the oration !

No answer ?   That was more than flesh and blood could stand.   Mr. Caldwell sat gasping for a moment, and then clutching the rail of the bench before him, drew himself up, and in tones more of sorrow than anger bewailed this act of contumacy. It was nothing to him. The newspaper reports would revenge him, and afterwards would come the pamphlet. But Mr. Caldwell, as a patriotic Scotchman, mourned with infinite pathos the action of a Lord Advocate who, replying on the debate, had utterly ignored his speech.

" There is," he said, with a ring of triumph rising above the notes of lamentation, " only one explanation. The right hon. gentleman did not answer my speech because he found he could not."

CHAPTER XXXIX.

MINISTERS *IN ESSE* AND *IN POSSE.*

The Long Session—Shattered Hopes—" Labby "—Diplomatist—Journalist— Politician—Minister?—Leaders in the Commons—" Old Morality "—Mr. Goschen.

Aug. 1. — The long Session.   THE Parliamentary Session now drawing to a close is in several respects a memorable one. It began as an experiment in the readjustment of long familiar arrangements of the sittings. Through the present century it has been customary for Parliament to meet on an early day in February and sit into August, with brief recesses at Whitsuntide and Easter. Up to the birth of the Home Rule Party in 1874 there was a certain pleasing regularity in the working of this scheme. Parliament was summoned on February 3rd or 5th, and, though the heavens fell, it adjourned in time for the opening of the other Session on the moors. When the Irish members, first under the leadership of Mr. Butt, more effectively under that of Mr. Parnell, took possession of the House, Parliament met early in the year, sat far past the once sacred 12th of August, and occasionally had a Winter Session. The custom of sitting in London through the summer months and going off for the long recess in the coolness of autumn has ever troubled a section of members. They recall the fact that it was not always so. In the time of the Georges, Parliament met in November, sat into May or June, and had a fair share of summer-time for its holiday. Last year Sir George Trevelyan, whose historical studies peculiarly impressed him with the absurdity and inconvenience of the arrangement, moved a resolution proposing to return to the old order of things. He was defeated, but by so narrow a majority that the Government, after their familiar manner, resolved to capitulate before they were actually beaten. It was decided that the present Session should commence in November, resume after a brief Christmas holiday, and wind up as early as possible in July.

Shattered hopes. The result has not been such as to encourage a repetition of the experiment. The movement is crushed in its infancy, and Parliament will certainly go back to its old habit of sweltering in London through the summer-time, and making holiday at a period when most holiday resorts are putting up their shutters. Of the proposed arrangement everything has been carried out except the prorogation in July. Up to a fortnight ago the hope was fondly cherished that at least it would take place on this the last day of July, and so the promise might be kept to the ear. But the House is sitting to-day, and will certainly sit through next week. The best now hoped for is that the prorogation may be accomplished on August 8, which is pretty much as it used to be, save that legislators have been on duty since November.

What makes the situation the more hopeless is knowledge of the fact that if this year the Session might not be closed early, there is nothing to be hoped for in the future. Never since the Session of 1874, when Mr. Disraeli came in with a large majority, and the political world craved for rest after the turmoil of Mr. Gladstone's protracted reign, have Ministers found themselves in such favourable circumstances as far as the conduct of public business is concerned. In the November Session Irish opposition was effaced, knocked to pieces, in the historical struggle in Committee Room No. 15. Two Bills crammed with explosive material—the Tithes Bill and the

Land Purchase Bill—passed their most critical stage within the space of a fortnight; when the Session was resumed on January 7, not only did no tedious debate on the Address block the way, but the two principal measures in the Ministerial programme were advanced as far as the committee stage.

Since then circumstances have combined to favour Ministers. The Irish Party, though slowly consolidating after the blow dealt it by Mr. Parnell, has not been in a position to revive its ancient glories of obstruction, whilst the Liberal Opposition, restrained by the authority of Mr. Gladstone, has been singularly docile.

Aug. 3.—"Labby." One of the minor but not least interesting questions discussed in view of the formation of a Liberal Ministry is—What will be done with Mr. Labouchere? There is no doubt he is in the House of Commons and out of it one of the most active agents of Liberalism, and Conservative authorities (for purposes of their own easily recognisable) take it as a matter of course that when Mr. Gladstone forms his Ministry some place must be found for the guerilla chief. That such speculation should form part of the ordinary political conversation of the day would, ten years ago, have seemed impossible. Mr. Labouchere—"Labby," to quote his more familiar cognomen—has for a quarter of a century filled a peculiar and increasingly prominent place in English life. But only within the last two or three years has he come to be regarded in a serious light as a politician. From earliest boyhood he has been connected with public affairs. He entered the diplomatic service during the Crimean War, a youth of twenty-three. He managed to see a good deal of life, and must have brought his immediate superiors into keen sympathy with the frame of mind described in Ecclesiastes, "when the grasshopper shall be a burden." After ten years' experience of diplomatic life he retired. But the memories of the period dwell with him, and furnish him in Committee of Supply on the Civil Service Estimates with many quaint, if occasionally apocryphal, stories and illustrations.

Diplomatic. One of the best known is of his journey from Dresden to Constantinople, which he quotes as illustrating the inoperative niggardliness which rules at the

Foreign Office in contrast with the wealth lavished on the
official residences of British Ambassadors. The young
attaché not putting in an appearance at Constantinople at the
appointed period, formal inquiry was made as to the reason for
the delay. After much trouble and considerable expense the
missive reached his hands, and in due course a letter arrived
at the Foreign Office stating that as inadequate provision had
been made for his travelling expenses, and as his private
means were limited, Mr. Labouchere was walking, and would
in due time reach the shores of the Bosphorus.

Another legend of his diplomatic career has its locality
fixed at Washington, where he was for some time stationed.
One day an aggressively irate countryman presented himself
at the office, and demanded to see the British Minister. He
was shown into Mr. Labouchere's room, who, with the suavity
which never deserts him in the most pressing moments,
explained that his Excellency was not in.

"Well," said the visitor, evidently suspecting subterfuge,
"I must see him, and will wait till he comes."

"Very good," said Mr. Labouchere, "pray take a chair,"
and he resumed his writing.

At the end of an hour the Britisher, still fretting and
fuming, asked when the Minister would be back. "I really
cannot say exactly," the attaché answered.

"But you expect him back?" the visitor insisted.

"Oh, certainly," said Mr. Labouchere, and went on writing,
as Madame Defarge, on a famous occasion, went on knitting.
At the end of another hour the irate visitor, bouncing up,
insisted on knowing what were the habits of the Minister at
that period of the day. Was he likely to be in in another
hour?

"I think not," said Mr. Labouchere, with increased bland-
ness; "the fact is, he sailed for Europe on Wednesday, and can
hardly yet have reached Queenstown. But, you know, you
said you would wait till he came in, so I offered you a chair."

Journalism   It was in 1864 that Mr. Labouchere retired from
the diplomatic service, and promptly turned his
attention to political life. By an odd coincidence, this extremest
of Radicals entered the House of Commons as member for the

Royal borough of Windsor, an anomaly promptly adjusted by his being unseated on petition, bribery and corruption being alleged against the blameless Senator. That was in 1866. In the following year he successfully contested Middlesex, but his tenure of the seat was equally brief. In the following year came the General Election, and though all over the country Liberals were returned in swarms, Middlesex left Mr. Labouchere out in the cold. Up to this period he had not secured wide recognition outside Parliament and club circles. The breaking out of the Franco-German war gave him the opportunity he has always been swift to seize. When the Germans closed around Paris, Mr. Labouchere voluntarily submitted to be shut up in the capital, and all the world, reading the *Daily News*, profited by the letters from "A Besieged Resident" who photographed with merciless severity and cynical humour daily life in the beleaguered city.

Probably it was this episode that turned Mr. Labouchere's attention to journalism. When a year or two later Mr. Edmund Yates established the *World*, he contributed to it a series of City articles which did much to concentrate public attention on the vigorous newcomer to weekly journalism. In 1876 Mr. Labouchere established *Truth*, which, instinct in every page with his brilliant individuality, was a success from the first, and now is a potent factor both in political and social life.

Politician. At the General Election of 1880 Mr. Labouchere found an ideal constituency to represent in the House of Commons. Politically, he was made for Northampton and Northampton for him. The accident of his having Mr. Bradlaugh for colleague served to bring him into prominence in the earliest days of the new Parliament. The Bradlaugh incident overshadowed everything, and Mr. Labouchere rode on the whirlwind, though, thanks to the defection of a number of Liberals who supported the Conservative Opposition in a course they have since done their best to retrace, he did not control the storm. Full justice has never been done to the loyalty of his conduct toward a colleague who possibly was not personally attractive. It is Mr. Labouchere's own fault that he is never taken seriously.

He was serious enough in the dogged, resourceful, implacable fight he made for Bradlaugh, a fight which ended in final victory only when the junior member for Northampton was on his death-bed.

Mr. Labouchere found in Parliamentary life, combined with the editing of *Truth*, precisely the outlet for his energy sought in various directions during a period of twenty-six years. When he first entered the House he was disappointing as a speaker. It is true he was handicapped by the often fatal condition that the House expected much from him. His writing was familiar to all; his brilliant conversational powers were widely known. When he rose on the dull flood of debate, people expected him to sparkle, and he failed, partly perhaps because, conscious of what was expected from him, he tried to live up to the standard. His speeches were too long and his impromptus bore evident marks of cogitation. There was a time, dangerously prolonged, when he threatened to be a Parliamentary failure. He improved as the Parliament of 1880 went on; but had his career closed in 1885 it could not have been regarded as strikingly successful.

Minister?

It is in the present Parliament that Mr. Labouchere has found his opportunity, and has won for himself a place not only in the House, but in the country, which makes it natural for everyone to be asking what post he shall have when the long fight is over and the battle won? Like Lord Randolph Churchill and Sir William Harcourt, his native air is that breathed on the Opposition benches. With his own political friends in office, his area of attack is limited, though to do him justice the limitation is not drawn at inconvenient points. In any circumstances he will have his joke, even if it contributes to the adversary acquiring his friend's estate. This is a natural and irresistible disposition it would be well to take into account in any speculation as to Mr. Labouchere's future in connection with the return of Mr. Gladstone to power. It is probable enough that office will be offered to him; but will he take it? It is not well to prophesy with respect to so versatile a personage, but I venture to think he will decline to sell his birthright for whatever alluring mess of pottage may be proffered. He has not lived through five years with the awful example of Mr. Ashmead Bartlett before his eyes without profiting by it.

There is no point of comparison between the two save this: that when the Conservatives were in Opposition, Mr. Ashmead Bartlett was an incessant participator in debate, a rough and irresponsible critic of things in general and the action of Mr. Gladstone in particular. Tempted by the offer of a minor post in the Ministry with a salary of £1,000 a year, he consented to be gagged, and has during the existence of the present Parliament honourably observed the conditions of his bargain. It would be impossible in any circumstances to gag Mr. Labouchere. But office must necessarily impose conditions that would be unbearably irksome. He has nothing to gain and much to lose by donning the livery of the Treasury bench, and has always displayed so shrewd an appreciation of his own well-being that he may be expected safely to pass through the coming temptation.

Aug. 5.— Leaders in the Commons. The House of Commons was prorogued to-day without seeing again the face of its old leader, and in some quarters there is doubt whether ever again his kindly face will beam from the Treasury bench. It is no new thing at the end of a Session to hear that Mr. Smith is about to retire, and seek in the House of Lords his well-earned rest. The report was current last year, and was not unknown the Session before. It has this material support in fact, that he is in very bad health, and would warmly welcome any opportunity of honourably retiring from the drudgery of leadership. But, as he says, with less frequency now, though people smile at the familiar phrase, "Duty to his Queen and country," is ever his lodestar. His appointment to the Leadership of the House of Commons was a desperate, despairing move, taken amid the cataclysm that followed on the resignation of Lord Randolph Churchill on the eve of Christmas, 1886. It turned out to be one of the happiest and most successful moves made by Lord Salisbury, in some respects recalling Disraeli's famous appointment of Lord Mayo to the Viceroyalty of India.

There is no post in English politics more important or more difficult to fill than that of Leader of the House of

Commons. Mr. Gladstone, with all his transcendent powers and heaven-born genius, never shone in it. He is too highly strung, too emotional, for the position. Disraeli was more successful, and Lord Palmerston better still. Six years ago Mr. Smith would have been much surprised to find his name bracketed in this list. Yet his enemies (if he has any) would readily admit that his leadership has been a tower of strength to his colleagues and his party. This is proved by the fact that, yielding to urgent solicitations, he has from time to time put off his retirement, being assured on all sides that the step would be followed by embarrassment, not to say calamity, to the Conservative Party.

"Old Morality." It would be difficult to define in a word, or even a sentence, the secret of Mr. Smith's astonishing success. Simplicity of manner has something to do with it, the more so, perhaps, as there is a growing conviction in the House of Commons that behind the innocence of the dove lurks some of the guile of the serpent. He is essentially of *bourgeois* standing, in looks, character, modes of thought, and even name. If he had chanced to be born with any other name than Smith there would have been something distinctly lacking in the symmetry of his individualism. He began by being exceedingly modest, almost suing *in forma pauperis* for the forbearance of the House. "Here I am," he seemed to say "by no fault of my own placed in a position where I come into comparison with my late lamented chief, Mr. Disraeli, and with the right hon. gentleman opposite. For goodness sake make the best of me whilst I am here, which is not likely to be very long."

The House of Commons, always generous to weakness, responded to this mute appeal. It is, after all, human, and it was pleased at being approached in this very proper manner. Then Mr. Smith amused it with his seriousness, his impressive utterance of commonplaces, and a disposition to cite little tags reminiscent of copybook heading literature, which earned for him the friendly nickname " Old Morality."

The critical audience which came to laugh has remained to praise. Mr. Smith is no genius, but he is a man of business habits, and is gifted with a certain shrewd insight

into public affairs, which, in his position, is worth more than
eloquence.   He has a way of conciliating opposition and
slipping through Government business not excelled by any
of his more famous predecessors since the days of Peel.   How
astute in his management, and how considerable his personal
influence, was not perceived till nearly a month ago he was
obliged to take to his bed.   Then Mr. Goschen took his seat
on the Treasury bench, and everything began to go wrong.

Mr. Goschen.   It has always been understood that part of the
price exacted by Mr. Goschen when, on Lord
Randolph Churchill's retirement, he went over to the Conservative ranks was that he should have the succession of the
leadership.   This story receives confirmation from the fact
that on all Mr. Smith's occasional absences from his post
the Chancellor of the Exchequer has been nominated to fill it.
A belated Premier may in secret conclave propose, but in such
a matter as the leadership it is the House of Commons that
disposes.   Mr. Goschen's chance of succeeding Mr. Smith
would have been much brighter if he had not had forced upon
him opportunities of showing what he would do with it.   He
has had rather a long spell of late, and it has absolutely confirmed the growing conviction that he will never do.   It is
a familiar saying, attributed to the Duke of Wellington, that
" Peel has no manners."   Mr. Goschen has manners, but they
are all bad.   It is a high tribute to his sterling ability that a
man so feebly equipped by the Graces should have attained so
prominent a place in public life.   Awkward in manner, not
goodly in appearance, nearly blind, and with a disagreeable
snuffle in his voice, he nevertheless fought his way to a front
place in the House of Commons without adventitious aid from
family or fortune.

CHAPTER XL.

MEN OF THE SALISBURY PARLIAMENT.

Lord Salisbury—Born out of Due Season—A Crisis in the Lords—His Parliamentary Presence—Mr. Arthur Balfour—Rapier and Bludgeon—Horoscope—Lord Randolph Churchill—A Leader in Opposition.

Lord Salisbury. THE premier man in the Parliament which, under curious, though not unprecedented, circumstances, brought Lord Salisbury into power in 1886 is, happily, the Prime Minister. Since Lord Beaconsfield died the Marquis of Salisbury has had no compeer, much less a rival, in the Conservative ranks. It is doubtful whether, for force of character and sheer ability, he was overtopped by his old enemy and later ally. That is a nice question which future historians, having the supreme advantage of perspective view, may be left to decide. It is enough for the present Parliament to reflect with satisfaction that the Premier of to-day holds his position not alone by title.

In recent times both Houses have known the inconvenience that pertains to the situation when we have had at the head of affairs men placed there rather as a matter of convenience than in submission to personal pre-eminence. The Lords had for a while their Duke of Richmond and the Commons their Stafford Northcote, both amiable and, in degree, capable men, but neither a born leader. To Lord Salisbury's pre-eminence everyone gladly pays homage, not the least readily his opponents, for there is nothing more embarrassing in political warfare than that the captain of the opposing host should be other than a man who is not only capable of conceiving a definite line of action, but strong enough to lead his united forces along it.

Lord Salisbury's misfortune in finally coming into a peerage was tempered by his experiences before, by unforeseen chance, he became heir-apparent to the marquisate. If he had been born eldest son, he would have lost distinct advantages by which he has long profited. A younger son, with no reasonable hope of reversion of the title, and, if report be true, not too richly endowed with pocket-money, he at the outset was faced by the necessity of carving out his own career. It is no secret that at one time he was a working member of that daily press for which he is now accustomed to spare some flashes of his illimitable scorn. Like another keen fighting man, to-day disguised under the title Lord Sherbrooke, he wrote articles for the papers, and was glad of the concomitant remuneration. He entered the House of Commons a comparative youth, and even as Lord Robert Cecil made his mark. When he became Lord Cranborne, he spoke with the added weight of the heir to an historic marquisate. But I have heard old *habitués* of the House of Commons say that for freshness and barb the irresponsible Lord Robert Cecil beat the graver Viscount Cranborne.

Whether fighting under one name or the other, his pet aversion was Mr. Disraeli, then pushing his way into recognised position in the Tory ranks, under the patronage of the late Lord Derby. The young man hated Mr. Gladstone with the bitter feeling with which a Tory of long lineage regards a champion of the masses; he despised Mr. Disraeli with the lofty scorn of a patrician for an adventurer. When from his seat in the House of Commons he used to assail Mr. Disraeli with "flouts and gibes and sneers"—his mastery of which arms that statesman on a memorable occasion pointedly acknowledged—he little dreamt that the time would come when he should share his enemy's homeward journey from Berlin, bringing Peace with Honour; still less that he should sit by his side on the Ministerial bench in the House of Lords, an apparently docile, certainly a faithful lieutenant.

Born out of due
season. Lord Salisbury's position in English political life, and especially in the House of Lords, is a peculiar one. He is a statesman born out of due season, and that he with increasing skill and success adapts himself to circumstances is crowning proof of his consummate ability. He should have lived in those spacious times when another Cecil was at the head of English affairs. He would have done much more as Minister to Queen Elizabeth than he is permitted to accomplish as Minister for Queen Victoria. With an almost total absence of sympathy with the people, he has fallen upon

a time when the people are more and more, and the Crown and
its appanages less and less. He is obliged in these days to
take into account the House of Commons and what he regards
as its vagaries and its prejudices. But he is never at pains to
disguise his dislike of it and all it represents.

This is a point on which Mr. Disraeli, with his keen in-
tuition of popular impulses, had the advantage over the friend
of his declining years. There is a story of Lord Melbourne
which is probably apocryphal, but if anything like it in
analogous circumstances were told of Lord Salisbury, it would
readily be believed. It was at the time of the Corn-Law
struggle, one of the phases of which had been discussed at a
Cabinet meeting, other topics intervening before the Council
broke up. As his colleagues were going away, Lord Melbourne
(according to the current story) leaned over the banisters of the
staircase and called out: "Is bread to go up or down? I don't
care which it is, you know, but we must all say the same thing
in the House."

A crisis in the Lords.

Just before the first Session of 1890 closed, Lord
Salisbury, with characteristic contempt for subterfuge, made in the House of Lords a speech conceived in the
very spirit of this off-hand remark over the banisters. A Bill
dealing with local rates, promoted by the Corporation of Dublin,
had come up from the Commons. It was a measure in charge
of the Chief Secretary, and in carrying the Bill through the
Commons Mr. Balfour had had the unwonted assistance of the
Irish members. That was sufficient to excite the ire of noble
lords like the Duke of Westminster, the Marquis of Waterford,
and Lord Wemyss. At the last moment they broke into
open revolt. The Bill had actually been read a third time,
and it was on the formal stage "that the Bill do pass" Lord
Wemyss moved an amendment which, if carried, would have
thrown out the measure. There was a strong whip out, and
the malcontent Lords mustered in numbers which surely pre-
saged a Government defeat. Lord Salisbury, sitting in his
favourite attitude, with his elbow on the back of the bench,
his head resting on his hand, and his back turned to the bishops,
listened to the impassioned debate. Members of the Commons,
leaving their own chamber, crowded at the Bar and in the

galleries over the pens where ladies sit, such of them as were Privy Councillors availing themselves of their privilege to stand on the steps of the throne. Among these was Mr. Balfour, smiling genially, whilst Lord Wemyss declaimed, and Lord Waterford, remaining seated in token of a terrible fall from his horse on the hunting-field, demonstrated how all was up with the Union if this iniquitous Bill passed.

To the Commons looking on its fate seemed sealed, and there was animated talk as to what line Mr. Balfour would take if he were thus openly and studiously flouted. When there appeared nothing left but the division, Lord Salisbury stirred his vast bulk and lounged up to the table. He did not trouble himself with any elaborate defence of the Bill. To him it was plainly a ludicrously insignificant thing whether rates were collected in Dublin under one system or another. What he had to point out was that here was an incidental feature in the Irish policy of the Government as carried out by Mr. Balfour. Did noble Lords approve that policy as a whole or did they not ? If they did—and the cheer that resounded through the House gave clear assurance of their feeling in the matter—they must take it as a whole. " You cannot," Lord Salisbury said, " be allowed to pick out a bit here and there, and say you won't have it."

Here was the unconscious echo of Lord Melbourne's remark dropped over the banister. " Are we," Lord Salisbury said, in effect, " to support Mr. Balfour's policy in Ireland, or are we to desert him and let in Home Rule and Mr. Gladstone ? I don't care which it is, you know, but we must stick to a definite line of action." It is an axiom cynically accepted in Parliament that a speech rarely, if ever, affects votes. On this occasion Lord Salisbury triumphantly proved the exception. Had he been accidentally absent, or, being present, had he refrained from taking part in the debate, the Bill would indubitably have been lost. As it was, the carefully marshalled majority silently melted away, and when the tellers returned from the division lobby the Bill was carried.

His Parliament-
ary presence. The delivery of this memorable speech afforded to those fortunate enough to hear it a fair idea of Lord Salisbury's oratorical style. Unlike Mr. Gladstone, the

Premier but slightly varies in the level excellence of his speech.
Never striking at the high flights at which Mr. Gladstone is

accustomed to soar, there is not the opportunity for comparative failure. Lord Salisbury, in addressing the Peers, does
not make speeches to them. He just talks, but with what
clearness of perception, what command of his subject, what
vigorous and well-ordered sentences, what irresistible argument, and now and then with what delicate, refreshing rain of
cynicism! Doubtless a Minister in his position must carefully
prepare his speeches on public affairs, but Lord Salisbury has in
peculiar degree the art of concealing his art. He rarely uses
manuscript notes even for the exposition of the most delicate
and important announcements. Just before Parliament rose
last Session he had occasion to explain the details of the arrangement concluded with Portugal for the settlement of contending claims with Africa. It was an exceedingly intricate
affair, the story involving an historical review and the adjust-
ment of nice points of latitude and longitude, not to mention
the recital of barbarous and unfamiliar geographical terms.
It was precisely the case in which the most practised speaker
would gratefully have taken refuge in a sheaf of notes.
The Premier had not a scrap of paper in his hand as he un-
wove the tangled skein, and when he sat down, after talking
for twelve minutes, he had made the whole case clear to the
perception of the dullest lord in the assembly.

Mr. Arthur Balfour. Next to the Premier in the quickly-exhausted
list of men who have made their mark in the
Salisbury Parliament stands Mr. Balfour. If any member who
had sat through a Session or two of the Parliament of 1880
had fallen asleep in the library and had, on any night when
the present House of Commons is sitting, returned to his old
place, he would not know this still slim young gentleman who
in Mr. Gladstone's Parliament was member for Hertford. Not
that in personal appearance Mr. Balfour is greatly altered. He
has at whiles the same languorous air, the same boyish smile
swiftly illumining his countenance, the same disposition to
discover how nearly he can sit on his shoulder-blades
when occupying a place on the front bench listening to Mr.
Gladstone or an Irish member. In other respects the met-
amorphosis is complete. The dilettante stripling that used
to lounge about the House, moved to what seemed the

just suffering the boredom of being interested when Lord Randolph Churchill was attacking somebody, has grown into the hardest-worked Minister of the Crown, the deviser and stern executer of an Irish policy as nearly Cromwellian as the prejudices of the nineteenth century will permit.

When, on the retirement of Sir Michael Beach in 1887, Mr. Balfour was appointed to the office of Chief Secretary, the arrangement was generally regarded as one of those temporary dispositions of a difficult post which mark the movement of a bewildered Premier. Though he had already a seat in the Cabinet as Secretary for Scotland, he had not yet developed any qualities that gave promise of his immediate future. The Irish members laughed at his pretty ways, inclined to regard his appointment as something like an echo of Mr. Disraeli's practical joke when he placed Mr. James Lowther at the same post. But before the Session closed members were fain to admit that there were unsuspected depths in the character of the young Minister. He trod gently as yet, but through the ordeal of the badgering to which Chief Secretaries are submitted at the question hour he passed with a skill and strength that extorted admiration.

There is no instance in English political life of a still young man making such rapid advance to a premier place. Lord Randolph Churchill had a meteoric flight, but he had been for several Sessions steadily forcing himself into prominence before he blossomed into Chancellor of the Exchequer and Leader of the House of Commons. Up to the day when all the world wondered to hear that Mr. Balfour had been appointed Chief Secretary for Ireland he was a person of no consequence. His rising evoked no interest in the House, and his name would not have drawn a full audience in St. James's Hall. Within twelve months, and in rapidly increasing degree within two years, he had gained for himself one of four principal places in debate in the House of Commons, and his name was one to conjure with in Conservative centres throughout the United Kingdom.

<p style="margin-left:2em; text-indent:-2em">Rapier and bludgeon. In personal appearance and in manner no one could less resemble Cromwell than the present ruler of Ireland. To look at Mr. Balfour as he glides with

undulous stride to his place in the House of Commons one would imagine rather he had just dropped in from an exercise on the guitar than from the pursuit of his grim game with the Nationalist forces in Ireland. His movements are of almost womanly grace and his face is fair to look upon. Even when making the bitterest retorts to the enemy opposite he preserves an outward bearing of almost deferential courtesy. Irish members may, if they please, use the bludgeon of Parliamentary conflict; for him the polished, lightly-poised rapier suffices for all occasions. The very contrast of his unruffled mien presented to furious onslaughts of excitable persons like Mr. W. O'Brien adds to the bitterness of the wormwood and gall his presence on the Treasury bench mixes for Irish members. But if he is hated by the men some of whom he has put in prison, he is feared and, in some sense, respected. In him is recognised the most perfect living example of the mailed hand under the silken glove.

Horoscope. As Mr. Balfour's earliest appearance on the Parliamentary scene was influenced by Lord Randolph Churchill, it is possible that future stages of his career may be constrained, if not controlled, from the same quarter. If Lord Randolph did not exist, it would not be difficult to cast the political horoscope of the Chief Secretary. He has no other rival in the succession to the leadership of a party who have had in distant succession two such chiefs as Peel and Disraeli. He is strong in something else than his Parliamentary position. The Conservative Party believe in him with a fulness of conviction withheld from Mr. Disraeli even after he had been received into the sanctified company of the House of Lords. Mr. Balfour at least knows what he means and what he intends to do, a great comfort to the large majority of a party who only want to be led. His succession to the Leadership on the retirement of Mr. W. H. Smith—an event which cannot long be postponed —would be hailed with approval by nine-tenths of the party in the House of Commons, and with a roar of acclamation by the party throughout the country. That the problem has not already been solved in this direction is due partly to the difficulty of finding a successor capable of continuing his policy in

Ireland, and partly to the apprehension of revolt in certain quarters on the Treasury bench if other claims were overlooked in favour of the brilliant nephew of the Prime Minister.

Lord Randolph Churchill If Mr. Balfour is to obtain this well-deserved promotion over the heads of his colleagues in the Cabinet as at present constituted, it will be necessary for the arrangement to be completed during the existence of the present Parliament. As far as its term is concerned, Lord Randolph Churchill's chance is played out. He is, as recent chapters in his history have proved, prone to hasty decisions. But it is too much even for his most sanguine enemy to hope that he will be so ill advised as to yoke himself with the falling fortunes of the present Ministry. If, indeed, he were invited to resume the Leadership of the House of Commons, with promise of free hand, the invitation might prove irresistible, and its acceptance would be well advised. He could not hope to avert the impending doom, but he would at least make a good fight, and might succeed in easing the fall. To take anything less than the Leadership at the present juncture would be an act of self-abasement no one has a right to expect at his hands.

Lord Randolph Churchill is not a man of the Salisbury Parliament in the sense that Mr. Balfour has won that distinction. His position was made in the Parliament of 1880, and was lost in that now nearing its close. During the past Session he has, even ostentatiously, withdrawn himself from Parliamentary affairs. He has given up to Newmarket what was meant for mankind. But no one with even elementary knowledge of political affairs, or the slightest acquaintance with his character, imagines he is finally out of the running. Though he has flung away Ministerial position and withdrawn himself from the councils of his party, his personal weight and influence in debate are not materially impaired. His command over the House, when he chooses to exercise it, is as complete as ever, and his influence in the country may be regained whenever he thinks it worth while to set himself the task. His time will come again when the present Government go into opposition and look around them for a Leader.

A Leader in Opposition. Lord Randolph Churchill is a model leader of Opposition; ready, resolute, inventive, audacious, and, if need be, unscrupulous. If it were only possible for Mr. Balfour to work with him in unity, Mr. Gladstone's next Ministry would have a sore time, whatever might be their numerical majority. The House of Commons likes to be shown sport, as one of its most successful Leaders said. Lord Randolph Churchill and Mr. Balfour working together in harmony on the front Opposition bench would show excellent sport. Whether such a combination be possible or not is one of the problems the near future will be called upon to solve. It does not in present circumstances appear probable, but adversity makes one acquainted with strange bedfellows, and in the gloom of Opposition these two old friends may come together again. Two things are, however, already certain. One is that Lord Randolph Churchill will be finally indispensable to the Conservative Party; the other, that he cannot hold a second place.

Whilst the Salisbury Parliament has not, with the curiously contrasted exceptions of Mr. Arthur Balfour and Mr. W. H. Smith, brought men from secondary positions into the very first rank, it has not been more productive in the direction of bringing out new men. One who has perhaps more than others advanced his position during the present Parliament is Mr. Henry Fowler. He has not only something useful to say on most topics that come up for discussion, but he has finally succeeded in the not less important task of catching the House-of-Commons-way of saying it. A man of wide information and business habits, he is a lucid speaker and an effective debater. When Mr. Gladstone's last Government came to an abrupt end, Mr. Fowler was Financial Secretary to the Treasury—a post, the importance of which is not appreciated outside the House of Commons. It, nevertheless, almost invariably leads to high cabinet office, and the precedent is not likely to be varied in the case of Mr. Fowler.

The present Government were fortunate in obtaining a successor to Mr. Fowler at the Treasury. When, on the formation of Lord Salisbury's Government in 1886, Mr. Jackson was appointed Financial Secretary, he was a dark horse. In   .

business he is a tanner, which does not seem to lead naturally
to the charge of Ministerial business in the House of Commons.
Probably Mr. Jackson's primary recommendation in the eyes
of Lord Salisbury was that he had won a seat for the Conservatives in an important centre of commerce. The appointment has, however, been amply justified on quite other
grounds. Mr. Jackson has turned out as great a success as
did Mr. W. H. Smith, when, sixteen years ago, he, also having
won an important seat, was made Financial Secretary, and
seemed to have reached with one bound the full height of his
reasonable ambition.

In a more prominent position than Mr. Jackson, Mr.
Ritchie has been the most successful Minister. Appointed
President of the Local Government Board at a time when a
Local Government Bill was the principal Ministerial measure,
he displayed an ability, an energy, and a tact which quickly
won for him a high position in the House and enabled him to
carry to happy issue the complex measure committed to his
charge. In Mr. Ritchie's hands the Local Government Bill
passed so smoothly that it seemed quite an easy thing to do.
The credit due to Mr. Ritchie will, however, become apparent
if we consider the probable fate of the measure had it been
entrusted to another Minister—say to Mr. Goschen.

Another member of official position, though not in Ministerial office, who has come to the front during the Salisbury
Parliament, is Mr. Courtney, who, by the way, also with great
credit, passed the honourable and exacting apprenticeship of
Financial Secretary to the Treasury. On the Home Rule
question Mr. Courtney, who once ranked as an uncompromising Radical, separated himself from the great body of the
Liberal Party and became a supporter of the Conservative
Government. Elected Chairman of Committees, he has by
common consent discharged the duties of that onerous
position with unfaltering judgment and unimpeachable impartiality. Always a post of extremest difficulty, Mr. Courtney's occupancy has been embarrassed by peculiar personal
circumstances. To a man of his political antecedents it could
not be agreeable to hold his office by favour of the Tory vote,
whilst he could not expect to be regarded with extreme favour
by the party whose ranks he had, on a question of conscience

temporarily but effectively quitted. He has surmounted these various difficulties, and has been so successful as Chairman of Committees that his promotion in due time to the Speaker's chair may be regarded as a certainty.

The names of new members who have made a mark in the present Parliament may be counted on the fingers of one hand. Mr. Louis Jennings has succeeded in commanding the attention of the House whilst performing the useful, but in other hands forbidding, task of discussing the details of administrativeexpenditure. Mr. Asquith, in more than one admirable speech, has established on the broader basis of the Parliamentary stage a reputation gained in the Law Courts. Mr. T. W. Russell has developed conspicuous debating power, and has sometimes risen to the height of eloquent declamation. On the other side, Colonel Saunderson has earned the gratitude of the House by relieving it from the apprehension that the peculiar humour which once endeared Irish members to a delighted senate is not finally extinct.

One of the most remarkable successes of the Salisbury Parliament is undoubtedly the First Lord of the Treasury, the Leader of the House of Commons. It does not disparage, but rather enhances, the merit disclosed by Mr. W. H. Smith in his high position, to remember that he was called to it not because he was regarded as the best man for the place, but because he was the best possible at the moment. He was Leader of the House *faute de mieux*. Lord Salisbury, stunned by the sudden resignation of Lord Randolph Churchill, and shrinking from determining the rival claims of colleagues who felt they were predestined for the place, hurriedly thrust Mr. Smith into it. It seemed a grim kind of jest to place in the seat lately vacated by Mr. Gladstone, once held in succession by Peel, Palmerston, John Russell, and Disraeli, the plain, unassuming, commonplace, *bourgeois* gentleman, with his admirably assorted plebeian name. It was not believed that the arrangement would last, and possibly it was not, in the first instance, designed as more than a temporary expedient. It has turned out to be one of the happiest episodes in the history of Lord Salisbury's Government. Mr. Smith has proved himself the very man for the place and hour. His kindly, honest nature, his trained business habits, his shrewd common sense, his modesty of mien, and even some grave comicalities of manner, have made him a personal favourite in the House, and have enabled him to do a priceless service to his party. Thus has the stone which builders in a less perturbed frame of mind would have rejected, become the head stone of the corner.

Aug. 5.   Prorogation.

SESSION OF 1890—91.

NOVEMBER, 1890.

25. Tues.—H.M. Speech. Address agreed to.

26. Wed.—Introduction of Bills.

27. Thurs.—Tithe Rent-charge, &c., Bill. Sir M. H. Beach. Read I°.

Purchase of Land, &c. (Ireland), Bill. Mr. A. J. Balfour. Read I°.

28. Fri.—Business of the House. Motion, Mr. W. H. Smith.

Perpetual Pensions. Motion, Mr. Brad-laugh.

DECEMBER.

1. Mon.—Tithe Rent-charge, &c., Bill. Bill committed.

2. Tues.—Purchase of Land, &c. (Ireland), Bill. 2nd Reading. First Debate.

3. Wed.—Ditto. Ditto. Second Debate. Bill committed.

4. Thurs.—Supply: Civil Services. Supplementary Estimates.

Tithe Rent-charge, &c., Bill. Committee: First Sitting.

5. Fri.—Purchase of Land, &c. (Ireland), Bill. Committee. First Sitting.

8. Mon.—Land Department (Ireland) Bill. Committed.

9. Tues.—Adjournment till 22nd January. Motion, Mr. W. H. Smith.

JANUARY, 1891.

22. Thurs.—Private Bill Procedure (Scotland) Bill. Committed to a Select Committee.

23. Fri.—Railway Servants (Hours of Labour). Motion, Mr. Channing.

26. Mon.—Tithe Rent-charge, &c., Bill. Committee: First Sitting.

27. Tues.—Parliamentary Oath (Mr. Bradlaugh). Motion, Mr. Hunter. Order that Resolution of 2nd June, 1880, be expunged from the Journal.

28. Wed.—Road and Streets, &c. (Scotland), Bill. Mr. S. Allison. Committed. Conspiracy Law Amendment Bill. Mr. K. Roberts. Put off six months.

29. Thurs.—Tithe Rent-charge, &c., Bill. Committee: Second Sitting.

30. Fri.—Land Tenure (Ireland). Motion, Mr. Shaw-Lefevre. Negatived.

FEBRUARY.

2. Mon.—Tithe Rent-charge, &c., Bill. Committee: Third Sitting. Bill reported.

3. Tues.—Marriage Bills. Motion, Mr. [illegible].

4. Wed.—Religious Disabilities Removal Bill. Mr. [illegible]. Bill put off six months.

5. Thurs.—Case of Walter Harvin. Adjournment. Motion, Mr. J. Lowther. Tithe Rent-charge, &c., Bill. Considered: First Sitting.

6. Fri.—Liverymen (City of London). Motion, Mr. J. Rowlands.

9. Mon.—Tithe Rent-charge, &c., Bill. Considered: Second Sitting.

10. Tues.—Ditto. Ditto. Tithe Read 3°.

11. Wed.—Marriage with a Deceased Wife's Sister Bill. Committed. Division on 2nd Reading—For, 238. Against, 158.

Thurs.—Tithe Rent-charge, &c., Bill. Read 3°. For, 250. Against, 141.

13. Fri.—Government Contracts. Motion, Mr. S. Buxton.

16. Mon.—Administration of the Law (Ireland). Motion, Mr. J. Morley.

17. Tues.—East India (Financial Statement). Motion, Mr. J. [illegible].

18. Wed.—Factory, &c., Bill. Mr. H. James. Committed.

19. Thurs.—Supply: Army Estimates.

20. Fri.—Church in Wales. Motion, Mr. P. [illegible]. For, [illegible]. Against, [illegible].

23. Mon.—Supply: Army Estimates.

24. Tues.—Income Tax. Motion, Mr. [illegible].

25. Wed.—Parochial Boards (Scotland) Bill. [illegible]. Bill put off six months.

26. Thurs.—Factories, &c., Bill. Mr. [illegible]. Committed.

27. Fri.—Taxation of Land. Motion, Mr. [illegible].

MARCH

2. Mon.—Supply: Navy Estimates.
3. Tues.—Parliamentary Franchise. Motion, Mr. Stansfeld.
4. Wed.—Conveyancing, &c., Amendment Bill. Mr. T. H. Bolton. Committed.
5. Thurs.—Conduct of the Police (Millwall). Adjournment. Motion, Mr. Graves. Supply: Army Estimates.
6. Fri.—Local Government. Motion, Dr. Clark.
9. Mon.—Supply: Naval and Civil Service Supplementary Estimates.
10. Tues.—Friendly Societies. Motion, Mr. B. Pickard.
11. Wed.—Small Holdings Bill. **Mr. J. Collings.** Committed.
12. Thurs.—Supply: Civil **Service Supple-**mentary Estimates.
13. Fri.—Local Taxation. Motion, **Mr. J.** Stuart.

16. Mon.—Morning Sittings. Motion, Mr. W. H. Smith. Supply: Civil Service Estimates.
17. Tues.—Savings Banks Bill, Committed. Betting, &c. Motion for a Select Committee. Mr. Fitzgerald.
18. Wed.—Liquor Traffic Local Veto (Wales) Bill. Mr. W. S. Caine, &c. For, 142. Against, 174. Bill committed.
19. Thurs.—Tithe Rent-charge, &c., Bill. Lords' Amendments considered.
20. Fri.—Ditto. Ditto. Second Sitting. Crofter Act, 1886. Motion, Mr. Shaw Lefevre.
23. Mon.—Supply: Debate on question. Adjourned.
24. Tues.—Tithe Rent-charge, &c., Bill. **Lords'** Amendments considered.

APRIL

6. Mon.—Supply: Civil Service Estimates.
7. Tues.—Public Health (London) &c., Bill. Considered.
8. Wed.—Burgh Bill. Committed.
9. Thurs.—Purchase of Land, &c., Ireland (Advance). Report of Resolutions. Considered.
10. Fri.—Purchase of Land, &c. **(Ireland)** Bill. Committee.
13. Mon.—Ditto. Ditto.
14. Tues.—Ditto. Ditto. Local Government in Rural Districts. Motion, Mr. A. Acland.
15. Wed.—Intoxicating Liquor (Ireland) Bill. Read 2. For, 174. Against, 61.
16. Thurs.—Purchase of Land (Ireland) Bill. Committee. First Sitting.
17. Fri.—Ditto. Ditto. Second Sitting. Administration of the Post Office. Motion, Earl Compton.

20. Mon.—Purchase of Land (Ireland) Bill. Committee. Third Sitting.
21. Tues.—Ditto. Ditto. Fourth Sitting.
22. Wed.—Places of Worship, &c., Bill. Committed.
23. Thurs.—Ways and Means. **Financial** Statement. Mr. Goschen.
24. Fri.—Purchase of Land (Ireland) Bill. Committee. Fifth Sitting. [illegible] Motion, Mr. A. Sutherland.
27. Mon.—Ways and Means. Committee.
28. Tues.—Purchase of Land (Ireland) Bill. Committee. Sixth Sitting. Intoxicating Liquors' Licenses. **Mr.** [illegible].
29. Wed.—Landholders' Enfranchisement Bill. Division on 2nd Reading—For, 166. Against, 151.
30. Thurs.—Purchase of Land (Ireland) Bill. Committee. Seventh Sitting.

MAY.

1. Fri.—Purchase of Land (Ireland) Bill. Committee. Eighth Sitting.
4. Mon.—Ditto. Ditto. Ninth Sitting.
5. Tues.—Ditto. Ditto. Tenth Sitting.
6. Wed.—Ditto. Ditto. Eleventh Sitting.
7. Thurs.—Ditto. Ditto. Twelfth Sitting.
8. Fri.—Ditto. Ditto. Thirteenth Sitting.
11. Mon.—Ditto. Ditto. Fourteenth Sitting.
12. Tues.—Ditto. Ditto. Fifteenth Sitting.
13. Wed.—Ditto. Ditto. Sixteenth Sitting.
14. Thurs.—Ditto. Ditto. Seventeenth Sitting.
15. Fri.—Ditto. Ditto. Eighteenth Sitting.

21. Thurs.—Purchase of Land (Ireland) Bill. Committee. Nineteenth Sitting.
22. Fri.—Ditto. Ditto. Twentieth Sitting. Bill reported.
25. Mon.—Supply: Vote on Account.
26. Tues.—Purchase, &c., Bill. Adjourned Debate on 2nd Reading. County Councils (Election of Women). Motion, Mr. Stuart.
28. Thurs.—Newfoundland Fisheries Bill. 2nd Reading put off: Resolution agreed to. Supply: Civil Service Estimates.
29. Fri.—Customs Bill. Committee. **First** Sitting.

JUNE.

1. Mon.—Seal Fishery Bill. Committed. Purchase of Land (Ireland) Bill. Considered. First Sitting.
2. Tues.—Ditto. Ditto. Second Sitting.
3. Wed.—Rating of Machinery Bill. Committed.
4. Thurs.—Purchase of Land (Ireland) Bill. Considered. Third Sitting.
5. Fri.—Ditto. Ditto. Fourth Sitting.
6. Mon.—Elementary Education (Free Grant). Committee.
8. Tues.—Elementary Education **Bill.** Read 1. Purchase of Land (Ireland) Bill. Considered. Fifth Sitting.

10. Wed.—Marriage with a Deceased Wife's Sister Bill. Committee.
11. Thurs.—Purchase of Land (Ireland) Bill. Considered. Sixth Sitting.
12. Fri.—Purchase of Land (Ireland) Bill. Considered. Seventh Sitting.
13. Mon.—Ditto. Ditto. Read 3.
16. Tues.—Railway, &c. Motion, Mr. W. Hayward.
17. Wed.—Supply: Navy Estimates.
18. Thurs.—Factories, &c., Bill. Considered. First Sitting.
19. Fri.—Ditto. Ditto. Second Sitting. Read 3.
22. Mon.—Elementary Education Bill. 2nd Reading. First Sitting.

JUNE (continued).

23. Tues.—Ditto. Ditto. Second Sitting.
24. Wed.—Ditto. Ditto. Third Sitting.
25. Thurs.—Supply: Army Estimates.
26. Fri.—Public Health (London) Bill. Considered.
29. Mon.—Elementary Education Bill. Committee. Instruction, Mr. H. Fowler.
30. Tues.—Ditto. Ditto. First Sitting.

JULY.

1. Wed.—Elementary Education Bill. Committee. Second Sitting.
2. Thurs.—Ditto. Ditto. Third Sitting.
3. Fri.—Ditto. Ditto. Fourth Sitting.
6. Mon.—Redemption of Rent (Ireland) Bill. Read 2°. County Councils Election Bill. Committee.
7. Tues.—Elementary Education Bill. Considered.
8. Wed.—Ditto. Read 3°.
9. Thurs.—Supply: Civil Service Estimates.
10. Fri.—Ditto. Ditto.
13. Mon.—Ditto. Ditto.
14. Tues.—Ditto. Ditto.
15. Wed.—Ditto. Ditto.
16. Thurs.—Supply: Civil Service Estimates.
17. Fri.—Ditto. Ditto.
20. Mon.—Ditto. Ditto.
21. Tues.—Ditto. Ditto. Post Office Acts Amendments Bill. Read 2°.
22. Wed.—Supply: Civil Service Estimates.
23. Thurs.—Purchase of Land (Ireland) Bill. Lords' Amendments considered.
24. Fri.—Supply: Civil Service Estimates.
27. Mon.—Ditto. Ditto.
28. Tues.—Ditto. Ditto.
29. Wed.—Ditto. Ditto.
30. Thurs.—Elementary Education Bill. Lords' Amendments considered.
31. Fri.—Supply: Civil Service Estimates.

AUGUST.

1. Sat.—Supply: Report considered.
3. Mon.—Appropriation Bill. Read 3°.
4. Tues.—East India (Revenue Accounts) Committee.
5. Wed.—Prorogation.

CHAPTER XLI.

THE RECREATIONS OF STATESMEN.

Lord Salisbury—Mr. Gladstone—Mr. Balfour's Day's Work —"Vastly Improved"—A Change—Lord Warden of the Cinque Ports—An Anniversary at Balmoral.

Aug. 19. AFTER a long and laborious Session, the brunt of which he has personally borne, and following close upon a couple of brilliant speeches delivered in the provinces, Mr. Arthur Balfour to-day set forth for Bayreuth to be present at the Wagner Festival. The concatenation of circumstances is certainly without political design. The Chief Secretary's holiday has come at last, and the Bayreuth Festival happening contemporaneously he has gone thither, as being the place where he is likely to find most pleasure. At the same time, there is no question that this particular holiday move has struck the public fancy and increased the personal interest in Mr. Balfour, which has grown apace within the last few years. That, after all he has gone through at Westminster, he should, with a light heart, voluntarily set out to spend a week with Wagner, passes the comprehension of some folk who have quite other views of the possible rest and joy of a holiday.

The British people always take a keen personal interest in the private recreations of their public men. Lord Palmerston's popularity was deeply built upon his fondness for field sports, including boxing, which does not strictly come under that head. The late Lord Derby owned racehorses and ran them. Mr. Disraeli was something of a failure in this direction, though that was not due to the lack of earnest endeavour to cope with accidental disadvantages. He did not ride, nor hunt, nor shoot, nor fish. He wrote novels, but in this connection the gift is not helpful. As early as circumstances permitted he made up as a country squire, had his place at Hughenden, where he grew peacocks, and whence he occasionally emerged in top-boots to attend farmers' ordinaries and talk learnedly about " crossing Southwolds."

Lord Salisbury.   Lord Salisbury has a laboratory at Hatfield and an engineer's workshop, where he planned and directed the lighting by electricity of the old mansion in which Queen Elizabeth was a guest. He is said to be much prouder of his electric-light arrangements than of the Berlin Treaty he helped to frame, or of the approach to settlement of the Newfoundland Fisheries Question he has brought about.

Mr. Gladstone.   Mr. Gladstone, as all the world knows, wields the woodman's axe and cuts down upas-trees in Hawarden Park with a success not excelled by his earlier exploits in Ireland. He could not in any circumstances of private life fail to fill a large place in the admiration and esteem of his countrymen. But it would be difficult to exaggerate, as it would be hard coolly to explain, the influence his wood-cutting has had in endearing him to the people. There is many a little cottage in Britain which counts as its chiefest treasure a chip of wood guaranteed to have fallen under the stroke of Mr. Gladstone's hatchet. If only it happens that the head of the household, making rare holiday, has joined one of the frequent excursions to Hawarden, and has with his own eyes seen Mr. Gladstone with bared arms and conveniently-disposed braces (*vide* one of the most popular of his photographs) assail the tree to which the chip once belonged, gold weighed out against it in the balance would not purchase the treasure.

Mr. Arthur Balfour, in his lean leisure time, plays golf; well enough in its way, but not, to the popular mind, an adequate set-off against Mr. Gladstone's wood-cutting. Golf, like Wagner, is certainly growing in favour, but to the average person it is too much like Wagner to create a general wave of enthusiasm round any one of its votaries. Amid much that is vague in popular information relating to the game, it is generally believed that the Chief Secretary is a crack player. Mr. Balfour says he is not, and I have found men accustomed to play with him too polite to contradict. However it be, he never loses an opportunity of retiring to some favoured spot where golf may be played, and indulging his fancy. But it appears, on this first opportunity when golf and Wagner compete for his presence, the minstrel wins.

Mr. Balfour's day's work. Even Mr. Balfour's enemies—a circle that has distinctly and significantly contracted within the last six months—will admit he has earned his holiday, in whatever form he may care to take it. He has toiled terribly through the Session, but his appearances in the House and his participation in its business are merely parts of his day's work. Before, at half-past three in the afternoon, he strolls into the House, he has already accomplished a day's work that would cause to stand aghast the labourer clamouring for an eight hour limit. He is Minister for Ireland, and he personally administers the affairs of Ireland. The Irish Office is a mean building, once a private house, almost within bowshot of the Houses of Parliament. Mr. Balfour is in his room at an hour in the morning as early as the average city merchant appears at his desk. Till he goes off to the House of Commons to begin a fresh phase of difficult and delicate work that will certainly not close before the stroke of midnight, he is grappling with an interminable series of problems, a mistake in dealing with any one being fraught with danger to the Ministry and possible disaster to the country. This tall, graceful stripling, with a face sometimes soft and beautiful as a woman's, is ruler of Ireland in a complete sense unknown in English history since the days of Cromwell. If anything is done in Ireland, it must be worked through him; and to him, as long as the doors of the Irish Office are open, repair representatives of the manifold interests struggling for predominance. He listens to all with engaging courtesy, but the polish of his manner is found to be developed upon a stratum of adamantine will. He is not to be cozened by political supporters any more than he is to be intimidated by the Irish Nationalists.

"Vastly Improved." The best sign discernible about the Chief Secretary just now, the one most hopeful for his future, is his development of a readiness to learn. This has been a slow process, and its accretion is accountable for the remarkable scenes witnessed in the House towards the close of the Session, when Mr. Tim Healy, Seagreen Incorruptible, admitted that Mr. Balfour's administration of the Relief Fund had been well planned and carefully carried out, and that, on

the whole, he had " vastly improved " since he first went to
the Irish Office. That is true, but it is not a truth expected
to be volunteered from the Irish camp, and that the tribute
was extorted is striking evidence to the weight of conviction.
When Mr. Balfour first became Chief Secretary the limit of his
duties was to his vision bounded by the resolve to put down
the Land League, and, to adopt his own formula, to re-establish
the reign of Law and Order. With his eye fixed on this goal,
he strode straight forward, caring nothing for any who might
chance to stumble under his iron heel. He began by system-
atically ignoring the right of Mr. Parnell and his then solid
phalanx to represent Ireland. "*L'etat, c'est moi*" was his motto
in all that related to the administration of the affairs of that
country. It is very much his motto to-day, but it works with
less friction because he knows more. When he took office he
was naturally in the hands of the permanent officials at
Dublin Castle. It was they who were the Estate, not he. In
the four years during which he has had to answer for Ireland
he has incidentally enjoyed the opportunity of learning something about the country, and in proportion as his knowledge
has increased, his relentless attitude toward the Parnell representatives of the masses of the people has softened.

A change.   There was a time when he went the length of
practically declining to hold personal communication with them across the floor of the House. Hapless Colonel
King-Harman had an office especially created for him, and to
him was left the daily duty of reading the manuscript containing
the answers prepared at Dublin Castle to questions put by the
National Party. That was a contemptuous proceeding, bitterly
resented by the men at whom it was flung. Night after night
there were stormy scenes at question time. "Balfour! Balfour!"
the Irish members shouted when King-Harman appeared at
the table to reply to a question addressed to the Chief
Secretary. Sometimes when the storm had raged for nearly
an hour Mr. Balfour strolled in, pale, defiant, contemptuous,
and presently descending into the arena whence his squire
had gratefully retired, he, single-handed, met the onrush of
the maddened enemy. It was more or less magnificent; it
certainly was not business; and when, presently, it helped to

hurry poor King-Harman into his grave, Mr. Balfour abandoned an unfortunate attitude and condescended to answer questions much as other Ministers did.

Those days have passed, and something like the Millennium has dawned. Mr. Balfour now pays the keenest attention to arguments advanced by the Irish members. Frequently in Committee on the Land Purchase Bill he accepted amendments submitted by them, and when he first made public promise of an Irish Local Government Bill for next year he paused and pointedly expressed the hope that he would have Mr. Healy's assistance in making it a really useful measure. The erstwhile truculent Tim, not to be outdone in chivalry, graciously intimated assent. This is a state of affairs calculated to make Mr. Biggar turn in his grave. But it is all to the good of Ireland.

Aug. 25.—Lord Warden of the Cinque Ports. Mr. W. H. Smith, who succeeded Lord Granville in the ancient post of Lord Warden of the Cinque Ports, has taken up his residence at Walmer Castle. Announcement of the event appears in a modest paragraph in the newspapers just such as might chronicle his temporary retirement to his villa at Henley-on-Thames. It is really an epoch-making event, honourable alike to Mr. Smith and to English public life. It is only twenty-three years since Mr. Smith entered public life, winning a seat at Westminster even when the flowing tide brought Mr. Gladstone into power in 1868 with a mission to disestablish the Irish Church. His name was then familiar in connection with the firm of newspaper agents whose flag flies over nearly every railway bookstall in the kingdom. Even at this day, in the latest edition of "Dod's Parliamentary Guide," he is described as "head of the firm of Messrs. William Henry Smith & Son, the well-know newspaper agents, etc." As a matter of fact, he is living retired from the active direction of the firm's business, content with drawing the princely revenues which keep up his house in Grosvenor Place, his yacht, and his riverside retreat. But the scent of the bookstall clings to him still, and now there is talk as to what title he shall take there comes tripping to the tongue the suggestion "Baron Bookstall of the Strand."

The House of Commons has long grown accustomed to see
him sitting in the seat where Mr. Gladstone sat of late, and
round which linger the shades of Peel and Palmerston, Lord
John Russell and Mr. Disraeli. Nevertheless there is something almost startling in finding him installed in the historic
castle on whose ramparts Pitt used to stand looking out for
the fleet that never sailed from Boulogne, where the Duke of
Wellington later lived, and was followed by Lord Palmerston
and Earl Granville. No salary is attached to the office of
Lord Warden, and the Castle is something of a white elephant
in the way of keeping up, as Lord Granville found to his cost.
But the post is one of the oldest and most honourable within
the gift of the Crown, its associations going back to Plantagenet
days. One of the pleasant things in connection with the new
incumbency is that no one grudges its bestowal upon plain
Mr. Smith or cavils at the honour done to him. This is
largely due to the personal popularity that has grown up
around his sterling worth and modest mien.

Aug. 29. — An
anniversary at
Balmoral.

Mr. Balfour arrived at Balmoral just too late
to be present at a quaint ceremony in which the
Queen takes keen personal interest. Shortly
after the Prince Consort died the tenants on the Balmoral,
Birkhall, and Abergeldie estates raised a stone cairn to his
memory. It stands on the hill above the castle, a huge
pyramid of stone, perpetuating his name and recording the
date of his death. There are other initials cut on the stone,
including the Queen's, and nearly all the members of the Royal
Family. The temptation to 'Arry to add his honoured
monogram has been irresistible; but the Obelisk, as it is
called, is jealously guarded, and only once did 'Arry, who
has cut his initials on all the historical buildings of the world
from the Pyramids to the innermost recesses of the Mammoth
Caves, succeed in getting his hand in, the inscription being
promptly and contumeliously erased. Thursday was the
seventy-second anniversary of Prince Albert's birth, and in
accordance with custom observed for nearly thirty years, a
procession wound its way up the hill to the Obelisk. First
came the gentlemen of Her Majesty's Household in attendance.
Then the principal tenants on the royal estates, with a troop

of the upper servants closing in the rear. The strange company formed a circle round the Obelisk; tumblers were produced, a generous jar of whiskey was fortuitously discovered in convenient proximity, bumpers were filled, and as noon clanged from the castle clock, the group silently drank to the memory of the long-dead Master.

CHAPTER XLII.

TWO DEAD MEN.

Mr. W. H. Smith—Mr. Parnell—His Short Way with Letters—His Aloofness —How the Work of Leadership was done—Dictator—Learning to Speak.

Oct. 9.—Mr. W. H. Smith. ON Monday afternoon the town was suddenly deeply stirred by news that the flag was flying at half-mast on Walmer Castle, for the Lord Warden of the Cinque Ports lay dead. Whilst this theme was on every tongue came news that Mr. Parnell had died at Brighton. It is impossible to conceive in English public life a coincidence more striking. Each man held a foremost place in Parliamentary life and English politics, and yet in all circumstances of position, character, and capacity they were wide as the poles asunder. There was something grimly characteristic in the time of Parnell's taking-off. All his political life—and it was only sixteen years long—he had been battling with staid respectability in politics, outraging Parliamentary usages, and defying constitutional authority. Of all these things Mr. W. H. Smith was the fleshly embodiment. He had, according to his chastened lights, so borne himself in public life as to have endeared himself to friend and political adversary. He died in what, according to the longevity of statesmen, may be regarded as the prime of life. The sorrow his sudden cutting-off created in the public mind was profound and sincere. At least a full week might well have been given up to his mourning and to the extolling of his sterling qualities.

At such a time, suddenly and unexpectedly, when no one was thinking of him, Parnell, obstructionist to the last, dies in

tho evening of tho very day Mr. Smith breathed his last,
and in tho newspaper press tho columns of appreciation and
criticism of the stormy career of the Irish chief jostle into
comparative obscurity the decent lamentation over tho bier of
tho amiable First Lord of tho Treasury. Abroad and at home
it is the same. The foreign newspapers teem with articles
discussing the disgraced and discarded Irish leader, and there

"OLD MORALITY."

is room only for a paragraph here and there about the First
Lord of the Treasury, Leader of the House of Commons, whom
the generality of men liked and applauded in much the same
degree that, in these latter days, Parnell was hated and
contemned.

Mr. Parnell.   This is, in its way, very sad. But there is no
doubt that history will justify contemporary
action in this matter. Years after dear "Old Morality" is quite

forgotten, the name of Charles Stewart Parnell will be familiar in schoolbooks, and his tall figure and pale, haggard face will stand out distinct in the portrait gallery of statesmen of the Victorian age. Parnell was not personally interesting in the sense that Disraeli was, and that Mr. Gladstone and Lord Randolph Churchill, in widely different fashion, remain. But there was about him that fascination which pertains to strong characters whom the public feel they do not thoroughly understand. Disraeli, at one epoch of his career, was known as the Mystery Man of Politics. That was a mocking phrase, used in a sense that implied full insight into the strings and motives of his double shuffling. About Parnell there really brooded an air of mystery that, in some subtle way, added to his power. One of his peculiarities was that he habitually concealed his address. Sometimes, as was disclosed in the proceedings in the

CHARLES STEWART PARNELL.

Divorce Court, he assumed a false name, being known in one place as "Mr. Fox," in another as "Mr. Preston." During

the most troublesome times of the campaign in the House of Commons his colleagues were sorely hampered by not knowing how to communicate with their chief. It is a matter of fact that for ten years his most intimate colleagues did not know where a letter would find him in or near London. When, after the judgment in the Divorce Court, Mr. John Morley was charged with delivery of a message from Mr. Gladstone to Mr. Parnell, he spent many precious hours in trying to reach him. Neither Justin McCarthy nor any other of his colleagues, not even Mr. Campbell, his private secretary, knew where a telegram would find him. Thus it came to pass that Parnell entered Committee Room No. 15 without having had Mr. Gladstone's message delivered to him, a circumstance that had momentous effect upon his future career and the constitution of the Irish party.

His short way with letters. Often at important crises in Parliamentary events I have seen Parnell suddenly enter the lobby of the House of Commons, walk with long stride to the Post Office, take his huge bundle of letters, and disappear towards the library, speaking to no one on the way, apparently seeing no one in his path. As for the letters, they might be, and probably were, the accumulation of a week or a fortnight. Many of them would not be opened, most of them would not be answered.

"It saves time," Parnell once said to a friend who remonstrated with him on this habit of dealing with his correspondence, a procedure which had at the moment led to some serious embarrassment. It is remarkable how many letters answer themselves in the space of a fortnight.

Having dealt with his letters, Parnell might or might not enter the House. Most often he did not, disappearing as rapidly and suddenly as he had arrived, neither coming nor going by the broad staircase with swinging brass-bound doors, through which the throng of legislators pass. There is another passage to the lobby, by a winding back staircase, used by messengers, policemen, and others having access. This Parnell always used, not from any more occult reason than that he was certain thereby to avoid meeting anyone who might speak to him, or would expect to be spoken to.

His aloofness. He was essentially non-gregarious. He shrank with equal solicitude from large crowds and small coteries. In the plenitude of his power he rarely visited Ireland to take part in public proceedings. It was one of the most striking alterations wrought by his fall that thereafter he immediately began to cultivate the populace. Nemesis was alert, and it was at a public meeting he was struck by the chill that brought on his death. On Sunday next he had an engagement to speak at Cork—Sunday, the day he will be laid to rest at Glasnevin Cemetery, at a spot not far distant from where O'Connell sleeps. During his last campaign in Ireland he amazed, even appalled, his associates by developing a jollity in public and a familiarity in private almost hysterical. Just as in the days of his prosperity he shrank from taking part in public meetings, so he shunned social gatherings. In the Parliamentary season London is given to abundant hospitality. The art of dining is cultivated in political circles with infinite solicitude. Parnell might, if he pleased, have dined out every night in company not lacking any of the delights, personal or material, of the dinner-table. If for sternly patriotic reasons he declined to join a party sure to be largely leavened by men who had voted against him, he might have met his own colleagues at their table in the dining-room of the House of Commons. In early days of his Parliamentary life, days that sometimes lengthened into all-night sittings, he used to dine frugally at the House. But it is years since he was seen at the table; where he dined, and how, being among the minor mysteries that brooded over his strange daily life.

How the work of leadership was done. How, with these habits, he managed to conduct the business of an exceedingly active party is a puzzle that affords only one solution. He did not conduct its business. That was settled in all its details by the lieutenants who bore the heat and burden of the day through the Parliamentary Session. Mr. Tim Healy, in one of his angry speeches, let some light upon this dark place by the assertion that for several years Parnell had practically withdrawn from the active direction of affairs, and that whatever had been done for Ireland had been accomplished by a small committee, consisting of himself, Mr. Dillon, Mr. O'Brien, and Mr. Sexton. He even added that when on rare occasions Mr. Parnell appeared on the scene, he was supplied with all the materials for speech to be made or letter to be written.

Dictator. That is probably true; but Parnell remained the absolute master of the party and its policy —a dictator from whose decision there was no appeal. The extraordinary relations that existed between him and his followers was strikingly illustrated at the end of last Session but one. Mr. Balfour's first attempt to deal with the Land Purchase question was still before the House. Parnell, unexpectedly appearing one evening, contributed to the debate an important speech, in the course of which he threw out certain suggestions materially modifying the Bill. His speech was listened to with rapt attention in a crowded House, being naturally accepted as the expression of the deliberately-arrived-at conclusions of the then undivided party that followed his lead. It was noted whilst he was speaking that no one followed his exposition with livelier interest than Mr. Healy, Mr. Sexton, Mr. Dillon, Mr. O'Brien, and others of the inner circle of his Cabinet. This was not unnatural, since, as one of these gentlemen told me later in the evening, they had never heard a word of the proposal till it was publicly made in the House of Commons. In the comparative leisure of his retirement at Eltham, Parnell had thought out this scheme (which, I may add, was in modified form finally adopted by Mr. Balfour, and is now embodied in the Act of Parliament), had run up to town, flashed it forth on an interested House and an astonished gathering of his colleagues, and then caught the last train for Eltham, probably on this very night meeting with the accident to his brougham that first led his trusting friend Captain O'Shea to believe that possibly something was wrong in the sylvan quiet of his Eltham home.

Learning to speak. Looking at the frantic, desperate way in which he clung to power, it seems a paradox to write that Parnell hated public life, with its necessity for joint action and its imposition of speech-making. Yet such is the fact. Public speaking was positively painful to him. His difference from the ordinary run of his colleagues in the House of Commons included a total lack of fluency. When, sixteen years ago, he first entered the House of Commons, he was so conscious of his infirmity that he remained silent for nearly two Sessions. He educated himself in a rough school, joining Mr. Biggar in talking against time: and the determination of the House of Commons not to give him a hearing, bad as it looked, was precisely the discipline that successfully schooled him. Had he risen amid an awful stillness, and been responsible for every sentence he uttered, he would have shrunk appalled from the ordeal. With a mob howling before and around him, it did not matter what he said or how he said it.

So he stood there with clenched hands, pale face, and closed teeth, literally hissing forth contumely and scorn in disjointed sentences. In time he came to be one of the most polished speakers in the House, delivering carefully-cut sentences in soft, mellow voice. That he was the same man to the end as he had been when he first wrestled with a majority of the House of Commons, was shown in Committee Room No. 15, when, once more at bay, with hands clenched, teeth closed, eyes flamed in fury, the soft voice was raised to the intonation of a furious scold. Mr. Biggar, had he lived to see the day, would have joyously recognised in Committee Room No. 15 his old colleague, the Parnell of 1877.

SESSION 1892.

. . . . .

CHAPTER XLIII.

MR. ARTHUR BALFOUR'S START IN THE LEADERSHIP.

Opening Day—A Death-roll—Lord Randolph—The Illiterate Voter—A Poser
for the Attorney-General—The Leader of the House—Mr. Webster's
Oratory—Calling Mr. De Cobain—Sir George Campbell—The New Leader
—A Contrast—Other Leaders.

Feb. 9.—Open-
ing Day.
WHEN at four o'clock this afternoon the Speaker took the Chair in the House of Commons, the front Opposition bench was so crowded that it seemed impossible to have found room for Lord Hartington if by any chance he had taken the wrong turning and, answering the summons for the opening of Parliament, had sought the chamber where he has been a familiar figure for nearly a quarter of a century. But Lord Hartington, transformed into the Duke of Devonshire, has found his way to the House of Lords, and was even in time to take the oath and his seat before other business intervened. Closely following the Speaker came Mr. Balfour, upon whom on the threshold of his new career the cares of high estate seem already to have told. Something of the bloom of youth is rubbed off. In respect of force and volume of cheering his entrance was a little disappointing, but that was due to the fact that the Conservative benches were only half filled. There was, indeed, at this stage of the proceedings a certain marked disinclination for enthusiasm, possibly connected with the funereal aspect of the gathering, nearly every member present being in deep mourning for the Duke of Clarence. Sir William Harcourt's entrance was unrecognised, whilst when Mr. Chamberlain appeared the Dissentient Liberals studiously concealed their approval of his succession to the leadership of Lord Hartington. Lord Randolph Churchill was not present.

A death-roll.   The Speaker, having read the formal resolutions pertaining to the opening of a new Session, went on to inform the House of the writs he had issued during the recess. This sadly partook of the character of a death-roll, the catalogue of names adding appreciably to the depression of the House. A new writ had been issued for the Strand in the room of " Mr. W. H. Smith, deceased." Dead also are Mr. Parnell, Sir John Pope Hennessy, Sir Charles Forster, Mr. Raikes, Mr. Bond, Sir J. P. Corry, and Mr. Richard Power. To the personal recollections invoked nothing was lost by the solemnity of tone with which the Speaker went through this ordinarily formal business. As he proceeded a crowd silently gathered at the Bar. These were the successors of the members from either side of the House gone over to the majority. Quite a crowd they grew, their number being reinforced by movers and seconders. The First Lord of the Treasury left his seat and walked to the Bar in readiness to act as sponsor to Mr. Jackson, who, happily, is his own successor, coming up after re-election on acceptance of office as Chief Secretary for Ireland. Escorted by Mr. Balfour and Mr. Akers Douglas, Mr. Jackson, on advancing to the table, was hailed with a cheer the unanimity of which testified to his personal popularity. After him came Sir James Fergusson, transferred to the Postmaster-Generalship; Lord Walter Lennox, re-elected on appointment to the Treasurership of the Household; and Mr. Graham Murray, the new Solicitor-General for Scotland, who, later, sitting on the Treasury bench with folded arms listening sedately to Sir William Harcourt, curiously recalled the personal appearance of Sir Stafford Northcote.

One new member, Mr. Holden, succeeded in importing some excitement into a hitherto doleful ceremony by endeavouring, in the excitement of the moment, to rush past the Clerk standing at the table waiting for him to sign the Roll of Parliament. But that official, experienced in the eccentricities of new members, dexterously stopped him on his unauthorised way to the Speaker, and the signature was duly appended. The appearance of Mr. Frederick Smith, approaching to take his seat for the Strand, in the room of his father, the late Leader of the House, first (after the welcome to Mr. Jackson) stirred the unaccustomed silence of the House. He was hailed with a hearty cheer, in which Opposition and Ministerialists joined. Immediately after came Mr. Lambert, who carried the Liberal flag triumphantly through South Molton. At his appearance the Opposition woke up and gave a rousing cheer, prolonged the full length of his passage up to the table. That was pretty well to begin with, but it was nothing to what followed on the appearance of Mr. Maden, Lord Hartington's successor in the representation of Rossendale. This good wine was kept to the last, and proved admirably to suit the palate of the crowded Opposition benches. Mr. Maden was not only cheered up to the table, where his escort left him, but was cheered all the while the clerk, in dumb show, administered the oath to him; again whilst he was signing the Roll of Parliament; and a third time, with growing enthusiasm, when he was introduced to the Speaker.

During this episode, Mr. Chamberlain, with folded arms, and a far-away look the late Mr. Disraeli might have envied, sat in the seat where Lord Hartington was wont to doze.

Feb. 14.—Lord Randolph. Lord Randolph Churchill appeared in the House to-day for the first time since the Session opened. He looks in excellent health, and much more civilised than the day he arrived from the Cape. His beard then was in a strangely loose condition. It is now trimmed, and shares with his moustache the friendly caress familiar in days when he sat below the gangway. In spite of this trimming of the beard, the great explorer, as a patrician member of the House observed to-night, has a decidedly "colonial" look. He is in high spirits, and discusses the political situation with delightful frankness. He does not intend to take a prominent part in such proceedings as may be possible to the present Parliament. He remained a couple of hours, holding something like a *levée* from his old corner seat above the gangway. He had a long conversation with Sir M. Hicks-Beach, a former colleague, with whom his friendly relations have not, as in many other cases, been interrupted.

Feb. 19.—The Illiterate Voter. The Angel of Death hovers over the House of Commons. You can almost hear the rustling of his wings. The talk is all of the coming dissolution. The

Irish Local Government Bill interests members not, nor Small Holdings either.   To-night Mr. Webster, with the acumen of a barrister-at-law and the trained strategy of one who has served for sixteen years in the 3rd Battalion South Lancashire Regiment, thought he had secured a subject to which the very circumstances of the case would lend a charm.   After the dissolution comes the General Election, and in the breasts of candidates a personal interest in the Illiterate Voter begins to glow.   Mr. Webster, accordingly, had secured a place for discussion of the delicate question whether the Illiterate Voter should, like the Irish Church, be abolished, or whether, like the Union up to the present moment, he should be retained.

It was not yet half-past seven, when, boldly springing up from a bench behind that on which Ministers should have been sitting, he exclaimed in trumpet tone, "Mr. Speaker!" The hour was perhaps drawing a little dangerously near to that at which members are accustomed to dine.   But the Illiterate Voter, cum the eloquence and military knowledge of the member for East St. Pancras, might surely be counted upon to keep an audience together even though the dinner-bell rang and the perfume of the waiting soup stole softly o'er the senses. At the moment the orator faced the House it was crowded in exhilarating fashion.   Over three hundred members had just passed through the division lobbies, and had gathered in their places to hear the result of what had suddenly threatened to become a narrow majority for the Government.   Mr. Lloyd George had brought forward a motion condemning the appointment of a certain County Court judge in Wales, on the ground that he was not able to speak the musical language of the Principality.   The debate did credit to the Welsh members, most of the speeches being to the point and all brief.

<table><tr><td>A power for the
Attorney-
General.</td><td>The interposition of the burly member for the Rhondda Valley stirred the current with fresh interest.   Mabon has a pretty habit, learned</td></tr></table>

amid the hills and dales and chapels of his native land, of varying his oratory by occasionally dropping into song.   To-night he had a fresh and scarcely less pleasing surprise in store.   The Attorney-General met the indictment in the resolution by affirming, first, that the offence of appointing a

non-Welsh-speaking County Court judge was not peculiar to
a Conservative Lord Chancellor: secondly, that, after all, the
practical inconvenience was not so great as had been pictured
by Cymric imagination. "Very well," said Mabon, in effect,
"let us consider the matter. Here we are in the County Court
House at Ynysymaengwyn. I'm the plaintiff. The Attorney-
General is the County Court judge. He, in the course of the
case, asks me if I am prepared to swear that the boots delivered to the defendant, for the price of which I sue, were
rights and lefts or otherwise as the defendant alleges. That is
a delicate question I, with my partial knowledge of English
do not trust myself to answer, except in my native tongue.
Therefore I say:—*Cymmer dau bwrch, ar gwastad dawshl
llaent twlch; pen-dre pistyll bwlch dwy hafod-tai bch wedd
Ympytty?* Now," thundered Mabon, whilst the House of
Commons held its breath and a cloud of embarrassment stole
over the ingenuous face of the Attorney-General, "what does
the honourable and learned gentleman say to *that?*"   .

<table><tr><td>The Leader of
the House.</td><td>The Leader of the House had evidently in-</td></tr></table>

The Leader of the House.   The Leader of the House had evidently intended at the outset to leave the conduct of the
case in the able hands of the Attorney-General. But after
this demonstration of its difficulties he found it necessary, or
desirable, to throw into the discussion the weight of his
personal authority and official position. His speech, apart
from other qualities, was interesting as illustrating the new
manner assumed by him since he came to the Leadership.
Those familiar with his bearing during the long Sessions he
was Chief Secretary would scarcely have recognised the
Minister laboriously and deferentially attempting to soothe
the ruffled feelings of the Welsh members. The light of
battle gleamed no more from his eyes. The quivering figure
was restful, almost staid in its pose. The smile with which
he was wont to launch his barbed arrows on their unerring
course played no longer round his lips. He was strictly
official, not to say surprisingly commonplace. Far be it from
him to question the intrinsic justice of the plaint uttered by
the Welsh members. As for the resolution on the subject
passed by the House of Commons in 1872, upon which Mr.
Lloyd George had built his proposition, Mr. Balfour was

almost lured into something of his pristine energy in asseverating his perfect approval of it.

"I am the last man in this House," he said, glancing quickly towards the third bench below the gangway opposite to see if by chance Mr. Tim Healy was in his seat, "to desire to introduce political controversy into such a question." But certainly Lord Halsbury in this particular appointment had the support of example set to him by Lord Chancellors acting under the Government of Mr. Gladstone; "and hon. gentlemen from Wales," he added, with winning smile, "will not be inclined to dispute the authority of the right hon. gentleman the member for Midlothian."

It was a pity Sir William Harcourt felt it his duty to interpose at this idyllic moment. What seemed more appropriate to the occasion was that Mabon should have risen, chanted a bar of "The March of the Men of Harlech," the Attorney-General (whose vocal parts are highly appreciated at Bar messes and in other social circles) should have sung the next verse, and, the resolution withdrawn, Mr. Webster might have found earlier opportunity of introducing the Illiterate Voter.

But Sir William Harcourt, as he once inferred, is almost human. Following Mr. Balfour to-night, he once again sounded the tocsin of war, and the Welsh members, shaking off the subtle influence of the Leader's melting mood, insisted upon going to a division, bringing down the Government majority to ominous repetition of the twenty odd votes by which the Address had been saved on Monday.

<table>
<tr><td>Mr. Webster's
oratory.</td><td>It was to the throng opposite, tumultuous with delight at this result, that Mr. Webster addressed</td></tr>
</table>

his speech. "Mr. Speaker," he cried aloud, with that stentorian voice with which he was accustomed to rally the 3rd Battalion South Lancashire Regiment in the stricken field. The immediate effect was oddly different from that it was wont to work upon the faithful 3rd Battalion. Instead of bringing the serried ranks to attention, it broke them up. With hilarious laughter and a mocking cheer the crowd streamed forth through the doorway, Mr. Webster finding it necessary to pause till the bustle of departure was stilled. Even

for an experienced orator it was embarrassing and disheartening to see what he had fondly hoped might be his audience
rapidly disappearing into space. In this dilemma, experience
and habits gained in his varied occupation as a barrister-at-
law, "also a magistrate for Middlesex," came to his assistance
and evaded disaster. He had observed the precaution of
writing out on brief paper his remarks about the Illiterate
Voter, and these he proceeded to read to the Speaker and the
Serjeant-at-Arms. Members furtively looking in from time to
time anxiously examined the decreasing bulk of the manuscript,
desirous of gauging the probable duration of the reading.
Happily the folios were not numerous, and Mr. Webster,
getting along at breathless rate, was permitted to conclude.
But when Mr. Kenny rose with obvious intention of making
this also an Irish question a count was moved. The bells rang
through empty corridors, and when the Speaker counted
heads, there were not forty within sight, and the House
adjourned.

Feb. 21.—Calling Mr. De Cobain.

Not many members were drawn to the House
to-day, even by the possibility of assisting at a
dramatic scene in connection with Mr. De Cobain, the fugitive member for Belfast. The first business of the sitting
was the reading of the order calling upon him to be in his
place. It was evidently empty to-night, and Mr. Balfour having
ascertained the fact by looking round, thought the road was clear.
The clerk at the table having read the order of the day, the
Leader of the House promptly followed with notice of his motion
to expel Mr. De Cobain. This was a curious blunder, something parallel to that committed by Mr. Goschen at the end of
the Session, when he attempted to expel Mr. De Cobain
forthwith. Mr. De Cobain should first have been cited to
appear, but the new Leader was in such a hurry to get rid of
his old follower that he did not await this ceremony, and went
on reading the terms of his motion. He was interrupted by
murmurs from the benches opposite, and stopped with a
sudden start, apparently apprehensive that at the last moment
the hunted member had turned up, and was making his way
to his place. There were cries of "Call him, call him," and the
Speaker rising, Mr. Balfour resumed his seat.

The Speaker added to the mystery by "putting the question," but no one heard what the question was, only the Speaker's declaration that "the ayes had it." The Speaker having resumed his seat, Mr. Balfour went on again. When he came to the statement in the resolution that Mr. De Cobain had failed to obey the orders of the House, there were cries of "Perhaps he's here." More than ever mystified, and beginning to suspect that members opposite had some special knowledge on the subject, Mr. Balfour stood and stared around him. Mr. Dillon came to his assistance by explaining that there was no evidence to show that Mr. De Cobain had failed to appear. Mr. Balfour once more re-seating himself, the Speaker in his sonorous voice called "Mr. De Cobain." There was no response, and at length Mr. Balfour succeeded in giving notice of his intention on Friday to move the expulsion of the member for Belfast.

Feb. 23. — Sir George Campbell. The misfortunes of the Parliamentary career of Sir George Campbell were crowned by the accident that news of his death reached the House of Commons on the night the Irish Local Government Bill was brought in. That event, and the circumstances attending it, were such as to engross conversation in the lobbies, and to fill the columns of next day's papers. Thus poor Sir George's removal from a scene through which he restlessly moved for sixteen Sessions received scarcely the notice it merited. On the whole he is spoken of kindly among his old associates at Westminster. He was, no one attempts to disguise it, a terrible bore, and this was the more lamented since his ability and capacity were unquestioned. He entered on the Parliamentary scene with a high reputation. There was at the time question in the newspapers at home and abroad as to how India would get along when he was no longer a member of its Council and Lieutenant-Governor of Bengal.

Possibly this high reputation had something to do with his melancholy fall. Long accustomed to autocratic position, he within a few days of entering the House of Commons fell a-lecturing it, proposing to personally direct its debates and proceedings, as, a few months earlier, he had ruled the Bengalese. He was genuinely surprised to find how different are men and things at Westminster. But, always sure he was right, he went on rubbing the House the wrong way, dogmatising in a rasping voice, the like of which was never heard on land or sea. Cocksure, indomitable, the more the House wouldn't listen to him the more frequently he spoke, till it came to pass in these later years that at the first sound of that unmistakable voice, however grave he might be, however serious his purpose, however important the occasion, it was instantly echoed by a shout of derisive laughter.

Feb. 26. — The new Leader. For not quite three weeks has Mr. Arthur Balfour held the office of Leader of the House of Commons, and already he is aweary. The light is fading from his eye, the ready smile from his lips: his temper is growing short, and his face grey. It seemed bad enough whilst he was Chief Secretary with back to the wall fighting, often singlehanded, the then United Irish Party. Two conditions then existent are absent now, which sadly vary the situation. Then he was on the war-path, might deal blow for blow, meet concentrated attack by a brilliant foray into the enemy's country. Also he had behind him an enthusiastically admiring host of backers. Whenever he stood up to do battle with Mr. Tim Healy, Mr. O'Brien, Mr. Dillon, or Mr. Sexton, he was sure to be inspirited by a hearty cheer, and every parrying stroke or skilful thrust was watched with keen delight and hailed with rousing cheers.

It is altogether different with the Leader of the House. Almost the last quality needed in him is that he should be a fighting man. This is illustrated in the case of Mr. W. H. Smith, and goes a long way to explain his remarkable success in the office into which accident and dire necessity thrust him. Mr. Smith instinctively recognised that the Leader of the House of Commons is something more than the chief of a political party. Gentlemen grouped on the right hand of the Speaker are his particular flock; but gentlemen opposite also form a component part of the House, and he is Leader of the House. Mr. Smith never forgot this in his lightest word or passing gesture. He carried the principle so far, that when proposing or discussing business arrangements, or the provisions of a measure, he habitually ignored the existence of his own side, addressing himself exclusively with painstaking courtesy and subtly winning deference to gentlemen opposite.

This habit, natural to a kindly, peaceable, unaggressive nature, worked wonders upon the Opposition. Mr. Smith was not a great statesman nor a brilliant Parliamentarian. He frequently stumbled into error, and was even more often drawn into embarrassing position by the blunders of his colleagues. But no Leader since Lord Palmerston's later day was so certain of friendly consideration from the Opposition. For the despatch of business, dependent as it is upon the equable temperament of the House, Mr. Smith as Leader was worth more to the Conservative Party than an addition of twenty votes on any one of their recorded majorities.

A contrast.   It is impossible to conceive two men more antipathic than Mr. W. H. Smith and Mr. Arthur Balfour. Where in given circumstances one succeeded, the other might be counted on as sure to fail. That does not necessarily follow in the matter of the Leadership of the House of Commons. But it points to an initial difficulty that faces Mr. Balfour, and with which he has been struggling, not successfully, through the three weeks of his novitiate. The House, grown accustomed to Mr. Smith's gentle sway, to the success of which it all unconsciously contributed, is startled into an attitude of censoriousness at the personal change. There was a great deal of human nature in the Black Country denizen who, being told that a passer-by on whom his eye had lighted was a new comer, promptly said, "Then let's 'eave arf a brick at 'im." The House of Commons, the sublimation of humanity, is not wholly free from this tendency to resent the intrusion of a new comer.

Mr. Balfour has the further disadvantage of being a new comer only in the sense that he is new to the prominent post he now fills. He brings to the discharge of his duties the recollection of bitter animosity born in the days when he was Chief Secretary. The curious thing notable in the House of Commons just now is that whilst these animosities evidently live on the benches opposite, the enthusiastic support from his

own side which buoyed up the Chief Secretary is chilled in
presence of the First Lord of the Treasury. Only last
Session Mr. Balfour's coming and going to and from the
Treasury bench, and his appearance at the table in debate,
were the sure signal of enthusiastic cheers from the serried
hosts of the Conservatives. Now, as far as these outward and
visible signs of personal admiration go, he is of no more
account than Mr. Goschen.

Other Leaders.   There happened to-night an incident that sharply
illustrated the curious change that has come
over the House in this personal matter. Early in the term of
his new office Mr. Balfour introduced a custom defensible
from certain narrow aspects, but decidedly grating on old traditions and the sense of the general fitness of things. There
is no unwritten law of Parliamentary procedure more peremptory or implacable than that the Leader of the House shall
be in his place from the time public business commences
till the cry "Who goes home?" echoes through the outer
lobby. It is a hard rule at which the British workman who
would have his daily toil strictly limited to eight hours would
scoff. It is, moreover, physically impossible that any man,
however hardy in mind and body, should bear the strain
pressing upon him night after night through six or seven
months in a year. Yet, within memory of the present
generation, the demand has been met with almost imperceptible lapse. Up to the very day when Mr. Disraeli, a
septuagenarian in years, worn with the incessant toil of half a
century, walked out of the House of Commons to enjoy
the fuller leisure of the Lords, he was, whilst Leader of
the House of Commons, rarely absent from the Treasury
bench for a full hour at a time, or for an aggregate of two
hours through a prolonged sitting. However empty the
House might be, however dull and commonplace the proceedings, there sat the passive figure on the Treasury bench
with arms folded, the skirt of his morning coat carefully
drawn over his crossed knees, head bent down, but eyes
keenly observant and ears ever open.

With Mr. Gladstone the daily habit was identical, save
that when on the Treasury bench he was rarely at rest,

showing by his gestures, sometimes by interpolation, constantly by whispered remarks to his companion, how closely he followed the most immaterial speech. During the troublous Sessions of 1881 and 1882 Mr. Gladstone had reduced the necessity of dining to an exact science. For health's sake he spent the necessary time in walking to Downing Street and back. But it was all done, dinner included, within a space that never exceeded forty minutes, and at grave crises was accomplished in half an hour. Early in his tenure of office Mr. W. H. Smith, foregoing the luxury of dining in Grosvenor Place, had a chop or a cut off the joint served in his room behind the Speaker's chair, eating it staff in hand and his loins girded as if the banquet were a Passover meal. He was always ready to rush into the House at sound of the division bell or on the arrival of a messenger with news of gathering complications.

In the cases of Mr. Disraeli and Mr. Gladstone, it must be remembered that, in addition to the cares of Leadership, they bore all the burden of the State on their shoulders. As Prime Minister, their anxious labours began with the mail on the breakfast-table, were pursued throughout the day, and when they took their seat on the Treasury bench they had already accomplished a task sufficient for the strength of a more than ordinary man. Yet it was but the prelude to a further course of from eight to ten hours' delicate work, performed in the fullest blaze of light that beats on public men, and in the presence of the most critical assembly in the world. Mr. Disraeli's Premiership, combined with the Leadership of the House of Commons, was marked by times compared with which those the House of Commons now drones through are midday siestas.

In addition to struggling against the growing force and aggressiveness of the newly-born Home Rule Party, the Leader of the 1874-80 House of Commons was confronted by the danger of Europe ablaze with war and Northern India in revolt. Later, Mr. Gladstone, beyond the Irish Land Bills and Coercion Bills, had Egypt and a war in South Africa on his hands.

Finally, the conditions under which, at these times, work was possible in the House of Commons were wholly different.

Procedure had not then been simplified, nor the authority of
the Chair strengthened, and, above all, there was not the
sweet certainty that, come what may, debate must, in ordinary
circumstances, close on the stroke of midnight. The Leader
of the present House of Commons may be, and it is to be
hoped often is, in bed at an hour when, in Mr. Disraeli's time,
and through Mr. Gladstone's last Leadership, the battle was
only beginning, with fair promise of continuance till break of
day. In such times and amid such manners these earlier
leaders, handicapped with the weight of nearly double Mr.
Balfour's years, contrived to be in their places when the
stream of questions began to flow. Mr. Balfour regards his
duty from a different point of view, lounging in when
questions are almost over, and then delegating to his colleagues
the task of answering those personally addressed to him.

To-night, when he returned after one of these absences,
upon which Mr. Dillon had meanwhile bitterly remarked, he
was hailed with ironical cheers from the Irish members.
Time was when this demonstration would have been met and
overpowered by a thunderous cheer from the Ministerialists.
To-night they made no response. It is, perhaps, a trifling
thing, not meriting the increasing attention growling round it
in the Commons. But small errors of conduct are sometimes
more fatal to success in high places than are breaches of the
Decalogue.

CHAPTER XLIV.

HARD TIMES FOR IRISH MEMBERS.

Mr. Gladstone nearing 83—His Personal Ascendency—His Second Speech—
"Gladstone's Up!"—Alphons Choophas—The Cue for the Closure—Mr.
Marjoribanks' Hobby—The Wearing of the Green—Changed Times—
Mr. Newton—Prison Experiences.

March 3.—Mr. Gladstone nearing 83.   THERE is a temptation to say of succeeding
speeches by Mr. Gladstone that the one just de-
livered is equal to any in the long series. This
tendency is justifiable on the ground that when a man has
passed the age of eighty any successful oratorical effort is a

marvel. That consideration apart, it must be admitted that his speech of Thursday night on the vote for the Mombasa Nyanza Railway was an effort which, had it stood alone, would

have established a Parliamentary reputation. It was a *tour de force* both intellectually and physically. Those who most widely differ from Mr. Gladstone in the view he takes of the question at issue may well be the loudest in their praises, since

to them comes the added marvel that having so little to work
upon he made it appear so much.

The night's oration, with its thrilling energy, lightning-like
brilliancy, and thunderous force, had the advantage of contrast with an afternoon's speech of widely distinct character.
The earlier effort was made upon the proposal submitted by
Mr. Balfour to take morning sittings on Tuesdays and Fridays
throughout the remainder of a Session just entered upon.
Private members (who so recently as Tuesday had testified to
the high value they place upon their possession by allowing
the House to be counted out at eight o'clock) were properly
aghast at the First Lord's audacity. Had Sir William
Harcourt still been in the place of the Leader of the Opposition he would have seized with alacrity upon this opportunity of illustrating the fact that the first duty of that
personage is to oppose. Champions of the privileges of private
members would have risen in all parts of the House to protest
against this new and unprecedented invasion of their rights.
Angry passions would have been aroused, half the sitting
wasted, a division taken, and morning sittings for the remainder
of the Session would have been decreed. The accident of Mr.
Gladstone's presence entirely changed the scene, and gave an
important turn to the issue.

His personal as-
cendency.
When he presented himself at the table he was
welcomed with an enthusiastic and prolonged
cheer, which testified to his final and absolute ascendency in
the House of Commons, achieved after many vicissitudes. It
was some moments before he found opportunity to speak.
After the thunder-clap of applause that had welcomed him his
voice sounded singularly musical. It is one of the signs of the
marvellous resuscitation of health completed during his sojourn by the Mediterranean that his voice has regained all its
rich organ-like tone.

Occasionally, when Mr. Gladstone assumes this attitude of
benignancy, and his voice in the opening sentences is sweet and
low, somebody chiefly concerned in what he has to say begins
to feel particularly uncomfortable. Often this attitude is the
prelude to a more than usually bitter attack. Mr. Balfour,
whose acquaintance with the Old Parliamentary Hand is

intimate and peculiar, looked uneasily across the table at the stately supple figure, with head slightly inclined in courteous reference to him in his new position as Leader of the House. This was all very well to begin with. But how would it end?

It ended very much as it had commenced, except perhaps with growing graciousness of manner and with notes of kindlier courtesy in the voice. It was, truly, Mr. Gladstone admitted—turning half in acquiescence towards his enthusiastic supporters, petrified now into silence at this unexpected attitude—a large order to come forward at the close of the third week of a Session and ask for morning sittings on Tuesdays and Fridays through all that was left of it. If the right hon. gentleman had asked for the concession up to Easter it would be a different thing. Mr. Gladstone, in this melting mood, would not do anything to embarrass gentlemen opposite, would not even move the amendment he had written out and deprecatingly held in his hand. He did not give utterance to the delicate thought everyone saw in the benevolent visage bent upon Mr. Balfour, that if he formally moved the amendment and the Government accepted it, it would be equivalent to something like a defeat. That he would not bring about by any means. Rather he would build a golden bridge for the adversary to retreat over, a convenience Mr. Balfour promptly accepted. And so, almost before the amazed Ministerialists and the still petrified Opposition had quite mastered the situation, it was amicably adjusted, and morning sittings up to Easter were placed at the disposal of the Government.

His second speech.

This was in the afternoon. Ere midnight struck "Linden saw another sight." When Mr. Gladstone was an older man, say last Session, he was ever careful to arrange matters so that when he took part in debate his speech should be delivered before the dinner-hour, he being thereafter free from the necessity of reappearing. Now that he is younger by the lapse of a year—for in his case the order of nature seems reversed—he is able to discard those precautions against fatigue, and rises to speak on the approach of midnight, as was his wont about the epoch of the Great Exhibition. It was ten minutes past eleven when he interposed in the debate on the vote to cover the cost of survey for the

proposed Mombasa railway. What he had to say must needs
be compressed within fifty minutes, since in these degenerate
days debate automatically closes at midnight. He pathetically
alluded to this condition at the outset of his remarks. "A
predicament" he called it. But it was one that happily
contributed to the success of his speech. There was no time
for diffusiveness or any beating about the bush. If it was
to be brought down within the allotted space of time the axe
must be driven at the root with every blow, and Mr. Gladstone set himself to the task with an energy that thrilled the
crowded House.

"Gladstone's up!" Hitherto, almost without exception since the
Session opened, the pulse of life has beat lan-
guidly at Westminster. Now it throbbed through every
artery. The cry "Gladstone's up!" echoed through the lobbies
and ran along the corridors. At sound of it smoking-room,
reading-room, all were deserted. Within a few minutes every
bench on the floor of the House had its occupant, and a throng
stood at the Bar, all eyes fixed upon the lithe figure at the
table carrying its burden of fourscore years as if it were a
featherweight. It is a long time since even Mr. Gladstone
held an audience so completely enthralled as he did through
this vigorous speech. The Opposition cheered incessantly,
whilst the Ministerialists, unconvinced, paid manifest tribute
to the masterful orator.

In the papers laid on the table relating to the proposed
survey was a letter from Sir Guilford Molesworth, in which he
makes reference to "the accompanying map." "There is no
accompanying map!" Mr. Gladstone cried, taking up the
unoffending Blue Book, seeming to scorch its cover with the
flash of indignation that blazed from his eyes. "Why is there
no accompanying map?" he thundered, bending over the
trembling table towards the shrinking forms of Mr. Balfour
and Mr. Goschen. That is an interrogation by which some
speakers would naturally sink to the level of bathos, inevitably
eliciting a shout of laughter. As Mr. Gladstone declaimed the
inquiry the effect upon the audience was even more striking
than when Mrs. Siddons in deepest tragedy tone once at a
dinner-table asked, "Where is the salt?" It is probable that

if at the moment he spoke there had been spread on the wall
behind him, as appears in committee rooms upstairs during
inquiries into railway projects, the very map he was asking for,
no one would have dared by calling his attention to the circumstance to break the spell that bound the House.

March 18.— When, in these days, debate in the House of
Alpheus Cleophas. Commons, having gone forward on devious lines
for several hours, seems to be reaching the end, there is invariably discovered standing below the gangway a tall, lean
figure with pale face steadily set towards the Chair. Attention is called to the new comer by a roar of execration
from the benches opposite. The hon. member seems to
have expected this, and accepts it as a part of the ordinary
Parliamentary proceedings. He does not attempt to stem the
current of contumely which dashes against him. He waits
till the force has spent itself, and then, in quiet voice, with
manner absolutely free from emotion, he calls attention to the
refreshment bar in the lobby, to the contract for the Parliamentary debates, or to the most recent development of the
native iniquity of the Home Secretary. This is Mr. Alpheus
Cleophas Morton, successor to the late Mr. Whalley in the
representation of Peterborough, an architect, a Common
Councilman of the City of London, a member of the City
Commission of Sewers, and a member of the Wandsworth
District Board of Works. It is a marvel how a man of affairs
so important and so diverse in their interest can manage to
devote so much time to Parliamentary duties. There is
sometimes an uneasy feeling in the House of Commons that
he is giving up to Imperial affairs what was meant for the
City Commission of Sewers. But that is their affair. It
suffices for the House to know that Alpheus Cleophas is
always with it, ready at any moment to interpose and
endeavour to give a fresh start to debate which, going forward
from one hour up to four, is evidently dying from sheer
inanition.

Alpheus Cleophas conducts his Parliamentary campaign on
clearly defined and admirably carried out principles. He is
the reserve force of Obstruction, and never wastes his strength
unnecessarily. He sits, as it were, on the pallid bust of Pallas

over against the chamber door, and just when the Minister in charge of a vote thinks he is at last about to get it he is startled by the croak " Never more!" and sinks back with a groan of despair. For a man who is fond of hearing himself talk and can go on indefinitely, like a tap drawing on the resources of the New River, it requires no small measure of self-control and trained discipline to remain silent by the hour waiting till everyone else is worn out, assisting at that nicely measured pause which gives the Speaker or Chairman opportunity of rising to put the question, and interposing not the billionth part of a second too soon or too late, and setting the ball rolling again. The weird influence Alpheus Cleophas exercises over the strongest forces of the House is as curious as it is unmistakable. He has behind him no social influence, nor any position won at the University or in other fields where men labour. He is not a born orator like Mr. Picton, nor has he the winning manner of Dr. Clark. This leads to the creation of a certain prejudice against him, which finds utterance in the moans, groans, and other evidences of acute personal suffering his appearance on the scene invariably elicits.

The cue for the Closure. Yet, somehow, the House refrains from adopting the implement lying to its hand, use of which would deliver it from the visitation. Mr. Conybeare's proposals to join in debate are received with manifestations much akin to those that greet Alpheus Cleophas. But in his case they are invariably the prelude to action. His appearance is as regularly followed by application of the Closure as night succeeds day. In the newspaper reports of the proceedings of Thursday, for example, there regularly appears at brief intervals the line " Mr. Conybeare was speaking when Mr. Balfour moved the Closure." It has come to be quite an automatic process. In theatrical parlance, Mr. Conybeare is the cue for the Closure. As soon as he appears on the stage the Leader of the House instinctively rises, and his lips involuntarily form the words—" I move that the question be now put." Personally this may be hard upon Mr. Conybeare. But he may at least cherish the assurance that when the accounts of the Session come to be made up, it will

appear that he has contributed more to the immediate settlement of current questions than any man in the House.
Alpheus Cleophas may have his compensatory reflections. But
they cannot include the credit of relieving the tedium of long-
drawn-out debate by the promptly invoked variety of a division.

March 22.—Mr. Marjoribanks' hobby. There are few men more charming in social life than Mr. Marjoribanks, and none more popular in the House of Commons. But, really, when
he appears at the table and lays upon it the new magazine
rifle members agree it is time to clear out. Last Session he
succeeded in endowing the subject with adventitious interest
by bringing down to the House a collection of arms of
precision, with which he stocked the Whips' Room. It was
reported that that sanctuary bore the appearance rather of a
place of arms than of an office where the affairs of an important but peaceful political party are overlooked. Persons
entering it on business were always afraid of something "going
off." Eventually (so common report ran at the time) Mr.
Marjoribanks was induced to remove his armament only upon
receipt of a Round Robin signed by his unnerved colleagues.

However that may be, it is certain that the hon. gentleman, having got his battery as far as the Whips' Room, was
to-night ready and anxious to bring a selection up to the table
of the House and there demonstrate his thesis. That would
have been an interesting and attractive performance, more
especially for those seated in the direction of the butt-end of
the rifle. But prejudice prevailed against enthusiasm, and
before getting up on his legs Mr. Marjoribanks was obliged to
lay down his arms. Deprived of the advantage of illustrating
his object lesson, weighed down by the prevailing atmosphere,
and handicapped by the admission, frankly made, that it was
the same lecture he had delivered last Session, Mr. Marjoribanks
did not in any appreciable degree contribute to the gaiety of
the sitting.

March 23.—The wearing of the green. The only gleam of sunlight shimmering through the heavy mist of depression that whelmed the morning sitting was contributed
by Private O'Grady of the Welsh Fusiliers. This now famous

soldier and his conversation on parade with his commanding officer had been formally brought to the knowledge of the House at the previous sitting. Mr. Stanhope had then read the report of the Colonel in command of the battalion, showing how Private O'Grady, mustering for duty on St. Patrick's morn, had been detected by the keen eye of his captain "wearing a bunch of green" in his cap, and had been ordered to remove it.

It was curious to note how, when the Secretary of State for War read thus far in the despatch, the crowded house bent forward with eager attention, expectant of Private O'Grady's response. Although Captain Tindal did not recognise the greenery, and was oblivious of the anniversary, the House of Commons well knew it was the shamrock the gallant Irishman sported in honour of the name-day of St. Patrick. Everyone expected Mr. Stanhope would go on to describe how Private O'Grady thus challenged stepped forward and, respectfully saluting, said: "When laws can kape the blades of grass from growin' as they grow, And when the leaves in summer-time their colour dare not show, Then I will change the colour that I wear in my caubeen; But till that day, plase God, I'll pray for the wearin' o' the green."

Probably these observations leaped to the lips of Private O'Grady as they lingered in the memory of the listening House. A shade of disappointment fell over the Irish members when they discovered that Private O'Grady had let slip this magnificent opportunity. He had simply, though emphatically, replied, "I'll not do't." On reflection it was perceived that this amounted to the same thing. It was a brief summary in prose of the sentiment of the musical melodious verse, and the Irish members, quickly recognising the fact, cheered again and again, almost rising in their seats with enthusiastic applause when Mr. Stanhope, proceeding with the reading of the despatch, told how Private O'Grady, taken in the rear by a non-commissioned officer, preferring a similar request, sternly repeated his watchword, "I'll not do't."

Changed times.   To the Irish members this springing up of the shamrock has been an unlooked-for mercy, tho discovery of a spring of running water in a thirsty land. The

Session, as far as it has gone, has been to them a dreary blank. They can make nothing out of Mr. Jackson, and Mr. Balfour is no longer their peculiar property. Racked by dissensions within, they have been deprived of opportunity of combined attack on the common enemy without. Mr. Tim Healy lingers in Ireland, arranging the amalgamation of morning newspapers. Mr. John Dillon, everyone is sorry to know, is confined to his house by the results of an accident. Mr. O'Brien, the ghost of his former self, forlornly hovers about the benches below the gangway, and on Monday, dissatisfied with an answer from the Treasury bench, announced his intention of "calling attention to the subject in Committee of Supply." That is the old familiar formula. But there was a hollow ring in the voice, a depression in the attitude, that marked the vast change that has taken place since yester year. Mr. O'Brien has never been the same man since he waved a damp pocket-handkerchief across the sympathetic Atlantic, no one being quite sure whether the friendly signal was meant for Mr. Parnell or for the men who had at the time taken their discredited leader by the throat in Committee Room No. 15. Attempting to sit on two stools, Mr. O'Brien finds himself forlornly seated on the ground, with no immediate prospect of getting up again.

Mr. Sexton.   Only Mr. Sexton is left, and it must be said to his credit that he does all a single tongue may do to strike the average of loquacity. Not nominally the leader of any section of the Irish Party, he is ready to answer for all. It was Colonel Nolan who discovered and played the trump card of Private O'Grady. But before the game had gone far the gallant Colonel was elbowed aside, and Mr. Sexton stood in the front, the representative of the implacable, un-purchasable Irishmen, righteously wrath at this fresh felon blow at his bleeding country. Irish members with com-paratively limited vision, like Mr. Flynn and Mr. Webb, are content to make long speeches about wronged post-mistresses on the Irish Establishment, bridges that ought to be built in Galway, or streams that should be dammed in County Cork. Mr. Sexton's more comprehensive mind and riper energy take the whole universe in his personal charge. Sure to deliver a prodigious speech on any question relating to Ireland, he may be counted upon for a few remarks on whatever subject comes before the House, ranging from China to Peru.

He has of late constituted himself in peculiar manner the guardian of law and order in Parliamentary procedure. Just as Sir William Harcourt has no chance of posing as the spokesman of the Opposition when Mr. Sexton is in his place, so is the Speaker being edged out of his chair by this new authority. Having corrected the grammar of a resolution decreeing the expulsion of one member, he stepped forward to instruct the House how it should proceed in the matter of the expulsion of a second. In this case he came in direct conflict with the Chair, a situation from which an old member like Mr. Gladstone carefully shrinks, or, finding himself approaching it by accident, deferentially withdraws. In the Hastings case Mr. Sexton calmly ignored the Speaker's dignified and more than usually emphatic ruling, insisted upon having his suggestion formally put as an amendment, and had the satisfaction of seeing it negatived, not a single voice being raised in its support.

Mar. 30.—Prison experiences. It is said Mr. Cuninghame Graham has prepared a lecture entitled "Six Weeks at Pentonville," being his experiences in gaol, whither he was, five years ago, sent in connection with the riots at Trafalgar Square. Mr. Graham is accustomed to regard that episode as one of the proudest events of his life; and, if his lecture prove as

CUNINGHAME GRAHAM.

interesting as his talk on the subject, he should make a success. He speaks of the epoch without bitterness. At first he found

the food unattractive and insufficient, but grew accustomed to
it, as he did to the prison dress. This was at least clean,
and it gratified his democratic instincts, inasmuch as all were
clothed exactly alike. He was, during his stay at Pentonville,
an object of keen and friendly interest to his fellow prisoners,
who liked to have the common standard of respectability
heightened by the arrival of a real member of Parliament.
Once in chapel, when the prayer for the High Court of
Parliament was read in the Litany, a burglar, seated by him,
nudged him in the ribs with his elbow, and winked at him as
who should say, " There you are, old pal. We're a praying for
you."

For a long time after his release Mr. Graham was subject
to embarrassing attentions from other manumitted criminals,
who had chanced to be " in " at the same time with him.
Recognition was not always mutual, and in course of time the
aggregate number seemed to exceed the total population of the
prison during the six weeks he was there. A peculiarity of the
conversation was that it invariably closed with the suggestion
thrown out by Mr. Graham's interlocutor that he would like,
just for the sake of old times, to drink the hon. member's
health.

—

CHAPTER XLV.

AT THE BAR OF THE HOUSE.

A Stirring Night—Stationmaster Hood—Mr M. Bench's Mistake—The real
Leader of the House—Revolt below the Gangway—An Irish Orator—In
Committee of Supply—Mr. Gladstone and Mr. Balfour—Mr. Blanc—
Speeches heard and read—A great Speech—The Tories and Mr. Gladstone
—Mr. Chamberlain's Friends.

April 8.—A
stirring night.
It is the fashion to speak of the present House
of Commons as moribund, and, truly, to observe
it at any period since it met in February has been sufficient
to secure acquiescence in the description. Looking upon it
a few hours ago, when the chime of midnight heralded the
approach of a new day, one felt there is life in the old dog

yet. Every bench was crowded. Members, finding no room elsewhere, sat on the gangway steps, whilst Ministers and ex-Ministers clustered on the steps of the Speaker's chair, as if they were engaged in forming a group for an enterprising photographer. The side galleries were thronged with members—a rare, sure sign of the highest pitch of excitement; whilst in the Strangers' Gallery the fortunate persons who had obtained admission were packed tier on tier, some of them sitting there without change of position, food, or drink for the full space of ten hours.

The incentive to this great gathering, the cause of this throbbing excitement, seemed scarcely adequate to the effect. It was, for example, not nearly so important as the vote in Committee of Supply upon which turns the policy and administration of the Army and Navy through the coming year, a business disposed of a few nights ago in the presence of some thirty listless members. It was the proceedings in a breach of privilege case that these people had come out for to see, and breaches of privilege import those personal aspects that ever prove irresistible to the House of Commons.

Stationmaster Hood.   There has been sitting for some time a Select Committee appointed to consider the question

of the hours of labour of railway servants. Last year there appeared in the witnesses' chair a man named Hood, a stationmaster on the Cambrian Railway. Evidence was drawn from him showing the existence in the service of some hard lines other than those upon which the trains run. There had been a railway accident, and Stationmaster Hood told how the signalman concerned was sometimes called upon to be at his post for thirty-six hours at a stretch. The Select Committee adjourned for the recess, met again for the new Session, and learned that in the meantime Hood, who had been in the service of the Cambrian Railway Company for more than twenty years, had been summarily dismissed, obviously as a consequence of the evidence he had given before the Committee. This was a serious matter as affecting the scope and usefulness of Parliamentary inquiry. The circumstances were investigated by the Committee, and a report was agreed upon calling the attention of the House to the breach of privilege.

Sir M. Beach's mistake. This did not of itself account for the crowded House and the animated proceedings which made the sometimes prosaic chamber fuller of dramatic interest than the ordinary theatre. It was swiftly perceived that underlying the transaction was the great question of the relations of master and man, much to the fore just now in anticipation of the General Election. Here was a great railway corporation resolved to put down anything like an attempt on the part of their workmen to appeal to Cæsar at Westminster on the question of long or short hours of labour. The position was accentuated by the blundering conduct of Sir M. H. Beach, who as chairman of the Select Committee had charge of the affair in the House of Commons. He began badly by endeavouring to postpone the hearing of the privilege case till alleged *laches* of a similar character committed by what he called "the other side" should be ready for simultaneous examination. The Amalgamated Association of Railway Servants had been parties to the inquiry before the Select Committee, and it was said that they also, offended by evidence given by two of their servants, had got rid of them. The too astute Sir Michael, thinking to play off man against master, proposed to defer proceedings in the House till they should stand side by side at the Bar. This manœuvre led to an angry scene on Monday night, with the result that the President of the Board of Trade was obliged to withdraw his proposal and hasten on the action against the Cambrian directors. Not profiting by this warning, he, in his speech last night, showed himself so tender towards the feelings of the railway directors that, as Sir George Trevelyan said, it was with something of surprise the House heard him conclude even with the studiously moderate resolution that the directors had been guilty of a breach of privilege, and should be called in and admonished by Mr. Speaker.

When Sir Michael Beach sat down the storm burst. The Radicals below the gangway insisted on an amendment calling upon the directors either to reinstate Hood or to compensate him for dismissal. The Chamber, through long weeks a scene of decorous dulness, became transformed into a veritable Babel. Members shouted at each other across the floor, jeered at Ministers, and loudly laughed at the portentous ceremony

of drawing forth from unsuspected receptacles the brass poles
which appear only once or twice in the history of a Parliament,
and, meeting across the gangway, form its veritable Bar.

The real Leader of the House. At the end of two hours' wrangle a mighty
cheer went up from the Opposition, and then a
dead silence fell on the crowded House. Mr. Gladstone was
discovered standing at the table, and passion was hushed in
anxiety to hear what he should say. It was an opportunity
that an ordinary leader of the Opposition—say Lord Randolph
Churchill or Mr. Arthur Balfour—might have been expected
to find irresistibly drawing him in one direction. The Minister
in charge of the business had woefully blundered. The
question had direct bearing on the General Election. Amid
the stillness that prefaced Mr. Gladstone's opening sentence
you could almost hear the murmur of the multitude of workmen listening at the doors, waiting to learn whether, as their
spokesmen below the gangway had put it, even-handed justice
was to be dealt out as between their employers and them. It
would have been so easy for Mr. Gladstone to have made
things uncommonly awkward for the Government, to have led
on the cheering pack below the gangway, and have won by a
speech the innumerable working-man vote. To do otherwise
was for one in his position as difficult as the task Socrates
depicts for the orator called upon to praise Athenians among
Peloponnesians, or Peloponnesians among Athenians. Mr.
Gladstone did not seem even to be aware of the existence of
the temptation. He is, above all things, a Parliamentarian,
jealous of the privileges of the House of Commons, resolved
to vindicate them, but anxious that it should be done with
dignity and with a deference to justice, untainted by passion
or prejudice. He doubtless had his opinion about Sir Michael
Beach's speech and his general bearing throughout the episode.
What the House had to deal with was the resolution submitted
to it, and that he showed, in a brief speech worthy of the
highest traditions of Parliamentary debate, was adequate and
in accordance with precedent.

Revolt below the gangway. This settled the matter as far as the main issue
was concerned. But the angry party below the

gangway broke away from their leader, when they found him differing from them, and hour after hour through the long night the fierce fire flamed.   Through it all passed, at stated times and in due and decorous order, the movements of the quaint comedy of procedure in privilege cases.   One of the accused directors was a member of the House, and was permitted to appear in his place.   The other three attended in the outer lobby, unmanacled, but conscious of the concentrated gaze of a dozen policemen and attendants posted at various coigns of vantage.

" Let the directors be called in," said the Speaker when the Order of the Day for consideration of the special report was reached.

The Serjeant-at-Arms, approaching the table, shouldered the Mace and went forth in search of the culprits.   Meanwhile, two attendants advanced to the cross-benches by the doorway and drew forth the Bar.   Presently the Serjeant-at-Arms, with the great Mace gleaming on his shoulder, appeared with the three prisoners in custody.   It was noted, with that delighted appreciation a habitually bored House discovers in odd details, that one of the directors had brought with him an umbrella in one hand and his hat in the other, which gave him quite a morning-caller appearance, grotesquely out of keeping with the solemnity of the scene and the dignity of the Mace borne aloft by the Serjeant-at-Arms.   The directors, having apologised and set down something in extenuation, were ordered to withdraw.   Then followed the long discussion, interspersed with exciting divisions.   Seven hours later, what was left of the depressed and storm-beaten directors was again brought up to the Bar, where they limply stood, whilst the Speaker, with awful mien and terrible voice, " most seriously admonished " them.

April 9. — An Irish orator.   Mr. Alexander Blane, member for South Armagh, is, perhaps, the only member of the House of Commons who invests a debate with reminiscences of antique oratorical gesture possibly familiar in the times of Demosthenes. If it has a fault, the prejudice of the day might urge that it smacks of the cheval glass.   In dull times between the seasons, when the nobility and gentry of Armagh are withholding orders

in anticipation of the arrival of newer fashion plates, one can
picture the hon. member alone in his establishment in Scotch
Street posing before the long glass and studying various
gestures wherewith, when the Session opens, he may the
better confound Mr. Balfour or strike terror into the soul
of Sir William Harcourt. Sometimes, if criticism be further
permitted, there is a lack of unity between the slow scornful
gesture of the right arm and the remark Mr. Blane is at the
moment making. It is said of an hon. member below the
gangway, whose interposition on questions of Imperial policy
are frequent and familiar, that his voice and all his gestures
are too big for him, that they were made for a man at least
six feet high, and were by some strange freak of Nature
conferred upon him. In the case of Mr. Blane the principle
of disproportion is not carried out in this wholesale and retail
manner. It is only when he rises to move for " Unopposed
Return No. 2," or to make some cognate remark, that the
impressive uplifting of the right elbow, the slow stretching
forth of the right hand, and the subtle indication of desire to
snap indignant thumb against scornful forefinger, seem as if
they belong to another speech.

In Committee of
Supply.   Mr. Blane's interposition in debate to-day followed upon Mr. Labouchere's inquiry as to
Ministerial intentions in respect of the dissolution. The vote
under discussion was that for the sustentation of the Royal
Palaces and Marlborough House. It did not at first blush
seem to lead up naturally to thoughts of dissolution. But an
old Parliamentary hand like Mr. Labouchere knows how to
bring his remarks within the limits of regulated debate. The
member for Northampton is nothing if not constitutional. He
came down bristling with precedents, requiring, firstly, that
Mr. Balfour should give a pledge that in the event of the
dissolution being postponed till September, October, or
November, a Bill should be introduced accelerating the
process of registration, so that the General Election should
take place on the new register. Further, he required that
whenever the dissolution took place, Parliament should
forthwith be summoned.

It was pretty to watch Mr Balfour's air of startled

surprise that this topic should have been suddenly sprung upon the House. They were gathered together with the ostensible purpose of considering the details of expenditure in the matter of the Royal Palaces. At the outset this natural condition of affairs had prevailed. Mr. Labouchere himself had, as it were, personally gone over Marlborough House and Buckingham Palace, tapping the drains, seeing that the windows were properly glazed, and that there had been no overflow in the bath-rooms. Mr. Alpheus Cleophas Morton had generously proposed that Buckingham Palace or Kensington Palace, he really didn't seem to care which, should be set aside for the purposes of a British gallery of art. Mr. Storey—*O Richard, O mon roi, L'univers t'abandonne!*—had genially observed that the Prince of Wales and the rest of the Royal Family were well able to pay for the maintenance of their residences, and it was shabby of them not only to take their palaces free, but to sponge upon the public to keep them in repair. Mr. Plunket had met these various objections with mingled courtesy and humour that disarmed everybody but Alpheus Cleophas, who, rising again and again, insisted upon knowing why Holyrood Palace, in which he told the Committee "he took a strong interest," was not kept in repair.

Mr. Gladstone
and Mr. Balfour.

Even Alpheus Cleophas was at length, though only temporarily, silenced, and on a division the proposed reduction of the vote was negatived. Then, when it seemed the vote might be passed, Mr. Labouchere came to the front with his constitutional question, plunging Mr. Balfour into the condition of puzzled surprise above noted. The First Lord of the Treasury had really nothing to say on the interesting subject broached. He was charmingly ignorant of historical facts bearing upon it. But taking, as he said, history from Mr. Labouchere, he was not able to find in the precedents cited any way to the conclusions arrived at in the amiable speech they had just listened to. Indeed, they led him in an exactly opposite direction.

Mr. Gladstone followed, and a quickened interest was manifested in the crowded assembly. Mr. Balfour's brief speech was exceedingly clever. He had appeared to reply to the

interpellation from the other side, and yet had said nothing—
sometimes the highest form of Ministerial speech. If Mr.
Gladstone chose to protest against its light, airy manner, and
insist on some definite declaration, the Opposition would only
too gladly take the cue, and an angry debate would follow.
Mr. Gladstone was, however, as he has been since his return
from sunny climes, in most benignant mood. He threw the
cloak of his supreme authority over the Minister, at the same
time dexterously managing to avoid irritation among his own
followers by suggesting that, though this might not be the
time to press for an answer to the questions put by Mr.
Labouchere, the time would surely come.

Mr. Blane   It was after attentively listening to this debate
               on constitutional practices, participated in by
eminent authorities, that Mr. Blane was moved to speech. He
desired to widen the scope of controversy by cross-examining
right hon. gentlemen on the front Opposition bench. Mr.
Labouchere had confined his questioning to the Ministers of
the day. Mr. Blane's keen perception glanced beyond this
limit, and his logical mind led him on to discuss a further
stage of the question opened up. It was tacitly and
generally admitted that the General Election would lead to
the installation of a new Ministry, and, as Mr. Blane said, it
was much more important to know what they would do in
certain relations than to ascertain what the present Government thought.

"Not," Mr. Blane added, bringing forth his right arm
with stately sweep, "that we care what Government is in
power after the General Election, regarding them only as they
may be of use to us."

Here Mr. Courtney interposed with gentle reminder that
this was straying somewhat beyond the scope of the question
before the House. Mr. Blane gazed silently and reproachfully
at the Chairman of Committees, making a movement with his
eloquent right arm that said things otherwise unutterable.
After a pause he went on again, resuming with professional
skill the thread of his discourse. His prophetic eye beheld
Mr. Gladstone seated on the Treasury bench after the General
Election, once more engaged upon the task of endeavouring

to settle Irish questions in conformity with British opinion and without estranging Irish allies. Catching sight of Mr. Gladstone (at present on the front Opposition bench) intently listening, Mr. Blane leaned forward as if to whisper in his ear. "We shall be hard taskmasters," he said, not without pleasing anticipation of days to come. The Conservatives cheered jubilantly at the prospect thus opened up; but Mr. Courtney, who resembles Heaven inasmuch as Order is his first law, again interrupted with increased sternness of manner. There was another pause on the part of the orator, who regarded the Chairman of Committees with some such look as he might have bestowed upon an importunate customer who twice in a season had made unfounded complaint of a misfit.

Thus again recalled to the question before the House, namely, that a vote of £20,850 be granted to Her Majesty for the supply and maintenance of the Royal Palaces and Marlborough House, Mr. Blane lapsed into a few comparatively inconsequential remarks bearing on Kew Gardens and the rapacity of turncocks at Windsor Castle. But this was only a parenthesis forced upon him by the scholastic discipline of the Chairman of Committees. Suddenly, without preface, and with one of his most majestic gestures, he said, "What we want to know is about the policy of the next Government—" Mr. Courtney was on his feet in a moment, and the Committee looked for the fall of the inevitable blow. The recalcitrant member, if he escaped the dire penalty of "naming," must surely be ordered to resume his seat. Before Mr. Courtney could open his mouth to deliver the judgment that evidently trembled on his lips, Mr. Blane, again leaning forward, as he had earlier bent over Mr. Gladstone, continued,"—— the policy of the next Government *about the vote now under discussion.*"

The House shouted with laughter at the happy turn that thus snatched the opportunity from the Chairman as he was in the act of reaching out his hand to seize it. It was some minutes before silence was restored, Mr. Blane meanwhile standing impassive, his arms now drooped at his side, his face wearing an aspect of gravity that gave the last touch to the humour of the situation. When the uproar ceased he went on again discussing the details of the vote, the crowded House watching and waiting for the inevitable head of Charles the First to reappear. Presently it peeped forth from under the orator's arms. Mr. Courtney, not again to be baffled, brought his ferrule sharply down on its pate, and Mr. Blane having resumed his seat when the Chairman rose, kept it, content that his sentence, like "the unfinished window in Aladdin's tower, unfinished must remain."

April 10.—
Speeches heard
and read.

Some speeches delivered in the House of Commons have fuller effect when read in the newspaper columns, whilst others suffer little from the change of medium of communication. In the former category were the speeches Lord Hartington was wont to deliver whilst yet he sat in the Commons. They were distinctly better to read than to hear. The reader who had also heard them was, indeed, sometimes surprised to find how lucid was the arrangement and how weighty the argument. Lord Hartington, at his best, never added to the liveliness of the House of Commons. But, to do him justice, no one was ever so bored with his speeches as he looked whilst he delivered them. Free from the weight of his personal depression, the ear not offended by the unmusical voice, and not wearied by constant effort to catch the full syllables of the conclusion of sentences, the student of Lord Hartington's Parliamentary speeches had full opportunity to realise the value of the sagacity and insight into public affairs which distinguished them.

Mr. Chamberlain's speeches come within the second and more fortunate category. It is an intellectual pleasure either to hear or to read them. The pleasure is, of course, the greater when one comes within the charm of a singularly clear voice and a perfect enunciation. But those who have not the opportunity of hearing the speeches may be well content to read a verbatim report. The same remark applies to Sir William Harcourt, and even with greater force to Mr. John Morley, who is often better to read than to listen to. Sir William Harcourt like Mr. Chamberlain inasmuch as his speeches read well, is also like him in adding in the delivery much to their force and charm.

A great speech.   Mr. Gladstone is the one living orator to whom no report, however faithful may be the transcript, can do justice. How true this is will be felt by those who, having had the good fortune to hear his speech in the House of Commons this afternoon, turn to read the report in the morning papers. For those who first make its acquaintance through the latter medium, it may, happily, appear impossible of improvement. They will recognise its lightness of touch, its sting, and its absolute felicity of phrasing. They will miss the picturesque figure, the richly modulated voice, and the dramatic, though natural, gestures. Also there will be lacking the scene in which the little comedy was set, the crowded House; the laughing faces all turned upon the orator; Mr. Chamberlain trying to smile back on the benevolent visage bent over him with just a flash of malice in the gleaming eyes; and, so that no touch might be missing to complete the perfectness of the scene just behind Mr. Chamberlain, sitting well forward on the bench, with folded arms and honest face broadened to a grin of perhaps qualified appreciation, Mr. Jesse Collings, "the hon. member for Bordesley, the faithful henchman of my right hon. friend, who would cordially re-echo that *or any other opinion*."

Mr. Gladstone has often, in various ways, delighted the House of Commons, sometimes stirring its emotions to its profoundest depths, often compelling its admiration by either skilfully evading an argument or irresistibly grappling with it. But it may safely be averred that never within recent memory has he suffused the House with such keen delight as moved it this afternoon. So uncontrollable was the laughter on the Liberal benches that it occasionally marred some of the points, breaking in too soon on an unfinished sentence. That was reasonable enough, and fully to be expected. The pleasure Mr. Gladstone's gently scathing speech gave on that side of the House was not purely intellectual. There was joy over the lost sinner in a sense quite other than that pertaining to the phrase in its original application. As Edgar Allan Poe loved his Annabel Lee "with a love that was more than love," so they hate their lost leader with a hate that is more than hate. Singly or in battalion, they are impotent against him in debate. There are, in truth, only three men in the House of Commons who can measure swords with Mr. Chamberlain, and here was the greatest of all slashing and cutting with infinite grace and skill, with effect all the greater because the onslaught was free from the slightest display of brutal force. Fighting practically single-handed, Mr. Chamberlain has held his own in the House of Commons through six turbulent Sessions. Now at last he was "getting it."

The Tories and Mr. Gladstone.   The merriment on the Opposition benches was natural enough, notable only for its exuberance. The aspect of hon. gentlemen watching the sport from the other side of the House was more interesting. They have had occasion more than once this Session—the memory of Thursday night was still fresh in their minds—to acknowledge Mr. Gladstone's ability and tendency to rise above considerations of party tactics, and stand before the House as the embodiment of its highest traditions, its most ennobling principles. There were some present who remembered the early Sessions of the Parliament of 1874, when the fallen Minister was the target of obloquy and derision, a position more hard to bear since there was no uncontrollable desire displayed on his own side to shield him from the darts. There may have been some who took part in the memorable scene in the division lobby, when Mr. Gladstone, going out to vote against the Government of the day, was greeted by the Conservative majority with a yell of execration that filled the lobbies and echoed through the empty chamber, startling the strangers in the gallery. That was only fourteen years ago, almost to a day. Regarding the attitude of the Conservatives in the House of Commons in this month of April, and comparing it with that assumed on the 12th of April, 1878, a century seems to stretch its limitless plain between the two dates in the calendar. On the several occasions he has spoken during the present Session, Mr. Gladstone has been listened to on the Ministerial benches with rapt, almost reverent attention, the situation being saved from absolute monotony in this respect by occasional signs of doubtful appreciation from below the gangway where the Radicals sit.

Mr. Chamberlain's friends. This afternoon, when Mr. Gladstone, regardless of etiquette, turned his back upon the Speaker and addressed himself personally to Mr. Chamberlain, good Conservatives on the benches opposite rolled about in their seats with uncontrollable laughter, whilst here and there some of the Old Guard did not feel it incompatible with the general terms of their new alliance to cheer a more than ordinary skilful thrust. What Mr. Balfour thought of it all can only be imagined. It is reported of him that once, when Mr. Goschen's finance was undergoing rough handling from the adversary opposite, he openly indulged in a merry chuckle. That was in days when he occupied the comparatively subordinate post of Chief Secretary to the Lord Lieutenant. Now he is the Leader of the House, and it would never do for him to pay the tribute of a smile to flashes of humour, however brilliant, indulged in at the expense of a powerful ally. So, whilst the House shook with laughter and rattled with hilarious cheering, Mr. Balfour sat with head bent down, toying with a paper, only a certain twitching at the corners of his mouth showing how deeply he was wounded by the castigation of a friend.

CHAPTER XLVI.

THE DERBY DAY.

More about the Letter to the Queen—The Beginning of the Correspondence—Mr. Cuninghame Graham Suspended—Sir Richard Temple—An Embarrassing Resolution—The Shadow of the Dissolution—Expectation—Despair—A Bishop in the Commons' Lobby—Dinner Dress—The Derby Day—Mr. Gedge's Opportunity—A new Record.

May 1. — More about the letter to the Queen. An impression exists in the House of Commons, and has never been contradicted, that Lord Beaconsfield delegated to Lord Barrington the task of writing the nightly letter to the Queen expected from the Leader of the House of Commons, and that he was imitated by Mr. W. H. Smith, who handed it over to Lord Lewisham. Lord Randolph Churchill assures me that this impression, which has come to be an article of belief in Parliamentary circles, is entirely erroneous. In no case has it happened that the letter to the Queen has been written by other hand than that of the Leader of the House. It is true Lord Barrington and Lord Lewisham, fulfilling one of the duties imposed upon the Vice-Chamberlain of the Household, were in nightly communication with Her Majesty whilst the House of Commons was sitting. What the Vice-Chamberlain

does is simply to draw up a bare summary of the course of proceedings, which every three hours during the sitting of the House is transmitted by telegraph to Her Majesty, whether at Windsor or Balmoral. The letter to the Queen is a different affair, being often of a private and confidential character, and it is written by the Leader.

Mr. Gladstone always at least commenced his letter whilst seated on the Treasury bench. Mr. Disraeli never wrote on the Treasury bench. The action would have interfered with his favourite attitude of folded arms, crossed legs, and Sphinx-like impassivity.   Mr. Smith followed Mr. Gladstone's example, writing on the Treasury bench, with both ears open to the debate going forward.   Mr. Balfour does the same, with the difference that he, with the enthusiasm of a beginner, commences earlier, describing events as they are enacted.

The beginning of the correspondence.

It was George III. who instituted this practice.   In his time there were no columns of reports of Parliamentary proceedings in the newspapers, and His Majesty commanded Lord North to despatch him nightly from the House a letter descriptive of the proceedings.   This was the first Parliamentary summary on record.   It has been abundantly supplemented during the Queen's reign, the private library at Buckingham Palace bulging with its record of fifty-five years. Here is a rich field of research for the historian, precious "copy" for the enterprising publisher.   The work, written by a rare series of eminent hands—Sir Robert Peel, Johnny Russell, Lord Palmerston, Disraeli, Gladstone, Randolph Churchill, to-day Mr. Balfour, yesterday the commonplaces and copybook-heading quotations of "Old Morality"—would be delightful and instructive reading, certainly too good to be wasted upon the desert air of Buckingham Palace.   The only peep the public have been permitted to obtain of this treasure trove is afforded in Sir Theodore Martin's "Life of the Prince Consort."   There are to be found a few passages of Mr. Disraeli's letters, written from the House of Commons during Lord Derby's second Administration.   Dizzy was then still in the prime of life, and was sedulously setting himself to overcome the strong personal dislike with which the Queen, influenced by the Prince Consort, regarded him.   Here was an opportunity of showing Her Majesty what potentiality of an interesting and sprightly correspondent lurked under the glossy curls of the new Chancellor of the Exchequer, and he was at pains to make the most of the opportunity.   His accounts of the Parliamentary proceedings doubtless lack the grim accuracy of Sir Robert Peel's communications.   But, judging from the specimens available, they sparkle with point and are full of graphic touches.

 The level flow of debate in the House of Commons was disturbed this afternoon in surprising,
even startling, fashion. Mr. Haldane's Bill
proposing to give compulsory powers to Town Councils to
acquire land for public purposes occupied the whole of the
sitting. Midway in the debate Mr. Asquith rose to support
the Bill, which he did in one of his closely-reasoned speeches.
The House was at the time as empty as usual, albeit the
Bill touched the sacred skirts of the property question. Mr.
Balfour did not think it worth while to be in his place. Mr.
Matthews and Mr. Ritchie had the Treasury bench all to
themselves. On the front Opposition bench Mr. Chamberlain was one of the two or three members present. Suddenly,
whilst Mr. Asquith was going forward in his quietly vigorous
fashion, Mr. Cuninghame Graham, who was sitting behind,
sprang to his feet, and, throwing up his arms, shouted in a
loud voice, "I want to know about the swindling companies
and their shareholders."

Mr. Asquith, startled by this roar of human voice sounding
in his ear, turned round and found Mr. Graham with clenched
fist and flashing eyes leaning over him. There was a moment's
pause in the astonished House. This was broken by the
Speaker's cry of "Order, order." When the Speaker rises, a
member on his feet is expected to sit down. Mr. Graham
had no such intention.

"Oh," he cried, wagging his head, "you can suspend me if
you like."

Upon this there were loud cries of "Order" from all parts
of the House, Mr. Graham turning from side to side like a
hound at bay. He went on to make further reference to the
"shareholders of a swindling company," at which there was
another shout of "Order."

The case evidently being one calling for swift decision, the
Speaker, without awaiting further development, "named" Mr.
Graham, who was provokingly undismayed. Mr. Matthews,
after a hasty consultation with the Clerk at the table, moved
his suspension, and the question was put and carried with
commendable celerity. Mr. Graham, of his own accord,
walked out of the House, genially declaring, as he went, that
the whole thing was a "swindle."

On the stroke of nine o'clock this evening Sir Richard Temple strode with glad step across Palace Yard, glancing up at the Clock Tower to see if the light was still on. It was burning brightly, in unison with the hope that flamed in his bosom. At the same time, ever eager in the public service, it occurred to the great legislator that here was an appreciable waste of public money. The sitting had been suspended at seven o'clock, not to be resumed till nine. The lengthening days had for the last fortnight made it unnecessary to flash forth during the morning sitting the beacon which comforts western London with the assurance that the Imperial Legislature is actually at work. Sir Richard's quick eye had noticed at earlier epochs of the Session that the light on the Clock Tower, burning when at seven the sitting was suspended, was left uselessly and ruinously expending its costly flame through the intervening two hours. In Committee of Supply on the vote for the expenses of the Houses of Parliament, Sir Richard would establish a fresh claim upon public confidence by questioning Mr. Plunket on this point.

Meanwhile it was cheering to have the light up there drawing towards it, as the candle allures the moth, hundreds of members, who, hurrying over their dinner, were even now making their way down to the House, hastening to singe their wings in the fire of Sir Richard's eloquence. It was not about India that on this occasion he proposed to address them. His subject was the injustice done to certain persons engaged upon the establishment at Kew Gardens, whose remunerations contrasted unfavourably with that received by colleagues in cognate positions under the State. What Sir Richard had to do with the Kew gardeners did not appear on the face of his amendment on going into Committee of Supply. He is, as all the world knows, member for the Evesham division of Worcestershire. On reflection it would be remembered that Sir Richard, feeling it invidious that he should concentrate his attention and his services upon a single constituency, had resolved to sever his connection with Evesham, and at the coming General Election to offer himself to the electors of the Kingston Division of Surrey. Now Kew is in this division. The workmen engaged in Kew Gardens are electors, and it was natural that they should look to the coming member for some token of sympathy, a look not cast in vain.

When Sir Richard reached the cloak room and divested himself of his overcoat, he carefully removed his hat and took from its recesses a dainty bunch of white chrysanthemums, which he inserted in the button-hole of his dress-coat. This was the offering of the Kew gardeners, his future constituents. He was their chosen knight, and he proudly wore their favour.

An embarrassing resolution. All through the morning sitting Sir Richard had plumed himself on the presence of mind which had secured for him this timely opportunity of commending himself to Kingston. For exactly a month there had stood in the first position on the Orders of the Day, placed there by that eminent statesman and orator Mr. Blane, a motion bluntly raising the question of Home Rule. The member for South Armagh, having drafted this critical motion and flung it in the face of the paralysed Liberal Opposition, had retired to his establishment in Scotch Street, Armagh, and gone on cutting out coats and trousers as unconcernedly as Charlotte cut bread and butter what time the love-light in Werther's eyes first beamed upon her. Probably never since Parliamentary institutions were created has there been presented such startling paradox as this—two great political parties anxiously discussing a proposition affecting the highest Imperial interests, planning attack, concerting defence, whilst the author of the resolution, the originator of the dilemma, unconcerned for, perhaps unconscious of, the turmoil he had created, was quietly measuring the nobility and gentry of a small Irish town for sixteen-shilling trousers.

Somehow it came to pass that Mr. Blane's masterly stroke was averted in the fall. Probably the approach of spring, naturally leading to an influx of business, made it inconvenient for him at this present juncture to leave the establishment in Scotch Street. However it be, on Thursday morning a letter bearing the Armagh postmark reached the Clerk at the table, asking him to withdraw from the Order Book the resolution which for four weeks had agitated the political world. Then

it was that Sir Richard Temple, with a readiness trained in the
Bengal Civil Service and a fertility of resource cultivated amid
the cares of the Government of Bombay, put down his resolution calling attention to the grievance of the Kew gardeners,
and so happily and unexpectedly found himself in command of
the time at the evening sitting.

The shadow of the dissolu-tion.   The talk that during the afternoon had buzzed
through the lobby, filled the library, and echoed
in the smoking-room, convinced Sir Richard
that he had been none too soon in seizing the opportunity.
Ever since the Session opened the engrossing topic of conversation has been the date of the dissolution. From day
to day and from week to week conjecture had varied in its
conclusion. One day everyone is agreed that things will run
their ordinary course well into June; that some time towards
the end of that month, the Small Holdings Bill having passed
all its stages, and an *impasse* being found in the Irish Local
Government Bill, Ministers will decide to go to the country,
so as to get the election over in July. Next day there is
talk of carrying on through the recess, meeting as usual in
February, and then seeing what may happen. Lord Cross,
it is whispered, is convinced it would be unpatriotic for him to
anticipate by a week or a month the natural term of his engagement at the India Office, and, of course, if the Government go
out, the Secretary of State for India cannot remain behind.
Between these two points rumour has moved in wide variety.

To-day there was noticeable in all parts of the House a
suddenly-born and surely-seated conviction that the end was
actually at hand. Men said to each other in confidential
whispers that it would all be over by Whitsuntide, if not before.
No one knew whence the scare started: everyone found it
prevalent, and helped to swell it. The peculiar direction given
to the course of public business had something to do with
it. Since the House re-assembled after the Easter recess,
it had been engaged in a sort of clearing-up arrangement.
Odds and ends, such as the Scotch Equivalent Grant and the
Indian Council Bill, had been sedulously cared for, whilst big
measures, like the Small Holdings Bill and the Local Government Bill, were kept back. Even more odd and significant

was the dealing with Supply. In ordinary times the Financial Secretary to the Treasury would have jumped at the opportunity presented by the withdrawal of Mr. Blane's motion to put down effective Supply on the chance of its being reached in time to get two or three votes. Members eagerly scanned the Orders to find Supply had not been put down. Then there was Mr. Balfour's frank confession that, in face of the objection taken by the Irish members, the Criminal Evidence Bill could not be passed this Session in the form in which it had been introduced. This Session! Why, it is only the 6th of May —a little early, if the Session were intended to run its ordinary course, to be throwing Government Bills on the fire.

Everyone knows that yesterday a Cabinet Council met. As the afternoon drew on it was made known that the Privy Council had been summoned to meet at Windsor Castle on Monday. What could be clearer? The Cabinet, resolutely facing the situation, had resolved straightway to go to the country. On Monday the Queen would sign the decree of dissolution, and at the sitting of that day Mr. Balfour, "rising to make a few remarks," as Sir Stafford Northcote had done on the 8th of March, 1880—that, by the way, was a Monday— would announce the dissolution.

Expectation.   Sir Richard Temple, tripping up the steps from the cloak-room, adjusting his white chrysanthemums, radiant in dinner-dress, thought of these things, and thanked his Star of India for the stroke of good luck that had befallen him, and would enable him, just in the nick of time, to secure the favour among his new constituents of the powerful Guild of Gardeners. The lobby seemed strangely empty as he passed through ; true, it yet lacked three minutes of nine. Dr. Tanner was buzzing about, which was at least a hopeful sign. If there were any danger of a count, he would make one to prevent the conspiracy triumphing. The House had a chillingly desolate look. The clerks were at the table ; the Serjeant-at-Arms was standing by his chair ; but certainly not more than a dozen members were in their places. Still they would come. At the worst they would miss the opening sentences of his speech, but dropping in hastily after their curtailed dinner, they would muster in crowded ranks in time to hear the peroration in which Sir Richard meant to bring in a passage dwelling on the similitude between the Garden of Eden and the Garden of Kew, and showing, on the authority of Milton, how the question of wages was never permitted to disturb the serenity of the former establishment.

Despair.   Promptly at nine the Speaker took the Chair, and Sir Richard Temple rose. Simultaneously, from the corner bench below the gangway, Dr. Tanner was on his feet, and said something about forty members not being present. Sir Richard, through dimmed eyes, beheld the Speaker rise, stretch forth his three-cornered hat, and slowly count. "Eighteen," he said, finally, pointing his hat towards Sir Richard ; "the House will now adjourn." And Sir Richard, gasping for breath, realised that he and the Kew gardeners were frozen out.

May 13. — A Bishop in the Commons' lobby.   The Bishop of London having business with the President of the Local Government Board, walked across to the Commons after the adjournment of the Lords, not delaying his visit by the time necessary to disrobe. Bishops are by no means infrequent visitors to the lobby of the House of Commons, but in an ordinary way they wear their black frock coat and gaiters. Dr. Temple's appearance in surplice and hood created a profound sensation in the busy centre of political life. A hush fell over the eager throng as the Bishop, halting within the doorway, crossed his hands and surveyed the scene. There was a general, vague impression that something was going to happen—a funeral, a wedding, or peradventure a confirmation service. For some moments no one approached the Lord Bishop, but the bold Maclure, chancing to quit the House at the moment, and finding his lordship standing there, went straight up and shook hands as if he were quite a common man. It was curious to see them as they stood there, emblematic of the union of Church and State. Mr. Maclure's instincts and habits are naturally bent upon hospitality. There was the refreshment bar close at hand. What more natural than to ask the Lord Bishop to take a glass of sherry, tempered with bitters if that were more conformable with

episcopal taste and usage ? In pauses in the long conversation
(chiefly carried on by Mr. Maclure) the hon. member almost
imperceptibly edged towards the bar, on which the sherry
decanter was plainly visible. The Bishop, seeming to divine

MR. MACLURE AND THE BISHOP.

his intention, almost as imperceptibly edged in the contrary
direction ; and so in course of time the two old friends parted.

May 27.—Dinner Dress. When at the commencement of the evening
sitting Mr. Balfour came in it was noticed that
he was in dinner dress, a rare departure from the unwritten
law that controls fashion in this matter. No one remembers to
have seen Mr. Disraeli in dinner dress when he was Leader of
the House, nor does memory recall similar laxity on the part
of Mr. Gladstone whilst he held the same position. The
assumption, comfortable for gentlemen who dine out at ease,
is that the Leader of the House is throughout its sittings
always at the post of duty, or at least within call. Mr. W. H.
Smith so scrupulously observed this rule that, though Grosvenor Place is within eight minutes' drive, and the domestic

cuisine at No. 3 was excellent, he rarely dined at home. In his room behind the Speaker's chair he shared the humble steak or the succulent chop with Mr. Jackson and Mr. Akers Douglas, always ready to obey the call that might summon him to the Treasury bench, to perform his duty to his Queen and country.

June 1. — The Derby day. The whole business of the debate on the motion for adjourning over the Derby day went hopelessly adrift from the lines on which Mr. Gedge planned it. When Major Rasch put his motion on the paper Mr. Gedge capped it with an amendment, carefully drawn up, by which he designed seriously to lead the thoughts of the House of Commons to the subject of betting, its illegality and its iniquitous consequences. Usually Sir Wilfrid Lawson came in at this juncture, and under guise of discussing the motion offered a series of flippant remarks, at which the House was wont to laugh. Mr. Gedge, anxious not to do injustice to any man, had been accustomed attentively to listen to Sir Wilfrid, and had the next morning continued his research by careful study of the report of his speech. But he never could see anything in it that might fairly excuse the House for indulging in the, to him, unaccountable and ungainly habit of laughter. The House, he felt, would like for once to be relieved from paying this tribute annually extorted, and would turn with unfeigned pleasure to consider with him the more serious aspects of the question.

Mr. Gedge's opportunity. For some days his amendment stood on the paper, the interval being occupied in diligent research among the ancient fathers and other authorities whose dicta would be likely to enliven a cheerful speech. An hour he felt sure might be usefully employed in discoursing to the House, and he was willing and prepared to devote that much time to the subject. At the last moment some godless man discovered that, as raising quite a distinct issue, his carefully prepared amendment was out of order, and so the Speaker ruled it. But if he might not move his amendment, he might deliver his speech, wedging it in somewhere amid the frivolity of the debate. He was on his feet as soon as Major Rasch

had finished his remarks on moving the adjournment over
the Derby day. But there was Captain Grice-Hutchinson
claiming precedence as being commissioned to second
the motion. Mr. Gedge resumed his seat, and awaited his
opportunity. Captain Grice-Hutchinson having somewhat
abruptly concluded when the House thought he was only just
beginning, Mr. Gedge, with alacrity remarkable in a man
who no longer rides at ten stone, was up again, and had
almost given out his text when Sir Wilfrid Lawson appeared,
and the frivolous majority insisted on preferring him.

When the Baronet had made an end of speaking, it seemed
that nothing could stand between the House and the luxury of
the address Mr. Gedge had prepared for its edification. Lord
Elcho was now competing with the member for Stockport, but
no mere newcomer could supersede a claim such as he had
established by his continued effort to catch the Speaker's eye.
On only one ground could Lord Elcho claim precedence, that
was as seconding Sir Wilfrid Lawson's amendment. But Lord
Elcho was notoriously the champion of the evil thing against
which Mr. Gedge was prepared to testify. On the last occasion
the House had proposed to sit over the Derby day, Lord Elcho
had moved and carried the adjournment. When Mr. Gedge
heard the Speaker ask the noble lord whether he rose to second
Sir Wilfrid Lawson's amendment, he for once in his life understood and almost sympathised with the peculiar physical impulse that contorts the aspect of an intelligent visage into an
expression vulgarly known as a smile. It was a slow process
with Mr. Gedge, and before it was quite accomplished he
heard Lord Elcho briskly answer in the affirmative, and sat
gasping for breath, whilst the House broke into a hilarious
roar of laughter.

This almost finished him. But an address such as he had
prepared is not to be lightly set aside, nor was the opportunity
of dealing a crushing blow at the illegal practice of betting to
be foregone because of a succession of strangely untoward
incidents. Whilst Lord Elcho, with intonation occasionally
reminiscent of a curate reading his first sermon, delivered a
speech continuously interrupted by shouts of laughter, there
were only two grave faces in the assembly. One was Lord
Elcho's, the other Mr. Gedge's. The member for Stockport

sat with lip pursed into a something more than usually stony
reproof of a flippant world. The recollection of the horrible
temptation that a few minutes earlier had nearly betrayed
him into a smile weighed on his conscience. He would atone
for that by adding another quarter of an hour to his address.

When Lord Elcho resumed his seat amid a fresh storm of
cheering and laughter, Mr. Gedge solemnly rose and faced the
hilarious crowd. Instantly the laughter merged into a cry
of horror, which, becoming articulate, angrily demanded the
division. Mr. Gedge, with the notes of his sermon tightly
rolled in his right hand, stonily stared before him, waiting till
the uproar should cease. The Opposition, noting the anguish
depicted on the faces opposite, began joyously to cry out,
"Gedge! Gedge!" Here at least was some ray of comfort, some
unexpected word of encouragement. Few men are prophets
in their own country. Scorned and insulted by his own party,
Mr. Gedge unexpectedly found appreciation from gentlemen
opposite—stranger than all, from the Radicals below the gangway. They evidently wanted to hear him, and the opportunity
should not be denied them. When they had shouted down
the cries for a division, Mr. Gedge found his opportunity and
began his address. But before he had got through a dozen
sentences the very men who had lured him on basely deserted
him, and the voices which but now had timefully called
"Gedge! Gedge!" hoarsely roared for the division. The cry
was taken up by friends near him, and, after battling for some
moments against the storm, Mr. Gedge dropped slowly into
his seat, nervously clutching his unread roll of sermon, and
marvelling more than ever at the madness men call humour.

June 2.—A me-
morable Derby
Day. The clerks at the table preparing the usual
entry for the journals of the House of Commons
were yesterday faced by a new duty. Every day entry is
made of a summary of the proceedings of the sitting.
It is done, like everything else, in strict accordance with
precedent. But no precedent could be found for a Wednesday
sitting with the curious experience of that which will in Parliamentary records ever be memorable—the Derby day of this
year. One of the highest authorities in the House, whose
recollection goes back as far as 1857, was haunted by the

recollection that in his early days there had been a failure to
make a House at four o'clock on a Wednesday, but no date
of reference was handy. A casual search failed to discover the
entry, and the clerks had accordingly to draw up a new form
of entry, which will appear in the journals, and will be added
to the innumerable volumes that line the walls in the long
corridor flanking the tea-room. This is the record as it
appears :—" The House met at twelve of the clock, and at
half-past twelve the House was told by Mr. Speaker, and
twelve members only being present Mr. Speaker retired from
the Chair until one of the clock, when the House was again
told by Mr. Speaker, nineteen members only being present.
Mr. Speaker again retired from the Chair until four of the
clock, when the House was again told by Mr. Speaker, and
thirty-five members only being present the House was adjourned by Mr. Speaker, without question put, till to-morrow.'

CHAPTER XLVII.

DISSOLUTION IMMINENT.

*A Crisis in the History of the Army—Sir H. Havelock-Allan—General Fraser's
Oration—The Archbishop goes out to Dinner—The Duke of York Sworn
In—Mr. Gladstone Roused—Sic vos non vobis—Pleasant Expectations—A
Thunderbolt.*

June 14.—A crisis
in the history of
the army.

Mr. STANHOPE'S regrettable but fortuitous illness
withdrew him from Westminster at a time when
it would have been otherwise difficult to resist
the increasingly imperative demand of military members for
opportunity to debate the evidence given before Lord Wantage's Committee and the recommendations of the Report.
In reply to questions, Mr. Balfour pointed out that it would be
inconvenient, not to say useless, to debate the subject in the
absence of the Minister for War. So the thing drifted on till
to-night, when, Mr. Stanhope being back again, the House
went into Committee of Supply, taking up the Army Estimates. Lord Randolph Churchill has withdrawn from the
scene, and Lord Curzon was not there to inquire whither he

had gone. When Sir Walter Barttelot rose to open the important debate, there were present (including the Speaker) just eighteen members. The front Opposition bench was tenantless, and only six members faced the orator.

This appearance of an audience, not in itself impressive or exhilarating, lost something by reason of accidental circumstances that environed Mr. Picton, that eminent military authority having, in view of an engagement about to take place, gone into laager. Borrowing an idea picked up in his studies of Boer campaigns, he had buttressed himself about with volumes of *Hansard* and Blue Books, from the centre of which Sir Walter Barttelot, standing in an elevated position behind the Treasury bench on the opposite side of the House, managed to catch sight of the top of his head. Colonel Nolan had all the front bench below the gangway to himself, and sat there visibly winding himself up for the speech which he began to let off an hour later, and which, as far as continuity of thought or argument was concerned, might equally well have run down half an hour earlier than it did, or rattled on for another hour. There was Viscount Ebrington with a carefully-prepared essay setting forth the entirely novel proposition that "recruits are taken on at too early an age." There was Dr. Farquharson gallantly struggling to keep out the opium question from a disquisition on the status of the Army and the misleading effect of posters inviting recruits to join the standard. Mr. Sinclair, everyone wondering what he did in this galley, rose to say, "What is wanted is a force on which we can rely in case of emergency to defend the Empire both at home and abroad."

Sir H. Havelock-Allan. The sixth member whom Sir Walter Barttelot had the privilege of addressing was Sir Henry Havelock-Allan, who, seated at the corner of the third bench above the gangway, aligned with Mr. J. A. Picton occupying a corresponding position below the gangway, was evidently a source of considerable embarrassment to that gentleman as he proceeded to set forth his views on the organisation of the Army and the administration of the War Office. When above his barricade the member for Leicester caught the Chairman's eye, and commenced the delivery of his pungent criticism, Sir

Henry turned and stared at him across the gangway with
eloquent though inarticulate inquiry, " What on earth do *you*
know about it ?" Mr. J. A. Picton, adroitly transferring to
this side, evidently a vulnerable point of attack, an additional
couple of volumes of *Hansard*, Sir Henry snorted in old
'war-horse fashion, and turned away from temptation.

Sir Henry is a soldier, accustomed to rough-and-tumble

JULIUS 'ANNIBAL PICTON.

expedients, and the attention of the Speaker has, on at least
two occasions, been called to his unconventional method of
conducting an argument. Once, finding an Irish member
strayed above the gallery, Sir Henry literally and physically sat
upon him. Purporting to plump down on a vacant seat next
to the visitor, he landed heavily on his lap, and it was a mere

flattened wreck of a member that presently appealed to the
Speaker to know if this sort of thing was in order. On a later
occasion he, in equally elaborately accidental way, came in
physical contact with another member from whom he differed
on the Home Rule question.

With a gentleman of these irregular debating habits
openly scowling at him across the narrow passage of the
gangway, Mr. Picton may be excused if his speech to-
night lacked something of his customary ease and command
over the sympathies of the House. There was something
painful in the frequency with which, glancing over the barricade at the gallant member for Durham persistently glaring
at him, he affirmed his entire freedom from desire to see a
standing army abolished. "We must have an army," he said :
"that I don't deny. Only let them keep it in a state of
efficiency."

"H'm !" said Sir Henry Havelock-Allan, tossing himself
about on the corner seat. It was a mere monosyllabic
exclamation ; but it sounded to Mr. Picton uncommonly like
the blood-curdling " Fee-fo-fi-fum " with which the man-
eating giant of the fable prefaced discovery of a toothsome
morsel.

General Fraser's oration.

These comprised the audience Sir Walter Barttelot addressed. Its lack of numbers and its
total freedom from appearance of profound interest abated
not one jot of the baronet's oratorical energy. His old
familiar battle cry, " Let me go one step further," rang out
as truculently as of yore, whilst his prepositions and his
conjunctions were still his most emphatic parts of speech.
Immediately in his rear sat General Fraser, having to himself
the full length of the top bench below the gallery. The
General had given up his nights and days to this question,
and had prepared a tremendous oration as contribution to
the debate. For greater accuracy, and with a view to the
convenience of posterity, he, regardless of expense, had had
it set up in type. He brought down with him a few dozen
copies, a number, as it turned out, in excess of the audience.
Private friends favoured with a present of a copy were interested to find how the ordinary custom of printing common

things had been departed from. Instead of running on in columnar mass of type, General Fraser's speech was printed in sentences, each standing in a generous margin of space. At first sight it looked like one of Walt Whitman's poems or a selection from Ossian. The whole was rounded off with a rhymed verse, the authorship of which was much discussed. Sir Lyon Playfair, who is well read in ancient and modern literature, and who, happening to look in in the course of the debate, had a copy of the oration presented to him, declared his ignorance of the authorship. This is not to be wondered at, since it was the General's very own, modesty inducing him to leave the authorship in that state of uncertainty which for a while varied the apathy of the House of Commons, called upon to discuss the condition and prospects of the British Army.

Members were at first surprised to find General Fraser addressing them from this unaccustomed place. In ordinary circumstances it is only when the House is crowded, and a member has no choice of seats, that he submits to the disadvantage of addressing the Speaker from beneath the shadow of the gallery. But General Fraser did not serve through the Indian Mutiny for nothing. Having had his speech printed he meant to read it, and, according to the rules of House of Commons debate, no member may take that course. If he deployed in the open, occupying his usual place in the centre of the benches above the gangway, the Chairman could not fail to see the pamphlet in his hand, and must needs call him to order. In the obscurity beneath the gallery he was safe, and there he stood with his right arm clinging round the post, his body limply resting against it as in dolorous tones he recited his melancholy story. In this attitude, the General, perhaps undesignedly, symbolised the British standard hanging at half-mast, flapping forlornly against the flag-post, oppressed with the consciousness that the Army that worked its way through the Peninsula to Waterloo had in these degenerate days gone hopelessly to the dogs.

June 15.—The Archbishop goes out to dinner.

Much sympathy is felt for the Archbishop of Canterbury in respect of the misfortune that attended his effort to dine out the other night. His host and hostess were an illustrious

statesman and his wife, and a select company were asked
to meet His Grace. The dinner-hour was fixed at eight
o'clock, at which time all were assembled except the Archbishop and Mrs. Benson. It was felt impossible to sit
down to dinner till they arrived, an event painfully delayed.
Quarter of an hour followed quarter of an hour, till nine o'clock
struck, when the host observed that on this occasion there were
only two courses open to them—either they must sit down to
dinner without the Archbishop, or must abstain altogether
from dining. It was resolved to go in to dinner; and when
the cruelly-spoiled repast was half-way through, the Archbishop
and Mrs. Benson arrived, with a tale sad enough to move the
hardest heart. The invitation to dinner had been written
on Dollis Hill paper, where host and hostess had of late been
staying, and it was naturally assumed that the feast would
be spread there. The Archbishop and his wife had accordingly set forth in good time from Lambeth and journeyed
to distant Dollis Hill, to discover that it was in Carlton
Gardens they were anxiously expected. There was nothing to
do but to drive back to town.

What the Archbishop said when he returned to the
brougham and the door closed upon him with a full
knowledge of the situation remains a secret. But there is a
strong human desire to know.

When, shortly after four o'clock this afternoon,
there emerged from the entrance below the bar
the thin red line of the procession leading the

June 17. — The
Duke of York
sworn in.

Duke of York up to the Lord Chancellor, the attendance of
peers was not promising for the important business that
awaits them next week. Lord Salisbury was on the Ministerial
bench, and Lord Cross had made a point of being present.
Other Ministers in their places were Lords Knutsford and
Cranbrook. The front Opposition bench was tenantless till
Lord Herschell dropped in, presently followed by Lord Kimberley; and these, whilst the ceremony went forward, had the
bench to themselves. The scarcity of attendance in this part
of the House was, it turned out, a fortunate event, seeing that
during the reading of the summons of the new peer and his
patent of peerage he and his escort stood at that side of the

table unembarrassed by the presence of the usual occupants of the bench that flanks it.   The most animated section of the House was found in the galleries, where a company of ladies in morning dress looked in to watch the ceremony. In the left-hand gallery, the crimson turbans of two dusky Indian princes broke the monotony of the prevailing colour, which still bears testimony to recent mourning.

The procession, in which the late comer to the House formed the principal figure, was led by the Yeoman Usher of the Black Rod. Behind him came the Lord Great Chamberlain and Garter King-at-Arms, the latter apparelled in crimson cloak embroidered with the Royal Arms.   The Prince of Wales walked next, in the scarlet robe slashed with ermine which Peers wear on State occasions.   The Duke of York, and his other sponsor, the Duke of Connaught, also wore the robes of a Peer of Parliament.   Black Rod piloted the procession up to the Woolsack, where the Lord Chancellor sat with a pretty air of nothing-particular-going-on.   When, prompted by the Prince of Wales, the new Peer proffered a roll of parchment, on which was engrossed his Patent of Peerage, the Lord Chancellor, not disposed irretrievably to commit himself before all was found to be in order, signalled the Reading Clerk to take it in hand.

This done, the procession, re-forming, walked back to the table, Black Rod, the Lord Great Chamberlain, and Garter King-at-Arms standing in a row at the foot, whilst the three Royal Princes stood at the side.   The Reading Clerk galloped at a tremendous pace through the phraseology of the documents of which he had taken charge, the only recognisable terms being those most frequently recurring, "the Duke of York" and "his heirs male aforesaid."   The reading completed, the Clerk of Parliaments came to the front and administered the oath; after which the new Peer signed the Roll of Parliament, the Prince of Wales standing close at hand, ready to meet any emergency in the way of prompting.

Once more the procession was re-formed, in the same order as before.   This time Black Rod went round by the cross benches between the bar and the table.   As each official or peer passed the Woolsack, he bent his head in mute salute. Still keeping up what seemed a rattling pace, Black Rod started off for the steps of the Throne, the procession following in close order. The gilt chair that serves for Throne was uncovered, as it is when the Queen is expected. On the left-hand side of it stood two lesser chairs. In the outer one the Duke of York seated himself and put on his hat. The Lord Chancellor, turning round on the Woolsack so as to present a side view to the new Peer, the Duke lifted his three-cornered hat, a salute acknowledged by the Lord Chancellor. Thrice the Duke lifted his hat and replaced it on his head; a distinct titter rippling through the crowded galleries when it was observed that the rapidity of his action left the Lord Chancellor a full salute behind.

When leeway had been made up the Duke returned to the Woolsack, and was formally presented to the Lord Chancellor by the Prince of Wales. All being now in order, the Lord Chancellor extended his hand to the Prince with an effusiveness that contrasted pleasantly with the studied coolness of his reception before the new Peer's credentials had been presented and examined. This completed the ceremony, and the latest Duke of York, having marched in through one door of the House of Lords, marched out at the other, and was seen no more through the sitting.

June 18, 1892.— *Mr. Gladstone roused.* Looking across the table to-night, Mr. Arthur Balfour, a keen observer familiar with Parliamentary portents, could not fail to note that the bow of Mr. Gladstone's necktie was set very nearly under his right ear. That was an arrangement familiar enough towards the close of the Parliament of 1880. Those were fighting days, in the course of which the Premier was accustomed to discover his most active foes amongst those of his own household. But of late, certainly not this Session, the well-known danger signal—the south cone of Parliamentary debate—has not been hoisted. Mr. Gladstone has, indeed, been so benevolent in his attitude towards the Ministry in general, and the First Lord of the Treasury in particular, as to excite the indignation of his following below the Gangway. He has encouraged them in well-doing, and only mildly hinted reproof when, in his opinion, they have shown a disposition to go astray. Nothing so nearly akin to millennium has been known in modern Parliamentary history. The novel relations established between Mr. Gladstone and honourable gentlemen opposite had been illustrated on the previous night by the charming little scene when the octogenarian Young Man, preparing for his mission Northward carrying the Fiery Cross over the Border, had suavely invited Mr. Balfour to give some definite indication of the date of the Dissolution. "It would be to the convenience of everyone," he said, adding with coquettish smile—"at least to those who have youth and vigour sufficient again to submit themselves to the judgment of their constituents." This little aside, with the personal reference everyone understood, was promptly taken up by the listening House; but none cheered so genially as the Ministerialists.

Twenty-four hours had elapsed and things were sorely changed. Mr. Gladstone's countenance no longer beamed with benevolent interest upon his young friend opposite, nor were his lips wreathed in smiles. They were, on the contrary, closely set, as if he could not for the moment trust himself to open them in ordered speech. His eyes flashed with indignation, and as he tossed about on the seat his necktie sympathetically stole round to the right till it reached the position Mr. Balfour, not without anxiety, had noted.

Sic vos non vobis. Sir William Harcourt sat by his side, also seething with indignation, but indicating the state of his mind in quite another way. He was serenely smiling at right hon. gentlemen opposite, as if no one enjoyed the little joke of the evening more than he. He certainly had a personal interest in it. All through the week he had been hard at work in the endeavour to leave the Government no excuse for postponing the dissolution beyond next Saturday. It would have been the easiest thing in the world to spread Supply over a week. In truth, any period less than that seemed trifling with important interests and imperative duties. Thanks chiefly to Sir William Harcourt, Supply was voted with both hands, and the other Government business on the paper had been put forward so rapidly that, as Mr. Balfour, speaking just now, had admitted, there really was nothing left to do. They might meet on Monday and Tuesday on the chance of something coming down from the Lords. But after Wednesday there would be nothing for it but to adjourn.

Almost alone Sir William Harcourt had done this. Left in charge of the Opposition, he had sat patient and watchful in his place, ready at any moment to interpose and deprecate discus-

sion. His start to his feet when one night Dr. Clarke proposed to recommit a Scotch Bill of innumerable clauses was irresistible. Even Dr. Clarke had nothing to say in reply to his pathetic protest against a proceeding that could not occupy less than an hour of the precious time of a dying Parliament. As for

Mr. Morton, he yielded after a struggle which few could regard without emotion. Sir William Harcourt, who had never before taken notice of his existence, walked about the corridors with him, asking for his valuable counsel as to how best to expedite the business of Supply, gently leading him to the conclusion that it would be the most dignified and patriotic course to leave to an already sin-burdened Government the full responsibility of their estimates. Alpheus Cleophas was finally brought to see matters in that light. But he frankly said he could not remain in the neighbourhood of the House and not make a casual speech or two in the course of a sitting. The only course open to him was to go away, a suggestion Sir William Harcourt, with apparent reluctance, approved, and since Tuesday the House of Commons has not seen Mr. Morton or heard his familiar voice.

Mr. Balfour, in common with his colleagues, had been a silent admirer of this self-sacrificing devotion on the part of a political adversary. Sir William Harcourt was working for them with a zeal that outstripped the service of their political friends, whether above or below the gangway. They had nothing to do but sit still and let him arrange matters. Never before had the close of a Session been so peaceful, but never before had a prominent and superlatively able leader of the Opposition laid himself out with so much zest to help the Government.

Pleasant expect-
ation. Now the labourer's task was o'er, and there remained for him only the fruition of his desire. There had been some talk early in the week of postponing the date of dissolution so as to carry it over Saturday, the 25th, and fix it on a day that would render it impossible for the Returning Officers to arrange for the polling in boroughs on a Saturday. Tuesday, the 28th, had been named with much confidence, and with the dissolution taking place on that date there would be no Saturday poll. That was a conclusion Sir William Harcourt felt he had rendered impossible. He had done his work so completely that the Government might, if they pleased, dissolve on Friday, the 24th, a date equally acceptable to him and his friends. Mr. Balfour's statement in reply to Mr.

Gladstone's request for information as to the definite prospects of the particular day for the dissolution of Parliament had through nearly its full length confirmed Sir William Harcourt, if confirmation were necessary, in his belief in the success of his mission. The First Lord of the Treasury, reviewing the position of public business, " saw no reason why we should not get through all the measures we have on the paper by Wednesday next."

That was definite enough, and members rapidly went through the mental process that carried the arrangement to its natural conclusion. The House having finished its work by Wednesday, there would be a formal meeting of both Houses on Thursday for the quaint ceremony of Prorogation by Royal Commission. On Friday a Council would be held for decreeing the dissolution. The evening's *Gazette* would proclaim the fact that Parliament was dissolved, and the night's post would carry the writs all over the country. Mr. Balfour's gracious and generous acknowledgment that for the forward state of business the House and the country were chiefly indebted to the efforts of the right hon. gentleman and hon. gentlemen opposite was only what was to be expected. As Sir William Harcourt sat and listened, caressing his chin with the quiet contentment of the moment, a faint blush overspread his countenance. It was not by stealth he had done good, since his figure had necessarily been prominent in the proceedings in the week as he went to and fro on his mission of peace. Still, he blushed to find it fame.

A thunderbolt.   Whether Mr. Balfour was deliberately having his joke or not, is a secret locked in his own breast. He is still young and light-hearted, and it must be admitted the temptation was great. However it be, nothing could have been better calculated than the form of his speech to confirm in the minds of the Opposition the conviction already filling it, that Saturday, the 25th, was the day finally fixed upon for the dissolution. Even when he introduced the House of Lords there was no suspicion of the truth. "There is," he said, " no prospect of a number of Bills sent to the Lords being probably, or even possibly, dealt with before the end of the week." This judicial deliberation of the Lords at the end of a Session was a little unusual; but if it pleased them, it did not threaten to hurt anyone else. If they sat till Friday they might get through the final stages of lingering measures by meeting at eleven in the morning, a not unusual arrangement in such circumstances. At two o'clock in the afternoon the Prorogation would take place, and on Saturday would come the dissolution and the posting of the writs.

Even whilst members opposite were doing this new sum in mental arithmetic, and contemplating with approval the way it worked out, the thunderbolt fell. It was the very last sentence in the speech, added casually just as the Leader of the House was about to resume his seat. "The dissolution," he said, "cannot possibly be later than Wednesday or Thursday in next week but one."

There was a moment's pause whilst men looked at each other with wondering eyes, mutely asking had their ears deceived them. Then there broke forth from the ranks of the Opposition a sharp prolonged cry, as of a body in acute physical pain. When it ceased, all eyes were turned towards the front Opposition bench, where Mr. Gladstone sat in eager conversation with Sir William Harcourt. Mr. Picton, always ready for any emergency, rose and inquired whether the Government really intended to pass the Archdeaconry of Cornwall Bill. The House cared nothing for Mr. Picton or the Archdeaconry either. No answer was forthcoming, and there was another pause. Probably not more than twenty might have been counted within its limits, but before it was broken it seemed stretching towards eternity. Since the leaders above the gangway were evidently not ready to act, another was forthcoming from below the gangway. Mr. Labouchere asked leave to move the adjournment of the House in order to call attention to a matter of urgent public importance—namely, the inconvenience the country was subjected to by the delay of the dissolution.

"Do forty members support the request?" the Speaker asked.

In an instant, as if he had touched some secret spring, there was an upheaval on the benches to the left. It seemed that every man in that part of the House was

on his legs, fiercely cheering. There was no question about
the necessary support, so leave was given, and to the animated
debate that followed Mr. Gladstone contributed a vigorous
speech, in the course of which his necktie completed the
segment of the circle over which it slowly but steadily
travelled.

CHAPTER XLVIII.

THE END.

Lord Denman—The Duke of Argyll—Lord Charles Beresford—Parliamentary
Portraits—Mr. Gladstone—Mr. Balfour—The Dead Parliament—Early
Closing—Improved Business Capacity—The Speaker.

June 21.—Lord
Denman.
WHAT is to be done with Lord Denman? It
has long been evident that a crisis is at hand,
and it seems to-night as if it were reached. When the Small
Holdings Bill came up for consideration on the third reading,
Lord Denman rose to move its rejection. He is, as he once
pathetically told the Lords, both blind and deaf. With the
object of securing fuller opportunities for taking part in
Parliamentary affairs, he has this Session formed the habit of
sitting at the table, shoulder to shoulder with Lord Balfour of
Burleigh, the Chairman of Committees. From this place, he
to-night anxiously kept watch on the Lord Chancellor, whom
he strongly suspects of designs to jockey him out of his birthright as a peer of the United Kingdom. Once or twice he
made a false start; but ticking off the Bills or the orders, he
was just in time to move the rejection of the Small Holdings
Bill before the Lord Chancellor could declare the third
reading carried.

A picturesque figure the old gentleman contributed
to the scene as he stood at the table in his scarlet
and black skull cap, his faded grey coat, in one hand his
ancient hat, held brim upmost and crammed with papers,
whilst in the other was a sadly-soiled pocket-handkerchief,
closed over a walking-stick.

Lord Salisbury seemed to have the advantage of the

rest of the audience, inasmuch as he caught the purport
of the words Lord Denman mumbled at the table. When
the noble lord had gone forward for something like ten
minutes, the Premier rose and declared that his remarks
had no bearing on the Bill before the House. Lord Denman
is used to interruptions of this kind. He had been taught

to expect the ignominy. Turning almost fiercely upon
Lord Salisbury, he cried aloud, in a voice this time heard
all through the chamber, "Does the noble lord want to
cloture me again?" Some other words he added, their
purport not easy to catch, but they were addressed to Lord
Salisbury, and were brought to a conclusion by Lord Denman
sharply smiting the table with his clenched fist and resuming
his seat. After which the Lord Chancellor made haste to put
the question, and declared the Small Holdings Bill read a
third time.

June 22.—The Duke of Argyll. When, if ever, the Marquis of Lorne returns to Parliament, he will find his father occupying a sadly different position from that he filled when father and son last represented the MacCallum Mores in the Legislature. Then the Duke of Argyll was one of the principal members of the Cabinet, and Secretary of State for India. Now he has retired to a back bench, whence he at not unfrequent intervals rises to scold the House of Lords and deal back-handed blows at his old friend and colleague, Mr. Gladstone. Once ranking as a statesman, he now fills in Parliament the position of a sort of coroneted Roebuck. Salisbury pleases him not, nor Gladstone either. He sits with the Liberals and votes with the Conservatives. A letter just turned up has been eagerly seized upon as presenting His Grace in a new light. It is in reply to a communication addressed to him by an American citizen in the year 1876. "Sir," wrote the Duke, with curious economy of the alphabet, "It wd: be very presumptuous in me to express any opinion on questions affecting domestic policy in the U. S. Public men have enough to do here with the difficulties of their own country, without being called upon to form decisive opinions on those affecting America, where many of the conditions are very different."

That was the diffidence of comparative youth, over which the Duke has absolutely triumphed. There is to-day no question under the sun upon which he wd: think it presumptuous to express an opinion.

The Duke of Argyll's failure in public life is due to causes diametrically opposed to those responsible for his son's less obtrusive discomfiture. The Duke is just as pragmatical as the Marquis is hesitating of speech, as obstinate as he is yielding. Father and son share a common leaning toward literature, but have developed it in characteristically different ways. While Lord Lorne has dallied with the Psalms of David, told how he took "A Trip to the Tropics," and murmured of the loves of "Guido and Lita," the Duke of Argyll at the same age fulminated a series of pamphlets designed to show how wrong other people were. In his nineteenth year he took the House of Lords in hand, writing to them a "Letter to the Peers from a Peer's Son." Then he wrote a trifle bearing the engaging title "On the Duty and

Necessity of Immediate Legislative Interposition in Behalf
of the Church of Scotland as Determined by Considerations
of Constitutional Law." In the same year the sky over
Scotland was darkened by "A Letter to the Reverend
Thomas Chalmers, D.D., on the Present Position of Church
Affairs in Scotland, and the Causes Which Have Led to It."

These compendious titles are drafted on the proportions of
the Duke's interposition in Parliamentary debate. He never,
as is Lord Salisbury's use and was Lord Granville's wont, listens
to debate and, at convenient opportunity interposing, replies to
arguments put forward by preceding speakers. A speech
from his place in Parliament by the Duke of Argyll is a
serious thing, and must be prepared for accordingly. When
he sees opportunity of benefiting a sadly indifferent world
by observations on public affairs he retires to Campden Hill
(or, if the effort is prodigious, to Inveraray), shuts himself up in
his study and produces sheaves of manuscript. His speeches
are lectures; and the Duke when addressing the House of
Lords scorns to hide the tell-tale foolscap notes.

It must be admitted that as lectures they are excellent,
glowing with fire, often rising to the height of eloquence,
irreproachable on the score of literary style. They are a
little long, and have no perceptible influence on opinion
whether in the Lords or outside the House. Still they are
interesting as examples of a style of Parliamentary debate
otherwise extinct; and the House of Lords has so little real
work to do that it cannot fairly complain if the Duke of Argyll
sometimes exquisitely delights himself by reciting polished
periods of his own composition through two full hours of a
summer afternoon.

June 23.
"Charlie"
Beresford.

There is talk to-day of Lord Charles Beresford
standing at the General Election as candidate
for North Kensington. His return to the House
would be welcome to both sides as a sea breeze on a sultry
afternoon. He is one of the most delightfully unconventional
men in English public life. Every inch a sailor, if he has a
foible it is a hankering after political life. He sat in the
House of Commons for his native county of Waterford through
the Parliament of 1874, losing his seat when, in 1880, the

National Party swept the board of the Conservatives. At the General Election of 1885 he came in for Marylebone, and sat for that borough till, a year or two ago, he was faced by the necessity of forthwith going to sea or losing his chances of promotion. It was a great wrench for him to leave the House of Commons, where from a back bench he kept a friendly eye on his "noble friend" who by grace of his father's dukedom rules the British Navy. In debate on the navy estimates, not of itself an engrossing occupation, members had full opportunity of reflecting on the strange disposition of public affairs in this country which made Lord George Hamilton First Lord of the Admiralty, and left this shrewd little sailor, with his wide experience, his keen intelligence, and his infinite knowledge of detail, on a back bench.

Lord Charles is still young, having only just passed his forty-fifth year. In that period he has seen a good deal of service, though, as he probably regrets, only one opportunity has been afforded him of taking part in actual warfare. Moreover, that was not a very glorious occasion, though he managed to illuminate it by a brilliant bit of pluck and seamanship. At the bombardment of the Alexandria forts he was in command of the gunboat *Condor*, and began the day's service by helping the great ironclad *Téméraire* off the shore, on to which she had drifted. Then, when Arabi opened fire from the Marabout batteries, which, served by British gunners, would have kept the fleet at bay, "Charlie" dashed in with the little *Condor* and gave the astonished Egyptians so much to do that they never found the range of the ironclads. "Well done, *Condor*," the Admiral in command signalled, while all the fleet looked on in admiration of a feat which showed that armour-plating, turreting, and torpedoing, had not fatally overlain the ancient spirit of the British tar who fought in wooden ships at Trafalgar and the Nile.

His tactics in the House of Commons were very much on the lines of his famous manœuvre off Alexandria. The little *Condor* was always bearing up against some massive fort of Admiralty incompetence and opening fire with a ruthless disregard of precedent and authority that gave much pain in official circles. The House of Commons in committee, whether on the army or navy estimates, presents a melancholy spectacle. The voting of millions of money may be under discussion, and, more important still, the dearest interests of the Empire as safeguarded by the army or fleet. What the stranger in the gallery sees is a dozen, or at most a score, of gentlemen scattered over the benches yawning or sleeping, while a colonel or an admiral recites a not always brief essay.

When news went round that "Charlie" Beresford was on his legs, the House filled as if by magic, and was always rewarded by hearing a man talking in brisk speech on a subject with which he was thoroughly familiar. There was as a preliminary to "Charlie's" contributions to Parliamentary debate an involuntary movement of the hands and hips as if he were about (saving the Speaker's presence) to hitch up his trousers. No one would have been in the least surprised or regarded it as out of keeping with the business of the moment if, during a brief pause while he was consulting his notes, he had broken into a step or two of the hornpipe. Not that he was frivolously inclined, for when discussing naval administration he was hotly in earnest, or that there was any tendency on his part to pose as a sailor. The fancy in the mind of the looker-on was born of association of ideas when listening to the sturdy, ruddy-faced tar talking in the vitiated atmosphere of the House of Commons.

June 24.—Parliamentary portraits. Last year there was shown at the Royal Academy a portrait of Mr. Gladstone by Sir John Millais. It was one of a series by the same artist, who has frequently painted Mr. Gladstone, and hitherto with success. He is, indeed, so familiar with his subject that four or five sittings suffice for the completion of his work. This picture of 1890, presumably the last, was intended to be the best. It was, in its way, to be an illustration of Coleridge's beautiful contrast of Youth and Age. Mr. Gladstone's little grandson was to have immortality bestowed upon him by being brought on to the canvas, standing at the knee of the octogenarian statesman. All this was done, and the picture turned out an astounding and lamentable failure. There sat on a chair a wooden-backed, sallow-visaged old gentleman, staring straight before him, and at his knee stood

L L

an exceedingly commonplace little boy, gazing upon the other wooden figure in a condition of almost cataleptic, and entirely pardonable, astonishment. Sir John has had the picture back at his studio, awaiting opportunity to alter it. Mr. Gladstone has at length found time to give him the necessary sittings, and there is much curiosity to see the result. It is difficult to conceive that the thing of last year could be tortured into anything resembling a success; and it is whispered that Sir John, acknowledging his failure, began again on a fresh canvas.

Mr. Gladstone.   It is to be hoped the misfortune may be retrieved, since Mr. Gladstone is immovable from his determination never to sit again. Five years ago, just after the split in the Liberal party opened, the Dissentient Liberals at the Reform set on foot a scheme to present the club with a portrait of Lord Hartington. Thereupon the Home Rulers opened a subscription for a portrait of Mr. Gladstone. Subscription was limited to a guinea, the list, of course, open only to members. An interesting and occasionally exciting race followed. Lord Hartington, having got the start, kept it for a few weeks. But the Gladstonians doggedly forged ahead, till the two favourites were running neck and neck, finishing, as a sporting member put it, so that an umbrella would have covered both. Then a fresh and unexpected difficulty arose. Lord Hartington consented to sit for his portrait to the artist nominated by the subscribers. But Mr. Gladstone steadily refused. He had not time, he said. The consequence has been that the Gladstonian committee were driven to pick up a portrait wherever they could find it. When Mr. Gladstone was last in Florence, a local artist made some fugitive sketches of him, which he elaborated into a full-length portrait. With this, a melancholy, almost unrecognisable portrait, the Reform Club has now been endowed.

Mr. Balfour.   Mr. Arthur Balfour, as he took occasion to say at Plymouth the other day, has not much in common with Mr. Gladstone. But he has of late shared his misfortune in the matter of portraiture. Last year he sat to Alma-Tadema, and the portrait had a place of honour in this season's show at the Royal Academy. Oddly enough, Tadema failed with the rising hope of the Tory party as completely as his fellow-R.A. had failed with Mr. Gladstone. Mr. Balfour was discovered seated on a sofa. Looking at the figure half starting to rise, and noting the flash of pained astonishment on the face, the observer could not resist the suspicion that a pin, point upward, had somehow found its way into the sofa-seat. Mr. Arthur Balfour is the very flower of graceful demeanour, and it will be perceived how incompatible with gracefulness of posture or ordinary facial expression is the circumstance hinted at.

The Chief Secretary has been much more successful this year in a far less ambitious effort. He has been giving sittings to a rising young artist, E. A. Ward, who has just completed a work Mr. Balfour declares to be the best portrait ever painted of him. He is indeed so delighted with it that he has ordered a replica, which he intends to present to his sister. The original picture was a commission for a private collection, which includes portraits of some of the best-known men of the day, of widely differing individuality. There are Lord Rosebery, Mr. Henry Irving and his dog, Mr. Chamberlain, Mr. Burnand, Mr. John Tenniel, Lord Randolph Churchill, Mr. Labouchere, Mr. John Morley, and Mr. Joseph Cowen, at one time Member for Newcastle, a man who for a period revived in the House of Commons the ancient standard of Parliamentary eloquence, and has now deliberately drifted into obscurity.

June 28.—The dead Parliament. Compared with its lusty brothers born in 1874 and 1880, the Parliament prorogued to-day has been deplorably dull. One or two memorable scenes stand forth in the retrospect of six years. But there has been nothing like the daily succession of stirring episodes that marked long stretches of the earlier Parliaments. We have seen the whole Liberal party, headed by Mr. Gladstone, leap to its feet to receive Mr. Parnell on the evening of the day following the flight of Pigott. Twelve months later we have beheld the same Parnell seated forlorn and forsaken in the very place whence he rose on that memorable evening, to stand silent for many moments waiting till the enthusiastic cheers of a united Opposition had died away.

There have been some passages of arms between Mr. Gladstone and Mr. Chamberlain, most perfect sword-play, watched with delight by a ring excited with varied emotions. Also, there has been an epidemic of expulsions. But in the matter of dramatic episodes the Parliament of 1886 has been to the Parliaments of 1874 and 1880 as a cycle of Cathay to twenty years of Europe.

Once or twice the House has stood breathless, apparently on the eve of an explosion. The dogged determination of Lord Hartington, Mr. Chamberlain, and Sir Henry James to claim and keep seats on the front Opposition bench seemed at one epoch a sort of slow match that sooner or later must inevitably fire the mine. More than once a crowded House has looked hungrily on, certain that the long-anticipated moment had arrived. By slight accident or act of personal forbearance and courtesy the climax has been averted. At one time there was current a blood-curdling rumour that pointed to Mr. Picton as the deliverer of right hon. gentlemen on the front Opposition bench from a distasteful and embarrassing companionship. It was said the Member for Leicester had roundly declared he had as much right to a seat on the front Opposition bench as had Lord Hartington or Mr. Gladstone. Some day he would come down bright and early, fling himself on one, or peradventure both, of the seats at the Gangway-end of the front bench, and see what would happen when Lord Hartington or Mr. Chamberlain came up to claim it. Somehow, the event never came off. St. George did not appear in the lists, and the Dragon slept on through the Sessions undisturbed.

One principal reason for the change wrought in Parliamentary life during the last six years has undoubtedly been the alteration of the hours of meeting and dispersing. In the older Parliaments, with the potential hour of adjournment stretching to doom, or at least to dawn, the fun did not commence till after eleven o'clock. About that hour gentlemen who had been out to dinner came back in white neck-ties, broad shirt fronts, and high spirits, in the words of a song of contemporary mode, "good for any game at night, my boys." The habitual order of debate favoured the fashion. In those

days the giants did not strip and step into the arena till
midnight approached. Up to the date of the present Parliament all Mr. Gladstone's fighting speeches were delivered
between ten o'clock at night and two in the morning. It was
the same with Mr. Disraeli. When a great debate had run its
appointed course of sittings, the Leader of the Opposition rose
at half-past ten or eleven o'clock, and amid thunderous cheers
from the crowded benches behind him, brought up all the
reserve of attack. The Leader of the House followed, and if
he were able to conclude his speech by one o'clock it was
thought a happy and convenient circumstance.

Frequently in the Parliament of 1880 an exciting half-hour,
or even an hour, intervened before the House was cleared for
a division. The sitting down of the Leader of the House with
the assumption that he had closed the debate was invariably
the signal for the appearance of Mr. O'Donnell on the scene.
With no closure nor any hour of automatic adjournment,
the hapless House was absolutely at the mercy of its most
inconsiderable member. It yelled and roared, clamouring
incessantly for the division. Mr. O'Donnell waited for a lull
in the storm, and then, having recovered and adjusted his
dropped eye-glass, continued the sentence that had been
interrupted. Reckless of ordinary conditions governing
debate, impervious to angry reproof, deaf to piteous entreaty,
he was painfully punctilious on one point. He respected the
House of Commons too much to look upon it with the naked
eye, and, whilst it tossed about with impotent fury, he was not
to be hurried in his search of his eye-glass, nor, till he had
found it, betrayed into advancing his speech by a syllable.

Early closing.   The New Rules have changed all that. The
whole course of debate is reversed. In these
days, with the House commencing business at half-past three
and the debate peremptorily adjourned at midnight, all the
big speeches are made before the dinner hour. This has,
obviously, become a necessity. There is no room for a final
tussle between the time of re-assembling after dinner and the
hour of adjournment. The two front benches have once or
twice in the course of the present Parliament been driven into
this dilemma, and have grievously suffered. The right hon.

gentleman who rises at half-past ten to deliver the final attack
is hampered throughout by chivalrous anxiety to leave his
opponent a fair share of the strictly limited time.   With the
best intentions he never quite hits it off, and his opponent,
speaking with his eye on the clock, is angered with the sense
of injustice done to him.   Recently Mr. Gladstone spoke
in such circumstances in an important debate. He complained that Mr. Goschen, who had immediately preceded
him, had evaded or scamped a particular branch of the argument. With eloquent gesture' of shrugged shoulders and
uplifted hand Mr. Goschen pointed to the clock, the hands of
which stood at a quarter to twelve.

   "The right hon. gentleman points me to the clock," said
Mr. Gladstone in a burst of Homeric rage. "I look and find
my opportunity is far more limited than was his."

Improved busi-
ness capacity.   Whilst the existing regulations have militated
against spectacular and dramatic effect in the
present Parliament, they have vastly improved its capacity as
a business assembly. The knowledge that a certain amount
of business has to be done by a stated hour goes a long way
towards its accomplishment. Men and the course of events
arrange themselves. There have been many nights in the
Session just closing on which, for all practical purposes, the
House might have adjourned at a quarter to eight, when, an
important speech closed, Members have trooped forth *en masse*
to dinner. It has, nevertheless, remained in Session till midnight, and Members have succeeded each other, reciting
strings of sentences echoing round empty benches, "thrice-
boiled colewort," the prevalence of which in Parliamentary
oratory Carlyle long ago deplored. Still, as St. Paul says,
all things are possible, but all things are not expedient. As
few stay to hear these supplementary speeches few suffer,
whilst individuals are made happy, and the light on the Clock
Tower testifies that the House of Commons is still sitting.

The Speaker.   Whilst the New Rules have worked admirably,
the present Parliament has had the further
advantage of supremely good direction from the Chair. It is
only fair to remember that Mr. Peel and Mr. Courtney have

wielded powers unknown to their predecessors. On the other
hand, the situation had the embarrassment of novelty, a
dangerous thing in an assembly which, in all that touches its
procedure, is doggedly conservative. In directing the proceedings under the New Rules, both Mr. Peel and Mr.
Courtney have from time to time been suddenly called upon
to solve knotty points, or to establish momentous precedents.
In the seven Sessions through which the life of Parliament
has run, there was one occasion when a ruling of the Speaker
was seriously challenged. Mr. Courtney's approval or ignoring
of demand for the Closure has often been angrily commented
upon. But as those who thought the Closure was not moved
often enough in Committee were exactly balanced by those
who complained that too free use was made of the privilege,
Mr. Courtney's constitutional content with himself was not in
danger of disturbance.

Apart from mere business direction, Mr. Peel has through
his term of Speakership graced the Chair with a dignity and
strengthened it with a personality worthy of its loftiest traditions. Of all public perches, the Chair of the House of
Commons is, perhaps, the most difficult and the most perilous
on which a man could find himself placed. To be inflexible
yet courteous ; to sink all personal feeling, be impervious to
all social or intellectual preference ; to sit through hours of
dreary verbiage and be alert at the eleventh to give judgment on a nice point of order ruled by precedents going back
two hundred years ; to be in some respects a simple member
of the House, having no rights and privileges other than
those possessed by the most inconsiderable unit of the 670,
yet to be habitually deferred to on every point ; colleague
and autocrat ; ever living in the fierce light beside which that
beating upon the Throne is as moonlight unto sunlight—this
is a unique position, requiring for its fulfilment the rarest
personal gifts. That Mr. Peel has proved equal to the task
is testified to by the admiration and personal esteem in which
he is held by a House of which he has been the chief corner-
stone these more than six years past.

INDEX.

Abercorn, Duke of, [illegible]
Abingdon, Lord, [illegible]
Acland, Mr. Arthur, [illegible]
Acton, Lord, 71
Addington, Lord, [illegible]
African missionaries in the House of Commons, 3[illegible]
Akers-Douglas, Mr., [illegible]; and the Licensing Bill, [illegible]
Albany, Duke of, [illegible]
All-night sittings, 17[illegible], [illegible]
Allotments Act, 3
Alma-Tadema, Mr., his portrait of Mr. Balfour, [illegible]
Amateur Artists in the House, [illegible]
Anderson, Mr., [illegible]
Anecdotes: Strangers flaying members, [illegible]; Mr. Chamberlain's desertion, and the Washington belle, [illegible]; Mr. Chamberlain and the Queen's photograph, [illegible]; Lord Leverson's indiscretion, [illegible]; Mr. Disraeli and his hat, [illegible]; Major O'Gorman and the child "Sophia," [illegible]; Lord Eversley and William Pitt, [illegible]; the Lord Chancellor and the cantered styles of Fox and Pitt, [illegible]; Rival notaries on Mr. Richard Webster and Sir E. Clarke, 141; Macaulay and the Duke of Newcastle, [illegible]; Lord George Bentinck's remark about John Bright, [illegible]; Lord Granville and the Carlton Club, [illegible]; Lord Rosebery and his Scottish guest, [illegible]; the Rev. H. Whitet and the burglar, [illegible]; the Irish priest and the Archbishop, [illegible]; Mr. Pym and his watch, [illegible]; Disraeli and Hannah, [illegible]; Biggar and his father, [illegible]; Mr. Gotchen and the Solicitor with the glass of grog, [illegible]; Disraeli and his Manchester speech, [illegible]; Mr. Delahanty and the contents of his black bag, [illegible]; Mr. Biggar and his will, [illegible]; Sir Wilfrid Lawson and the Billy goat, [illegible]; Lord Bessmer and the Manitoba Franchise Bill, [illegible]; Lord R. Churchill and the Oxford tutor, [illegible]; Lord Granville and the "at home," [illegible]; Lord Granville and the birth of Browning's child, [illegible]; Wordsworth and Westmorland, [illegible]; the candidate for a diplomatic appointment, [illegible]; the Rugby school scholar and Mr. Jesse Collings, [illegible]; Mr. Labouchere at Washington, [illegible]; Lord Salisbury and the price of bread, [illegible]; Mr. Cunninghame Graham and the burglar at Pentonville, [illegible]; the Archbishop of Canterbury and the dinner at Carlton Gardens, [illegible]
Appropriation Bill, Discussion on the, [illegible]
Argyll, Duke of, [illegible]; his speech on the Isle of Lewis, [illegible]; and his failure in public life, [illegible]; his literary work and style, [illegible]
Army, A crisis in the history of the, [illegible]
Ascension Day, [illegible]
Ashbourne, Lord, once Lord Chancellor of Ireland, 4

Ashmead-Bartlett, Mr., [illegible]
Asquith, Mr., 160, 161, 243; on the Report of the Parnell Commission, 151, 213; his success in Parliament, 231, 27, 439, 443
Atkinson, Mr., 103, 404, 441
"Attleaw," 147
Aveland, Lord, 235

D

Baillie, Mr. Cochrane, 205
"Baker Pasha," 13
Balfour, Mr. Arthur, made Secretary for Scotland, 4; introduces the Crimes Bill, 7; made Chief Secretary for Ireland, 9, 14, 18, 22; speech on Address, [illegible]; his reply to Mr. O'Brien's speech after his imprisonment, 35; makes Col. King-Harman his secretary, 41; his increasing influence in the House, 77; Lord Randolph Churchill's attitude towards him, 87; answering questions, 77; changes in his manner, [illegible]; his before-the-congress attitude, 101; his reception by the House at the opening of Session, 1889, 109, 192; and Tory, [illegible]; and the spray of roses, 194, 195; and the motion to abolish the House of Lords, 205; and the Scotch University Bill, 211; on the Land Bill, 211; his arrest of Messrs. Dillon and O'Brien, 217; reply to Mr. Healy with reference to Lord Colland's Fund, 242; his indifference to attacks, 267; his taste for a "Life" of Pitt, 285; attacked by Mr. Keay, 406; his parliamentary prowess, 435; qualities for leadership, 435; goes to Bayreuth, 484; his recreations, 485; his less severe attitude towards the Irish Party, 221; at Balmoral, 499; and Mr. De Cobain, 499; as leader, 435, 441; and royal palaces, 479; and Mr. Gladstone, 484; and the chancellorship, 505; his portrait, 531
Baillie of Inchiloch, Lord, and the Chairmanship of Committees in the Lords, 183
Balmoral, Queen's centenary to the serenery of the Prince Consort at, 439
Baring, Lord, 289
Barrington, Lord, a confidant of Disraeli's, 304, 305
Barristers in Parliament, 543
Barclay, Mr., 205, 206; and a fall of snow in London, 506
Bartlett, Sir Walter, 193, 259; and the Army Estimates, 459
Basing, Lord, 13
Beaumont, Mr., the "Demosthenes of Park Lane"; his speech on overtime-work in Government factories, 44, 45
Beaconsfield, Lord, (see Disraeli, Mr.)
Beauchamp, Earl, 131, 243; his Parliamentary life, 311
Beresford, Mr., 205
Beresford, Lord George, 103; and Mr. Bright, 104
Beresford, Lord Charles, and the Civil Lords,

[illegible]; Parliamentary career, and tactics in the House, [illegible]
Biggar, Mr., [illegible] and the new Procedure Rules, [illegible]; called "The Admiral," [illegible]; altered, [illegible] and the flight to Paris, [illegible]; his watchful attitude, [illegible]; opposition to Government Bills, [illegible]; illustrative tactics and gestures, [illegible]; his affinity, [illegible]; [illegible]; his vote on Royal Grants, [illegible]; his sudden death and character, [illegible]; and Mr. Disraeli, [illegible]; and obstruction, [illegible]; his four hours' speech, [illegible]; now the Irishman's favourite, [illegible]; and his father, [illegible]; his "[illegible]" and the "Admiral," [illegible]; his will, [illegible]; his association with Mr. Parnell, [illegible]
Bills, Bringing in, [illegible]
Birmingham, Representation of, and Lord R. Churchill, [illegible]
Bishops, the method of their introduction to the House of Lords, [illegible]
Bismarck, Prince, and his letter to Mr. Morley, [illegible]
"Black Rod," [illegible]
Blaine, Mr., [illegible]
Blake, Mr., [illegible]; his story of a correspondence with his uncle, [illegible]
Blane, Mr. [illegible], his [illegible]; and Royal Palaces, [illegible]
Blücher, Waterloo, and Wellington, [illegible]
Boileau and Cromwell's Horses, [illegible]
Bolton, Mr., and State railways, [illegible]
Bond, Mr., and the [illegible], [illegible]; his death, [illegible]
Boulogne, Irish members at, [illegible]
Bourke, "Bobby." (See Connemara, Baron.)
Brabourne, Lord, [illegible]
Bradlaugh, Mr., and the oath, [illegible] and the Oaths Bill, [illegible]; defends the Conservative Government, [illegible]; his industry, [illegible]; an example of the triumph of natural ability against prejudice, [illegible]; on foreign politics, [illegible]; brings in Bills on prosecutions for matters of religion, [illegible]; makes [illegible] for the table, [illegible]; amendments on Royal Grants, [illegible]; his legal knowledge, [illegible]; his death, his conflicts with Parliament, and work, [illegible]
Bradlaugh difficulty, The, [illegible]
Brand, Sir Henry. (See Hampden, Lord.)
Bright, Mr. Jacob, [illegible]
Bright, Mr. John, [illegible]; his death, [illegible]; proposed reconciliation with Mr. Gladstone, [illegible]; tributes to his memory from Mr. Gladstone, Mr. Smith, and Mr. Morley, [illegible]; reminiscences of his appearances in the House, [illegible], and Dr. Kenealy, [illegible]; Lord George Bentinck's remark about him, [illegible]; his patience in the House, [illegible]
Bright, Mr. J. A., 182
Broadhurst, Mr., [illegible]
Brodrick, Mr., and the House of Lords, [illegible]
Browning, Robert, and the birth of his child, [illegible]
Bryce, Mr., [illegible]
Bryce, Professor, [illegible]
Budget Bill of 1885, [illegible]
Budget night (1889), [illegible]; (1890), [illegible]
Burdett-Coutts, Mr., and Mr. Lockwood's humorous sketch, [illegible]
Burghley, The Lord of, [illegible]
Butt, Mr., [illegible]
Butt, Isaac, [illegible]; contrasted with Parnell, [illegible]; decline of his influence, [illegible]; and the O'Gorman Mahon, [illegible]

Buxton, Mr. Sydney, raises a storm in the House, 120-122, [illegible]

C

Cæsar, Julius, and his contribution to Mr. John Morley, [illegible]
Caine, Mr., [illegible]
Cairns, Sir Hugh, [illegible]
Caldwell, Mr., on the educational condition of Scotland, [illegible]
Calendar of Parliamentary events: Session of 1886, [illegible]; Session II. (1886), [illegible]; Session 1887, [illegible]; Session 1888, [illegible]; Session of 1889, [illegible]; Session of 1890, [illegible]; Session of 1890-91, [illegible]
Cambridge, Duke of, [illegible]
Campbell, Sir George, and the "[illegible] creatures" on the staircase, [illegible]; exercises a strategy respecting the Scotch University Bill, [illegible]; and the "[illegible]," [illegible]; and St. George and the Dragon, [illegible]; his death and high reputation, [illegible]
Campbell-Bannerman, Mr., [illegible]
Camperdown, Earl of, and Lord Tyrone's maiden speech, [illegible]
Canning, [illegible]
Canterbury, Archbishop of, [illegible]; goes out to dinner, [illegible]
Carlton Club, Meeting of Conservatives at the, [illegible]; and Lord Granville, [illegible]
Carlyle, Mr. Harrison's reference to, [illegible]
Carmarthen, Marquis of, [illegible]
Carnarvon, Lord, [illegible]
Cavan, Earl of, [illegible]; and Sir Henry James's speeches, [illegible]
Cavendish, Lord Frederick: his assassination, [illegible]
Cavendish-Bentinck, Lord H., [illegible]; his death, [illegible]; his Toryism, [illegible]
Cavendish-Bentinck, Mr., [illegible]
Cetewayo, [illegible]
Chairman of Committees, Duties of, [illegible]
Chamberlain, Mr. Joseph, made President of the Local Government Board, [illegible]; his resignation, [illegible]; presented by the Queen with her photograph, [illegible]; a Washington belle's opinion of his dancing, [illegible]; attacked by Sir W. Harcourt, [illegible]; consults with Lord Randolph Churchill on Local Government in Ireland, [illegible]; attacked by Mr. Parnell, [illegible]; defence against Mr. Parnell's charges, [illegible]; the best debater in the House, [illegible]; his imitation of Mr. Gladstone, [illegible]; congratulations on his marriage, [illegible]; expostulated with, by Mr. Gladstone, [illegible]; and Lord R. Churchill's proposed candidature for Central Birmingham, [illegible]; and the Land Bill, [illegible]; his resemblance to Pitt, [illegible]; and the Liberals, [illegible]; and Lord Hartington, [illegible]; goes to Germany, [illegible]; success in social world, [illegible]; his speeches heard and read, [illegible]; and Mr. Gladstone, [illegible]
Channel Tunnel Bill, Second reading of the, [illegible]
Chaplin, Mr., and the fatal [illegible] of [illegible], [illegible]; congratulates Mr. Chamberlain on his marriage, [illegible]; and Lord R. Churchill, [illegible]; and Mr. Gladstone, [illegible]
Childers, Mr., and his Budget of 1885, [illegible]
Churchill, Lord Randolph, nominates Mr. Matthews for the Home Secretaryship and is made Chancellor of the Exchequer and Leader of the House, [illegible]; reminiscences and

characteristics and habits in the House, [illegible]; and Mr. [illegible], [illegible]
[illegible] Club, The, [illegible]
Kirton, Lord, [illegible] (See also Wemyss, Earl.)
[illegible], Lord, [illegible]
Electric-light arrangements at Hatfield House, [illegible]
Elliot, Sir George, takes the floor, [illegible]
Elphinstone, Sir James, [illegible]
Emperor of Germany, Death of the, [illegible]
Errington, George, [illegible]
[illegible], Sir Thomas, [illegible]
[illegible], Mr., 210
Eversley, Lord, his death, [illegible]

F

Farquharson, Dr., [illegible]
Father of the House of Commons, The, [illegible]
Fay, Mr., [illegible]
Fenwick, Mr., [illegible]
Ferguson, Sir James, [illegible]; compared with Lord Strathcona and Campbell [illegible]; a model Under-Secretary, [illegible]; made Postmaster-General, [illegible]
Field, Admiral, [illegible]
Fife, Duke of, [illegible]
Flanigan, Lynach, [illegible]
Flowery Commission and Mr. Chamberlain, [illegible]
"Flag of truce," Sir W. Hart-Dyke's, [illegible]
Flynn, Mr., [illegible]
Fog in the House of Commons, Battle with the, [illegible]
Folkestone, Lord, and his strictures of Members, [illegible]; and Mr. Healy, [illegible]; succeeds to the Radnor peerage, [illegible]. (See also Radnor, Earl of.)
Forster, Mr., Death of, [illegible]
Forster, Sir Charles, in a dilemma, [illegible]; his death, [illegible]
Fourth Party, The, [illegible]
Fowler, Mr. Henry, [illegible]; his position in the House, [illegible]
Fox and Pitt, Oratory of, [illegible]
Fraser, General, on the Army, [illegible]
Free Education Bill, The, [illegible]
Fulton, Mr. Forrest, [illegible]

G

Gedge, Mr., [illegible]
General Election of 1886, [illegible]
George, Mr. Lloyd, [illegible]
Gibson, Mr. (See Ashbourne, Lord.)
Giffard, Sir Hardinge. (See Halsbury, Lord.)
Gilhooly, Mr., wanted by the police, [illegible]; arrested, [illegible]
Gill, Mr., [illegible]
Gladstone, Mr., his majority in 1886, 1; members of his Government of 1886, [illegible]; unfolds his scheme of Home Rule (1886), [illegible]; his defeat and resignation, [illegible]; and the Crimes Bill, [illegible]; moves for a Select Committee to inquire into the charges of the Times against Mr. Parnell, [illegible]; at the head of a majority, [illegible]; his reception at the opening of Session (1888), [illegible]; speech on the Address (1888), [illegible]; reply to Mr. Balfour on the O'Brien episode, [illegible]; and the new Procedure Rules, [illegible]; at the Speaker's dinner, [illegible]; and the Affirmation Bill, [illegible]; on State railways, [illegible]; tireless of speech-making, [illegible]; a phenomenon, [illegible]; and the wrongs of Mr. Tayler, of Point, [illegible]; on the Channel Tunnel Bill, [illegible]; his English vivacity at [illegible]; on Mr. Parnell's charges against Mr. Chamberlain, [illegible]; his demeanour in the House, [illegible]; and

the death of Lord Eversley, [illegible]; the only orator in the House, [illegible]; Mr. Chamberlain's tribute to his greatness, [illegible]; speech on the Irish Question (Mr. Morley's amendment to the Address), [illegible]; relations with John Bright, and his tribute to Bright's memory, 176–177, [illegible]; his letters to the Queen, [illegible]; his historic letter to the Queen, [illegible]; his patience in the House, [illegible]; and Royal Grants, [illegible]; origin of his appellation, the "Grand Old Man," [illegible]; also called "Mr. G.," [illegible]; his reception at the opening of Session (1890), [illegible]; on the Report of the Parnell Commission, [illegible]; in a tight place, [illegible]; and his "pound his peck," [illegible]; on Mr. Parnell's Land speech, [illegible]; "saving himself up," [illegible]; on the Address (1890-91), [illegible]; his letter on the Parnell leadership, [illegible]; invites Parnell to Hawarden, [illegible]; disappointed by the position taken by Parnell, [illegible]; declines a proposal of compromise on the Parnell question, [illegible]; on the Religious Disabilities Bill, [illegible]; his stock of energy, [illegible]; his personal preponderance in the House, [illegible]; a powerful item, [illegible]; his Home Rule Bill, [illegible]; and the death of Lord Granville, [illegible]; and Mr. Seymour Keay, [illegible]; his representations, [illegible]; his appearance at, [illegible]; personal controversy, [illegible]; speech on the Mombasa Railway, [illegible]; and the hours of railway servants, [illegible]; on Royal Palaces, [illegible]; his speeches heard and read, [illegible]; attention paid to him by the Tories, [illegible]; his castigation of Mr. Chamberlain, [illegible]; and the question of dissolution, [illegible]; his portrait by Millais, [illegible]; and the hours of labour, [illegible]
"Gladstone's up!" [illegible]
"God bless the Duke of Argyll!" [illegible]
"God save Ireland!" and Dr. Tanner's suture, [illegible]
Goldsmid, Sir Julian, [illegible]
Goldsworthy, General, [illegible]
Gorst, Sir John, [illegible]; and Lord Randolph Churchill, [illegible]; the "utility man" of the Treasury Bench, [illegible]; his report on Mr. S. Smith, [illegible]; and Privilege, [illegible]
Goschen, Mr., his speech in reply to Mr. Gladstone on the O'Brien incident, [illegible]; his style of oratory, [illegible]; and Mr. Bums's will, [illegible]; his worries, [illegible]; his Budget of 1889, [illegible]; his Budget of 1891, [illegible]; and the leadership, [illegible]; as Leader, [illegible]; and the clock, [illegible]
"Goschen's room," [illegible]
Graham, Mr. Cunninghame, suspended from attendance in the House, [illegible]; "one of the proudest events in his life," [illegible]; suspended, [illegible]
Graham, Sir James, [illegible]
Granby, Marquis of, takes his seat in the House of Commons, [illegible]
"Grand Old Man," The, [illegible]
Granville, Lord, appointed Colonial Secretary, [illegible]; and Lord Lorne, [illegible]; letter from "Carlton House Terrace," 177, [illegible]; and the Chairmanship of Committees, [illegible]; walks into the Carlton Club by mistake, [illegible]; characteristics, [illegible]; and Lord Tryphon, [illegible]; his death and his successors, [illegible]; and Mr. Gladstone, [illegible]; his leadership in the Lords, [illegible]; and the Eastern Question, [illegible]; fencing with Lord Salisbury, [illegible]
Graphic, The, and Lord R. Churchill's letters from Africa, [illegible]

Gries Ratcliffe, Captain, [illegible]
Grissell, Mr., [illegible]
Grosvenor Gallery, Sketch in the, and Mr. Burdett-Coutts, [illegible]
"Gummidge, Mrs.," and the Irish Party, [illegible]
Gunpowder Plot, 107

H

Hanlane, Mr., [illegible]; and his Town Councils Bill, [illegible]
Halsbury, Lord, made Lord Chancellor, 4; his patronage, [illegible] visits the House of Commons, [illegible]; his loss of the [illegible] since by his wife, [illegible]; his resignation appearance to war and down, [illegible]; possibility of his catching the Speaker's eye, [illegible]; and the re-introduction of the Duke of Fife, [illegible]
"——," and Mr. Healy, [illegible]
Hamilton, Lord George, made First Lord of the Admiralty, 4, [illegible]; his asent of paper, [illegible]; thinks a man cleverer he than not of a duke, [illegible]; and the Navy Estimates, [illegible]
Hampden, Lord, [illegible]
Hanbury, Mr., [illegible]
Harcourt, Sir W., appointed Chancellor of the Exchequer, 4, 11; interrupts Mr. Goschen in his speech on Irish matters, [illegible]; attacks Mr. Chamberlain during the Local Government Bill debate, [illegible]; his style of oratory, [illegible]; repeats the apposition, the "Grand Old Man," [illegible]; and the Tithes Bill, [illegible]; and the Irish members, [illegible]; change of temper, [illegible]; sadness in Parliament, [illegible]; on Welfare, [illegible]; and Mr. Ray, [illegible]; as leader of the Opposition, [illegible]; his speeches bitter and cruel, [illegible]; and the question of dissolution, [illegible]
Hardy, Mr. Gathorne, [illegible]
Hartington, Mr. E., suspended from attendance in the House, [illegible]
Harringtons, The, [illegible]
Hart-Dyke, Sir William, [illegible]; made Chief Secretary to the Lord-Lieutenant, [illegible]; made Vice-President of the Council, [illegible]; speech on the proposal to appoint a Minister of Education, [illegible]; his "flag of truce," [illegible]; a wine bottle, [illegible]
Hartington, Lord, [illegible]; leads the dissentient Liberal party, [illegible]; offered the Premiership by Lord Salisbury, [illegible]; promises to support the Conservative Government, 4, 14, [illegible]; and the Speaker's dinner, [illegible]; and Lord R. Churchill's proposed candidature of Birmingham, [illegible]; on the Land Bill, [illegible]; takes his seat in the Liberal Union (Duke of Devonshire, [illegible]; his speeches heavy and dull, [illegible]; his portrait, [illegible]
Havelock-Allan, Sir, [illegible]
Healy, Mr. Maurice, on Mr. Parnell's repudiation of [illegible]
Healy, Mr. Tim, [illegible]; and the new Procedure Rules, [illegible]; his cleverness as a debater, [illegible]; his improved manners—now the "boys, and learned gentlemen," [illegible]; and the Parnell leadership, [illegible]; as "Buss," [illegible]; his question with reference to Lord Iveagh's report, [illegible]; honored by Mr. Parnell, [illegible]; and the Irish leadership, [illegible]; his nickname, [illegible]; and Mr. Balfour, [illegible]; and Irish newspapers, [illegible]
Heaton, Mr. Henniker, [illegible]; and advertising on postage, [illegible]
Heligoland, Transfer of, [illegible]

Heneage, Mr., [illegible]
Hennessy, Sir John Pope, his return to Parliament, [illegible]; changes in the House since his first election, [illegible]; his death, [illegible]
Henry, Mitchell, 84
Herbert, Mr. Auberon, [illegible]
Herschell, Sir Farrer (afterwards Lord), made Lord Chancellor, 7; on Mr. Parnell and the Times, [illegible]; his asceticism in Parliament, [illegible]
Hicks-Beach, Sir Michael, and the Newbridge difficulty, 1; made Chief Secretary for Ireland, 4; temporary withdrawal from Parliamentary life, 6; his amendment to Mr. Childers' Budget Bill, [illegible]; and Main railway, [illegible]; and the hours of railway servants, [illegible]
Hill, Lord Arthur, [illegible]
Hogg, Sir James M'Garel. (See Magheramorne, Lord.)
Holker, Mr., [illegible]
Holker, Sir John, and the stronger's eye, [illegible]
Home Rule, Mr. Gladstone's scheme of, 8, 9; rejection of Mr. Gladstone's scheme, 10; and Mr. Parnell, [illegible]; and Mr. Parnell's visit to Hawarden, [illegible]
Hood, Stationmaster, [illegible]
Hope, Beresford, 19, 73, [illegible]
Horner, Cornelius, and Railway, [illegible]
Hornby, Mr., [illegible]
Horsman, Mr., [illegible]
Hours of labour, Bill, [illegible]
House of Commons, Changes in the, [illegible]; under the new rules, 21; the appeal with members in disorder drink, [illegible]; Mr. Sydney Buxton and Mr. Jackson cabbage order, [illegible]; sittings of, [illegible]; the best debaters in, [illegible]; waste of time in, [illegible]; behaving in Bills, [illegible]; all-night sittings, [illegible]; the lamp lit of, [illegible]; a dinnerless to, [illegible]; daily letter to the Queen from the Leader of, [illegible]; a quiet time, [illegible]; a comic scene, [illegible]; battle with the bag, [illegible]; sleepiness, [illegible]; a dull state of things, [illegible]; the Long Session, [illegible]; a stirring scene, [illegible]; the question of dissolution, [illegible]
House of Lords, The, with no work to do, [illegible]; its architectural arrangements, [illegible]; "another place," [illegible]; Mr. Labouchere's motion for its abolition, [illegible]; Lord Salisbury's motion to add thirty life peers to, [illegible]; re-introduction of the Duke of Fife by the Prince of Wales, [illegible]; Lord Teynham's maiden speech, [illegible]; Lord Denman and the Municipal Franchise Bill, [illegible]; and the Duke of Hamilton and Argyle, [illegible]; time of adjournment, [illegible]; a mess with an Irish Bill, [illegible]
Hubbard, Mr. J. G. (See Addington, Lord.)
"Hodibras" quoted by Sir J. Gorst, [illegible]
Hudson, George, and his railway to Scotland, [illegible]
Hughes, Colonel, the "Woolwich infant," [illegible]; and a fall of snow, [illegible]
Hughes-Hallett, Colonel, 21, 25, 62
Humour, Scottish, 66, 73
Hunt, Mr. Ward, [illegible]

I

Iddesleigh, Lord, made First Lord of the Treasury, 4; his death, 4, 14; his reputation in the House of Commons, 17, 24
Imprisonment of Irish members, 21
Income-tax, Mr Robert Peel and Mr. Goschen on the, 24

Mithen, speech of Lord Tyndham, [illegible]
Majoribanks, Mr. [illegible]; his bishop in the Election, [illegible]
Manners, Lord John, made Chancellor of the Duchy of Lancaster, [illegible]; succeeds to the Rutland peerage, [illegible]
M'Arthur, Mr. William, [illegible]
Martin, Sir Theodore; his "Life of the Prince Consort," and Disraeli's letters to the Queen, [illegible]
"Master of the Rolls," The, [illegible]
Matthews, Mr. Henry, made Home Secretary, [illegible]; confirmed by Lord Randolph Churchill, [illegible]; on a speech of Mr. Gladstone's, [illegible]; on the Penal Servitude Bill, [illegible]; and Mr. Graham's [illegible], [illegible]
Mavis, Lord, [illegible]
M'Carthy, Mr. Justin, [illegible]; and the Irish Leadership, [illegible]; elected Leader of the "Nationalist" section of the Irish Party, [illegible]; his meeting with reference to Messrs. Dillon and O'Brien, [illegible]; as "[illegible]," [illegible]; his relations with Mr. Parnell, [illegible]; and the Irish Leadership, [illegible]
M'Kenna, Sir Joseph, [illegible]
M'Laughton, Lord, [illegible]
Merchandise Marks Act, [illegible]
Metge, Mr., [illegible]
Millais, Sir John; his portrait of Mr. Gladstone, [illegible]
Mines Regulation Act, [illegible]
Molesworth, Sir Guilford, and the Mombassa Railway, [illegible]
Molloy, Mr., [illegible]
Mombassa Railway, [illegible]
Monk Bretton, Lord, [illegible]
Morgan, Osborne, Mr., [illegible]
Morley, Lord, elected to the Chairmanship of Committees in the Lords, [illegible]
Morley, Mr. Arnold, [illegible]
Morley, Mr. John, appointed Secretary for Ireland, [illegible]; reply to Mr. Balfour on the debate on the Address (1886), [illegible]; speech on the proposal to appoint a Minister of Education, [illegible]; his retirement from Parliament, [illegible]; and the death of John Bright, [illegible]; his resemblance to Julius Cæsar, [illegible]; and the Parnell Leadership, [illegible]; his speeches heard and read, [illegible]
Morning sittings for the Government, [illegible]
Morton, Mr. A. C., [illegible]; his battle in the House, [illegible]; and Buckingham Palace, [illegible]
Meeting in the House for the Purpose of Germany, [illegible]
Mouse in the dock, The, [illegible]
Mundella, Mr., [illegible]
Municipal Franchise (Ireland) Bill, [illegible]
Murphy, Mr., [illegible]
Murray, Mr. Graham, [illegible]

N

National Debt, The, and Mr. Damer's will, [illegible]
Nelson, Rev. Mr., [illegible]
Neville, Mr., [illegible]
Newdegate, Mr., [illegible]
Nolan, Colonel, [illegible]
Norfolk, Duke of, [illegible]
Northcote, Sir Stafford, [illegible] (see also Iddesleigh, Lord.)

O

Oaths Bill, The, [illegible]
O'Brien, Mr. J. F. X., [illegible]; wrongly accused by Mr. Courtney, [illegible]

O'Brien, Mr. Patrick; arrested in mistake for Mr. O'Brady, [illegible]
O'Brien, Mr. W., imprisoned, [illegible]; speech on his liberation from prison, [illegible]; his oratory, [illegible]; and the Parnell Leadership, [illegible]; at Boulogne, [illegible]; his temporary retirement, [illegible]; his travel, [illegible]; in acquittancy, [illegible]
O'Connell, [illegible]; contrasted with Parnell, [illegible]
O'Connor, Mr. Arthur, [illegible]
O'Connor, Mr. T. P., [illegible]
O'Donnell, Mr. F. H., [illegible]
O'Donnell v. Walter, [illegible]
O'Donoghue, The, [illegible]
O'Gorman, Major, [illegible]; his death, and some of his characteristics, [illegible]; and the House of Lords, [illegible]; and Obstruction, [illegible]
O'Grady, Private, [illegible]
O'Hanlon, Mr., [illegible]
O'Hea, Mr., [illegible]
O'Kelly, Mr., his eventful career, [illegible]
"Old Mortality," [illegible]
O'Leary, Dr., [illegible]
O'Brien, M., [illegible]
One-pound notes, [illegible]
Oratory in the House of Commons, low standard of, [illegible]; modern style, [illegible]
O'Shea, Captain, [illegible]
O'Sullivan, "Whisky," [illegible]
Oswald, Mr., Lord, [illegible]

P

Palaces, Royal, [illegible]
Palmerston, Lord, [illegible]; his letters to the Queen, [illegible]; fondness for field sports, [illegible]
Parliament of December, 1885, [illegible]; of 1886-1892, [illegible]; opening of Session of 1887, [illegible]; opening of Session of 1888, [illegible]; opening of Session of 1889, [illegible]; opening of Session of 1890, [illegible]; opening of Session of 1890-91, [illegible]; opening of Session of 1893, [illegible]
Parliament, The late, compared with many of its predecessors, [illegible]; hours of debate, [illegible]; the new rules, [illegible]
Parnell, Mr., challenges the policy of the Government, [illegible]; and the Coercion Bill, [illegible]; and the charges brought him by the Times, [illegible]; and the Eighty Club, [illegible]; pleads "not guilty" to the charge of being accessory to murder, [illegible]; and the Members of Parliament Bill, [illegible]; attacks Mr. Chamberlain, [illegible]; his charges against Mr. Chamberlain, [illegible]; influence upon him of the disruption of the House, [illegible]; his style, [illegible]; his hour of triumph, [illegible]; and Royal grants, [illegible]; and a Times letter, [illegible]; and the Report of the Commission, [illegible]; on the Land Purchase Bill, [illegible]; contrasted with Mr. Isaac Butt, [illegible]; his reconciliation with O'Connell, [illegible]; his influence in the House, [illegible]; his position as Leader of the Irish Party in view of the proceedings in the Divorce Court, [illegible]; his visit as His master, [illegible]; his statement to Mr. Davitt, [illegible]; his motion with reference to Messrs. Dillon and O'Brien, [illegible]; attack on the idea of United Ireland, [illegible]; the instant results on politics of the Divorce Court proceedings, [illegible]; his relations with Mr. M'Carthy and Mr. Healy, [illegible]; his advances from the throne, [illegible]; and the mighty Closing Bill, [illegible]; Mr. Maurice Healy's challenge to him, [illegible]; retention his old seat, [illegible]; his sacred blindness, [illegible]; his

Q

R

N

[...], and the Irish **Leadership**, [illegible]; on Irish questions, [illegible]

Shaw, Mr. W., [illegible]

Shaw-Lefevre, Mr. (*See* Eversley, **Lord**.)

Sheridan, R. L., 10

Signing the Roll, [illegible]

Sinclair, Mr., [illegible]

Sleep, Mr., motion on Tuition Policy, 41

Smith, Mr. Frederick, takes his seat for the Strand, [illegible]

Smith, Mr. Samuel, 101, 168

Smith, Mr. W. H., made War Secretary, 4; takes the Leadership of the House and moves the Closure, 8; greeted in the House, 34; and the new Procedure Rules, 38-41; his appointments as Leader of the House, 54, 66; and the Parnell Commission, 94, 101; makes a joke; 118, 141; his reception by the House at the opening of Session 1889, 149, 150; rumoured retirement to the House of Lords, 172; and the death of John Bright, 178; and the array of peers, 183; and Royal Grants, 221; his admirable capacity for leading the House, 228, 266; and the Titles Bill, 283; and the Parnell Commission Report, 313, 314; his proxy sermon, 324; his work in the House and his reputation as Leader, 354-361; made Lord Warden of the Cinque Ports, 378; illness, 385; as Leader, 417; "Old Morality," 417; his high tariff, 430; installed at Walmer, 431; his death, 443; contrasted with Mr. Balfour, 446; illness, 436

Smyth, P. J., [illegible]; his oratory, [illegible]

Somers, Mr., [illegible]

Somers, The, 11, 97

Southwark, Liberal victory in, 2

Sovereigns, The, stamp on, and Sir George Campbell, 387

Speaker, The, and all-night sittings, [illegible]

Speaker's Gallery, The, 49

Spencer, Earl, appointed Lord President of the Council, 3; and the Leadership in the Lords, 129

Spencer, Mr. Herbert, and the Duke of Westminster, 82, 211, 212

Staniels, Captain, 212

Stalbridge, Lord, 54

Stanhope, Mr., made Colonial Secretary, 4; reply to Mr. Baumann, 42, 43; and Private O'Grady, 46; and the Army Estimates, 106

Stanhope, Mr. Philip, as Whig, 214, 215

Stanley, Lord, made President of the Board of Trade, 3, 13

Stansfeld, Mr., 168

Stewart, Mr. Mark, 89

"Stop-gap Government," The, 303

Stuart, Mr., moves to reduce the vote for the Board of Works, 213, 289, 306; on royal palaces, 219

Stranger breaks the rules, A, 213

Strangers' Gallery, Regulations for admission to the, 98

Strathcona and Campbell, Lord, appearance and habits in Parliament, 334-336

Sullivan, Mr. A. M., tipped by a stranger, 23, 25; and Mr. Lowther, 332

Sullivan, Mr. T., 16, 21

Swinburn, Mr., 86

Sunday Closing Bill, and the ladies' prayer meeting, 352

Sunday Closing Bill (Ireland), 303

Swinburne, Sir John, vanishes peacefully, 167

Sykes, Mr. Christopher, and his patience with "small beer," 338

Syria, Missions in, [illegible]

T

Talbot, Mr., "Miller of the **House of Commons**," 29

Tanner, Dr., 28, 91; his escort of "boys" from the House to his hotel, 138, 141; his arrest, 145; and the Speaker, 192, 221, 259

Taylor, Mr., The wrongs of, 21

Temple, Sir Richard, on Intemperance in India, 122, 164; and the ladies, 224, 259, 317, 348; and the Kew Gardeners, 322, 325, 345, 350

Teynham, Lord, and his maiden speech, 139-140

"The usual time!" 136

Times, The, and the charges against **Mr.** Parnell, 10, 157, 162, 173, 261, 340

Tips paid by strangers to the Sergeant-at-Arms and messengers of Parliament, 38, 39

Tobacco, Mr. Gardner's missing notes about tobacco, 259

Tottenham, Colonel, 18, 19

Trevelyan, Sir George, appointed Secretary for Scotland, 3; his resignation, 3; and the Land Bill, 196, 265; on the duration of the Session, 411; and the hours of railway servants, 172

Truck Act, 8

Truck, 418

Tuite, Mr., 85

U

Unionists, their meeting after General Election (1886), 3; said by Lord Randolph Churchill to be a "crutch" for the Government, 3; alliance with the Conservatives, 157

V

Vere, Trotty, 24

Victoria, Queen, and the letters **of Lord** Sackville, 278

Villiers, Mr., 274, 352

Vivian, Sir Hussey, 206

Volunteers, The, and Mr. Goschen's **Budget** of 1889, 308

W

Waddy, Mr., 166; and "Black Rod," 362

Wakefield, Bishop of, his introduction in the House of Lords, 321

Wales, Prince of, re-introduces the Duke of Fife to the House of Lords, 166, 341; and Lord Teynham's speech, 230; on Budget night, 255, 258, 306, 401; and the swearing-in of the Duke of York, 341

Wallace, Dr., and the motion to abolish the House of Lords, 321

Walmer Castle and Lord Granville, 304

Walter, Mr., and the Parnell Commission Bill, 101; and Mr. Healy, 158

Wantage, Lord, 430

Ward, Mr. E. A., portrait of Mr. Balfour by, 445

Waterford, Marquis of, 471

Watkin, Sir Edward, and the Channel Tunnel Bill, 41

Wales, Mr., and State railways, 41, 42

Wearing of the green, The, by Private O'Grady, 416, 417

Welch, Mr., 464

Webster, Mr., and illiterate votes, 446, 448

Webster, Sir Richard, 159, 161; a reply to Sir W. Harcourt, 105, 106; tables a map, 311; and the Titles Bill, 313; on the Report of the Parnell Commission, 316, 348, 349; a poser from Mr. Maloney, 450

Welsh Members, 69
Wemyss, Earl, 18, 779; his motion on Socialistic legislation, 290, 421
Westminster, Duke of, and Mr. Robert Spencer, 96; and the Duke of Fife, 762, 821
Weymouth, Lord, 222
Whalley, Mr., 179
Whips, their duties in the House, and their habitual absence, 55, 56
White, Rev. Henry, and the dying burglar, 212
" Who gave him up?" 197, 457
Wilkes and Bradlaugh, 159
Winn, Mr. Rowland. (See Oswald, St., Lord.)
Wolff, Sir Henry, and the mission to Persia, 18, 42, 144, 348

Wolmer, Lord, 224
Wolverton, Lord, 56
Wood, Sir Charles, 221
Woolsmouth, 283
Working man, The, 233

Y

Yates, Mr. Edmund, and the World, 114
York, Duke of, sworn in, 349
" Young England " school, 33

Z

Zulus in the House of Commons, 330–344

MR. GLADSTONE WALKS IN.

PRINTED BY CASSELL & COMPANY, LIMITED, LA BELLE SAUVAGE, LONDON, E.C.
10·1292